# THE NEVER GAME

"With a twisty plot, riveting characters, and relentless suspense, *The Never Game* fires on every single cylinder. Readers will delight in this compelling new character from one of the finest suspense writers in the field. I always look forward to the new Deaver, but this one tops them all." —Karin Slaughter

"Lightning-fast and loaded with twists, *The Never Game* is a thrill a minute from one of the best. Don't miss it." —Harlan Coben

"Jeffery Deaver is one of our most exciting storytellers, and *The Never Game* pulls off the remarkable feat of intertwining a devilish plot with unforgettable characters, fascinating disquisitions with propulsive action, every element conspiring to make it almost impossible to not turn the page. I absolutely loved it." —Chris Pavone

"Jeffery Deaver knows how to deliver exactly what a reader wants. He has a gift for place and character and, here, the tension ratchets up, page by page, as we follow the exploits of a new hero. Crisply plotted and fraught with danger." —Steve Berry

"Terrific writing, vivid and raw, Deaver grips from the very first line and never lets up. He is, hands-down, one of the finest thriller writers of our time." —Peter James

"*The Never Game* is the very definition of a page-turner." —Ian Rankin

## SHORT FICTION

### Collections
*A Hot and Sultry Night for Crime* (Editor)
*Trouble in Mind*
*Triple Threat*
*Books to Die For* (Contributor)
*The Best American Mystery Stories 2009* (Editor)
*More Twisted*
*Twisted*

### Stories
"Buried"
"The Second Hostage"
"Verona"
"The Debriefing"
"Ninth and Nowhere"
"Captivated"
"The Victims' Club"
"Surprise Ending"
"Double Cross"
"The Deliveryman"
"A Textbook Case"

# THE
# NEVER
# GAME

## JEFFERY
## DEAVER

G. P. PUTNAM'S SONS
NEW YORK

**PUTNAM**
— EST. 1838 —

G. P. PUTNAM'S SONS
*Publishers Since 1838*
An imprint of Penguin Random House LLC
penguinrandomhouse.com

The Library of Congress has catalogued the G. P. Putnam's Sons hardcover edition as follows:

Names: Deaver, Jeffery, author.
Title: The never game / Jeffery Deaver.
Description: New York, New York : G. P. Putnam's Sons, [2019]
Identifiers: LCCN 2019003019 | ISBN 9780525535942 (hardback) |
ISBN 9780525535966 (epub)
Subjects: | BISAC: FICTION / Mystery & Detective / General. |
FICTION / Crime. |
GSAFD: Mystery fiction. | Suspense fiction
Classification: LCC PS3554.E1755 N48 2019 | DDC 813/.54—dc23
LC record available at https://lccn.loc.gov/2019003019

First G. P. Putnam's Sons hardcover edition / May 2019
First G. P. Putnam's Sons international edition / May 2019
First G. P. Putnam's Sons premium edition / March 2020
First G. P. Putnam's Sons mass market international edition / March 2020
G. P. Putnam's Sons premium edition ISBN: 9780525535959

Printed in the United States of America
1  3  5  7  9  10  8  6  4  2

*To M and P*

Gaming disorder is defined . . . as a pattern of gaming behavior ("digital-gaming" or "video-gaming") characterized by impaired control over gaming, increasing priority given to gaming over other activities to the extent that gaming takes precedence over other interests and daily activities, and continuation or escalation of gaming despite the occurrence of negative consequences.

—The World Health Organization

Video games are bad for you? That's what they said about rock 'n' roll.

—Nintendo game designer Shigeru Miyamoto

# THE
# NEVER
# GAME

# LEVEL 3:

# THE
# SINKING
# SHIP

Sunday, June 9

Sprinting toward the sea, Colter Shaw eyed the craft closely.

The forty-foot derelict fishing vessel, decades old, was going down by the stern, already three-fourths submerged.

Shaw saw no doors into the cabin; there would be only one and it was now underwater. In the aft part of the superstructure, still above sea level, was a window facing onto the bow. The opening was large enough to climb through but it appeared sealed. He'd dive for the door.

He paused, reflecting: Did he need to?

Shaw looked for the rope mooring the boat to the pier; maybe he could take up slack and keep the ship from going under.

There was no rope; the boat was anchored, which meant it was free to descend thirty feet to the floor of the Pacific Ocean.

And, if the woman was inside, take her with it to a cold, murky grave.

As he ran onto the slippery dock, avoiding the most rotten pieces, he stripped off his bloodstained shirt, then his shoes and socks.

A powerful swell struck the ship and it shuddered and sank a few more inches into the gray, indifferent water.

He shouted, "Elizabeth?"

No response.

Shaw assessed: there was a sixty percent chance she was on board. Fifty percent chance she was alive after hours in the waterlogged cabin.

Whatever the percentages, there was no debate about what came next. He stuck an arm beneath the surface and judged the temperature to be about forty degrees. He'd have thirty minutes until he passed out from hypothermia.

Let's start the clock, he thought.

And plunges in.

An ocean isn't liquid. It's flowing stone. Crushing.

Sly too.

Shaw's intention was to wrestle open the door to the cabin, then swim out with Elizabeth Chabelle. The water had a different idea. The minute he surfaced for breath he was tossed toward one of the oak pilings, from which danced lacy flora, delicate thin green hairs. He held up a hand to brace himself as he was flung toward the wood. His palm slid off the slimy surface and his head struck the post. A burst of yellow light filled his vision.

Another wave lifted and flung him toward the pier once more. This time he was just able to avoid a rusty spike. Rather than fighting the current to return to the boat—about eight feet away—he waited for the outflow that would carry him to the vessel. An upward swell took him and this time he gigged his shoulder on the spike. It stung sharply. There'd be blood.

Sharks here?

*Never borrow trouble . . .*

The water receded. He kicked into the flow, raised his head, filled his lungs and dove, swimming hard for the door. The salty water burned his eyes but he kept them wide; the sun was low and it was dark here. He spotted what he sought, gripped the metal handle and twisted. The handle moved back and forth yet the door wouldn't open.

To the surface, more air. Back under again, holding himself down with the latch in his left hand, and feeling for other locks or securing fixtures with his right.

The shock and pain of the initial plunge had worn off, but he was shivering hard.

Ashton Shaw had taught his children how to prepare for cold-water survival—dry suit, number one. Wet suit, second choice. Two caps—heat loss is greatest through the skull, even with hair as thick as Shaw's blond locks. Ignore extremities; you don't lose heat through fingers or toes. Without protective clothing, the only solution is to get the hell out as fast as you can before hypothermia confuses, numbs and kills.

Twenty-five minutes left.

Another attempt to wrench open the door to the cabin. Another failure.

He thought of the windshield overlooking the bow deck. The only way to get her out.

Shaw stroked toward the shore and dove, seizing a rock big enough to shatter glass but not so heavy it would pull him down.

Kicking hard, rhythmically, timing his efforts to the waves, he returned to the boat, whose name he noticed was *Seas the Day*.

Shaw managed to climb the forty-five-degree incline to the bow and perch on the upward-tilting front of the cabin, resting against the murky four-by-three-foot window.

He peered inside but spotted no sign of the thirty-two-year-old brunette. He noted that the forward part of the cabin was empty. There was a bulkhead halfway toward the stern, with a door in the middle of it and a window about head height, the glass missing. If she were here, she'd be on the other side—the one now largely filled with water.

He lifted the rock, sharp end forward, and swung it against the glass, again and again.

He learned that whoever had made the vessel had fortified the forward window against wind and wave and hail. The stone didn't even chip the surface.

And Colter Shaw learned something else too.

Elizabeth Chabelle was in fact alive.

She'd heard the banging and her pale, pretty face, ringed with stringy brown hair, appeared in the window of the doorway between the two sections of the cabin.

Chabelle screamed "Help me!" so loudly that Shaw could hear her clearly though the thick glass separating them.

"Elizabeth!" he shouted. "There's help coming. Stay out of the water."

He knew the help he promised couldn't possibly arrive until after the ship was on the bottom. He was her only hope.

It might be possible for someone else to fit through the broken window inside and climb into the forward, and drier, half of the cabin.

But not Elizabeth Chabelle.

Her kidnapper had, by design or accident, chosen to abduct a woman who was seven and a half months pregnant; she couldn't possibly fit through the frame.

Chabelle disappeared to find a perch somewhere out of the freezing water and Colter Shaw lifted the rock to begin pounding on the windshield once more.

# LEVEL 1:

# THE ABANDONED FACTORY

Friday, June 7, Two Days Earlier

# 1.

He asked the woman to repeat herself.

"That thing they throw," she said. "With the burning rag in it?"

"They throw?"

"Like at riots? A bottle. You see 'em on TV."

Colter Shaw said, "A Molotov cocktail."

"Yeah, yeah," Carole was saying. "I think he had one."

"Was it burning? The rag part?"

"No. But, you know . . ."

Carole's voice was raspy, though she wasn't presently a smoker that Shaw had seen or smelled. She was draped with a green dress of limp cloth. Her natural expression seemed to be one of concern yet this morning it was more troubled than usual. "He was over there." She pointed.

The Oak View RV park, one of the scruffier that Shaw had stayed at, was ringed with trees, mostly scrub oak and pine, some dead, all dry. And thick. Hard to see "over there."

"You called the police?"

A pause. "No, if it wasn't a . . . What again?"

"Molotov cocktail."

"If he didn't have one, it'd be embarrassing. And I call the cops enough, for stuff here."

Shaw knew dozens of RV park owners around the country. Mostly couples, as it's a good gig for middle-aged marrieds. If there's just a single manager, like Carole, it was usually a she, and she was usually a widow. They tend to dial 911 for camp disputes more than their late husbands, men who often went about armed.

"On the other hand," she continued, "fire. Here. You know."

California was a tinderbox, as anybody who watched the news knew. You think of state parks and suburbs and agricultural fields; cities, though, weren't immune to nature's conflagrations. Shaw believed that one of the worst brush fires in the history of the state had been in Oakland, very near where they were now standing.

"Sometimes, I kick somebody out, they say they'll come back and get even." She added with astonishment, "Even when I caught them stealing forty amps when they paid for twenty. Some people. Really."

He asked, "And you want me to . . . ?"

"I don't know, Mr. Shaw. Just take a look. Could you take a look? Please?"

Shaw squinted through the flora and saw, maybe, motion that wasn't from the breeze. A person walking slowly? And if so, did the pace mean that he was moving tactically—that is, with some mischief in mind?

Carole's eyes were on Shaw, regarding him in a particular way. This happened with some frequency. He was a civilian, never said he was anything else. But he had cop fiber.

Shaw circled to the front of the park and walked on the cracked and uneven sidewalk, then on the grassy shoulder of the unbusy road in this unbusy corner of the city.

Yes, there was a man, in dark jacket, blue jeans and black stocking cap, some twenty yards ahead. He wore boots that could be helpful on a hike through brush and equally helpful to stomp an opponent. And, yes, either he was armed with a gas bomb or he was holding a Corona and a napkin in the same hand. Early for a beer some places; not in this part of Oakland.

Shaw slipped off the shoulder into the foliage to his right and walked more quickly, though with care to stay silent. The needles that had pitched from branch to ground in droves over the past several seasons made stealth easy.

Whoever this might be, vengeful lodger or not, he was well past Carole's cabin. So she wasn't at personal risk. But Shaw wasn't giving the guy a pass just yet.

This felt wrong.

Now the fellow was approaching the part of the RV camp where Shaw's Winnebago was parked, among many other RVs.

Shaw had more than a passing interest in Molotov cocktails. Several years ago, he'd been searching for a fugitive on the lam for an oil scam in Oklahoma when somebody pitched a gas bomb through the windshield of his camper. The craft burned to the rims in twenty minutes, personal effects saved in the nick. Shaw still carried a distinct and unpleasant scent memory of the air surrounding the metal carcass.

The percentage likelihood that Shaw would be attacked by two Russian-inspired weapons in one lifetime, let alone within several years, had to be pretty small. Shaw put it at five percent. A figure made smaller yet by the fact that he had come to the Oakland/Berkeley area on personal business, not to ruin a fugitive's life. And while Shaw had committed a transgression yesterday, the remedy for that offense would've been a verbal lashing, a confrontation with a beefy security guard or, at worst, the police. Not a firebomb.

Shaw was now only ten yards behind the man, who was scanning the area—looking into the trailer park as well as up and down the road and at several abandoned buildings across it.

The man was trim, white, with a clean-shaven face. He was about five-eight, Shaw estimated. The man's facial skin was pocked. Under the cap, his brown hair seemed to be cut short. There was a rodent-like quality to his appearance and his movements. In the man's posture Shaw read ex-military. Shaw himself was not, though he had friends and acquaintances who were, and he had spent a portion of his youth in quasi-military training, quizzed regularly on the updated *U.S. Army Survival Manual FM 21-76*.

And the man was indeed holding a Molotov cocktail. The napkin was stuffed into the neck of the bottle and Shaw could smell gasoline.

Shaw was familiar with revolver, semiautomatic pistol, semiautomatic rifle, bolt-action rifle, shotgun, bow and arrow and slingshot. And he had more than a passing interest in blades. He now withdrew from his pocket the weapon he used most frequently: his mobile, presently an iPhone. He punched some keys and, when the police and fire emergency dispatcher answered, whispered his location and what he was looking at. Then he hung up. He typed a few more commands and slipped the cell into the breast pocket of his dark plaid sport coat. He thought, with chagrin, about his transgression yesterday and wondered if the call would somehow allow the authorities to identify and collar him. This seemed unlikely.

Shaw had decided to wait for the arrival of the pros. Which is when a cigarette lighter appeared in the man's hand with no cigarette to accompany it.

That settled the matter.

Shaw stepped from the bushes and closed the distance. "Morning."

The man turned quickly, crouching. Shaw noted that he didn't reach for his belt or inside pocket. This might have been because he didn't want to drop the gas bomb—or because he wasn't armed. Or because he was a pro and knew exactly where his gun was and how many seconds it would take to draw and aim and fire.

Narrow eyes, set in a narrow face, looked Shaw over for guns and then for less weaponly threats. He took in the black jeans, black Ecco shoes, gray-striped shirt and the jacket. Short-cut blond hair lying close to his head. Rodent would have thought "cop," yet the moment for a badge to appear and an official voice to ask for ID or some such had come and gone. He had concluded that Shaw was civilian. And not one to be taken lightly. Shaw was about one-eighty, just shy of six feet, and broad, with strappy muscle. A small scar on cheek, a larger one on neck. He didn't run as a hobby but he rock-climbed and had been a champion wrestler in college. He was in scrapping shape. His eyes held Rodent's, as if tethered.

"Hey there." A tenor voice, taut like a stretched fence wire. Midwest, maybe from Minnesota.

Shaw glanced down at the bottle.

"Could be pee, not gas, don'tcha know." The man's smile was as tight as the timbre of his voice. And it was a lie.

Wondering if this'd turn into a fight. Last thing Shaw wanted. He hadn't hit anybody for a long time. Didn't like it. Liked getting hit even less.

"What's that about?" Shaw nodded at the bottle in the man's hand.

"Who are you?"

"A tourist."

"Tourist." The man debated, eyes rising and falling. "I live up the street. There's some rats in an abandoned lot next to me. I was going to burn them out."

"California? The driest June in ten years?"

Shaw had made that up but who'd know?

Not that it mattered. There was no lot and there were no rats, though the fact that the man had brought it up suggested he might have burned rats alive in the past. This was where dislike joined caution.

*Never let an animal suffer . . .*

Then Shaw was looking over the man's shoulder— toward the spot he'd been headed for. A vacant lot, true, though it was next to an old commercial building. Not the imaginary vacant lot next to the man's imaginary home.

The man's eyes narrowed further, reacting to the bleat of the approaching police car.

"Really?" Rodent grimaced, meaning: You *had* to call it in? He muttered something else too.

Shaw said, "Set it down. Now."

The man didn't. He calmly lit the gasoline-soaked rag, which churned with fire, and like a pitcher aiming for a strike, eyed Shaw keenly and flung the bomb his way.

# 2.

Molotov cocktails don't blow up—there's not enough oxygen inside a sealed bottle. The burning rag fuse ignites the spreading gas when the glass shatters.

Which this one did, efficiently and with modest spectacle.

A silent fireball rose about four feet in the air.

Shaw dodged the risk of singe and Carole ran, screaming, to her cabin. Shaw debated pursuit, but the crescent of grass on the shoulder was burning crisply and getting slowly closer to tall shrubs. He vaulted the chain-link, sprinted to his RV and retrieved one of the extinguishers. He returned, pulled the pin and blasted a whoosh of white chemical on the fire, taming it.

"Oh my God. Are you okay, Mr. Shaw?" Carole was plodding up, carrying an extinguisher of her own, a smaller, one-hand canister. Hers wasn't really necessary, yet she too pulled the grenade pin and let fly, because, of course, it's always fun. Especially when the blaze is nearly out.

After a minute or two, Shaw bent down and, with his palm, touched every square inch of the scorch, as he'd learned years ago.

*Never leave a campfire without patting the ash.*

A pointless glance after Rodent. He'd vanished.

A patrol car braked to a stop. Oakland PD. A large black officer, with a glistening, shaved head, climbed out, holding a fire extinguisher of his own. Of the three, his was the smallest. He surveyed the embers and the char and replaced the red tank under his front passenger seat.

Officer L. Addison, according to the name badge, turned to Shaw. The six-foot-five cop might get confessions just by walking up to a suspect and leaning down.

"You were the one called?" Addison asked.

"I did." Shaw explained that the person who'd thrown the cocktail had just run off. "That way." He gestured down the weedy street, handfuls of trash every few yards. "He's probably not too far away."

The cop asked what had happened.

Shaw told him. Carole supplemented, with the somewhat gratuitous addendum about the difficulty of being a widow running a business by herself. "People take advantage. I push back. I have to. You would. Sometimes they threaten you." Shaw noted she'd glanced at Addison's left hand, where no jewelry resided.

Addison cocked his head toward the Motorola mounted on his shoulder and gave Central a summary, with the description from Shaw. It had been quite detailed but he'd left out the rodent-like aspect, that being largely a matter of opinion.

Addison's eyes turned back to Shaw. "Could I see some ID?"

There are conflicting theories about what to do when the law asks for ID and you're not a suspect. This was a question Shaw often confronted, since he frequently found himself at crime scenes and places where investigations were under way. You generally didn't have to show anybody anything. In that case, you'd have to be prepared to endure the consequences of your lack of cooperation. Time is one of the world's most valuable commodities, and being pissy with cops guarantees you're going to lose big chunks of it.

His hesitation at the moment, though, was not on principle but because he was worried that his motorbike's license had been spotted at the site of yesterday's transgression. His name might therefore be in the system.

Then he recalled that they'd know him already; he'd called 911 from his personal phone, not a burner. So Shaw handed over the license.

Addison took a picture of it with his phone and uploaded the details somewhere.

Shaw noted that he didn't do the same with Carole, even though it was her trailer court that had tangentially been involved. Some minor profiling there, Shaw reflected: stranger in town versus a local. This he kept to himself.

Addison looked at the results. He eyed Shaw closely.

A reckoning for yesterday's transgression? Shaw now chose to call it what it was: theft. There's no escape in euphemism.

Apparently the gods of justice were not a posse after

him today. Addison handed the license back. "Did you recognize him?" he asked Carole.

"No, sir, but it's hard to keep track. We get a lot of people here. Lowest rates in the area."

"Did he throw the bottle at you, Mr. Shaw?"

"Toward. A diversion, not assault. So he could get away."

This gave the officer a moment's pause.

Carole blurted: "I looked it up online. Molotov secretly worked for Putin."

Both men looked at her quizzically. Then Shaw continued with the officer: "And to burn the evidence. Prints and DNA on the glass."

Addison remained thoughtful. He was the sort, common among police, whose lack of body language speaks volumes. He'd be processing why Shaw had considered forensics.

The officer said, "If he wasn't here to cause you any problem, ma'am, what was he here about, you think?"

Before Carole answered, Shaw said, "That." He pointed across the street to the vacant lot he'd noted earlier.

The trio walked toward it.

The trailer camp was in a scruffy commercial neighborhood, off Route 24, where tourists could stage before a trip to steep Grizzly Peak or neighboring Berkeley. This trash-filled, weedy lot was separated from the property behind it by an old wooden fence about eight feet tall. Local artists had used it as a canvas for some very talented artwork: portraits of Martin Luther King, Jr., Malcolm X and two other men Shaw didn't recognize. As the three got closer, Shaw saw the names printed below the pictures: Bobby Seale and Huey P. Newton, who'd been connected with the Black Panther Party. Shaw remembered cold nights in his television-free childhood home. Ashton would read to Colter and his siblings, mostly American history. Much of it about alternative forms of governance. The Black Panthers had figured in several lectures.

"So," Carole said, her mouth twisted in distaste. "A hate crime. Terrible." She added, with a nod to the paintings, "I called the city, told them they should preserve it somehow. They never called back."

Addison's radio crackled. Shaw could hear the transmission: a unit had cruised the streets nearby and seen no one fitting the description of the arsonist.

Shaw said, "I got a video."

"You did?"

"After I called nine-one-one I put the phone in my pocket." He touched the breast pocket, on the left side of his jacket. "It was recording the whole time."

"Is it recording now?"

"It is."

"Would you shut it off?" Addison asked this in a way that really meant: Shut it off. Without a question mark.

Shaw did. Then: "I'll send you a screenshot."

"Okay."

Shaw clicked the shot, got Addison's mobile number and sent the image his way. The men were four feet apart but Shaw imagined the electrons' journey took them halfway around the world.

The officer's phone chimed; he didn't bother to look at the screenshot. He gave Carole his card, one to Shaw as well. Shaw had quite the collection of cops' cards; he thought it amusing that police had business cards like advertising executives and hedge fund managers.

After Addison left, Carole said, "They're not going to do winkety, are they?"

"No."

"Well, thanks for looking into it, Mr. Shaw. I'd've felt purely horrid you'd gotten burned."

"Not a worry."

Carole returned to the cabin and Shaw to his Winnebago. He was reflecting on one aspect of the encounter he hadn't shared with Officer Addison. After the exasperated "Really?" in reference to the 911 call, Rodent's comment might have been "Why'd you do that shit?"

It was also possible—more than fifty percent—that he'd said, "Why'd you do that, Shaw?"

Which, if that had in fact happened, meant Rodent knew him or knew about him.

And that, of course, would put a whole new spin on the matter.

# 3.

I nside the Winnebago, Shaw hung his sport coat on a hook and walked to a small cupboard in the kitchen. He opened it and removed two things. The first was his compact Glock .380 pistol, which he kept hidden behind a row of spices, largely McCormick brand. The weapon was in a gray plastic Blackhawk holster. This he clipped inside his belt.

The second thing he removed was a thick 11-by-14-inch envelope, secreted on the shelf below where he kept the gun, behind condiment bottles. Worcestershire, teriyaki and a half dozen vinegars ranging from Heinz to the exotic.

He glanced outside.

No sign of Rodent. As he'd expected. Still, sometimes being armed never hurt.

He walked to the stove and boiled water and brewed a ceramic mug of coffee with a single-cup filter cone. He'd selected one of his favorites. Daterra, from Brazil. He shocked the beverage with a splash of milk.

Sitting at the banquette, he looked at the envelope, on

which were the words *Graded Exams 5/25*, in perfect, scripty handwriting, smaller even than Shaw's.

The flap was not sealed, just affixed with a flexible metal flange, which he bent open, and then he extracted from the envelope a rubber band–bound stack of sheets, close to four hundred of them.

Noting that his heart thudded from double time to triple as he stared at the pile.

These pages were the spoils of the theft Shaw had committed yesterday.

What he hoped they contained was the answer to the question that had dogged him for a decade and a half.

A sip of coffee. He began to flip through the contents.

The sheets seemed to be a random collection of musings historical, philosophical, medical and scientific, maps, photos, copies of receipts. The author's script was the same as on the front of the envelope: precise and perfectly even, as if a ruler had been used as a guide. The words were formed in a delicate combination of cursive and block printing.

Similar to how Colter Shaw wrote.

He opened to a page at random. Began to read.

> *Fifteen miles northwest of Macon on Squirrel Level Road, Holy Brethren Church. Should have a talk with minister. Good man. Rev. Harley Combs. Smart and keeps quiet when he should.*

Shaw read more passages, then stopped. A couple sips of coffee, thoughts of breakfast. Then: Go on, he chided himself. You started this, prepared to accept where it would lead. So keep going.

His mobile hummed. He glanced at the caller ID, shamefully pleased that the distraction took him away from the stolen documents.

"Teddy."

"Colt. Where am I finding you?" A baritone grumble.

"Still the Bay Area."

"Any luck?"

"Some. Maybe. Everything okay at home?" The Bruins were watching his property in Florida, which abutted theirs.

"Peachy." Not a word you hear often from a career Marine officer. Teddy Bruin and his wife, Velma, also a veteran, wore their contradictions proudly. He could picture them clearly, most likely sitting at that moment where they often sat, on the porch facing the hundred-acre lake in northern Florida. Teddy was six-two, two hundred and fifty pounds. His reddish hair was a darker version of his freckled, ruddy skin. He'd be in khaki slacks or shorts because he owned no other shade. The shirt would have flowers on it. Velma was less than half his weight, though tall herself. She'd be in jeans and work shirt, and of the two she had the cleverer tattoos.

A dog barked in the background. That would be Chase, their Rottweiler. Shaw had spent many afternoons on hikes with the solid, good-natured animal.

"We found a job close to you. Don't know if you're interested. Vel's got the details. She's coming. Ah, here."

"Colter." Unlike Teddy's, Velma's voice was softly pouring water. Shaw had told her she should record audiobooks for kids. Her voice would be like Ambien, send them right to sleep.

"Algo found a hit. That girl sniffs like a bluetick hound. What a nose."

Velma had decided that the computer bot she used (Algo, as in "algorithm") searching the internet for potential jobs for Shaw was a female. And canine as well, it seemed.

"Missing girl in Silicon Valley," she added.

"Tipline?"

Phone numbers were often set up by law enforcement or by private groups, like Crime Stoppers, so that someone, usually with inside knowledge, could call anonymously with information that might lead to a suspect. Tiplines were also called dime lines, as in "diming out the perp," or snitch lines.

Shaw had pursued tipline jobs from time to time over the years—if the crime was particularly heinous or the victims' families particularly upset. He generally avoided them because of the bureaucracy and formalities involved. Tiplines also tended to attract the troublesome.

"No. Offeror's her father." Velma added, "Ten thousand. Not much. But his notice was . . . heartfelt. He's one desperate fellow."

Teddy and Velma had been helping Shaw in his reward operation for years; they knew desperate by instinct.

"How old's the daughter?"

"Nineteen. Student."

The phone in Florida was on SPEAKER, and Teddy's raspy voice said, "We checked the news. No stories about police involvement. Her name didn't show up at all, except for the reward. So, no foul play."

The term was right out of Sherlock Holmes yet law

enforcement around the country used it frequently. The phrase was a necessary marker in deciding how police would approach a missing-person situation. With an older teen and no evidence of abduction, the cops wouldn't jump on board as they would with an obvious kidnapping. For the time being, they'd assume she was a runaway.

Her disappearance, of course, could be both. More than a few young people had been seduced away from home willingly only to find that the seducer wasn't exactly who they thought.

Or her fate might be purely accidental, her body floating in the cold, notoriously unpredictable waters of the Pacific Ocean or in a car at the bottom of a ravine a hundred feet below sidewinding Highway 1.

Shaw debated. His eyes were on the four hundred–odd sheets. "I'll go meet with the father. What's her name?"

"Sophie Mulliner. He's Frank."

"Mother?"

"No indication." Velma added, "I'll send you the particulars."

He then asked, "Any mail?"

She said, "Bills. Which I paid. Buncha coupons. Victoria's Secret catalog."

Shaw had bought Margot a present two years ago; Victoria had decided his address was no secret and delivered it unto her mailing-list minions. He hadn't thought about Margot for . . . Had it been a month? Maybe a couple of weeks. He said, "Pitch it."

"Can I keep it?" Teddy asked.

A thud, and laughter. Another thud.

Shaw thanked them and disconnected.

He rebanded the sheaf of pages. One more look outside. No Rodent.

Colter Shaw lifted open his laptop and read Velma's email. He pulled up a map to see how long it would take to get to Silicon Valley.

# 4.

As it turned out, by the estimation of some, Colter Shaw was actually in Silicon Valley at that very moment.

He'd learned that a number of people considered North Oakland and Berkeley to be within the nebulous boundaries of the mythical place. To them, Silicon Valley—apparently, "SV" to those in the know— embraced a wide swath from Berkeley on the east and San Francisco on the west all the way south to San Jose.

The definition was largely, Shaw gathered, dependent on whether a company or individual wanted to be in Silicon Valley. And most everyone did.

The loyalists, it seemed, defined the place as west of the Bay only, the epicenter being Stanford University in Palo Alto. The reward offeror's home was near the school, in Mountain View. Shaw secured the vehicle's interior for the drive, made sure his dirt bike was affixed to its frame on the rear and disconnected the hookups.

He stopped by the cabin to break the news to Carole and

a half hour later was cruising along the wide 280 freeway, with glimpses of the suburbia of Silicon Valley through the trees to his left and the lush hills of the Rancho Corral de Tierra and the placid Crystal Springs Reservoir to the west.

This area was new to him. Shaw was born in Berkeley— twenty miles away—but he retained only tatters of memories from back then. When Colter was four, Ashton had moved the family to a huge spread a hundred miles east of Fresno, in the Sierra Nevada foothills—Ashton dubbed the property the "Compound" because he thought it sounded more forbidding than "Ranch" or "Farm."

At the GPS guide's command, Shaw pulled off the freeway and made his way to the Westwinds RV Center, located in Los Altos Hills. He checked in. The soft-spoken manager was about sixty, trim, a former Navy man or Merchant Marine, if the tattoo of the anchor signified anything. He handed Shaw a map and, with a mechanical pencil, meticulously drew a line from the office to his hookup. Shaw's space would be on Google Way, accessed via Yahoo Lane and PARC Road. The name of the last avenue Shaw didn't get. He assumed it was computer-related.

He found the spot, plugged in and, with his black leather computer bag over his shoulder, returned to the office, where he summoned an Uber to take him to the small Avis rental outfit in downtown Mountain View. He picked up a sedan, requesting any full-sized that was black or navy blue, his preferred shades. In his decade of seeking rewards he'd never once misrepresented himself as a police officer, but occasionally he let the impression stand. Driving a vehicle that might be taken for a detective's undercover car occasionally loosened tongues.

On his mission over the past couple of days, Shaw had ridden his Yamaha dirt bike between Carole's RV park and Berkeley. He would ride the bike any chance he got, though only on personal business or, of course, for the joy of it. On a job he always rented a sedan or, if the terrain required, an SUV. Driving a rattling motorbike when meeting offerors, witnesses or the police would raise concerns about how professional he was. And while a thirty-foot RV was fine for highways, it was too cumbersome for tooling about congested neighborhoods.

He set the GPS to the reward offeror's house in Mountain View and pulled into the busy suburban traffic.

So, this was the heart of SV, the Olympus of high technology. The place didn't glisten the way you might expect, at least along Shaw's route. No quirky glass offices, marble mansions or herds of slinky Mercedeses, Maseratis, Beemers, Porsches. Here was a diorama of the 1970s: pleasant single-family homes, mostly ranch-style, with minuscule yards, apartment buildings that were tidy but could use a coat of paint or re-siding, mile after mile of strip malls, two- and three-story office structures. No high-rises—perhaps out of fear of earthquakes? The San Andreas Fault was directly underneath.

Silicon Valley might have been Cary, North Carolina, or Plano, Texas, or Fairfax County, Virginia—or another California valley, San Fernando, three hundred miles south and tethered to SV by the utilitarian Highway 101. This was one thing about midwifing technology, Shaw supposed: it all happens inside. Driving through Hibbing, Minnesota, you'd see the mile-deep crimson-colored iron mine. Or Gary, Indiana, the fortresses of steel mills. There were no scars of geography, no unique superstructures to define Silicon Valley.

In ten minutes he was approaching Frank Mulliner's house on Alta Vista Drive. The ranch wasn't designed by cookie cutter, though it had the same feel as the other houses on this lengthy block. Inexpensive, with wood or vinyl siding, three concrete steps to the front door, wrought-iron railings. The fancier homes had bay windows. They were all bordered by a parking strip, sidewalk and front yard. Some grass was green, some the color of straw. A number of homeowners had given up on lawns and hardscaped with pebbles and sand and low succulents.

Shaw pulled up to the pale green house, noting the FORECLOSURE SALE sign on the adjoining property. Mulliner's house was also on the market.

Knocking on the door, Shaw waited only a moment before it opened, revealing a stocky, balding man of fifty or so, wearing gray slacks and an open-collar blue dress shirt. On his feet were loafers but no socks.

"Frank Mulliner?"

The man's red-rimmed eyes glanced quickly at Shaw's clothes, the short blond hair, the sober demeanor—he rarely smiled. The bereft father would be thinking this was a detective come to deliver bad news, so Shaw introduced himself quickly.

"Oh, you're . . . You called. The reward."

"That's right."

The man's hand was chill when the two gripped palms.

With a look around the neighborhood, he nodded Shaw in.

Shaw learned a lot about offerors—and the viability,

and legitimacy, of the reward—by seeing their living spaces. He met with them in their homes if possible. Offices, if not. This gave him insights about the potential business relationship and how serious were the circumstances giving rise to the reward. Here, the smell of sour food was detectable. The tables and furniture were cluttered with bills and mail folders and tools and retail flyers. In the living room were piles of clothing. This suggested that even though Sophie had been missing for only a few days, the man was very distraught.

The shabbiness of the place was also of note. The walls and molding were scuffed, in need of painting and proper repair; the coffee table had a broken leg splinted with duct tape painted to mimic the oak color. Water stains speckled the ceiling and there was a hole above one window where a curtain rod had pulled away from the Sheetrock. This meant the ten thousand cash he was offering was hard to come by.

The two men took seats on saggy furniture encased in slack gold slipcovers. The lamps were mismatched. And the big-screen TV was not so big by today's standards.

Shaw asked, "Have you heard anything more? From the police? Sophie's friends?"

"Nothing. And her mother hasn't heard anything. She lives out of state."

"Is she on her way?"

Mulliner was silent. "She's not coming." The man's round jaw tightened and he wiped at what remained of his brown hair. "Not yet." He scanned Shaw closely. "You a private eye or something?"

"No. I earn rewards that citizens or the police've offered."

He seemed to digest this. "For a living."

"Correct."

"I've never heard of that."

Shaw gave him the pitch. True, he didn't need to win Mulliner over, as a PI seeking a new client might. But if he were going to look for Sophie, he needed information. And that meant cooperation. "I've got years of experience doing this. I've helped find dozens of missing persons. I'll investigate and try to get information that'll lead to Sophie. As soon as I do, I tell you and the police. I don't rescue people or talk them into coming home if they're runaways."

While this last sentence was not entirely accurate, Shaw felt it important to make clear exactly what he was providing. He preferred to mention rules rather than exceptions.

"If that information leads to her you pay me the reward. Right now, we'll talk some. If you don't like what you hear or see, you tell me and I won't pursue it. If there's something I don't like, I walk away."

"Far as I'm concerned, I'm sold." The man's voice choked. "You seem okay to me. You talk straight, you're calm. Not, I don't know, not like a bounty hunter on TV. Anything you can do to find Fee. Please."

"Fee."

"Her nickname. So-*fee*. What she called herself when she was a baby." He controlled the tears, though just.

"Has anybody else approached you for the reward?"

"I got plenty of calls or emails. Most of 'em anonymous. They said they'd seen her or knew what had happened. All it took was a few questions and I could tell they didn't have anything. They just wanted the money.

Somebody mentioned aliens in a spaceship. Somebody said a Russian sex-trafficking ring."

"Most people who contact you'll be that way. Looking for a fast buck. Anybody who knows her'll help you out for free. There's an off chance that you'll be contacted by somebody connected with the kidnapper—if there is a kidnapper—or by somebody who spotted her on the street. So listen to all the calls and read all the emails. Might be something helpful.

"Now, finding her is our only goal. It might take a lot of people providing information to piece her whereabouts together. Five percent here. Ten there. How that reward gets split up is between me and the other parties. You won't be out more than the ten.

"One more thing: I don't take a reward for recovery, only rescue."

The man didn't respond to this. He was kneading a bright orange golf ball. After a moment he said, "They make these things so you can play in the winter. Somebody gave me a box of them." He looked up at Shaw's unresponsive eyes. "It never snows here. Do you golf? Do you want some?"

"Mr. Mulliner, we should move fast."

"Frank."

"Fast," Shaw repeated.

The man inhaled. "Please. Help her. Find Fee for me."

"First: Are you sure she didn't run off?"

"Absolutely positive."

"How do you know?"

"Luka. That's how."

# 5.

S haw was sitting hunched over the wounded coffee
table.

Before him was a thirty-two-page, 5-by-7-inch
notebook of blank, unlined pages. In his hand was a
Delta Titanio Galassia fountain pen, black with three orange rings toward the nib. Occasionally people gave him
a look: Pretentious, aren't we? But Shaw was a relentless
scribe and the Italian pen—not cheap, at two hundred
and fifty dollars, yet hardly a luxury—was far easier on
the muscles than a ballpoint or even a rollerball. It was
the best tool for the job.

Shaw and Mulliner were not alone. Sitting beside
Shaw and breathing heavily on his thigh was the reason
that father was sure daughter had not run away: Luka.

A well-behaved white standard poodle.

"Fee wouldn't leave Luka. Impossible. If she'd run
off, she would've taken him. Or at least called to see how
he was."

There'd been dogs on the Compound, pointers for

pointing, retrievers for retrieving—and all of them for barking like mad if the uninvited arrived. Colter and Russell took their father's view that the animals were employees. Their younger sister, Dorion, on the other hand, would bewilder the animals by dressing them up in clothing she herself had stitched and she let them sleep in bed with her. Shaw now accepted Luka's presence here as evidence, though not proof, that the young woman had not run off.

Colter Shaw asked about the details of Sophie's disappearance, what the police had said when Mulliner called, about family and friends.

Writing in tiny, elegant script, perfectly horizontal on the unlined paper, Shaw set down all that was potentially helpful, ignoring the extraneous. Then, having exhausted his questions, he let the man talk. He usually got his most important information this way, finding nuggets in the rambling.

Mulliner stepped into the kitchen and returned a moment later with a handful of scraps of paper and Post-it notes containing names and numbers and addresses—in two handwritings. His and Sophie's, he confirmed. Friends' numbers, appointments, work and class schedules. Shaw transcribed the information. If it came to the police, Mulliner should have the originals.

Sophie's father had done a good job looking for his daughter. He'd put up scores of MISSING flyers. He'd contacted Sophie's boss at the software company where she worked part-time, a half dozen of her professors at the college she attended and her sports coach. He spoke to a handful of her friends, though the list was short.

"Haven't been the best of fathers," Mulliner admitted with a downcast gaze. "Sophie's mother lives out of state, like I said. I'm working a couple of jobs. It's all on me. I don't get to her events or games—she plays lacrosse—like I should." He waved a hand around the unkempt house. "She doesn't have parties here. You can see why. I don't have time to clean. And paying for a service? Forget it."

Shaw made a note of the lacrosse. The young woman could run and she'd have muscle. A competitive streak too.

Sophie'd fight—if she had the chance to fight.

"Does she often stay at friends' houses?"

"Not much now. That was a high school thing. Sometimes. But she always calls." Mulliner blinked. "I didn't offer you anything. I'm sorry. Coffee? Water?"

"No, I'm good."

Mulliner, like most people, couldn't keep his eyes off the scripty words Shaw jotted quickly in navy-blue ink.

"Your teachers taught you that? In school?"

"Yes."

In a way.

A search of her room revealed nothing helpful. It was filled with computer books, circuit boards, closetsful of outfits, makeup, concert posters, a tree for jewelry. Typical for her age. Shaw noted she was an artist, and a good one. Watercolor landscapes, bold and colorful, sat in a pile on a dresser, the paper curled from drying off the easel.

Mulliner had said she'd taken her laptop and phone with her, which Shaw had expected but was disappointed that she didn't have a second computer to browse through, though that was usually not particularly helpful. You rarely found an entry: *Brunch on Sunday, then I'm going to run away because I hate my effing parents.*

And you never have to search very hard to find the suicide note.

Shaw asked for some pictures of the young woman, in different outfits and taken from different angles. He produced ten good ones.

Mulliner sat but Shaw remained standing. Without looking through his notebook, he said, "She left at four in the afternoon, on Wednesday, two days ago, after she got home from school. Then went out for the bike ride at five-thirty and never came home. You posted an announcement of the reward early Thursday morning."

Mulliner acknowledged the timing with a tilt of his head.

"It's rare to offer a reward that soon after a disappearance—absent foul play."

"I was just . . . you know. It was devastating. I was so worried."

"I need to know everything, Frank." Shaw's blue eyes were focused on the offeror's.

Mulliner's right thumb and forefinger were kneading the orange golf ball again. His eyes were on the Post-it notes on the coffee table. He gathered them, ordered them, then stopped. "We had a fight, Fee and I. Wednesday. After she came home. A big fight."

"Tell me." Shaw spoke in a softer voice than a moment ago. He now sat.

"I did something stupid. I listed the house Wednesday and told the broker to hold off putting up the For Sale sign until I could tell Fee. The Realtor did anyway and a friend up the street saw it and called her. Fuck. I should've thought better." His damp eyes looked up. "I tried everything to avoid moving. I'm working those two jobs. I borrowed money from my ex's new husband. Think about that. I did everything I could but I just can't afford to stay. It was our family house! Fee grew up in it, and I'm going to lose it. The taxes here in the county? Jesus, crushing. I found a new place in Gilroy, south of here. A long way south. It's all I can afford. Sophie's commute to the college and her job'll be two hours. She won't see her friends much."

His laugh was bitter. "She said, 'Great, we're moving to the fucking Garlic Capital of the World.' Which it is. 'And you didn't even tell me.' I lost it. I screamed at her. How she didn't appreciate what I did. How my commute'll be even longer. She grabbed her backpack and stormed out."

Mulliner's eyes slid away from Shaw's. "I was afraid if I told you, you'd be sure she ran off, and wouldn't help."

This answered the important question: Why the premature reward offer? Which had raised concerns in Shaw's mind. Yes, Mulliner seemed truly distraught. He'd let the house go to hell. This testified to his genuine concerns about his daughter. Yet murderous spouses, business partners, siblings and, yes, even parents sometimes post a reward to give themselves the blush of innocence. And they tend to offer fast, the way Mulliner had done.

No, he wasn't completely absolved. Yet admitting the

fight, coupled with Shaw's other conclusions about the man, suggested he had nothing to do with his daughter's disappearance.

The reason for the early offer of a reward was legitimate: it would be unbearable to think that he'd been responsible for driving his daughter from the house and into the arms of a murderer or rapist or kidnapper.

Mulliner said now, his voice flat as Iowa and barely audible, "If anything happens to her . . . I'd just . . ." He stopped speaking and swallowed.

"I'll help you," Shaw said.

"Thank you!" A whisper. He now broke into real tears, racking. "I'm sorry, I'm sorry, I'm sorry . . ."

"Not a worry."

Mulliner looked at his watch. "Hell, I have to get to work. Last thing I want to do. But I can't lose this job. Please call me. Whatever you find, call me right away."

Shaw capped his pen and replaced it in his jacket pocket and rose, closing the notebook. He saw himself out.

# 6.

I n assessing how to proceed in pursuing a reward—or, for that matter, with most decisions in life—Colter Shaw followed his father's advice.

"Countering a threat, approaching a task, you assess the odds of each eventuality, look at the most likely one first and then come up with a suitable strategy."

The likelihood that you can outrun a forest fire sweeping uphill on a windy day: ten percent. The likelihood you can survive by starting a firebreak and lying in the ashes while the fire burns past you: eighty percent.

Ashton Shaw: "The odds of surviving a blizzard in the high mountains. If you hike out: thirty percent. If you shelter in a cave: eighty percent."

"Unless," eight-year-old Dorion, always the practical one, had pointed out, "there's a momma grizzly bear with her cubs inside."

"That's right, Button. Then your odds go down to really, really tiny. Though here it'd be a black bear. Grizzlies are extinct in California."

Shaw was now sitting in his Chevy outside the Mulliners' residence, notebook on lap, computer open beside him. He was juggling percentages of Sophie's fate.

While he hadn't told Mulliner, he believed the highest percentage was that she was dead.

He gave it sixty percent. Most likely murdered by a serial killer, rapist or a gang wannabe as part of an initiation (the Bay Area crews were among the most vicious in the nation). A slightly less likely cause of death was that she had been killed in an accident, her bike nudged off the road by a drunk or texting driver, who'd fled.

That number, of course, left a significant percentage likelihood that she was alive—taken at the hands of a kidnapper for ransom or sex, or pissed at Dad about the move and, the Luka poodle factor notwithstanding, was crashing on a friend's couch for a few days, to make him sweat.

Shaw turned to his computer—when on a job he subscribed to local news feeds and scanned for stories that might be helpful. Now he was looking for the discovery of unidentified bodies of women who might be Sophie (none) or reports over the past few weeks of serial kidnappers or killers (several incidents, but the perpetrator was preying on African American prostitutes in the Tenderloin of San Francisco). He expanded his search around the entire northern California area and found nothing relevant.

He skimmed his notes regarding what Frank Mulliner had told him, following his own search for the girl Wednesday night and yesterday. He'd called as many friends, fellow students and coworkers whose names he could find. Mulliner had told Shaw that his daughter had not been the target of a stalker that any of them knew of.

"There is someone you ought to know about, though."

That someone was Sophie's former boyfriend. Kyle Butler was twenty, also a student, though at a different college. Sophie and Kyle had broken up, Mulliner believed, about a month ago. They'd dated off and on for a year and it had become serious only in early spring. While he didn't know why they split he was pleased.

Shaw's note: *Mulliner: KB didn't treat Sophie the way she should be treated. Disrespectful, said mean things. No violence. KB did have a temper and was impulsive. Also, into drugs. Pot mostly.*

Mulliner had no picture of the boy—and Sophie had apparently purged her room of his image—but Shaw had found a number on Facebook. Kyle was a solidly built, tanned young man with a nest of curly blond hair atop his Greek god head. His social media profile was devoted to heavy metal music, surfing and legalizing drugs. Mulliner believed he worked part-time installing car stereos.

*Mulliner: No idea what Sophie saw in him. Believed maybe Sophie thought herself unattractive, a "geek girl," and he was a handsome, cool surfer dude.*

Her father reported that the boy hadn't taken the breakup well and his behavior grew inappropriate. One day he called thirty-two times. After she blocked his number, Sophie found him on their front yard, sobbing and begging to be taken back. Eventually he calmed down and they flopped into a truce. They'd meet for coffee occasionally. They went to a play "as friends." Kyle hadn't pushed hard for reconciliation, though Sophie told her father he wanted desperately to get back to-gether.

Domestic kidnappings almost always are parental ab-ductions. (Solving one such snatching, on a whim, in fact, had started Shaw on his career as a reward seeker.) Occasionally, though, a former husband or boyfriend would spirit away the woman of his passion.

Love, Colter Shaw had learned, could be an endlessly refillable prescription of madness.

Shaw put Kyle's guilt at ten percent. He might have been obsessed with Sophie, but he also seemed too nor-mal and weepy to turn dark. However, the kid's drug use was a concern. Had Kyle inadvertently jeopardized her life by introducing her to a dealer who didn't want to be identified? Had she witnessed a hit or other crime, maybe not even knowing it?

He gave this hypothesis twenty percent.

Shaw called the boy's number. No answer. His mes-sage, in his best cop voice, was that he had just spoken to Frank Mulliner and wanted to talk to Kyle about Sophie. He left the number of one of his half dozen active burn-ers, with the caller ID showing Washington, D.C. Kyle might be thinking FBI or, for all Shaw knew, the Na-tional Missing Ex-girlfriend Tactical Rescue Operation, or some such.

Shaw then cruised the three miles to Palo Alto, where he found the boy's beige-and-orange cinder-block apart-ment complex. The doors were, inexplicably, baby blue. At 3B, he pounded on the door, rather than using the ringer, which he doubted worked anyway, and called out, "Kyle Butler. Open the door."

Cop-like, yet not cop.

No response, and he didn't think the boy was dodging him, since a glance through the unevenly stained curtain showed not a flicker of movement inside.

He left one of his business cards in the door crack. It gave only his name and the burner number. He wrote: *I need to talk to you about Sophie. Call me.*

Shaw returned to his car and sent Kyle's picture, address and phone number to his private investigator, Mack, requesting background, criminal and weapons checks. Some information he wanted was not public but Mack rarely differentiated between what was public and what was not.

Shaw skimmed the notebook once more and fired up the engine, pulling into traffic. He'd decided where the next step of the investigation would take him.

Lunch.

# 7.

Colter Shaw walked through the door of the Quick Byte Café in Mountain View.

This was where Sophie had been at about 6 p.m. on Wednesday—just before she disappeared.

On Thursday, Mulliner had stopped in here, asking about his daughter. He'd had no luck but had convinced the manager to put up a MISSING flyer on a corkboard, where it now was pinned beside cards for painters, guitar and yoga instruction and three other MISSING announcements—two dogs and a parrot.

Shaw was surveying the place and smelling the aroma of hot grease, wilty onions, bacon and batter (BREAKFAST SERVED ALL DAY).

The Quick Byte, EST. 1968, couldn't decide if it wanted to be a bar, a restaurant or a coffee shop, so it opted to be all three.

It might also function as a computer showroom, since most of the patrons were hunched over laptops.

The front was spattered plate glass, facing a busy commercial Silicon Valley street. The walls were of dark paneling and the floor uneven wood. In the rear, backless stools sat in front of the dim bar, which was presently unmanned. Not surprising, given the hour—11:30 a.m.—though the patrons didn't seem the alcohol-drinking sort; they exuded geek. Lots of stocking caps, baggy sweats, Crocs. The majority were white, followed by East Asian and then South Asian. There were two black patrons, a couple. The median age in the place was about twenty-five.

The walls were lined with black-and-white and color photographs of computers and related artifacts from the early days of tech: vacuum tubes, six-foot-high metal racks of wires and square gray components, oscilloscopes, cumbersome keyboards. Display cards beneath the images gave the history of the devices. One was called Babbage's Analytical Engine—a computer powered by steam, one hundred and fifty years old.

Shaw approached the ORDER HERE station. He asked for green huevos rancheros and a coffee with cream. Cornbread instead of tortilla chips. The skinny young man behind the counter handed him the coffee and a wire metal stand with a numbered card, 97, stuck in the round spiral on top.

Shaw picked a table near the front door and sat, sipping coffee and scanning the place.

The unbusy kitchen served up the food quickly and the waitress, a pretty young woman, inked and studded, brought the order. Shaw ate quickly, half the dish. Though it was quite good and he was hungry, the eggs were really just a passport to give him legitimacy here.

On the table he spread out the pictures of Sophie that her father had given him. He took a shot of them with his iPhone, which he then emailed to himself. He logged on to his computer, through a secure jetpack, opened the messages and loaded the images onto the screen. He positioned the laptop so that anyone entering or leaving the café could see the screen with its montage of the young woman.

Coffee in hand, he wandered to the Wall of Fame and, like a curious tourist, began reading. Shaw used computers and the internet extensively in the reward business and, at another time, he would have found the history of high technology interesting. Now, though, he was concentrating on watching his computer in the reflection in the display case glass.

Since Shaw had no legal authority whatsoever, he was present here by the establishment's grace. Occasionally, if the circumstances were right and the situation urgent, he'd canvass patrons. Sometimes he got a lead or two. More frequently he was ignored or, occasionally, asked to leave.

So he often did what he was doing now: fishing.

The computer, with its bright pictures of Sophie, was bait. As people glanced at the photos, Shaw would watch them. Did anyone pay particular attention to the screen? Did their face register recognition? Concern? Curiosity? Panic? Did they look around to see whose computer it was?

He observed a few curious glances at the laptop screen but they weren't curious enough to raise suspicion.

Shaw could get away with studying the wall for about five minutes before it looked odd, so he bought time by pulling out his mobile and having an imaginary conver-

sation. This was good for another four minutes. Then he
ran out of fake and returned to his seat. Probably fifteen
people had seen the pictures and the reactions were all
blasé.

He sat at the table, sipping coffee and reading texts
and emails on his phone. The computer was still open for
all to see. There were no tugs on the fishing line. He
returned to the ORDER HERE counter, now staffed by a
woman in her thirties, a decade removed from the waitress who had served him but with similar facial bones.
Sisters, he guessed.

She was barking orders and Shaw took her to be the
manager or owner.

"Help you? Your eggs okay?" The voice was a pleasant
alto.

"They were good. Question: That woman on the bulletin board?"

"Oh, yeah. Her father came in. Sad."

"It is. I'm helping him out, looking for her."

A statement as true as rain. He tended not to mention
rewards unless the subject came up.

"That's good of you."

"Any customers say anything about her?"

"Not to me. I can ask people who work here. Anybody knows anything, I'll call you. You have a card?"

He gave her one. "Thanks. He's anxious to find her."

The woman said, "Sophie. Always liked that name. It
says 'student.' The flyer does."

Shaw said, "She's at Concordia. Business. And codes
part-time at GenSys. According to her father, she's good
at it. I wouldn't know a software program if it bit me."

Colter Shaw was quiet by nature, yet when working a job he intentionally rambled. He'd found that this put people at ease.

The woman added, "And I like what you called her."

"What was that?"

"*Woman*. Not *girl*. She looks young and most people would've called her girl." She glanced toward the waitress, willowy and in baggy brown jeans and a cream-colored blouse. She nodded the server over.

"This's my daughter, Madge," the manager said.

Oh. Not sister.

"And I'm Tiffany." Mom read the card. "Colter." She extended a hand and they shook.

"That's a name?" Madge said.

"Says so right here." Tiffany flicked the card. "He's helping find that missing woman."

Madge said, "Oh, girl on the poster?"

Tiffany gave a wry glance toward Shaw.

*Girl . . .*

Madge said, "I saw her pictures on your computer. I wondered if you were a policeman or something?"

"No. Just helping her dad. We think this is the last place she was at before she disappeared."

The daughter's face tightened. "God. What do you think happened?"

"We don't know yet."

"I'll check inside," said Tiffany, the mother—the generation-bending names of the women were disorienting. He watched her collect the flyer from the corkboard and disappear into the kitchen, where, presumably, it was displayed to cooks and busboys.

She returned, pinning up the flyer once more. "Nothing. There's a second shift. I'll make sure they see it." She sounded as if she definitely would, Shaw thought. He was lucky to have found a mother, and one close to her child. She'd sympathize more with the parent of missing offspring.

Shaw thanked her. "You mind if I ask your customers if they've seen her?"

The woman seemed troubled and Shaw suspected she wouldn't want to bother clientele with unpleasant news.

That wasn't the reason for the frown, however. Tiffany said, "Don't you want to look at the security video first?"

# 8.

Well. This was interesting news. Shaw had looked for cameras when he'd first walked in but had seen none. "You've got one?"

Tiffany turned her bright blue eyes away from Shaw's face and pointed to a small round object in the liquor bottles behind the bar.

A hidden security camera in a commercial establishment was pointless, since the main purpose was deterrence. Maybe they were getting . . .

Tiffany said, "We're getting a new system put in. I brought mine from home for the time being. Just so we'd have something." She turned to Madge and asked the young woman to show Sophie's picture to customers. "Sure, Mom." The waitress took the flyer and started on her canvass.

Tiffany directed Shaw into the cluttered office. She said, "I would've told her father about the tape but I wasn't here when he brought the poster in. Didn't think about it again. Not till you showed up. Have a seat."

With a hand on his shoulder, Tiffany guided Shaw into an unsteady desk chair in front of a fiberboard table, on which sat stacks of paper and an old desktop computer. Bending down, her arm against his, she began to type. "When?"

"Wednesday. Start at five p.m. and go from there."

Tiffany's fingers, tipped in lengthy black-polished nails, typed expertly. Within seconds a video appeared. It was clearer than most security cams, largely because it wasn't the more common wide-angle lens, which encompass a broader field of view yet distort the image. Shaw could see the order station, the cash register, the front portion of the Quick Byte and a bit of the street beyond.

Tiffany scrubbed the timeline from the moment Shaw had requested. On the screen patrons raced to and from the counter, like zipping flies.

Shaw said, "Stop. Back up. Three minutes."

Tiffany did. Then hit PLAY.

Shaw said, "There."

Outside the café Sophie's bike approached from the left. The rider had to be the young woman: the color of the bike, helmet, clothes and backpack were as Mulliner had described. Sophie did something Shaw had never seen a cyclist do. While still in motion she swung her left leg over the frame, leaving her right foot on the pedal. She glided forward, standing on that foot, perfectly balanced. Just before stopping, she hopped off. A choreographed dismount.

Sophie went through the ritual of affixing the bike to a lamppost with an impressive lock and a thick black wire. She pulled off her red almond-shell helmet and entered the Quick Byte and looked around. Shaw had hoped she might wave to somebody whom a staff member or patron could identify. She didn't. She stepped out of sight, to the left. She returned a moment later and ordered.

On the silent tape—older security systems generally didn't waste storage space or transmission bandwidth with audio—the young woman took a mug of coffee and one of the chrome number-card holders. Shaw could see her long face was unsmiling, grim.

"Pause, please."

Tiffany did.

"Did you serve her?"

"No, it would have been Aaron working then."

"Is he here?"

"No, he's off today."

Shaw asked Tiffany to take a shot of Sophie on her phone, send it to Aaron and see if he recalled anything about her, what she said, who she talked to.

She sent the shot to the employee, with the whooshing sound of an outgoing text.

Shaw was about to ask her to call him, when her phone chimed. She looked at the screen. "No, he doesn't remember her."

On the video Sophie vanished from sight again.

Shaw then noticed somebody come into view outside. He, or she, was of medium build and wearing baggy dark sweats, running shoes, a windbreaker and a gray stocking cap, pulled low. Sunglasses. Always damn sunglasses.

This person looked up and down the street and stepped closer to Sophie's bike and crouched quickly, maybe to tie a shoelace.

Or not.

The behavior earned Shaw's assessment that it was possibly the kidnapper. Male, female, he couldn't tell. So Shaw bestowed the gender-neutral nickname, Person X.

"What's he doing?" Tiffany asked in a whisper.

Sabotage? Putting a tracking device on it?

Shaw thought: Come in, order something.

He knew that wouldn't happen.

X straightened, turned back in the direction he had come and walked quickly away.

"Should I fast-forward?" Tiffany asked.

"No. Let it run. Regular speed."

Patrons came and went. Servers delivered and bused dishes.

As they watched the people and drivers stream past, Tiffany asked, "You live here?"

"Florida, some of the time."

"Disney?"

"Not all that close. And I'm not there very often."

Florida, he meant. As for Disney, not at all.

She might have said something else but his attention was on the video. At 6:16:33, Sophie left the Quick Byte. She walked to her bike. Then remained standing, perfectly still, looking out across the street, toward a place where there was nothing to look at: a storefront with a sun-bleached FOR LEASE sign in the window. Shaw noted one hand absently tightening into a fist, then relaxing, then tightening again. Her helmet slipped from the other and bounced on the ground. She bent fast to collect and pull it over her head—angrily, it seemed.

Sophie freed her bike and, unlike the elegant dismount,

now leapt into the seat and pedaled hard, to the right, out of sight.

Staring at the screen, Shaw was looking at passing cars, his eyes swiveling left to right—in the direction Sophie'd headed. It was, however, almost impossible to see inside the vehicles. If stocking-capped, sunglasses-wearing Person X was driving one, he couldn't see.

Shaw asked Tiffany to send this portion of the tape, depicting X, to his email. She did.

Together they walked from the office into the restaurant proper and made their way back to the table. Madge, the daughter with the mother name, told him that no one she'd showed the picture to had seen the girl. She added, "And nobody looked weird when I asked."

"Appreciate it."

His phone sang quietly and he glanced at the screen. Mack's research into Kyle Butler, Sophie's ex-boyfriend, revealed two misdemeanor drug convictions. No history of violence. No warrants. He acknowledged the info, then signed off.

Shaw finished his coffee.

"Refill? Get you anything else? On the house."

"I'm good."

"Sorry we couldn't help you more."

Shaw thanked her. And didn't add that the trip to the Quick Byte had told him exactly where he needed to go now.

# 9.

Colter Shaw, fifteen, is making a lean-to in the north-west quadrant of the Compound, beside a dry creek bed, at the foot of a sheer cliff face, a hundred feet high.

The lean-to is in the style of a Finnish *laavu*. The Scandinavians are fond of these temporary structures, which are found commonly on hunting and fishing grounds. Colter knows this only because his father told him. The boy has never been outside California or Oregon or Washington State.

He's arranged pine boughs on the sloping roof and is now collecting moss to provide insulation. The campfire must remain outside.

A gunshot startles him. It's from a rifle, the sound being chestier than the crack of a pistol.

The weapon was fired on Shaw property because it could not have been fired anywhere else; Ashton and Mary Dove Shaw own nearly a thousand acres, and from here it's more than a mile's hike to the property line.

Colter pulls an orange hunting vest from his back-pack, dons the garment and walks in the direction of the shot.

About a hundred yards along, he's startled when a buck, a small one, sprints past, blood on its rear leg. Colter's eyes follow it as it gallops north. Then the boy continues in the direction the animal came from. He soon finds the hunter, alone, hiking deeper into the Shaw property. He doesn't see or hear Colter approach. The boy studies him.

The broad man, of pale complexion, is wearing cam-ouflage overalls and a brimmed cap, also camo, over what seems to be a crew-cut scalp. The outfit seems new and the boots are not scuffed. The man is not protected with an orange vest, which is a hugely bad idea in thick woods, where hunters themselves can be mistaken for game or, more likely, bush. The vests don't alert deer to your presence; the animals are sensitive to the color blue, not orange.

The man wears a small backpack and, on his canvas belt, a water bottle and extra magazines for his rifle. The gun is a curious choice for hunting: one of those black, stubby weapons considered assault rifles. They're illegal in California, with a few exceptions. His is a Bushmaster, chambered for a .223 bullet—a smaller round than is usually chosen for deer hunting and never used for big-ger game. The shorter barrel also means it is less accurate at a distance. These guns are semiautomatics, firing each time the trigger is pulled; that aspect is perfectly legal for hunting, but Colter's mother, the marksman in the fam-ily, has taught the children to hunt only with bolt-action rifles. Mary Dove's thinking is that if you can't drop your target fast with a single shot you (a) haven't worked hard enough to get closer or (b) have no business hunting in the first place.

And, also odd, the Bushmaster isn't equipped with a scope. Using iron sights to hunt? Either he's an amateur's amateur or one hell of a shot. Then Colter reflects: he only wounded the deer. There's the answer.

"Sir, excuse me." Colter's voice—even then, a smooth baritone—startles the man.

He turns, his clean-shaven face contracting with suspicion. He scans the teenager. Colter is the same height then as now, though slimmer; he won't put on bulking muscle until college and the wrestling team. The jeans, sweatshirt, serious boots and gloves—the September day is cool—suggest the boy is just a hiker. Despite the vest, he can't be a hunter, as he has no weapon.

Colter is teased frequently by his sister for never smiling, yet his expression is usually affable, as it is now.

Still, the man keeps his hand on the pistol grip of the .223. His finger is extended, parallel to the barrel and not on the trigger. This tells Colter there is a bullet in the chamber and that the hunter is familiar with weapons, if not the fine art of hunting. Maybe he was a soldier at one time.

"How you doing?" Colter asks, looking the man straight in the eye.

"Okay." A high voice. Crackly.

"This is our property, sir. There's no hunting. It's posted." Always polite. Ashton has taught the children all aspects of survival, from how to tell poisoned berries from safe, to how to stymie bears, to how to defuse potential conflicts.

*Never antagonize beast or man . . .*

"Didn't see any signs." Cold, cold dark eyes.

Colter says, "Understood. It's a lot of land. But it is ours and there's no hunting."

"Your dad around?"

"Not nearby."

"What's your name?"

Ashton taught the children that adults have to earn your respect. Colter says nothing.

The man tilts his head. He's pissed off. He asks, "Well, where *can* I hunt?"

"You're a mile onto our land. You would've parked off Wickham Road. Take it east five miles. That's all public forest."

"You own all this?"

"We do."

"You're kind of like a *Deliverance* family, aren't you? You play banjo?"

Colter doesn't understand; he would later.

"I'll head off then."

"Wait."

The man stops, turning back.

Colter's confused. "You're going after that buck, aren't you?"

The man gives a look of surprise. "What?"

"That buck. He's wounded." Even if the man is inexperienced, everyone knows this.

The hunter says, "Oh, I hit something? There was just a noise in the bushes. I thought it was a wolf."

Colter doesn't know how to respond to this bizarre comment.

"Wolves hunt at dusk and night," he says.

"Yeah? I didn't know that."

And pulling a trigger without a sure target?

"Anyway, sir. There's a wounded buck. You've got to find him. Put him down."

He laughs. "What is this? I mean, who're you to lecture me?"

The teenager guesses that this man, with his ignorance and the little-worn outfit, had been asked to go hunting with friends and, never having been, wanted to practice so he wouldn't be embarrassed.

"I'll help you," Colter offers. "But we can't let it go."

"Why?"

"A wounded animal, you track it down. You don't let it suffer."

"Suffer," the man whispers. "It's a deer. Who cares?"

*Never kill an animal but for three reasons: for food or hide, for defense, for mercy.*

Colter's father has given the children a lengthy list of rules, most of them commencing with the negative. Colter and his older brother, Russell, who call their father the King of Never, once asked why he didn't express his philosophy of life with "always." Ashton answered, "Gets your attention better."

"Come on," Colter says. "I'll help. I can cut sign pretty well."

"Don't push me, kid."

At that point the muzzle of the Bushmaster strays very slightly toward Colter.

The young man's belly tightens. Colter and his siblings practice self-defense frequently: grappling, wrestling, knives, firearms. But he's never been in a real fight. Home-schooling effectively eliminates the possibility of bullies.

He thinks, Stupid gesture by a stupid man.

And stupid, Colter knows, can be a lot more dangerous than smart.

"So what kind of father you have that lets his son mouth off like you do?"

The muzzle swings a few degrees closer. The man certainly doesn't want to kill, but his pride has been thumped like a melon and that means he may shoot off a round in Shaw's direction to send him rabbit-scurrying. Bullets, though, have a habit of ending up in places where you don't intend them to go.

In one second, possibly less, Colter draws the old Colt Python revolver from a holster in his back waistband and points it downward, to the side.

*Never aim at your target until you're prepared to pull the trigger or release the arrow.*

The man's eyes grow wide. He freezes.

At this moment Colter Shaw is struck with a realization that should be shocking yet is more like flicking on a lamp, casting light on a previously dark place. He is looking at a human being in the same way he looks at an elk that will be that night's dinner or at a wolf pack leader who wishes to make Colter the main course.

He is considering the threat, assigning percentages and considering how to kill if the unfortunate ten percent option comes to pass. He is as calm and cold as the pseudo-hunter's dark brown eyes.

The man remains absolutely still. He'll know that the teenager is a fine shot—from the way he handles the .357 Magnum pistol—and that the boy can get a shot off first.

"Sir, could you please drop that magazine and un-chamber the round inside." His eyes never leave the intruder's because eyes signal next moves.

"Are you threatening me? I can call the police."

"Roy Blanche up in White Sulphur Springs'd be happy to talk to you, sir. Both of us in fact."

The man turns slightly, profile, a shooter's stance. The ten percent becomes twenty percent. Colter cocks the Python, muzzle still down. This changes the gun to single-action, which means that when he aims and fires, the trigger pull will be lighter and the shot more accurate. The man is thirty feet away. Colter has hit pie tins, center, at this distance.

A pause, then the man drops the magazine—with the push of a button, which means it is definitely an illegal weapon in California, where the law requires the use of a tool to change mags on semiauto rifles. He pulls the slide and a long, shiny bullet flies out. He scoops up the magazine but leaves the single.

"I'll take care of that deer," Colter says, heart slamming hard now. "If you could leave our property, sir."

"Oh, you bet I'll leave, asshole. You can figure on me being back."

"Yessir. We will figure on that."

The man turns and stalks off.

Colter follows him—silently, the man never knows he's being tailed—for a mile and a half, until he gets to a parking lot beside a river popular with white-water rafters. He tosses his weapon into the back of a big black SUV and speeds away.

Then, intruder gone, Colter Shaw gets down to work.

*You're the best tracker of the family, Colter. You can find where a sparrow breathed on a blade of grass . . .*

He starts off in search of the wounded animal.

*For mercy . . .*

There isn't much blood trail and the ground on this part of the property is mostly pine-needle-covered, where it isn't rock; hoof tracks are nearly impossible to see. The classic tried-and-true techniques for sign cutting won't work. But the boy doesn't need them. You can also track with your mind, anticipating where your prey will go.

A wounded animal will seek one of two things: a place to die or a place to heal.

The latter means water.

Colter makes his way, silently again, toward a small pond named—by Dorion, when she was five—Egg Lake, because that's the shape. It's the only body of water nearby. Deer's noses—which have olfactory sensors on the outside as well as within—are ten thousand times more sensitive than humans'. The buck will know exactly where the lake is from the molecules off-gassed by minerals unique to pond water, the crap of amphibians and fish, the algae, the mud, the rotting leaves and branches, the remains of frogs left on the shore by owls and hawks.

Three hundred yards on, he locates the creature, blood on its leg, head down, sipping, sipping.

Colter draws the pistol and moves forward silently.

---

And Sophie Mulliner?

Like the buck, she too would want solace, comfort, after her wounding—her father's decision to move and the hard words fired at her through the smoke of anger. He recalled on the video: the young woman standing with shoulders arched, hand clenching and unclenching. The fury at the fallen helmet.

And her Egg Lake?

Cycling.

Her father had said as much when Shaw had interviewed him. Shaw recalled too the horseman's elegant dismount as Sophie pulled up to the Quick Byte, and the powerful, determined lunge as she sped away from the café, feet jamming down on the pedals in fury.

Taking comfort in the balance, the drive, the speed.

Shaw assessed that she'd gone for the damn hardest bike ride she could.

Sitting in the front seat of the Malibu, he opened his laptop bag and extracted a Rand McNally folding map of the San Francisco Bay Area. He carried with him in the Winnebago a hundred or so of these, covering most of the United States, Canada and Mexico. Maps, to Colter Shaw, were magic. He collected them—modern, old and ancient; the majority of the decorations in his house in Florida were framed maps. He preferred paper to digital, in the same way he'd choose a hardcover to an ebook; he was convinced the experience of paper was richer.

On a job, Shaw made maps himself—of the most important locations he'd been to during the investigation. These he studied, looking for clues that might not be obvious at first but that slowly rise to prominence. He had quite a collection of them.

He quickly oriented himself, outside the Quick Byte Café, in the middle of Mountain View.

Sophie's launch had been to the north. With a finger he followed a hypothetical route in that direction, past the 101 freeway and toward the Bay. Of course, she might have turned toward any compass point, at any time. Shaw saw, though, that if she continued more or less north she would have come to a large rectangle of green: San Miguel Park, two miles from the café. He reasoned that Sophie would pick a place like that because she could shred furiously up and down the trail, not having to worry about traffic.

Was the park, however, a place where one could bike? Paper had served its purpose; time for the twenty-first century. Shaw called up Google Earth (appropriately, since the park was only a few miles from the company's headquarters). He saw from the satellite images that San Miguel was interlaced with brown-dirt or sand trails and was hilly—perfect for cycling.

Shaw started the Malibu and headed for the place, wondering what he'd find.

Maybe nothing.

Maybe cyclist friends who'd say, "Oh, Sophie? Yeah, she was here Wednesday. She left. Headed west on Alvarado. Don't know where she was going. Sorry."

Or: "Oh, Sophie? Yeah, she was here Wednesday.

Pissed at her dad about something. She was going to her friend Jane's for a few days. Kind of sticking it to him for being a prick. She said she'd be home Sunday."

After all, happy endings *do* occur.

As with the buck at Egg Lake.

It turned out that the fast but thin bullet had zipped into and out of the deer's haunch with no bone damage and had largely cauterized the wound.

Standing ten feet from the oblivious, drinking animal, Colter had replaced the pistol in his holster and withdrawn from his backpack the pint bottle of Betadine disinfectant he and his siblings kept with them. Holding his breath, he stepped in utter silence to within a yard of the deer and stopped. The creature's head jerked up, alerted by a few molecules of alien scent. The boy aimed the nozzle carefully and squirted a stream of the ruddy-brown antiseptic onto the buck's wound, sending the animal two feet into the air, straight up. Then it zipped out of sight like a cartoon creature. Colter had had to laugh.

And you, Sophie? Shaw now thought as he approached the park. Was this a place for you to heal? Or a place for you to die?

# 10.

San Miguel Park was divided evenly, forest and field, and crisscrossed by dry culverts and streambeds, as well as the paths that Shaw had seen thanks to the mappers of Google. In person, he observed they were packed dirt, not sand. Perfect for hard biking: both Sophie's muscular variety and his own preferred petrol.

Owing to the drought, the place was not the verdant green that Rand McNally had promised, but was largely brown and beige and dusty.

The main entrance was on the opposite side of the park but Sophie's route would have brought her here, to the bike paths off the broad shoulder of Tamyen Road. While not familiar with the area, he knew the avenue's name. Hundreds of years ago the Tamyen, a tribe of Ohlone native people, had lived in what was now Silicon Valley. Their lands had been lost in a familiar yet particularly shameful episode of genocide—not at the hands of the conquistadors but by local officials after California achieved statehood.

Shaw's mother, Mary Dove Shaw, believed an ancestor to be an Ohlone elder.

He killed the engine. Here were two openings in the line of brush and shrubbery that separated the shoulder from the park proper. The gaps led down a steep hill to trails, imprinted with many footprints and tire tread marks.

Climbing from the car, Shaw surveyed the expansive park. He heard a sound he knew well. The whine of dirt bikes, a particular pitch that gets under the skin of some but to others—Shaw, for one—is a siren's song. Motorbiking was illegal here, a sign sternly warned. If he hadn't been on a job, though, Shaw'd have had his Yamaha off the rack in sixty seconds and on the trails in ninety.

So: One, assume kidnapping. Two, assume it was Person X, in the gray stocking cap and sunglasses. Three, assume X put a tracker on Sophie's bike and followed her.

How would it have gone down?

X would snatch her here, before she got too far into the park. He'd worry about witnesses, of course, though the area around Tamyen Road wasn't heavily populated. Shaw had passed a few companies, small fabricators or delivery services. But the buildings had no view of the shoulder. There was little traffic.

The scenario? X spots her. Then what? How would he have approached? Asking for directions?

No, a nineteen-year-old honors student and employee of a tech company wouldn't fall for that, not in the age of GPS. Exchanging pleasantries to get close to her? That too didn't seem likely. X would see she was strong and athletic and probably suspicious of a stranger's approach. And she could zip into the park, away from him, at twenty miles an hour. Shaw decided there'd be no ruse, nothing subtle. X would simply strike fast before Sophie sensed she was a target.

He began walking along the edge of the shoulder nearest the park. He spotted a tiny bit of red. In the grass between the two trail entrances was a triangular shard of plastic—that could easily have come from the reflector on a bike. With a Kleenex he collected the triangle and put it in his pocket. On his phone he found the screen-shot of Sophie's bike outside the Quick Byte—lifted from Tiffany's security camera video. Yes, it had a red disk reflector on the rear.

Made sense. X had followed Sophie here and—the moment the road was free of traffic—he'd slammed into the back of her bike. She'd have tumbled to the ground and he'd have been on her in an instant, taping her mouth and hands and feet. Into the trunk with her bike and backpack.

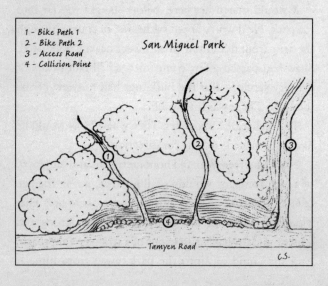

1 - Bike Path 1
2 - Bike Path 2
3 - Access Road
4 - Collision Point

San Miguel Park

Tamyen Road

C.S.

Some brush had been trampled near the plastic shard. He stepped off the shoulder and peered down the hill. He could see a line of disturbed grass leading directly from where he was standing to the bottom of a small ravine. Maybe the plan hadn't gone quite as X had hoped. Maybe he'd struck Sophie's bike too hard, knocking her over the edge, and she'd tumbled down the forty-five-degree slope.

Shaw strode down one path to the place where she would have landed. He crouched. Broken and bent grass, and gouges in the dirt that might have come from a scuffle. Then he spotted a rock the size of a grapefruit. There with a smear on it: brown, the shade of dried blood.

Shaw pulled out his phone and dialed a number he'd programmed in several hours ago. He hit CALL. About ten feet up the hill came a soft sound, repeated every few seconds. It was the Samsung whistling ringtone.

The phone number he'd dialed was Sophie's.

# 11.

Now, time for the experts.

Shaw called Frank Mulliner and told him what he'd found. The man greeted the news with a gasp.

"Those sons of bitches!"

Shaw didn't understand at first. Then he realized Mulliner was referring to the police.

"If they'd gotten on board when they should have . . . I'm calling them now!"

Shaw foresaw disaster: a rampaging parent. He'd seen this before. "Let me handle it."

"But—"

"Let me handle it."

Mulliner was silent for a moment. Shaw imagined the man's mobile was gripped in white, trembling fingers. "All right," Sophie's father said. "I'm heading home."

Shaw got the names of the detectives whom Mulliner had first spoken to about Sophie's disappearance: Wiley and Standish of the Joint Major Crimes Task Force, based in nearby Santa Clara.

After disconnecting with Mulliner, Shaw called the JMCTF's main number and asked for either of them. The prim-voiced desk officer, if that was her job title, said they were both out. Shaw said it was an emergency.

"You should call nine-one-one."

"This is a development in a case Detectives Standish and Wiley are involved in."

"Which case?"

Of course, there was none.

"Can you give me your address?" Shaw asked.

Ten minutes later he was headed for the JMCTF headquarters.

There's no shortage of law enforcement in California. Growing up in the eastern wilderness of the state, the Shaw family had contact with park rangers—the Compound abutted tens of thousands of acres of state and federal forest. The family was no stranger to other agencies either: state police, the California Bureau of Investigation and, on rare occasion, the FBI. Not to mention Sheriff Roy Blanche.

The JMCTF was new to Colter Shaw. In a brief online search he'd found that it was charged with investigating homicides, kidnappings, sexual assaults and larcenies in which an injury occurred. It had a small drug enforcement group.

He was now approaching the headquarters: a large, low '50s-style building on West Hedding Street, not far from the Santa Clara County Sheriff's Office. He steered the Chevy into the lot and walked along the curving sidewalk bordered with succulents and red flowers, hearing the persistent rush of traffic on the Nimitz Freeway.

At the front desk, he walked up to the window behind which a blond uniformed officer sat.

"Yessir?"

He knew the voice. It was the same young woman who'd fielded his earlier call. She was calm and stodgy. Her face was pert.

He asked again for either Detective Wiley or Detective Standish.

"Detective Standish is still out. I'll see if Detective Wiley is available."

Shaw sat in an orange-vinyl-and-aluminum chair. The waiting room was like a doctor's office, without the magazines . . . and with bulletproof glass protecting the receptionist.

Shaw opened his computer bag, extracted his bound notebook and began to write. When he was done, he walked to the desk officer. The woman looked up.

"Could you please make me a copy of this? It's for an investigation Detective Wiley's running."

Or, is soon to be running.

Another pause. She took the notebook, did as he'd requested and returned the notebook and copies to him.

"Many thanks."

As soon as Shaw sat down, the door clicked open and a large man in his mid-forties stepped into the waiting area.

The plainclothes officer was an inverted pyramid: broad shoulders and a solid chest, testing the buttons of his shirt, tapering to narrow hips. Had to have played football in school. His salt-and-pepper hair was thick and swept back from a high forehead. The proportioned bulk, hair, along with the eagle's beak nose and solid jaw, could have landed him a role as a detective in a thriller movie. Not the lead but the dependable—and often expendable—sidekick. His weapon was a Glock and it rode high on the hip.

His eyes, muddy brown, looked Shaw up and down. "You wanted to see me?"

"Detective Wiley?"

"Yes."

"Colter Shaw." He rose and extended his arm, forcing a handshake. "You got a call from Frank Mulliner about his daughter, Sophie. She disappeared on Wednesday. I'm helping him find her. I've found some things that make it clear she was kidnapped."

Another pause. "'Helping him find her.' You're a friend of the family?"

"Mulliner offered a reward. That's why I'm here."

"Reward?"

Wiley was going to be a problem.

"You're a PI?" the detective asked.

"No."

"BEA?"

"Not that either." Bond enforcement agents are highly regulated. One reason not to go down that road. Also, Shaw had no desire to chase Failure to Appears in Piggly Wiggly parking lots, cuff them and haul their sweaty bodies to the grim receiving docks of sheriffs' departments.

Shaw continued: "This is urgent, Detective."

Another scan. Wiley waited a moment and said, "You're not armed?"

"No."

"Come on back to the office. We'll just have a look in that bag first."

Shaw opened it. Wiley prodded and then turned and walked through the security doorway. Shaw followed him along the functional corridors, past offices and cubicles populated with about fifteen men and women—slightly more of the former than latter. Uniforms—all gray—prevailed. There were suits too, as well as the scruffy casual garb of those working undercover.

Wiley directed him into a large, austere office. Minimal décor. On the open door were two signs: DET. D. WILEY and DET. L. STANDISH. The desks were in the corners of the rooms, facing each other.

Wiley sat behind his, the chair creaking under his weight, and looked at phone message slips. Shaw sat across from him, on a gray metal chair whose seat was not molded for buttocks. It was extremely uncomfortable. He supposed Wiley perched suspects there while he conducted blunt interrogations.

The detective continued to adeptly ignore Shaw and studied the message slips intently. He turned away and typed on his computer.

Shaw grew tired of the pissing game. He took Sophie's cell phone, wrapped in Kleenex, from his pocket and set it on Wiley's desk. It thunked, as he'd intended. Shaw opened the tissue to reveal the cell.

Wiley's narrow eyes narrowed further.

"It's Sophie's mobile. I found it in San Miguel Park. Where she'd been cycling just before she disappeared."

Wiley glanced at it, then back to Shaw, who explained

about the video at the Quick Byte Café, the possibility of the kidnapper following her, the park, the car's collision with the bike.

"A tracker?" That was his only response.

"Maybe. I've got a copy of the video and you can see the original at the Quick Byte."

"You know Mulliner or his daughter before this reward thing?"

"No."

The detective leaned back. Wood and metal creaked. "Just curious about your connection with all this. It's Shaw, right?" He was typing on his computer.

"Detective, we can talk all about my livelihood at some point. But right now we need to start looking for Sophie."

Wiley's eyes were on the monitor. He'd probably found some articles in which Shaw was cited for helping police find a fugitive or locate a missing person. Or checking his record, more likely, and finding no warrants or convictions. Unless, of course, the powers that be at Cal had learned he was behind the theft of the four hundred pages yesterday from their hallowed academic halls, and he was now a wanted man.

No handcuffs were forthcoming. Wiley swung back. "Maybe she dropped it. Didn't want to go home because Dad'd paid eight hundred bucks for it. She went to stay with a friend."

"I found indications there'd been a scuffle. A rock that might have blood on it."

"DNA is taking us twenty-four hours minimum."

"It's not about confirming it's Sophie's. It suggests that she was attacked and kidnapped."

"Were you ever law enforcement?"

"No. But I've assisted in missing-person cases for ten years."

"For profit?"

"I make a living trying to save people's lives."

Just like you.

"How much is the reward?"

"Ten thousand."

"My. That's some chunk of change."

Shaw extracted a second bundle of tissue. This contained the small triangular shard of red reflector, which he believed had come from Sophie's bike.

"I picked them both up with tissues, this and the phone. Though the odds of the perp's prints being on them are low. I think after she fell down the hill she was trying to call for help. When the kidnapper came after her, she pitched the phone away."

"Why?" Wiley's eyes strayed to a file folder. He extracted a mechanical pencil and made a note.

"Hoping that when a friend or her father called, somebody'd find it and they could piece together that she'd been kidnapped." He continued: "I marked where I found it. I can help your crime scene team. Do you know San Miguel Park? The Tamyen Road side?"

"I do not."

"It's near the Bay. There aren't a lot of places a witness might've been but I spotted some businesses on the way to the park. Maybe one of them has a CCTV. And there's a half dozen traffic cams on the route from the Quick Byte to San Miguel. You might be able to piece together a tag number."

Wiley jotted another note. The case or a grocery list?

The detective asked, "When do you collect your money?"

Shaw rose and picked up the phone and the bit of plastic, put them back in his bag. Wiley's face flashed with astonishment. "Hey there—"

Shaw said evenly, "Kidnapping's a federal offense too. The FBI has a field office here, in Palo Alto. I'll take it up with them." He started for the door.

"Hold on, hold on, Chief. Take it easy. You gotta understand. You push the kidnap button, a lot of shit happens. From brass down to the swamp of the press. Take a bench there."

Shaw paused, then turned and sat down. He opened his computer bag and extracted the copy of the notes he'd jotted while waiting for Wiley. He handed the sheets to the detective.

"The initials FM is Frank Mulliner. SM is Sophie. And the CS is me."

Obvious, but in Wiley's case Shaw wasn't taking any chances.

- *Missing individual: Sophie Mulliner, 19*

- *Site of kidnapping: San Miguel Park, Mountain View, shoulder of Tamyen Road*

- *Possible scenarios:*

  - *Runaway: 3% (unlikely because of her phone, the reflector chip and evidence of struggle; none of her close friends—8 interviewed by FM—give any indication she's done this).*

- *Hit-and-run: 5% (driver probably would not have taken her body with him).*

- *Suicide: 1% (no history of mental issues, no previous attempts, no suicidal communication, doesn't fit with scene in San Miguel Park).*

- *Kidnapping/murder: 80%.*

  - *Kidnapped by former boyfriend Kyle Butler: 10% (somewhat unstable, possibly abusive, drug history, didn't take breakup well; hasn't returned calls of CS).*

  - *Killed in gang initiation: 5% (MT-44 and several Latino gangs active in area, but crews generally leave corpses in public as proof of kill).*

  - *Kidnapped by FM's former wife, Sophie's mother: <1% (Sophie is no longer a minor, the divorce happened seven years ago, criminal records and other background check of mother make this un-likely).*

  - *For-profit kidnapping: 10% (no ransom demand, they usually occur within 24 hours of abduction; father isn't wealthy).*

  - *Kidnapped to force FM to divulge sensitive infor-mation from one of his two jobs: 5% (one, middle management in automotive parts sales; the other, warehouse manager with no access to sensitive or valuable information or products). Would expect contact by now.*

- *Kidnapped to force Sophie to divulge information about her part-time job as coder at software development company, GenSys: 5% (does work not involving classified information or trade secrets).*

- *Killed because she witnessed a drug sale between boyfriend, Kyle Butler, and dealer who didn't want identity known: 20% (NOTE: Butler is missing too; related victim?).*

- *Kidnapped/killed by antisocial perpetrator, serial kidnapper or killer; SM raped and murdered or kept for torture and sex, eventual murder: 60%–70%.*

- *Unknown motive: 7%.*

- *Relevant details:*

  - *SM's credit cards have not been used in two days; FM is on cards and has access.*

  - *Quick Byte Café has video of possible suspect following her. Manager has preserved original and uploaded to cloud. Tiffany Monroe. CS has copy.*

  - *Under expectation-of-privacy laws, FM cannot access her phone log.*

  - *Perpetrator possibly put tracking device on bike to follow her.*

- *Mulliner's house just on market, no prospective buyers yet to case the location for kidnapping potential.*

The detective's carefully shaved face wore a frown. "The hell all this come from, Chief?"

The nickname rankled but Shaw ignored it; he was making headway. "The information?" He shrugged. "Facts from her father, some legwork of mine."

Wiley muttered, "What's with the percentages?"

"I rank things in priority. Tells me where to start. I look at the most likely first. That doesn't pan out, I move to the next."

He read it again.

"They don't add up to a hundred."

"There's always the unknown factor—that something I haven't thought of's the answer. Will you send a team to the park, Detective?"

"Alrightyroo. We'll look into it, Chief." He smoothed the copy of Shaw's analysis and shook his head, amused. "I can keep this?"

"It's yours."

Shaw set the cell phone and the chip of reflector in front of Wiley.

His own phone was humming with a text. He glanced at the screen, noted the word *Important!* Slipped the mobile away. "You'll keep me posted, Detective?"

"Oh, you betcha, Chief. You betcha."

# 12.

At the Quick Byte Café, Tiffany greeted him with a troubled nod.

It was she who'd just texted, asking if he could stop by.

*Important!* . . .

"Colter. Come here." They walked from the order station to the bulletin board on which Frank Mulliner had tacked up Sophie's picture.

The flyer was no longer there. In its place was a white sheet of computer paper, 8½ by 11 inches. On it was an odd black-and-white image, done in the style of stenciling. It depicted a face: two eyes, round orbs with a white glint in the upper-right-hand corner of each, open lips, a collar and tie. On the head was a businessman's hat from the 1950s.

"I texted as soon as I saw, but whoever it was might've taken it anytime. I asked everybody here, workers, customers. Nothing."

The corkboard was next to the side door, out of view of the camera. No help there.

Tiffany gave a wan smile. "Madge? My daughter? She's pissed at me. I sent her home. I don't want her here until they find him. I mean, she bikes to work three, four times a week too. And he was just here!"

"Not necessarily," Shaw said. "Sometimes people take Missing posters for souvenirs. Or, if they're after the reward themselves, they throw it out to narrow the field."

"Really? Somebody'd do that?"

And worse. When the rewards hit six digits and up, reward seekers found all sorts of creative ways to discourage competition. Shaw had a scar on his thigh as proof.

This eerie image?

Was it an intentional replacement, tacked up by the kidnapper?

And if so, why?

A perverse joke? A statement?

A warning?

There were no words on it. Shaw took it down, using a napkin, and slipped it into his computer bag.

He looked over the clientele, nearly every one of them staring at screens large and screens small.

The front door opened and more customers entered, a businessman in a dark suit and white shirt, no tie, looking harried; a heavyset woman in blue scrubs; and a pretty redhead, mid-twenties, who looked his way quickly, then found an empty spot to sit. A laptop—what else?—appeared from her backpack.

Shaw said to Tiffany, "I saw a printer in your office."

"You need to use it?"

He nodded. "What's your email?"

She gave it to him and he sent her Sophie's picture. "Can you make a couple of printouts?"

"Sure." Tiffany did so and soon returned with the sheets. Shaw printed the reward information at the bottom of one and tacked it back up.

"When I'm gone, can you move the camera so it's pointed this way?"

"You bet."

"Be subtle about it."

The woman nodded, clearly still troubled about the intrusion.

He said, "I want to ask if anybody's seen her. That okay?"

"Sure." Tiffany returned to the counter. Shaw detected a change in the woman; the thought that her kingdom here had been violated had turned her mood dark, her face suspicious.

Shaw took the second printout Tiffany had made and began his canvass. He was halfway through—with no success—when he heard a woman's voice from behind him. "Oh, no. That's terrible."

Shaw turned to see the redhead who'd walked into the café a few minutes ago. She was looking at the sheet of paper in his hand.

"Is that your niece? Sister?"

"I'm helping her father find her."

"You're a relative?"

"No. He offered a reward." Shaw nodded toward the flyer.

She thought about this for a moment, revealing nothing of her reaction to this news. "He must be going crazy. God. And her mother?"

"I'm sure. But Sophie lives here with her father."

The woman had a face that might be called heart-shaped, depending on how her hair framed her forehead. She was constantly tugging the strands, a nervous habit, he guessed. Her skin was the tan of someone who was outside frequently. She was in athletic shape. Her black leggings revealed exceptional thigh muscles. He guessed skiing and running and cycling. Her shoulders were broad in a way that suggested she'd made them broad by working out. Shaw's exercise was also exclusively out of doors; a treadmill or stair machine, or whatever they were called, would have driven a restless man like him crazy.

"You think something, you know, bad happened to her?" Her green eyes, damp and large, registered concern as they stared at the picture. Her voice was melodic.

"We don't know. Have you ever seen her?"

A squint at the sheet. "No."

She shot her eyes down toward his naked ring finger. Shaw had already noticed the same about hers. He made another observation: she was ten years younger than he was.

She sipped from a covered cup. "Good luck. I really hope she's okay."

Shaw watched her walk back to her table, where she booted up her PC, plugged in what he took to be serious headphones, not buds, and started typing. He continued canvassing, asking if the patrons had seen Sophie.

The answer was no.

That took care of all those present. He decided to get back to San Miguel Park and help the officers that Detective Dan Wiley had sent to run the crime scene. He thanked Tiffany and she gave him a furtive nod— meaning, he guessed, that she was going to start her surveillance.

Shaw was heading for the door when he was aware of motion to his left, someone coming toward him.

"Hey." It was the redhead. Her headset was around her neck and the cord dangled. She walked close. "I'm Maddie. Is your phone open?"

"My—?"

"Your phone. Is it locked? Do you need to put in a passcode?"

Doesn't everybody?

"Yes."

"So. Open it and give it to me. I'll put my number in. That way I'll know it's there and you're not pretending to type it while you really enter five-five-five one-two-one-two."

Shaw looked over her pretty face, her captivating eyes—the shade of green that Rand McNally had promised, deceptively, to be the color of the foliage in San Miguel Park.

"I could still delete it."

"That's an extra step. I'm betting you won't go to the trouble. What's your name?"

"Colter."

"That has to be real. In a bar? When a man's picking up a woman and gives her a fake name, it's always Bob or Fred." She smiled. "The thing is, I come on a little strong and that scares guys off. You don't look like the scare-able sort. So. Let me type my number in."

Shaw said, "Just give it to me and I'll call you now."

An exaggerated frown. "Oh-oh. That way I'll have captured you on incoming calls and stuck you in my address book. You willing to make that commitment?"

He lifted his phone. She gave him the number and he dialed. Her ringtone was some rock guitar riff Shaw didn't recognize. She frowned broadly and lifted the mobile to her ear. "Hello? . . . Hello? . . ." Then disconnected. "Was a telemarketer, I guess." Her laugh danced like her eyes.

Another hit of the coffee. Another tug of her hair. "See you around, Colter. Good luck with what you're up to. Oh, and what's my name?"

"Maddie. You never told me your last."

"One commitment at a time." She slipped the headphones on and returned to the laptop, on whose screen a psychedelic screen saver paid tribute to the 1960s.

# 13.

S haw couldn't believe it.

Ten minutes after leaving the café he was pulling onto the shoulder of Tamyen Road, overlooking San Miguel Park. Not a single cop.

*Alrightyroo. We'll look into it, Chief...*

Guess not.

Shaw approached the only folks nearby—an elderly couple in identical baby-blue jogging outfits—and displayed the printout of Sophie. As he'd expected, they'd never seen her.

Well, if the police weren't going to search, he was. She'd—possibly—flung the phone, as a signal to alert passersby when someone called her.

Maybe she'd also scrawled something in the dirt, a name, part of a license plate number, before X got her. Or perhaps they'd grappled and she'd grabbed a tissue or pen or bit of cloth, rich with DNA or decorated with his fingerprints, tossing that too into the grass.

Shaw descended into the ravine. He walked on grass

so he wouldn't disturb any tracks left by the kidnapper in sand and soil.

Using the brown-smeared stone as a hub, Shaw walked in an ever-widening spiral, staring at the ground ahead of him. No footprints, no bits of cloth or tissue, no litter from pockets.

But then a glint of light caught his eye.

It came from above him—a service road on the crest of the hill. The flash now repeated. He thought: a car door opening and closing. If it was a door, it closed in compete silence.

Crouching, he moved closer. Through the breeze-waving trees, he could make out what might indeed have been a vehicle. With the glare it was impossible to tell. The light wavered—which might have been due to branches bending in the wind. Or because someone who'd exited the car had walked to the edge of the ridge and was looking down.

Was this a jogger stretching before a run, or someone pausing on a long drive home to pee?

Or was it X, spying on the man with a troubling interest in Sophie Mulliner's disappearance?

Shaw started through the brush, keeping low, moving toward the base of the ravine, above which the car sat—if it was a car. The hill was quite steep. This was nothing to Shaw, who regularly ascended vertical rock faces, but the terrain was such that a climb would be noisy.

Tricky. Without being seen, he'd have to get almost to the top to be able to push aside the flora and snap a cell phone picture of the tag number of the jogger. Or pee-er. Or kidnapper.

Shaw got about twenty feet toward the base of the hill before he lost sight of the ridge, due to the angle. And it was then, hearing a snap of branch behind him, that he realized his mistake. He'd been concentrating so much on finding the quietest path ahead of him that he'd been ignoring his flank and rear.

*Never forget there are three hundred and sixty degrees of threat around you . . .*

Just as he turned, he saw the gun lifting toward the center of his chest and he heard a guttural growl from the hoodie-clad young man. "Don't fucking move. Or you're dead."

# 14.

Colter Shaw glanced at the attacker with irritation and muttered, "Quiet."

His eyes returned to the access road above them.

"I'll shoot," called the young man. "I will!"

Shaw stepped forward fast and yanked the weapon away and tossed it into the grass.

"Ow, shit!"

Shaw whispered sternly, "I told you: Quiet! I mean it." He pushed through a knotty growth of forsythia, trying to get a view of the road. From above came the sound of a car door slamming, an engine starting and a gravel-scattering getaway.

Shaw scrabbled up the incline as fast as he could. At the top, breathing hard, he scanned the road. Nothing but dust. He climbed back down to the ravine, where the young man was on his knees, patting the grass for the weapon.

"Leave it, Kyle," Shaw muttered.

The kid froze. "You know me?"

He was Kyle Butler, Sophie's ex-boyfriend. Shaw recognized him from his Facebook page.

Shaw had noted the pistol was a cheap pellet gun, a one-shot model whose projectiles couldn't even break the skin. He picked up the toy and strode to a storm drain and pitched it in.

"Hey!"

"Kyle, somebody sees you with that and you get shot. Which entrance did you use to get into the park?"

The boy rose and stared, confused.

"Which entrance?" Shaw had learned that the quieter your voice, the more intimidating you were. He was very quiet now.

"Over there." Nodding toward the sound of the motorbikes. The main entrance to the east. He swallowed. Butler's hands rose fast, as if Shaw presently had a gun on him.

"You can lower your arms."

He did so. Slowly.

"Did you see that car parked on the ridge?"

"What ridge?"

Shaw pointed to the access road.

"No, man. I didn't. Really."

Shaw looked him over, recalling: surfer dude. The boy had frothy blond hair, a navy-blue T-shirt under the black hoodie, black nylon workout pants. A handsome young man, though his eyes were a bit blank.

"Did Frank Mulliner tell you I was here?"

Another pause. What to say, what not to say? Finally: "Yeah. I called him after I got your message. He said you said you found her phone in the park."

The excess of verbs in the last sentence explained a lot to Shaw. So, the lovesick boy had conjured up the idea that Shaw had kidnapped his former girlfriend to get the reward. He remembered that Butler's job was bolting big speakers into Subarus and Civics and his passion was riding a piece of waxed wood on rollicking water. Shaw decided that the percentage likelihood of Kyle Butler being the kidnapper had dropped to nil.

But there was that related hypothesis. "Was Sophie ever with you when you scored weed, or coke, or whatever you do?"

"What're you talking about?"

First things first.

"Kyle, does it make sense that I'd kidnap somebody hoping her father would post a reward? Wouldn't I just ask for a ransom?"

He looked away. "I guess. Okay, man."

The sound of the motorbikes rose and fell, buzz-sawing in the distance.

Butler continued: "I'm just . . . It's all I can think about: Where is she? What's happening to her? Will I ever see her again?" His voice choked.

"At any time was she with you when you scored?"

"I don't know. Maybe. Why?"

He explained that a dealer might have been concerned that Sophie was a witness who could identify him.

"Oh God, no. The dudes I buy from? They're not players. Just, like, students or board heads. You know, surfers. Not bangers from East Palo or Oakland."

This seemed credible.

Shaw asked, "You have any idea who might've taken her? Her dad didn't think she had any stalkers."

"No . . ." The young man's voice faded. His head was down, slowly shaking now. Shaw saw a glistening in his eyes. "It's all my fault. Fuck."

"Your fault?"

"Yeah, man. See, Wednesdays we always did things together. They were like our weekend, 'cause I had to work Saturday and Sunday. I'd go out and new-school— you know, trick surf at Half Moon or Maverick. Then I'd pick her up and we'd hang with friends or do dinner, a movie. If I hadn't . . . If I hadn't fucked up so bad, that's what we would've done last Wednesday. And this never would've happened. All the weed. I got mean, I was a son of a bitch. I didn't want to; it just happened. She'd had enough. She didn't want to be with a loser." He wiped his face angrily. "But I'm clean. Thirty-four days. And I'm switching majors. Engineering. Computers."

So Kyle Butler was the knight coming to San Miguel Park with a BB gun to confront the dragon and rescue the damsel. He'd win her back.

Shaw looked toward the shoulder of Tamyen Road. Still no cops. He called the Task Force. Wiley was out. Standish was out.

"Find me a bag," Shaw said to Butler.

"Bag?"

"Paper, plastic, anything. Look on the shoulder. I'll look here."

Butler climbed the hill to Tamyen Road and Shaw walked the trails, hoping for a trash can. He found none.

Then he heard: "Got one!" Butler trotted down the hill. "By the side of the road." He held up the white bag. "From Walgreens. Is that okay?"

Colter Shaw was a man who smiled rarely. This drew a faint grin. "Perfect."

Sticking to the grass once more, he walked to the bloodstained rock and picked it up with the bag.

"What're you going to do with it?"

"Find a private lab to do a DNA test—I'm sure it's Sophie's blood."

"Oh, Jesus."

"No, it's just from a scrape. Nothing serious."

"Why're you doing that? Because the cops aren't?"

"That's right."

Butler's eyes flashed wide. "Yo, man, let's look for her together! If the cops aren't doing shit."

"It's a good idea. But I need your help first."

"Yeah, man. Anything."

"Her father's on his way home from work."

"His weekend job's over in the East Bay." Butler's face showed pity. "Two hours each way. Got another job during the week. And he still couldn't afford to keep their house, you know?"

"When he gets back, I need you to find out something."

"Sure."

"Sorry, Kyle. Might be kind of tough. I need to find out if she's been dating anybody. Go through her room, talk to friends."

"You think that's who it is?"

"I don't know. We have to look at every possibility."

Butler gave a wan smile. "Sure. I'll do it. It's just a stupid dream I had anyway, us getting back together. It's not going to happen." The young man turned and started up the hill. Then he stopped and returned. He shook Shaw's hand. "I'm sorry, man. I didn't mean to go all *Narcos* on you. You know?"

"Not a worry."

He watched Butler hike back toward the far entrance.

On his mission.

His futile mission.

From his interview with her father and examination of her room, Shaw didn't believe that Sophie was seeing anyone, not seriously, much less anyone who might have kidnapped her. But it was important for the poor kid to be elsewhere when Shaw discovered what he was now sure he'd find: Sophie Mulliner's body.

# 15.

Shaw was driving along winding Tamyen Road, having left San Miguel Park behind.

A serial kidnapper stashing his victims in a dungeon for any length of time wasn't an impossible likelihood. It did seem rare enough, though, that he focused on a more realistic fate: that Sophie'd been the victim of a sexual sociopath. In Shaw's experience, the majority of rapists might be serial actors, but almost always with multiple victims. The rapist's inclination was to kill and move on.

This meant Sophie's corpse lay somewhere nearby. X was clearly not stupid—the tracker on her bike, the obscuring clothing, the selection of a good attack zone. He wouldn't drive any distance with a body in his trunk. There might be an accident or traffic violation or a checkpoint. He'd do what he wanted, near San Miguel Park, and flee. In this southwest portion of San Francisco Bay were acres and acres of wet, sandy earth soft enough to dig a quick, shallow grave. But the area was open, with good visibility for hundreds and hundreds of yards; X would want his privacy.

Shaw came to a large, abandoned self-storage operation of about a hundred compartments. The facility was in the middle of an expanse of weeds and sandy ground. He parked and noted that the gap in the chain-link gate was easily wide enough for two people to slip through. He did so himself and began walking up and down the aisles. It was an easy place to search because the paneled overhead doors to the units had been removed and lay in a rust-festering pile behind one of the buildings, like the wings of huge roaches. Maybe this was done for safety's sake, the way refrigerator doors are removed upon discarding so a child can't get trapped inside. Whatever the reason, this practice made it simple to see that Sophie's body wasn't here.

Soon the Malibu was cruising again.

He saw a feral dog tugging something from the ground about thirty feet away. Something red and white.

Blood and bone?

Shaw braked fast and climbed out of the Chevy. The dog wasn't a big creature, maybe forty or fifty pounds and rib-skinny. Shaw approached slowly, keeping a steady pace.

*Never, ever startle an animal . . .*

The creature moved toward him with its black eyes narrowed. One fang was missing, which gave it an ominous look. Shaw avoided eye contact and continued forward without hesitating.

Until he was able to see what the dog was tugging up.

A Kentucky Fried Chicken bucket.

He left the scrawny thing to its illusory dinner and returned to the car.

Tamyen Road made a long loop past more marshes and fields, and with San Francisco Bay to his left he continued south.

The cracked and bleached asphalt led him to a row of trees and brush, behind which was a large industrial facility, seemingly closed for decades.

An eight-foot-high chain-link fence encircled the weed-choked facility. There were three gates, about thirty yards apart. Shaw pulled up to what seemed to be the main one. He counted five—no, six—dilapidated structures, marred with peeling beige paint and rust, sprouting pipes and tubing and wires. Some walls bore uninspired graffiti. The outlying buildings were one-story. In the center was an ominous, towering box, with a footprint of about a hundred by two hundred feet; it was five stories high and above it soared a metal smokestack, twenty feet in diameter at the base, tapering slightly as it rose.

The grounds abutted the Bay and the skeleton of a wide pier jutted fifty yards into the gently rocking water. Maybe maritime equipment had been fabricated here.

Shaw edged the car off the driveway. There was nowhere to hide the vehicle completely, so he parked on the far side of a stand of foliage. Difficult to see from the road. Why risk a run-in with local cops for violating the old yet unambiguous NO TRESPASSING signs? Shaw was mindful too of the individual twenty minutes ago possibly surveilling him from the ridge above San Miguel Park. Person X, he might as well assume. He placed his computer bag and the bloody rock in the trunk. He scanned the road, the forest on the other side of it, the grounds here. He saw no one. He believed that a car had driven through the main gate at some point in the recent past. The grounds were tall grass and bent in a way that suggested a vehicle's transit.

Shaw walked to the gate, which was secured by a piece of chain and a lock. He wasn't looking forward to scaling the fence. It was topped with the upward-pointed snipped-off ends of the links, not as dangerous as razor wire but sharp enough to draw blood.

He wondered if there was any give to the two panels of this gate, as there had been at the self-storage operation. Shaw tugged. The two sides parted only a few inches. He took hold of the large padlock to get a better grip. He pulled hard and it opened.

The lock was one of those models without keys; instead they have numbered dials on the bottom. The shank had been pushed in. Whoever had done it had not spun the dials to relock the mechanism. Two things intrigued Shaw. First, the lock was new. Second, the code was not the default—usually 0-0-0-0 or 1-2-3-4—but, he could see by looking at the dials, 7-4-9-9. Which meant someone had been using it to secure the gate and had neglected to lock it the most recent time he had been here.

Why? Maybe the laziness of a security guard?

Or because the visitor had entered recently, knowing he'd be leaving soon.

Which meant that perhaps he was still here.

Call Wiley?

Not yet.

He'd have to give the detective something concrete.

He opened the gate, stepped inside and replaced the lock as it had been. He then walked quickly over the weed-filled driveway for twenty yards to the first building—a small guardhouse. He glanced in. Empty. He scanned two other nearby buildings, Warehouse 3 and Warehouse 4.

Keeping low, Shaw moved to the closest of these, eyes scanning the vista, noting the vantage points from which a shooter could aim. While he had no particular gut feeling that he was in fact in any crosshairs, the lock that should have been locked and wasn't flipped a switch of caution within him.

*Bears'll come at you pushing brush. You'll hear. Mountain lions will growl. You'll hear. Wolf packs're silver. You'll see. You know where snakes'll be. But a man who wants to shoot you? You'll never hear, you'll never see, you'll never know what rock he's hiding under.*

Shaw looked into each of the warehouses, pungent with mold and completely empty. He then moved along the wide driveway between these buildings and the big manufacturing facility. Here he could see faded words painted on the brick, ten feet high, forty long, the final letters weathered to nothing.

AGW INDUSTRIES, INC.—FROM OUR HANDS TO Y

Shaw stepped across the driveway and into the shadows of the big building.

*You're the best tracker in the family . . .*

Not his father's words, his mother's.

He was looking for a trail. In the wild, cutting for sign is noting paw prints and claw marks, disturbed ground, broken branches, tufts of animal coat in brambles. Now, in suburbia, Colter Shaw was looking for tire treads or footprints. He saw only grass that might have been bent by a car a month ago—or thirty minutes.

Shaw continued to the main building—the loading dock in the back, where the vehicle might have stopped. He quietly climbed the stairs, four feet up, and walked to a door. He tried to open it. The knob turned yet the door held fast.

Someone had driven sharp, black Sheetrock screws into the jamb. He checked the door at the opposite end of the dock. The same. At the back of the dock was a window of mesh-impregnated glass and that too was sealed. The screws appeared new, just like the lock.

This gave Shaw a likely scenario: X had raped and killed Sophie and left the body inside, screwed the doors and windows shut to keep trespassers from finding her.

Now, time to call the police.

He was reaching for his phone when he was startled by a male voice: "Mr. Shaw!"

He climbed off the loading dock and walked along the back of the building.

Kyle Butler was approaching. "Mr. Shaw. There you are!"

What the hell was he doing here?

Shaw was thinking of the open gate, the likelihood that the kidnapper was still here. He held his finger to his lips and then gestured for the boy to crouch.

Kyle paused, confused. He said, "There's somebody else here. I saw his car in a parking lot back over there."

He was pointing to the line of trees on the other side of which was one of the outlier structures.

"Kyle! Get down!"

"Do you think Sophie's—" Before he finished his sentence, a pistol shot resounded. Butler's head jerked back and a mist of red popped into the air. He dropped straight to the ground, a bundle of dark clothing and limp flesh.

Two shots followed—make-sure bullets—striking Butler's leg and chest, tugging at his clothing.

Think. Fast. The shooter would've heard Butler calling him and would know basically where Shaw was. And to make the headshot, he would have been close.

But the shooter—most likely X—would also be cautious. He would have seen Shaw at San Miguel Park and suspected he wasn't the law but he couldn't be sure. And would be assuming Shaw was armed.

Shaw glanced at Kyle Butler.

Dead, glazed eyes and shattered temple. Much blood.

And then, for the moment, Shaw forced himself to forget about him entirely.

He backed away, crouching, heading for the drive where he'd spotted the bent grass. As he did, he punched in 911 and reported an "active shooter" at the old AGW plant off Tamyen Road.

He whispered to the dispatcher, "Do you know where that is?"

"Yessir, we'll have units responding. Stay on the line, please, and give me your—"

He disconnected.

All Shaw had to do now was find cover and avoid getting shot. He guessed that X would figure that he, whether civilian or cop, would have called for help. The kidnapper would flee.

Except, apparently, X hadn't done that at all.

Above Shaw came a crash of shattering glass and around him shards fell to the ground as he crouched and covered his head with his arm.

X wasn't finished yet. He'd gotten into the factory and climbed to an upper floor where he'd have a clearer shot at Shaw. He was now about to stick his head and arm out the window he'd just smashed and pepper Shaw with rounds.

There was no cover here, not for fifty feet.

Shaw turned and began sprinting toward the closest warehouse, waiting for the pop, then the slam of the slug in his back.

That didn't happen.

Instead, he heard from inside a woman's fierce scream. He stopped and looked back.

It was Sophie Mulliner who stood at the shattered window, her face turned toward the bloody body of Kyle Butler.

Then she looked at Shaw. A look of pure rage filled her face. "What've you done? What've you done?"

She vanished inside.

# 16.

Colter Shaw stood on a mesh catwalk inside the dim, cavernous manufacturing space. He crouched, listening.

Sounds, echoing from everywhere. Footsteps? Dripping water? The ancient structure settling? And then the roar of jet engines overhead. The factory was along the final approach path to San Francisco Airport. The gassy howl made it momentarily impossible to hear anything else.

Like someone coming up behind you.

Shaw had found one door that had not been secured with Sheetrock screws. He'd opened it and quickly stepped inside, closing it after him. He climbed to the third-floor catwalk so he could get an overview of the space below.

He saw no sign of Sophie or of X. Was the kidnapper still here? He would've guessed Shaw called for help. But he also might risk remaining for some minutes to find and murder Shaw, who might have some incriminating information, like his license tag number. Sophie Mulliner, of course, would die too.

He climbed down metal staircases to the ground floor, the labyrinth he'd surveyed from above, a network of offices, workstations, concrete slabs and machinery, presumably still here because technology had made the equipment obsolete, not even worth parts.

All surreal, in the gloom. Shaw was dizzy too; this, he guessed, was from air infused with the astringent fumes of diesel oil, grease and vast colonies of mold.

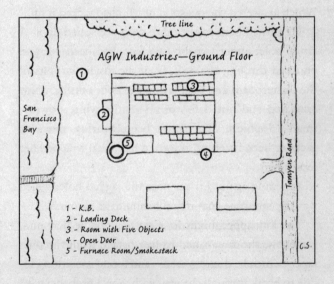

AGW Industries—Ground Floor

San Francisco Bay

Tree line

Tamsyen Road

1 - K.B.
2 - Loading Dock
3 - Room with Five Objects
4 - Open Door
5 - Furnace Room/Smokestack

C.S.

He spotted the window Sophie had broken—beside another catwalk on the fourth level—but there were no hiding spots there. She'd have gone to cover somewhere on the main floor. Shaw started through that level now, weaving around slabs and bins and machinery and workstations. He passed rows of rooms—ROTOR DESIGN II, ENGINEERING SUPERVISION, WAR DEPARTMENT LIAISON. Shaw paused beside each, listening—for breathing, for gritty scrapes underfoot, for that altered echo when a human takes up space in a room.

No, they were empty.

But one office was different from the others. Its door was closed and sealed with the same Sheetrock screws that held fast the outer doors. Shaw stopped. On the wall nearby was a crude painting—an approximation of the eerie stenciled face on the flyer in the Quick Byte Café. Which answered the question of who had tacked it up.

He turned back to the office with the sealed door. A crude hole, about two by two feet, had been cut and punched through the wall, from the inside out; bits of the plasterboard and dust lay on the floor outside. Shaw crouched and noted footprints in the white powder, small—Sophie's? She hadn't been wearing shoes or socks or been barefoot. It looked like she'd wrapped her feet in rags.

Listening again, his ear near the jagged hole, which was big enough—just—for a person to fit through.

The kidnapper might have stashed Sophie here and, somehow, she'd managed to free herself from the duct tape—which he'd surely used—and found something inside to break through the wall with. She'd probably tried to get out of the building and hadn't found a door that wasn't screwed shut.

He was debating his next steps when he heard a faint click to his right, followed by what might have been a low muttering sound, as if someone were angry he'd accidentally given himself away. It came from the end of a nearby corridor, between long metal walls lined with pipes and conduit. A sign read DON'T "BUCK" THE RULES: HARD HAT OR FINE. YOU CHOOSE!

At the end of the corridor were racks holding fifty-five-gallon oil drums and piles of lumber.

The muttering sound once more.

Sophie or X?

Then, his eyes growing yet more sensitive to the dimness, he could make out, at the end of the corridor, a shadow on the factory floor. It was moving slightly, cast by someone standing just out of sight, to the left at the T intersection of aisles.

Shaw couldn't pass up the advantage. He'd ease slowly to the corner and step around fast. If the shadow belonged to X he'd secure the gun hand and take him down. He knew a number of ways to get someone onto the floor such that they weren't inclined to get up anytime soon.

He moved closer. Twenty feet. Ten. Five.

The shadow shifted slightly, rocking back and forth.

Another step.

And Shaw walked right into the trap.

A tripwire. He went down fast and hard, getting his hands up just in time. The agonizing pushup saved his jaw from fracture. He rose, crouching, found himself looking at a sweatshirt hanging on a hook. To it was tied a piece of fishing line.

Which meant . . .

Before he could rise fully, an oil drum rolled from the rack and slammed into his shoulders. It was empty but the impact toppled him. He heard a voice, Sophie's, screaming, "You son of a bitch! You killed him!"

The young woman was advancing on him, hair disheveled, eyes wide, her T-shirt stained. In her hand was what seemed to be a shiv, a homemade glass knife, the handle a strip of cloth wrapped around it.

Shaw muscled the drum off—it bounced loudly on the concrete. With that sound and the scream, X would know more or less where they were.

"Sophie!" Shaw whispered, climbing to his feet. "It's okay! Don't say anything."

Her courage broke and she turned and fled.

"Wait," he called in a whisper.

She vanished into another room and swung a solid-metal door shut behind her. Shaw followed, thirty feet away. He stuck to her path, where there'd be no more traps. He pushed open the door and found himself in a boiler or smelting room. Coal bins lined the walls, some still half filled. There was dust, ash and soot everywhere.

And light at the far end of a long row of furnaces.

Shaw followed her footsteps, toward the cool illumination, whose source filtered down from a hundred feet above him; Shaw stood at the base of the smokestack. With less concern about the environment in the factory's working days, the furnaces would have spewed fumes into the air throughout the south Bay Area. In the middle of the base was a pit, fifteen feet across, filled with a gray-brown muck, presumably ancient ash and coal dust mixed with rainwater.

Shaw was looking for Sophie's footprints.

Which had simply vanished.

And then he saw why. Mounted into the inside of the smokestack's wall were rectangular rungs, like large staples, protruding about eight inches from the brick: a ladder for daredevil workers climbing to the top to replace aircraft warning lightbulbs, he guessed.

She was thirty feet up and climbing. A fall from there would kill or paralyze her.

"Sophie, I'm a friend of your father's. I've been looking for you." Shaw saw a glint and jumped back fast as something she'd flung fell toward him.

It was what he'd guessed—the shiv—and it just missed him, shattering at his feet. He glanced toward the entrance to the furnace room. No sign of the kidnapper. Yet.

Her voice was unsteady and she was crying. "You killed him! I saw you!"

"I was there. But the shot came from whoever kidnapped you."

"You're lying!"

"We have to be quiet! He could still be here." Shaw was speaking in a harsh whisper. He remembered her father's nickname for her. "Fee! Please."

She stopped.

Shaw added, "Luka. Luka's your poodle. A white standard."

"How do you know . . . ?" Her voice fading.

"You named yourself Fee when you were a baby. Your father offered a reward to find you. That's what I'm doing."

"He did?"

"I went to your house. Alta Vista Drive. Luka sat next

to me on the couch with the gold slipcover. The ugly gold slipcover. In front of the coffee table with the broken leg."

"What color is Luka's collar?"

"Blue with white rhinestones," Shaw said, then added, "Or maybe diamonds."

Her face went still. Then a faint smile. "He offered a reward?"

"Come on down, Fee. We've got to hide."

She debated for a moment.

Sophie began the climb to the floor. Shaw saw that her legs were trembling. Heights could do that to you.

More rungs. When she was about fifteen feet above the brick floor, Sophie released the grip with her right hand and wiped her palm on her thigh, drying the sweat.

Before she could take the rung again, though, her left hand slipped off the one she was gripping. Screaming, she made a desperate lunge for the rung but missed. She pitched backward, headfirst, tumbling exactly toward the spot on the brick where the glass knife had shattered into razor-sharp splinters.

# 17.

U nlike at San Miguel Park, the law had arrived fast
and en masse. Ten official cars, a carnival of flashing lights.

The medical examiner technician had just finished
with Kyle Butler; that team had been the first to get to
work. This always seemed odd to Shaw. You'd think
corpses could wait—once you'd confirmed they were indeed corpses, of course—while evidence might dry up or
blow away or change in composition. But they were the
experts.

The heart and brain of the investigation seemed to be
the Task Force, specifically Dan Wiley. The imposing
man was conferring with others, some local, some Santa
Clara County, and a few plainclothes who, Shaw overheard, were from the Bureau of Investigation—California,
not federal. Shaw was mildly surprised the FBI was not
present. As he'd reminded Wiley, kidnapping is a federal
crime as well as state.

Shaw was standing near the loading dock, where he'd

been directed to wait by Wiley. He had told the detective about Kyle Butler's words and suggested that X—though using the preferred police term *unsub*, for "unknown subject"—had fled south on Tamyen Road.

"At Highway 42 and Tamyen, there might be CCTVs. I don't know the make or color of the car. He'll be driving carefully. Stopping for red lights, not speeding."

Wiley had grunted and wandered off to deliver this information to minions—or not.

He was now barking to a young woman officer, her hair in a constricted blond bun, "I said to search it. I meant to search it. Why would I not mean for you to search it?"

The woman reluctantly deflated her defiant gaze. She walked away to search it, whatever *it* was.

Shaw glanced at the pair of ambulances, forty feet in front of him. One of the boxy vehicles held the deceased Kyle Butler, the other Sophie Mulliner, whose condition he didn't yet know. He'd managed to avert her landing on the glass-strewn floor by leveraging her into the ash pit— disgusting but softer than brick. He'd felt a bone pop with this maneuver—hers, not his—and she'd veered into the unpleasant soup. He pulled her out immediately as she moaned in pain and retched. The cleanest water he could find was standing rainwater, more or less clear, and he scooped up handfuls, draining it into her mouth and telling her, like a dentist, to rinse and spit. The chemicals in the pit could not be good. The fracture was bad, both radius and ulna, though not a through-the-skin fracture.

Shaw had not heard her account of the kidnapping; their time together in the smokestack had been devoted to first aid. He now saw the medical technician who'd been attending to Sophie walk away, speaking on his cell phone.

Shaw pushed off the loading dock wall and started toward the ambulance to speak to the young woman.

Wiley saw him. "Don't wander too far, Chief. We need to talk."

Shaw ignored him and continued toward the ambulances. To his right, on the far side of the chain-link, he could see a gaggle of news vans and maybe thirty reporters and camera operators. Some spectators.

He found Sophie, sitting up, groggy, eyes glazed. Her right arm, the broken one, was in a temporary cast. She'd be on the way to the hospital soon. Shaw was familiar with breaks; surgery would be involved. The medics had apparently used an emergency wash to clean off what chemicals they could.

She blinked in Shaw's direction. "Is he really . . ." Her voice was harsh and she coughed. "Kyle?"

"He's gone. I'm sorry."

She lowered her head and cried, covering her eyes. Catching her breath, she asked, "Did they . . . Have they found him?"

"No."

"Jesus." She tugged a tissue from a box and used that to wipe her eyes and nose.

"Why Kyle?"

"He saw the kidnapper's car. He could identify it."

"Did he come with you?"

"No. I told him to go to your house, to see your father. But he was worried about you. He wanted to help me search."

More sobbing. "He just . . . He was so sweet. Oh, his mom. Somebody'll have to tell her. And his brother." Eyes easing into and out of focus. "How did you . . . How did you find me?"

"Checked places near San Miguel Park you might've been."

"That's where this is?" She looked up at the towering building.

"Did you get a look at him, recognize him?" Shaw asked.

"No. He had a mask on, like a ski mask, and sunglasses."

"Gray? The mask?"

"I think. Yes."

The stocking cap.

Shaw's phone hummed. He looked at the screen. He hit ANSWER and handed the unit to her.

"Your father."

"Daddy! . . . No, I'm okay. My arm. I broke my arm . . . Kyle's gone. Daddy, he killed Kyle. He shot him . . . I don't know . . . That man . . . Mr. . . . ."

She looked his way.

"Shaw."

"Mr. Shaw. Daddy, he found me. He saved me . . . Okay . . . Where are you? . . . I love you too. Call Mom. Can you call her? . . . Love you."

She disconnected and handed the phone back. "He's on his way."

Her eyes looked past Shaw to the building where she'd been held captive. She whispered, "He just left me there." Her voice revealed bewilderment. "I woke up in this dark room. Alone. That was almost scarier than if he'd tried to rape me. I would've fought him. I would've fucking killed him. But he just left me there. Two days. I had to drink rainwater. Disgusting."

"You found that glass and cut your way out with it?"

"There was a bottle inside. I broke it and made a knife."

Another voice, from behind him: "Mr. Shaw?"

He turned to the blond officer who'd been dressed down by the detective earlier.

"Detective Wiley asked me to bring you to see him."

Sophie reached out with her good arm and gripped Shaw's shoulder. "Thank you," she whispered. And her eyes began to well with tears.

The officer said, "Please, Mr. Shaw. Detective Wiley said *now*."

# 18.

S haw followed the officer to where Wiley stood, by the loading dock, lording over the crime scene, snapping at yet another young deputy.

Shaw wished Detective Standish had drawn the case. However obnoxious, he couldn't be as insufferable as his partner.

As they approached, Wiley gave a nod and said to the officer who'd brought Shaw to him, "Kathy, dear, do me a solid. I sent Suzie out front. See if she's got anything for me. Hop hop."

"Suzie? Oh, you mean Deputy Harrison."

Wiley was oblivious to the snap of the correction whip. He simply added, ominously, "And don't talk to a single reporter. Am I clear on that?"

The blond officer's face grew dark as she too reined in her anger. She disappeared down the broad driveway between the manufacturing building and the warehouses.

The detective turned to him now and patted one of the stairs on the loading dock. "Take a pew, Chief."

Remaining standing, Shaw crossed his arms—Wiley lifted an eyebrow, as if to say, *Whatever*—and Shaw asked, "Did they find any CCTV at that intersection, Tamyen and Forty-two?"

"It's being looked into." Wiley pulled out a pen and pad. "Now, whole ball of wax. Tell me from when you left my office."

"I went back to the Quick Byte. Somebody'd taken the Missing poster Sophie's father'd put up."

"Why'd they do that?"

"And replaced it with this." He patted his pocket.

"Whatcha got there, Chief? Tobacco chaw? A fidget stick?"

"You have a latex glove?"

Wiley hesitated, as Shaw knew he would. But—also as Shaw anticipated—handed him one. Shaw pulled it on and fished in his pocket. He extracted the sheet of paper from the Quick Byte. The eerie stenciled image of the man's face. He displayed it.

"So?" Wiley asked.

"This image?"

"I see it." A frown.

"In the room where he put Sophie? The same thing— or close to it—was graffitied on the wall."

Wiley pulled on his own gloves. He took the sheet and gestured a crime scene tech over. He gave her the paper and asked her to run an analysis. "And check in the databases if it means anything."

"Sure, Detective."

Bullying and talent, Shaw reminded himself, are not mutually exclusive.

"You were in the café. And after that?"

"I went back to San Miguel Park. I thought you were going to send a team there."

Wiley set the pad and pen down on the chest-high loading dock. For a moment Shaw actually believed Wiley was planning to deck him. The detective removed a metal container, like a pill bottle, from his front slacks pocket. He unscrewed the top and extracted a toothpick. Shaw smelled mint.

"Better if you stay on message here, Chief." He pointed the toothpick at Shaw and then slipped it between his teeth. He wore a thick, engraved wedding ring. He reversed the ritual of the container and picked up his writing implement once more.

Shaw continued with his chronology: Kyle approaching him and the car on the ridge.

"Was it you?" Shaw asked. "In the car?"

Wiley blinked. "Why'd I do that?"

"Was it?"

No answer. "You see that vehicle?"

"I didn't."

"Lot of invisible cars around here," Wiley muttered. "Go on."

Shaw explained his conclusion that Sophie had been raped and killed and the body disposed of. He went looking for the most logical places where that might have been and ended up here. "I told Kyle to go to Sophie's house. He didn't."

"Why do you think the kidnapper didn't come after you?"

"Thought I was armed, I'm guessing. Detective, all the doors on the ground level were screwed shut, except one. Why would he leave it open?"

"The whole point, Chief. He came back to rape her."

"Then why not put a lock on that too, like he did the gate?"

"This's one sick pup, Chief. Can't hardly expect people like that to behave like you and me, can we now?" The toothpick moved from one side of his mouth to the other, via tongue only. It was a clever trick. "I suppose you'll be getting that reward."

"That's between me and Mr. Mulliner, a business arrangement."

"Arrangement," the officer said. His voice was as impressive as his bulk. Shaw could smell a fragrance and thought it was probably from the ample hairspray with which he froze his black-and-white mane in place.

"At least tell me how you heard about it, Chief."

"My name's Colter."

"Aw, that's just an endearment. Everybody uses endearments. Bet you do too."

Shaw said nothing.

The toothpick wiggled. "This reward. How'd you hear about it?"

"I'm not inclined to talk about my business anymore," Shaw said. Then added, "You might want to get security video from the Quick Byte and go through the past month. You could find a clearer image of the perp—if he was staking it out."

Wiley jotted something, though whether it was Shaw's suggestion or something else, Shaw had no idea.

The young woman officer Wiley'd sent to search for "it" returned.

Wiley raised a bushy eyebrow. "What'd you find, sweetheart?"

She held up an evidence bag. Inside was the Walgreens plastic bag containing the rock stained with what Shaw now knew was Sophie's blood.

"It was in his car, Detective."

Wiley clicked his tongue. "Hmm, stealing material evidence from a scene? That's obstruction of justice. Do the honors, sweetheart. Read him his rights. So, turn around, Mr. Shaw, and put your hands behind your back."

Shaw courteously complied, reflecting: at least Wiley'd dropped the "Chief."

# 19.

In the sprawling cabin on the Compound, where the Shaws lived, several rooms, *large* rooms, were devoted to books. The collection came from the days when Ashton and Mary Dove were academics—he taught history, the humanities and political science. She was a professor in the medical school and was also a PI—principal investigator, overseeing how corporate and government money was spent at universities. Then there was Ashton's flint-hard devotion to survivalism, which meant yet more books—hard copies, of course.

*Never trust the internet.*

This one too was so obvious Ashton didn't bother to codify it in his Never rulebook.

Colter, Dorion and Russell read constantly, and Colter was drawn to the legal books in particular, of which there were hundreds. For some reason, on the exodus from Berkeley to the wilderness east of Fresno, Ashton had brought along enough jurisprudential texts to open a law firm. Colter was fascinated with the casebooks—

collections of court decisions on topics like contracts, constitutional law, torts, criminal law and domestic relations. He liked the stories behind each of the cases, what had led the parties to court, who would prevail and why. His father taught his children the rules for physical survival; law provided the rules for social survival.

After college—he graduated cum laude from the University of Michigan—Shaw returned to California and interned in a public defender's office. This taught him two things. First, he would never, ever work in an office again, thus ending any thoughts of law school and a legal career. Second, he'd been right about the law: it was a brilliant weapon for offense and defense, like an over-under shotgun or a bow or a slingshot.

Now, sitting in an interview room in the sterile lockup attached to the Joint Major Crimes Task Force, Colter Shaw was summoning up what criminal law he knew. He'd been arrested more than a few times in his career. Though he'd never been convicted of any crime, the nature of his work meant he occasionally butted heads with the police, who, depending on their mood and the circumstances, might haul him in front of a booking desk.

He massaged his right arm, which had taken the brunt of deflecting the tumbling Sophie Mulliner, and calmly, in an orderly way, prepared his defense. This didn't take long.

The door opened and a balding man, slim, in his fifties, walked inside. His scalp was shiny, as if it had been waxed, and Shaw had to force himself not to look at it. The man wore a light gray suit, with a badge on his belt. His tie was a bold floral, the knot perfectly symmetrical. Colter Shaw had last worn a tie . . . Well, he couldn't exactly remember. Margot had said he looked "distinguished."

"Mr. Shaw."

A nod.

The man introduced himself as "Joint Task Force Senior Supervisor Cummings," a mouthful that spoke more about the man's nature than about the job description. "Fred" or "Stan" would have painted him better.

Cummings sat across the table from Shaw. The table, like the benches, was bolted down and made of sturdy metal. Cummings had a notebook and a pen. Shaw couldn't spot the cameras, but they'd be here.

"The detention officer said you wanted to talk to me. So you've changed your mind about waiving your right to speak to us without an attorney."

"I didn't change my mind. I wouldn't speak to Detective Wiley, with or without an attorney. I'll speak to you."

The lean man digested this, tapping the end of the Bic against a notepad. "I'm at a disadvantage here. This happened pretty fast and I don't have all the facts. There's something about a reward that the victim's father was offering? You're trying to get that?"

While Shaw preferred "earn," he nodded.

"That's your job?"

"It is. And it's not relevant to our conversation."

Cummings processed once more. "Dan Wiley can be a difficult person to deal with. But he's a good officer."

"Have there ever been complaints against him? Women officers, for instance?"

Cummings gave no response. "He tells me that you

stole evidence from a crime scene. With the evidence missing, it would have looked like you were the only one who found the girl. And that meant you'd be entitled to the reward."

Shaw had to give Wiley credit. Clever.

"Now, what we'll do—and Detective Wiley's on board with this—is knock down the obstruction to tampering. Misdemeanor. You forget about that reward and leave the area—you live in the Sierra Nevadas, right?"

"That's my residence."

"We'll do recognizance. And you can walk now. The prosecutor's got the paperwork ready."

Shaw was tired. A long day—from Molotov cocktail to murder—and it was only 6 p.m.

"Supervisor Cummings, Detective Wiley arrested me because he needs to steer this whole ship in a different direction. If I don't pursue the reward and I leave town, it doesn't look like Wiley screwed up and a civilian solved his case."

"Hold on, Mr. Shaw."

But Shaw didn't hold on. "Wiley had all the information he needed to realize this was an active kidnapping. He should've had twenty-five uniforms in and around San Miguel Park to search for Sophie Mulliner. And if he had, they would've found her—because I found her by myself in a half hour—and Kyle Butler'd be alive right now and, likely, you'd have your unsub in custody."

"Mr. Shaw, the fact is you removed evidence from a crime scene. That's an offense. The law is black-and-white on that."

Cummings had helpfully walked right into Shaw's trap.

Shaw leaned forward ever so slightly. "One, I took that rock to have a DNA test done, at my own expense, to prove that Sophie'd been kidnapped—because none of you believed it. Two"—Shaw held up a hand to silence Cummings's impending sputter—"San Miguel Park wasn't a crime scene. Dan Wiley never declared it one. I picked up a piece of granite in a county park. Now, Supervisor Cummings, I'm ending our conversation. You can discuss all this with your DA or I'll call my attorney and she'll take it from there."

# 20.

Shaw opted for one of those packets of peanut butter crackers.

All the other snacks in the Joint Major Crimes Task Force lobby were of the sweet variety, other than some unpopped cheddar popcorn, though how a visitor might prepare it was a mystery, there being no microwave that he could see.

He bought a bottled water too. The coffee, he figured, would be undrinkable.

He'd just finished the delicacy when Cummings's assistant, a sharp-eyed young man, entered the lobby through the submarine-quality security door and said that, unfortunately, Shaw's car had been towed to the pound.

Shaw didn't bother to ask why. So while he'd been released, his wheels were still in detention.

"I'm not being charged."

"I know that, sir."

"But I can't get my car?"

"No, sir. Some evidence was found in the car. I need a detective to sign off on it."

"Supervisor Cummings will."

"Well, he's gone home. We're looking for a supervising detective who can authorize the release."

"How long do you think it will take?"

"There's paperwork. Usually four, five hours."

It was a rental; maybe he'd just leave it and get a new one. Then he decided there might be some penalty. He always bought the collision damage waiver option. On the other hand, rental contracts had a lot of fine print. There was possibly a provision that voided the protection if a customer intentionally abandoned the car at the police pound.

"We have your phone number. We'll call when it's ready to be released."

"Do you know if the suspect has been identified?"

"Suspect?" The tone: *Which one?*

"The Sophie Mulliner abduction."

"I wouldn't know." The assistant was swallowed up through the doomsday door, which clicked shut with reverberation.

Shaw looked out the front of the Task Force headquarters. Four news station vans were there. Reporters and camera operators jockeyed. Shaw had been cleared as a suspect in the heinous crime of putting evidence in a Walgreens bag and there would be no indictment or arraignment details in public records featuring his name. But he was a participant and had been spotted, surely, by a keen-eyed reporter or two at the crime scene. With his gunslinger kind of job and his resemblance to a movie star, even if a generic one, Colter Shaw could be media fodder.

He returned to the officer behind the bulletproof glass—not the one who'd made the copy for him—and said to her, "You have a side entrance here?"

She debated, eyeing the reporters outside and assuming he'd been booked for something and didn't want his wife to see him on the eleven o'clock news. She pointed to a windowless door not far from the vending machines.

"Thanks."

Shaw left via this side corridor. A flash of brilliant early-evening sunlight fired into his eyes as he stepped out. He walked up the street, passing bail bond storefronts and the small offices of hardscrabble lawyers. He was about to summon an Uber to hitch a ride to the Winnebago when he found a bar. Mexican-themed, which appealed to him.

A few minutes later a freezing can of Tecate was in his hand. He worked a lime wedge through the opening. He never squeezed the fruit juice in; Shaw thought a float in the can was enough.

A long swallow. Another, as he looked over the menu.

His phone hummed and he recognized the number. "Mr. Mulliner?"

"Make it Frank. Please."

"Okay, Frank."

"I don't know where to begin." Breathless.

"How's Sophie?"

"She's home. Really shaken up, you can imagine. The break's bad. But the cast doesn't cover her fingers, so she can still use a keyboard. And text her friends." The laugh went quiet quickly. He would be deciding how to control the sudden urge to cry. "They checked her out at the hospital. Everything else is okay."

A euphemism, "everything else." There'd been no sexual assault, words a father would find so very difficult to utter.

"But . . . you? How are you?"

"Fine."

"The police said somebody helped them find her. Sophie said you were the only one."

"The cops played cavalry."

"She said they took you away, they arrested you!"

"Not a worry. It got worked out. Is her mother coming?"

A pause. "She'll be here in a couple of days. She had a meeting—a board meeting. She said it was important." Which told Shaw all about the former Mrs. Mulliner. "Mr. . . . Colter, I owe you everything . . . I just can't describe it. Well, you've probably heard that before."

He had.

"But . . . Kyle." Frank's voice had lowered and Shaw supposed Sophie was nearby. "Jesus."

"That was a shame."

"Listen, Colter. I have your reward. I want to give it to you in person."

"I'll come over tomorrow. The police must've debriefed Sophie?"

"A detective was here, yes. Detective Standish."

The elusive partner had surfaced—now that the case had proved to be real.

"Do they have any leads?"

"No."

Shaw said, "Did the Task Force leave a car out front of your house, Frank?"

"A squad car? Yes."

"Good."

"Do you think he'll come back?"

"No. But better to be safe."

They arranged a time to meet tomorrow and disconnected.

Shaw was about to order the *carne asada* when his iPhone buzzed once more. He recognized this number too. He hit ACCEPT. "Hello."

"It's me. Pushy Girl."

The redhead from the café. "Maddie?"

"You remembered! I saw the news. They found that girl you were looking for. The police saved her. They said a 'concerned citizen' helped. That was you, right?"

"It was me."

"Somebody was killed. Are you all right?"

"Fine."

"They didn't catch him, I heard."

"Not yet, no."

A pause. "So. You're wondering, what's up with stalker chick?"

He said nothing.

"Do you like Colter or Colt?"

"Either."

"It's Poole, by the way. Last name."

*Commitment* . . .

"Did you get the reward?"

"Not yet."

"They pay in cash? I'm just wondering." Maddie's mind seemed to dance like a water droplet on a hot skillet. "Okay, I'm getting a feel for you. You don't like to answer pointless questions. Noted and absorbed. What've you been up to since you saved her?"

Jail. And Tecate with lime.

"Nothing much."

"So you're not doing anything now? This minute? Immediately?"

"No."

"There's something I want to show you. You game?"

Shaw pictured her angelic face, the wispy hair, the athletic figure.

"Sure. I don't have wheels."

"That's cool. I'll pick you up."

He asked the bartender for a card and gave Maddie the address of the restaurant.

"Where are we going?" he asked.

"I just gave you a clue," she said breezily. "You can figure it out." The line went dead.

# 21.

Colter Shaw had never seen anything like it in his life. He stood at the entrance to an endless convention center—easily a half mile square—and was being assaulted by a million electronically generated sounds, from ray guns to automatic weapons to explosions to chest-drumming music to the actorly voices of demons and superheroes—not to mention the occasional dinosaur roar. And the visuals: theatrical spotlights, LEDs, backlit banners, epilepsy-inducing flashers, lasers and high-definition displays the size of school buses.

*You game?*

Maddie Poole's clue: Not as in "Are you game?" but "*Do* you game?"

Clever.

For this, apparently, was ground zero of the video gaming world, the international C3 Conference at the San Jose Convention Center. Tens of thousands of attendees moved like slow fish in a densely inhabited aquarium. The light here was eerily dim, presumably to make the images on the screens pop.

Beside him Maddie was a kid in a candy store, gazing around in delight. She wore a black stocking cap, a purple hoodie with UCLA on the chest, jeans and boots. She had a small tat of three Asian-language characters on her neck; he hadn't noticed them earlier. As at the café, she tugged at her lush hair—those strands that escaped the cap. Her unpolished nails were short, the flesh of her fingertips was wrinkled and red—he wondered what profession or hobby had done that. She wore no makeup. On her cheeks and the bridge of her nose was a dusting of freckles that some women would have covered up. Shaw was glad she didn't.

Maddie had given him the rundown on the drive here. Video gaming companies from around the world came to exhibit their wares at elaborate booths, where attendees could try out the latest products. There'd be tournaments between teams for purses of a million dollars, and cosplay competition among fans dressing up as their favorite characters. Film crews would roam the aisles for live streaming broadcasts. A highlight would be press conferences where company executives would announce new products—and field questions from journalists and fans about the minutiae of the games.

They eased past the booths, filled with players at gaming stations. He saw signs above some of them. TEN-MINUTE LIMIT. THERE'S A LOT OF OTHER SHIT TO SEE. And: MATURE 17+ ESRB. Presumably a rating board designation for games.

"What're we doing here?" he shouted. He foresaw a raspy throat by the end of the evening.

"You'll see." She was being coy.

Shaw was not a big fan of surprises. But he decided to play along.

He paused at a huge overhead monitor, which glowed white with blue type:

WELCOME TO C3

WHERE TODAY MEETS THE FUTURE . . .

Below that, stats scrolled:

DID YOU KNOW . . .

THE VIDEO GAMING INDUSTRY REVENUES WERE $142 BILLION LAST YEAR, UP 15% FROM THE YEAR BEFORE.

THE INDUSTRY IS BIGGER THAN HOLLYWOOD.

180 MILLION AMERICANS REGULARLY PLAY VIDEO GAMES.

135 MILLION AMERICANS OVER 18 REGULARLY PLAY.

40 MILLION AMERICANS OVER 50 REGULARLY PLAY.

FOUR OUT OF FIVE HOUSEHOLDS IN AMERICA OWN A DEVICE THAT WILL PLAY GAMES.

THE MOST POPULAR CATEGORIES ARE:

—ACTION/ADVENTURE: 30%
—SHOOTERS: 22%

—SPORTS: 14%

—SOCIAL: 10%

THE MOST POPULAR PLATFORMS ARE:

—TABLETS AND SMARTPHONES: 45%

—CONSOLES: 26%

—COMPUTERS: 25%

SMARTPHONE GAMING IS
THE FASTEST-GROWING SEGMENT.

Shaw'd had no idea about the industry's size and popularity.

They made their way through a crowd clustering around the booth for *Fortnite*, which seemed to attract the most attention in this portion of the hall. Some attendees within the cordoned-off portion of the booth were at computers, playing the game, in which avatars ran around the landscape and homemade structures—forts, he assumed. The characters would blast away at creatures and occasionally break into a bizarre dance.

"This way," Maddie said. "Come on." She clearly had a mission. She called, "What was your favorite game growing up?"

His turn to be wry. He said, "Venison."

A brief moment passed. Maddie laughed, a light, high voice, as she got the joke. Then she eyed him. "Serious? You hunt too?"

Too? One of those something-in-common moments? He nodded.

"My father and I'd go out every fall for duck and pheasant," she said. "Kind of a tradition." They dodged a pair of Asian women in bobbed wigs, one of which was bright green, one yellow. They wore snakeskin bodysuits.

Maddie asked, "You didn't play games?"

"No computers in our house."

"So you played on consoles?"

"None of the above," he said.

"Hmm," she said. "Never met anybody who grew up on Mars."

On the Compound, in the rugged Sierra Nevadas, the Shaw family had two basic cell phones—prepaid, of course, and for use in emergencies only. There was a shortwave radio, which the children could listen to, but like the phones it could be used for transmission only in dire straits. Ashton warned that "fox hunters"—people with devices to locate the source of radio signals—might be roaming the area to find him. When the family made the trip to the nearest town, White Sulphur Springs, twenty-five miles away, Ashton and Mary Dove had no problem with the children's logging on to the antiquated computers in the town library, or using them at their aunts' and uncles' homes during their summer visits to "civilization"— Portland and Seattle. But when your daily routine might find you rappelling down cliffs or confronting a rattlesnake or moose, vaporizing fictional aliens was a bit frivolous.

"Oh, oh, oh! . . . Come on." Maddie charged off toward a large monitor on which a gamer—a young man in stocking cap and sweats and an attempt at a beard— was firing away at bulky monsters, blowing most of them up.

"He's good. The game's *Doom*," she said, shaking her head, sentimental. "A classic. Like *Paradise Lost* or *Hamlet* . . . Caught you almost looking surprised there, Colter. I have a B.A. in English lit and a master's in information science."

She picked up a controller. She offered it to him. "Try your hand?"

"I'll pass."

"You mind if I do?"

"Go right ahead."

Maddie dropped into a seat and began to play. Her eyes were focused and her lips slightly parted. She sat forward and her body swayed and jerked, as if the world of the game were the only reality.

Her movement was balletic, and it was sensuous.

Speakers behind Shaw roared with the sound of a rocket and he turned, looking across the jammed aisle. He gazed up at the monitor, on which a preview of this company's game was displayed. In *Galaxy VII* the player guided an astronaut piloting a flying ship over a distant planet. The craft set down and the gamer directed the character to leave the vehicle and walk into a cave, where he explored tunnels and collected items like maps, weapons and "Power Plus wafers." Which sounded to Colter like a marathon runner's food supplement.

The game was calmer and subtler than the shoot-'em-up carnage of *Doom*.

Maddie appeared beside him. "I saved the world. We're good." She gripped his arm and leaned close, calling over the noise, "The gaming world in a nutshell." She pointed back to *Doom*. "One, where it's all from your perspective and you mow down the bad guys before they mow you down. They're called first-person shooters." Then she turned to the game he'd been looking at. "Two, action-adventure. They're third-person role playing, where you direct your character—avatar—you know *avatar?*" He nodded. "Direct your avatar around the set, overcoming challenges, collecting things that might help you. You try to stay alive. Not to worry, you can still use a pulse laser to fry Orc butt."

*"Lord of the Rings."*

"Hey." She laughed and squeezed his arm. "Hope for you after all."

When there's no TV, you gravitate toward books.

"One last lesson." She pointed up to the *Galaxy VII* screen. "See the other avatars walking around? Those are players somewhere else in the world. It's not just a role-playing game but a 'multiplayer online role-playing game,' a MORPG. The other gamers might be on your side or you might be fighting them. At any given moment in the popular games—like *World of Warcraft*—there could be a quarter million people online playing."

"You game a lot?"

She blinked. "Oh, I never told you: it's my job." She dug into her pocket and handed him a business card. "I'll introduce myself proper. My real name is GrindrGirl88." And she shook his hand with charming formality.

# 22.

Maddie Poole didn't design games, didn't create their graphics, didn't write their ad campaigns.

She played them professionally.

Grinding—as in her online nickname—was when one played hour after hour after hour for streaming sites like Twitch. "I'm going to give up asking if you know any of this, okay? Just go with it. So what happens is people log on to the site and watch their favorite gamers play."

It was a huge business, she explained. Gamers had agents just like sports figures and actors.

"You have one?"

"I'm thinking about it. When that happens, you end up committed to a gig. You're not as free to play where you want, when you want. You know what I mean?"

Colter Shaw said nothing in response. He asked, "The people who log on? They play along?"

"No. Just watch. They see my screen while I'm gaming, like they're looking over my shoulder. There's also a camera on me so they see my cute face. I have a headset and mic and I explain my gameplay, what I'm doing, why I'm doing it, and crack jokes, and chat. A lot of guys—and some girls—have crushes on me. A few stalkers, nothing I can't handle. We gaming girls gotta be tough. Almost as many women play games as men, but grinding and tournaments're a guys' world, and the guys give us a lot of crap."

Her face screwed up with disgust. "A gamer I know—she's a kid, eighteen—she beat two assholes playing in their loser basement in Bakersfield. They got her real name and address and SWAT'd her. You know it? Capital S-W-A-T."

Shaw didn't.

"When somebody calls the police and says there's a shooter in your house, they described her. The cops, they've gotta follow the rules. They kicked in the door and took her down. Happens more than you'd think. Of course, they let her go right away and she traced the guys who did it, even with their proxies, and they ended up in jail."

"What's your tat?" A glance toward her neck.

"I'll tell you later. Maybe. So. Here's your answer, Colt."

"To what question?"

"What we're doing here. Ta-da!"

They were in front of a booth in the corner of the convention center. It was as big as the others yet much more subdued—no lasers, no loud music. A modest electronic billboard reported:

HSE PRESENTS

*IMMERSION*

THE NEW MOVEMENT IN VIDEO GAMING

This booth featured no play stations; the action, whatever it might be, was taking place inside a huge black-and-purple tent. A line of attendees waited to get inside.

Maddie walked up to a check-in desk, behind which sat two Asian women in their thirties, older than most employees at the other booths. They were dressed in identical conservative navy-blue business suits. Maddie showed her ID badge, then a driver's license. A screen was consulted and she was given a pair of white goggles and a wireless controller. She signed a document on a screen and nodded toward Shaw.

"Me?"

"You. You're my guest."

After the ID routine, Shaw received his set of the toys too. The document he'd signed was a liability release.

They walked toward the curtained opening to the tent, lining up in a queue of other people, mostly young men, holding their own controllers and goggles.

Maddie explained, "I'm also a game reviewer. All the studios hire us to give them feedback about the beta version of new games. *Immersion*'s one I've been waiting for for a long time. We'll just try it out here for the fun of it, then I'll take it home for a serious test drive."

He studied the complicated goggles, which had a row of buttons on each side and earpieces.

The line moved slowly. Shaw noted that a pair of

employees—large, unsmiling men dressed in the male version of the women's somber suits—stood at the entryway, admitting a few people at a time, only after the same number had left by a nearby exit, handing back their goggles to yet another employee. Shaw noted the expressions on the faces of those leaving. Some seemed dumbfounded, shaking their heads. Some were awestruck. One or two looked troubled.

Maddie was explaining, "HSE is 'Hong-Sung Enterprises.' A Chinese company. Video gaming's always been international—the U.S., England, France and Spain all developed games early. Asia's where it really took off. Japan, in particular. Nintendo. You know Nintendo?"

"Mario, the plumber." Once off the Compound for college, then work, Shaw's education in modern culture took off exponentially.

"It was a playing card company in the eighteen hundreds and eventually pioneered console gaming—those're like arcade games for the home. The name's interesting. Most people say it means 'leave luck to Heaven.' Sort of a literal translation. But I was playing with some Japanese gamers. They think it has a deeper meaning. *Nin* means 'chivalrous way,' *ten* refers to 'Tengu,' a mythical spirit who teaches martial arts to those who've suffered loss, and *do* is 'a shrine.' So, to me, Nintendo means a shrine to the chivalrous who protect the weak. I like that one better.

"Now, back to history class. Japan soared in the video gaming world. China missed the party entirely—that's a joke. Because the Communist Party didn't approve of gaming. Subversive or something. Until, natch, they realized what they were missing out on: money. Two hundred million Americans play video games. *Seven* hundred million play in China.

"The government got involved and Beijing had a problem: players sit on their asses all day long. They get fat; they're out of shape. They're in their thirties and they have heart attacks. So HSE, Hong-Sung Enterprises, did something about it." Maddie waved her hand at the *Immersion* sign. "When you play, you actually move—everywhere, not just standing in front of your TV, swinging a fake tennis racket. You walk around, you run, you jump. Your basement, your living room, your backyard. The beach, a field. There's a version you can play on a trampoline and they're working on one you can use in a pool."

She held up the goggles and pointed. "See, cameras in the front and on the sides? You put it on, get a cellular or Wi-Fi connection and go out into your backyard, but it's not your backyard anymore. The game's algorithms change what you see. The tricycle, the barbecue, the cat— everything's been turned into something else. Zombies, monsters, rocks, volcanoes.

"I'm pretty into sports and exercise, which is why it's totally my kind of game. *Immersion*'s going to be the NBT—the next big thing. The company's already donating thousands of the units to schools, to hospitals to help with rehab, to the Army. There's software to replicate battlefields, so soldiers can train anytime. In the barracks, at home, wherever."

They were next to go in. "Okay, this's it, Colter. Put the goggles on." He did. It was like looking through lightly tinted gray sunglasses.

"The controller's your weapon." She smiled. "Umm,

you've got it backward. You fire that way, you'll shoot yourself in the groin."

He turned the thing around. It was like a remote control and felt comfortable in his hand.

"Just press that button to shoot."

Then Maddie took his left hand and lifted it to that side of the goggles. "This is the on switch. Press it for a second or so after we get inside. And this button. Feel it?"

He did.

"If you die, hit it. It resets you back to life."

"Why do you think I'm going to die?"

She only smiled.

# 23.

When they walked inside the tent, an employee directed them down a corridor to Room 3.

The thirty-by-thirty-foot space looked like a theater's backstage: walkways, stairs, platforms, furniture, a fake rubber tree, a large sprawl of tarp, a table on which sat bags of potato chips and cans of food, a grandfather clock. He and Maddie had the room to themselves.

Just a game, of course, but Shaw felt himself go into set mode. Just like before rappelling off a cliff, or streaking up a hill on the Yamaha fast enough to go airborne, you have to ready yourself.

*Never be unprepared physically or mentally . . .*

A voice from on high said: "Prepare for combat. On one, engage your goggles. Three . . . two . . . one!"

Shaw pressed the button Maddie had indicated.

And the world changed.

Astonishing.

The grandfather clock was some sort of bearded wizard, the platforms were icy ledges, the rubber plant a campfire burning with green flame. The tarp was now a rocky coast overlooking a turbulent ocean in which whirlpools swirled and sucked ships into dark spirals. There were two suns in the sky, one yellow and one blue, and they cast a faint green haze over the world. The walls were no longer black curtains but instead distant vistas of snowcapped peaks and a towering volcano, which was erupting. All in stunning 3-D.

He glanced to his right and saw Maddie, now dressed in black armor. He then looked at his own legs and found he was wearing the same. His hands were in black metallic gloves, and in his right the controller had become a ray gun.

A consuming experience.

*Immersion* was aptly named.

"Colt," Maddie called, though it wasn't her voice. The tone was husky.

"I'm here," he said. His voice too had changed from its easy baritone to a rugged bass.

He noted her climbing up a rocky ledge, which had been a simple scaffolding before putting on the goggles. She was crouched low, head sweeping back and forth. "They're coming. Get ready."

"Who's—"

He gasped. A creature pounced on the ledge beside her. The glistening blue thing had a human face—with the minor addition of saber teeth and an extra eye, glowing red. The creature swung a sword at Maddie. She blasted it. It didn't die right away but kept coming after her, taking the sparking hits from her weapon. It swung a second glowing sword. She had to dodge, leaping off the rocks onto a grassy field. Here too there was an elegance to her moves.

*Sensuous* . . .

Which is when a flying pterodactyl dropped from the sky and ripped Shaw's heart out of his chest.

YOU'VE JUST DIED! a sign in the goggle screen announced.

He remembered which button to hit.

*RESET* . . .

He was alive once more. And, now, his survival upbringing returned.

*Never lose sight of your surroundings* . . .

He spun around—just in time to dodge a squat creature attacking with a fiery hammer. It took five shots of the laser to kill it and he had to leap back from a final swing of its weapon before it died.

The goggle message was YOU'VE JUST EARNED A LAVA HAMMER. A small picture of one popped up in the lower-right-hand corner of the screen. The window was called WEAPONS STASH.

A shadow appeared on the grassy field in front of him.

Shaw's heart thudded and he looked up fast, just in time to kill one of those damn flying things. It too had a human face.

He found himself sweating, tense. He felt an urge to be trigger-happy, blasting creatures through weeds and trees, shooting when he had no clear line of sight.

He thought of the hunter, all those years ago, shooting the buck through a stand of brush.

*I hit something? There was just a noise in the bushes. I thought it was a wolf* . . .

Shaw calmed and took control of his tactics. He zapped a slew of running, flying and slithering things—

until an alien unsportingly dropped a boulder off a hill-top and crushed him.

*RESET.*

He saw Maddie Poole taking on three creatures at once, ducking for cover behind a downed tree trunk, laden with bags of corn and peasant bread—it was the table on which sat the chips and soup cans. Shaw had a good shot at one and killed it. She didn't acknowledge the aid. Like a real soldier, she wouldn't let her attention waver.

An Asian-inflected voice came through the speakers: "Your *Immersion* experience will end in five minutes."

After Maddie killed her other two assailants, she hit a button on her goggles and walked up to Shaw and pressed the same on his. While the fantasy world remained, the aliens had vanished. It was suddenly quiet, aside from the make-believe sound of the ocean and the wind. There were no laser guns in their hands any longer.

"Hell of an experience," he told her.

She nodded. "Totally. Notice how all the creatures had variations on human faces."

He said he had.

"Hong Wei, the CEO of the company, ordered focus groups to help select villains. Gamers are much more comfortable killing anything that resembles people than animals. We're fodder; Bambi's safe."

Shaw looked around. "Where's the exit?"

She said coyly, "We've got a few minutes left. Let's fight some more."

He was tired, after the eventful day. But he was enjoying the time with her. "I'm game."

She smiled, then took his hand and put it on yet another button on his goggles.

"On three, press this one."

"Got it."

"One . . . two . . . three!"

He pushed where instructed and, from the controller, a red-hot glowing sword blade emerged. One appeared in her hand too. This time there were no other creatures, just the two of them.

Maddie Poole didn't waste a second. She leapt at him, swinging the sword overhead, bringing it down fast. While Shaw knew knives well, he'd never held a sword. Still, combat with the weapon was instinctual. He effectively parried her blow and, finding himself irritated that she'd withheld what this portion of the game would entail, he charged forward. She deflected each of his thrusts and swings or dodged out of the way. As soon as he missed her, she was back, coming at him. His advantages were longer legs and strength, hers were speed and being a smaller target.

He was breathing hard . . . and only partly from the effort of climbing on the ledges and rocks.

They received a two-minute warning from the heavens. The deadline seemed to energize Maddie. She charged forward repeatedly. He took a cut on his leg, and she one on the upper arm. Blood appeared in the wound, an eerie sight. A meter on his goggles reported that he had ninety percent life left.

He feinted and Maddie fell for it. She dodged too late to miss a slash on her upper thigh, a shallow wound, and he could hear her low, murky voice: "Son of a bitch."

Shaw pressed forward and Maddie backed up. She tried to make a leap onto a low ledge—a platform about eighteen inches off the ground—misjudged and fell hard. Though the floor was padded with foam, her side had collided with the edge of the platform. She dropped to her knees and gripped her ribs. He heard her grunt in pain.

Standing straight, he lowered the sword and walked forward to help her up. "You all right?"

He was about three feet away when she sprang to her feet and plunged her blade into his gut.

YOU'VE JUST DIED!

It had all been a trick. She'd fallen on purpose, landing in a particular way—with her feet under her so she could leverage herself up and lunge.

The overlord in the ceiling announced that their time was up. The fantasy world became a backstage once more. He and Maddie pulled their goggles off. He started to give her a nod and say, "That was a low blow"—not a bad joke—but he didn't. She wiped sweat from her forehead and temple with the back of her sleeve and looked about with an expression that wasn't a lot different from that of the creatures that had killed him. Not triumph, not joy in victory. Nothing. Just ice.

He recalled what she'd said before they stepped inside the booth.

*We'll just try it out here for the fun of it* . . .

As they walked to the exit, it was as if she grew aware suddenly that she wasn't alone. "Hey, you're not mad, are you?" she said.

"All's fair."

The awkward atmosphere leveled but didn't exactly vanish as they walked outside. What did disappear was his intention to ask her to dinner. He would—might—later. Not tonight.

They handed their goggles to the HSE employee, who put them in a bin for sanitizing. At the desk, Maddie was given a canvas bag, which he assumed contained a new game for her to take home and review.

His phone hummed.

A local area code.

Berkeley police, to arrest him for the transgressing larceny? Dan Wiley and Supervisor Cummings deciding to arrest him anew after changing their minds about the Great Evidence Robbery?

It *was* from JMCTF, though just the desk officer, telling him his car was available to be picked up at the pound.

Exhausted and having died three times in ten minutes—or was it four?—Shaw thought: Give it a shot. "Can somebody deliver it to me?"

The silence—which he imagined was accompanied by a look of bewilderment on the officer's face—lasted a good three seconds. "I'm afraid we can't do that, sir. You'll have to go to the pound to pick it up."

She gave him the address, which he memorized.

He eased a glance Maddie's way. "My car's ready."

"I can drive you."

It was obvious that her preference was to stay. Which was fine with him.

"No, I'll get an Uber."

He hugged her and she kissed his cheek.

"It was fun—" he started.

"'Night!" Maddie called. Then she was off, tugging at her hair and striding toward another booth—with the marauding aliens, the swords and Shaw himself completely erased, like data dumped from a hard drive's random access memory.

# 24.

No logical reason in the world to pay one hundred and fifty dollars to retrieve a car that should never have been held hostage in the first place.

But there you have it.

Adding insult, the charge was five percent more if you used a credit card. Colter checked his cash: one hundred and eighty-seven dollars. He handed over the Amex, paid and walked to the front gate to wait.

The pound was a sprawling yard in a seedy part of the Valley, on the east side of the 101. Some of the cars had been there for months, to judge from the grime. He counted airliners on final approach to San Francisco Airport, thinking of how the sound of the planes had unsettlingly masked the noise of any attackers when he was searching for Sophie at that old factory. Now he gave up at sixteen jets. The vehicle arrived five minutes later. Shaw examined it. No scratches or dents. His computer bag was still in the trunk and had probably been searched, yet nothing had been damaged or taken.

The crisp voice of the GPS guided him back into a

tamer part of Silicon Valley, quieted in the late evening. He was headed toward his RV park in Los Altos Hills. Colter Shaw had, however, chosen a circuitous route, ignoring the electronic lady's directives—and her patient recalculating corrections.

Because someone was following him.

When he'd left the pound, he'd been aware of car lights flicking on and the vehicle to which they were attached making a U-turn and proceeding in his direction. Maybe a coincidence? When Shaw stopped abruptly at a yellow light that he could easily have rolled through without a ticket, the car or truck behind him swerved quickly to the curb. He couldn't tell the make, model or color.

A random carjacker or mugger? Two percent. A Chevy Malibu wasn't worth the jail time.

Detective Dan Wiley, planning to beat the crap out of him? Four percent. Satisfying but a career ender. The man was a narcissist, not a fool.

Detective Dan Wiley, hoping to catch him score some street pot or coke? Fifteen percent. He seemed like a vindictive prick.

A felon Shaw had helped put inside or a hitman or leg breaker hired by said felon? Ten percent. No shortage of those. It would have been hard for someone to have traced him to the police pound yet not impossible. Shaw gave it double digits because he tended to skew the number higher when the consequences of what might occur were particularly painful. Or fatal.

The more likely possibility, Person X—whose plans for Sophie Mulliner had been spoiled and who'd come for revenge: sixty percent.

He muted the GPS lass, turned off the automatic braking system and steered down a quiet street. He hit the gas hard, as if trying to run, spinning tires. The pursuer sped up too. At fifty mph he crunched the brake pedal and turned into a left-hand skid. Almost lost it—the asphalt was dew-damp—then steered in the direction of the car's veering rear end. He controlled the flamboyant maneuver just in time and the Malibu zipped neatly into the entrance of a darkened parking garage. Twenty feet inside he made a U-turn, the sound a teeth-setting squeal due to the concrete acoustics. He goosed the accelerator and sped back to the entrance.

Shaw's phone was up, camera videoing, car lights on high beam. Ready to capture an image of the tail.

His prey never appeared. A minute later he gunned the engine and exited, turning right, expecting his pursuer to be waiting.

The street was empty.

He continued to the RV park, this time obeying Ms. GPS to the letter. He paused at the entrance to the trailer park and looked around. Traffic, but the vehicles streamed by, their drivers uninterested in him. He continued into the park, turned on Google Way and parked.

He climbed out, locked the car and walked quickly to the Winnebago door. Inside, leaving the lights off, he retrieved his Glock from the spice cabinet. For five minutes he peered through the blinds. No cars.

Shaw went into the small bathroom, where he took a hot, then ice-cold, shower. He dressed in jeans and a sweatshirt, and made dinner of scrambled eggs with some of the gun-cabinet herbs (tarragon, sage), buttered toast and a piece of salty country ham, along with an Anchor Steam. Eleven p.m. was often his dinnertime.

He sat at the banquette to dine and perform his nightly check of the local news feeds. Another woman had been attacked—in Daly City—the perp arrested before Shaw had rescued Sophie. Some irrelevant stories: a popular labor organizer denying corruption claims, a terrorist plot thwarted on the Oakland docks, a surge in voter registration as Californians prepared to go to the polls on some special referenda.

As for the Sophie Mulliner kidnapping, the anchors and commentators didn't provide any news that Shaw wasn't aware of, while still doing what they did best: ramping up the paranoia. "That's right, Candy, my experience has been that kidnappers like this—'thrill kidnappers,' we call them—often go after multiple victims."

Shaw had made the news as well.

Detective Dan Wiley said that a concerned citizen, Colter Shaw, pursuing the reward offered by Mr. Mulliner—making him sound particularly mercenary—had provided information that proved helpful in the rescue.

He logged off and shut down computer and router.

*Proved helpful . . .*

Nearly midnight.

Shaw was ready for sleep but sleep was not on the immediate horizon. He returned to the kitchen cabinet and once more removed the envelope he'd stolen from the Cal archives, the one with the elegant penmanship emblazoned on the front: *Graded Exams 5/25*. Inside were the documents he'd skimmed earlier. He opened a blank notebook and uncapped his fountain pen.

A sip of beer and he began to read in earnest, wondering if in fact he'd find an answer to the question: What had actually happened in the early-morning hours of October 5, fifteen years ago, on bleak Echo Ridge?

# LEVEL 3:

# THE SINKING SHIP

### Sunday, June 9

The rock had had no effect on the windshield of the foundering *Seas the Day.*

Shaw tossed it back into the grim, turbulent Pacific and pulled the locking-blade knife from his pocket. He'd use it to try to remove the screws securing the window frame to the front of the cabin.

He heard, over the gutsy roar of waves colliding with rock and sand, Elizabeth Chabelle shouting something.

Probably: "Get me the fuck out of here!"

Or a variation.

Gripping a scabby railing with his left hand, he began on the screws. There were four—standard heads, not Phillips. He fitted the blade in sideways and rotated counterclockwise. Nothing for a moment. Then, with all his strength, he twisted and the hardware moved. A few minutes later the screw was out. Then the second. The third.

He was halfway through the fourth screw when a large swell smacked the side of the boat and sent Shaw over the railing backward, between the ship and a pylon.

Instinctively grabbing for a handhold, he let go of the knife and saw it vanish in a graceful spiral on its way to the ocean floor. He kicked to the surface and muscled his way once more onto the forward deck.

Back to the window, loosened but not free.

Okay. Enough. Angrily Shaw gripped it with both hands, planted his feet on the exterior side wall of the cabin and pulled—arm muscles, leg muscles, back muscles.

The frame broke away.

Shaw and the window went over the side.

Oh, hell, he thought, grabbing a breath just before he hit.

Kicking to the surface again. The shivering was less intense now and he felt a wave of euphoria, hypothermia's way of telling you that death can be fun.

Scrabbling back onto the foredeck, he dropped into the front portion of the cabin and slid to the bulkhead separating this part from the aft. The vessel was now down by the stern at a forty-five-degree angle. Below him, exhausted Elizabeth Chabelle had left her bunk bed perch in the half-flooded aft section of the cabin. She gripped the frame of the small window in the door. He saw wounds on her hands; she would have shattered the glass and reached through to find the knob.

Which had been removed.

She sobbed, "Why? Who did this?"

"You'll be fine, Elizabeth."

Running his hands around the perimeter of the interior door, Shaw felt the sharp points. It had been sealed from the other side with Sheetrock screws, just like at the factory where Sophie had been stashed.

"Do you have any tools?"

"No! I l-looked for f-fucking tools." Stuttering in the cold.

Where was the hypothermia clock now? Probably ten minutes and counting down.

Another wave crashed into the boat. Chabelle muttered something Shaw couldn't understand, her shivering was so bad. She repeated it: "Wh-who . . . ?"

"He left things for you. Five things."

"It's so f-fucking c-cold."

"What did he leave you?"

"A kite . . . th-there was a kite. A PowerBar. I ate it. A f-flashlight. Matches. They're all wet. A p-p-pot. F-flowerpot. A f-fucking f-flowerpot."

"Give it to me."

"Give—?"

"The pot."

She bent down, feeling under the surface, and a moment later handed him the brown-clay pot. He shattered it against the wall and, picking the sharpest shard, began digging at the wood around the hinges.

"Get back on the bunk," Shaw told her. "Out of the water."

"There's n-no . . ."

"As best you can."

She turned and climbed to the top of the bed. She managed to keep most of her body, from ample belly up, above the surface.

Shaw said, "Tell me about George."

"Y-you know m-my boyfriend?"

"I saw a picture of you two. You ballroom dance."

A faint laugh. "He's t-terrible. But he t-tries. Okay with f-fox-trot. Do you . . ."

Shaw gave a laugh too. "I don't dance, no."

The wood was teak. Hard as stone. Still he kept at it. He said, "You get to Miami much, see your folks?"

"I—I . . ."

"I've got a place in Florida. Farther north. You ever get to the 'Glades?"

"One of those b-boats, with the airplane p-propellers. I'm going to d-die, aren't I?"

"No you're not."

While the glass knife might have cut through plaster to free Sophie, the pottery shard was next to useless. "You like stone crabs?"

"Broke my t-tooth on a . . . on a shell one time." She began sobbing. "I d-don't know who you are. Thank you. Get out. Get out now. S-save yourself . . . It's t-too late."

Shaw looked into the dim portion of the cabin where she clung to the post of the bunk.

"P-please," she said. "Save yourself."

The ship settled further.

# LEVEL 2:

# THE DARK FOREST

Saturday, June 8, One Day Earlier

# 25.

At 9 a.m. Colter Shaw was in one of the twenty-five million strip malls that dotted Silicon Valley, this one boasting a nail salon, a Hair Cuttery, a FedEx operation and a Salvadoran restaurant—the establishment he was now sitting in. It was a cheerful place, decorated with festive red-and-white paper flowers and rosettes and photos of mountains, presumably of the country back home. The restaurant also offered among the best Latin American coffee he'd ever had: Santa Maria from the "microregion" of Potrero Grande. He wanted to buy a pound or two. It wasn't for sale by the bag.

He sipped the aromatic beverage and glanced across the street. On his drive to the mall he'd passed imposing mansions just minutes away, but here were tiny bungalows. One was in foreclosure—he thought of Frank Mulliner's neighbor—and another for sale by owner. Two signs sat in the parking strips of houses. VOTE YES PROPOSITION 457. NO PROPERTY TAX HIKES!!! And a similar message with the addition of a skull and crossbones and the words SILICON VALLEY REAL ESTATE—YOU'RE KILLING US!!

Shaw turned back to the stack of documents he'd removed from the university the other day. Stolen, true, though on reflection he supposed an argument might be made that the burglary was justified.

After all, they had been written or assembled by his father, Ashton Shaw.

Two of whose rules he thought of now:

> *Never adopt a strategy or approach a task without assigning percentages.*

> *Never assign a percentage until you have as many facts as possible . . .*

That, of course, was the key.

Colter Shaw couldn't make any assessment of what had happened on October 5, fifteen years ago, until he gathered those facts . . . What in these pages addressed that? There were three hundred and seventy-four of them. Shaw wondered if the number itself were a message; after all, his father had been given to codes and cryptic references.

Ashton had been an expert in political science, law, government, American history, as well as—an odd hobby—physics. The pages contained snippets of all those topics. Essays started but never completed and essays completed but making no sense whatsoever to Shaw. Odd theories, quotations from people he'd never heard of. Maps of neighborhoods in the Midwest, in Washington, D.C., in Chicago, of small towns in Virginia and Pennsylvania. Population charts from the 1800s. Newspaper clippings. Photographs of old buildings.

Some medical records too, which turned out to be from his mother's research into psychosis for East Coast drug companies.

Too much information is as useless as too little.

Four pages were turned down at the corner, suggesting that his father, or someone, wished to return to those pages and review them carefully. Shaw made a note of these and examined each briefly. Page 37 was a map of a town in Alabama; page 63, an article about a particle accelerator; page 118 was a photocopy of an article in *The New York Times* about a new computer system for the New York Stock Exchange; page 255 was a rambling essay by Ashton on the woeful state of the country's infrastructure.

And Shaw reminded himself that it was possible these documents had no relevance whatsoever. They'd been compiled not long before October 5, yes, yet look by whom they'd been compiled: a man whose relationship with reality had, by that time, grown thread-thin.

As Shaw stretched, looking up from examining a picture of an old New England courthouse, he happened to see a car moving slowly along the street, pausing at his Malibu. It was a Nissan Altima, gray, a few years old, its hide dinged and scraped. He couldn't see the driver— too much glare—though he did notice that he or she didn't sit tall in the seat. Just as Shaw was rising, phone ready for a picture of the tag, the vehicle sped up and vanished around the corner. He hadn't seen the tag number.

The person from last night? The person spying on him from above San Miguel Park? Which begged the all-important question: Was it X?

He sat down once again. Call the Task Force?

And, then, what would he tell Wiley?

His phone hummed. He looked at the screen: Frank Mulliner. They weren't scheduled to meet for an hour.

"Frank."

"Colter." The man's voice was grim. Shaw wondered if the young woman's health had taken a bad turn; maybe the fall had been worse than it seemed originally. "There's something I have to talk to you about. I'm . . . I'm not supposed to but it's important."

Shaw set down the cup of superb coffee. "Go ahead."

After a pause the man said, "I'd rather meet in person. Can you come over now?"

# 26.

A white-and-green Task Force police cruiser sat like a lighthouse in front of the Mulliners'. The uniformed deputy behind the wheel was young and wore aviator sunglasses. Like many of the officers Shaw had spotted in the HQ, his head was shaved.

The deputy had apparently been told that Shaw was soon to arrive, along with a description. A glance Shaw's way and he turned back to his radio or computer or—after Shaw's indoctrination into the video gaming world yesterday—maybe *Candy Crush*, which Maddie Poole had told him was considered a "casual" game, the sort played to waste time on your phone.

Mulliner let him in and they walked into the kitchen, where the man fussed over coffee. Shaw declined.

The two men were alone. Sophie was still sleeping. Shaw saw motion at his feet and looked down to see Luka, Fee's standard poodle, stroll in, sip some water and flop down on the floor. The two men sat and Mulliner cupped his mug and said, "There's been another kidnapping. I'm not supposed to tell anybody."

"What're the details?"

The second victim was named Henry Thompson. He and his marriage partner lived south of Mountain View, in Sunnyvale, not far away. Thompson, fifty-two, had gone missing late last night, after a presentation at Stanford University, where he was speaking on a panel. A rock or a brick had crashed into his windshield. When he stopped, he'd been jumped and kidnapped.

"Detective Standish said there weren't any witnesses."

"Not Wiley?"

"No, it was just Detective Standish."

"Ransom demand?"

"I don't think so. That's one of the reasons they think it's the same man who kidnapped Fee," he said, then continued: "Now, Henry Thompson's partner got my name and number and called. He sounded just like I did when Fee was missing. Half crazy . . . Well, you remember. He'd heard about you helping and asked me to get in touch with you. He said he'd hire you to find him."

"I'm not for hire. But I'll talk to him."

Mulliner wrote the name and number on a Post-it: Brian Byrd.

Shaw bent down and scratched the poodle on the head. While the dog wouldn't, of course, understand that Shaw had saved his mistress, you might very well think so from its expression: bright eyes and a knowing grin.

"Henry Thompson." Shaw was typing into Google on his phone. "Which one?" There were several in Sunnyvale.

"He's a blogger and LGBT activist."

Shaw clicked on the correct one. Thompson was round and had a pleasant face, which was depicted smiling in almost every picture Google had of him. He wrote two blogs: one was about the computer industry, the other about LGBT rights. Shaw sent the man's web page to Mack, asking for details on him.

The reply was typical Mack: "'K."

Shaw said to Mulliner, "Can I see Fee?"

He left and returned a moment later with his daughter. She wore a thick burgundy robe and fuzzy pink slippers. Her right arm was embraced by quite the cast, pale blue. And there were bandages on the back of her other hand.

Her eyes were hollow, red-rimmed.

Sophie leaned into a gentle hug from her father.

"Mr. Shaw."

"How does it feel? The break?"

Expressionless, she looked at her arm. "Okay. Itches under the cast. That's the worst." She walked to the refrigerator and poured some orange juice, then returned to the stool and sat. "They put you in a police car. I told them you saved me."

"Not a worry. All good now."

"Did you hear? He kidnapped somebody else?"

"I did. I'm going to help the police again."

A fact the police did not yet know.

Shaw told her, "I know it might be tough but would you tell me what happened?"

She sipped the orange juice, then drank half the glass down. Shaw guessed she was on painkillers that made her mouth dry. "Like, sure."

Shaw had brought one of his notebooks and opened it. Sophie looked at the fountain pen, again without expression.

"Wednesday. You got home."

In halting words, Sophie explained that she'd been angry. "About stuff."

Frank Mulliner's mouth tightened but he said nothing.

She'd biked to Quick Byte Café for a latte and some food—she couldn't remember what now—and called some friends to check on lacrosse practice. Then to San Miguel Park. "Whenever I get pissed or sad, at anything, I go there to bike. To shred, rage. You know what I mean 'rage'?"

Shaw knew.

Her voice caught. "What Kyle used to do on his board. Half Moon Bay and Maverick." Her teeth set and she wiped a tear.

"I pulled onto the shoulder of Tamyen to tighten my helmet. Then this car slammed into me."

The police would have asked and he did as well: "Did you see it?" Shaw thinking gray Nissan, though he'd never lead a witness.

"No. It was, like, *boom*, the fucker slammed me."

She'd lain stunned at the bottom of the hill and heard footsteps coming closer. "I knew it wasn't an accident," she said. "The shoulder was really wide—there was no reason to hit me unless he wanted to. And I heard the car spin its wheels just before it hit, so he was, like, aiming. I got my phone to call nine-one-one but it was too late. I just threw it, so they could track it maybe and find me. Then I tried to get up but he tackled me. And kicked me or hit me in the back, the kidney—so I was, like, paralyzed. I couldn't get up or roll over."

"Smart, tossing your phone. It's how I found out what happened to you."

She nodded. "Then I got stabbed in the neck, a hypodermic needle. And I went out."

"Did the doctors or police say what kind of drug?"

"I asked. They just said a prescription painkiller, dissolved in water."

"Any more thoughts about their appearance?"

"Did I tell you . . . ? I was telling somebody. Gray ski mask, sunglasses."

He showed her the screenshot from the security video at the Quick Byte.

"Detective Standish showed it to me. No, I never saw anybody like that before." She rose, found a chopstick in a drawer and worked it under the cast, rubbing it up and down.

"If you had to guess, a man or a woman?"

"Assumed a man. Not tall. It could've been a woman but if it was she was strong, strong enough to carry me or drag me to the car. And, I mean, kicking me in the back when I was down? You wouldn't think a woman would do that to another woman." She shrugged. "I guess we can be as messed up as a man."

"Did they say anything?"

"No. Next thing, I woke up in that room."

"Describe it."

"There was a little light but I couldn't see much." Her eyes now flared. "It was just so fucking weird. I thought, in the movies, somebody's kidnapped and there's a bed and a blanket and a bucket to pee in, or whatever. There *was* a bottle of water. But no food. Just a big empty glass bottle, this wad of cloth, a spool of fishing line and matches. The room was really old. Moldy and everything. The bottle, the rag—that stuff was new."

Shaw told her again how smart she was, breaking the bottle to make a glass blade and cutting through the Sheetrock.

"I started looking for a way out. The only windows that weren't boarded up were on the top floor. I couldn't just break one and climb out. I started looking for a door. They were locked or nailed shut."

Screwed shut, actually, Shaw recalled. Recently. He told them that he too had looked and found only one open—in the front.

"Didn't get that far." She swallowed. "I heard the gunshots and . . . Kyle . . ." She sobbed quietly. Her father approached and put his arm around her and she cried against his chest for a moment.

Shaw explained to him how Sophie had made a trap from the fishing line and had used another piece to tie it to her jacket and made it move back and forth so there'd be a shadow on the floor. To lure the kidnapper closer. And nail him with an oil drum.

Mulliner was wide-eyed. "Really?"

In a soft voice she said, "I was going to kill you . . . him. Stab him. But I just panicked and ran. I'm sorry if you got hurt."

"I should've figured it out," Shaw said. "I knew you'd be a fighter."

At this she smiled.

Shaw asked, "Did he touch you?"

Her father stirred, but this was a question that needed to be asked.

"I don't think so. All he took off was my shoes and socks. My windbreaker was still zipped up. Your handwriting's really small. Why don't you just write on a computer or tablet? It'd be faster."

Shaw answered the young woman. "When you write something by hand, slowly, you own the words. You type them, less so. You read them, even less. And you listen, hardly at all."

The idea seemed to intrigue her.

"Anybody at the Quick Byte try to pick you up recently?"

"Guys flirt, you know. Ask, 'Oh, what're you reading?' Or 'How're the tamales?' What guys always do. Nobody weird."

"This was in the Quick Byte." On his phone Shaw displayed a photo of the sheet that had been left in place of her MISSING poster. The stenciled image of the eerie face, the hat, the tie. "There was also a version on the outside wall of the room where you were held."

"I don't remember it. The place was so dark. It's creepy."

"Does it mean anything to either of you?"

They both said it did not. Mulliner asked, "What's it supposed to be?"

"I don't know." He'd searched for images of men's faces in hats and ties. Nothing close to this showed up.

"Detective Standish didn't ask you about it?"

"No," Sophie said. "I would have remembered."

A ringtone sounded from inside her robe pocket. It was the default. She hadn't had time to change it on her new phone. The old was in Evidence and would probably die a silent death there. She looked at the screen and answered. "Mom?"

She glanced toward Shaw, who said, "I have enough for now, Fee."

Sophie embraced him and whispered, "Thank you, thank you . . ." The young woman shivered briefly and, with a deep inhalation, walked away, lifting the phone. "Mom." She picked up the glass of orange juice in her other hand and walked back to her room, Luka following. "I'm fine, really . . . He's being great . . ."

The corner of Mulliner's mouth twitched. He glanced at Shaw's naked ring finger. "You married?"

"No. Never." And, as happened occasionally when the topic was tapped, images of Margot Keller's long, Greek goddess face appeared, framed by soft dark blond curls. In this particular slideshow she was looking up from a map of an archaeological dig. A map that Shaw himself had drawn.

Then Mulliner was offering an envelope to him. "Here."

Shaw didn't take it. "Sometimes I work out payment arrangements. No interest."

"Well . . ." Mulliner looked down at the envelope. His face was red.

Shaw said, "A thousand a month for ten months. Can you swing that?"

"I will. Whatever it takes. I will."

Shaw made this arrangement with some frequency

and it drove business manager Velma Bruin to distraction. She'd delivered many variations on the theme: "You do the job, Colt. You deserve the money when it's due."

Velma was right, but there was nothing wrong with flexibility. And that was particularly true on this job. He'd gotten the lesson about the financial stresses of Silicon Valley.

The Land of Promise, where so very many people struggled.

# 27.

Halfway to Henry Thompson's address, Colter Shaw noted that his pursuer was back. Maybe.

He'd twice seen a car behind him making the same turns he'd made. A gray sedan, like the one outside Salvadoran coffee heaven. The grille logo was indiscernible six or seven car lengths back. Nissan? Maybe, maybe not.

He believed, to his surprise, that the driver was a woman.

Shaw had been keeping an eye on the car when the driver blew through a red light to make a turn in his direction. He caught a glimpse of a silhouette through the driver's-side window. He saw again the short stature and frizzy hair tied in a ponytail. Not exclusive to women, of course, but more likely F than M.

*You wouldn't think a woman would do that to another woman. I guess we can be as messed up as a man . . .*

Shaw made two unnecessary turns and the gray car followed.

Eyeing the street, the asphalt surface, measuring angles, distances, turning radii.

Now . . .

He slammed on the brake and skidded one hundred and eighty degrees, to face the pursuer. He earned a middle finger or two and at least a half dozen horns blared.

A new sound joined the salute.

The bleep of a siren. Shaw hadn't noticed that he'd U-turned directly in front of an unmarked Chrysler.

A sigh. He pulled over and readied license and rental contract.

A stocky Latino in a green uniform walked up to him.

"Sir."

"Officer." Handing over the paperwork.

"That was a very unsafe thing you did."

"I know. I'm sorry."

The cop—his name was P. ALVAREZ—wandered back to his car and dropped into the front seat to run the info. Shaw was looking at the space where the gray car had been and was no longer. At least he'd confirmed that it was the same vehicle as at the Salvadoran restaurant—a Nissan Altima, the same year, with the same dings and scrapes. He hadn't caught the license tag.

The man returned to the driver's window and gave Shaw back the documents.

"Why'd you do that, sir?"

"I thought somebody was following me. Was worried about a carjacker. I heard they go after rental cars."

Alvarez said slowly, "Which is why rental cars don't have any markings to indicate they're rental cars."

"That right?"

"You troubled by something, call nine-one-one. That's what we're here for. You're from out of town. You have business here?"

A nod. "Yep."

Alvarez seemed to ponder. "All right. You're lucky. It's my court day and I don't have time to write this up. But let's not do anything stupid again."

"I won't, Officer."

"Be on your way."

Shaw restowed the papers and started the engine, driving to the intersection where he'd last seen the Nissan. He turned left, in the direction where she would logically have escaped. And, of course, found no trace.

He returned to the GPS route and in fifteen minutes was at the complex where Henry Thompson shared a condo with his partner, Brian Byrd. A police car, unmarked, sat in front of the building. Unlike with Sophie's kidnapping, the Task Force, or whoever was running the disappearance, would know for certain that Henry Thompson had been kidnapped, having found the man's damaged car. The officer—maybe the elusive Detective Standish—would be with Byrd, waiting for the ransom demand that Shaw knew would never come.

His phone hummed with a text. He parked and read it. Mack had discovered no criminal history in the lives of Thompson or Byrd. No weapons registrations. No security clearances or sensitive employment that might suggest motive—Thompson was the blogger and gay rights activist that Wikipedia assured Shaw he was. Byrd worked as a financial officer for a small venture capital firm. No domestic abuse complaints. Thompson had been married for a year to a woman, but a decade ago. There seemed to be no bad blood between them. Like Sophie, he appeared to have been picked at random.

Very wrong time, very wrong place.

After leaving the Mulliners, Shaw had texted Byrd to make sure he was home, asking if they could meet. He immediately replied yes.

Shaw now called the number.

"Hello?"

"Mr. Byrd?"

"Yes."

"Colter Shaw."

Byrd was then speaking to someone else in the room: "It's a friend. It's okay."

Then back to Shaw: "Can we talk? Downstairs? There's a garden outside the lobby."

Neither of them wanted the police to know that Shaw was involved.

"I'll be there." Shaw disconnected, climbed from the Malibu and strolled through manicured grounds to a bench near the front door. A fountain shot mist into the air, the rainbow within waving like a flag.

He scanned the roads beyond the lovely landscaping looking for gray Nissans.

Byrd appeared a moment later. He was in his fifties, wearing a white dress shirt and dark slacks, belly hanging two inches over the belt. His thinning white hair was mussed and he hadn't shaved. The men shook hands and Byrd sat on the bench, hunched forward, fingers interlaced. He arranged and rearranged the digits constantly, the way Frank Mulliner had toyed with the orange golf ball.

"They're waiting for a ransom call." He spoke in a weak voice. "Ransom? Henry's a blogger and I'm a CFO, but the company's nothing by SV standards. We don't even do tech start-ups." His voice broke. "I don't have any money. If they want some, I don't know what I'm going to do."

"I don't think it's about money. There might not even be a motive. It could be he's just deranged." Shaw was going with *he*; no need to muddy the conversation with talk about gender.

Byrd turned his red eyes to Shaw. "You found that girl. I want to hire you to find Henry. Detective Standish seems smart . . . Well, I want you. Name your price. Anything. I may have to borrow but I'm good for it."

Shaw said, "I don't work for a fee."

"Her father . . . He paid something."

"That was a reward."

"Then I'll offer a reward. How much do you want?"

"I don't want any money. I have an interest in the case now. Let me ask you some questions. Then I'll see what I can do."

"God . . . Thank you, Mr. Shaw."

"Colter's fine." He withdrew his notebook and uncapped the pen. "With Sophie, the kidnapper spotted her ahead of time and followed her. It's logical that he'd have done the same with Henry."

"You mean, staking him out?"

"Probably. He was very organized. I want to check all

of the places Henry was, say, thirty-six hours before he was kidnapped."

Byrd's fingers knitted once more and the knuckles grew white. "He was here, of course, at night. And we had dinner at Julio's." A nod up the street. "Two nights ago. The lecture at Stanford last night. Other than that, I have no idea. He drives all over the Valley. San Francisco, Oakland too. He must drive fifty miles a day for research. That's why the blogs are so popular."

"Do you know about any meetings in the past few days?"

"Just the lecture he was driving home from when he was kidnapped. Other than that, no. I'm sorry."

"What articles was he working on? We can try to piece together where he was."

Byrd looked down at the sidewalk at their feet. "The one he was most passionate about was an exposé about the high cost of real estate in SV—Silicon Valley, you know?"

Shaw nodded.

"Then there was an article about game companies data-mining players' personal information and selling it. The third was about revenue streams in the software industry.

"For the real estate blog, he drove everywhere. He talked to the tax authorities, zoning board brokers, homeowners, renters, landlords, builders . . . For the data-mining and revenue-stream stories, he went to Google and Apple, Facebook, a bunch of other companies; I don't remember which." He tapped his knee. "Oh, Walmart."

"Walmart?"

"On El Camino Real. He mentioned he was going there and I said we'd just been shopping. He said no, it was for work."

"The panel at Stanford last night? What facility?"

"Gates Computer Science Building."

"Did he go to any LBGT rights meetings lately?"

"No, not recently."

Shaw asked him to look over Thompson's notes and any appointment calendars he could find to see where else Thompson might have gone. Byrd said he would.

"Would Henry have gone to the Quick Byte Café in Mountain View recently?"

"We've been there, but not for months." Byrd couldn't sit still. He rose and looked at a jacaranda tree, vibrantly purple. "What was it like for the girl? Sophie. The police wouldn't tell me much."

Shaw explained about her being locked in a room, abandoned. "There were some things he left. She used them to escape and rigged a trap to attack him."

"She did that?"

Shaw nodded.

"Henry would hate that. Just hate it. He's claustro-phobic." Byrd began to cry. Finally he controlled him-self. "It's so quiet in the condo. I mean, when Henry's away and I'm home, it's quiet. Now, I don't know, it's a different kind of quiet. You know what I mean?"

Shaw knew exactly what the man meant but there was nothing he could say to make it better.

# 28.

Shaw was making the rounds of places Henry Thompson had been prior to his kidnapping.

Apple and Google were big and formidable institutions and without the name of an employee Thompson had contacted there, Shaw had no entrée to start the search. And there'd be no chance to reprise any Quick Byte scenario in which a Tiffany would help him play spy and give him access to security videos.

Stanford University was a more logical choice. The kidnapper was likely to have followed Thompson from the lecture, then passed him on a deserted stretch of road, stopped a hundred or so yards ahead and, when Thompson caught up, flung the brick or rock into his windshield.

But the Gates Computer Center, the site of the panel, was in a congested part of the Stanford campus. There was no parking nearby and Thompson might have walked as far as two hundred yards in any direction to collect his car. He shared Thompson's picture with a handful of employees, guards and shopkeepers; no one recognized him.

Shaw knew the road where Thompson had been taken. He drove past it. The car had been towed but a portion of the shoulder was encircled by yellow tape. It was a grassy area; probably picked by X to avoid leaving tire prints, like at the factory. There were no houses or other buildings nearby.

Then there was the Walmart that Byrd had said Thompson had driven to. Why had the blogger's research taken him to a superstore?

He set the GPS for the place and piloted the Malibu in that direction. Over the wide streets of sun-grayed asphalt. Past perfectly trimmed hedges, tall grass, sidewalks as white as copier paper, blankets of radiant lawns, vines and shaggy palms. He noted the stylish and clever buildings that architects might put on page one of their portfolios, with mirrored windows like the eyes of predatory fish, uninterested in you . . . though only at the moment.

Then, just as had happened on his drive from his camper to the Salvadoran restaurant, Shaw left behind the mansions and glitzy corporations and suddenly entered a very different Silicon Valley. Small residences, stoic and worn, reminiscent of Frank Mulliner's house. The owners had made the choice between food and fresh paint.

He now pulled into the parking lot of Walmart, a chain with which he was quite familiar. A dependable source of clothing, food, medical supplies and hunting and fishing and other survival gear—and, just as important, last-minute presents for the nieces—his sister's children, whom he saw several times a year.

What could have brought Henry Thompson here?

Then he understood the blogger's likely mission. In a far corner of the parking lot were a number of cars, SUVs and pickups. Sitting in and around the vehicles—front seats and lawn chairs—were men in clean, if wrinkled, clothing. Jeans, chinos, polo shirts. Even a few sport coats. Everyone, it seemed, had a laptop. Ninety years ago, during the Great Depression, they would have gathered around a campfire; now they sat before the cold white light of a computer screen.

A new breed of hobo.

Shaw parked the Malibu and climbed out. He made the rounds, displaying Thompson's picture on his phone screen and explaining simply that the man had gone missing and he was helping find him.

Shaw learned to his surprise that none of these men— and it was men exclusively—was in fact homeless or unemployed. They had jobs here in the Valley, some with prestigious internet companies, and they had residences. Yet they lived miles and miles away, too far to commute daily, and they couldn't spare the money for hotel or motel rooms. They'd stay here for two, three or four days a week, then drive back to their families. At night, Shaw learned, the camp was more crowded; this group worked evening or graveyard shifts.

This would be why Henry Thompson had come here: to interview these men for his blog about the hardship of owning or renting property in the Valley.

A lean, wiry Latino living out of his Buick crossover

told Shaw, "This is a step up for me. I used to spend all night riding the bus to Marin, then back. Six hours. The drivers, they didn't care, you buy a ticket, you can sleep all night. But I got mugged twice. This's better."

Some were janitorial, some maintenance. Others were coders and middle management. Shaw saw one young man with an elaborate hipster mustache and filigree gold earrings drawing on a large artist's pad, sketching out what seemed to be a trade ad for a piece of hardware. He was talented.

Only one man remembered Henry Thompson. "A couple days ago, yessir. Asked me questions about where I lived, the commute, had I tried to find someplace closer? He was interested if I'd been pressured out of my house. Had somebody tried to bribe me or threaten me? Especially government workers or developers." He shook his head. "Henry was nice. He cared about us."

"Was anybody with him or did you see anybody watching him?"

"Watching?"

"We think he might've been kidnapped."

"Kidnapped? Are you serious? Oh, man. I'm sorry." He gazed around. "People come and go here. I can't help you."

Shaw surveyed the lot. There was a security camera on the Walmart building itself but too distant to pick up anything here. And there was the No Tiffany factor.

He climbed back into the Malibu. Just as he did, his phone hummed and he answered.

"Hello?"

"Oh, Colter. It's Brian Byrd."

"Have you heard anything?"

"No. I did want to tell you I looked everywhere and couldn't find any more notes of Henry's. You know, where he might've been if that guy was watching him. Henry must've had everything with him. You had any luck, anything at all?"

"No."

"Who does something like this?" Byrd whispered. "Why? What's the point? There's no ransom demand. Henry never hurt anybody. I mean, Jesus. It's like this guy's playing some goddamn sick game . . ." Shaw heard a deep sigh. "Why the hell's he doing this? You have any idea?"

After a moment Colter Shaw said, "I might, Brian. I just might."

# 29.

Shaw sped back toward the Winnebago. He kept an eye out for cops but at the moment he didn't care about a ticket.

Once in the camper he went online and began his search.

He was surprised that it didn't take very long to find what he hoped he might. And the results were far better than he'd expected. He called the Joint Major Crimes Task Force and asked for Dan Wiley.

"I'm sorry. Detective Wiley's not available."

"His partner?"

"Detective Standish's not available either."

The message of the woman at the JMCTF desk was getting as familiar as her voice.

Shaw hung up. He'd do what he did before: go to the Task Force in person and insist on seeing Wiley or Standish, if either of the men was in the office. Or Supervisor Cummings, if not. Better in person anyway, he decided. Getting the police to accept his new hypothesis of the case would take some persuasion.

He printed out a stack of documents, the fruits of his research, and slipped them into his computer bag. He stepped outside, locked the door and turned to the right, where he'd parked the Malibu. He got as far as the electrical and water hookups and froze.

The gray Nissan Altima had blocked in his rental. Its driver's seat was empty, the door open.

Back to the camper, get your weapon.

Dropping his computer bag, he pivoted and strode to the door, keys out.

Three locks. Fastest way to get them undone: slowly.

*Never rush, however urgent . . .*

He never got to the last lock. Twenty feet in front of him, a figure holding a Glock pistol stepped from the shadows between his Winnebago and the neighboring Mercedes Renegade. It was the driver of the Nissan—yes, a woman, African American, her hair in the ragged ponytail he'd seen in silhouette. She wore an olive-drab combat jacket—of the sort favored by gangbangers—and cargo pants. Her eyes were fierce. She raised the weapon his way.

Shaw assessed: nothing to do against a gun that's eight paces distant and in the hand of somebody who clearly knows what to do with a weapon.

Odds of fighting: two percent.

Odds of negotiating your way out: no clue, but better.

Still, sometimes you have to make what seem like inane decisions. The wrestler in him lowered his center of gravity and debated how close he could get before he passed out after a gunshot to the torso. After all, lethal shots are notoriously difficult to make with pistols. Then he recalled: if this was the kidnapper, she'd killed Kyle Butler with a headshot from much farther away than this.

The grim-faced woman squinted and moved in, snapping with irritation, "Get down! Now!"

It wasn't get down or I'm going to shoot you. It was get down, you're in my goddamn way.

Shaw got down.

She jogged past him, her eyes on a line of trees that separated the trailer camp from a quiet road, the gun aimed in that direction. At the end of the drive, she stopped and peered through a dense growth of shrubs.

Shaw rose and quietly started for the Winnebago's door again, pulling the keys from his pocket.

Eyes still on the trees, both hands on the gun, ready to shoot, the woman said in a blunt voice, "I told you. Stay down."

Shaw knelt once more.

She pushed farther into the brush. A whisper: "Damn." She turned around, holstering her weapon.

"Safe now," she said. "You can get up."

She walked to him, fishing in her pocket. Shaw wasn't surprised when she displayed a gold badge. What he didn't expect, though, was what came next: "Mr. Shaw, I'm Detective LaDonna Standish. I'd like to have a talk."

# 30.

Shaw collected his computer bag from the clump of grass where he'd dropped it.

As he and Standish approached the Winnebago door, an unmarked police car squealed to a stop in front of the camper. Shaw recognized it. It was the same vehicle that had lit him up after the dramatic U-turn on his way to Henry Thompson's condo. Officer P. Alvarez.

Shaw looked from the detective to the cop. "You were both following me?"

Standish said, "Double team tailing. The only way it works. Ought to be triple, but who can afford tying up three cars these days?" She continued: "Budget, budget, budget. Had to follow you myself last night. Peter here was free this morning."

Alvarez said, "I didn't want to have to pull you over but it'd been more suspicious if I didn't. Was an impressive turn, Mr. Shaw. Stupid, like I said, but impressive."

"I hope I don't need to do it again." He cast a dark

glance toward Standish, who snickered. Shaw nodded to the bushes. "So, who'd you spot?"

"Don't know," she said with some irritation in her voice. "Had a report of somebody near your camper, possible trespasser. Smelled funky to me, all things considered."

Her radio clattered. Another officer, apparently also cruising the area, had not spotted the suspect. Then came one more transmission, from a different patrolman. She told them to continue to search. She told Alvarez to do the same. When he drove off, she nodded toward the Winnebago. After Shaw unlocked the last lock, she preceded him inside.

The word *warrant* glanced off his thoughts. He let it go. He closed and locked the door behind them.

"You've got a California conceal carry," she said. "Where's your weapon? Or weapons?" She walked to his coffeepot and poked through the half dozen bags of ground beans in a basket bolted to the counter.

"The spice cabinet," he said. "My carry weapon."

"Spice cabinet. Hmm. And it's a . . . ?"

"Glock 42."

"Just leave it there."

"And under the bed, a Colt Python .357."

She lifted an eyebrow. "Must be doing well in the reward business to afford one of those."

"Was a present."

"Other CCPs?"

A concealed carry permit in California is available only to residents. The California ticket doesn't let you carry in many other states. He had a nonresidence permit

issued by Florida and that was good in a number of juris-
dictions. Shaw, though, rarely went around armed; it was
a pain to constantly pay attention to where you could and
couldn't carry—schools and hospitals, for instance, were
often no-gun zones. The laws varied radically from state
to state.

Shaw said, "You thought I might be the kidnapper."

"Crossed my mind at first. I confirmed your alibi,
what you told Dan Wiley. Didn't mean you weren't
working with somebody, of course. But snatching some
soul and hoping her daddy'll hand over a reward? Well,
there's stupid and then there's stupid. I checked you out.
You're not either variety."

He then understood why she'd been tailing him. "You
were using me as bait."

A shrug. "You went and ruined a play date for the
perp. Got Sophie home safe. Pissed that boy off in a large
way, I'm thinking. Pissed him off enough that he went
out and did it again—with Henry Thompson."

"That was the kidnapper following me?" A nod outside.

"Big mug of coincidence if it wasn't. And if it's like
Sophie's case he'd just leave Thompson on his own. Have
himself plenty of free time to come visit you. If he was so
inclined. As maybe he was. Unless you have other folks
might want to have a few words with you? As I suspect
might be the case, given your career."

"Some. I've got people who keep an eye on that. And
no reports of anything."

Shaw's friend and fellow rock climber Tom Pepper,
former FBI, ran a security company in Chicago. He and

Mack kept track of those felonious alumni of Shaw's successful rewards jobs who'd threatened him.

He continued: "Description of the perp here?"

"Dark clothing. Nothing else. Nothing on the vehicle."

"You said *him*."

"Ah. Him or her."

"Is Detective Wiley at Brian Byrd's condo?"

She paused. "Detective Wiley is no longer with the Criminal Investigations Division of the Task Force."

"He's not?"

"I rotated him to Liaison."

"You rotated him?"

Standish angled her head slightly. "Oh, you thought he was the boss and that I worked for him? Why would that be, Mr. Shaw? Because I'm"—there was a fat pause—"shorter?"

It was because she was younger but he said, "Because you're so bad at surveillance."

The touché moment landed and her mouth curved into a brief smile.

Shaw continued: "Wiley's gone because he arrested me?"

"No. I would've done that. Oh, his grounds for the collar were wrong—like you told Cummings. Tampering with evidence we missed and you secured? My oh my, the JMCTF would look mighty bad if you mentioned that to the press. Which you would have done."

"Maybe."

"I would've taken you in as a material witness and not behind Plexiglas, thank you very much. Just till we checked you out properly. No, Dan got kicked down 'cause he didn't follow up on that memo of yours. You've got good handwriting. Bet you've heard that before. He should've jumped on the case with both feet. You ever work in law enforcement?"

"No. What's Liaison? That you sent him to?"

"We're a Task Force, right? We come from eight different agencies and there's a lot of back-and-forth. Dan'll get reports to where they belong."

A messenger. Shaw thought, Tough break, Chief.

Standish said, "Dan's not a bad guy. Had a bad spell recently. He was admin for years. Good at it, real good. Then his wife passed away. It was sudden. Thirty-three days from diagnosis to the end. He wanted to try something new. Get out, away from the desk. He thought the field would help. Man sure looks like a cop, doesn't he?"

"Central casting."

"He was out of his league on the street. Insecurity and authority—bad combo. There were other complaints too."

*What'd you find, sweetheart? . . .*

Standish was looking over a map of a trail in the Compound. "That's . . . ?"

"My family home. Not far from Sierra National Forest."

"You grew up there?"

"I did. My mother still lives on the family place. I was heading there for a visit until this happened."

Her finger followed a red marker line on the map.

He said, "Was going for a rock climb there."

Standish exhaled a brief laugh. "You do that for the fun of it?"

He gave a nod.

"Your mom? Lives there? Middle of nowhere?"

Shaw didn't give Standish too much history, just explained that Mary Dove Shaw had become a sort of Georgia O'Keeffe—both in spirit and, with her lean sinewy figure and long hair, in appearance. With her background as a psychiatrist, med school professor and principal investigator, she had turned the Compound into a retreat for fellow doctors and scientists. Women's health was a popular theme of the get-togethers. Hunting parties too. One needs to eat, after all.

Shaw added that he made it a point to visit several times a year.

"That's the way," Standish said, and his impression was that she was devoted to her parents too.

Shaw asked, "Anything new about Henry?"

"Henry Thompson? No."

He asked, "Forensics?"

Shaw guessed she wouldn't share with a civie. Standish instead spoke without hesitation. "Not good. No touch DNA on Sophie's clothes. Too early to tell with Thompson's car and the rock that got pitched into his windshield, but why would the unsub turn careless now? No prints anywhere. Wore cloth gloves. Can't source anything—the screws he sealed the door with, the water, the matches and the other stuff he left. Tire treads're useless, thanks to the grass, which I guess you knew. Oh, and I did have a team look over that access road where you said somebody was watching you."

When he met Kyle Butler. Shaw nodded.

"That was gravel. So: useless encore. And I ran the traffic cams on Tamyen en route to the park from the

Quick Byte . . ." She furrowed her brow, staring at his face. "You told Dan to check them out too?"

"I did."

"Hmm. Well, nothing, sorry to report. No cars parked near the café were tagged on Tamyen."

A good job, Shaw was thinking.

"With Thompson, he picked another place with a grassy field—no tire tracks there. Now, our unsub's shoes're men's size nine and a half Nikes. That means he—or she—was wearing men's size nine and a half Nikes. Doesn't mean they have size nine and a half feet. No security camera footage except for what you found at the Quick Byte Café. Had an unfortunate rookie spend hours scrubbing through the tape. Nobody seemed interested in Sophie, going back for two weeks. Other stores, bars and restaurants? Nothing. Was it you or Dan thought of the CCTV at Tamyen and Forty-two?"

"Did it show anything?"

Standish seemed amused Shaw wouldn't say. "There wasn't one. Weapon was a Glock nine. And he took the brass with him. While he *was* a ways from Kyle Butler, he made a clean headshot. He's done some range time in his day. I'd say he was a pro, but pros don't do weird things like lock people in rooms. They shoot them or promise *not* to shoot them if the family coughs up the bucks."

"You?" Shaw said.

"Me what?"

"Combat." Shaw nodded at the OD jacket.

"No. It's cozy. I chill easy."

"You canvassed for the gray stocking cap?"

"From the Quick Byte tape? Yep. Nothing yet. I've got another rookie looking at about ten hours of security video from the parking lots at Stanford."

Shaw said, "The lots on Quarry Road would be best. The ones closer to the Gates Center are small and they fill up fast."

"What I was thinking too."

He added that he had canvassed stores and security guards on the campus. She smiled when he used the cop term.

"Anybody talk to you?"

"Most of them did. Nobody saw Thompson."

"And what about the poster?" Shaw asked.

She frowned quizzically.

"That I gave to Wiley. Of the face."

She flipped through her notebook. "Something about a sheet of paper left at a café. The lab ran it and it was negative DNA and prints. I didn't see it."

Explained why she hadn't shown it to Sophie.

Shaw opened his computer bag and withdrew the sheets he'd printed earlier. On top was the image of the stenciled face, which he turned her way.

"What's this?"

"It's the Whispering Man."

"Why's it important?" she asked.

"Because it might be the key to the whole case."

# 31.

Shaw was explaining. "I was looking into some leads that Brian Byrd gave me. Places that Henry had been over the past day or so. I wanted a witness who'd seen somebody following him, maybe find another security video. Nothing panned out. I told that to Brian. And he said it made no sense to kidnap Henry. It was somebody playing a sick game."

Standish grunted, though it was a benign grunt. She looked up from the printout.

Shaw continued: "You know the C3 Conference in town?"

"Computers. Gamers, right? Screwing up traffic. But that's in San Jose, so I don't care in particular. What's that got to do with the unsub?"

"He could've raped or killed Sophie anytime. He didn't. He left her in that room in the factory with things she could use to survive. Five things: fishing line, matches, water, a glass bottle and a strip of cloth."

"Okay."

He sensed she was guessing where this was going and the skeptic's flag was starting to go up.

"I was at the conference yesterday."

"You were? You into games?"

"No. I went with a friend."

*I had time to kill after your people hijacked my car* . . .

He said, "And I saw a game where you collect objects you can use to play. Like weapons, clothes, food, magic power things."

"Magic."

"What if Byrd was right? This *is* a sick game? I went online and looked for video games where players are given five things and have to use them to survive. I found one. *The Whispering Man*."

She fanned out the top few sheets. While the stenciled image of the Whispering Man was crudely done, Shaw had downloaded a number of pictures that were professionally drawn or painted, most from promotions or ads for the game. Some from rabid fans.

"Is he a ghost?" she asked. "Or what?"

"Supernatural, who knows? In the game he knocks you out. You wake up barefoot—like Sophie—and all you have are the five things. You can trade them, use them as weapons to kill other players and steal what they have. Or players can work together—you've got a hammer and somebody else has nails. You play online. At any given time, there're a hundred thousand people playing, all over the world."

"Mr. Shaw," she began, the cynic's flag wholly unfurled now.

He continued: "There're ten levels of play, going from easier to harder. The first is called The Abandoned Factory."

Standish remained silent.

"Look at this." He turned to his Dell and loaded You-Tube. They leaned close to the screen. He typed into the search block and scores of videos depicting scenes from *The Whispering Man* came up. He clicked one. The video began with a first-person view, strolling down a sidewalk in pleasant suburbia. The music soundtrack was soft, under which you could hear what might be footsteps behind you. The player stopped and looked back. Nothing except the sidewalk. When he turned to continue, the Whispering Man was blocking the way, a faint smile on his face. A pause, then the creature lunged forward. The screen went black. A man's voice, high-pitched and giddy, whispered, "You've been abandoned. Escape if you can. Or die with dignity."

The screen slowly lightened, as if the player were growing conscious. Looking around, you could see it was an old factory, with five objects sitting in view—a hammer, a blowtorch, a spool of thread, a gold medallion and a bottle of some kind of blue liquid.

As they watched, the point-of-view character looked up to see a woman avatar walking stealthily closer, about to reach for his gold medallion; he picked up the hammer and beat her to death.

"Lord." This from Standish.

A line of text appeared: *You have just earned water purification tablets, a silk ribbon, and what appears to be a clock but might not be.*

"At the factory? The unsub gave Sophie enough tools to escape, if she could figure out how. He screwed all the doors shut except for one. He was giving her a chance to win."

She said nothing for a moment. "So your theory is he's basing the kidnappings on the game."

"It's a hypothesis," Shaw corrected. "A theory is a hypothesis that's been verified."

Standish glanced at him, then turned back to the screen. "I don't know, Mr. Shaw. Most crime's simple. This's complicated."

"It's happened before. With the same game." He handed Standish another sheet, an article from a Dayton newspaper. "Eight years ago, two boys in high school got obsessed with the game."

"This game? *The Whispering Man?*"

"Right. They played it in real life and kidnapped a girl classmate. A seventeen-year-old. They hid her in a barn, tied up. She was badly injured trying to escape. Then they decided they'd better kill her. They tried to but she got away. One of the boys went to a mental hospital, the other was sentenced to twenty-five years in prison."

This got her attention. She asked, "And are they . . . ?"

"They're both still in the system."

She looked at the printouts and folded them.

"Worth looking into. 'Preciate it. And I appreciate what you did for Sophie Mulliner, Mr. Shaw. You saved her life. Dan Wiley didn't. I didn't. My experience is, though, that civilians can . . . muddy an investigation. So, with all respect, I'll ask you to fire up this nifty camper of yours and get on with that visit to your mother. Or see the sequoias, see Yosemite. Go anywhere else you want. As long as it isn't here."

# 32.

Colter Shaw was not on his way to the Compound to see his mother, nor en route to marvel at millennia-old trees nor planning a climb up towering El Capitan in Yosemite.

Nor anywhere else.

He was still smack in the middle of Silicon Valley—at the Quick Byte Café, to be specific. He was sipping coffee that was perfectly fine, though it didn't approach the Salvadoran beans from Potrero Grande, wherever that was.

He glanced at the bulletin board; the picture of Sophie he had pinned up yesterday was still there. Shaw wondered if that was because of the video camera now aimed at the board. He returned to yet more printouts—material that private eye Mack had just sent him in response to his request. He looked for Tiffany to thank her for the help, but she and her daughter were not in at the moment.

A woman's sultry voice from nearby: "I rarely get calls from men after I kill them. I'm glad you don't wear grudges, son."

Maddie Poole was approaching. Her pretty, appealing face, sprinkled with those charming freckles, was smiling. She dropped into the chair opposite him. The green eyes sparkled.

*Son* . . .

Shaw thought of Dan Wiley's reference to him as "Chief" and reflected that one's tolerance for endearments depends largely on the person doing the endearing.

"Get you something?" he asked.

She glanced at a neighboring table. Two young men in baggy sweats and jackets were sitting with Red Bulls and coffees. They were bleary-eyed. Shaw remembered that this was a hub of the computing and gaming world. The hour—10:30 a.m.—was probably savagely early for them. Maddie's eyes too were red-rimmed. "That," Maddie said. "RB and coffee. Not mixed together, of course. That would be strange. And no milk or anything that might upset the caffeine. Oh, and something sweet maybe? You mind?"

"Not a worry."

"You like sweet stuff, Colt?"

"No."

"Pity poor."

At the counter he perused the pastries, under plastic domes. He called, "Cinnamon roll?"

"You read my mind."

These choices didn't require a numbered card. The kid heated the half-pound roll, dripping with icing, for thirty seconds, then placed it and the beverages on a tray. A second cup of coffee for Shaw too.

He carried the tray to the table.

Maddie thanked him and drank down the entire Red Bull and took a fast slug of coffee. The giddiness vanished. "Look. Yesterday—at the Hong-Sung game, *Immersion*? It's hard to explain. The thing is, I get sort of possessed when I play. Any game. I can't control myself. Or sports. I used to downhill-ski, and race mountain bikes too. You ever race?"

"Motocross. AMA. Too much work to pedal. I've got a gas engine."

"Then maybe you know: you just *have* to win. No other option."

He did know. No further explanation necessary.

"Thanks," she said. Now the tense, troubled mood was jettisoned. "Sure you don't want a bite?"

"No."

She tore off a hunk of the excessive roll with a fork. It sped to her mouth and, as she chewed, she closed her eyes and exhaled extravagantly.

"Do I look like a commercial? Those restaurant ads where somebody takes a bite of steak or shrimp and they get all orgasmic."

Shaw didn't see many commercials. And he'd definitely seen no commercials like that.

"You've been back to the conference?" he asked.

"I go back and forth. There, then my rental, where my rig's set up. GrindrGirl's gotta make a living." She took another bite and on its heels another slug of coffee. "Sugar rush. I've never done coke. No need when you've got icing. You agree?"

Was she asking about his interest in drugs? He had none, never had. Other than the occasional painkiller when there was a need. This was a question on the road to Relationship. Now was not the time.

"There's been another kidnapping."

Her fork went to the plate. The smile vanished. "Shit. By the same guy?"

"Probably."

"Have they found this victim?"

"No. He's still missing."

"He? So it's not a pervert?" Maddie asked.

"Nobody knows."

"There a reward again?"

"No, I'm just helping the police. And I could use some help from you."

"Nancy Drew."

"Who?"

"You have a sister, Colt?"

"Three years younger."

"She didn't read Nancy Drew?"

"A kid's book?"

"A series, yeah. Girl detective."

"I don't think so." The Shaw children had read a great deal yet children's fiction was not to be found in the substantial library in the cabin at the Compound.

"I read them all growing up . . . We'll save the date talk for another time . . . You don't smile much, do you?"

"No, but I don't mind date talk."

She liked that. "Ask away."

"The kidnapper might've based the crimes on a video game. *The Whispering Man*. Do you know it?"

Another bite of roll. She chewed, thoughtful. "Heard of it. Been around for a long time."

"You ever played it?"

"No. It's an action-adventure. NMS." She noted his blank reaction. "Sorry. 'Not my style.' I'm a first-person shooter, remember? I think the gameplay for that one is you're trapped somewhere and you have to escape. Something like that. It's the Survival subcategory of action-adventures. You think some psycho dude's acting out the game in real life for kicks?"

"One possibility. He's smart, calculating, plans everything out ahead of time. He knows forensics and how not to leave evidence. My mother's a psychiatrist. I've talked to her about some of the jobs I've worked. She told me that sociopaths—serial killers—are very rare and even the organized ones aren't usually this organized. Sure, he could be one. I'm guessing that's only a ten percent option. Somebody this smart might be acting crazy, to cover up what he's really doing."

"Which is what?"

Shaw sipped coffee. "Not many ideas there. One possibility? Drive the manufacturer of *The Whispering Man* out of business."

He went on to explain about the incident of the schoolgirl in Ohio, the classmates who played the game in real life. Maddie said she hadn't heard of it.

He continued: "Maybe those crimes gave the perp the idea. When word gets out that for the second time somebody's been inspired to re-create the game, the publicity might ruin the company." He tapped some of the printouts. "You probably know this, but there's a lot of concern about violence in video games. Maybe the perp's harnessing that."

"The debates've been going on forever. Back to the seventies. There was an early arcade game called *Death Race*, published by a company right here, I think, in Mountain View. It was cheesy: monochrome, two-D, stick figures. And it caused an uproar. You drove a car around the screen and ran over these characters. When you did, they died and a tombstone popped up. Congress, I mean everybody, freaked out. Now there's *Grand Theft Auto* . . . One of the most popular games ever. You get points for killing cops or just walking around and shooting people at random." She touched his arm and looked into his eyes. "I kill zombies for a living. Do I look disturbed?"

"The question is: Who'd have a motive to ruin the company?"

"Ex-wife of the CEO?"

"Thought of that. His name's Marty Avon and he's been happily married for twenty-five years. Well, I'm adding the *happily*. Let's just say there's no ex in the picture."

"Disgruntled employee," Maddie suggested. "Plenty of those in the tech world."

"Could be. Worth checking out . . . There's another thought too. What's the competition like in the gaming world? I mean, competing companies, not players."

Maddie gave a sardonic laugh. "More combat than competition." Her eyes seemed wistful. "Didn't used to be that way. In the old days. Your days, Colter."

"Funny."

"Everybody worked together. They'd write code for you for free, no bullshit about copyright. They'd donate computer time, give away games for nothing. The one that got me started was *Doom*—remember from C3 yesterday? Ground zero for first-person shooters. It was originally shareware. Free to anybody who wanted it. That didn't last long. Once the companies figured out they could make money in this business . . . Well, it was every shooter for himself."

Maddie told him about the famous "Console Wars," the battle between Nintendo and Sega, Mario the plumber versus Sonic the hedgehog. "Nintendo won."

*A shrine to the chivalrous who protect the weak . . .*

"Nowadays, you can't look at the news out of SV without seeing stories about theft of trade secrets, ripping off copyrights, spies, insider trading, piracy, sabotage. Buying up companies, then firing everybody and burying their software because it might compete with yours." She glanced at the remnants of the roll and pushed it away. "But murdering somebody, Colter?"

Shaw had pursued rewards for fugitives who'd killed for less than the value of a businessman's second Mercedes. He recalled the welcome screen at the conference.

> *THE VIDEO GAMING INDUSTRY REVENUES WERE*
> *$142 BILLION LAST YEAR, UP 15% FROM THE*
> *YEAR BEFORE . . .*

Plenty of motive with that kind of money.

"*The Whispering Man*'s made by—"

"Oh, Colt. We say *published*. A game's published, like a book or a comic. By a studio, like Hollywood. Games actually are just like movies now: the avatars and creatures are real actors shot against green screens. There are directors, cinematographers, sound designers, writers, CG people, of course."

Shaw continued: "Published by Destiny Entertainment. Marty Avon and Destiny have been sued a dozen times. All the suits were settled or dismissed. Some complaints alleged that Avon stole source code. I'm not sure what that is but it seems important."

"Just the way your heart and nervous system are important."

"Maybe one of the plaintiffs got kicked out of court and wanted to get revenge against Destiny his own way." Shaw slid a stack of sheets toward her. "This's a list of lawsuits against Destiny for the past ten years. My private eye pulled them together."

"You've got a private eye?"

"Can you see if there are any plaintiffs that publish games like *The Whispering Man* and were around ten years ago?"

Reading, Maddie said, "It'd have to be an independent company. None of the big public companies—Activision Blizzard, Electronic Arts, id—are going to hurt anybody. That'd be crazy."

Shaw didn't necessarily agree—thanks for the paranoia about corporate America, Ashton—but he decided to stick to private companies for the moment.

Maddie read for no more than two minutes before stopping. "Well. Think I just earned my Cinnabon," she said, and brought her index finger down hard on a name.

# 33.

Tony Knight was the founder and CEO of Knight Time Gaming Software.

He'd been creating video games and other programs for years. He'd been hugely successful, hobnobbing with politicians and venture capitalists and Hollywood. He'd also been down-and-out, bankrupt three times. Once, like the Walmart residents Shaw had spoken to, he'd lived out of his car in an abandoned lot in Palo Alto and written code on a borrowed laptop.

Maddie had ID'd Knight as a possible suspect because his company published a survival action-adventure game in the same vein as *The Whispering Man*. Knight's product was called *Prime Mission*.

"Let's see if it came first. If it did, maybe Knight believes Marty Avon stole his source code. He tried to sue and lost and now he's getting even."

It took only a few minutes to find that, yes, *Prime Mission* preceded *The Whispering Man* by a year.

Maddie reminded Shaw that she wasn't particularly

familiar with either game—they were action-adventures, which were too slow for her—but she did know that Tony Knight was known in the industry to have a raging ego, a ruthless nature and a short fuse . . . and a long memory for slights.

"How close are the games?" Shaw asked.

"Let's find out." She nodded to his computer and scooted her chair close to his.

Lavender? Yes, he smelled lavender. Freckles and lavender seemed like a good combination.

And what was that tattoo?

She logged on to a website and an image of a labyrinth appeared—the Knight Time logo—then the words *Tony Knight's Prime Mission.*

A window appeared. Shaw expected ads for insurance or discount hotels. It was an actual news broadcast. Two attractive anchors—a man and a woman, both with fastidious hair and wearing sharp outfits—were reporting on the news of the day: a trade meeting of the G8 in Europe, a CEO of a Portland, Oregon, company under fire for suggesting the government was justified in interring U.S. citizens of Japanese descent during World War II, a shooting at a school in Florida, a Washington congressman under investigation for texting a gay teenage prostitute, an "alarming" study about the cancer risks of a brand of soft drinks . . .

Cable news at its finest . . .

She nodded at the screen. "Most video games're cheap to buy but you can't really play without the add-ons— things to help you win or just be cool—power-ups, costumes for your avatars, armor, weapons, spaceships, advanced levels . . . You can spend a ton of money."

"The razor's free," he said, "but the razor blades . . ."

"Exactly. Knight Time never charges for anything—the game, the extras. You've just got to sit through this." The newscast faded to a public service announcement encouraging voter registration. Maddie then pointed. "See?" The announcer said players could get five hundred "Knight points," to be used to buy accessories for any Knight Time game, if they did in fact register.

Whether or not Tony Knight was in some way behind the kidnappings, Shaw had to give him credit for the public service. As a professor of politics, Ashton Shaw believed it was a travesty that the U.S. didn't have mandatory voting like many other countries.

And, finally, the logo for the game *Prime Mission* appeared.

"Watch," Maddie said, nodding as type scrolled onto the screen.

YOU ARE THE PILOT OF A UNITED TERRITORIES XR5 FIGHTER SHIP. YOU HAVE CRASH-LANDED ON THE PLANET PRIME 4, WHERE UT FORCES HAVE BEEN BATTLING THE OTHERS. YOU HAVE LIMITED AIR AND FOOD AND WATER. YOU MUST REACH SAFE STATION ZULU, TWO HUNDRED KILOMETERS TO THE WEST.

The rest of the crawl revealed, in effect, that the character must take three items from the spaceship to use to survive on the trek. It ended with the admonition:

*You're on your own. Choose wisely. Your life depends upon it.*

"It's *The Whispering Man* in space," Shaw said. "Even those lines at the end are similar. In *The Whispering Man*, it's 'You've been abandoned. Escape if you can. Or die with dignity.' I want to see more about Knight."

He logged out of the game and called up more articles about the CEO and the company.

Shaw learned that Knight Time fell into the mold of several big tech companies—cofounded by two men in a garage. Like Bill Gates and Paul Allen, Steve Jobs and Steve Wozniak, and Bill Hewlett and Dave Packard. Knight's partner was Jimmy Foyle, both from Portland, Oregon. Knight handled the business side of the company; Foyle designed the games.

The press accounts of the company revealed details that echoed what Maddie had told him about Knight's nature.

The stories pointed to Jimmy Foyle as the model of a professional tech industry expert, who'd spend eighty-hour weeks perfecting the code for the company's gaming engines. He was described as a "gaming guru."

This was in sharp contrast to Tony Knight. The handsome, dark-haired CEO had a legendary temper. He was paranoid, petty. Twice, police were called to the company headquarters in Palo Alto when employees claimed Knight had physically hurt them—shoving one to the floor and flinging a keyboard into the face of another. No charges were filed and "generous" settlements were offered. Knight would sue for what he thought was a breach of a nondisclosure or noncompete, even if there was little reason to do so. He had also been arrested outside of the company for incidents like a pushing match over a parking space and a lawn worker who he believed had stolen a shovel from his garage.

The industry was always anticipating a breakup between the partners because of their differing personalities. One inspired profile writer described the two as the "Black Knight" and the "White Knight" because Foyle had once been a well-known white hat hacker—someone hired by companies and the government to try to break into their IT systems and expose vulnerabilities.

Knight's lawsuit against Destiny had been dismissed and both parties moved to have the records sealed, claiming that the court documents connected to the case contained trade secrets. A Freedom of Information Act request could be made, but that would take months. Shaw would proceed on the assumption that Destiny Entertainment had in fact stolen Knight's code. And he'd make the assumption that Knight was egotistical and vindictive enough to exact revenge.

He said to Maddie, "Still, it's a big risk for a man who's already rich."

She replied, "There's another piece. Knight Time's flagship game is *Conundrum*. It's an alternative reality game. Spectacular to watch. Too brainy for me, I'm not fast enough. The new installment is six months late. That's a no-no in the gaming world."

Shaw added, "And Knight waited until tens of thousands of gamers descend into the Valley. He hired somebody to be a psychotic player. Police wouldn't look past that. Great smoke screen."

"You going to tell the police?"

"The detective wasn't impressed with my idea in the first place. When I suggest a famous CEO might be the perp, it'll make her even more skeptical. I need facts."

Maddie was looking over his face. She said, "I'd go hunting with my father sometimes, remember?"

He did, an interest they shared—though it was a sport for her while something else entirely for him.

"And there was this look he'd get. He wasn't really himself. He was in a different place. All that mattered was getting that deer or goose or whatever. That's what you're looking like now."

Shaw knew what she was talking about—he'd seen the same expression in her face while she was stabbing him to death yesterday.

"Knight Time Gaming would have a booth at the C3 Conference?" he asked.

"Oh, yeah. One of the biggest."

Shaw started assembling the printouts. "I'm going to go pay a visit."

"You want some company? Always more fun to hunt with somebody else."

Shaw couldn't argue with that, thinking of the times he'd go out with his father or his brother into the forests and fields of the Compound. His mother too, who was the best shot in the family.

This, however, was different.

*Most crime's simple. This's complicated . . .*

"Think it's better for me to go on my own." Shaw took one last hit of coffee and headed out the door, pulling out his phone to make a call.

# 34.

T ruth is a curious thing.

Often helpful, sometimes not.

Colter Shaw had learned in pursuing rewards that there usually was nothing to be gained by lying. It might get you a few quick answers, but if you were found out, as often happened, sources would dry up.

Which didn't mean that there weren't times when it was helpful to let the impression settle that you were someone other than who you were.

Shaw was once again strolling the chaotic aisles of the C3 Conference, wandering through the mostly young, mostly male audience.

He passed Nintendo, Microsoft, Bethesda, Sony and Sega. The same carnage as before yet also bloodless games, like soccer, football, race cars, dance, puzzle solving and, well, the just plain bizarre. One featured green squirrels wearing toreador outfits and armed with nets as they chased worried bananas.

Shaw thought, People actually spent their time this way?

Then: Was obsessively cruising the country in a battered camper any worthier?

You disregard others' passions at your peril.

The Knight Time booth was larger but more austere and somber than the others. The walls and curtains were black, the music eerie, not thumping in your chest. No flashing lights or spots. Of course, the booth boasted ten-foot-long high-def screens—those seemed to be requisite at C3. The displays showed trailers for the delayed installment *Conundrum VI*. The text promised *Coming Soon!*

Shaw watched the action on the big screen for a while. Planets, rockets, lasers, explosions. In the booth fifty or so young people sat at stations and tried their hand at Knight Time games. In front of him a young woman wearing stylish red glasses, her hair in a ponytail, was intently playing *Prime Mission*.

"Well, that sucks." A teenager was talking to his friend. Waiting for a Knight Time game to start, he was gazing at the ad and news broadcast window Shaw remembered. On-screen was a pair of anchors, two young, geeky men. They were reporting on the fact that a congressman had supported a proposal to tax users' internet traffic over a certain number of gigabytes per day.

The gamer's friend lifted a middle finger to the screen.

They both relaxed when the game loaded and they could start to shoot aliens.

Shaw wandered up to an employee.

"Got a question," Shaw said to the man, who was in black jeans and a gray T-shirt, which had KNIGHT TIME GAMING across the chest. The letters began at the left in solid black, then dissolved into pixels, graying so that the final ING was hard to see. He noted that all Knight-Time employees wore the same outfit.

"Yessir?"

The man was six or seven years younger than Shaw. About Maddie Poole's age, he thought.

"I get games for my nieces—you know, birthdays and Christmas. I'm checking some out here."

"Great," said the man. "What're they into?"

"*Doom. Assassin's Creed. Soldier of Fortune.*" Maddie Poole had briefed him.

"Classic. Hmm, girls? How old are they?"

"Five and eight."

This gave the man pause.

"I've heard about *Conundrum*." He nodded at the screen.

"I was going to say, it's a bit old for them. But if they play *Doom* . . ."

"The eight-year-old's favorite. What about your game *Prime Mission*? They like *The Whispering Man*."

"I've heard of that one. Never played it. Sorry."

"*Prime Mission*'s good, right?"

"Oh, a big winner at The Game Awards."

"I'll take them both. *Conundrum* and *Prime Mission*." Shaw looked around. "Where do I buy the discs?"

The employee said, "Discs? Well, we're download only. And it's free."

"Free?"

"All our software is."

"Well, that's a deal." He glanced at the impressive monitor overhead. "I've heard that the head of the company's a genius."

Reverence dusted the kid's face. "Oh, there's nobody in the business like Mr. Knight. He's one of a kind."

Shaw looked up at the screen. "That's the new installment? *Conundrum VI*?"

"That's it."

"Looks good. How's it different from the current one?"

"The basic structure is the same, ARG."

"ARG?"

"Alternative reality game. In Installment 6 we're upping the galaxies to explore to five quadrillion and the total planets to fifteen quadrillion."

"*Quadrillion*? You mean, a player can visit that many planets?"

With geek pride, the man said, "Theoretically, if you spent just one minute per planet, it would take you—I'm rounding—twenty-eight billion years to finish the game. So . . ."

"Pick your planet carefully."

The employee nodded.

"It's been delayed, right? The new installment?"

He grew defensive. "Just a little. Mr. Knight has to make sure it's perfect. He won't release anything before its time."

"Should I wait for that one, for *VI*?" Another nod at the screen.

"No, I'd get *V*. Here." He handed Shaw a card:

### CONUNDRUM
#### KNIGHT TIME GAMING
##### EVER FREE . . .

On the back was a link for downloads. Into Shaw's back jeans pocket.

He thanked the employee and walked slowly past the players. He posed similar questions to a couple of other employees in the booth and got many of the same answers. Nobody seemed to know anything about *The Whispering Man*. He tried too to find out where Knight was presently and some things about his personal life. Nobody answered the specific questions, though the same message was often repeated: Tony Knight was a visionary, the paternal god atop the Olympus of high technology.

Smacked of cult, to Shaw.

He'd done all he could do here, so he headed to the booth's exit, walking past a curtained wall. He was half-way along it when he startled as a hundred lasers and spotlights positioned around the twenty-foot monitors towering over the booth shot fiery beams toward the ceiling. Amid a deafening blare of electronic music, a booming voice cried, "*Conundrum VI*, the future of gaming . . . Ever free . . ." And on the screen, a death beam blew to pieces one of the fifteen quadrillion planets.

Everyone nearby turned to the display and the light show.

Which is why not a single person noticed when a flap in the curtains opened and two fiercely strong men yanked Colter Shaw into the darkness on the other side.

# 35.

As he stood in a dim alcove, being expertly frisked in silence, he reflected on the flaw in his plan. Which had otherwise been a good one, he believed.

After a half hour of playing the role of naïve attendee, asking seemingly pointless yet probing questions, he'd assumed the Knight Time employees would realize he surely had to be here for some purpose other than buying children video games that were utterly inappropriate.

And so he would head outside the convention center to see if Knight's minders would take the bait: Shaw himself. As soon as he was in the parking lot, headed for the deserted corner where he'd left the Malibu, he would hit Mack's phone number and open a line. His PI would hear who and how many, if any, of Knight's men had come after him. If that happened and it sounded like he was endangered, the PI would call the JMCTF and the Santa Clara County Sheriff's Office. Shaw had also slipped his Glock into the glove compartment of the Malibu, just in case.

A good plan on paper, flushing Knight or his people as potential suspects.

But a plan based on the assumption that they wouldn't dare move on him at the convention center itself.

Got that one wrong.

He was now quick-marched a good thirty feet into the black heart of the Knight Time booth, through more shrouds of soundproof cloth. He'd heard the distant bass of the *Conundrum VI* ad. Then, once it had served its distractive purpose, the speaker volume dropped.

Shaw didn't bother to say anything. His bald minders wouldn't have answered anyway. He knew they were pros. Was the shorter one Person X? Sophie had said her kidnapper was not tall.

*Size nine and a half shoes . . .*

When they arrived at a proper door—not a fabric flap—they halted, then put everything Shaw had in his pockets into a plastic box, including, of course, the phone on which Mack's number was front and center but as yet undialed.

The box was handed off to someone else and the two men holding his arms escorted Shaw through the door and dropped him into a comfortable black chair, one of eight surrounding an ebony table. The walls had been constructed with baffles, the ceiling acoustical tile. All these surfaces were painted black or made from matte-black substances. The space was deathly silent. The only illumination came from a tiny dot at the bottom of one wall, like a night-light. Just enough to make out a few details: the chamber—the word came to mind automatically—was about twenty feet square, the ceiling about eight feet high.

No telephones, no screens, no laptops. Just a room and furniture. Private, and secure from the outside world.

His father would have appreciated it.

The shorter guard left, the other remaining at the door. Shaw could see some features of his captor. No jewelry. The earpiece of the Secret Service and TV commentators. Dark suit, white shirt, striped tie that seemed to be clip-on—an old trick—so that it couldn't be used as a garrote in a fight. His face in the shadows so Shaw couldn't see any expressions. He guessed there'd be none. He knew men like this.

Shaw debated next steps.

Ninety percent odds that he'd come to no harm here because of the inconvenience of dealing with the aftermath—smuggling his damaged or dead body out of the convention center. He supposed that logic didn't mean much to abusive and temperamental Tony Knight, who, if he was behind the kidnappings, was risking everything over a vindictive whim to destroy a competitor who'd wronged him.

Suddenly a ceiling light came on, a downward-pointing spot. Cold. The door opened. Shaw squinted against the flare of illumination.

Tony Knight entered. The CEO was leaner and shorter than he'd appeared in the pictures Shaw had found online, though he was still a substantial man. And it occurred to Shaw: Why assume he'd farmed out the kidnapping job, if he was in fact behind it? With his temper and vengeful nature, he might very well have enjoyed snatching Sophie Mulliner and Henry Thompson himself.

The man's dark eyes were fixed and didn't waver as they met Shaw's blue. The shadows from the light above made his gaze all the more sinister. The executive wore expensive-looking black slacks and a white dress shirt, two buttons undone at the top revealing thick chest hair, which added to his animal intensity. His hands were large and kept flexing in and out of fists. Shaw was gauging where to roll to minimize the damage from the first blow.

Knight sat at the head of the table. Shaw, at the opposite end, noted that the chair he himself had been deposited in, and six of the others, were about two inches shorter than the eighth, Knight's. This room would be used for sensitive negotiations and the short CEO would want to be at eye level with, not looking up at, the others.

Knight withdrew his phone, plugged a bud into his ear and stared at the screen.

Survival, Ashton Shaw taught Russell, Colter and Dorion, is about planning.

*Never be caught off guard.*

Plan how you're going to avoid or eliminate a threat. Shaw'd assume the guard was armed and that Knight was not. While Shaw knew little about boxing or martial arts, his father had taught all the children grappling skills . . . And there *were* all those wrestling trophies from his Ann Arbor days.

Taking down the minder by the door would be relatively easy. Knight—and his ego—would have instructed the muscle to expect threats to their boss's life, not their own.

Shaw planted his feet on the floor and casually put a hand on the edge of the table. From the corner of his eye, he saw that the minder had missed the maneuver. Shaw's legs—strong from hiking and rock climbing—tensed and he adjusted his balance. Ten feet to the guard. Lunge and, at the same time, shove the table toward Knight. Body-slam the minder, maybe a palm to the jaw, an elbow to the solar plexus. Get the weapon, pull the slide to make sure a round was chambered, even if it meant ejecting one. Control the two men in the room. Get a phone, go out the way he came in, call LaDonna Standish.

Grim-faced, Knight now rose angrily.

Revise slightly. When he got close, grab his lapels and drive him back into the guard, get the weapon.

One . . .

The CEO strode to Shaw and leaned down, close, hands continuing to flex and unflex.

Two . . .

Shaw readied himself, judging distances. Apparently no video cameras here. Good.

It was then that Tony Knight, at an ear-ringing decibel, raged, "*Conundrum VI* is not vaporware. Can't you get that through your fucking skulls?"

He returned to his chair and sat down, crossing his arms and fixing Shaw with a petulant glare.

# 36.

Colter Shaw had been accused of committing any number of offenses in his life, real and imagined.

The word *vaporware* had never figured in any of them.

There were many arrows of reply available in Shaw's quiver. He chose the most accurate: "I don't know what you're talking about."

Knight licked his lip, just the tip of his tongue. The flick wasn't exactly serpentine but wasn't far off.

"I heard it all." The accent placed his roots in Ontario. He tapped his phone. "The questions you were asking my people . . . You're not a gamer. We tagged your face and went back to the video, checked you out from the minute you entered the convention center. No interest in any other booths but mine. And asking bullshit questions, playing dumb, just to get information. You think this hasn't happened before? Trying to get somebody to turn? An employee? Turning against *me*? Do you really think that would ever fucking happen?"

Knight gestured in the general direction of the front of the booth. "You saw the promo outside. Did it look like vaporware to you? Did it?"

The door opened again and the other minder, the bigger one, stepped inside. He bent down to Knight and whispered. Knight's eyes remained on Shaw. When the guard stood up, his boss asked, "Verified?"

The muscle nodded. When Knight waved his hand, the man left. The other remained where he'd been, in Tower of London Beefeater mode.

Knight's anger had morphed to confusion. "You're like a private eye?"

"No. Not a PI. I make my living collecting rewards."

"You were the one who found that girl'd been kidnapped?"

A nod.

"You don't have any tech background."

"No."

"So nobody hired you to play corporate spy."

"I don't even know what vaporware is."

It would be dawning on Knight that Shaw wasn't a threat. It was dawning on Shaw that his hypothesis about Knight plotting to destroy a competitor might have a few holes.

"Vaporware's when a software company announces a new product that's either fake or won't be ready for a while. It's a tactic to gin up excitement, get some press. And keep the hordes at bay when you need more time to tweak the install. Because your fans can also be your biggest enemies if you don't deliver what you promised when you first promised it."

Shaw said, "That's the rumor about *Conundrum VI*? Vaporware?"

"Yeah." Knight's voice was sardonic. "It's just taken a little longer than I'd planned."

Fifteen quadrillion planets would understandably require some time.

Knight gazed at Shaw closely. "So, what's going on here?"

Sometimes you don't play the odds. Sometimes your gut gives you direction.

"Can we get out of here?" Shaw asked.

Knight debated. He nodded and the guard opened the door. The three of them stepped into a larger, brighter room, the inner sanctum of the booth. Two young women and a young man, wearing the corporate T-shirt and jeans uniform, labored away furiously at computer terminals. They shot wary looks toward their boss when he emerged and then their attention snapped back to their clattering tasks.

Shaw and Knight sat at the only table that didn't have an impressive computer perched upon it. A young woman with a crew cut brought Shaw the box containing his personal effects. He slipped them where they belonged.

Knight barked, "So?"

"You sued Marty Avon a few years ago."

Knight digested this with a frown. "Avon? Oh, Destiny Entertainment? Did I? Probably. When somebody tries to fuck me over, I sue them. You're not answering my question."

"That young woman who was kidnapped the other

day, Sophie Mulliner? The kidnapper was re-creating *The Whispering Man.*"

Not a flicker of reaction, other than the appropriate confusion. Which effectively deflated Shaw's hypothesis about Knight to low single digits. "Destiny's flagship game . . . What do you mean 're-creating'?"

Shaw explained about the room in the factory, the five objects, the chance to survive.

"That's one sick fuck. Why?"

"Maybe a disturbed gamer . . . I have another idea." He explained that the crime was intended to get even with Marty Avon or bring down Destiny. "When word gets out that a kidnapper was inspired by the game, the company would be sued and boycotted by the anti–violent video game crowd. It goes out of business. Destiny's already been through this before."

Shaw told him about the two teenagers who'd kidnapped their classmate and nearly killed her.

"I remember that. Sad story." Then he scoffed. "And you thought I was behind it? Because I had some grudge against Marty Avon for stealing code? Or I wanted him closed down because *The Whispering Man* competes against *Prime Mission*?"

"We need to explore every option. There's been another kidnapping."

"Another one? Shit." Knight asked, "When was that first incident? The boys who hurt that girl?"

Shaw told him.

Knight stood and walked to a terminal where one of the uniformed employees sat. She glanced up with wide eyes and, when Knight lifted his palm abruptly, leapt up and held the chair for him. He sat and spent a few minutes keyboarding. Behind Shaw came humming and *ca-shhh* from a printer. Knight rose and collected several sheets of paper, which he placed before Shaw. Knight withdrew a pen from his pocket. It was a ballpoint, but an extremely expensive one—made from platinum, Shaw believed.

"We subscribe to a marketing data service that tracks the sales of products and services all over the world. Did Cheerios outsell Frosted Flakes in March of last year? In what regions? In the places where Cheerios won, what was the average household income? What are the ages of the schoolchildren in those homes? On and on and on. You get the idea." He tapped the top sheet before Shaw with the pen. "This chart tracks Destiny Entertainment's sales of *The Whispering Man*."

Knight circled a flat line. "That period was the two months following the Ohio girl's attack, when, we can assume, the protests were the loudest, the press was the worst. Somebody tries to murder a girl because of the game and what happens? No effect on sales whatsoever. People don't care. If there's a game they like, they'll buy it, and they don't give a shit if it inspires psychos or terrorists."

Shaw noted that the data confirmed what Knight was telling him. He didn't ask if he could keep the sales stats; he folded the pages and slipped them in his pocket to verify them later, though he didn't doubt the figures were accurate.

The CEO said, "What happened with Destiny is, the suit? I think they might've tried to poach some retailers

I had an exclusive with. Penny-ante stuff. But I had to come down hard. You can't let people get away with anything. And Marty Avon? He's no threat. He's the mom-and-pop corner store of the gaming world." Knight looked him over. "So. We cool with everything? My guys got too rough?"

"Not a worry." Shaw rose and looked for the door.

"There." Knight was pointing.

Shaw was almost to the exit when Knight said, "Hold up."

Shaw turned.

"There's somebody you should talk to." He sent a text and then nodded to the table and the two men sat once more. "I want some coffee. You want coffee? I fly the beans in directly from Central America."

"El Salvador?"

"No way. It's my own farm in Costa Rica. Better than Salvadoran, hands down."

Shaw said, "Why not?"

# 37.

Jimmy Foyle, the cofounder of Knight Time, was in his mid-thirties.

Shaw recalled that he was also the chief game designer, the "gaming guru." Whatever that meant.

The compact man had straight black hair in need of a trim. His face was boyish and chin dusted with faint stubble. His blue jeans were new, his black T-shirt ancient and the short-sleeved plaid overshirt, faded orange and black, was wrinkled. No corporate uniform for him, presumably because, as the creator of fifteen quadrillion planets, he could wear whatever the hell he wanted to.

Shaw decided the look was Zuckerberg-inspired, though more formal, owing to the overshirt.

Foyle was fidgety, not in an insecure way but in the manner of those who are intensely smart and whose fingers and limbs move in time to their spiraling minds. He had joined Knight and Shaw at the table in the workstation room, and the three were alone. Knight had cleared the room of the keyboarding employees by shouting, "Everyone, get out!"

Shaw sipped the coffee, which was a fine brew, yet the Costa Rican beans didn't live up to their claim of overshadowing the Salvadoran.

Foyle was listening to Shaw's explanation about the kidnappings, sitting forward at an acute angle. The man seemed shy and had made no pleasantries, offered no greetings; he had not shaken Shaw's hand. A bit of Asperger's, maybe. Or perhaps because software code looped through his thoughts constantly and the idea of social interaction emerged briefly, if at all. He wore no wedding ring or other jewelry. His loafers needed replacement. Shaw recalled the article about the game designer and assumed if you spent eighty hours a week in a dark room, it was because you enjoyed spending eighty hours a week in a dark room.

When Shaw finished, Foyle said, "Yes, I heard about the girl. And on the news this morning the other kidnapping. The journalists said it was likely the same man but they weren't sure." A Bostonian lilt to his voice; Shaw supposed he'd acquired his computer chops at MIT.

"We think probably."

"There was nothing about *The Whispering Man*."

"That's my thought. I told the investigators but I'm not sure how seriously they took it."

"Do the police have any hope of finding the new victim?" His language was stiff, formal in the way that Shaw supposed computer codes were formal.

"They didn't have any leads as of an hour ago."

"And your thought is that either he's some troubled

kid who's taken the game to heart, like those boys a few years ago, or—alternatively—someone has hired him to pretend he's a troubled kid to cover up something else."

"That's right."

Knight asked, "What do you think, Jimmy?" Unlike his dictatorial attitude toward the other minions, with Foyle the CEO was deferential, almost obsequious.

Foyle drummed his fingers silently on his thigh while his eyes darted about. "Masquerading as a troubled gamer to cover up another reason for a kidnapping? I don't know. It seems too complicated, too much work. There'd be too many chances to get found out."

Shaw didn't disagree.

"A troubled player, though, stepping over the line." The man nodded thoughtfully. "Do you know Bartle's categorization of video game players?"

Knight offered a gutsy laugh. "With all respect, he doesn't know shit about games."

Which wasn't exactly true but Shaw remained silent.

Foyle went into academic mode. His eyes widened briefly—his first display of emotion, such as it was. "This is significant. There are four personality profiles of gamers, according to Bartle. One: Achievers. Their motivation is accumulating points in games and reaching preset goals. Two: Explorers. They want to spend time prowling through the unknown and discovering places and people and creatures that haven't been seen before. Three: Socializers. They build networks and create communities."

He paused for a moment. "Then, fourth: Killers. They come to games to compete, to win. That's the sole purpose of gaming to them. Winning. Not necessarily to take lives; they enjoy race car and sports games too. First-person shooters are their favorites, though."

*Killers . . .*

Foyle continued: "We spend a lot of time profiling who we're creating games for. The profile of Killers is mostly male, fourteen to twenty-three, who play for at least three hours a day, often up to eight or ten. They frequently have troubled family lives, probably bullied at school, loners.

"But the key element of Killers is they need someone to compete against. And where do they find them? On-line."

Foyle fell silent and his face revealed a subtle glow of satisfaction.

Shaw didn't understand why. "How does that profile help us?"

Both Knight and Foyle seemed surprised at the question. "Well," the game designer said, "because it might just lead you straight to his front door."

# 38.

Detective LaDonna Standish was saying, "Don't mind admitting when I'm wrong."

She was referring to her advice that Shaw leave Silicon Valley for home or to do some sightseeing.

They were in her office at the Task Force, only one half of which showed any signs of occupancy. The other hemisphere was completely vacant. There'd been no replacement found for Dan Wiley, who'd now be shuffling files to and from the various law enforcement agencies throughout Santa Clara County, a job that, to Shaw, would be a level of hell unto itself.

When Standish had stepped into the JMCTF reception area twenty minutes ago, Shaw had been amused to see her stages of reaction when he told her what he'd found: (1) confusion, (2) irritation and (3) after he'd shared what Jimmy Foyle had told him, interest.

Gratitude—reaction 3½?—had followed. She'd invited him to the office. Her desk was covered with documents and files. On the credenza pictures of friends and family, as well as several commendation plaques, were daunted by more files.

Jimmy Foyle's idea was that if the suspect were a Killer he would be online almost constantly.

"His online presence defines him," the designer had said. "Oh, he probably goes to school or a job, sleeps—though probably not much of that. He'll be obsessed with the game and play it constantly." Foyle had then sat forward with a slight smile. "But when do you know for certain the times he *wasn't* playing?"

A brilliant question, Shaw had realized. And the answer: he wasn't playing when he was kidnapping Sophie Mulliner and Henry Thompson and when he was shooting Kyle Butler.

He now told Standish, "*The Whispering Man* is a MORPG, a multiplayer online role-playing game. Players have to pay a monthly fee, which means Destiny, the publisher of the game, keeps credit cards on file."

Standish's thinking gesture was to touch an earring, a stud in the shape of a heart, an accessory in stark contrast to her outfit of cargo pants, black T and combat jacket. Not to mention the big-game Glock .45 on her hip.

"Foyle said we could use the credit card information to get a list of all the subscribers in the Silicon Valley area. Then we find out from the company who, among those, play obsessively but who weren't online at the times of the kidnappings and Kyle's murder."

"That'll work. I like it."

"We need to talk to the head of Destiny, Marty Avon. Can you get a warrant?"

She chuckled. "Paper? Based on a video game? I'd be

laughed out of the magistrate's office." She then turned her eyes his way. They were olive in color, and very dark, two tones deeper than her skin. Hard too. She added, "One thing I'm hearing, Mr. Shaw."

"How about we do 'Colter' and 'LaDonna.'"

A nod. "One thing I'm hearing: 'we.' The Task Force doesn't deputize."

"I'm helpful. You know it."

"Rules, rules, rules."

Shaw pursed his lips. "Upstate New York one time, I was visiting my sister. A boy'd gone missing, lost in the woods near his house, it looked like. Five hundred acres. The police were desperate, blizzard coming on. They hired a local consultant to help."

"Consultant?"

"A psychic."

"For real?"

"I went to the sheriff too. I told him I had experience sign cutting—you know, tracking. I said I'd help them for free. The psychic was charging. They agreed." He lifted his palms. "Don't deputize me, LaDonna. Consultize me. Won't cost the state a penny."

A finger to the earlobe. "Out of harm's way. No weapon."

"No weapon," he agreed, and could see, from the tightening of her lips, that she was aware he'd offered only half agreement.

They walked out of the Task Force building and into the parking lot, heading for her gray Altima. Standish asked, "How'd it turn out, that missing boy? Did she help?"

"Who?"

"The psychic."

"How'd you know it was a woman?" Shaw asked.

"I'm psychic," Standish said.

"She said she had a vision of the boy near a lake, making shelter under the trunk of a fallen walnut tree, four miles from the family house. A milk carton was nearby. And there was an old robin's nest in a maple tree next to him."

"Damn. That was one particular vision. Was she in the ballpark?"

"No. Took me ten minutes to find him. He was in the loft of the family's garage. He'd been hiding there the whole time. He didn't want to take his math test."

# 39.

"Y our first name?" Standish asked Shaw. They were driving through Silicon Valley in her rickety car. Something was loose in the rear. "Never heard of it."

"I'm one of three children," Shaw told her. "Our father was a student of the Old West. I was named after the mountain man John Colter, with the Lewis and Clark Expedition. My kid sister's Dorion, after Marie Aioe Dorion, one of the first mountain women in North America. She and her two kids survived for two months in the dead of winter in hostile territory—Marie Aioe, not my sister. My older brother, Russell, he was named after Osborne Russell, a frontiersman in Oregon."

"They do this reward stuff too?"

"No."

Though the apples didn't fall far, at least in Dorion's case. She worked for an emergency preparedness consulting company. Maybe in Russell's too. But no one in the family knew where he was or what he was up to. Shaw had been trying to find him for years. Both hoping to and worried that he might succeed.

*October 5, fifteen years ago . . .*

Sometimes Shaw thought he should simply let it go.

He knew he wouldn't.

*Never abandon a task you know you must complete . . .*

They were cruising along the 101, southbound, and had left the posh Neiman Marcus Silicon Valley behind, as well as the more modest yet tidy neighborhoods where the Quick Byte Café squatted and Frank Mulliner lived. Here, on either side of the freeway, badly in need of resurfacing, was hard urban turf, banger turf, city projects housing, abandoned buildings and overpasses dolled up with gang-sign graffiti.

According to GPS, the Destiny Entertainment Inc. offices were not far away. Shaw recalled Foyle telling him that *The Whispering Man* was the company's main game. Maybe they hadn't had any other big hits and the failures had kept the company on the wrong side of the tracks.

Shaw mentioned this to Standish as she pulled off the highway onto surface streets. "But it's my wrong side of the tracks."

He glanced her way.

"Home sweet home. EPA. East Palo Alto. Grew up here."

"Sorry."

She scoffed. "No offense taken. EPA . . . Doesn't that confuse everybody? It's really north of the other Palo Alto. Place so far on the wrong side you couldn't even hear any train whistle. Your father liked his cowboys.

Well, this was Tombstone back in the day. Highest murder rate in the country."

"In Silicon Valley?"

"Yessir. It was mostly black then, thank you, because of the redlining and racial deed restrictions in SV." She chuckled. "When I was growing up here, there was gunfire every night. We kids—I have three brothers—we'd hang out in Whiskey Gulch. Stanford was dry and didn't allow any liquor within a mile of campus. And what was one mile and one block away? Yep, a strip mall in EPA, with package stores and bars galore. That's where we'd play. Until Daddy came looking and dragged us home.

"'Course, the Gulch all got torn down and replaced with University Circle. Lord, there's a Four Seasons Hotel there now! Just imagine that sacrilege, Colter. Last year, the murder rate was one—and that was a murder/suicide, some computer geek and his roommate. My daddy'd roll over in his grave."

"You lose him recently?"

"Oh, years ago. Daddy, he didn't benefit from the new and improved statistics. He was shot and killed. Right in front of our apartment."

"That why you went into policing?"

"One hundred percent. High school, college in three years and into the academy at twenty-one, the minimum age. Then signed on with EPA police. I worked street while I got my master's in criminal justice at night. Then moved to CID. Criminal investigation. Loved the job. But . . ." A wan smile.

"What happened?"

"Didn't work out." She added, "I didn't blend. So I asked for a transfer to the Task Force."

Shaw was confused. The population he was looking at was mostly black.

She noted his expression. "Oh, not that way. I'm talking 'bout my father. I didn't explain. Yes, I went into policing because of him. But not because he was some poor innocent got gunned down in front of Momma and me. He was an OG."

Shaw could imagine how her fellow cops would respond to working with the daughter of an original gangster whose crew might've shot at or even killed their friends.

"He was a captain in the Pulgas Avenue 13s. Warrant team from Santa Clara Narcotics came after him and it went south. After I was in, I snuck his file. My oh my, Daddy was a bad one. Drugs and guns, guns and drugs. Suspect in three hits. They couldn't make two of the cases. The one where they had a good chance, the witness disappeared. Probably in the Bay off Ravenswood."

A click of her tongue. "Wouldn't you know it, my brothers and I would come home from school and, damn, if Momma was sick he'd have dinner ready and be reading us *Harry Potter*. He'd take us to the A's games. Half my girlfriends didn't have a father. Daddy was there. Until, yeah, he wasn't."

They continued in silence for five minutes, driving over dusty surface streets, wads of trash and soda and beer cans on the sidewalks and curbside. "It's over there." She nodded at a three-story building that seemed to be about fifty, sixty years old. This structure, along with several others nearby, wasn't as shabby as the approach suggested they'd be. Destiny Entertainment's headquarters was freshly painted, bright white. Shaw could see some smart storefront offices: graphic design and advertising agencies, a catering company, consulting.

Tombstone as reimagined by Silicon Valley developers.

They parked in the company's lot. The other cars here were modest. Not the Teslas, Maseratis and Beemers of the nearby Google and Apple dimension. The lobby was small and decorated with what seemed to be artists' renditions of the Whispering Man, ranging from stick drawings to professional-quality oils and acrylics. They'd have been done, he supposed, by subscribers. Shaw looked for the stenciled image that the kidnapper was fond of but didn't see it. Standish seemed to be doing the same.

The receptionist told them Marty Avon would be free in a few minutes. A display caught Shaw's eye and they walked to a waist-high table, six by six feet, that held a model of a suburban village. A sign overhead read WEL-COME TO SILICONVILLE.

A placard explained that the model was a mock-up of a proposed residential development that would be built on property in unincorporated Santa Clara and San Jose counties. Marty Avon had conceived of the idea in reaction to the "excruciatingly expensive" cost of finding a home in the area.

Shaw thought of Frank and Sophie Mulliner's exodus to Gilroy, the Garlic Capital of the World. And the Walmart hoboes whom Henry Thompson was writing about in his blog.

Eyes on the sign, Standish said, "Have a couple open cases in the Task Force. Some of the big tech companies, they run their own employee buses from San Francisco or towns way south or east. They've been attacked on the road. People're pissed, thinking it's those companies that're responsible for everything being so expensive. There've been injuries. I told them, 'Take the damn name off the side of the bus.' Which they did. Finally." Standish added with a wry smile, "Wasn't rocket science."

Avon had created a consortium of local corporations, Shaw read, who would offer the reasonably priced housing to employees.

A generous gesture. Clever too: Shaw suspected that the investors were worried about a brain drain—coders moving to the Silicon Cornfields of Kansas or Silicon Forests in Colorado.

He wondered if because Destiny Entertainment wasn't in the same stratosphere as Knight Time and the other big gaming studios, Avon had chosen to expand into a new field—one with a guaranteed stream of revenue: real estate.

The receptionist then said that Avon would see them. They showed IDs and were given badges and directed to the top floor. Once off the elevator they noted a sign: THE BIG KAHUNA THATAWAY →.

"Hmm." From Standish.

As they proceeded thataway, they passed thirty workstations. The equipment was old, nothing approaching the slick gadgets at Knight Time Gaming's booth; Shaw could only imagine what that company's headquarters was like.

Standish knocked on the door on which a modest sign read B. KAHUNA.

"Come on in!"

# 40.

Gangly Marty Avon rose from his chair and strode across the room. He was tall, probably six foot five. Thin, though a healthy thin that probably came from a racehorse metabolism. Avon strode forward, hands dangling, feet flopping. His mass of curly blond hair—very '60s—jiggled. Shaw had expected the creator of *The Whispering Man* to be dressed gothic, in black and funereal purple. Nope. A too-large beige linen shirt, untucked, and, of all things, bell-bottoms in a rich shade of rust. His feet were in sandals because what else could they be in?

Shaw looked around the office, as did Standish. Their eyes met and he raised a brow. While the reception area may have featured pictures of the crazy psychopath, the Whispering Man, here the décor was kids' toy store: Lionel trains, plastic soldiers, dolls, building blocks, stuffed animals, cowboy guns, board games. Everything was from before the computer era. Most of the toys didn't even seem to need batteries.

Standish and Shaw shook his hand, and he directed them to sit on a couch in front of a coffee table on which sat a trio of plastic dinosaurs.

"You like my collection?" His high voice was dusted with a rolling Midwestern accent.

"Very nice," Standish said noncommittally.

Shaw was silent.

"Did you both have a favorite toy growing up? I always ask my visitors that."

"No," they both answered simultaneously.

"You know why I love my collection? It reminds me of my philosophy of business." He looked fondly at the shelves. "There's one reason and one reason only that video games fail. Do you want to know why that is?"

He picked up a wooden soldier, an old one, resembling the nutcracker from the ballet. The CEO looked from the toy to his visitors. "The reason games fail is very simple. Because they aren't fun to play. If they're too complicated or too boring, too fast, too slow . . . gamers will walk away."

Setting down the toy, he sat back. "Nineteen eighty-three. Atari is stuck with nearly a million cartridges of games that nobody wanted, including the worst video game in history: *E.T.* Good movie, bad game. Supposedly, the games and consoles were buried in a secret landfill in New Mexico. Not long after that the entire industry collapsed. The stock market had the Great Crash of '29. Video gaming had '83."

Standish steered the meeting back on track. She asked if Avon knew about the recent kidnapping.

"The girl from Mountain View? Yes." Behind him was a huge poster for Siliconville. His desk was littered with maps, many official-looking documents, some photocopies and some with seals and original signatures. The real estate project seemed to be taking more time than his gaming business.

"There was another one too, late last night."

"Oh, I heard about that! It's the same kidnapper?"

"We think so."

"My God . . ." Avon looked genuinely distraught. Though, understandably, his was probably a double-duty frown, the second meaning being: What does this have to do with me?

"And he appears," Standish said, "to be modeling the crimes after *The Whispering Man*."

"No, no, no . . ." Avon closed his eyes briefly.

She continued: "We know about the incident in Ohio a few years ago."

His head was hanging. "Not again . . ."

Shaw explained what Sophie Mulliner had found in the room she'd been sealed into.

"Five objects." Avon's voice was hollow. "I came up with five because my daughter was learning to count. She used her fingers. She'd do the right hand and then, when she went to the left, she started over again."

Shaw explained, "One possibility is that the kidnapper's a player who's obsessed with the game and is acting it out. Like the boys in Ohio. If so, we want to try to trace him."

The detective said, "Mr. Shaw here had a conversation with Tony Knight and . . ." A glance Shaw's way.

"Jimmy Foyle."

"*Conundrum*. It's a real phenomenon. Supposedly the longest source code ever written for a game."

*Fifteen quadrillion planets . . .*

Avon added, "Alternative reality. I've thought about publishing one but you really need supercomputers for them to work right. You should see their servers. Well, what can I help with?"

Shaw explained what Foyle had suggested. How they wanted to locate local gamers who were online frequently—obsessed with the game—as well as offline at three specific times: when Sophie was kidnapped, when she was rescued and when Henry Thompson was taken.

Now would come the battle. Avon would say, Sure. And you don't get user logs without a warrant.

And he was indeed shaking his head.

"Look," Standish said, "I know you'll want a warrant. We're hoping you'll cooperate."

Avon scoffed. "Warrant. I don't care about that."

Standish and Shaw regarded each other.

"You don't?"

The CEO chuckled. "Do you know what an EUA is?"

Shaw said he didn't. The detective shook her head.

"'End user agreement.' Whenever anybody subscribes to *The Whispering Man*, they have to agree to the EUA. Every software and hardware company makes you agree or you don't get the goods. Nobody reads 'em, of course. Ours has got a clause that gives us permission to use their data any way we want—even give it to the police without a warrant.

"No, we have other problems. We'll have to track the user—your suspect—through his IP address. We get hacked all the time—all game companies do—so we separate online presence from personal information. All our gaming servers know is that User XYZ has paid, but we don't know who he is. That might not be a problem, tracking IP to the user's computer. But most of our subscribers—at least the younger ones—use proxies."

"Masks that hide their real location when they're online," Shaw said. He did too in all of his online activity.

"Exactly. ID'ing somebody using a proxy is time consuming and sometimes impossible. But let's give it a shot. When was he offline?"

Shaw displayed his notebook.

"Now, we'll want subscribers who play for, let's say, twenty-five hours a week or more but were offline then." Nodding at the notebook. "Quite some handwriting." Avon hunted and pecked and, as he did, he mused, "Did you know that in China they're considering legislation to limit the hours you can play? And the World Health Organization just listed video gaming addiction as a disease. Ridiculous. That's like saying lawyers who work more than forty hours a week are dysfunctional. Nurses, surgeons." He fiddled with a pencil that had a clown's head topper. He glanced at the screen. "Okay. Here we go."

Standish sat forward. "You have results already?"

Shaw, familiar with the speed of Velma Bruin's rewards-finding algorithm, Algo, wasn't surprised.

Reading the screen, Avon said, "The answer is a yes, with a caveat. There are about two hundred and fifty-five people who play the game at least twenty-five hours a week and they meet the offline timing criteria. Of those, sixty-four aren't anonymous—no proxies. But none of them are within a hundred miles of here. The others? They're behind proxies. So we have no idea where they are—maybe next door, maybe Uzbekistan." He gazed at the list. "Most of them are off-the-shelf proxies, not very righteous. They can be cracked but it'll take some time."

He tapped out another request. Hit RETURN. "There," he said, "I've got somebody on it."

And then Marty Avon went into a different place mentally. Finally he asked, "Where was the girl hidden?"

Shaw said, "The Abandoned Factory. Level 1."

"You know the game? You play it?"

"No. You're thinking he put Henry Thompson—that's the new victim—at a different level?"

Avon said, "The kidnapper's a gamer, obviously, and it'd be a fail to repeat a level and a cheat to play out of order."

Shaw, who embraced technology in his work, had been amused to learn that geeks often swapped verbs for nouns: A *fail* was "a loss," an *ask* was "a question."

"The second level's called The Dark Forest."

"So Henry Thompson's being held in the woods somewhere."

Standish grimaced. "Got a few acres of those around here."

Shaw's eyes fell on the set of toy soldiers. They were about three inches high, dark green, in various combat poses. Troops from the Second World War, probably. Nowadays, what would the manufacturer produce? Men or women sitting at drone command stations? A cybersecurity expert at a desk, hacking into Russian defenses?

The CEO leaned back, lost in thought, eyes closed. They popped open. "What were the five objects he left with the girl?"

Shaw told him: "Water, glass bottle, a book of matches, fishing line, a strip of cloth."

Avon said, "Good."

# 41.

For all his traveling, the restless man had never been in a helicopter.

Now that he was, he wasn't enjoying it.

The altitude wasn't the problem, not even with the open door. Canvas and steel, in the proper configuration, are substances that you can depend on, and the harness in the Bell was intimately snug. Shaw and his siblings had gotten over any fear of heights early—Ashton again—by learning to climb before they were thirteen. When no challenging jobs beckoned, Shaw would find a nice vertical face and ascend (always free-climbing—using ropes to prevent falls, not to aid in the climb). Earlier in the day he'd looked fondly over Standish's shoulder at the trail map leading to the site of the climb he'd been planning while visiting his mother at the Compound.

No, the five hundred feet between him and the tree line was not a problem. Shaw simply didn't want to puke. That, he hated more than pain. Well, most pain.

Maybe inevitable, maybe not. Teeter-totter. He inhaled deeply. Bad idea; exhaust and fuel fumes were co-conspirators.

LaDonna Standish was strapped in beside him. They were riding backward, facing two tactical officers, dressed in black, with matching body armor. POLICE was printed in white on their chests—their backs too, Shaw had seen, in larger type. They were holding Heckler & Koch machine guns. Standish was not enjoying the trip either. She refused to look out the open door, and she kept swallowing. She clutched an airsickness bag and Shaw hoped she didn't start in with that. He *really* hoped she didn't. The power of suggestion is formidable.

She wore body armor and had only her sidearm. Shaw too was in a Kevlar vest, without weapon, per the rules. The out-of-harm's-way dictate had obviously gone to hell.

How they happened to be here was thanks to the creator of *The Whispering Man*, Marty Avon. The CEO had explained that the game's algorithm randomly assigned three of the five items that players were abandoned with, like Sophie's fishing line, scarf and glass bottle. The other two items might vary but fell into two categories: sustenance and communication. Food or water—Sophie had been given the latter—and some way to signal for help, to let an ally know where you were, or to warn about danger. Matches, in her case. Players sometimes got a flashlight or signal mirror. More often, they received a way to start a fire. If not matches, a cigarette lighter or a flint-and-steel kit. This could also help players stay alive in some of the colder game settings, like mountaintops and caves.

"If the victim's in a forest and he has matches or a cigarette lighter, he might try to start a fire," Avon had suggested.

Shaw had said, "A brush fire in northern California? That's one thing that'd be sure to get somebody's attention."

Drought, heat and winds had helped fires ravage part of central and northern California lately. Shaw and his family had battled one on the Compound years ago and nearly lost the cabin.

"He won't be a fool," Standish had said. "He'll control it. Probably set a small bonfire in a clearing or on rock, where it'll be noticed but won't spread."

Standish had called the Park Service, which used drones and satellites mounted with thermal sensors to see if any of the systems had registered flames. She learned that, yes, the service had monitored a small blaze on a rocky hilltop in Big Basin Redwoods State Park. It had flared up about midnight, burned for a brief time and then went out. Infrared scans showed that by 1 a.m. the ground was fire- and ember-free once more. They'd marked the site to check it out later but sent no crews at that time.

Shaw had looked up the location on the map. It was a forty-minute drive from where Henry Thompson had been kidnapped.

Via speakerphone, the ranger had explained that it was curious there'd been a fire at that location at that time of the morning, since it wasn't near any hiking trails, and the only road nearby, an old logging way, was chained off. Odd too that there was a fire at all, since there'd been no lightning strikes and the blaze was limited to a rocky shelf that didn't seem to have any natural brush growing from the cracks in the stone. "Best we could figure, some campers went off road."

Standish had then asked, "Satellite images of the site?"

The ranger had sent some and she, Shaw and Avon huddled over the game maker's high-def monitor.

They were looking at what might have been a configuration of rocks or shadows but also might have been a human form, standing near the fire.

"Good enough for me," Standish had said and grabbed her phone, pressing a single button to make a call.

Standish and Shaw had sped to Moffett Field, an old military air base north of Sunnyvale and Mountain View—only ten minutes from Destiny Entertainment. At least, ten minutes the way Standish had been driving. Shaw had held on to the armrest and enjoyed the NASCAR ride.

The military air functions of the field, Standish had explained, were shrinking, though an air-rescue operation remained. Google leased much of the field and the internet company was involved in the restoration of Hangar 1, which was one of the largest wooden structures in the world, built in the '30s to house dirigibles and other lighter-than-air craft.

There they had climbed into the Task Force's Bell chopper, which was now—after only a twenty-minute flight—closing in on the spot where the fire had been tagged. Four other tac officers were in an Air National Guard Huey, old and olive-drab, presently thumping away fifty yards to the starboard.

Through his headphone, Shaw heard Standish's throat making tiny retching sounds and he pulled the unit off. It helped.

The hazy suburban sprawl of the valley became hills and trees, then the landscape turned tough, with lush, spiky redwoods giving way to rocky terrain, skeletal trees, dry riverbeds. This was the heart of Big Basin. Shaw had thought the rugged land would send updrafts skyward, making the ride worse. Oddly, though, the air was smooth; the bumpiness had been severe when they were over suburbia.

Standish's head tilted slightly. She must have heard the pilot say something. Shaw put his headset back on and entered the conversation.

"Negative," Standish called.

The pilot: "Copy. I'll find an LZ."

Shaw looked at Standish, who said, "Pilot asked if I wanted a flyby of the site. I told him no. Don't imagine the perp's here after all these hours, but he came back to the first site with a weapon. He'll hear us land, but I don't want him to see us."

The odds he was back at this particular time? Shaw figured them to be low. Yet still vivid in his memory was the horrible collapse of Kyle Butler as the bullet struck him.

Two craft hovered over a clearing atop a plateau, two hundred feet from the valley floor, then touched down in tandem. Shaw was out fast, ducking his head unnecessarily—even though the rotors were high, you did it anyway. Almost immediately his gut felt better. And he didn't react when Standish jumped out the other side and bent over, vomiting. She then stood up, spitting. She rinsed her mouth with water from a bottle the pilot handed her, as if he kept them on hand for that very purpose.

She joined Shaw. "At least there's nothing left for the ride home."

They and the two officers with them jogged to the edge of the clearing, where they were joined by the four-man team from the Huey, also in tactical gear. They nodded to Standish and Shaw, who was examined with glancing side looks. The detective didn't introduce him. The Bell pilot joined them and unfurled a map of the area. He'd been given the coordinates of the site of the fire and had marked it in red pen. He looked around, trying to judge where exactly they were in relation to it. Shaw glanced at the map, then the surrounding hills. He'd done orienteering on the Compound and, in college, had competed in the sport, a timed trek through the wilderness, following a route using only a compass and a map.

Shaw pointed. "The fire was there, about five hundred yards. Over that ridge. Straight line."

Everyone was staring at him. He in turn looked to Standish. This was, after all, her hunt.

"Your supervisors brief you?" She was talking to the four men from the other helicopter. They weren't Task Force, Shaw could see, different uniforms. Maybe county, maybe state. Their equipment was shiny, their boots polished, their guns hardly dinged.

One of these officers, a man with bulbous, dumbbell-lifting arms, said, "No, ma'am. Other than a hostage sit, possible HT on the scene."

"At the last taking—the Mulliner girl—the unsub came back to the scene with a weapon. That ended up a homicide." Two of the men nodded, recalling. "Weapon's a nine-millimeter handgun. Glock. Long barrel probably—the accuracy. He knows how to shoot. It's not likely he's here—we've done sat and drone surveillance and didn't see any vehicles—but, well, you can see the canopy. Lots of places to hide. Watch for shooters."

Standish turned to Shaw. "Best routes?"

He borrowed the pilot's red pen and drew lines, like parentheses, from where they stood to the ridge where the fire had been. "The north one? You'll have to be careful."

A SWAT officer asked, "Umm, which one's north?"

Shaw touched it. "When you get to the cedar, there'll be a drop-off."

A pause. "What's a cedar look like?"

Shaw pointed one out.

"A drop-off you won't see until you're almost on it. And once you crest the ridge, you'll have exposure to shooters from the high ground here and here. The sun's in a good spot. It'll be in his eyes. And if he's got binoculars or a scope, there'll be lens flare."

Standish took over. "The hostage won't have shoes. He may've made covering for his feet, but I don't think he's gone very far."

Shaw added, "And he was brought here unconscious, so, for all he knows, he's in the midst of Yosemite or the Sierra Madres. He's not an outdoorsman, so I don't think he'll try to hike out. I was him, I'd look for water and shelter in place."

Standish: "Secure the scene first and then we look for him. You probably gathered Mr. Shaw here's done some tracking work. He'll help us. He's a consultant with the Task Force."

She then asked Shaw where the logging road was. He glanced at the map and turned and pointed.

"He and I'll go this way," Standish said, nodding. "The unsub wouldn't've dragged the vic that far—the ridge where the fire was. He would've left him near the road. Mr. Shaw and I'll look for that scene and secure it." She looked at them all in turn. "You good with that?"

Nods all around.

"Questions?"

"No, Detective."

Standish started in the direction of the logging road while Shaw reviewed the map, deciding where would be the most logical place for the Whispering Man, playing Level 2 of the game, to have abandoned Henry Thompson.

*The Dark Forest* . . .

The officers clustered, talking among themselves, presumably selecting who wanted to go with whom. Someone barked a brief laugh. Shaw folded the map carefully and walked over to them. As he hadn't known who'd spoken the words he'd just heard, he let his eyes tap them all. He nodded.

They nodded back. Discomfort settled like fog.

"I don't know if Detective Standish's a lesbian or not," he whispered, having heard their infantile comment. "I'm pretty sure if you're not part of the team you don't say 'dyke.' I know for a fact that 'nappy-headed' is just plain wrong."

They looked back, their eyes various degrees subzero. Two then examined the ground carefully.

He'd thought it would be the big one who'd push back; he had "bully" written in his furrowed brow and bulky arms. It was the slightest of the officers who said, "Come on, man. Doesn't mean anything. The way it is in Tactical. You know, combat. You joke. We live on the edge. Burn off steam."

Shaw glanced down at the man's pristine weapon, which they both knew had been fired on the range only. The officer looked away.

Shaw scanned the rest of them. "And I do have a little Native American blood in me, my mother's side. Great-great-grandmother. But you know my name. And it's not Geronimo."

The look of disgust on several officers' faces was meant to convey that this untidy incident was Shaw's fault for not playing along. Shaw turned to follow Standish, to look for the nest where the unsub had left Henry Thompson to escape if he could.

Or to die with dignity.

# 42.

By the time he'd caught up with her, he glanced back. The teams were deploying along the routes he had set out.

Beside him, Standish said, "I get it some."

"You heard?"

"No, but I saw you turn back. Was it about being gay or about being black?"

"A bit of both. Wondering if you're gay. And your hair."

She laughed. "Oh, not 'nappy' again. Seriously? Those boys."

"Struck me as odd, them saying it. It was about something else?"

Standish, still smiling. "You got that right."

Shaw was silent.

"I moved in from EPA police direct to the Task Force, I was telling you. Moved up to gold shield fast. And I mean months."

"How'd that happen?" Shaw was surprised.

She shrugged. "Ran some ops that ended okay."

The modesty told Shaw that they were big, critical operations and they ended much better than okay. He remembered the commendations on the credenza behind her desk, including some actual medals, on ribbons, still in their plastic cases.

"Got me twenty K more salary." She nodded toward the other officers. "You probably figured, Shaw, there're two Silicon Valleys."

"You're from north of the 101. They're from the south."

"That's it. They're soccer dads who play golf when they're not out at an air-conditioned gun range. Barbecues and boats. God bless 'em. Never the twain shall meet. They don't want to take orders from somebody like me. And it doesn't help I'm younger than the youngest." She glanced at Shaw; he could feel her eyes. "I don't need protecting."

"I know. Just can't help myself sometimes."

A nod. He believed it meant she was exactly the same.

"Was that your partner? The picture on your desk?" Shaw had seen a photo in her office of Standish with a pretty white woman, their heads together, smiling.

"Karen."

Shaw asked, "How long you been together?"

"Six years, married four. You were probably wondering about the name. Standish."

Shaw shrugged.

"I took her name. She and I have something in common, you know? The rumors are that Karen's family came over on the *Mayflower*. You know, Myles Standish?"

"*That* Standish? What do you have in common?"

"My ancestors came over on a boat too." Standish couldn't restrain her laugh. Shaw had to smile.

"Kids?"

"Two-year-old. Gem's her name. Karen's the birth mother. We're going to—"

Suddenly, Shaw lifted a hand and they stopped. He scanned the dense forest. Where they stood was particularly congested, a soupy tangle of pine, oak, vines. A good place for a shooter to hide.

Standish's hand dropped to her holster. "You see something?"

"Heard something. Gone now." He scanned the trees and shrubbery, the rocks. Motion everywhere but no threat. You learn the difference early.

They continued toward the logging road, looking for where Henry Thompson had been abandoned. Had to be here somewhere. Shaw was searching for marks left by shoes, either walking or being dragged.

She asked, "You married?"

"No."

"Sounds like you prefer I don't ask if there's anybody you're with."

"No preference. But there isn't. Not at the moment."

Another image of Margot began to form. It remained silent and opaque. Then, fortunately, disappeared.

"How 'bout kids?"

"No."

They continued on for another fifty yards. Standish cocked her head—she'd gotten a transmission and was listening through her earbud. She lifted the Motorola mic and said, "Roger. Join up with the other teams."

She hooked the radio back on her belt. "They're at the clearing where the fire was. No sign of the unsub. Or Thompson."

He crouched. Crushed grass. Caused by animal hooves and paws, not leather soles. Rising, he scanned the terrain. His head dipped and he said, "There. He walked that way."

It was a faint trail that led toward the logging road. They started along it.

Standish said, "You know, we need a name for him."

"Who?"

"The unsub. We sometimes do that. We get a lot of unsubs and it helps keep 'em separate. A nickname. Any ideas?"

With a reward, you usually knew the name of the missing person or fugitive you were after. Even if you didn't, you didn't give them a nickname. At least, Shaw didn't. He told her, "No."

Standish said, "The Gamer. How's that?"

It seemed self-conscious. Then again, it wasn't his case and he wasn't a cop with a lot of unsubs that needed telling apart. "Why not?"

Ten feet farther along the logging road, Standish stopped. "There," she said.

Shaw looked down at a circular indentation in the pine needles, right beside the old logging road. Within the circle were a plastic bag of marbles like children play with, a coil of laundry line, a box of double-edged razor blades and a large package of beef jerky.

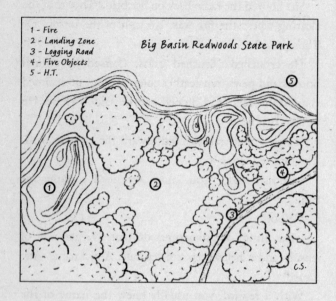

"Look." Shaw was pointing at a flat surface of rock a few feet above where the Gamer had left the five items. Those, and the matches or lighter he'd used to start the fire, were this victim's infamous five items from *The Whispering Man*.

"Is that . . . ?"

It was. A version of the face on the sheet at the Quick Byte and graffitied on the wall near the room where Sophie Mulliner had been left.

The stark image of the Whispering Man.

She took a step forward, when Shaw stopped and closed his hand around her muscular biceps. "Don't move. And quiet."

Standish had good training. Or instinct. She didn't look at Shaw. But as she crouched to make herself a smaller target, she scanned for a threat.

It wasn't the kidnapper that Shaw had heard. The slow crackling of branches and a low vibration—a sound unlike any other on Earth—told him exactly who the visitor was.

Thirty feet away, a mountain lion—a big male, one hundred and thirty pounds—stepped into view and looked them over with fastidious eyes.

# 43.

"Oh, man," LaDonna Standish whispered. She stood straight and reached for her weapon.

"No," Shaw said.

"We got a protocol in Santa Clara. They're not endangered. We can shoot."

"We don't know if the Gamer's nearby. Do you really want to tell him where we are?"

She hadn't thought about this and withdrew her hand. Then said, "It *is* a fucking mountain lion."

The creature's muzzle was red with blood. Was it Henry Thompson's?

"Look him in the eyes. And stand as tall as you can."

"This's as tall as I get," she whispered.

"Don't bend over. The more you look four-legged, the more you seem like prey to him."

"It's a boy?"

"Male, yeah. And open your jacket."

"Showing him my weapon's not going to make him go away, Colter. I'm just saying."

"Makes you look bigger."

"I shouldn't have to be worried about this shit." She opened the windbreaker slowly and held the zipper ends outward. She resembled one of those young folks Shaw occasionally saw when rock-climbing, wearing wingsuits, leaping into the void and arcing through the air like diving falcons.

He added, "And don't run. Whatever happens, even if he approaches, don't run."

The animal, with perfect muscles and a rich tan coat, sniffed the air. His ears were low—a bad sign—and his long fangs, yellow and bloody and three times the length of his other teeth, were prominently displayed. Another mean growl emanated from his throat.

"What exactly does that purr mean?"

"He's getting information. He wants to know our story. Are we strong or weak? Are *we* predators?"

"Who the hell'd mess with him?"

"Bear. Wolves. Humans with guns."

She gave her own mean growl. "*I'm* a human with a gun."

Keeping his eyes locked onto the animal's, Shaw slowly crouched and, after a brief glance down, picked up a rock about the size of a grapefruit. He rose, an inch at a time. Confident, calm. Not aggressive.

*Never display fear.*

"You can fight. Just have to keep them away from your face and neck. That's what they go for."

"You're not going to . . . ?" Her voice sounded astonished.

"Rather not, but . . ." Then Shaw said, "Open your mouth."

"You want me to . . . ?"

"You're breathing fast and loud. Open mouths're quieter. You sound scared."

"That can't come as a surprise." She did as he'd instructed.

Shaw continued: "They're not used to anything fighting back. He's debating now. Is this dinner going to be worth it? He sees two. The size difference—he might be thinking you're my young. You'd be vulnerable and tasty, yet he'd have to go through me and he knows that I'd fight till the end to save you. He's already eaten so he's not driven by hunger. And we're not running, we're defiant, so he's uneasy."

"*He's* uneasy?" She scoffed. "Is my jacket big enough?"

"You're doing fine. By the way, if he does come after us and I can't stop him, then you can shoot him."

The creature's head lowered.

Shaw gripped the rock, kept his eyes on the predator, and arched his shoulders. The black feline pupils surrounded by yellow remained fixed on Shaw. He really was a magnificent creature. His legs were like flexing metal. The face gave off what seemed to be an evil glare; of course, it was nothing of the kind. It was no more evil than Shaw's when he was about to tuck into a bowl of stew for dinner.

Assessing. Odds that he'd attack: fifty percent.

He really hoped it wouldn't come to shooting. He didn't want the beautiful creature to die.

*For food or the hide, for defense, for mercy . . .*

Gripping the stone.

Decision made. The animal backed away, then turned

and vanished. Shaw was aware of the faint crackling of underbrush once more, like the sound of distant fire, muted in humid air. It lasted only a second or two. For all their size, mountain lions had perfected the art of entering and leaving the stage quietly.

"Jesus." Standish slumped, eyes closed. Her hands were shaking. "He going to come back?"

"Not likely."

"But that doesn't mean no."

"Correct," he said.

"Shot at by punks and junkies, Shaw." She paused. "Sorry, *Colter*."

"Know what? 'Shaw' and 'Standish' are fine. I think we've graduated. Mountain lions can do that."

Margot had called him by his last name. He'd always liked it.

She continued: "Had an informant turn, halfway through a set, and come at me with a razor. That was a day's work, I'm saying. Mountain lions're not a day's work."

Depends on the day and depends on the work, Shaw supposed.

Standish had brought a roll of yellow tape and now spent a few minutes running it from tree to tree, encircling the crime scene.

"So, the blood?" she asked.

"Thompson's?" Shaw replied. "A possibility." He walked in the general direction the animal had vanished—cautiously. He climbed a rock formation and examined the tableau before him.

He returned.

Standish glanced his way. "You found something?"

"A deer carcass. He'd eaten most of it. That's why he wasn't so interested in us."

She finished stringing the tape. Then rose.

Shaw studied the ground. "I can't tell if Henry walked that way or not. I think so." He was looking at a limestone shelf that led to a line of trees. On the other side there seemed to be a deep valley.

Shaw climbed onto the rock and helped Standish up. Together they walked toward the edge of the cliff.

There, they paused.

A hundred feet below lay Henry Thompson's crumpled, bloody body.

# 44.

Ten minutes later two tactical officers were on the floor of the canyon, having rappelled down the sheer face—and doing a smart job of it.

"Detective?" one of them radioed.

"Go ahead, K," Standish said.

"Have to tell you. Cause of death wasn't the fall. He's been shot."

She paused. "Roger."

Shaw was not surprised. He muttered, "Explains it."

"What?"

"Why the Gamer comes back to the scenes. *The Whispering Man*—the game—it isn't only about escaping. It's also about fighting." He reminded Standish about the gameplay: the players might form alliances or they might try to kill one another. And the Whispering Man himself, in his funereal suit and dapper hat, roams the game, ready to murder for the fun of it.

Shaw remembered that the character would come up behind you and whisper advice—which might be real or might be a trick. He might also attack, shooting you with an old-time flintlock pistol or slicing your throat or plunging a blade into your heart, whispering a poem as your screen went black and eerie music played.

*Say good-bye to the life you've known,*
*to your friends and lovers and family home.*
*Run and hide as best you can.*
*There's no escaping the Whispering Man.*
*Now, die with dignity . . .*

The Gamer was simply following the storyline as written. He'd returned to the scene of Sophie Mulliner's captivity to pursue her. He'd done the same here. He'd left Henry Thompson alone for a time, let him build the signal fire—the way he'd given Sophie a chance to escape. Then it was time to return and finish the game.

Standish said nothing but walked along the rocky ground to the clutch of tactical officers who'd joined them here. Shaw sat on a rocky ledge. He received a text from Maddie Poole.

So, you de-looped me?? Is Knight in jail? Are you still alive?

Shaw's inclination was not to reply. But he did, texting that he was with the police. He'd be in touch.

The forensic officers weren't here yet. There was no such thing as a Crime Scene Unit helicopter, so the vans would be driving up the logging trail the long way around to avoid contaminating the shorter way to the highway on the assumption that the kidnapper had taken that route. Yet finding helpful tire tracks seemed an impossible task; the trail was largely covered with a thick carpet of leaves and where it was bare it was baked dry. Why would the Gamer turn careless now?

Standish and the tactical officers were staying clear of the immediate scenes—here and in the nest of pine needles where the Gamer had originally left Thompson. They were visually perusing the site and gauging where the kidnapper might have stalked Thompson. Everyone was a pro now; whatever resentments lingered, they weren't interfering with the mission of solving this crime to prevent others.

"This boy's enjoying himself," one of the officers muttered grimly. "He ain't going to stop."

A SWAT cop suggested Shaw go back to the chopper, not wanting a civilian on the scene. But Standish pointed out that he wasn't armed and that there was at least one hostile in the vicinity—the mountain lion. It also wasn't absolutely certain that the killer was gone. There was some logic to this, though scant; a tac cop, armed for big game, could have accompanied him. Shaw sensed that Standish wanted him here, perhaps to offer insights. Unfortunately, at the moment, he had none.

He gazed down at Thompson's body. There was no blessing in it but at least the man had died quickly, not thanks to the ripping teeth and claws of a wild animal. The shot was to his forehead. Thompson would have returned from setting the fire and made his way back to the nest, for the beef jerky and to rest, awaiting rescue. There, the Gamer would have been waiting. Thompson would have run. His bare feet would have slowed his escape.

Shaw stepped away from the crime scene and walked farther along the stone ridge. He stopped a few feet from the edge. Eyeing the rock face, he noted that it would be a good climb. Lots of cracks and outcroppings. Challenging, with its nearly ninety-degree surfaces, but doable. An overhang that would take quite some strategy to surmount.

Looking down, he didn't plot out, as usual, a route to the bottom.

Nor did he think about poor Henry Thompson.

No, seeing the cliff and the creek bed below, he thought of one thing only.

Echo Ridge.

# 45.

Colter's eyes instantly open when the cabin floor creaks.

He sometimes thinks his father has taught him to sleep light, though that doesn't seem possible. Must've been born with the skill.

The sixteen-year-old's hand dips to the box beneath the bed where his revolver rests. Hand around the grip. Thumb on the trigger to cock it to single action.

Then he sees his mother's silhouette. Mary Dove Shaw, a lean woman, hair always braided, standing in his doorway. No religion in the Shaw household. When he's older, Colter will come to think of his mother in saintly terms, a woman taking comfort in her husband's good moments and sheltering her children from the bad. Protecting Ashton for himself too.

Her nature was clothed in kindness. Underneath was iron.

"Colter. Ash is missing. I need you."

Everyone awakes early on the Compound, but this

hour is closer to night. Not quite 5 a.m. That it's his mother in the doorway doesn't stay his hand from touching the cold steel and rough grip of the .357 Python. Intruders?

Then, swimming closer to wakefulness, he sees in her face concern, not alarm. He rises, leaving the weapon under the bed.

"Ash went out after I fell asleep, about ten. He hasn't come back. The Benelli's gone."

His father's favorite shotgun.

Camping and expeditions in the Compound are always planned and, in any event, there is no reason for Ashton to go out at that hour, much less to stay out all night.

*Never hike anywhere without telling at least one person where you'll be.*

The way his mind had been sputtering recently, Mary Dove had made sure she or one of the children accompanied him on the longer forays within the Compound. Chaperoning was especially essential when he went into White Sulphur Springs because on those outings he'd taken to carrying a weapon. Two in fact: in the car and on his person. There'd been no incidents but Mary Dove thought it best to have a family member with him. Even thirteen-year-old Dorion has the grit and intelligence to defuse what might become a confrontation.

Only three people in the Compound tonight, apart from Ashton: Dorion, Colter and Mary Dove. Colter's older brother, Russell, is in Los Angeles. He is starting to become a recluse, a role he will perfect in later years. Even if he had been here, though, Mary Dove would have come to her middle child for help.

"You're the best tracker of the family, Colter. You can find where a sparrow breathed on a blade of grass. I need you to find him. I'll stay here with your sister."

"He take anything else?"

"Nothing that I could tell."

In five minutes Colter is dressed for the predawn wilderness. October in eastern California can be fickle, so he wears thermals and two shirts under his canvas jacket. Jeans, thick socks and boots he broke in when he stopped growing two years ago; they feel like cotton on his feet. He has a night bag with him: clothes, flashlights, flares, food, water, sleeping bag, first aid, two hundred feet of rope, rappelling hardware, ammunition. For weapons: the Ka-Bar Army knife, ten-inch, and the Python. Ashton, who carries a .44 Magnum revolver, says that mud and water and tumbles won't affect a revolver's action the way they might a semiautomatic like a Glock, despite the gun manufacturer's assertions to the contrary.

"Wait," Mary Dove says. She goes to the mantel and opens a box, from which wires sprout, connected to the wall outlet. She removes one of the mobile phones inside, powers it on and gives it to Colter. He hasn't held the phone in two years and he's never used it.

In his hand the unit feels alien. Taboo. He places it in the bag as well.

Colter slips on gloves and a stocking cap that can pull down to a ski mask. He steps out into the bracing, damp chill, feeling the sting of cold in his nose. As soon as he steps off the porch he catches a break. A handful of trails lead from the cabin into the fields and woods on the property and beyond. One of these paths is rarely hiked and it's on this one that the boy sees fresh boot prints—his father's, which he knows well. The stride is curious. It's longer than that of a man leisurely strolling into the woods. There is urgency in it. There's purpose in it.

Colter continues cutting for sign in the direction his father took about five or six hours previously, to judge from the snapped grasses. It's an easy track, since there are no forks or cross-paths. He can move quickly, stopping only sporadically to confirm that Ash came this way.

A mile from the cabin he spots another boot print in soft earth, paralleling his father's route. He can't tell its age. It might have been made months ago, by one of his father's friends who'd come to visit—friends from the old days before he fled the Bay Area. They would frequently trek out together, just the two or three of them, for the day. His mother too has colleagues from her teaching days who visit.

But this is not a likely route for a leisurely walk with acquaintances. Being in a valley, there's nothing to see. And here it's a chore to hike—the angle, the rocks and pits and gravelly slopes. He continues along the trail, confirming again that his father came this way. Confirming too that the Second Person did as well.

Onward. Until he comes to a fork and sees that his father has turned left and that means only one destination: Crescent Lake, a large body of water that resembles either a smile or a frown, depending.

In twenty minutes Colter comes to the mucky shore. He looks across, a half mile at the widest. The water is black now, though the sky is going to a soft glow. The surface is mirror-still. The distant shore rises in forest to ragged peaks. He assumes his father has gone there because the family's canoe is missing.

Why would he cross? It's a warren of thickets and rocks on the other side.

He looks for signs of the Second Person's prints and can find none. Widening his search circle, he finally does locate the sign. The man stood on the shore, perhaps looking around for Ashton. He then started up the steep trail to Echo Ridge, from which he can gaze over the whole terrain and possibly spot the man.

The ground is soft here, so Colter can see the Second Person's prints clearly.

And something else.

His father's prints. On top of the other man's.

Ashton knew he was being followed. He probably hid in the canoe until the man started up the trail and then followed.

The pursuer became prey.

The trail isn't so very fresh—the men were here some hours ago—yet an urgency ignites within Colter and he muscles up the trail, quickly, after the two men, a thirty-degree incline through rocks and over small, sandy ledges. He has never been to Echo Ridge, a craggy rise in the foothills of the Sierra Nevadas. The terrain is unforgiving. Echo Ridge was one place on the Compound that the children were not allowed to go.

Yet it was to Echo Ridge that Ashton Shaw followed someone who had been pursuing him. And Echo Ridge is the place to which his son is climbing now.

Ten minutes later a breathless Colter crests the summit and stands against a rock face, sucking in air. In his hand is the Colt Python.

He's looking over the tree- and brush-covered plateau of the ridge. To his left—west—is a pelt of forest and a layered maze of rock formations and caves, where your assumption is: bears in the big ones, snakes in the small.

To Colter's right—east—is a cliff face, ninety degrees, a hundred feet or more straight down to a dry creek bed on the valley floor.

The same creek bed where last year Colter had the confrontation with the hunter, who'd blindly shot into a bush and wounded the buck.

He now looks east again, at the brightening morning sky, and sees the sharp black silhouette of the Sierra Nevada peaks, a massive jaw of broken teeth.

As for his father's footsteps? The other man's? He can't see either. The plateau is rock and gravel. No cutting for sign here.

Now the sun rises over the mountains and pastes orangey light on the rock and the forest of Echo Ridge.

The light also pings off a shiny object fifty yards away.

Glass or metal? It's not too early for ice, but the glint is coming from the floor of pine needles, where there would be no standing water to freeze.

Colter cocks the pistol and lifts it as he walks forward. The gun is a heavy one, weighing two and a half pounds, but he hardly notices the weight. He proceeds toward the flash, eyeing the forest to his left; no threat could come from the cliff edge on his right, except from that hundred-foot drop to the creek bed below.

When he's still about twenty feet from the light

source, he sees what it is. He stops, gazing around him. He doesn't move for a moment, then slowly he walks in a circle, which ends at the cliff's edge.

Colter swaps the gun for the cell phone. He flips it open and takes a moment to remember how it works. Then he dials a number he memorized years ago.

N ow, fifteen years later, Colter Shaw was looking at a configuration of rock so very similar to Echo Ridge.

He gazed at the crime scene tape around the place where Henry Thompson lay.

Shaw thought about the button on the Hong-Sung goggles—the one you pushed to be resurrected.

RESET . . .

Over the crest of the rise, four newcomers walked slowly, carrying and wheeling large cases—like professional carpenters' toolboxes. The Joint Major Crimes Task Force crime scene team wore blue jumpsuits, the hoods pulled low around their necks. The day was not particularly hot but the sun was relentless and wearing the contamination-proof coveralls would be unbearable after any length of time.

Standish approached and offered Shaw a bottle of water. He took it and drank down half, surprised at how thirsty he was. "We'll leave it to Crime Scene and the ME. No hurry to get back. I'm going to hitch a ride in the vans. Not in an airborne mood at the moment."

Shaw agreed.

The detective was staring over the cliff. After a moment she asked, "You see that big cat again?"

"No."

Absently she said, "You know, there were a couple of them in Palo Alto the other day. I read the story in the *Examiner*. Safeway parking lot. Roughhousing like kittens. Then they ran off into the woods and disappeared. They interviewed somebody. He said, 'The mountain lion you can't see is worse than the one you can.' Is that the truth about life or what, Shaw?"

His phone vibrated. He read the text.

A moment of debate as he stared down the rock face. He typed and sent a reply.

He slipped the phone away and said to Standish that he'd changed his mind and would take the chopper back after all.

# 46.

Six p.m., and Colter Shaw was back in the Quick Byte Café.

He tilted the beer bottle back, drank long. It was a custom of his to drink locally brewed beer whenever he traveled. In Chicago, Goose Island. In South Africa, Umqombothi, which smelled and looked daunting but tricked you with a three percent alcohol content. In Boston, Harpoon—not that other stuff.

And in the San Francisco Bay Area: Anchor Steam, of course. Tiffany, back on duty, had given it to him on the house, delivered with a wink.

He set down the bottle and closed his eyes briefly, seeing Henry Thompson's body, the gradient colors of his blood on the rock, as white and flat as that creek bed below Echo Ridge.

In ten years of seeking rewards Shaw been successful the majority of the time. Not a landslide but respectable nonetheless.

He might have given his success rate a percentage number. He never did. It seemed flippant, disrespectful.

He could remember some of the victories—the tricky ones, the dangerous ones, the ones occasioned by desperation and despair on the part of loved ones whose lives crashed when their child or spouse went missing and that Shaw pieced back together—like the final scenes in time travel movies when disaster is miraculously reversed.

Other than those, though, most jobs were just that: assignments, assignments like a plumber or an accountant might take on. They drifted down into the recesses of the brain, some lost forever, some filed away to be recalled if needed, which was rarely.

The losses? They stayed forever.

This one would. That there'd been no reward offered to find Henry Thompson was irrelevant. Because the truth was, for Colter Shaw it was never about the money. The reward was important mostly because it was a spotlight illuminating a challenge that no one else had yet been able to meet. What mattered was finding the child, the elderly parent addled by dementia, the fugitive. What mattered was saving the life.

Sophie Mulliner was safe, but that was no solace at all. Kyle Butler was dead. Henry Thompson was dead. And at times like this the restlessness grew and became a person itself, following Shaw, close behind. Like the Whispering Man.

He sipped more of the ripe, rich beer. The cold was more of a comfort than the alcohol. Neither was much of a balm.

He walked back to the counter and asked Tiffany for

the remote. He wanted to change the station on the set above the bar. She handed it to him. They had a brief conversation about TV programs, to which he couldn't contribute much. She would have liked to continue talking to him, Shaw could tell, but an order was ready. He was relieved when she went to deliver it and he sat down at his table once more. Shaw changed the channel from a sports game no one was watching—not a lot of jocks in the Quick Byte Café—to a local news channel.

A minor earthquake had troubled Santa Cruz; a labor organizer was fighting cries for removal, claiming the rumors that he'd paid money under the table for a green card were false; a whale had been saved at Half Moon Bay; a Green Party congressman in L.A., running for reelection, had withdrawn after stories surfaced he'd been allied with ecoterrorists who'd burned down a ski resort at Tahoe a few years before. He vehemently denied his involvement. "A man's career can be ruined based on lies. That's what it's come to . . ."

His attention waned until finally: "And in local news, a Sunnyvale blogger and gay rights activist was found murdered today in Big Basin Redwoods State Park. Police reported that Henry Thompson, fifty-two, was kidnapped on the way home from a lecture at Stanford last night, taken to the park and murdered. No motive has been established. A spokesperson for the Joint Major Crimes Task Force in Santa Clara said that the crime may be related to the kidnapping of a Mountain View woman on June fifth. Sophie Mulliner, nineteen, was rescued unharmed by the Task Force two days later."

The story ended with a scroll at the bottom of the

screen of the hotline to call if anyone was on the block when Thompson was kidnapped or was hiking in Big Basin today.

Behind him, in the Quick Byte, a woman's strident voice interrupted Shaw's thoughts.

"Well, I didn't message you. I don't know you."

Shaw and other patrons looked toward the source of the shrill words. An attractive woman of about twenty was sitting in front of her Mac and holding a mug of coffee. Her long chestnut hair was tinted purple near the tips. She was dressed like a model or an actress: studied casual. The blue jeans were close-fitting and intentionally torn in places. The white T-shirt was baggy and off the shoulder, revealing purple undergarment straps. The nails were oceanic blue, the eye shadow autumnal shades.

Standing over her was a young man about her age, on the other end of the style spectrum. The baggy cargo pants were well worn, and the loose red-and-black-checked shirt too large; this made him seem smaller than his frame, which was probably five-eight or -nine, slim. He had straight hair that was none too clean and was self-cut or clipped by a mother or sister. His dark brows nudged close over his fleshy nose. A big gray laptop, twice as thick as Shaw's, was clutched in his hands. His face was bright red with embarrassment. Anger was in his eyes too. "You're Sherry 38." He shook his head. "We instant-messaged in *Call to Arms IV*. You said you'd be here. I'm Brad H 66."

"I'm not Sherry anybody. And I don't know who the hell you are."

The man lowered his voice. "You said you wanted to

hook up. You said it!" He muttered. "Then here I show up and you don't like what you see. Right?"

"Oh, excuse me. You really think I'm the sort of loser who plays *Call to Arms*? Fuck off, okay?"

Once more a scan of the room. The young man surrendered and walked to the order station.

The perils of the internet. Had the poor kid been set up by bullies? Shaw recalled what Maddie Poole had told him about SWAT'ing. And what Marty Avon had told him about the ease of hacking gaming servers.

Or was the kid right, that the description he'd sent the woman online didn't match the in-person geek version, so she'd bailed on him?

The kid placed an order, paid and took the number on the wire metal stand to a table in the back, dropped into a chair and opened his computer. He plugged in a bulky headset and began pounding away on the keys. His face was still red and he was muttering to himself.

Shaw pulled out a notebook and opened his fountain pen. From memory he sketched a map of where Hank Thompson had been killed. His sure hand completed the drawing in five minutes. He signed it with his initials in the lower-right-hand corner, as he always did. He was waiting for the ink to dry when he looked up. Maddie Poole was walking in. Their eyes met. She smiled; he nodded.

"Lookit you," she said, possibly meaning his posture. He was leaning back in his chair, his feet stretched out in front of him, the Ecco tips pointed ceilingward.

Then the smile faded. She'd scanned his face. The eyes, in particular.

She sat down, took the bottle of beer from him and lifted it to her own lips. Drank a large mouthful.

"I'll buy you another one."

"Not a worry," he said.

"What is it? And you'd better not say 'Nothing.'"

He hadn't texted or spoken about Thompson's murder.

"We lost the second victim."

"Colt. Jesus. Wait. Was it that murder in the state park? The guy who was shot?"

A nod.

"*The Whispering Man* thing again?"

"The police still aren't talking about that in the news—they don't want the Gamer to know how much they know."

"Gamer?"

"That's what they're calling him." He sipped the beer. "He took Thompson into the mountains and left him with the five objects. Thompson came to and started a signal fire. That's how we got onto him. But the Gamer came back to hunt him. That's part of the game too."

She looked over the map, then up at his eyes, a frown of curiosity on her face. He explained about his custom of drawing the maps.

"You're good."

Shaw happened to be looking at the spot on the map that represented the foot of the cliff where Henry Thompson had died. He closed the notebook and put it away.

Maddie touched his forearm firmly. "I'm sorry. What about Tony Knight? You didn't tell me what happened. I was worried until I got your text."

"Things got busy. And Knight? I was wrong. It wasn't him. He's been helpful."

"Do the police have any ideas who it is?"

"No. If I had to guess, a sociopath. Nothing I've ever seen before—this elaborate modeling on the game. My mother might have known people like that."

"You said she was a psychiatrist."

He nodded.

Mary Dove Shaw had done a lot of research into medications for treating the criminally insane and as a principal investigator had funneled a lot of grant money to Cal and other schools.

That was earlier in her career—before the migration east, of course. In the later years her practice was limited to family medicine and midwifing in and around White Sulphur Springs and the management of paranoid personality and schizophrenia, though the latter practice involved only one patient: Ashton Shaw.

Shaw had yet to share with Maddie much about his father.

She asked, "Are the police offering a reward?"

"Maybe, I don't know. I'm not interested in that. I just want to get him. I—"

The rest of the sentence was never uttered. Maddie had lunged forward and kissed him, her strong hands gripping his jacket, her tongue probing.

He tasted her, a hint of lipstick, though he hadn't seen any color. Mint. He kissed back, hard.

Shaw's hand slipped to the back of her head, fingers splayed, entwined in her sumptuous hair. Pulling her closer, closer. Maddie leaned in and he felt her breasts against his chest.

They began to speak simultaneously.

She touched his lips with a finger. "Let me go first. I live three blocks from here. Now what were you going to say?"

"I forgot."

# 47.

Shaw led a nomadic life and didn't have a large inventory of possessions. But the Winnebago was downright cluttered compared with Maddie Poole's rental.

True, it was temporary; she was only in town for C3, had driven up from her home outside L.A. Still . . .

One aspect exaggerated the emptiness: the ancient place was huge, five bedrooms, possibly more. A cavernous dining room. A living room that could be a wedding venue.

It was occupied by few possessions; her big desktop computer—a twenty-something-inch monitor dominating the table it sat on. On either side of the big Dell were cardboard cartons serving as end tables; they held books and magazines, DVDs and boxes of video game cartridges. An office chair rested before it. Surrounding the workstation were shopping bags from computer companies—giveaways, he guessed, from the conference.

A mountain bike, well-used, sat in the corner. The

brand was SANTA CRUZ. Shaw didn't bike but when hiking or climbing he came across bikers often. He knew this make could go for nine thousand dollars. Also, there were free weights—twenty-five-pounders—and some elastic exercise contraption.

In the bedroom, to the right, was a double-sized mattress and box spring, sitting on the floor. The sheets were atop it, untucked and swirled like a lazy hurricane.

In the living room an unfortunate beige couch rested before a coffee table that made Frank Mulliner's limb-fractured model look classy. The laminated dark wood top of Maddie's was curling upward at the ends.

The kitchen was empty of furniture and appliances other than those built in: a range, a fridge, an oven and a microwave. On the counter was a box of cornflakes and two bottles of white wine, a six-pack of Corona beer.

Shaw dated the huge house around the 1930s. It was sorely in need of paint and repair. Water damage was prevalent and the plaster walls cracked in a dozen places.

"Out of *The Addams Family*, right?" Maddie said, laughing.

"True."

Last Halloween, Shaw had taken his nieces to an amusement park; it had featured a haunted house that looked a lot like this.

She went on to explain that she'd found it through an Airbnb kind of service. It was available only because its days were numbered; next month it was being demolished, thanks to Siliconville. The stained wallpaper was of tiny, dark flowers on a pale blue background. The dotted effect was oddly disconcerting.

"Wine?"

"Corona."

She got a cold bottle from the refrigerator and poured herself a tall glass of wine, returned to the couch, handed him the beer and curled up. He sat too; their shoulders touched.

"So . . . ?" From her.

"This is where you ask if there's anybody in my life."

"Good-looking *and* a mind reader."

"Wouldn't be here if there was."

Clinking glasses. "Lot of men say that but I believe you."

He kissed her hard, his hand around the back of her neck once more, surprised that the tangles of her rust-shaded hair were so soft. He thought they'd be more fibrous. She leaned in and kissed back, her lips playful.

She took a large sip of wine. A splash hit the couch.

"Oops. Good-bye, security deposit."

He started to take the glass from her. She had one more hit and then relinquished it. The glass and his beer ended up on the wavy coffee table. They were kissing harder yet. Her legs straightened from their near-lotus fold and she eased back onto the cushions. His right hand descended from her hair to her ear to her cheek to her neck.

"Bedroom?" Shaw whispered.

A nod, a smile.

They rose and walked inside. Just past the threshold Shaw kicked off his shoes. Maddie lagged, diverting momentarily, shutting out the living room and kitchen lights. He sat on the bed and tugged his socks off.

"Got something that might be fun," her voice whispered seductively from the dark space on the other side of the doorway.

"Sure," he said.

When Maddie appeared in the doorway, she was wearing the Hong-Sung *Immersion* goggles.

"Lord, Colter, I got what I think is the first smile out of you in two days."

She pulled them off and set them on the floor.

Shaw reached out a hand and tugged her to him. He kissed her lips, the tattoo, her throat, her breasts. He started to pull her into the bed. She said in a soft voice, "I'm a lights-out girl. You okay with that?"

Not his preference but under the circumstances perfectly fine.

He rolled across the bed and clicked the cheap lamp off and, when he turned back, she was on him and their hands began undoing buttons and zippers.

Naturally, it was played as a competitive game.

This one ended in a tie.

# 48.

Nearly midnight.

Colter Shaw rose and walked into the bathroom. He turned the light on and in his peripheral vision he saw Maddie scrambling, urgently, to pull a sheet up to her neck.

Which explained the lights out. And explained the cover-up clothing of sweats and hoodies; many of the women at C3 wore tank tops and short-sleeved T's.

He'd gotten a glimpse of three or four scars on Maddie's body.

He recalled now that, earlier, as his hands and mouth roamed, she would subtly direct him away from certain places on her belly and shoulder and thigh.

He guessed an accident.

As they'd driven from the Quick Byte Café, she'd done so carelessly, speeding sometimes twenty over the limit, then slowed to let him catch up. Maybe she'd been in a car crash or biking mishap.

Making sure to shut out the bathroom light before he

opened the door, Shaw returned to bed, a towel wrapped around his waist. He passed her by and went into the kitchen, fetched two bottles of water from the fridge and returned. He handed her one, which she took and set on the floor.

He drank a few sips, then lay back on the lumpy mattress. The room was not completely dark and he could see that she'd pulled a sweatshirt on while he was in the kitchen. The shirt had some writing on the front. He couldn't read the words. She was sitting up, checking texts. Shaw could see the light from her phone on her face—a ghostly image. The only other illumination was the faint glow from her monitor's screen saver bleeding through the door to the living room.

He moved closer to her, sitting up too. His fingers lightly brushed her tattoo.

*I'll tell you later. Maybe . . .*

Maddie stiffened. It was very subtle, almost imperceptible.

Yet not quite.

He put distance between them, propping the pillow up and sitting against it. He'd been here often enough—on both sides of the bed, so to speak—to know not to ask what was wrong. Words that came too fast were usually worse than no words at all.

Head on the pillow, he stared at the ceiling.

A moment later Maddie said, "Damn air conditioner. Makes a racket. Wake you up?"

"Wasn't asleep." He hadn't noticed. Now he did. And it was noisy.

"I'd complain but I'll be gone in a few days. And this place'll be in a scrapyard by next week. That Siliconville thing."

Silence between them, though the groaning AC was now like a third person in the room.

"Look, Colt, the thing is . . ." She was examining words, discarding them. She found some: "I'm pretty good with the before part. And I think I'm pretty good with the during part."

That was true. But the rules absolutely required him to not respond.

"The after part? I'm not so good with that."

Was she wiping away tears? No, just tugging at the tangle of hair in front of her face.

"Not a big deal. It's not, like, get the hell out of my life. Just, it happens. Not always. Usually." She cleared her throat. "You're lucky. I got pissed at you for bringing me water. Imagine what would've happened, you'd asked to meet the family. I can really be a bitch."

"It's good water. You're missing out."

Her shoulders slumped and she twined hair around her right index finger.

He said, "Here's where I say we're a lot alike and that pisses you off more."

"Fuck you. Quit being so nice. I want to throw you out."

"See? Told you. We're a lot alike. I'm not so good with the after part either. Never have been."

Her hand squeezed his knee, then retreated.

Shaw told her, "Had two siblings, growing up. We fell

out in three different ways. Russell, oldest, was the reclusive one. Dorie, our kid sister, was the clever one. I was the restless one. Was then, still am."

The laugh from Maddie's mouth was barely perceptible but it was a laugh. "You know, Colter, we should start a club."

"A club."

"Yeah. Both of us, good with before and during, not after. We'll call it the Never After Club."

This struck home.

*The King of Never . . .*

Which he didn't share with her.

"I'll go," he said.

"No way. You've gotta be beat. This's a hiccup, is all. Only don't plan on spooning till noon tomorrow and then make plans to take BART to an art museum and a waffle brunch."

"The likelihood of that happening I'd put at, let's see, zero percent."

Maddie gave a smile. A whatever happens, it's been good smile. "Curl up or stretch out. Or whatever you do."

"You going to . . ."

"Kill some aliens. What else?"

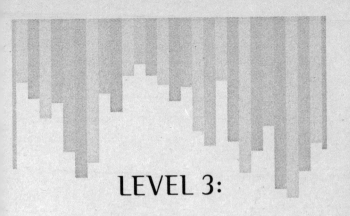

# LEVEL 3:

# THE SINKING SHIP

Sunday, June 9

# 49.

W e're calling it an accident. No other thing fits."

Colter Shaw awoke, lying in Maddie Poole's disheveled bed, his eyes on the overhead fan, a palm frond design, one blade sagging, and though the room was hot he didn't think it was a good idea to flick the unit on.

*Accident* . . .

Maddie was not in bed nor was she in the living room, killing or maiming aliens. The big house creaked, the sounds from its infrastructure, not inhabitants.

Apparently the woman took the "never after" part seriously.

The hour was close to 4 a.m.

Sleep was an illusion. He wondered if he'd had a nightmare. Maybe. *Probably.* Because he kept hearing the voice of White Sulfur Springs sheriff Roy Blanche.

"We're calling it an accident. No other thing fits."

This was the opinion too of the county coroner, regarding the death of Ashton Shaw. He'd lost his footing and tumbled off the eastern side of Echo Ridge, a hundred-foot-plus plummet to the dry creek bed where Colter spotted him, that rosy-dawn morning, October 5, fifteen years ago. The boy had rappelled as fast as he'd ever descended in the hope that he might save his father. While he didn't know it at the time, a person falling from that height will reach a speed of about sixty-five miles per hour. Anything over forty-five or fifty is fatal.

The death occurred around six hours earlier—1 a.m. Sheriff Blanche found a patch of wet leaves that might have been slick with an early frost. One step on them, with the incline, and Ashton would have gone over.

The glint that Colter had seen was the sun striking the chrome receiver of the Benelli Pacific Flyway shotgun. It was lying on the ground, ten feet from the edge, where it had flown after Ashton made a frantic grab for nearby branches to arrest his tumble.

Another possibility was in everyone's mind but on no one's tongue: suicide.

To Colter, though, both theories were flawed. Accident? Twenty percent. Suicide? One percent.

Ashton was a survivalist and outdoorsman and conditions like slippery foliage would have been just one more factor he'd have tucked into the equation on a trek, like gauging the dependability of ice on a pond or how fresh a bear paw print was and how big the creature that had left it.

As for suicide, Ashton Shaw's essence was survival and Colter couldn't envision any universe in which his father would have taken his own life. Mental issues? Sure. Yet as mad as he could be, his affliction was paranoia—which is, of course, all about protecting yourself from threats.

He was also carrying a 12-gauge shotgun. If you want to end your life, why not just use a beloved weapon, like Papa Hemingway? Why tumble over and hope the fall will kill you? Colter and his mother had discussed it. She was as sure as her son that the death was not self-inflicted.

So, an accident.

To the world.

But not to Colter Shaw, who believed—around eighty percent—his father had been murdered. The killer was the Second Person, who had followed Ashton from the cabin and who had then become the pursued—after Ashton's clever canoe trick at Crescent Lake. The two had met atop Echo Ridge. There'd been a fight. And the killer had pushed Ashton over the edge to his death.

Yet Colter had said nothing to the police, to anyone, much less to his mother.

The reason? Simple. Because he believed that the Second Person was Colter's older brother, Russell.

Ashton would have been following the shadowy figure along the rocky ground of the ridge, the bead sight of his weapon on his back. He'd have demanded to know who he was. Russell would have turned and a shocked Ashton Shaw would have seen his eldest son. Dumbfounded, he would have lowered the gun.

Which is when Russell would have grabbed it, flung it away and pushed his father over the cliff.

Unthinkable. Why would a son do that?

Colter Shaw had an answer.

A month before his father died, Mary Dove was away; her sister was ill and she'd traveled to Seattle to help her brother-in-law and nieces and nephews while Emilia was in the hospital. So very aware of her husband's troubles, she had asked Russell to drive up to the Compound from L.A., where he was in grad school at UCLA and working, to look out for her younger children in her absence. Colter was sixteen, Dorion thirteen.

Colter's brother, then twenty-two, sported a full beard and long dark hair—just like the mountain man he was named after—but wore city slicker clothes: slacks, dress shirt and sport coat. When he'd arrived, he and Colter had embraced awkwardly. Quiet as always, Russell deflected questions about his life.

One evening, Ashton looked out the window and said to his daughter, "Graduation night, Dorion. Crow Valley. Suit up."

The girl had frozen.

Colter thought: She was no longer "Button." Ashton's daughter was, in his mind, an adult now.

"Ash, I've decided. I don't want to," Dorion said in an even voice.

"You can do it," Ashton said calmly.

"No," Russell said.

"Shh," their father had whispered, waving his hand to silence his son. "Mark my words. When they come, it's not going to do any good to say, 'I don't want to.' You'll have to swim, you'll have to run, you'll have to fight. You'll have to climb."

Graduation was a rite of passage Ashton had decided upon: an ascent, at night, up a sheer cliff face, rising a hundred and fifty feet above the floor of Crow Valley.

Ashton said, "The boys did it."

That wasn't the point. When they were thirteen, Colter

and Russell had wanted to make the climb. Their sister didn't. Colter was aware too that Ashton had only proposed this when Mary Dove was away. She supported her husband, she sheltered him. But in addition to being his wife, she was his psychiatrist too. Which meant there were things he couldn't get away with when she was present.

"There's a full moon. No wind, no ice. She's as tough as you." He started to pull Dorion to her feet. "Get your ropes and gear. Change."

Russell had then stood, removed his father's arm from his sister's and said in a low voice, "No."

What happened next seared itself into Colter's memory.

Their father pushed Russell aside and grabbed Dorion's arm once more. The older son had learned well and, in a flash, he slammed his open palm into their father's chest. The man stumbled back, shocked. And as he did, he reached for a carving knife on the table.

Everyone froze. A moment later Ashton took his hand off the knife. He muttered, "All right. No climb. For now. For now." And walked to his study, lecturing an invisible audience. He closed the door behind him.

A burning silence ensued.

"He's a stranger." Dorion looked toward the study. Her eyes were as steady as her hands. The incident appeared to have affected her far less than it had her brothers.

Russell muttered, "He's taught us how to survive. Now we have to survive him."

It was two weeks later that Mary Dove awakened her middle child in the predawn hours.

*Colter. Ash is missing. I need you . . .*

Yes, Colter suspected Russell had killed their father.

That was only circumstantial speculation. The hypothesis would move closer to theory, if not certainty, at their father's funeral.

Mary Dove arranged for a modest ceremony three days after her husband's death, attended by close family and colleagues from their former lives as academics at Berkeley.

Russell had flown back to L.A. after his mother returned from her sister's hospital stay. He then returned to the Compound for the funeral. And it was when the family had gathered for breakfast before the memorial that Colter heard a brief exchange.

A relative asked Russell if he'd flown in from L.A. and he said no, he'd driven. And then he mentioned the route.

Colter actually gasped, a reaction nobody else heard. Because the route Russell had described had been closed recently because of a rockslide; it had been clear on the day of Ashton's murder. This meant that Russell had been in the area for several days. He'd driven up earlier, hiding out nearby, maybe because his reclusive nature kept him from seeing family. Maybe to murder their father in the chill morning hours of October 5, for the purpose of saving his younger sister from any mad and dangerous "graduations."

And for another reason too: to put his father out of his misery.

*For food or hide, for defense, for mercy.*

Colter resolved at the funeral to wait and confront his brother later. Later never came, because Russell had left abruptly after the service and then went off the grid entirely.

The thought of patricide haunted Colter for years, a

constant wound to the soul. But then, a month ago, some hope emerged that perhaps his older brother might not have been the killer after all.

He was at his house in Florida, sorting through a box of old pictures his mother had sent. He found a letter addressed to Ashton with no return address. The postmark was Berkeley and the date three days before he died. This caught Shaw's attention.

Ash:

*I'm afraid I have to tell you Braxton is alive! Maybe headed north. Be CAREFUL. I've explained to everybody that inside the envelope is the key to where you've hidden everything.*

*I put it in 22-R, 3rd floor.*

*We'll make this work, Ash. God bless.*

—Eugene

What could he make of this?

One conclusion was that Ashton—indeed "everybody" in Eugene's note—was at risk.

And who was Braxton?

First things first. Find Eugene. Colter's mother said Ashton had a friend at Cal by that name, a fellow professor, but she couldn't remember his last name. And she'd never heard of a Braxton.

Shaw's search of staff at UC Berkeley fifteen years ago

uncovered a professor Eugene Young, a physicist, who'd died, in a car crash, two years after Ashton had. The death itself seemed suspicious: driving off a cliff near Yosemite on a safe stretch of road. Shaw tracked down Young's widow, who had remarried. Shaw had called her, explaining who he was and adding that he was compiling material about his father. Did she have anything—correspondence or other documents—relating to Ashton? She said she'd disposed of all her late husband's personal documents over the years. Shaw gave her his number and told her he'd be in an RV park in Oakland for the next few days if she thought of anything.

Then Colter Shaw did what he was good at: tracking. Eugene Young was a professor on the Cal campus and he'd hidden something at a place designated as 22-R. It took Shaw two days to learn that only the Cal Sociology Department archives, located on the third floor, had a Room 22, with a stack *R*.

Which was where, three days ago, he found—and stole—the magic envelope.

*Graded Exams 5/25 . . .*

If there was any proof that someone other than Russell Shaw had killed Ashton—this Braxton or possibly an associate—it would be that cryptic stack of documents the envelope contained.

Now, in Maddie's bed, he heard Sheriff Roy Blanche's words.

*We're calling it an accident. No other thing fits . . .*

Except, to his great relief, Colter Shaw had realized that perhaps something else did.

Braxton is alive!

The AC unit outside Maddie's window grew more temperamental yet. Returning to sleep was not an option, Shaw realized, so he rose and dressed. Opened another bottle of water and walked outside, extending the deadbolt so that the door wouldn't lock behind him. He sat down on an orange plastic deck chair, the sole bit of furniture in a porch space that could accommodate twenty times that. He sipped. On his phone, he found the local news to see if there'd been any more developments in the Henry Thompson case. As he waited for the story to appear, he saw another story that sounded familiar . . . Oh, right. It was about the congressman accused of texting young interns; he'd first heard the story on the broadcast within Tony Knight's game, *Prime Mission*. The politician, a representative named Richard Boyd, from Utah, had committed suicide, his note proclaiming innocence and citing a life in tatters due to the rumors. The story was more than just a tragic death. His seat in Congress could tip the party balance in the next election.

Shaw's father had been fascinated with politics, but this was a paternal gene that had not been passed down to Colter.

Nothing in the news about Henry Thompson, so he shut the channel off and slipped his phone away.

The street was quiet, no insects, no owls. He heard the shush of traffic from a freeway, a few horns. While there were a half dozen airports nearby, this would be a no-fly time.

He looked over the avenue and saw one house in the process of being torn down and, next to it, a vacant lot recently bulldozed. Signs in both front yards read FU-TURE HOME OF SILICONVILLE!

Shaw was amused that spacey, frizzy-haired Marty Avon, the man who loved toys, was engaged in such a serious project as real estate development. Shaw guessed he'd had more fun designing and building the mock-up of Siliconville in the Destiny lobby than he would watching construction of the real thing.

Shaw finished the water and wandered back inside. He stepped to Maddie's thirty-inch computer monitor, on which a three-dimensional ball bounced slowly over the screen, its colors changing from purple to red to yellow to green, all rich shades.

He glanced at her desk—everything Maddie Poole owned was devoted to the art and science of video gaming: CD and DVD jewel cases, the circuit boards, RAM cards, drives, mouses and consoles. Game cartridges were everywhere. And cables, cables, cables. He picked up a few of her books, flipped through them. The word *Gameplay* figured in most of the titles. And, in some, *Cheats* and *Workarounds*. He skimmed *The Ultimate Guide to Fortnite*, recalling the company's booth at the C3 Conference. The complexity of the instructions was overwhelming. He started to set it back and he froze.

There was a booklet beneath the *Fortnite* guide. With a pounding heart, he picked it up and thumbed through the pages. Passages were circled and starred. And there were margin notes, references to knives, guns, torches, arrows. The title was:

### GAMEPLAY GUIDES. VOL. 12
#### THE WHISPERING MAN

The game Maddie Poole had claimed she'd never played and knew virtually nothing about.

# 50.

She'd lied to him.

Why?

Certainly, there might be innocent explanations. Maybe she'd played a long time ago and forgotten.

Were the notes even hers?

He found some Post-its with her handwriting on the small pink squares.

Yes, she'd made the notes in *The Whispering Man* book.

The implications: Maddie knew the Gamer. They'd learned Shaw was involved and the Gamer told her to pick him up at the Quick Byte and stay close to find out what the investigators knew.

*Do the police have any ideas who it is?*

Then he decided there was a problem with this hypothesis: the lack of evidence that a Second Person was involved in the Gamer's crimes.

Which left him with the heart-wrenching possibility: Maddie Poole was herself the Gamer.

Shaw stepped outside to his car and retrieved his computer bag. He returned to the house and extracted one of his notebooks and his fountain pen. Writing down the facts not only let him analyze the situation more clearly, it was a comfort. Which he needed at the moment.

Was this idea even feasible?

His first thought was that she perfectly fit the Killer category of gamer that Jimmy Foyle had told him about—supercompetitive, playing to win, to survive, to defeat, at all costs.

As he read through the facts and chronology, the percentage of her guilt edged upward. Maddie had come into the Quick Byte just after he had, on the day they'd met. She could have followed him from his meeting with Frank Mulliner. Then, after he'd left her at the café, he'd seen somebody spying on him at San Miguel Park. Had she followed him there, and to the old factory afterward?

She'd certainly come on to him, charming and flirtatious, called him to congratulate him on saving Sophie and invite him to the conference. To work her way into his life.

He reflected: the two victims had been taken by surprise, slammed to the ground and injected with the drug, then dragged to a car. Maddie was strong enough for that—he knew this for a fact from their time in bed a few hours ago. He thought of the ruthlessness he'd seen on her face when they'd played *Immersion* in the Hong-Sung booth. Her wolf eyes, triumphant in the act of killing him. And as a hunter, she'd know firearms.

This hypothesis he put at twenty-five percent.

That number didn't last long. It rose to thirty, then

more, when he thought of a motive. He'd recalled her scars and how she'd tried to hide them from him. Was this from modesty or because she didn't want Shaw to suspect who she really was?

The high school girl kidnapped eight years ago by those teens who'd grown obsessed with *The Whispering Man* and tried to kill her. The news stories hadn't said how. It was possible they'd used knives—another of the Whispering Man's weapons.

Perhaps Maddie had come here to destroy the company that had published the game, drive it out of business. Of course, she wouldn't have known what Tony Knight had told him: that the attack had had no effect on sales.

He went online and searched for the earlier incident once more; the first time had been a cursory examination. There were many references to the crime. Because the girl was then seventeen, though, her name and photo had been redacted. He doubted that even Mack could get juvie reports. LaDonna Standish could, of course, and he'd have to tell her as soon as possible.

Shaw told himself to slow down.

Thirty-five percent isn't one hundred.

*Never move faster than the facts . . .*

He'd spent time with Maddie—in and out of bed. She simply didn't seem to be a murderer.

Then, scanning one article, Shaw learned that the teenager—Jane Doe—had suffered serious PTSD as a result of the attack. There'd been breaks with reality, a condition Shaw was more than familiar with thanks to his father. She'd been committed to a mental hospital.

Maybe Maddie decided that the victims, Sophie Mulliner and Henry Thompson, were no more than avatars, easily sacrificed on her mission to destroy the Whispering Man himself, Marty Avon.

He swiped her mouse and the screen saver vanished. The password window came up. Shaw didn't bother to try. He rose and conducted a fast search of the house, looking for the gun, bloody knives, any maps or references to the locations where the victims had been taken. None. Maddie was smart. She'd have them hidden somewhere nearby.

*If* she was the perp.

Now the number edged up to sixty percent. Because Shaw was in Maddie's bathroom and looking at the bottles of opioid painkillers. Possibly the sort that had been used to knock out the Whispering Man's victims. Forensics would tell. He took a picture of the labels with his phone.

Just as he was slipping his phone away, it hummed.

Standish.

He answered and said, "I was about to call you."

Silence. But only for a brief moment. "Shaw, where are you?"

He paused. "Out. I'm not at my camper."

"I know. I'm standing next to it. There's been a shooting. Could you get over here as soon as possible?"

# 51.

A full-fledged crime scene.

Shaw accelerated fast along Google Way within the Westwinds RV park, aiming for the yellow tape, noting two uniformed officers turning toward him. One lowered her hand toward her service weapon. Braking, he kept his hands on the steering wheel, statue-still, until Standish called to the cops nearby, "His camper. It's okay."

The JMCTF forensic van was parked within the yellow tape and robed and masked technicians were paying attention to the wall of a small shower/restroom in the middle of the park. They were digging at a black dot—extracting a slug, he guessed. Others were packing up evidence bags, concluding the search.

One uniform was rolling up the yellow tape. No press, Shaw noted. Maybe a shot or two didn't warrant a cam crew. Residents of the park, though, were present, standing well back from the scene as instructed.

The detective, in her ubiquitous combat jacket and

cargo pants, gestured him to where she stood by the door to the Winnebago. She was wearing latex gloves.

"Camper and the ground here've been released. They're still mining for slugs." A nod to the restrooms and tree. Shaw noticed that another team of gowned officers was at a maple, cutting into the trunk with a wicked-looking saw. How had they found the slug there? Metal detectors, he supposed. Or a really sharp eye.

"So. Here's what we've put together," Standish said. Her eyes were red and her posture slumped. He wondered if she'd gotten any sleep last night. At least he'd had a few hours' worth. "About an hour ago one of your neighbors saw somebody come through those bushes there." She pointed to a sloppy hedge separating the camp from a side street. "Look familiar?"

"Where you saw that visitor the other day."

"Exactly the place. Yeah. The wit—means 'witness,' which I guess you know—didn't see more than dark clothes and a dark hat. Well, look at the lights. Which there aren't many of. He walked toward your camper. The wit lost sight and when she looked again he was gone. And, frankly, playing stupid, she went up close to the window and saw a flashlight inside. Your car wasn't here and where your locks used to be was shambles."

Shaw looked over the remnants.

"Local uniforms from Traffic took the call, but"—she grimaced—"wonderful, they kept their lovely illumination on, all red, white and blue and flashy." She lowered her voice. "Because what they're really good at is traffic and only traffic. Anyways, the perp saw the lights and opened up with his weapon. Took out a headlight and let fly another half dozen rounds.

"Our boys and gals hit the deck—did I mention the Traffic detail?—and by the time backup and SWAT got here, he was gone. No description. Even the wit called nine-one-one didn't see anything useful. We need you to spot if he took anything."

Shaw said nothing yet about the gender she'd assigned. He'd tell her about Maddie Poole in a moment.

He was looking at the wrecked door.

"Dent puller," she said.

A tool with a screw at one end and a sliding weight on a shaft. It's used, yes, for pulling dents out of car bodies, but you can also screw the tip into a lock, nice and tight, then slam the weight back. Pops the whole cylinder out. Shaw had one lock that couldn't be pulled that way. The intruder had come equipped and used a pry bar to bend the tempered-steel flanges on the body of the camper. Winnebago makes a fine vehicle but titanium doesn't figure in the construction.

"There's something else you should know," Standish said. She was pulling her phone from one of the pockets in her cargo pants. She called up an image. It was the stenciled drawing of the Whispering Man's face.

"That the one I gave to Dan Wiley?"

"No. It was left for me." She paused, her face again a grimace. "Actually, left for Karen, on her car. She was going to take Gem for ice cream and found it on the windshield. I sent them to my mother's. Maybe it was just to spook me. I wasn't going to take a chance, though."

Shaw asked, "Any forensics?"

"No. Like everything else."

The black eyes, the slightly open mouth, the jaunty hat . . .

The RV park manager came by to see if Shaw was all right. Shaw told the old salt he was fine and asked if he'd be so kind as to get an emergency locksmith to take care of the Winnebago. He gave the manager one of his credit cards and a hundred dollars.

Then he and Standish stepped inside to survey the damage, which, on the surface, didn't seem too bad. First, of course, pantry and bed. His weapons were where he'd left them: spice cabinet for the Glock, the Colt Python under the bed.

Standish nodded to a small gun safe beside the bed, bolted to the floor. This couldn't be opened with a dent puller or much else, other than a diamond saw or a two-thousand-degree cutting stick. "Anything in there?"

He explained that it contained only a rattrap. If he was ever forced to open the safe, the intruder would be rewarded with one or, ideally, two broken fingers. Shaw would then have time to reach under the bed and pull out his revolver.

"Hmm."

For twenty minutes, Shaw conducted a step-by-step examination of the camper. Drawers had been opened and notebooks and clothes and toiletries disturbed. They were mostly about other jobs and some personal materials. All his notes on the kidnappings and on the Gamer were in his computer bag in the rental car, hidden under the passenger seat.

Some coins were on the floor, as were Post-it notes and pens, phone chargers and cables. The detritus from the junk drawer, identical to the one that every household has: batteries, tools, wire, aspirin bottles, hotel key cards, loose nuts and bolts and screws.

Shaw also kept petty cash here. A few hundred dollars, U.S. and Canadian, was gone.

He told Standish this and added, "Tossing the junk drawer was a cover. This wasn't a random break-in." He pointed to the front of the vehicle. In the storage sleeve beside the driver's seat were two GPS units—a TomTom and a Garmin. He'd found that some brands worked better than others in different areas of the country. Any thief would have seen them while rifling the glove compartment.

Standish said, "Wasn't really thinking a methhead anyway."

"No. It's the Gamer. Wanted to take a look at my notes. And anything else on the case."

"Taking a chance that you'd be out?"

Shaw picked up the Post-its and coins. "No risk at all, Standish. She knew exactly where I'd be."

"She?" Then the curiosity on Standish's face faded as she fielded his meaning.

# 52.

Shaw walked to a drawer in the kitchenette and took out a plastic storage bag. He wrapped it around his hand as Standish looked on with curiosity. With this improvised glove, he extracted from his pocket the business card that Maddie Poole had given him.

*GrindrGirl88* . . .

"Here. In case there's a print on the brass or slug. Or maybe she got careless. See if there's a match."

"Explain, Shaw."

"Ohio. Eight years ago. The teenager attacked by her classmates playing *The Whispering Man*. Maddie could be that girl. Trying to close down Marty Avon and the game that ruined her life."

"And this insight, which is a bizarre one, is based on what?"

He offered the analysis he'd hammered out just forty minutes before, including finding *The Whispering Man* book hidden in her house, a game she claimed she'd never played. "And she left me in her house, knowing I'd stay—exactly when the break-in happened." He nodded around the camper. "To see what I'd found on the case." He chose not to mention her edginess, her ruthless gaze when she'd stabbed him to death in the game. Stick with the objective.

"And here." Shaw lifted his phone and displayed the pictures of the opioids and other drugs in Maddie's medicine cabinet.

"Powerful stuff. Send them to me. We'll check them against what was in Sophie Mulliner's and Henry Thompson's blood."

Shaw uploaded the pictures to her phone and she in turn forwarded them onward.

"I'll check out that Ohio case." She Googled it, read, then tucked her phone away. "I'm going to call the sheriff in Cincinnati and the OSP. They get me the girl's name and picture. Might take a while. Juvie records usually need a magistrate's okay."

He noted the time from the microwave. "I'm going back."

"Back . . . ?"

"To her place. I know some law. Maddie invited me in. I've got permission to be there. I only did a fast search before you called. There're suitcases, a couple of gym bags."

"You'd be pushing the line there, Shaw. Permission to be in someone's residence . . . for one thing, that doesn't mean permission for others."

"I'm not Crime Scene, Standish. I just want to know."

Shaw's gut clenched again at Maddie's possible betrayal. Seeing her come up to him at the Quick Byte, taking his arm at the C3 Conference, her body against his. The flirt. And then tonight . . . In bed. Was that only to give herself a chance to go through his camper?

"I need to be back now. If I don't, she'll suspect something and vanish."

Standish pointed to the woman's business card in the plastic bag. "We can find her."

"That's an email address and a post office box."

Colter Shaw knew very well that if you want not to be found, you can make sure you're not found.

Standish wasn't pleased. She debated. "'K. But with a team outside, I don't have time to wire you. Open up curtains, if you need to, so we can get eyes in." She then summoned to the door of the camper the woman officer who'd accompanied him here and a male detective, plainclothes, and told them to go with Shaw and stage nearby.

To Shaw she said, "You thinking odds on this one? Maddie?"

"Probably over fifty somewhere. I'm leaning toward less than that but that's because I want to lean toward less."

*Never rely on your heart when it comes to survival . . .*

For good or bad, thank you, Ash.

He walked to the spice cabinet and removed the gray plastic inside-the-waistband holster for the Glock, which he mounted on his right hip. Dropping the gun's magazine, he checked to make sure it was loaded with the full six rounds, plus one in the chamber. He slipped the gun away.

LaDonna Standish watched him. She said nothing about the Glock. Now both the out-of-harm's-way rule and the no-weapons rule were history. As he walked to the door with a grim face she offered, "I hope it's not her, Shaw."

He stepped outside and climbed into the Malibu. He was thinking that if Maddie had returned while he was away she might wonder about his absence.

So he stopped and bought breakfast at an all-night deli.

This confused the cops driving behind him but it was a logical thing for a man to do when he'd awakened to find his lover no longer in bed beside him. Making breakfast would have been too domestic and would have irritated a card-carrying member of the Never After Club. Buying it was a fine balance. He got scrambled eggs and bacon on rolls, fruit cups and two coffees. And a Red Bull for her, the selecting of which troubled him, recalling their meeting at the Quick Byte.

*Think I just earned my Cinnabon . . .*

Though the king of percentages reminded himself: a hypothesis is just a hypothesis until it's proven true.

Back in the car he sped to Maddie's house, with dawn tempering the sky. The air was rich with dew and pine-fragrant.

She had not yet returned.

Shaw parked quickly and walked to the officers' sedan.

"Her car's not here. If she comes back, text me." He gave the woman officer his number and she put it into her mobile.

He then took the tray of aromatic food and coffee and walked into the house. Setting the tray on the counter in the kitchen, he turned to the basement door. It was unusual for houses to have cellars in California but this was an old structure—dating back to early in the prior century, he estimated. Shaw had decided that if Maddie Poole had any secrets she didn't wish to be discovered—the murder weapon, for instance—the basement was as good a place as any to hide them.

He paused at the door, glancing back at her fancy computer setup.

Could it really be her?

*You've been killed . . .*

Well, don't waste any more time. Find out yes, find out no.

He pulled open the basement door and was greeted with a complex scent of old and something sweet, something familiar—cleanser, he guessed.

He left the lights off—maybe there were windows to the outside and she might see the overhead basement lights when—or if—she returned. He chanced using the flashlight on his iPhone, shining it downward, to make his way along the rickety stairs.

Standing on the damp concrete slab floor, he swung the beam around him to see if there were any windows. No, he spotted none. He flicked the only light switch he could see, then noted there were no bulbs in the sockets.

The phone would have to do. He scanned the basement. There was nothing at all in the main room here, a roughly square twenty-by-twenty-foot area. But to his left was a corridor that led to what seemed to be storerooms. He searched them one by one; they were all empty.

Well, what had he been expecting to find?

A map of Basin Redwoods Park? Sophie Mulliner's bike and backpack?

One the one hand, this was absurd.

On the other, Sophie had admitted the kidnapper might have been a woman. And the forensics were inconclusive.

He turned the flashlight off and climbed the stairs.

He was turning from the kitchen into the living room when he stopped, inhaling a fast breath.

Maddie Poole was standing in front of him. She held a long kitchen knife in her hand. Her eyes looked him up and down, as if at a deer she was preparing to gut.

# 53.

ind anything interesting?"

There was no point in lying. There was no point in reaching for his weapon. The Glock was far more efficient than her blade but she could plant the Henckels between his ribs or in his throat before he could pull the trigger.

"Lose something? Get lost after going out to buy breakfast? Which would have been a charming gesture after sleeping with somebody—except it's pretty clear you had a different agenda."

Her hand tightened its grip on the handle of the knife. In her eyes was a glaze of hysteria and he wondered how close he was to being stabbed.

The Maddie Poole of the *Immersion* game was back, with a very real blade, not one made up of a hundred thousand bytes of data. The tip now turned closer to him. Killing with a knife is hard work, and lengthy. Blinding or slashing tendons, though, can be done in an instant.

"Relax," he said in a soft voice.

"Shut the hell up!" she raged. "Who are you really?"

"Who I said I was."

With her free hand, she tugged her hair, hard, fidgeting. The knife hand's digits continued to clench and unclench. She shook her head, hair whipping back and forth. "Then why spy on me? Go through all of my things?"

"Because I thought there was a chance you might be the kidnapper. Or, if not, be working with him. Keeping an eye on me to see where the investigation was."

*No point in lying . . .*

"Me?"

"The facts suggested it was a possibility. I had to check it out. I was looking for any evidence that connected you to the crimes."

Her face twisted into a dark, unbelieving smile. "You can't be serious."

"I didn't think it was likely. But—"

"You had to check it out." Bitter sarcasm. "How long've you been spying on me? From the beginning, from our night at the conference?"

"You have the gameplay guide for *The Whispering Man*. You told me you'd never played, didn't know anything about it. I found it this morning."

He told her his thought: that she was that girl in Ohio who was attacked by classmates who took the game to heart.

"Ah, the scars," she said. "You saw them."

He added that she'd come up to him at the Quick

Byte Café. "After I'd started looking for Sophie. You might've followed me there."

She held the knife up closer to him. Shaw tensed, judging angles.

Maddie spat out, "Fuck." And flung the blade across the room.

Her expression alone was evidence enough of her innocence—along with the fact that she hadn't hidden behind the door when he ascended the stairs and slashed him to death.

She was breathing hard. And, it seemed, trying to keep tears at bay. "You're wondering how I knew. Well, take a look." Her voice choked yet she had a sardonic smile on her face, just the lips. The eyes were a blend of sorrow and ice. She walked to her computer and sat down heavily in the seat. "I've got a new video game, Colt. A hard one. I don't mean difficult. I mean it makes you feel shitty. I call it the *Judas Game*. Take a look."

Onto the screen came not a game but a video, a wide-angle view, like that taken by a security cam. It was of this very living room and had been filmed within the past couple of hours. Colter Shaw was rifling through her books, opening drawers, reaching onto the tops of bookcases. He'd been looking for the gun. You couldn't see him photograph the medicine bottles—that was in the bathroom—but you could see the flash from his phone.

She shut off the clip. "I told you about Twitch and the other streaming game sites where your fans want to see you playing? I was online earlier and forgot to shut the camera off. It wasn't broadcasting, just recording. I don't use a webcam. It's a wide-angle security camera. Better night vision. There's no red record light on it."

Same thing he'd done at the Quick Byte, the first time there, to record anyone who was particularly interested in Sophie Mulliner's pictures.

Maddie reached for her backpack. She rummaged for a moment, then withdrew a small slip of paper. She handed it to him. It was a purchase receipt.

"A used-book store near Stanford. Specializes in gaming books. Check the date on the receipt. I bought it for you today and made some notes in it about the game, things I thought might be helpful. I didn't have a chance to give it to you." She looked to the bedroom.

"As for hitting on you? No, I wasn't following you, I didn't track you into the Quick Byte. Believe it or not, Colter, I saw a handsome dude, kind of a cowboy, tough, quiet, on a mission, looking for this missing girl. My sort of guy." She swallowed. "No motives, no agendas. It's a lonely life. Don't we all try to make it less lonely?

"And the scars . . . Sure, the scars . . . May as well have everything out. You've bought yourself the lurid details. I got married when I was nineteen. Love of my life. Joe and I lived outside of L.A., owned an athletic outfit store, ran day trips—you know, biking, hiking, rafting, skiing. It was heaven. Then a customer turned into a stalker. Totally psychotic. One night when my sister and her boyfriend were visiting he broke in and shot my husband and sister. Killed them both. I ran into the kitchen and got a knife. He took it away and stabbed me fourteen times before my sister's boyfriend tackled him.

"I almost died. A couple of times. Had nine surgeries.

In the hospital and housebound for a year and two weeks. Video games were the only things that kept me from killing myself. See, for me, Colter, the Never After Club is real. It's not a commitment thing. There is no 'after' for me. Literally. I died four years ago.

"Look me up. It was all over the press in southern California. Maddie Gibson was my name then. I changed back to my maiden name because that asshole kept sending me love letters from prison." She shook her head. "I got back a half hour ago and saw the video. What the hell were you up to? I was thinking, maybe doing this reward stuff, the people you go after—like the kidnapper here—maybe that pushed *you* over the edge. Maybe *you* were a killer, a thief. It wasn't logical. But you go through what I did, it makes you a little paranoid, Colt.

"So. I had to find out. I moved my car around the corner and grabbed that"—she glanced to the floor where the knife lay—"and waited for you to come back." Some tears now.

"Look . . ." Shaw began. He stopped when she lifted a brow. Now her eyes were the cold green of a dull emerald.

He fell silent. What was there to say?

That his restless mind sometimes took over and drove him to find the answers no matter what the cost?

That fragments of his father's paranoia and suspicion were lodged in his genes?

That he couldn't quite eradicate the images of Kyle Butler's and Henry Thompson's bodies, still and bloody?

Those were all true. They were also excuses.

He offered a faint nod—a flag signifying both his crime and the utter inadequacy of any remedies.

Colter Shaw walked to the door and, without a look back, let himself out.

At his car, he was startled by the squeal of tires coming his way. His hand dropping toward his weapon, he glanced to his left. It was the unmarked car that had accompanied him, speeding forward, now with its blue-and-white grille lights flashing. It skidded to a stop abruptly, directly beside him, the passenger window coming down.

The uniformed woman officer said, "Mr. Shaw, Detective Standish just radioed. There's been another kidnapping. Can you follow us to the Task Force?"

# 54.

The conference room was populated with fifteen or so men and women from various law enforcement agencies. Shaw saw the uniforms of deputies and police and the plainclothes suits and ensembles of agents and detectives. They stood in clusters, looking at a whiteboard on which were written details of the recent kidnapping.

Shaw walked up to LaDonna Standish, who said, "What'd you find? About Maddie?"

Without expression Shaw said, "I was wrong."

As soon he arrived at the Task Force headquarters he'd confirmed Maddie's story. The picture accompanying one article was an image of the woman, younger, on top of a mountain with her husband, both in ski gear, both smiling, taken a few months before the murders.

He nodded at the new bodies present. "FBI?"

"California Bureau. Not the feds."

Heading the show was a tall, chiseled B of I agent, dark-haired and wearing a gray suit a shade darker than his partner's—a man who was not tall, not thin, not good-looking. The name of the tall one was Anthony Prescott. Shaw had missed the other's.

Prescott said, "Detective Standish, could you brief us on the latest taking?"

She explained how the vic was kidnapped in a parking lot in Mountain View about an hour ago on her way to work. "Municipal lot. No video. We canvassed and a wit saw a person in gray sweats and a gray stocking cap. Like on the Quick Byte Café security cam."

Standish had created a file and made copies for everyone on the case. She handed Shaw one. Inside was a bio of the victim, which Shaw read through. There were pictures too.

The detective fired off other facts—the absence of fingerprints, the lack of DNA for tracing through the CODIS database, every piece of physical evidence the Gamer'd left behind being untraceable, the homemade knockout potion, his weapons, the inability to identify his vehicle because he drove on grass or other ground cover and left no tread marks.

"In the files I gave you are security webcam shots of the suspect that Mr. Shaw here obtained at the Quick Byte. It doesn't show much but it might be helpful."

Prescott asked, "And who are you?" Then to Standish, "And who is he?"

"A consultant."

"Consultant?" the shorter CBI agent asked.

"Hmm," Standish confirmed.

"Wait. The bounty hunter?" Prescott asked.

Shaw said, "Frank Mulliner offered a reward to find his missing daughter."

"Which he did," Standish offered.

"Is there a fee to us involved?" Prescott's partner asked Shaw.

Shaw said, "No."

Perhaps Prescott wanted an explanation about why Shaw was doing this. He didn't indulge.

Standish touched her copy of the folder. She continued: "Another fact you need to know. The victim—her name's Elizabeth Chabelle—is seven and a half months pregnant."

"Jesus!" from somebody. Gasps too. An obscenity.

"And one more thing: the unsub hid her on a ship. A sinking ship."

Colter Shaw took over.

"It appears that the unsub is basing the crimes on a video game."

Void reaction from the room.

"It's called *The Whispering Man*. That's the villain in the game. He hides his victims in an abandoned place. They have to escape—before other players, or the character himself, kill them."

Someone in the back—an older male uniformed officer—called, "That's pretty bizarre. You sure?"

"His kidnapping M.O. lines up with the gameplay. And he's left graffiti or printouts of the character at the scenes."

"Photos are in the file," Standish said.

Shaw: "Any of you know how levels work in video games?"

Some nodded. Others shook their heads. The majority simply gazed at him the way they'd observe, with more or less interest, a lizard in a pet shop terrarium.

Shaw said, "A video game's about meeting increasing challenges. You start out on the simple level, saving some settlers, trekking to a certain place, killing X number of aliens. If you're successful you move to a more difficult level. The Gamer's placed his victims in the first two levels of *The Whispering Man*."

Standish added, "The Abandoned Factory. That was Sophie Mulliner. Henry Thompson's was The Dark Forest. The third level is The Sinking Ship."

The last level, the tenth, Shaw had learned, was hell itself—where the Whispering Man lives. No player in the history of the game had ever made it that far.

Prescott said slowly, "An interesting theory." Slowly and uncertainly.

There was enough corroboration that Shaw could *accept* theory over hypothesis in this case.

One officer, a uniform from Santa Clara, pointed to the whiteboard. "That's why he's the Gamer?"

Shaw said, "Correct."

Prescott's partner said, "Supervisor Cummings said you're profiling him as a sociopath."

Standish cleared her throat. "I said the likelihood of that diagnosis was about seventy percent." She glanced at Shaw, who nodded.

"But no sado-sexual activity?" someone pointed out. "Which you almost always see in the case of a male unsub."

"No," Standish said.

Shaw continued: "We've been working with the company that publishes *The Whispering Man*—they're cooperating. The CEO is trying to track down suspects in the customer database. He'll call Detective Standish as soon as he finds some likely names."

Standish said, "All this is in the file."

Prescott said, the fiber of doubt in his voice, "If it *is* a ship, you know where?"

Shaw said he did not. Then added, "He'll've left five objects she can use to save herself. One is food or water. Another will probably let her signal for help. Maybe a mirror or—"

One of the other suited agents said, "We gotta lot of boats here. We don't have the resources to send drones and choppers over anything that floats."

Ignoring the obvious, as usual, Shaw said, "Or start a signal fire."

Standish: "We need to tell all the public safety offices to let us know if there're any fires or smoke on docks or boats themselves. It'll be a deserted place too."

Prescott stepped forward. "All right, Detective, Supervisor Cummings. We appreciate your work," he said. "We'll keep you posted on the developments."

Two sentences that Shaw guessed were patently false.

Standish's face was emotionless, though her eyes settled. She was mad at the downgrading. But the CBI was state, the JMCTF was local. And if the FBI were here, they'd rule the roost. The way of the world.

While this ping-pong discussion had been going on, Shaw was wondering how much time Elizabeth Chabelle had until she perished from exposure. Or drowned.

Or until the Gamer, playing *The Whispering Man* with relish, returned to pursue her through the vessel or on the dock and shoot or stab her.

Prescott said, "We'll consider what Detective Standish and her consultant have suggested. Somebody perverted by these video games."

Which wasn't the theory at all.

The agent continued: "Though, you ask me, I think anyone who plays them is a bit off."

Shaw noted several of the officers staring at him without any reaction. The gamers in the room, he figured.

"We'll pursue that lead. We'll also follow standard protocol for an abduction. Get taps on all Ms. Chabelle's phones. She have a boyfriend, husband?"

Standish said, "Boyfriend. George Hanover."

"Taps on his too and her parents', if they're alive."

"They are," Shaw said. "They live in Miami. All in the report."

"Look at financial resources of the boyfriend and her parents to see if they might be ransom targets. Get a list of registered sex offenders in the area. See if she has any stalkers." The Bureau of Investigation agent kept talking, but Shaw had stopped listening. He was watching a man in the corridor approach the glass-walled conference room.

It was Dan Wiley, now in a green uniform. The man still looked like a cop right out of a movie.

The detective—or whatever he was now that he'd been rotated to Liaison—was holding a large envelope. He knocked and, when nodded in by Prescott, spotted Detective Standish and walked over to her.

Prescott said, "Officer, is that related to the Chabelle kidnappings?"

"Well, it's the ME's report on the latest vic. Henry Thompson."

"I'll take it. BI's running the case."

With a glance to Standish, Wiley handed the envelope to the tall agent and left.

Nearly to the door, he paused, looking back toward Shaw. A rueful smile crossed his face and, if Shaw's translation was correct, its meaning was that the cop was offering an apology.

Shaw nodded in return.

*Never waste time on anger.*

Prescott opened the envelope and read to himself. Then he announced to the room: "Nothing new here. Henry Thompson died of a single gunshot, a nine-millimeter, determined to be from the same gun used in the Kyle Butler murder, a Glock 17. TOD was between ten p.m. and eleven p.m. Friday. He had also suffered blunt force trauma to the skull, resulting in a bone fracture and brain concussion. This was prior to the gunshot and prior to the fall from the cliff. He—"

Shaw asked, "Where was the fracture?"

Prescott looked up, his head askew. "I'm sorry?"

Standish asked, "Where was the fracture?"

"Why?"

Standish added, "We'd like to know."

Prescott skimmed the report. "Left sphenoid." He glanced up. "Anything else?"

Standish looked at Shaw, who shook his head. She said, "Nope. We're good."

Prescott kept his eyes on her for a moment longer. He continued: "He'd been injected with OxyContin suspended in water. Nonlethal, just enough to sedate him temporarily." He handed the report to one of the two uniformed women officers. "Make copies for the team, would you? Then transcribe it on the board. You probably have better handwriting than the boys."

The officer took the report with a faint tightening of her lips.

Standish said to Shaw in a soft voice, "So, why did I want to know where he got hit?"

"Can we leave?" Shaw whispered.

She looked over the room. "Don't see why not. We're invisible anyway."

As they walked to the door they happened to pass Cummings. He held up a hand. Standish and Shaw paused.

Was an issue looming?

Keeping his eyes on Prescott and the whiteboards, the supervisor whispered, "I do not want to know what you two have in mind. But get to it. And get to it fast. Good luck."

# 55.

They were back in the Quick Byte.

Shaw was getting to recognize some of the regulars. Sitting nearby was the kid in the red-and-black-checked shirt whose potential romance with the beautiful young woman had been derailed either by her change of mind or as a cruel joke. He spotted a dozen others who seemed to treat the place as their home away from home. Some were talking to one another; some were on phones; most were communing with their laptops.

Shaw was browsing the internet, looking through medical sites, on his mobile. He showed Standish a diagram. A picture of the human skull, each of the bones composing it named. The sphenoid was just behind the eye socket.

"That's the bone?" She was silent for a moment. "Okay. Next question: Is the Gamer right-handed?"

"That's *exactly* the next question. Because if he is, that means he hit Thompson from the front. And that's prob-

ably what happened because lefties make up only ten percent of the population."

Standish's eyes swept slowly through the café. "Let's
think about this. Thompson's driving down the street,
the Gamer's following. He passes Thompson, parks and
waits, then pitches a rock into his windshield. Thompson
gets out. And up comes the Gamer, holding a gun on
him. Thompson thinks it's a carjacking. Rule one: Give
up the keys. You can always get another car."

"But the Gamer slugs him with the gun, cracking his
facial bone. Which means he didn't care if Thompson
saw him or not. Even if he was wearing the mask,
Thompson would get *some* description. So the Gamer
meant all along to kill him."

Standish said, "The time of death in the report Dan
Wiley brought Prescott. That's what tipped you."

Shaw nodded. "It was just an hour or so after Thompson was taken. The Gamer drove him to Redwoods
Park, walked him out on the ledge and shot him right
away. The Gamer's the one who set the fire to get our
attention so we'd find the body—and the Whispering
Man graffiti."

"None of this is about playing a scary-ass game in
real life."

"No," Shaw said. "He was using the game to cover up
murdering Thompson. That was my original idea. I
thought that Tony Knight hired somebody to play a psycho to bring down Marty Avon. I got that wrong. That
doesn't mean the hypothesis in general is wrong."

"Sophie Mulliner was just part of the misdirection?"
Standish asked.

"I'd think so."

"And Elizabeth Chabelle?"

"Probably the same."

"So she might be alive."

Shaw: "He'll want to make sure the game plays out. So we'll assume she is."

Standish: "The big question: Who'd want to kill Henry Thompson?"

"He was a gay rights activist. Was he controversial?"

Standish said, "Karen and I are involved in the community, I never heard of him. Gay in the Bay Area? Unless you're a cop, nobody cares." She gave him a wry smile. "What was he blogging about? Bet he stumbled on somebody's secret."

Shaw found the notebook in which he'd recorded Brian Byrd's comments about his partner. He skimmed. "Henry was working on three stories at the moment. Two of them don't seem very controversial—revenues in the software industry and the high price of real estate in Silicon Valley."

"Tell me about it." Standish puffed air from her mouth.

"But the third?" he said, reading. "It's how gaming companies are illegally stealing gamers' data and selling it."

Standish had not heard of this trend.

"There must be hundreds of gaming companies that collect data."

"True. I have a place where we can start, though."

"You going to put one of your fancy percentages on it?"

"Ten, I'd say."

"That's ten percent better than anything else we've got. Let's hear it."

"Hong-Sung Enterprises."

Shaw explained about the goggles and how the game turned your house and backyard into imaginary battlegrounds. "Most companies data-mine information from things you do actively: fill out forms, answer questionnaires, click on products to buy. Hong-Sung collects data without your knowing it. The goggles have cameras. They upload everything you look at when you play."

Standish was interested. "Products in your house, the clothes you wear, how many kids you've got, a sick or elderly relative, if you've got pets—they sell that to datamining companies? Smart. And Henry Thompson was going to write about it . . . Is that really a reason to kill somebody, Shaw? Conspiracy to mail me coupons for diapers for Gem? Or oil changes for that fancy camper of yours?"

"I think it's more than that. Maddie told me the company was giving the game and the goggles away to the U.S. military. When the soldiers or sailors play, they might look at something classified—maybe a weapon, an order for deployment, information about troop movements— and the goggles could capture and upload it."

"Maybe audio recordings too?"

Shaw nodded. He replaced phone with laptop and looked up Hong-Sung. "They've got links to the Chinese government. Anything the goggles scanned could go directly to the Chinese Ministry of Defense. Or whatever their military operation's called."

Standish's phone pinged with a text. She sent one in reply. Shaw wondered if it had to do with the case. She put the phone away. "Karen. We got good news. The last hurdle. We're adopting. Always wanted two."

"Boy, girl?"

"Girl again. Sefina. She's four. I took her out of a hostage sit in EPA and got her into foster about eighteen months ago. Mother was brain-damaged from all the drugs and her boyfriend was warranted up his ass."

"Sefina," Shaw said. "Pretty name."

"Samoan."

Shaw asked, "We tell Prescott about Hong-Sung?"

"What would they do with it? Nothing. Remember, Shaw: simple. That's what they like. Ransom demands, bullets and drugs and lovers running amuck." She frowned. "Is there such a thing as 'running muck'? Is that what you run when everything's calm and good?"

Shaw was taking quite the liking to Detective La-Donna Standish. He powered down his laptop and slipped it and his notebook back into the bag. "I'll try to find a way into Hong-Sung."

"Could your friend Maddie help?"

"That's not going to happen. I'll see Marty Avon myself."

Standish's tongue tsked. "What happened to the *we*?"

"Got a question," Shaw said.

"Which is?"

"Who's going to stay home with Sefina and Gem?"

"Karen. She writes her cooking blog from home. Why?"

"So you can't afford to lose this job, right? That doesn't require an answer."

Her lips pursed. "Shaw, you—"

"I've been shot at, I've abseiled off a burning tree. I've decapitated a rattler halfway into his strike—"

"You did not."

"Truth. And we can all agree that I can face down a mountain lion."

"I'll give you that."

"I can handle myself. If that's what you were going to say."

"I was."

"Anything I find pans out, I'll call you. *You* call SWAT."

# 56.

"The Astro Base."

Marty Avon was speaking to Shaw but was gazing at an eighteen-inch toy on his desk. A red-and-white globe atop landing legs. His beloved gaze reminded Shaw of how his sister, Dorie, and her husband would look adoringly at their daughters.

"Nineteen sixty-one. Plastic, motors. See the astronaut." A little blue guy, dangling from a crane, about to be lowered to the surface of Avon's desk. "We didn't have space stations then. No matter. The toy companies were always a generation ahead. You could fire a ray gun. You could explore. Batteries required. Lasted about two weeks before the rush wore off. That's the nature of toys. And chewing gum. And cocaine. You just have to make sure there's a new supply available.

"I don't have much time," Avon added, focusing on Shaw. "I'm meeting with some people about Siliconville. We're getting some resistance from traditional real estate developers. Imagine that!" He gave a wink. "Affordable housing, subsidized by employers—not popular!"

Like the company towns of the late-nineteenth and early-twentieth centuries, which Shaw knew about from his father's reading to the children about the Old West. Railroads and mines often built villages for their workers—who paid exorbitant prices for rent, food and necessities, often running up huge debts, which bound them forever to their employers.

He suspected Avon's apparent socialist bent would lead him to run Siliconville in a very different way.

"There's been another kidnapping. We think it's related. We need your help again."

"Oh, no. Who?"

"A woman, thirty-two. Pregnant."

"My God, no."

Shaw had to give Avon credit that the first words out of his mouth weren't something to the effect of: more bad publicity for me and my game.

"We're doing everything we can with the proxies to find you a suspect. But it's taking more time than I'd hoped. We've cracked eleven. None of them are in the area."

"Only eleven?"

A grimace. "I know. It's slow. We don't have supercomputers. And some proxies are just so righteous you can't trace them back. That's why they exist in the first place, of course."

Shaw said, "Add these times too, when he wouldn't have been online." He displayed his notebook and pointed to the hour Chabelle disappeared.

Avon typed fast and, with a flourish, hit RETURN. "It's on its way."

"I need something else. We have another hypothesis. Hong-Sung Entertainment."

The CEO corrected, "No, it's 'Enterprises.' Hong Wei sets his sights high. Gaming's just a part of his businesses. Small part, actually."

"You familiar with *Immersion*?"

Avon laughed, his expression saying, Who isn't?

"So you know how it works?"

The lanky man's fidget fingers maneuvered the cerulean astronaut back into the Astro Base. "Here's where you might ask: Do I wish I'd thought the game up? No. Virtual reality and motion-based game engines sound good. The fact is, of the billion-plus gamers in the world, the vast majority sit on their asses in dark rooms and pound away on a keyboard or squeeze their console controller. Because they *want* to sit on their asses in dark rooms and pound away on keyboards. *Immersion*'s a novelty. Hong-Sung's poured hundreds of millions into *Immersion*. Hong's less of a prick than some in Silicon Valley but he's still a prick. I don't have any problem with the game taking him to the cleaners when people get tired of hopping around like bunnies in their backyards. Which is going to happen. Why? Because it's not . . ." His eyebrow rose.

"Fun?" Shaw said.

*"Exactement!"* Offered in a curious French accent.

And this grinning, goofy fellow had created one of the creepiest video games in history.

"What if *Immersion*'s more than a game?"

Avon's squinting eyes moved from the space station back to Shaw, who explained his idea about the cameras on the goggles sucking up images from players' houses or apartments as they roamed their homes and uploading the data to Hong-Sung's servers for later sale.

Avon's eyes widened. "Jesus. That is solid gold brilliant. Okay, now ask if I wish I'd thought *that* one up."

"There's another what-if," Shaw said. "Hong-Sung's giving away goggles to U.S. military personnel. Presumably other government workers too."

"To capture classified data, you're thinking?"

"Maybe."

"My." Avon considered this. "You're talking a huge amount of data to process. Private companies couldn't handle it. You know what the Chinese government has? The TC-4. Thirty-five petaflops. Most powerful supercomputer in the world. They might be able to handle the load. But, I have to ask, how does this involve my game?"

Shaw: "The second victim? Henry Thompson? He was writing a blog about how companies steal data from gamers. Maybe Hong-Sung—or some other game company—didn't want the story to appear and somebody mimicked a psycho gamer and killed him."

"How can I help?"

"I need to talk to somebody who's got a connection to the company. Best if he works there. Can you make that happen?"

The implication being that since it was, after all, his game that was the hub of the crime, even if it wasn't Avon's fault, a little cooperation wouldn't be a bad idea.

"I don't know anybody there personally. Hong is secretive, to put it mildly. But it's a small world, SV is. I'll make some calls."

# 57.

Though he was inherently restless, Colter Shaw was not necessarily impatient. Now, however, with Elizabeth Chabelle missing and in grave danger and with the Gamer prepared to play out the final act in his *Whispering Man* game, he wanted Eddie Linn to show up.

Avon had made a half dozen calls and found a connection to Hong-Sung; a man named Trevor, whose further identity Avon didn't share, would put Shaw in touch with Linn, who was an employee of HSE. This cost Avon something significant; it was clear that he would license some software to Trevor, at a discount, in exchange for setting up a rendezvous between Shaw and Linn.

Shaw was presently in the appointed place at the appointed time: a park, carefully planned and maintained. Serpentine sidewalks of pebbled concrete, bordered by tall, wafting grasses and reeds, flower beds, trees. The grass as bright as an alien's skin in a C3 game. A tranquil pond was populated with sizable fish, red and black and white.

The grounds were balanced in color, laser-cut trim, perfectly symmetrical.

Setting Colter Shaw on edge. He liked his landscapes designed by the foliage and water and dirt and rocks themselves.

As he walked along the path he caught a small glimpse of Hong-Sung Enterprises' U.S. headquarters. The building was a glistening mirrored copper doughnut. To the side were four huge transmission antennas.

Presumably, just what was needed to beam stolen data into the ether.

Linn had told him to sit on a particular bench, in front of a weeping willow, or one nearby if this one was occupied. Shaw noted why: it was out of sight of the company's offices. The preferred bench was free. Behind it was a stand of thick boxwood, a plant that smelled of ammonia.

Now the impatience factor was cresting and Shaw, thinking of Elizabeth Chabelle on a sinking ship, was glancing at his phone for the time when he heard a man's tense, tenor voice. "Mr. Shaw."

Eddie Linn was a tall, narrow man of about thirty. Asian features. He wore a polo shirt with an HSE logo on the left chest and dark gray slacks that were slightly baggy.

He sat down next to Shaw, whom Trevor would have described to Linn. The man didn't offer his hand. Shaw had the ridiculous thought that Linn didn't want to transfer DNA, which might be used for evidentiary purposes.

"I just have a few minutes." He frowned. "I have to get back to my office. I'm only doing this because . . ." His voice was fading.

Because Trevor had something on Linn. Extortion is a distasteful yet often very effective tool.

"Did you hear about the kidnappings?"

"Yeah, yeah, yeah. All over the news. Terrible. And one victim killed." Speaking high and quickly.

Shaw continued: "That man was working on an article about stealing data from gamers. We're speculating that he was looking into *Immersion*."

"Oh God. You don't think Mr. Hong had anything to do with it?"

"We don't know, but a woman's life's at risk. We're following up every lead. This is one of them."

Linn fiddled with his collar. "Who are you? Mr. Trevor said you were like a private eye."

"I'm working with the police."

He wasn't listening; he stiffened instantly as footsteps sounded, the faint grit of soles on sidewalk. Shaw had heard it only after Linn's reaction.

Linn put his hands on the seat of the bench and Shaw believed he was about to sprint away.

The threat, however, turned out to be two women, one pregnant and pushing a baby carriage that held a tiny sleeping child. They chatted and sipped iced-drink concoctions. The friend was younger and Shaw caught her glancing into the carriage with hints of envy in her eyes. The two women—one an accountant, he gathered, the other the mother—sat down on the neighboring bench and talked about how few hours of sleep they each got.

Linn, visibly calming, continued, though whispering now: "Hong is a tough man. Ruthless. But killing someone?"

"You write code," Shaw said. "That's what Marty Avon told me."

"Yes."

"For *Immersion*?"

His eyes scanned the park. Seeing no threat, he leaned closer to Shaw and said, "A while ago. For an expansion pack."

"I want your impression of an idea we're looking at."

Linn swallowed. Shaw realized he'd been doing that a lot since he sat down. "Okay."

He gave Linn his hypothesis about stealing data via the *Immersion* goggles. "Could that be done?" Shaw asked.

Linn seemed stunned as he digested this. His first reaction was to shake his head. "The cameras on the goggles are high-resolution. It would be too much data . . . unless . . ." A near smile crescented his thin lips. "Unless they didn't upload video, but screenshots, JPEGs, compressed some more into an RAR archive. Yes, yes, it could work! Then up it goes along with the other information to the mainframe here. It could then be processed and sold or used by the company itself. We have divisions that do advertising, marketing, consulting."

"I think there's also a risk that Hong is stealing sensitive government information," Shaw said. "He's giving away thousands of copies of *Immersion* to soldiers."

Alarmed, the HSE employee flicked his fingers together. He'd just fallen down the rabbit hole of government intrigue.

"What is it?" Shaw said. He'd noticed the man's eyes faintly squint.

After a moment: "There's a facility in the basement of the building. In the back. No regular employees are allowed in there. It's got a whole separate staff. Visitors show up by helicopter, go in, do whatever they do and leave. We heard it's called the Minerva Project. But no one knows what it's about."

"I need you to help me," Shaw said.

Before Linn could respond, though, Shaw was aware of a rustling sound behind them.

No, no, Shaw realized suddenly: a woman four, five months pregnant isn't going to have a newborn. She's pushing a doll in the carriage. He stood and gripped Linn's arm and said, "Get out of here now!"

Linn gasped.

But it was too late.

The pregnant woman was pushing aside the carriage and rising. Her "friend" was speaking into a microphone on her wrist and the source of the noise behind them turned out to be two minders, bursting from the boxwoods. The large Asian men's motions were perfectly choreographed. One held a Glock on Linn and Shaw and the other emptied their pockets.

Chill-eyed momma-to-be took the items. When she opened her Coach bag, Shaw saw that she too was armed. It was a Glock, nine-millimeter. The same brand of weapon that had killed Kyle Butler and, presumably, been used to pistol-whip and murder Henry Thompson.

A black SUV screeched to a stop on the wide sidewalk, feet away from them. One of the security men gripped Shaw by the arm and the other grabbed Linn. Both were shoved into the back, the middle-row seats, which were separated from the front by a Plexiglas divider. There were no door handles.

"Look, I can explain," Linn cried. "You don't understand!"

A second vehicle pulled up, a black sedan. The two women got inside, the one who was not pregnant held the door for the other, who, Shaw deduced, was the mastermind of the admittedly brilliant takedown operation.

The driver got out, folded up the baby carriage and placed it in the trunk, tossing the doll in afterward.

# 58.

"Where are you taking me?" Eddie Linn asked, his voice vibrating like an off-balance washing machine. The SUV paused at an elaborate security gate, which then opened, and the vehicle sped through.

Shaw had two reactions to the question. First, the man's concern was solely about himself. Shaw supposed Linn would happily throw him to the wolves. Second, it was pointless to ask. Even if the guards in the front seat had been able to hear it through the Plexiglas, they wouldn't have answered.

When the Suburban stopped at the back door of Hong-Sung's futuristic headquarters, the guards nodded them out and directed them inside, where the group descended a flight of stairs. Shaw looked back, wondering if the pregnant woman's limo was behind them. It wasn't.

"Don't look around. Walk." This from the bigger guard, who took Shaw's arm. Gripping tighter than even Tony Knight's men, who really knew how to grip.

"Don't push it," Shaw said.

And was rewarded with a crushing squeeze.

Linn didn't need a jerk of the leash. He walked passively beside the smaller guard.

They were taking the prisoners down a lengthy, dim corridor. It might have been in the basement but it was spotless. The walls were bare. Somewhere, not far away, machinery hummed.

A two-minute trek took them to an elevator, in which they ascended to the fifth—and top—floor. It opened into a small, plain office. The receptionist, a woman of about forty, sitting at a wooden desk, nodded to the guards. Shaw and Linn were led through the wide double doors behind her. This room was larger yet just as austere as the receptionist's, hardly the place for the CEO of a multibillion-dollar conglomerate to work.

For that's whom they were looking at: Hong Wei, whom Shaw recognized from the internet stories he'd downloaded. The dark-haired Asian was about fifty. He wore a suit, white shirt and blue shimmery tie. The jacket was buttoned. Shaw and Linn were deposited in chairs facing him. The guards stood a respectful distance back but also close enough to step forward and break necks in a fraction of a second.

The doors through which they'd entered opened again and the pregnant woman walked in. She carried a file folder and handed it to the man behind the desk. "Mr. Hong."

"Thank you, Ms. Towne."

Shaw noted something odd. The man's desk contained no computer, other electronic device or telephone, either mobile or landline.

Hong opened the file and read studiously for a moment.

Linn was close to whimpering. Shaw had decided that while there might be consequences to his furtive meeting with Eddie Linn, dismemberment and being fed to the aquatic life in San Francisco Bay probably was not going to be one of them. Largely because it would have happened already.

Which meant his hypothesis of Hong's involvement shrank a few percentage points.

Hong read. Very slowly. And he seemed not to move a muscle. Shaw didn't even see him blink.

To Hong's right, lined up side by side like logs at the lumber camp where Shaw had worked summers during college, were a number of yellow wooden pencils and, to his left, a half dozen more. Those on the right had needle-sharp points. The ones on the left were duller. Did the CEO appreciate the dangers of digital communication so much that he relied on paper and carbon?

Hong read without any acknowledgment of the two men in front of him.

Linn took a breath to say something. Then apparently thought the better of it.

*Waste of time . . .*

Shaw waited. What else was there to do?

Finally Hong finished reading and looked at Shaw. "Mr. Shaw, you are here because you were trespassing on private property. This park where you were sitting is owned by Hong-Sung Enterprises. There are signs."

"Conveniently invisible."

"You had a reasonable expectation that this was private property."

"Because the landscaping outside the fence matches the landscaping inside?"

"Exactly."

"That'd be a tough one for a jury to buy."

"And since we were able to hear your conversation we had a reasonable expectation that Mr. Linn here was in the process of divulging trade secrets to you and—"

"My God, no, I wasn't!" The high voice rose even higher yet. "I was just helping—"

"Which justified our taking you into custody, as if you were shoplifters at a grocery store."

Shaw glanced at Ms. Towne. Her face was calm and confident and he bet she'd be a loving and huggy mother when off the clock. She continued to stand, despite a nearby empty chair.

Hong tapped the folder. "You make your living with these rewards, do you?"

"That's right."

"What do you call yourselves? Rewardists?"

"I've heard that. I don't call myself anything."

"And I understand you are not a private investigator; nor are you a bond enforcement agent. You assist in finding missing persons and escaped fugitives, and suspects who have not yet been identified or located, for rewards, traveling around the country from, say, Indiana to Berkeley, in your recreational vehicle."

Shaw had some public presence but Hong had assembled that information in record time. And how the CEO knew that his most recent job was in Indianapolis and Muncie, and that he was at the university on his personal mission, was an utter mystery. "That's all correct."

Hong's face brightened, only just slightly. "Then like PIs and like the police and like bounty hunters, which you would prefer not to be called, you solve puzzles for a living. You analyze situations and make decisions and to do this you must prioritize. And sometimes you need to do all of those at once and do them very quickly. Lives might be hanging in the balance."

Shaw had no idea where this steamship of thought was bound for, though he was struck by the word *prioritize*, which was the reason his percentage technique existed. He said, "True."

"Mr. Shaw, do you play video games?"

Aside from once? Resulting in his stabbing death by a beautiful woman he would never see again? "No."

"I ask because playing games would enhance those very skills you need in your job."

He reached into his desk.

Shaw didn't bother to tense. He wasn't fishing for a gun or knife.

Hong retrieved a magazine and set it before Shaw, *American Scientist*, a layperson monthly he was familiar with. Ashton, as an amateur physicist, had read it religiously. Hong opened it to the page marked with a Post-it note. He pushed it forward.

"No need to read it. I'll tell you. This article, from several years ago, was the inspiration for my Minerva Project."

Shaw glanced down at the title: "Can Video Games Be Good for You?"

Hong: "It's a report from several prestigious universities about the physical and mental benefits of video gaming. Since we are about to announce it to the world, there is no longer the need for secrecy regarding the Minerva Project. It's the code name for our Therapeutic Gaming Division." He tapped the article. "These studies show that video games can create vast improvement in patients with attention deficit disorder, autism, Asperger's and physiological conditions like vertigo and vision issues. Older patients in the trials report significantly improved memory and concentration.

"And even individuals with no disease can benefit. I'm thinking of your career, Mr. Shaw, as I said a moment ago. Game playing results in improved cognition, faster response times, the ability to switch between various tasks quickly, assess spatial relationships, visualization, many other skills."

*Prioritizing* . . .

"That's the mysterious room, Mr. Linn. Minerva, the Roman Goddess of Wisdom. Or, I prefer to say, the Goddess of Cognitive Functioning. Now, I run a business and as the CEO I'm charged with making HSE money. The engine for Therapeutic Gaming, I decided, could easily be used for lucrative action-adventure and first-person shooter games. Hence, *Immersion*.

"Now, let me dispose of your concern—the reason you recruited Mr. Linn. About *Immersion*. Which I note that you've played, Mr. Shaw, despite what you told me earlier."

Shaw tried not to register surprise. He would just assume, from now on, that Hong Wei knew everything about him.

"Yes, it is a goal to get young people around the world off their behinds and exercise. I myself am a black belt in karate and tae kwon do and I practice Afro-Brazilian capoeira. I engage in those sports because I enjoy them. You cannot talk someone into exercising if they don't want to. But you can encourage them to pursue their passion. And if exercise is a necessary consequence, then they will exercise. That is *Immersion*.

"I have two recordings of conversations you've had about your concern we are stealing confidential data and giving it to the Chinese government. Military data in particular."

Two? Shaw wondered.

"To address that concern, which is not unreasonable, considering you're trying to save the life of a young woman, let me say this: from the moment I envisioned *Immersion* and the forward-facing cameras we were developing, I knew that privacy would be a concern. I personally supervised the algorithms to make certain that every written word, every letter, every chart or graph, every photograph that the cameras scanned would be pixelated beyond recognition. The same with human figures in the slightest stage of undress. No toilets, no personal hygiene products. Dogs urinating, much less mating, would not make it into the *Immersion* system. Obscene language is filtered out.

"We've worked with law enforcement, military and government regulators around the country to guarantee that no one's privacy has been invaded. You can confirm this." His eyes flicked to Ms. Towne. The glance was fast as a viper's bite. She stepped forward and gave Shaw a piece of paper with four names on it, along with their law enforcement affiliation and phone number. The first was FBI, the second Department of Defense.

Shaw folded the paper and put it away.

Hong turned to Eddie Linn. In a voice just as calm and flat as that with which he'd addressed Shaw, Hong said, "Mr. Linn. At first, when Ms. Towne told me about your conversation with Mr. Trevor today, about insisting you meet with Mr. Shaw . . . Oh, no need to look confused. Your contract with us allows us to intercept all your communications."

"I didn't know that."

"You didn't *read* that. Which is on you. I was saying when Ms. Towne first told me about your disloyalty—"

"It wasn't—"

The marble gaze from Hong silenced him.

"I believed you would be doing what you'd done at Andrew Trevor's company: selling code you'd written based on his copyrights to third parties."

So that was Trevor's leverage over Linn: this theft.

"It was nothing," Linn said. "Really. It was code that was just easier for me to write. Anybody could have done it."

"But *anybody* didn't. You did. I've always been aware that you might be willing to sell me up the river." Hong frowned. "Is it 'up the river' or 'down the river'?"

"Down the river," Shaw said. "From the slave trade. New Orleans. Up the river is something else."

"Ah." A look of satisfaction from learning a new fact. "Today, your transgression wasn't theft of copyrighted material. But it was a betrayal. So your career with HSE is now terminated."

"No!"

"Since there was the blush of good cause in this whole matter, I will not do what I first thought: to make certain you never work in the tech world again."

Linn's eyes widened. Tears glistened. "Will you give me a month? Just to give me a chance to find something new. Please?"

Hong's steadfast face registered a splinter of disbelief. He glanced at Ms. Towne, who had a hand on her burgeoning stomach. She nodded. Hong continued: "Your office has already been cleaned out and your personal effects are in a van on the way to your house in Sunnyvale. They'll be left on your back porch, so you'll want to get there straightaway. After you leave my office, you'll be escorted to your car and shown off the grounds."

"My mortgage . . . I'm already overdue."

Shaw began to speak. Hong lowered his head and said, "Please, Mr. Shaw. You knew this was a possibility, didn't you?"

He'd put it about twenty percent.

"Since this incident has had a happy ending and I have lost no secrets or been the victim of sabotage, I'm inclined to help you out, Mr. Shaw. Thinking that this Mr. Thompson, your blogger, was going to expose some secret in the data-mining world, a secret worth killing for? That's infinitely unlikely. Stealing one's data? Everyone these days soaks up your data as if using a sponge. The boy making your submarine sandwich at the local franchise, your car repair garage, your coffee shop, your pharmacy, your internet browser—and I'm not even up to credit rating companies, insurers and your doctors. Data is the new oxygen. It's everywhere. And what happens with an abundance of any product? Its value diminishes. No one would murder for it. You should look elsewhere for your kidnapper. Now, good day."

He picked up a pencil, examined the tip with approval and pulled an overturned document toward him. He said to himself, "Up the river, down the river." Another nod.

Hong waited until Shaw and Linn were at the door and could not read the words before turning the sheet faceup.

# 59.

Shaw and Standish were in Joint Major Crimes Task Force Annex No. 1.

The Quick Byte Café.

Standish hung up her phone. "Hong. And the company. Clean as a whistle. Homeland Security, the Bureau, DoD."

"The Santa Clara County Middle School Board of Supervisors too."

"The . . ." Frowning, Standish cast a quick glance. "Oh. A joke. You don't joke much, Shaw. Well, no. You do. You just don't smile, so it's hard to tell."

She tossed down her pen, with which she'd been recording the results of her calls—doodling, really. She toyed with the heart-shaped earring. "I've got to say, we've struck out a few times here. Knight. Hong-Sung. You don't seem as upset as I thought you'd be."

"Struck out?" Shaw was confused. "Knight got us to Avon. Hong Wei gave us the idea that Thompson probably wasn't killed because of the data-mining story."

Her phone hummed. And from the timbre of her voice when she spoke, he knew it was her partner, Karen.

Shaw pulled out his laptop, logged on and ran through the local news feeds once more. His notebook was ready. Of the stories he skimmed, none were relevant to Elizabeth Chabelle's kidnapping.

There is a little-discussed aspect of survivalism that some people call destiny and some call fate and some, the more earthbound, call coincidence. You're in a bad way. There is no solution to the crisis you face, one that seems certain to kill you or de-toe you, say, thanks to frostbite.

But then? You survive. With your ten little appendages intact.

Because someone or something intervenes.

Colter Shaw himself learned of this concept when he was on a survival run, alone, in December. Fourteen years old. His father had driven him to a remote corner of the Compound and let him out of the truck, to make his way back over the course of two days. He had everything he needed: food, matches, maps, compass, sleeping bag, weapon. The sky was blue, the weather cold yet above freezing, the trek that lay ahead unchallenging and through spectacular scenery.

An hour later, he was crossing a fast-moving stream on a fallen oak that would have been a solid bridge had it not been a host to termites and carpenter bees, who'd been dining on its insides for years. In he went.

Gasping from the cold, Colter scrabbled up the stream bank, shivering fiercely.

He didn't panic; he assessed. The matches, in a waterproof container, and the knife were on him. He'd had to jettison the backpack when it dragged deep below the surface. He gathered leaves and cut pine boughs and soon had a fire going. In forty minutes or so his core temperature was stable. But he was ten miles from the Compound, now without his compass or map or pistol, and by the time he was safely warm and his clothes and boots dry it would be too late to hike. He needed to spend the time until nightfall building a lean-to big enough to take the fire inside; the air smelled like rain.

This he did. And while it was still light enough to see, Colter watched squirrels as they searched for nuts they'd hoarded. He followed only the gray squirrels; the reds don't bury. He found several stashes in abandoned burrows and collected walnuts; acorns are edible yet too bitter to eat without boiling to remove the tannins. He drank stream water and ate and fell asleep confident the trails he'd spotted before the dunking would lead him in the general direction of the Compound.

He woke up about six hours later to the blizzard. Two feet of snow were on the ground.

Colter's head had sunk with despair. The snow covered the trails he'd noted yesterday. He had four walnuts left.

Would he die here?

As he surveyed the rolling white landscape, he noticed something beside the lean-to: a large orange backpack. He yanked it inside and, with trembling fingers, opened the zipper. It contained energy bars, a wire saw, extra matches, a map and a compass, a thermal sleeping bag. Also: a weapon—the Colt Python .357 that he carried still. The gun that was his father's pride.

Ashton Shaw had not returned to the cabin after dropping Colter off. He'd been following the boy all along.

*Intervention . . .*

Which is what happened now.

Shaw's phone hummed. It was the toy man, Marty Avon.

"We still have a way to go with the proxies. For what it's worth, one of the subscribers logged on a few hours ago without turning on his VPN—his proxy, you know. His real IP address popped up. He fit our criteria about being an obsessive player but had been offline when the crimes occurred. We traced him to a house in Mountain View."

"May have something," he told the detective. "It's Marty."

Standish disconnected her personal call and took the phone and had a brief conversation, at the conclusion of which she gave Avon her email address. It was only a moment after they disconnected that the detective's phone chimed. She read: "I'll DMV him and see what our databases have to say." She typed: "Okay. Forwarded."

They sat in silence for a moment. Shaw looked around the café, focusing on the computer history wall. Mario the plumber and Sonic the hedgehog. Hewlett and Packard. ENIAC, an ancient computer as big as a semitruck. Then his eyes took in the front door of the café and he recalled seeing Maddie Poole for the first time as she walked inside, twining her red hair around a finger.

*So. You're wondering, what's up with stalker chick . . .*

Standish's phone sang out once more.

The detective read quickly. "His name is Brad Hendricks. No warrants, no arrests. He was detained frequently in high school. Bullying incidents. Don't know which end of it he was on. No charges filed. Here he is."

He glanced down and must have stiffened.

"What is it, Shaw?"

"I've seen him."

It was the boy in the red-and-black-checked shirt who'd been so harshly rejected by the pretty girl right here in the Quick Byte Café, two tables away from where Shaw and Standish now sat.

# 60.

Brad Hendricks, nineteen, was attending community college part-time and lived with his parents in a lower-income area of Mountain View. He also worked in a computer repair shop about fifteen hours a week. In the high school fights Brad had been the one bullied and had then ambushed several of his tormenters. Bones had not been broken and noses were only slightly bloodied. All parties being in the wrong, the parents had chosen to let the matters go without police intervention. Brad played *The Whispering Man* and other Destiny Entertainment games forty or so hours a week—and presumably spent many hours at other companies' games too. He had minimal social media presence, apparently preferring gaming to posting on Facebook, Instagram or Twitter.

LaDonna Standish had started canvassing in the Quick Byte, displaying the picture of the young man, who'd been there earlier in the day and was not present at the moment.

Shaw was presently pursuing a related lead: browsing

Santa Clara County and California State records—using Standish's secure log-in. What he learned—and it was quite interesting—he recorded in one of his case notebooks.

He sat back, staring at the now-blank screen.

"What?" Standish said as she joined him. "You're looking like the cat that got the cream."

Shaw asked, "Doesn't the cat get the canary?"

"Cream sounds better than a dead bird. Brad hasn't been here since you saw him earlier." She went on to explain that none of the patrons now in the café knew him. A few recalled seeing him have the fight with the young woman he claimed he'd met online but couldn't remember seeing him before that.

Standish was tucking something into her wallet. She said to Shaw, "Took a liking to me 'cause I'm a cop."

"Who?"

"Tiffany. I'm now a lifetime member of the QB Koffee Discount Klub. You're one too, aren't you?"

"Invite's in the mail, I guess."

"Work it. She's sweet on you, you know."

Shaw didn't reply.

Standish's face grew solemn. "So. We're talking cream and cat . . . What'd you come up with, Shaw? There any chance to save Elizabeth?"

"Maybe."


Shaw parked on a street of old houses, probably built not long after World War II.

Cinder block and wood frame. Solid. He wondered if that was because of earthquake danger. Then decided:

No, there wouldn't have been that much forethought put into these children's toy blocks of homes. Plop 'em down and sell 'em. Move on.

This was a different Mountain View from where the rich lived. Different from even Frank Mulliner's place. Not as dingy as East Palo Alto but plenty grim and shabby. The persistent hiss of the 101 filled the air, which was aromatic with exhaust.

The yards, which would be measured in feet, not acreage, were mostly untended. Weeds and patches of yellowing grass and sandy scabs. No gardens. Money for watering the landscape—always expensive in the state of California—had gone for necessities and the crushing taxes and mortgage payments.

He thought of Marty Avon and his dream, Siliconville, recalling what he'd just read online a half hour ago.

> For decades, Silicon Valley has always looked for the "Next Big Thing"—the internet, http protocol, faster processors, larger storage, mobile phones, routers, browser search engines. That search goes on and always will. The message that everybody has missed in the Valley: Real Estate is the true Next Big Thing . . .

The house Shaw focused on was typical of the bungalows here. Green paint touched up with a slightly different shade, stains descending from the roof along the siding like rusty tears, discarded boxes and pipes and plastic containers, rotting cardboard, a pile of newspaper mush.

An ancient half-ton pickup sat in the driveway, the color sun-faded red. It listed to the right from shocks that had long ago lost enthusiasm.

Shaw climbed out and was walking toward the door when it opened. A burly man, balding and in gray dungaree slacks and a white T-shirt, approached. Looking at Shaw ominously, he strode forward and stopped a few feet away. He was about six-two. Shaw could smell sweat and onion.

"Yeah?" the man snapped.

"Mr. Hendricks?"

"I asked what you wanted."

"I'd just like a few minutes of your time."

"If you're repo, that's bullshit. I'm only two months behind." He nodded toward the junker.

"I'm not here to repossess your truck."

The man processed, looking up and down the street. And at Shaw's car. "I'm Minnetti. My wife's name was Hendricks."

"Brad's your son?" Shaw asked.

"Stepson. What's he done now?"

"I'd like to talk to you about him."

"Brad ain't here. Supposed t'be in school."

"He is in school. I checked. I want to talk to you."

The big man's eyes went squinty. "You're not a cop. You'd've said so. They gotta do that; it's the law. So what's the little shit done now? He can't've fucked your little sister. Not unless she's a computer." He grimaced. "Over the line. About your sister. Sorry. He owe you money?"

"No."

He sized Shaw up. "He couldn'ta beat you up or anything. Not that boy."

"I just have a few questions."

"Why should I tell you anything about Brad?"

"I've got a proposition for you. Let's go inside."

Shaw walked past Brad's stepfather toward the front door. There, Shaw paused, looking back. The man slowly walked toward him.

The air within the bungalow was heavy with the scent of mold and cat pee and pot. If Frank Mulliner's décor was a C, this was a grade below. All the furniture was shabby and couch and chairs indented with the impression of bodies sitting for long periods on the ratty cushions. Cups and plates encrusted with food sat stacked on the coffee and end tables. At the end of a corridor, Shaw believed he saw the fast passage of a heavyset woman in a yellow housedress. He guessed it was Brad Hendricks's mother, startled that her husband had let an unexpected visitor into the home.

"So? Proposition?"

No offer to sit.

Didn't matter. Shaw wouldn't be here very long. "I want to see your son's room."

"I don't know why I should help you. Whoever the fuck you are."

The woman's face—a round pale moon—peered out. Below the double chin was the burning orange dot of a cigarette tip.

Shaw reached into his pocket and extracted five hundred dollars in twenties. He held it out to the man. He stared at the cash.

"He doesn't like anybody to go down there."

This wasn't a time for bargaining. He glanced at the man, his meaning clear: take it or leave it.

Brad's stepfather looked into the hallway—the woman had disappeared again—and he snatched the bills from Shaw's hand and stuffed them into his pocket. He nodded to a door near the cluttered, grimy kitchen.

"Spends every minute down there. Fucking games're his whole life. I'd had three girlfriends, the time I was his age. I tried him on sports, wasn't interested. Suggested the Army. Ha! Figure how that went. You know what me and the wife call him? The Turtle. 'Cause every time he gets outside, he goes into this shell. Closes down. Fucking games did that. We took the washer and dryer and moved 'em to the garage. He wouldn't let Beth go down there for laundry. Sometimes I think it's booby-trapped. You be careful, mister."

The unspoken adjunct to that sentence was: I don't want the inconvenience of having to call the police if you touch something that blows your hand off.

Shaw walked past him, opened the door and descended into the basement.

The room was dim and it seemed to be the source of the mold stench, which stung Shaw's eyes and nose. Also present was the scent of damp stone and of heating oil, unique among petrochemical products. Once smelled, never forgotten. The place was cluttered with boxes, piles of clothing, broken chairs and scuffed tables. And countless electronics. Shaw paused halfway down the creaky stairs.

The center of the room was a computer workstation, featuring a huge screen and keyboard and a complicated trackball. He recalled what Maddie had told him about those who had preferences for playing on computers, versus those who liked consoles, but Brad also had three Nintendo units, beside which were cartridges of Mario Brothers games.

Nintendo.

*A shrine to the chivalrous who protect the weak. I like that one better . . .*

Ah, Maddie . . .

A half dozen computer keyboards lay in the corner, many of the letters, numbers and symbols worn away, some keys missing altogether. Why didn't he throw them out?

Shaw continued down the uneasy stairs. Nails were needed in three, maybe four, places to keep the structure safe. Some boards sagged with rot. Shaw clocked in at about one hundred and eighty pounds. Brad's stepfather was clearly two hundred and fifty or more. He presumably didn't come down here much.

The cinder-block walls were unevenly painted and gray stone showed through the swaths of white and cream. Posters of video games were the only decorations. One was of *The Whispering Man*. The pale face, the black suit, the hat from a different era.

*You've been abandoned. Escape if you can. Or die with dignity.*

There was a flowchart on the wall—measuring three by four feet. In handwriting as small as Shaw's yet much more careless, Brad had detailed his progress through the levels of *The Whispering Man*, jotting hundreds of notes about tactics and workarounds and cheats. He'd gotten as far as Level 9. The top of the chart, Level 10, Hell, was blank. The level no one had ever attained, in the history of the game, Shaw recalled.

A sagging mattress sat on the box spring, with no frame. The bed was unmade. Empty plates of food and cans and bottles of soft drinks sat near the pillow. A stack of music CDs rested beside a decades-old boom box. All the boy's disposable income went into gaming gear, it seemed.

Shaw sat in Brad's chair and watched the screen saver, a dragon flying in circles. He followed the hypnotic motion for a full three minutes. Then he pulled out his phone and made two calls. The first was to LaDonna Standish. The second was to Washington, D.C.

# 61.

mean, people want to come here? For the fun of it?"

Colter Shaw and LaDonna Standish walked through the chaos of the C3 Conference. Shaw carried a backpack over his shoulder. A woman security guard at the entrance had examined the contents carefully, using what looked like large chopsticks to probe. Standish's gold shield had not exempted him.

The detective's head was swiveling, left to right, then back, then up, to take in the huge high-def screens.

"I got a headache already."

As before, there were a hundred different blaring sounds: spaceship engines, alien cries, machine guns, ray blasters . . . and the never-ending electronic soundtracks with the ultra-bass pedal tones that seemed to exist unrelated to any game. It was as if the conference organizers were worried that a few seconds of silence might creep in like mice in a bakery.

Shaw shouted, "We're not even in the loudest part."

They dodged their way through the crowds of intense youngsters, passing by the Hong-Sung booth.

HSE PRESENTS

*IMMERSION*

THE NEW MOVEMENT IN VIDEO GAMING

Shaw glanced at the queue of excited attendees, goggles in hand.

He didn't see Maddie Poole.

Standish called, "I'm going to tell you one thing, Shaw. Our daughters are not getting involved in this game shit."

He wondered what games would be available when Gem and Sefina were old enough to play. Wondered too how on earth Standish and Karen would keep them from the console controller or the keyboard.

In a few minutes they came to the Knight Time Gaming booth, where Tony Knight's developer, Jimmy Foyle, greeted them at the entrance.

He shook Shaw's hand and, after introductions, Standish's.

"Let's go inside," Foyle said, nodding them in.

They followed him into the working area of the booth, where Shaw had met with Knight and Foyle the day before. The three sat at the conference table. Foyle pushed aside promotional materials for the new installment of *Conundrum*. Three employees sat at the three computer stations. Shaw couldn't tell if they were the same ones as before; all Knight Gaming workers were oddly identical.

The detective said to Foyle, "It was your idea how to

find the subscriber to *The Whispering Man*, the one who's a suspect. We really appreciate it."

"I had some thoughts, that's all," Foyle said modestly. He was as shy as the other day. Shaw remembered the press described him as a "backroom kind of guy."

Shaw had called earlier and told him there'd been another kidnapping and that they had a suspect, could he help once again? He'd agreed.

Shaw now explained about Brad Hendricks.

Standish added, "We think it's him but we're not sure. There's no grounds for a warrant . . ." She looked to Shaw.

"Brad lives at home with his parents," Shaw said. "I went to see them—he's in class now. I . . . convinced his stepfather to help us."

The game designer asked, "Turning against his own stepson?"

"For five hundred dollars. Yes."

Foyle's brow furrowed.

"He let me take all of this." Shaw hefted the backpack onto the table. Foyle peered inside at the scores of external drives, disks, thumb drives, SD cards, CDs and DVDs, along with papers, Post-it notes, pencils and pens, rolls of candy. "I just scooped up what was on the boy's desk."

Standish said, "We looked through some of it. The drives and cards we could figure out how to plug in. All we got was gibberish."

"You need somebody to decrypt it," Foyle said, "and you can't go to your own Computer Crimes people because you can't get a warrant."

"Exactly."

"Because what you're doing is . . ."

"Irregular." Standish leaned forward and said evenly, "We'll lose the chance to present any evidence we recover in court. But I don't care about that. All that matters is saving the victim."

Foyle asked, "If he's following *The Whispering Man* gameplay, what level would it be?"

"The Sinking Ship."

Foyle winced. "Around here? Hundreds of tankers and containerships, a lot of them have to be abandoned. Fisherman's Wharf, Marin. Pleasure boats everywhere . . ."

Shaw said, "Your *Conundrum*'s an ARG, alternate reality game. Marty Avon told us that it only works because your servers're supercomputers."

"That's right."

"Can you use them to break the passcodes?"

"I can try." The man peered into the backpack. "SATA drives, three-and-a-halfers without enclosures, SDs . . . thumb drives. Some he's made on his own. I don't recognize them." He looked up, his eyes eager at the idea of a challenge, it seemed. "You know, I might find a symmetric back door. And if he uses first-gen DES, then anyone can crack that."

Shaw and Standish regarded each other, exceptions to the "anyone" rule.

"If that's the case, I could have readable text or graphics in hours. Minutes, maybe."

Standish eyed her phone for the time. "Brad Hendricks's going to be out of class soon. Colter and I are going to follow him. He might lead us to Elizabeth. If he's just left her to die, though, you're the only hope."

# 62.

A half hour later, LaDonna Standish was piloting her Nissan Altima along an increasingly deserted region of western Santa Clara County, keeping a safe distance behind the car they were following.

Shaw texted Jimmy Foyle:

Brad Hendricks is on the road—not going home. We are following. Maybe on way to kidnap site but can't tell. Success with encryption?

A moment later the game designer texted back.

First SATA drive, can't crack. He used 2-fish algorithm. Working on SD cards now.

Shaw read this to her.

Standish gave a wry laugh. "Two-fish. Computer stuff. Who comes up with those names? Why Apple? Why Macintosh?"

"Google makes sense to me."

A glance his way. "You gotta smile sometime, Shaw. It's like a contest now. I'm going to make it happen." She steered the Nissan around two more turns, then slowed at the top of a hill, keeping far enough back so they wouldn't be spotted in the rearview mirrors.

In the distance was the hazy blue of the Pacific Ocean. From here, it lived up to its name.

"And our backup?" Shaw asked.

A glance at her phone. "Nothing yet."

Both Shaw and Standish had understood they couldn't request tactical backup from the California Bureau of Investigation, given their "renegade" investigation. They'd be closed down in an instant or would have to talk their way up through the ranks to find someone senior to support them. No time for that. Standish had sent some texts, to see if she might "improvise" backup. Apparently with no success. She sent another message.

Shaw opened *The Whispering Man* gameplay booklet that Maddie Poole had bought for him. He was skimming to look for anything to help them when—if—they found where Elizabeth Chabelle had been abandoned.

### Level 3: The Sinking Ship.

*You've been abandoned on a Forrest Sherman–class destroyer, the USS Scorpion, which has been struck by an enemy torpedo and is sinking in shark-infested waters, a hundred miles from land. You're in a cabin with a bottle of water, a cotton*

*handkerchief, a double-sided razor blade, an acet-*
*ylene torch and a container of engine lubricant.*

*There are a number of crew members on the*
*vessel and only one life raft remaining, hidden on*
*board. You must find the raft before the ship goes*
*under.*

*Gameplay clues:*

*1. The more members of the crew who die, the*
*more resources will be left for the others.*

*2. The ship is rumored to be haunted by the*
*ghosts of the crew of a World War II destroyer,*
*also named the Scorpion, that went down in*
*1945. A ghost can achieve his final rest by tak-*
*ing the life of a sailor on your vessel.*

*3. There is something large cruising nearby un-*
*derwater. It might be a megashark—or might*
*be a submarine, though whether it's friendly or*
*enemy is not known. The radio gear on the*
*Scorpion was destroyed by the torpedo strike.*

*You've been abandoned. Escape if you can. Or*
*die with dignity.*

Shaw read Maddie Poole's margin notes: In the chap-
ter on Level 3, The Sinking Ship, she'd written: *More*
*stabbings on this level than the others. Knives, razors? Gas-*
*oline too. Look out for flares.*

He spotted a passage in the front:

CS:

*You game.*
*I game.*
*We both game . . .*

*Xo,*
*MP*

Standish asked, "Shaw?"

He set the booklet down.

She continued: "Got a question. Your impression? Brad Hendricks's homelife? His parents?"

"Bad, *A* to *Z*. A stepfather happy to sell the boy out even before he knew the facts. Mom all but comatose in an armchair, watching TV. Smell of pot in the air. The way she looked at her husband, you couldn't help seeing *bad choice* written in her eyes. Couldn't tell about physical abuse. Probably not. The house was a mess."

"That's why he gets lost in the games. His social life is make-believe."

*The Turtle . . .*

The route was taking them through increasingly deserted hills and forest. The road was serpentine, working to their advantage. They were hidden from view by trees and brush but were able to follow glints of chrome and glass ahead of them.

"You have your weapon?"

"I do."

"Don't shoot him, okay?" Standish said. "The paperwork for something like that . . ." She clicked her tongue.

"You've got a sense of humor too."

"I wasn't being funny."

Ahead of them, the car turned onto a dirt road.

Standish braked and they consulted the GPS. The unnamed road ended about two miles ahead, at the ocean. There was no other exit. She drove on, remaining some distance behind now yet not too far. It was a balance. They couldn't take him too early; he had to lead them to Chabelle. They couldn't lag too much either, because he was here to kill the woman and they'd have to move in fast.

At ten miles per hour, they rocked along the unsteady road.

"I'm going to see about starting a new division."

"In the Task Force?"

She nodded. "It's a different kind of street in SV, different from EPA and Oakland. But it's still street. Look at Brad. I want to get to kids like him early. So they have a chance. I can do just what I did back in the 'hood. Talk to the parents, teachers. It puts a frame around the kids, people see them differently, for the first time."

"Were you in a crew, Standish?" Shaw asked.

A smile on her face as she tugged on the heart earring. "A mascot. I was a mascot." A laugh. "My daddy, badass. Frankie Williamson. You can look him up. Oh, Lord, that man was a tough one. At home, he was the best father you could want. All of us kids, he took care of us. I'll show you pictures sometime. His crew'd come around and bring us stuff." She shook her head, nostalgic. "In the den they'd do their business, exchange the envelopes—you know what I'm saying? With us, they brought us Legos and board games. Cabbage Patch dolls! I was thirteen and had a crush on Devon Brown you wouldn't believe and Daddy's crew was giving me dolls! They were all so proud, though, so of course I made a fuss. Why, I've got pictures of me sitting on the knee of Dayan Cabel. The hitman? That boy'll never see the outside of San Quentin in twenty lifetimes.

"I'm going to start that program. It's in the works. Street Welfare Education and Excellence Program. SWEEP."

"Like it."

She watched the dust trail of the car ahead of them settle. "This is weird crime, Shaw, fantasy crime. Like the Zodiac, Son of Sam. I don't want fantasy anymore. Helping kids stay alive. That's real. How about you, Shaw? You run with a crew? I could see you in a blackleather jacket, smoking behind the gym."

"Homeschooled with my brother and sister."

"You're kidding." She then nodded out the windshield. "Road ends up there. We can't go any farther; he'll see us." Standish steered into a stand of trees and cut the engine.

They climbed out and, without communicating, both left the doors open for the silence. They started forward on ground that Shaw pointed toward: pine needles. They moved about thirty feet into the dunes and crouched not far from the car they'd been pursuing.

A moment later the driver climbed out, the man Shaw and Standish had concluded two hours ago at the Quick Byte was the Gamer: not Brad Hendricks at all but the brilliant if shy game designer Jimmy Foyle.

# 63.

Silhouetted against a haze-dulled sun, Foyle turned toward the ocean and stretched.

Shaw and Standish eased lower into the congregation of brush and yellow grass. The man would undoubtedly be armed with the Glock with which he'd killed Kyle Butler and Henry Thompson, though at the moment he held only his key fob in one hand and, in the other, a small bag. Inside the sack would be some of the items from the backpack Shaw had given him—the detritus from Brad's gaming station desk in the family's pungent, dank basement. Pens, batteries, Post-it notes.

Foyle had returned here, to the place where he'd stashed Elizabeth Chabelle, as Shaw had anticipated, to plant these things as evidence implicating the innocent boy; they'd have his fingerprints and DNA on them.

The kidnapper's next step, Shaw was sure, would be to head straight to the Hendrickses' house and hide the murder weapon in the backyard or garage. He'd then call in an anonymous tip as to where Elizabeth Chabelle was, giving a description of Brad, maybe a partial tag number of his car. The police would find her body and the evidence here, which would eventually lead to the family house.

This had been a gamble on Shaw's part but a rational one, a sixty or seventy percent one. He concluded that Brad Hendricks was innocent and that it was Jimmy Foyle who was the Gamer, so he'd set up the trap, pretending to enlist his help in the decryption, hoping he'd the take the bait: the contents of the backpack.

It was Foyle, whom Shaw and Standish had just been following, texting the man occasionally to make him believe they were elsewhere tailing Brad Hendricks.

And where was the sinking ship?

Foyle walked between two dunes and disappeared.

Shaw nodded in that direction and he and Standish rose and followed. At the crest of a dune they crouched, looking down at an old pier that jutted fifty feet into the choppy Pacific. Midway along it was an ancient fishing boat, half sunk.

1 - Sinking Ship with Five Objects
2 - L.S.
3 - Pier South of Pedro Point

Pacific Ocean

"Your armor snug, Shaw?"

They were both in bulletproof vests. He nodded.

"You know how to cuff somebody?"

"I can. Better with restraints."

Standish handed him two zip ties. "I'll cover him. You get his weapon and get his hands." She drew her Glock, rose and walked forward silently to the sand. Twenty feet from Foyle, she raised her weapon and aimed. "Jimmy Foyle! Police. Don't move. Hands in the air."

Foyle jerked to a stop, turning slowly.

"Drop the bag. Hands up."

Shocked, he stared their way. Dismay flooded his face.

"Drop the bag!"

He did and lifted his hands as he looked from Shaw to Standish and back to Shaw, no doubt understanding how this had come together. The great computer game strategist had been outplayed. Bewilderment morphed to anger.

"Get on your knees. Knees! Now!"

Just then, from behind them, came the blaring sound of a car horn.

Shaw realized then that the key fob was still in Foyle's hand. He'd hit the panic button.

Instinctively, the detective started to turn at the sound.

"Standish, no!" Shaw shouted.

Foyle crouched and drew his Glock. A series of ragged flashes sprouted from his right hand. Standish gave a high yelp as slugs tore into her body.

# 64.

Shaw dove for her, squinting against the sand spitting into the air from Foyle's gunshots.

He drew his own Glock, raising the weapon in both hands, steadying it, scanning for a target.

Foyle had circled to the left, sprinting flat out through the trees, and Shaw had no clear shot. Foyle's car started up and sped away.

Shaw returned to Standish, who was writhing in agony. "Okay, they don't teach you this shit. Hurt, hurts."

He assessed the damage: Two slugs had hit the vest. She'd taken one in the forearm, which had nicked the suicide vein, and one low in the belly.

Shaw slipped his gun into his jacket pocket and put pressure on the wounds, saying, "Had to be sensitive, didn't you, Standish? Couldn't shoot a man armed with a BMW key fob?"

"Get to the boat, Shaw. If Elizabeth's still . . . Go!" A gasp.

"This's going to hurt."

He put pressure on Standish's abdominal wound, pulled her locking knife from its holder and, gripping the blade, used the weight of the handle to flick it open, one-handed. He lifted his bloody palm away from the wound only long enough to cut a strip of his shirttail and tie a tourniquet. This went around her biceps. He used a branch to tighten the cloth. The fierce bleeding in Standish's shattered lower arm slowed. He closed the blade and slipped the knife into his pocket.

"Hurt, hurts . . ." Standish repeated, gasping. "Call it in, Shaw. Don't let him get too far."

"I will. Almost there."

There wasn't much to do with the gut shot, except pressure. He gathered some leaves and placed them on the wound and then found a rock that weighed about five pounds. He set this on top. Standish groaned in pain, arched her back.

"No. Stay still. I know it's tough, but you've got to stay still."

He wiped his hands on his jacket and slacks so he could use his phone. He dialed.

"Police and fire emergency. What's—"

"Code 13. Officer shot," Standish said weakly.

He repeated this, then looked at his GPS and gave the longitude and latitude.

"What's your name, sir?"

"Colter Shaw. Supervisor Cummings at the JMCTF'll know me. Armed suspect. Fleeing from location I gave you. Might be headed east in white late-model BMW, California plate, first numbers 9-7-8. Didn't get the rest. Suspect is Jimmy Foyle, employed by Knight Time Gaming. Wounded officer is Detective LaDonna Standish, also with the Task Force."

The dispatcher was asking more questions. Shaw ignored her. He left the line open and set the iPhone next to Standish. Her eyes were dim, lids low.

Shaw released the tourniquet for a moment. Then tightened it again. He pulled a pen from Standish's breast pocket and wrote on her wrist, slightly lighter than the ink, the time he'd twisted it tight. It would let the med techs know that it had been binding the arm for some time and that they should relax it to get blood circulating, to minimize the risk she'd lose the arm.

No words passed between them. There was nothing to say. He set the pistol next to the phone, though it was clear the woman would be unconscious in a few minutes.

And probably dead before help arrived. Yet leave her he had to.

He pulled off his jacket and vest and covered her with them, then stood. Then:

Sprinting toward the sea, Colter Shaw eyed the craft closely.

The forty-foot derelict fishing vessel, decades old, was going down by the stern, already three-fourths submerged.

Shaw saw no doors into the cabin; there would be only one and it was now underwater. In the aft part of the superstructure, still above sea level, was a window facing onto the bow. The opening was large enough to climb through but it appeared sealed. He'd dive for the door.

He paused, reflecting: Did he need to?

Shaw looked for the rope mooring the boat to the pier; maybe he could take up slack and keep the ship from going under.

There was no rope; the boat was anchored, which meant it was free to descend thirty feet to the floor of the Pacific Ocean.

And, if the woman was inside, take her with it to a cold, murky grave.

As he ran onto the slippery dock, avoiding the most rotten pieces, he stripped off his bloodstained shirt, then his shoes and socks.

A powerful swell struck the ship and it shuddered and sank a few more inches into the gray, indifferent water.

He shouted, "Elizabeth?"

No response.

Shaw assessed: there was a sixty percent chance she was on board. Fifty percent chance she was alive after hours in the waterlogged cabin.

Whatever the percentages, there was no debate about what came next. He stuck an arm beneath the surface and judged the temperature to be about forty degrees. He'd have thirty minutes until he passed out from hypothermia.

Let's start the clock, he thought.

And plunged in.

# 65.

lease. Save yourself."

Twenty minutes later Colter Shaw was inside the
sinking ship's cabin, at the bulkhead door separating
him from Elizabeth Chabelle. With the flowerpot shard, he
continued to try to chip away the wood around the hinges.

"You with me, Elizabeth?" Shaw called.

The *Seas the Day* settled further. The water was now
streaming in through the gap in the front of the cabin.
Soon it would be cascading in.

"My baby . . ." She was sobbing.

"Keep it together. Need you to. Okay?"

She nodded. "You're nah . . . nah . . . not police?"

"No."

"The . . . then . . . ?"

"Boy or girl?"

"Wha . . . what-t-t?"

"Baby. Boy or girl?"

"Girl."

"You have a name for her?"

"Buh . . . Buh . . . Belinda."

"Don't hear that much.

"You need to get as high as you can on the bunk."

"And your . . . ?" Whispering. "Name?"

"Colter."

"Don't . . . Don't hear that much." She smiled. Then began to cry again. "You . . . you . . . you've done everything you . . . you can. Get . . . out. You have a family. Get out. Thank you. Bless you. Get out."

"Farther, climb farther! Do it, Elizabeth. George wants to see you. Your mom and dad in Miami. Stone crabs, remember?"

Shaw squeezed her hand and she did as he'd asked, paddling to the bunk and climbing it. He tossed away the useless ceramic shard.

Time left on the hypothermia clock? It would've run out. Of course.

"Go!" she called. "Get out!"

Just then gray water, flecked with kelp, poured into the forward cabin through the gap where the window had been.

"Go! Puh . . . Please . . ."

*Die with dignity . . .*

Shaw scrabbled to the front window frame and, with a look back toward Chabelle, vaulted through and outside, into the ocean. Dizzy from the cold, disoriented.

A wave hit the boat, the boat hit him, and Shaw was shoved again toward a pylon. His foot found a deck railing and he pushed himself out of the way just before he was crushed.

He heard, he believed, Chabelle's sobs.

Hallucination?

Yes, no . . .

Shaw turned toward the submerged stern of the boat and swam hard for it. He'd stopped shivering, his body saying, That's it. No point in trying to keep you warm.

With the forward window gone, the water rushed inside as if flowing through a rent in a broken dam. The ship was going down fast.

When the cabin was almost entirely underwater, Shaw took a deep breath and dove straight down.

At about eight feet below the surface, he held on to a railing and, remembering where the door handle was located, gripped it hard. Bracing his feet on the cabin wall, he slowly extended his legs.

The door resisted, as before. But then, at last, it slowly swung outward.

A gamble of his, paying off. With Sophie, the Gamer had left one door open. The rules of *The Whispering Man* stated there was always a way to escape if you could figure it out.

Here, the only way out was the cabin door. It wasn't sealed with screws; it was held fast by the unequal pressure: water outside, air within. Shaw had speculated that as soon as the water was the same height on the inside as on the outside, it could be wrestled open. And it could.

The transit of the door seemed to take forever. Finally there was enough of a gap for him to kick inside, grab the nearly unconscious Chabelle and pull her out. Together they floated free of the *Seas the Day*, which disappeared beneath them, rolling to the starboard as it sank. The suction following the ship pulled them after it, but only momentarily. Soon they broke again to the surface, both gasping hard.

Shaw, kicking, looked around, orienting himself.

They were still thirty feet from the shore. The pier was five feet above them yet featured no ladder. The pylons, slick and green, couldn't be climbed.

"You with me?" Shaw shouted.

Chabelle spat out water. A cough. A nod. She was very pale.

Kicking to keep them on the surface, Shaw used one hand to fend off the pylons as the indifferent waves shouldered them toward the pier.

The only way out was the shore . . . What he saw wasn't encouraging. The sharp-edged stone—fossil gray—was also covered in the green moss-like growth. There were places where he could get a grip, it seemed, but to get close meant being at the mercy of the ocean, which surged against the rocks. It would fling them against the rocks too, breaking them the way the water itself broke.

"Muh . . . my baby, baby . . ."

"Buh . . . Belinda's going to be just fine. Guh . . . got you out of the *Tuh* . . . *Titanic*, didn't I?"

"Baby . . ."

Okay. It had to be the rocks. No time left.

As he turned them both toward the shore, Elizabeth Chabelle screamed. "He's back! He's come back!"

Shaw looked up and saw the silhouette of a figure running toward the pier.

However fast the 911 responders were, they couldn't possibly be here by now, unless via helicopter, and no helicopter was near. It would be Jimmy Foyle. He'd returned to take out witnesses.

Shaw kicked hard, fighting to turn toward the pier. They'd hide under it and risk the rise and fall of the water, trying to avoid the spikes and nails and sharp barnacles on the pylons.

Once more the cold arms of the ocean didn't cooperate. They kept Shaw and Chabelle nice and centered, six feet away from the pier. A bull's-eye for Jimmy Foyle, who was, Shaw knew very well, a fine shot.

Shaw blinked water from his eyes and looked up . . . to see the figure dropping to his belly on the rotting pier and extending a hand.

Which held not a pistol but something . . . Yes, something cloth, a rope of bulky cloth . . .

"Come on, Shaw, grab it!" The figure was Detective Dan Wiley.

So their backup had made it after all. He was the one Standish had texted for assistance. Since they weren't on the case, they needed someone unofficially, and the only person Standish could think of was the Liaison officer.

After two tries, Shaw managed to grip what Wiley'd lowered.

Ah, clever. Wiley had bound Shaw's jacket and his own together. He'd tied his belt onto the end, like a rescue harness.

"Under her arms!" Wiley shouted. "The belt."

While the cop held his end firmly, Shaw worked the belt over Elizabeth Chabelle's head.

The big man pulled her upward. She disappeared onto the top of the dock. The improvised device was lowered again and Wiley tugged while Shaw's feet found some purchase on the pilings. A moment later he too scrabbled onto the pier.

# 66.

*ever hesitate to improvise . . .*

Which was, of course, one of the rules in Ashton Shaw's voluminous *Book of Never*.

At the moment, his son Colter was thinking of a more specific variation:

*Never hesitate to use the efficient heater of a dinged-up gray sedan to warm the core temperature of a hypothermia victim.*

Shaw was reflecting that this was a pretty good rule as he sat in LaDonna Standish's Nissan Altima. Parked nearby were eight or nine police cars, representing various agencies, and the ambulance where Elizabeth Chabelle was being examined.

Shaw's shivering had lessened and he turned the heat down some. He was in a change of clothing provided by the Santa Clara Fire Department, a dark blue jumpsuit.

Shaw's bloodstained phone hummed with an email. It was from Mack, his private eye, and was in response to the call he'd made in Brad Hendricks's den just before he'd begun collecting drives and other tidbits from the desk with a tissue.

He read the email carefully.

Hypothesis became theory.

Shaw noted a medical technician stepping from the ambulance and, frowning into the glare, looking around. He spotted Shaw and approached. Shaw climbed out of the Nissan. The tech reported that Chabelle's multiple heartbeats—the one emanating from her chest, the other from her belly—were both strong. The medics had assured her that the amount of drug Foyle had used to sedate her would have no lasting effect on mother or child. Both would be fine.

For LaDonna Standish, however, the same could not be said.

Shaw had steeled himself to the fact that she had died from the terrible wounds. But no. The detective was alive, in critical condition, and had been medevacked to a hospital in Santa Clara, which had a trauma center specializing in gunshot wounds. She'd lost much blood, though Shaw's tourniquet and his jotting down the time had probably saved her life, at least temporarily. The technician told Shaw she was still in surgery.

Dan Wiley was standing near his car, speaking with Ron Cummings, the JMCTF supervisor. Prescott and the unnamed shorter agent from the CBI were present too, but Cummings now was in charge.

Because, Shaw guessed, it was his officer and not theirs who'd found the perp and rescued the victim.

With help from the concerned citizen.

Shaw could see another participant in the festivities.

Thirty feet away, Jimmy Foyle sat in the backseat of a police cruiser, head down.

It was Dan Wiley who'd collared him. The detective had been on the narrow road to the beach where Standish had texted him they'd be, when he found Foyle's white BMW speeding toward him.

While the man may have been a lousy detective, he'd proved he had a cool head under fire. With his unmarked car he'd played a game of chicken, driving Foyle into a ditch. When the game designer leapt out and began firing, blindly, Wiley had simply squatted behind his car, holding yet not firing his weapon until the man's magazine was empty, and then went after him. The tackle must have been a hard one. Foyle showed evidence of a bloody nose and his left hand was deformed by a thick beige elastic bandage. The protruding fingers were purple.

Cummings noted that Shaw had emerged from his hot lodge of a sedan and the supervisor walked his way. Prescott and the other agent started after him. Cummings uttered something and they stopped.

"You okay?" Cummings asked.

A brief nod.

The Task Force commander said, "Foyle isn't talking. And I'm at sea."

Some irony in the comment, considering that they were standing thirty yards from the Pacific Ocean, where Shaw and one extremely pregnant woman had nearly drowned.

The setting sun flared atop Cummings's shiny head. "So?"

Shaw explained, "Marty Avon told me he'd found someone who fit the perfect profile of the Gamer: Brad Hendricks had been spotted at the Quick Byte Café, he was obsessed with *The Whispering Man* and he was offline when the kidnappings occurred."

"You thought he was too perfect." Cummings would not have risen to be Joint Task Force Senior Supervisor Cummings without being shrewd. "Like he was being set up."

"Exactly. His proxy was suddenly shut down and his name conveniently appeared. Oh, Brad was worth checking out as a suspect. And I did. I went to see his parents, went through his room. It was a pretty grim place. But I've searched for plenty of missing teenagers and a lot of their rooms are grim too. I noticed something he had on the wall. It was a chart of his progress through *The Whispering Man*. I realized it was the *game* Brad was obsessed with. Not the violence the game represented.

"That kid had absolutely no desire to get out into the real world—and, frankly, do much of anything, let alone go to the trouble to kidnap anybody."

*The Turtle . . .*

"So I settled on the idea he was most likely innocent. Somebody wanted him to take the fall for killing Henry Thompson. Who? I looked at what Thompson was blogging. We'd already considered the data-mining blog. That turned out to be unlikely. I also considered his story about the high cost of property and rentals in Silicon Valley."

A scowl. "Real estate here? Tell me about it."

"Marty Avon created a syndicate to buy up property and create low-cost housing for workers. Was the syndicate guilty of kickbacks or bribes? Was Thompson onto them? I used LaDonna's account to get into the county and state databases. Avon's syndicate is nonprofit. None of the principals will make a penny on it. There was nothing for Thompson to expose there. Maybe he'd come across another real estate scam but I didn't have any leads there.

"Then I stepped back. I thought about how we got onto Brad Hendricks in the first place. Jimmy Foyle. I remembered that Marty Avon—with Destiny Entertainment—told us that game companies' databases could be hacked easily. Foyle was a talented white hat hacker."

Cummings shook his head and Shaw explained what the term meant.

"I guessed he hacked *The Whispering Man* server and changed Brad's log-in times to make it look like he was out when the crimes occurred. Brad was at the Quick Byte recently, which would link him to Sophie, but nobody'd seen him before. He'd gotten a text from a young woman who said she wanted to meet him there. I'm sure it was Foyle pretending to be her so people would spot Brad, associate him with the café. Then today, since he'd done what he needed to—kill Thompson—he shut off Brad's proxy and we got his address."

"But why kill Thompson?"

"Because his blog about a new revenue source for software companies was going to expose what was really going on."

"What was that?"

"Tony Knight and Jimmy Foyle were using their games to spread false news stories for profit."

# 67.

Shaw said to Cummings, "Earlier, my private eye opened a subscription to the video game *Conundrum*."

He explained that he'd asked Mack to go back and look over broadcasts that appeared in the few minutes before the game loaded. The PI found a number of stories in those broadcasts that were blatantly false, spreading rumors about businesspeople and politicians.

Shaw lifted his phone and paraphrased Mack's notes about several stories that he himself remembered from the past few days: "Congressman Richard Boyd, suicide because of rumors of texting young gay prostitutes. No reports of such activity prior to the 'story' appearing in Knight's game. Boyd's wife had just died and he was reported by family members to be in unstable condition. His death may throw the balance of power in Congress up in the air.

"Arnold Farrow, CEO of Intelligraph Systems, Portland, was forced to step down after rumors he spoke favorably about interring Japanese American citizens during the Second World War. No reports of such incident prior to the story appearing in Knight's game.

"Thomas Stone, Green Party candidate for mayor of Los Angeles, rumored to have been affiliated with eco-terrorists and to have participated in arson and vandalism. He denies it and no charges were filed.

"Senator Herbert Stolt, Democrat-Utah, subject of hate mail campaign for proposing a tax on internet usage. First reported in Knight's game. Stolt denies any such proposal and no record of such a proposal exists."

Shaw tucked his phone away. "Tony Knight's offered his games and add-ons for free, provided you sat through news broadcasts and public service spots. And he didn't dare let Thompson find that out. For three or four years, the company's revenues had been declining. Their one big game—*Conundrum*—wasn't doing well; and Foyle, the designer, couldn't come up with any new ideas. Knight was desperate. He was sort of a player—in the traditional sense of the word. I'd guess he contacted lobbyists, politicians, political action committees, CEOs, floating the idea of offering a platform to broadcast whatever they wanted: lies, rumors, defamatory and phony news stories."

"Video games as a way to get propaganda in front of an audience." Cummings was both appalled and impressed, it seemed.

Shaw added, "A young audience. An impressionable audience. And it goes a lot deeper."

"How so?"

"You got game add-ons for registering to vote. And

there were plenty of suggestions about who to vote for—some subtle, some not so subtle."

He noticed Wiley walk to the car where Foyle was handcuffed in the backseat. He opened the door and bent down, spoke to him.

Cummings said, "And all under the radar. It's just an add-on to a video game. Who'd even think about it? No regulation. No FCC, no Federal Election Commission. All fake news and opinion. How big an audience?"

"Tens of millions of subscribers in the U.S. alone. Enough to sway a national election."

"Jesus."

Shaw and Cummings watched Dan Wiley close the back door of the car. He walked forward, the handsome, unflappable TV cop.

Cummings asked, "He going to talk?"

Wiley: "He looked at me like I was a bug. Then said he wanted a lawyer and that was that."

# 68.

Brad Hendricks was hunched forward, sitting in front of the high-definition computer screen in his basement lair.

The young man, motionless, ears enwrapped in large headphones, typed frantically, yet with dead eyes fixed on the Samsung screen. Nothing existed but the game, which was, Shaw noted without surprise, *The Whispering Man*.

Shaw continued to the basement but stopped at the foot of the stairs, peering at the computer screen.

A window reported that Brad now had eleven objects in his KEEP BAG.

A memory came to Shaw. Ashton had made him, Russell and Dorion prepare GTHO bags, near the back door—the door facing the mountains. The bags—intended, yes, for a get-the-hell-out situation—contained everything you would need to survive for a month or so under even the most extreme circumstances. (When older, Colter had learned the real acronym among surviv-

alists was GTFO. Ashton Shaw would never have con-
doned such language in front of the children.)

Shaw approached, wide and slow.

*Never surprise an animal or a human . . . unless you
need to surprise them for your own survival.*

Brad turned his head, saw Shaw and turned back to
the game.

Subtitles appeared at the bottom of the screen.

THE HYDRAULIC PRESS WILL BE OPENING IN FIVE MINUTES.
GET THROUGH IF YOU CAN. A REWARD AWAITS ON THE
OTHER SIDE.

But, Shaw recalled, the Whispering Man himself was
the coach. The master of the game sometimes helped
you. Sometimes, he lied.

The boy turned his ruddy face to Shaw, pulling off the
headphones and pausing the game. He brushed his
straight, shiny hair from his eyes.

"Brad? Colter Shaw."

He handed the young man the backpack, containing
most of the items he'd taken to Jimmy Foyle.

Peering inside, Brad said, "Never liked *Conundrum*."

"Ads, infomercials."

Brad gave a frown, as if at something so obvious it
hardly needed stating. "No, no. Jimmy Foyle's smart—
*too* smart. We don't need a quadrillion planets. He used
to be good but he forgot what gaming's all about. He
made a game for himself, not for players."

*Fun*, Shaw recalled Marty Avon telling him. A game
has to be fun.

Brad pulled out the disks and drives and arranged them on the desk. He looked affectionately at one as if happy a dog that had wandered out of the yard had now returned.

He arranged them in some harmonious order. "Do you know why silicon is used? Silicon? Used in computer chips?"

"I don't, no."

"There are three types of materials. Conductors let electrons through all the time. Insulators don't let any through. Semiconductors . . . Well, you get it. That's what silicon is. They let electrons through sometimes and not others. Like gates. That's the reason computers work. Silicon's the most common. There's germanium. Gallium arsenide's better. This whole area could have been called Gallium Arsenide Valley." He picked up the headphones. He wanted to get back to the game. The screen pulsed impatiently in its waiting state.

Before he could put them on, though, Shaw asked, "You ever get outside?"

"No. Too much glare on the screen."

Shaw, of course, had meant something else.

"Why don't you grind? On Twitch?"

If Brad was surprised that Shaw knew the term, he gave no indication. The boy offered a smile but a sad one. "That's for the pretty people. In nice rooms. With fun things on the walls and made beds and clean windows. You're on webcam all the time. The subscribers expect that. They expect you to be cool and funny. And talk out your gameplay. I don't do that. It's instinct, the way I play. Only twenty-two people in the world have gotten to

Level 9. I'm one of them. I'm going to get to 10. I'm going to kill the Whispering Man."

"I want to give you something."

No response.

"It's the name of somebody you might want to call."

Still silence. Then the hands lowered the headphones.

"Marty Avon. The CEO of Destiny Entertainment."

Now a flicker of emotion.

"You know him?"

"I do."

"To talk to?"

Shaw found the number on his phone, lifted a pen from Brad's desk and wrote it on a Post-it. He placed the yellow square near an empty yogurt container and five books about *Minecraft* gameplay. "Tell him I wanted you to call. If you're interested in a job, he'll talk to you."

Brad glanced at the slip of paper quickly and his attention wavered to the screen.

Then the headphones were back on. The avatars were in motion. The knives were drawn. Laser guns powered up.

Shaw turned and walked up the stairs. In the living room he glanced at the parents, mother on a couch, stepfather in an armchair, both focused on a crime show on TV.

Without a word, Shaw passed them by and stepped outside. He fired up his dirt bike and rode far too fast through the damp evening.

# 69.

This's him."

Helmet in hand, Colter Shaw was standing in the doorway of Santa Clara Memorial Hospital, the third word in the name ever curious to him in connection with a house of healing because it suggested the place had had its share of failures.

He nodded to the woman who'd just spoken, in a whisper worthy of the Whispering Man. LaDonna Standish.

From her elaborate bed, surrounded by elaborate machines, she continued: "Colter, this is Karen."

He recognized her from the picture on Standish's desk. She was a solid woman, tall and with a farm girl look about her. Her hair, which had appeared blond in the photo, was a vibrating tone of orange-red, two shades brighter than Maddie Poole's.

A pretty girl of about two studied him; she held a stuffed rabbit, made from the same material as her red gingham dress. She had her mother's blue eyes. This would be Gem.

"Hello," Shaw said. He saved his smiles for moments like this—with his nieces, mostly.

The girl waved.

Karen rose and shook Shaw's hand firmly. "Thank you." Her eyes were wide and radiated gratitude.

Shaw sat. He noted flowers and cards and candy and a balloon. He was not a bring-a-present kind of person. Not averse to the idea; he just tended not to think about it. If he came back, maybe he'd bring her a book. That seemed practical; you couldn't do much with balloons.

"What do they say?" He glanced at Standish's vastly bandaged arm and was surprised they'd been able to save the limb. The belly wound was hidden under functional blankets.

"Broken arm, nicked spleen—I'll probably get to keep it. You don't need a spleen, Shaw. You know that?"

He recalled something about that from his father's lectures on emergency medicine in the field.

"If they take it out, you can get infections. My doctor"—she floated away for a moment, the painkillers—"he said the spleen is like a bush league pinch hitter. Not vital but better to have one. I can't believe I fell for that, Shaw. A car horn." A faint smile. "The doctor said you knew what you were doing. You treated gunshots before?"

"I have."

It was one of the first lessons their father gave them in emergency first aid: pressure points, tourniquets, packing wounds. Other advice too:

*Never use a tampon in a bullet wound. People say you ought to. Don't. It'll expand and cause more damage.*

Ashton Shaw was a wealth of wisdom.

"When're you getting sprung?"

"Three, four days."

Shaw asked, "You heard the whole story?"

"Dan told me. It's about disinformation, propaganda, lies, getting the kids to vote . . . and vote certain ways. Starting rumors. Last thing in the world we need now. Destroy lives, careers . . . Lies about affairs, crimes. Bullshit." Standish drifted away, then back. "And Knight?"

"Vanished. They locked down his airplane and detained his minders—conspiracy. But no sign of him."

Which is why a Task Force officer was stationed outside her door.

Karen handed a picture book to Gem, who was growing restless. She'd brought a bag filled with books and toys. Shaw's sister did the same and had taught him the art of distraction for the times he babysat. He didn't do so often but when he was called for duty, he made sure he was prepared.

He knew survivalism under all circumstances.

Then the tears appeared in Standish's eyes.

Karen leaned forward. "Honey . . ."

Standish shook her head. She hesitated. "I called Cummings," she said.

Karen said, "Looks like Donnie's going to administration."

Standish said, "He didn't want to tell me. Not now, when I'm laid up. But I had to know. He said my job's safe. Just no street work. It's policy. He said nobody wounded this bad's ever gone back in the field."

Shaw thought of her plan to get onto the street, which would now apparently be permanently derailed.

Or not. The tears stopped and she roughly wiped her face. There was something in her olive-dark eyes that suggested there would be future conversations with the JMCTF about the topic. His nod said *Good luck*.

Karen said to Shaw, "When Donnie's back home, if you're still here, you'll come for dinner? Or will you be on the road?"

"She's a"—Standish whispered the adjective—"cook." Because her lips didn't move much when she spoke the censored syllables, Shaw assumed they were "kick-ass."

"I'd like that."

Wondering where the stack of his father's documents would lead him in his search for the answer to the secret of October 5. Maybe he'd still be here. Maybe he'd be gone.

They talked for a bit longer and then a nurse came in to change dressings.

Shaw rose and Karen threw her arms around him and whispered once more, "Thank you."

Standish, bleary-eyed, just waved. "I'd do that too. But I don't think . . . you'd appreciate the screaming."

He stepped to the door. Standish whispered, "Hold on, Shaw." Then to her partner, she said, "You bring it?"

"Oh. Yeah." The woman dug into her purse. And handed him a small brown paper bag. He extracted a disk of cheap metal about four inches in diameter. In the center was a five-pointed star embossed with the words:

OFFICIAL

DEPUTY SHERIFF

# 70.

"You're a hero."

This was from she's-sweet-on-you Tiffany.

"TV and everything. Channel 2 said they invited you in for an interview. You didn't respond."

Shaw ordered a coffee and deflected the adoration. He did, however, say, "Was a big help—the video. Thank you."

"Glad for it."

He looked around. The man he was going to meet hadn't yet arrived.

A pause. Tiffany napkin-wiped her hands, looking down. "Just . . . I thought I'd put this out there. I'm off later. Around eleven. That's pretty late, I know. But, maybe, you want to get a bite of dinner?"

"I'm beat."

The woman laughed. "You look it."

True. He *was* tired, to his soul. He'd taken a fast shower at the camper, changed clothes and then headed here. If he hadn't gotten the phone call, he'd be asleep by now.

"And I imagine you're headed out of town pretty soon."

He nodded. Then glanced at the door.

Ronald Cummings pushed through it. He surprised Shaw by nodding with familiarity to Tiffany, who gave him a smile. "Officer. The usual?"

Shaw raised an eyebrow.

The supervisor said to him, "We people get out too . . . Yes, please, the usual, Tiff. How's Madge?"

"Doing well. Still training. I tell her a half triathlon is as good as a whole. She's, like, no it isn't. Kids these days."

She fixed him a latte, or some other frothy concoction, and both Cummings and Shaw sat. Not many free tables. Open laptops were scattered throughout the place like cherry blossoms in April.

Cummings sipped and diligently wiped away his white mustache. "I have to tell you something and I wanted it to be in person."

"I gathered." Shaw drank a bit of his coffee.

Tiffany appeared with what seemed to be an oatmeal cookie. She set it before Cummings.

"You?" she asked Shaw.

"I'm not a sweet guy. Thanks anyway."

A smile, more affectionate than flirtatious.

When she'd walked away, Shaw looked over at the supervisor.

"It's really good. Tiffany makes them herself." He nodded at the cookie.

Shaw said nothing.

"Okay. There's a hold on the operation against

Knight. This, by the way, I am absolutely *not* telling you."

"Hold?"

"There's a warrant, but the feds're sitting on it." Cummings looked around and leaned forward. "It looks like one of Knight's clients—who hired him to break a fake-news story or two—was a lobbyist working for a certain politician. Maybe there's a link to this individual, maybe not. But if Knight's arrested and his name surfaces, then his future plans're derailed. I mean, plans for a trip to Washington. A trip that would last four or eight years."

Shaw sighed. He now understood why the feds had not been at the Elizabeth Chabelle briefing.

Cummings chewed some cookie. "And you're about to ask: What about us? The Task Force or the California B of I. Making a state case against Knight."

"I was."

"We have to stand down too. That word came from Sacramento. Only for twenty-four hours. Make it look like we're marshalling evidence or following up leads or some nonsense. Then we all—feds too—hit his last-known locations. Flashbangs, tanks, big splash."

"By then he'll be on the beach in an extradition-free country."

"Pretty much. We caught one plum—Foyle. And we've closed down his operation."

"And the Whispering Man gets away."

"The . . . Oh, the game. Standish told me you were . . . bothered about Kyle Butler. And Henry Thompson. You wanted Knight arrested."

Or dead.

"You've called in all your favors?"

Cummings had lost interest in his heavy-duty baked good. The coffee too. "Favors I didn't even have. And word is, we sit tight."

"Twenty-four hours?"

The man nodded.

"And there's nothing you can do?"

"I'm sorry. The only way Knight's going to prison is if he strolls into the Task Force with his hands up, says, 'I'm sorry for everything,' and surrenders." He gave a tired smile. "LaDonna told me you do this percentage thing? Well, you and I both know the odds of that happening, now don't we?"

Shaw asked, "You, or the feds, have any idea where Knight is?"

"No, we don't. And I wouldn't tell you if I did." Cummings glanced into Shaw's eyes and must've seen something in them that was troubling. "I know how you feel, but don't do anything stupid here."

"Tell that to Kyle Butler and Henry Thompson." Shaw rose and picked up his helmet and gloves. He nodded to Tiffany and headed for the door.

"Colter," Cummings said. "He's not worth it."

The supervisor said something more but by then Shaw was outside into the cool evening and didn't hear a word.

# 71.

Jimmy Foyle might've been expecting a visitor but he clearly wasn't expecting this one.

He blinked as Colter Shaw walked into the interview room at the Joint Major Crimes Task Force. Coincidentally, it was the room where Shaw and Cummings had had their get-together a day or so ago. To Shaw it felt like ages.

Foyle sat down across from him. While there were rings cemented into the floor, the man wasn't shackled. Maybe the turnkeys had assessed Shaw as being able to deflect an attack.

The designer muttered, "I have nothing to say to you. This is a trick. They want to get a confession. I'm not saying anything." The man's lips tightened.

Shaw had to admit he felt some sympathy for him. What would it have been like to throw your entire life into your art and then, at his young age, to realize that you'd lost your spark? The muse had deserted you?

"This is just for me. What you're going to tell me doesn't go anywhere else."

"I'm not going to tell you anything. Go to hell."

Calmly Shaw said, "Jimmy, you know what I do for a living."

He said uncertainly, "You go after rewards . . . or something."

"That's right. Sometimes it's finding a missing child or a grandfather with Alzheimer's. Mostly, I track down fugitives and escapees. There's a fair number of people I've put into prison. People who're not very happy with me. Now, I checked your incarceration schedule. You'll be in San Quentin until your trial. I've put four prisoners in the Q. If you don't help me, I'm going to talk to a screw or two I know. Those're guards, by the way. You'll learn that soon enough. They'll spread the word that you're a friend of mine and—"

"What?" Foyle stiffened.

Shaw held his hand out, palm first. "Calm, there . . . And I guarantee that word'll spread fast."

"You son of a bitch." He sighed, then leaned forward. "If I say anything, they'll hear." A nod at the ceiling, where presumably hidden microphones were hard at work.

"That's why I'm going to write down the questions and you're going to write down the answers."

He removed from his bag one of his case notebooks and opened it, then he uncapped a pen. It was a cheap, flexible plastic one provided by the guards, who had explained that the Delta Titanio Galassia, with its sharp point, was not a wise implement to take into an interview with a suspected murderer.

# 72.

I t's easy to *not* die," Ashton Shaw is saying to Colter, then fourteen. "Surviving is hard."

His son doesn't bother to ask what he means. The professor always gets to his point.

"Lying on a couch in front of a TV. Sitting in your office typing reports. Walking on the beach. You're avoiding dying . . . Say, hand me another piton."

Even at that age Colter notes the irony in his father's comment about the ease of not dying since they are presently one hundred and twenty feet in the air, on Devil's Notch, a sheer rock face just across the boundary of the Compound.

Colter hands him the piton, and, using the tethered hammer, Ashton whacks the metal spike into a crack, tests it and hooks in the carabiner with a sharp click. Parallel on their course, father and son chalk their hands and move several feet higher. The summit is only ten feet away.

"Not dying isn't the same as being alive. You're only alive when you're surviving. And you only survive when there's a risk there's something you can lose. The more you risk losing, the more you're alive."

Colter waits for this to be translated into a Never rule.

His father says nothing more.

And so this becomes Colter Shaw's favorite advice from his father. Better than all the Never rules put together.

Ashton's words were in Shaw's mind now as he down-shifted the Yamaha YZ450FX bike and pounded along a dirt road on the way to Scarpet Peak, between Silicon Valley and Half Moon Bay. As at Basin Redwoods Park, where Henry Thompson had been murdered, this might have been an old logging trail but was now apparently the means of transit for hikers. He hit fifty-five, caught air, then landed like waterfowl in autumn skimming down to the surface of a lake.

Minutes counted. He twisted the throttle higher.

Soon he came to the clearing. Ten acres of low grass, ringed by pine and leafy trees.

He steered the bike out of the woods and killed the engine. This model of dirt bike—the 499cc version—came with a kickstand, a necessity for a street-legal conversion since you could hardly rest it on its side when you went shopping. He propped the bike up and removed his helmet and gloves.

How crazy was this?

Shaw decided: Doesn't matter. It was inevitable.

*Not dying isn't the same as being alive . . .*

The clearing reminded him of the meadow behind the cabin on the Compound—the place where Mary Dove had presided over her husband's funeral. Ashton had anticipated—one might say overanticipated—his death and had made funeral arrangements long before the fact. His mind was sharp and clever then and rich with a wicked sense of humor. In his instructions he'd written: *It's my wish that Ash's ashes be scattered over Crescent Lake.*

Shaw gazed across the clearing. On the far end of the moonlit expanse were two cat's eyes of windows, glowing yellow. Just dots from here. The illumination was radiating from a vacation cabin, whose location was the information that Shaw had wrung out of Jimmy Foyle.

The jog to the cabin took him no more than five minutes. Thirty yards away he paused, looking for security. There might be cameras, there might be motion sensors. Shaw was relying on speed to his target and the element of surprise.

Tony Knight wouldn't be expecting anyone to come a'calling. After all, he had immunity.

Shaw wondered who the client was, the politician who'd hired Knight's broadcast anchors to spread phony rumors about his opponent and destroy his chances in a forthcoming election. Some senator? A representative?

He drew his Glock and—habit—eased the slide back against the tight spring to confirm a round was chambered, then reholstered the weapon. Crouching, he moved to the front of the rustic cabin, not unlike the one Shaw and his brother and sister had grown up in, though this one was much smaller. The rough-sided house, Nantucket gray, would have three or four bedrooms. There was a separate garage and Shaw could see an SUV and a Mercedes parked out front.

This told Shaw that there were at least two minders

with Knight. The man would be departing via helicopter; an orange wind sock sat nearby in the clearing. Two men would remain behind to drive the cars back.

Smelling pine on the cool, damp air, Shaw crept closer to the cabin, lifted his head briefly and dropped back to cover.

The image he'd seen was of Tony Knight on his mobile, pacing, gesturing with his other hand.

The CEO was dressed in weekend casual. Tan slacks, a black shirt and a dark gray jacket. On his head was a black baseball cap with no logo or team designation. This suggested his departure was imminent. He wasn't alone. There were two minders nearby. They were the same ones who'd abducted him from the floor of the C3 Conference while all eyes were on the pyrotechnic announcement about *Conundrum VI* overhead. One was on his phone and the other watching a tablet, earbud plugged in. He laughed at something.

Shaw waited three long minutes and looked again.

The tableau had not changed.

He circled the building, planting his feet only on pine needles and bare earth, and checked what other rooms he could see into. It appeared that just the three men were inside.

He stepped to the front door and tried the knob. Locked. A window, then.

Except that he never got to a window.

A fourth man now joined the party, walking from the garage with a backpack over his shoulder and a duffel bag in both hands; he was squat and bulky, with a crew cut and long arms. Stopping quickly, he shucked the backpack, dropped the bag and started to reach for his hip. Shaw lunged; the man gave up on the gun—he couldn't get to it in time—and drew back a fist. But he had no target; Shaw dropped his center of gravity, ducked low and executed a passable single-leg takedown, a classic college wrestling move.

The minder was heavy yet he went down hard, flat on his back, gasping, his face contorted. The wind had been knocked from his lungs. Shaw drew his own pistol and kept it pointed toward, but not at, the man.

He wasn't stupid. He nodded quickly. Shaw pocketed the pistol, also a Glock, and patted him down for other weapons. There were none. He powered off the man's phone and took a set of keys. Shaw moved his finger in a circle. The minder nodded again and rolled onto his belly.

Shaw zip-tied his wrists and ankles and turned back to the house.

Key in the lock. He turned it—silent—and, drawing his gun, he opened the door and stepped into the hallway, aromatic with the smells of cooking: onions and grease. A glance around the dim place. The bedrooms, to the left, were dark. He'd have to take a chance on the kitchen. To look inside would expose him—because of a pass-through bar—to the men in the living room. The odds that there were five men here?

Small.

So, with a two-handed grip on his gun, Shaw stepped fast into the room, where the trio was sitting and pacing.

Knight dropped his phone and the "Jesus Christ!" he uttered was nearly a shout. The minders spun around, starting to stand.

"No. Down."

They complied slowly.

Shaw had noted how each held his phone or tablet. "You." Nodding to one. "Left hand, thumb and forefinger. Weapon out. Pitch it toward me." The other was told to do the same with his right hand.

There was no opportunity here for heroics or clever tactics, only foolishness, and they did as instructed.

Shaw tossed zip ties to them.

"How do we . . ." one began.

Shaw offered a wry glance. "Just figure it out."

Using their teeth to hold and tighten the plastic ties, they bound their own wrists.

Shaw spotted a light panel against the far wall and walked to it, then flipped the switches. The grounds were brilliantly illuminated. Then he stepped to a spot near the kitchen, where he could stand and have complete cover of the room and a view out to the yard.

"Is anyone else here, other than the one tied up outside?"

"Listen, Shaw—"

"Because if there is and he makes a move, he's going to get shot. And that means there might be other shots."

Knight said, "There sure is somebody. And you better . . ."

Shaw looked at one of the minders—the one who'd been enjoying his comedy on the tablet until the interruption. The man shook his head.

Knight growled, "The fuck're you doing?" Odd how anger negates handsome.

"Lift up your jacket and shirt and turn around, then empty your pockets."

After a defiant moment the CEO did. No weapons.

Shaw picked up the man's phone and disconnected the call.

"How'd you find me? Was it Foyle? That fucker. Well, so what? You can call all the cops you want but nobody's going to touch me. I'm out of the country in an hour. I've got a get-out-of-jail card."

"Sit down, Knight."

"I'm sorry that kid got killed. Kyle Butler. That wasn't supposed to happen." The man's eyes were widening with fear as he looked from Shaw's weapon to his cold eyes.

"I don't care. He did get killed. And so did Henry Thompson. And Elizabeth Chabelle and her baby almost died too."

"Foyle was an idiot to kidnap a pregnant woman." The legendary temper flared and Shaw believed he actually shivered with rage. "So, what is this? You can't turn me in to the cops. You going to shoot me? Just like that? Vengeance is mine—that kind of bullshit? They'll figure out it was you. You won't get away with it."

"Shh," Shaw said, tired of the sputtering. He withdrew his cell phone, unlocked it, opened an email and set the cell on the coffee table. He stepped back, keeping his aim near Knight. "Read that."

Knight picked up the unit—his hands were none too steady—and read. He looked up. "You've got to be kidding."

# 73.

As Shaw steered the dusty, streaked Yamaha into the entrance of the Westwinds RV Center in Los Altos Hills, Colter Shaw noticed a sign he hadn't been aware of earlier. It was some distance from the park, maybe two football fields' worth, but the stark black letters on a white billboard were easily read: MAKE YOUR NEW HOME SILICONVILLE . . . VISIT OUR WEBSITE NOW!

To think he'd suspected the toy aficionado of being the Whispering Man . . .

He drove along Apple Road. Anywhere else in the world, the name would refer to the fruit. Here, of course, in SV, it meant only one thing and that bordered on the religious. It would be like Vatican Drive or Mecca Avenue. He turned right, on Google Way, toward his Winnebago and, arriving there, braked more harshly than he'd intended. He killed the engine. After a pause he removed his helmet and gloves.

He joined Maddie Poole, who was leaning against her car's front fender, drinking a Corona. Without a word, she reached into the car and picked up another bottle. She opened it with a church key and handed the beer to him.

They nodded bottlenecks each other's way and sipped.

"Damn. You saved somebody else, Colt. Heard the news."

He glanced toward the camper and she nodded. The night was chill. He unlocked the door and they walked inside. He hit the lights and got the heat going.

Maddie said, "She was pregnant. She going to name the baby after you?"

"No."

Maddie clicked her tongue. "Hey, was that the bullet hole from the other night? By the door?"

Shaw tried to recall. "No, that was a while ago. In better light you can see it's rusty."

"Where'd it happen?"

You'd think someone takes a shot at you, you'd recall instantly where it was, along with the weather, the minute and hour and what you were wearing.

Probably that job in Arizona.

"Arizona."

"Hmm."

Maybe New Mexico. Shaw wasn't sure so he let the neighboring state stand.

She smoothed her dark purple T-shirt, on which only the letters AMA and, below, ALI were visible beneath a thin leather jacket. She wore pale blue sandals, shabby, and he noticed a ring on her right middle toe, a red-and-gold band. Had it been there the other night? That's right, he couldn't tell. The lights had been out.

She looked around the camper. With her attention on a map mounted to a wall near the bedroom—a portion of the Lewis and Clark Expedition—Shaw quickly slipped his Glock back into the spice cabinet resting place.

"I never asked, Colt. What's with the reward thing? Funny way to make a living." She turned back.

"Suits my nature."

"The restless man. In body and mind. So, I got your message." She took a long sip of her beer. There was silence, if you didn't count the whoosh of traffic, audible even here, inside. In Silicon Valley, always, always traffic. Shaw recalled the Compound on windless days. A thousand acres filled with a clinging silence, which could be every bit as unsettling as a mountain lion's growl. He noticed the fingers of Maddie's left hand—her free hand—were twitching. Then he realized, no, they were air-keyboarding. She didn't seem aware of it.

Shaw said, "I drove by the house. You were gone."

"Conference is over. All us gaming nomads, packing up our tents. I'm getting a head start on the drive south." The hour was late, 11 p.m., but for grinders like Maddie Poole it was midafternoon. "I'm not much of a phone person. Thought I'd come by in person."

Shaw sipped. "Wanted to apologize. That's all. Not worth much. It never is. Still . . ."

She was looking over another map.

Shaw said, "I had a thought. About our organization."

"Organization?"

"Renaming it," he said. "From the Never After Club to the On Rare Occasions Club. What do you think?"

She finished her beer.

"Trash is there," he said, pointing.

She dropped the bottle in. "Couple years ago a friend of mine, she told me she was breaking up with this guy. I knew him pretty well too. She told me he hit her and pushed her down a flight of stairs. She went all drama on me, sobbing. So, naturally, I drove over to his place and beat the crap out of him. I mean, what else was there to do?"

As good an answer as any.

"Only, it turned out, she lied to me. Can you believe it? He dumped her and she wasn't used to that. She was spreading rumors that he was abusive so it wouldn't look so bad for her." A shake of her head. "And you know what? If I'd thought about it, I'd've known in my heart that boy'd never do any such thing. I jumped too fast. After, I tried to patch it up but, uh-uh, didn't work."

Shaw said, "No reset button."

"No reset."

"Anyway, Colt, even if you hadn't called I was going to come by. I've got this rule. Life's short. Never miss a chance to say hello to somebody, never miss a chance to say good-bye . . . Hey, look at that. I finally got a smile out of you. Okay, better hit the road."

They embraced, briefly, and then she walked out the door. He watched her through the window as she slid into her car. A moment later she left two black, wavy tread marks, accompanied by ghosts of blue smoke, as she fishtailed onto Google Way and vanished.

Shaw let the curtain fall back, thinking: Never did find out what the tattoo meant.

# 74.

The story was already on the air.

Shaw had turned on the TV to a local station.

> *Tony Knight, the cofounder of Knight Time Gaming, has turned himself in to the Joint Major Crimes Task Force headquarters in Santa Clara. Knight was wanted for questioning in connection with the kidnappings and murders that terrorized Silicon Valley this past weekend. James Foyle, the other cofounder of the company and its chief game designer, was arrested earlier tonight . . .*

Shaw shut down the feed. That was all he needed to know. He wondered what conversations were going on in the offices of law enforcers around the state and in Washington at the moment. He suspected heated words, high blood pressures and very worried hearts.

He could still hear Knight's voice in the cabin off the clearing as he stared at the screen of Shaw's phone.

"You've got to be kidding me."

Shaw had nodded at the mobile. "Tomorrow morning at six a.m. that gets uploaded to the web and sent to fifty newspapers and feeds around the world."

**$1 MILLION REWARD**

FOR INFORMATION LEADING TO THE WHEREABOUTS OF
ANTHONY ("TONY") ALFRED KNIGHT,
WANTED FOR MURDER, KIDNAPPING, ASSAULT
AND CONSPIRACY IN CALIFORNIA.

Below were a number of pictures of Knight—some Photoshopped to represent him with a changed appearance—and other information about him that might lead a reward seeker to him. There were details too on how to claim the money.

"I don't . . . I don't understand. Who's offering this? Not the police? They agreed . . ." He fell silent, probably deciding it best not to shine a light on the deal he'd arranged.

"I'm offering it," Shaw told him.

"You?"

He was personally funding the reward through one of his LLCs. When he said he made his living by seeking rewards, a more accurate way to phrase it was that he made *some* of his living with rewards. Colter Shaw had resources beyond that.

"Let me explain something to you, Knight. As soon as that hits the news, hundreds of people're going to be making plans to track you down. All over the world. Wherever you think you might want to go. No extradition laws? That doesn't mean a thing. A mercenary'll find you, smuggle you back to the States and claim the money.

"I've crossed paths with a lot of these folks and they aren't the nicest kids on the block. For that kind of money, some'll be thinking: bounty. And even if the announcement doesn't say dead or alive, that's what they're reading. You'll spend every minute of every day for the rest of your life looking over your shoulder."

The man glanced at his helpless minders in disgust.

Shaw said, "Only I can stop that from being uploaded. If anything happens to me, six o'clock, off it goes to the world."

"Fuck."

"You've got your friends in high places, Tony. Your clients. If they can put a hiatus on the investigation, they can put in a recommendation for a sentence. Something less than life. Now, put the phone down."

He read the announcement once more and set the iPhone on the table.

"Back up."

When he had, Shaw retrieved and pocketed the unit.

"Six a.m., Knight. Your move."

Shaw had backed out of the house, crouched to make sure the minder on the ground was all right—he was—and jogged back to the far side of the clearing to retrieve his bike.

He now stepped outside and secured the Yamaha to the rack on the rear of the camper, locked it in place and returned. Just as he walked inside his phone hummed and he glanced at the screen.

He'd been expecting a call from this number, though the caller was a surprise.

"Colter? Dan Wiley."

"Dan."

"Say, people ever call you Colt?"

"Some do."

"You know Colt's a brand of gun."

"So I've heard," he said. Like the one sitting under his bed at the moment.

Shaw glanced out the window at the charcoal tread marks Maddie's feisty car had left on Google Way. Had an image of meeting her in the Quick Byte. He filed it away in the same room where he kept the images of Margot Keller. He closed the door.

"So. Have some news. It's about Tony Knight. Ron Cummings—you remember him?"

"I do."

"He asked me to give you a call and tell you."

"Go on."

"Just thought you'd want to hear this. Well, we—at the Task Force—were kind of wrangling with the feds about an op to find Knight?"

"Were you?"

"Yes, we were. And nobody was getting anywhere. Then all of a sudden, who walks into our office and surrenders?"

"Knight?"

"That's right. We booked him in on homicide, kidnapping and, everybody's favorite, conspiracy. Nobody knows why the hell he gave it up."

"Good news, then." He wasn't surprised that Cummings had delegated to Wiley the task of calling Shaw. Joint Task Force Senior Supervisor Cummings would want to distance himself from all things Knight. He wondered if the meeting at the Quick Byte had been a way of suggesting that Shaw might want to take matters into his own hands while decidedly warning him not to. This one clocked in at fifty-fifty.

Wiley said, "Oh, a whole n'other thing. We're getting Crime Scene stuff in. And I was looking over ballistics. The slugs that killed Kyle and that hit LaDonna were from the same gun, that Glock we found on Foyle. But the bullets the metro CS team dug out of the wall and tree near your camper yesterday came from a Beretta, probably. A forty-cal. You find any other weapon Foyle might've had?"

The beer bottle stopped halfway to Shaw's mouth. "No, Dan. Never did . . . I've got to go. I'll be in touch."

He disconnected without hearing Wiley's farewell.

Because Shaw doubted very much that Foyle had another gun—and even if he did, why would he switch from one to the other and back again?

No, somebody else broke into the Winnebago last night.

Three steps across the camper and he was pulling open the spice cabinet door, thrusting his hand through the jars of sage, oregano and rosemary for his Glock.

Which was no longer there. It had been removed while he was outside affixing the Yamaha to the camper.

Shaw heard the door to his bedroom open. He turned, expecting to see exactly what he saw: the intruder stepping forward, holding the Beretta pistol in his hand.

What he hadn't been expecting to see, though, was that his visitor was the man from Oakland—Rodent, the one who'd been carting around a Molotov cocktail, apparently hell-bent on committing a hate crime, burning down the graffitied homage to early political resistance. Shaw now understood that his mission was a very different one.

# 75.

S it, Shaw. Make yourself comfy."

The same voice. High. Amused. Confident. Clearly Minnesota or Dakota.

Shaw tried to make sense, then just gave up.

He sat.

Rodent pointed to the table. "Unlock that phone of yours and set it down. Thank'ee much."

Shaw did.

The man picked it up, his hand encased in black cloth gloves, with light-colored finger pads, which he used to swipe his way through the iPhone. His eyes flicked from the screen to Shaw—up, down, fast.

Yes, Jimmy Foyle was the one following Shaw at San Miguel Park and who delivered the eerie stencil drawings of the Whispering Man. That didn't mean, of course, that someone else wasn't conducting surveillance too.

*Never focus too narrowly.*

Rodent asked, "This last call, incoming. Who was it from?"

Easily discovered. "Joint Major Crimes Task Force. Silicon Valley."

"Well, some kettle of fish that is, don'tcha know."

"Doesn't concern you. It was about the kidnapping case I was involved in."

Rodent nodded. He flipped through the log, surely noting the time stamp, which indicated that Shaw disconnected before Rodent had shown up with his fine Italian gun. Rodent set the phone down.

"Where're my weapons?" Shaw asked.

"Snug in my pocket. That little tiny thing. And the Python too. Under the bed. That's smart. And a fine piece of gun making, that model is, as I'm sure you appreciate."

Confused, yes. But one thing Shaw understood: the man wasn't here because he was pissed off Shaw had ruined his bonfire in Oakland. That attempted arson had been about creating a diversion so that Rodent could break into Shaw's Winnebago.

He probably *had* uttered the words, during the confrontation, "Why'd you do that, Shaw?"

The further question—what did he want in the camper?—was not yet answerable.

In the light within the camper Shaw could see the man's pocked face more clearly than the other day. He noted too a scar on the side of his neck, in roughly the same position as the one on Shaw. Rodent's wound had been more serious and the scar looked like the twin disfigurement caused by a grazing bullet: troughing skin and burning with the slug's heat at the same time.

The man was too much of a professional to hold his own pistol out toward Shaw. A fast person might slap aside the gun with one hand and strike flesh with the other. Shaw had done so more than once. No, Rodent kept the glossy black weapon close to his side, the muzzle trained forward.

Shaw said, "You broke in last night, dent puller and crowbar. Sloppy. To make it look like it was some meth-head. Tonight you were subtler."

Rodent had picked the repaired locks with a deft touch. Shaw, who had occasion to break into secure locations, was impressed.

The first time, Rodent had looked for whatever it was he'd wanted—and hadn't found it. He had done reconnaissance, finding the lockbox—which would take heavy equipment to remove or open—and the location of the weapons. Then waited until tonight to return for a visit in person—hiding until Maddie Poole had left.

With his left hand, Rodent fished in a pocket and extracted jingling handcuffs. These he tossed to Shaw, who dropped them on the floor.

A pause.

"Lookie, got to establish a rule or two."

Shaw said, "No cuffs. I don't know karate. You have my only firearms. I do know how to throw knives but I only have Sabatiers for cooking in the camper and they're badly balanced."

"Rules, don'tcha know. For your safety and my peace of mind. Now, yessir, yessir, I've killed a soul'r two, though mostly in self-defense. Death isn't helpful . . . What's that word? Death's counterproductive. It draws attention, makes my life complicated. And that, I don't need. So I'm going to kill you? Nope. Unless, naturally, something you do requires me to kill you.

"I do hurt people. I like hurting people. And I hurt in ways that change them. Forever. A man who loves art, blind him. A woman who loves music, her ears. You can see where this is going. We know about you, Shaw. You wouldn't do very well hanging out in a wheelchair the rest of your life, don'tcha know."

Shaw gazed at the wiry man and kept his face a mask, while his heart was slamming in his chest, his mouth dry as cotton.

*Never reveal fear to a predator* . . .

"This is a forty-caliber gun. That's a big old bullet. Which I'm guessing you're familiar with."

Shaw was.

"Elbows, ankles, then knees. There'd be virtually nothing left to repair. And I've got this thing that'll make the sound like a cough. Another one over your mouth for the screams. So. Put the cuffs on. I do not need to worry about you, Shaw. Cuffs or elbow?" He took wads of black plasticized cloth from his pocket. Some kind of silencer?

Shaw retrieved the bracelets and put them on.

"Now, we'll do our business and I'll be on my way. Is the envelope in the lockbox in your bedroom?"

"The . . . ?"

Patiently: "I know you're not being—what's that word?—coy. You're in the dark here. I want the envelope your father's friend Eugene Young hid in the School of Sociology archives at Berkeley. That you stole a couple days ago."

Shaw tried but couldn't process the change in direction.

"No, no, don't wan'ta hear 'Don't know what you're

talking about.' We know you called Young at home, not knowing he was dead. Now, there's a look for you, Shaw. You usually give the great stone face. The answer to your question: we had a tap on his line."

They'd been monitoring his father's colleague, and now his widow, for fifteen years? And this was accompanied by a queasy sense of invasion. They'd been monitoring him as well.

Why on earth?

Rodent said, "You found out about the envelope. Looking through Daddy's old stuff, maybe. And it sent you to the Sociology archives, where you 'borrowed it.'" His face tightened into a rat smile. "Sociology. My goodness. One of the few places—really few—we didn't look. Because why would we? A subject your daddy had no interest in."

"I—"

"Remember, don'tcha know. None of that 'confused' stuff."

How had Rodent found out about the theft at Berkeley? Shaw thought back. He'd told Young's widow that he was staying at an RV camp in Oakland. Would have been easy to trace him to Carole's. Rodent had followed Shaw to Berkeley. Shaw hadn't seen him tailing. Because it's a good rule when riding a motorcycle to look ahead and to the side, not behind, flashing lights being the exception.

However, such logistics faded from Shaw's thoughts. More important: the word *we*, mysterious documents and a fifteen-year-old wiretap. Shaw realized that his father had maybe not been as crazy or as paranoid as he seemed.

*Never dismiss conspiracies too quickly . . .*

Shaw thought back to the letter Eugene Young had

written to his father. He asked Rodent, "So where's Braxton now?"

Touché. A wrinkle in the pasty flesh between Rodent's eyes. "What do you know about her?"

Well, one thing more than he'd known a few seconds ago.

*Her* . . .

The man's mouth tightened slightly. He'd been gamed. He said nothing else about Ms. Braxton, whoever she might be.

"Lockbox. Let's look inside."

"Just a trap. Empty." Being cuffed defeated Shaw's tactic of disarming the intruder when he reached in and broke a finger. He thought of the irony, given his nickname for the intruder. The trap was a big one, meant for rats.

"I guessed. Could be a reverse trap. Not sure that makes sense but you get the idea."

Shaw opened it.

Rodent'd already pulled out a small halogen flashlight, which he now used to peer into the safe. He seemed impressed with the booby trap.

Back into the kitchenette. "Where's the envelope? Or we start with the pain. This is entirely up to you."

"My wallet."

"Wallet? . . . On the floor. Facedown."

Shaw did as told and felt the man lay something soft against the back of his knee, then apply pressure.

"It's the weapon."

Shaw had guessed. It must be some kind of truly magic cloth if it could dull the sound of a .40 caliber pistol.

The man extracted the wallet and rolled Shaw over and upright.

"Behind the driver's license."

Rodent fished. "A claim check for a FedEx store on Alameda?"

"That's it. They have the original of my father's documents and two copies."

It was in the strip mall that also contained the Salvadoran restaurant of the other day, with the coffee from Potrero Grande. After he'd left, on his way to Frank Mulliner's, he'd taken the manuscript in to have the copies made. He'd decided to leave the job there for a few days just in case the police, at the behest of the Sociology Department, came a'calling. Plausible deniability.

"Any other copies?"

"None that I made."

Eyes leaving Shaw for only a second at a time, Rodent extracted his phone and placed a call, explaining to whoever was on the other end about the FedEx store. He recited the claim number. He disconnected.

"It's closed now," Shaw said.

Rodent smiled. Silence, as he sent a text, presumably to someone else. His eyes scanned Shaw as if, were he to look away for a whole second, his captive would strike like a snake.

Finally, Shaw could wait no longer. He said, "October fifth. Fifteen years ago."

Rodent paused, looking up from his phone, not a twitch of surprise in his eyes. His voice was no longer high as a taut violin string as he said, "We didn't kill your father, Shaw."

Shaw's heart was thudding for reasons that had nothing to do with the fact that he was looking down the barrel of a large pistol.

"This is all a big soup of a mystery to you, that's pretty clear. And it should stay that way. I'll tell you this: Ashton's death was a . . . problem . . . for us. Pissed us off as much as you . . . Well, okay. That's not fair . . . But you get my drift."

Rodent texted some more.

Shaw was dismayed. His heart sank. Because this meant his nightmare had come true: his brother, Russell, was their father's killer. He closed his eyes briefly. He could hear his brother's voice as if the lanky man were in the room with them.

*He's taught us how to survive. Now we have to survive him . . .*

Russell had committed the murder to save his siblings—and his mother too. She and Ashton had been virtually inseparable ever since they met forty years ago in the Ansel Adams Wilderness on the Pacific Crest, a National Scenic Trail extending from the Mexican border to Canada. Yet as his mind dissolved, the year or so before his death, Ashton grew suspicious of his wife too, occasionally thinking she was part of the conspiracy, whatever that was.

And what if saving his siblings and mother wasn't the only motive? Shaw had long wondered too if there was a darker one. Had Russell's resentment finally boiled over? Dorie and Colter were very young when the family moved. Neither remembered much, if anything, about life in civilization. Russell was ten; he'd had time to experience the frenetic, marvelous San Francisco Bay Area.

He'd made friends. Then, suddenly, he was banished to the wilderness.

Angry all those years, never saying anything, the resentment building.

*Russell was the reclusive one . . .*

Rodent lowered his phone. "For what it's worth, it was an accident."

Shaw focused.

"Your father. We wanted him alive, Braxton wanted him dead—but not yet, not till she had what she wanted. She sent somebody to, well, talk to him about the documents."

Talk. Meaning: torture.

"Near as we can piece it together, your father knew Braxton's man was on his way to your Compound. Ashton tipped to him and led him off, was going to kill him somewhere in the woods. The ambush didn't work. They fought. Your father fell.

"That was the second time Braxton's man screwed up, so he's no longer among the living—if it's any consolation." Then Rodent tilted his head and gave a faint smile. "The first time was he got kicked off the property by some kid. A teenager. A kid who drew down on him, some old revolver . . . My goodness, would that've been you, Shaw?"

*You're kind of like a* Deliverance *family, aren't you?*

The hunter . . . That's what he had been doing there, gunning for his father. Ashton Shaw, who—everybody believed—possessed a mind so troubled it invented spies and forces set against him.

Ashton Shaw, who had been right all along.

Oh, Russell . . .

Colter Shaw had never felt his brother's absence more than at this moment. Where are you?

And why have you vanished?

He said, "You know a lot. What about my brother, Russell? Where is he?"

"Lost his trail years ago. Europe."

Overseas . . . This surprised Shaw. Then he wondered why that should, since he'd had virtually no contact since the funeral. Paris was no more far-fetched than the Tenderloin in San Francisco or a tract house in Kansas City.

"What's this all about?"

Rodent answered, "I told you. Not your concern, don'tcha know."

"What *is* my concern is Braxton. Accident or not. She's responsible."

"No, that's none of your concern either. And, believe me, you don't want it to be your concern."

Shaw wondered where the facial pocks had come from. Youthful acne? An illness later in life? Rodent had the wiry build and staccato glances of a military man or soldier of fortune. Maybe a gas attack?

Rodent's phone hummed. Lifted it to his ear. "Yes . . . Okay. Back at the place."

The FedEx caper had apparently been successful.

He disconnected. "Alrighty, then." He put away the black silencing handkerchief and, moving back to the far side of the camper, slipped his Beretta away. "I'll leave the cuff keys under your car, the Glock and the Colt in the trash can by the front entrance. Don't try to find us. For your own sake, don'tcha know."

# 76.

Fifteen minutes of contortions on unforgiving blacktop to fish the keys out from under the Malibu with his feet. The duration of the discomfort expanded because he needed to field questions from a ten-year-old boy.

"What'chu doing, mister? That's funny."

"Got an itch on my back."

"You do not."

After freeing his wrists, it took another five minutes to find the Glock and Colt. He was particularly irritated that Rodent had dropped them in a trash can containing the remnants of a Slurpee. Shaw would have to strip both weapons and apply heavy dosages of Hoppe's cleaner to remove the cherry-flavored syrup.

Back in the camper, he prescribed a Sapporo beer to dull the pain from the pulled thigh and neck muscles. Then he transferred his contacts, photos and videos from his iPhone to his computer, checked them for viruses and placed the mobile in a plastic bag and took a hammer to it. He texted the new number to his mother at the Compound, his sister and Teddy and Velma.

He then dialed Mack's number in D.C.

"Hello?" the woman's sultry voice said.

"I'll be on burners till I get a new iPhone."

"'K."

Charlotte McKenzie was six feet tall, with a pale complexion and long brown hair, her brows elegantly sculpted. During the day she wore a stylish but dull-colored suit, cut to conceal her weapon if she was wearing her weapon, and flats, though not because of her height; her job occasionally required her to run and when it did she had to run fast. Shaw had no clue what she'd be wearing now, presumably in bed. Maybe boxers and a T. Maybe a designer silk negligee.

Shaw loved the way she made lobbyists cry, the way she sheltered whistle-blowers, the way she found facts and figures that, to anyone else, were as invisible as cool spring air.

Those who knew both of them wondered, Shaw had heard, why they'd never gotten together. Shaw occasionally did too, though he knew that, like his heart, Mack's was accessed only by negotiating an exceedingly complex and difficult ascent, rather like Dawn Wall on El Capitan in Yosemite.

"Need some things," he said.

"Ready."

"There's a picture on its way. I need facial recognition. Probably a California connection but not certain." From his computer he sent her an email containing an attachment of a screenshot of Rodent from the video he'd taken during the Molotov cocktail incident.

A moment later: "Got it. On its way." Mack would be sending it to a quarter million dollars' worth of facial recognition software running on a supercomputer.

"Be a minute or two."

A pause, during which clicks intervened. Mack made and received her phone calls with headset and stalk mic so she could knit. She quilted too. In anyone else these would jar with her other hobbies—of wreck scuba diving and extreme downhill skiing. With Mack, they were elegantly compatible.

"Something else. I'll need everything you have on a Braxton. Probably last name. Female, forties to sixties. She might've been behind my father's death."

The only response was "B-R-A-X-T-O-N?"

In the years he'd worked with her Mack had registered not a single breath of surprise at anything he asked her to do.

"That's it." He thought back to the note that Eugene Young had written to his father:

*Braxton is alive!*

"May have been an attempted hit on her fifteen years ago."

This introduced the unsettling thought that his father was a member of a murderous conspiracy too.

"Anything else?"

He thought about asking for the address of one Maddie Poole, a grinder girl who lived somewhere in or around Los Angeles.

"No. That'll do it."

*Click, click, click.* Then silence and a different tap— that of a computer keyboard.

"Got him on facial recognition."

"Go ahead."

"Ebbitt Droon." She spelled it for him.

Shaw said, "*That's* a name, for you."

"I'm sending you a picture."

Shaw reviewed the image on his screen. A twenty-something version of Rodent.

"That's him."

*Droon?*

"His story?"

Mack said, "Virtually no internet presence but enough fragments that tell me he—or, more likely, some IT security pro—scrubs his identity off the 'net regularly. He missed a pic I found in an old magazine article about vets. It was a JPEG of the page, not digitized, so a bot would miss it. Boyhood in upper Midwest, military—Army Rangers—then discharged. Honorable. Vanished from public records. I sent the one-twenty to someone. They'll keep looking."

An enhanced facial recognition search—based on one hundred and twenty facial points, double the usual. That "someone" would probably mean a security agency of some sort.

Mack said, "Now. Second question. Braxton, female. Nothing. That wasn't much to go on. I can keep searching. I'll need people."

"Do it. Take what you need from the business account."

"'K."

They disconnected.

Colter Shaw stretched back on the banquette. Another sip of Sapporo.

*What's this all about?*

From a stack of old bills—in which he kept his important documents—he extracted the note Professor Eugene Young had sent his father. He'd hidden it in a resealed power company envelope.

*Ash:*

*I'm afraid I have to tell you Braxton is alive! Maybe headed north. Be CAREFUL. I've explained to everybody that inside the envelope is the key to where you've hidden everything.*

*I put it in 22-R, 3rd Floor.*

*We'll make this work, Ash. God bless.*

—Eugene

The two Cal professors, his father and Eugene Young, were involved in something obviously dangerous, along with "everybody," whoever they might be. Rodent's side wanted Ashton alive; Braxton's people wanted him— presumably the others too—dead. But only after finding the envelope.

The stack of pages was the key to something that his father had hidden somewhere. He went back to his notebook and skimmed through the pages he'd jotted at the Salvadoran café. Precious little. He found only a notation of the pages whose corners had been turned down.

*37, 63, 118 and 255.*

He hadn't bothered at that time to jot their contents.

He tried to recall: an article from the *Times*, one of his father's incoherent essays . . . Wasn't one a map?

Staring at the numbers, trying to recall.

Then it struck him. There was something familiar about the numbers. What was it?

Colter Shaw sat upright. Was it possible?

*37, 63, 118 and 255* . . .

He rose and found his map of the Compound, the one LaDonna Standish had been looking over, on which he'd pointed out the climb he had planned when he visited his mother.

Spreading the unfolded chart in front of him, he ran his finger down the left side, then along the top. Longitude and latitude.

The coordinates, 37.63N and 118.255W, were smack in the middle of the Compound.

In fact they delineated a portion of the caves and forest on Echo Ridge.

The man of few smiles smiled now.

His father had hidden something there, obviously something important—worth dying for. And he'd left the envelope as a key to its whereabouts. The caves of Echo Ridge.

*Bears in the big ones, snakes in the smaller* . . .

The coordinates didn't pinpoint a very specific place; without other degrees in the numbers, they defined an area about the size of a suburban neighborhood. Even if Rodent and his crew made the deduction as to what the numbers represented—quite unlikely—they would never find what Ashton had hidden. Shaw could. He'd know the man's habits, his trails. His cleverness.

On his burner, he took a picture of the coordinates,

encrypted the image, sent Mack and his former FBI agent friend, Tom Pepper, a copy, telling each to keep it safe.

Then he ripped the sheet from his notebook and soaked it in the sink until it turned to pulp.

What did you hide, Ashton? What is this all about?

With his Colt Python in his jacket pocket, he opened another beer and, holding it in one hand and a bag of peanuts in the other, walked outside. Not in the mood for conversation from neighbors curious about the recent O.K. Corral scene at his camper, he carried a lawn chair to the back, set it down and dropped into it.

The chair was his favorite, upholstered in the finest of brown-and-yellow plastic strips, unreasonably comfortable. This spot in the RV camp offered a pleasant view: waving grass and what might pass for a stream meandering by on its way through never-sleeps Silicon Valley. He kicked his shoes off. The grass was spongy, the sound of the water seductive and the air rich with eucalyptus scent. If a crazy man with the face of a rat and an impressive Italian gun hadn't just threatened life and limb, Shaw might very well have spent the night in his sleeping bag here. Clearing the senses by passing dusk to dawn this way in the forest. Or riding a dirt bike at top speed. Or roped onto a ledge five hundred feet up a cliff face. These were perhaps acts of madness. To Colter Shaw, they were an occasional necessity.

Half a beer and thirteen peanuts later, his phone hummed.

"Teddy," Shaw said. "What're you doing up at this hour?"

"Velma couldn't sleep. Algo spotted something you might be interested in."

"Hey, Colter."

Shaw said to the woman, "Mulliner'll start sending the checks in the next month or so."

"Plural?" Velma said. "Did I hear plural checks? You didn't do installments again?"

"He's good for it."

Teddy said, "Made the news here, even. Saving that pregnant lady. And you caught the Gamer to boot. Don't you just love the media, coming up with names like that?"

Shaw didn't tell him that the moniker had been invented not by a news anchor but by a diminutive police detective whose married name was derived from a Pilgrim—and a famous one at that.

"What've you got?" Shaw asked. Now that he knew his father's documents were smoke and mirrors, there was no reason to remain in the Bay Area.

Teddy asked, "You inclined to go to Washington State?"

"Maybe."

Velma said, "Hate crime. A coupla kids went on a spree and painted swastikas on a synagogue and a coupla black churches. Set one church on fire. It wasn't empty. A janitor and a lay preacher ran out and got themselves shot up. Preacher'll be okay, the janitor's in intensive care. Might not wake up. The boys took off in a truck and haven't been seen since."

"Who's the offeror?"

"Well now, Colter, that's what makes it interesting. You've got yourself a choice of two rewards. One's for fifty thousand—that's joint state police and the town. The other's for nine hundred."

"Not nine hundred thousand, I'm assuming."

"You're a card, Colt," Velma offered.

Shaw sipped more beer. "Nine hundred. That's what one of the boy's families scraped together?"

"They're sure he didn't do it. The whole town thinks otherwise but Mom and Dad and Sis are sure he was kidnapped or forced to drive the getaway car. They want somebody to find him before the police or some civilian with a gun does."

"I'm hearing something else," Shaw said.

Teddy replied, "We heard Dalton Crowe's going after it—the fifty K reward, of course."

Crowe was a dour, hard-edged man, in his forties. He had grown up in Missouri and, after a stint in the Army, had opened a security business on the East Coast. He found that he too was restless by nature and closed the operation. He now worked as a freelance security consultant and mercenary. And, from time to time, he too sought rewards. Shaw knew this about him because the men had had several conversations over the years. Their paths had crossed in other ways, Crowe being responsible for the scar on Shaw's leg.

Their philosophies about the profession differed significantly. Crowe rarely went after missing persons; he sought only wanted criminals and escapees. If you gun down a fugitive using a legal weapon and in self-defense, you still get the reward. This was Crowe's preferred business model.

"Where're we talking?"

"Little town, Gig Harbor, near Tacoma. I'll send you the particulars, you want."

"Do that." Shaw added that he'd think about it, thanked them and disconnected.

He tucked in the earbud and called up a playlist of

tunes by the acoustic guitarist Tommy Emmanuel on his music app.

A sip of beer. A handful of peanuts.

He was thinking of the options: the nine-hundred-dollar reward in Tacoma, Washington, for tracking down perpetrators of a hate crime. No, he reminded himself.

*Never judge without the facts . . .*

Two suspects who'd allegedly defaced religious buildings and shot two men. Maybe supremacists, maybe a love triangle, maybe a dare, maybe an innocent boy taken hostage by a guilty one, maybe a murder for hire under the guise of a different crime.

We've certainly seen that lately, haven't we?

The other option: Echo Ridge, searching for the secret treasure.

So. Gig Harbor? Or Echo Ridge?

Shaw took a quarter from his pocket, a fine disk, with its profile of greatness and its regal bird.

He flipped it into the air and it glistened as it spun, a sphere in the blue glow of the streetlight lording over Google Way.

In his mind Shaw called it: Heads, Echo Ridge. Tails, Gig Harbor.

By the time the silver disk came to rest in the sandy soil beside his lawn chair, though, Colter Shaw didn't bother to look. He picked up the coin and pocketed it. He knew where he was going. The only things to figure out were what time he would leave in the morning and what was the most efficient route to get him to his destination.

# Author's Note

Writing a novel is, for me at least, never a one-person operation. I'd like to thank the following for their vital assistance in shaping this book into what you have just read: Mark Tavani, Tony Davis, Danielle Dieterich, Julie Reece Deaver, Jennifer Dolan and Madelyn Warcholik; and, on the other side of the Pond, Julia Wisdom, Finn Cotton and Anne O'Brien. And my deepest gratitude, as always, to Deborah Schneider.

For those who would like to learn more about the fascinating world of video gaming, you might want to take a look at these works: *Replay: The History of Video Games*, Tristan Donovan; *The Ultimate Guide to Video Game Writing and Design*, Flint Dille and John Zuur Platten; *The Video Game Debate*, Rachel Kowert and Thorsten Quandt; *A Brief History of Video Games*, Richard Stanton; *Game On!: Video Game History from Pong and Pac-Man to Mario, Minecraft, and More*, Dustin Hansen; *Blood, Sweat, and Pixels: The Triumphant, Turbulent Stories Behind How Video Games Are Made*, Jason Schreier; *Console Wars: Sega, Nintendo, and the Battle That Defined a Generation*, Blake J. Harris. You might also enjoy a novel by William Gibson (who coined the term *cyberspace*) and Bruce Sterling: *The Difference Engine*, which mixes fact and fiction in a tale about building a steam-powered computer in 1855.

Oh, and while you're at it, take a look at a thriller called *Roadside Crosses,* in which video games also figure prominently. One of the investigators actually analyzes the body language of an avatar in the game to get insights into a possible murderer. The author is some guy named Deaver.

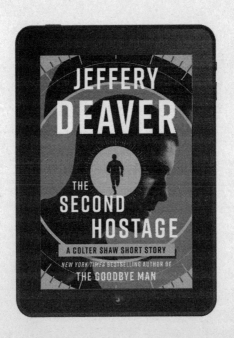

# 1.

O kay. We've got a situation."

The slim, tanned deputy, of upright posture, had just hung up the phone and was addressing the room. "That was Sally, dispatch. There's a hostage situation and gunshots. Kiowa Lake."

The half dozen fellow law enforcers, in tan slacks and dark green shirts, were essentially frozen in time, looking his way. Five men and one woman, ages mid-twenties to mid-forties. Four men were white. The other a light-skinned African American. The woman was indigenous.

Their collective expression was one of surprise.

The words *hostage situation* and *gunshots* were not uttered here very often, Colter Shaw supposed.

He was sitting across the desk from the man who'd uttered them.

Deputy Peter Ruskin—Shaw pegged him about thirty-five—continued, "One of those vacation houses. Renter said a guy pulls up in a car, wanders around the dock, talking to himself, then pulls a gun and breaks in."

"Type of weapon?" one deputy, about Ruskin's age, heavier, asked. H. Garner. The law enforcers all wore name tags. Convenient.

"Unknown. Renter gets into the bathroom, calls nine-one-one. Dispatch heard the door getting kicked in and a voice saying, 'Get into the living room, sit down. Shut up.' Phone went dead. Then neighbors called in and said they heard a shot. Wasn't the hostage got hit, looks like. The taker was aiming out the window."

The Cimarron County Sheriff's Department was functional, typical of dozens of public safety offices Shaw had been in. Small too. Their jurisdiction—in south central Kansas—was large geographically but not in population.

"The renter say if he'd recognized him?"

Ruskin said, "It's a vacation house, Jerry."

J. Briscoe.

"Oh, right. He's from out of state."

"Injuries?" B. Harper asked. The woman. She was short of stature, with broad shoulders. Her stylish glasses bore a faintly blue tint.

"No. Was shooting at a tree, seems. Sally called the sheriff. He's on his way. Okay, let's get to it." Ruskin seemed to have some seniority over the others, even though he was in the middle of the years-on-earth bell curve. He looked over the cramped room. "George, Devon and E.J.'re on patrol. I'll have dispatch get 'em over. I want some of you with me. Who here's run a hostage case? Anybody?"

The deputies regarded one another but said nothing.

Colter Shaw said, "I have."

# 2.

He'd come to Kansas pursuing a reward.

Colter Shaw's profession.

A mother in a suburb of Topeka was offering $3K to locate her runaway daughter. The small amount—and the fact the young woman was nineteen—had generated little interest among rewards seekers. Kids who take off from home? Tracking them was usually more trouble than they were worth.

Emma Cummings had come home from college, and a day or two later Mom had found some drugs in her jeans pocket. Not much, but enough to create a domestic explosion. The don't-I-have-any-privacy side battling the I-was-only-doing-your-laundry-thank-you-very-much side. The next morning Emma had split, taking her backpack and computer.

After several fretful days, Emma's mom had scraped together what cash she could and posted the reward announcement on the internet. Shaw's associates in Florida, who scanned the web regularly for offers, sent the info his way, knowing his soft spot for runaways. He'd piloted his Winnebago to Kansas and met with Mom.

Shaw always approached domestics warily. Sometimes you could put the disappearance down to impulsive youth. Sometimes the kids ran for a reason, in which case Shaw chose not to continue or, upon finding the kid, went to the authorities. But in the Cummings household, he spotted no abuse, just an overly protective mother with a churchgoing, conservative background, shocked about a baggie in Emma's Levi's. For her part, it seemed, Emma had just broken up with her boyfriend the day she'd left for home. Bad moods all around would have been a factor, as were issues about her parents' recent divorce, Shaw was sure.

One aspect of the job was unique; the mother didn't actually want him to report Emma's location. He was to make a delivery. The business-sized envelope contained not only a letter but a lump. A charm or a necklace? Shaw wondered. A silly toy?

She'd preempted his next question: "I trust you. Come back and tell me you've delivered it. I'll give you the check."

His search had begun, interviewing Emma's friends. It had gone smoothly up to a point. A lead sent him to Prescott, Kansas, thirty miles away, where one of Emma's high school classmates lived. Emma had spent the night with her. The teen had been willing to talk to Shaw; she'd thought the mother-daughter fight was "stupid" and encouraged Emma to return home. But, no, she had continued southwest into the hinterland. The only clue: Emma was planning to stop at a renowned fried chicken place in Humble, Kansas. That was all she knew.

So on to the curiously named burg, population eight thousand.

Downtown Humble was exactly what one would expect: a diorama of 1950s Middle America. In late July, the streets had a dusty feel. Shaw had the chance to buy plenty of souvenirs bearing the town's name, which he declined, to sample the Southern-fried chicken, which he indulged in. It was the best he'd ever eaten. The establishment was Ling Yu's Chicken Shack, whose name initially seemed to require an explanation. Then Shaw reflected: But why? He ordered seconds.

He displayed Emma's picture to the owner and the servers. One waitress vaguely remembered the young woman, but couldn't help with later destinations. She'd been quiet while she'd eaten, texting the entire time. It was moments like these that Shaw regretting not having a law enforcement agency behind him, and the magic bullet of a warrant to get his hands on texts.

Where had she gone after Humble?

The trail didn't exactly end; it diverged: in the middle of the town was a roundabout with four roads branching off in different directions.

Colter Shaw had a vast collection of Rand McNally maps, and as he ate he studied Kansas. Two of the routes would have taken Emma to even more remote parts of the state—and places beyond. A third was the paved version of the old Dodge City Turnpike—a covered wagon route. The last of them would have taken her directly to

I-35. This latter would have been unfortunate from Shaw's point of view, as it was a major north–south thoroughfare, from which she could access thousands of destinations from Mexico to Canada.

So, Emma, Shaw thought, finishing the not-terrible coffee, which was it?

Or had you turned around and headed back in the direction of home via the route on which you'd come after finishing Luncheon Special 2, half chicken, slaw and biscuit?

He had then glanced out the window of the restaurant.

Oh.

There's an idea.

Shortly thereafter, Shaw was sitting in the Cimarron County Sheriff's Department, a five-minute walk from Ling Yu's. Deputy P. Ruskin was cautiously happy to hear him out.

"The traffic cam, hmm?" the man asked.

The "idea" had been viewing the video from a camera that looked down over the intersection.

"Rewards?" asked another deputy. He had massive biceps and forearms, and his name tag read T. THORN-TON. He was laughing. "Can't be your job."

"It is."

"You make a living at it?"

Of sorts.

"I do."

He would hardly explain that rewards-seeking, for him, wasn't exactly about the money. It was that a reward represented a puzzle that no one else had been able to solve. Growing up among the three Shaw siblings, Colter was known as the "restless one." Restless in body, also restless in mind. Traveling around the country untying Gordian knots was the perfect vocation for him.

"Not a bounty hunter, bond enforcement agent?" Ruskin asked.

"Nope. Not a private investigator either. I'm not licensed."

"Would you be armed?"

"There're two handguns in my camper, yes. I have a conceal carry permit. It's valid here."

No one in the room gave any reaction. You'd think police might be concerned about the number of citizens toting guns in pockets and hidden holsters. Not the case. What the cops knew was that in order to get a CCP, you needed to pass a comprehensive criminal and mental health background check.

Ruskin seemed sympathetic, but rules, apparently, were not to be breached in Humble. "I'm sorry, sir. Can't help you. Maybe if you contacted a law enforcement agency in Topeka, they could come to us. And we'd see what we could do."

Shaw sighed. Out the window, he could see the camera, lording over the intersection like a UFO. He was trying to think of some way to persuade Ruskin to help, when the deputy's phone had rung.

He answered and said, "Hey, Sal." Then, frowning, he had a conversation.

After he hung up, he looked over at the other deputies in the office, and said, "Okay. We've got a situation."

# 3.

The car was speeding through cornfields.

The stalks were adolescent at this time of year: several feet high, with leaves and husks bright green, the tassels shiny brown and white.

Colter Shaw, in the passenger seat of the sheriff's department cruiser, watched the endless blue sky of America's breadbasket.

The route was straight and flat, given the two-dimensional geography of this part of the state. Occasionally, and for no apparent reason, Deputy Peter Ruskin slowed to eighty. Maybe he knew of unofficial deer crossings.

Ruskin and Shaw were in the lead; two more Chrysler police sedans trailed.

"What's this experience you've had, sir? Hostages?"

"Two times now. A reward was offered for a runaway, like the job I'm on now."

"Only she hadn't run away."

"Was a kidnapping. The perp made it look like she'd left on her own. I found them in a shack in the mountains."

"You track?" Ruskin asked.

"I do. Called the state police but it was an hour before they could get there. I talked him into letting her go. He did and took off—not my job to arrest anyone. I got her home safe. He was picked up a few days later.

"The other was a reward for an escaped prisoner. I found him hiding in a barn behind an abandoned house outside of Portland."

"Who was the hostage? He get somebody from the house?"

"That's what I assumed. Turned out to be a cow."

Ruskin laughed, then saw Shaw wasn't joking.

"And?"

"Talked him out. All species were safe."

"Hmm."

Fifteen minutes into the drive, the geography and landscape changed to trees and houses, and the road began a gentle sidewind. Ruskin eased off the gas. Ahead, through growths of oak and maple Shaw could see the shimmer of water, blue and white. Kiowa Lake. He recalled it from his map. The body of water was big, around a thousand acres, and defined by complicated, rough edges. Natural, augmented by a dam.

Ruskin's radio crackled.

"Fuck's this about?" came a gruff voice. "Barricade in a lake house? Are there kids in there?"

"We'll be there in five, Sheriff," Ruskin said. "I'll know more then. How's that situation in Farmington?"

"Was nothing. Waste of time. I'm leaving now."

A faint frown crossed Ruskin's brow; Shaw recalled that the dispatcher had said he'd left earlier.

"What's your ETA?" Ruskin asked.

No answer.

"Sheriff . . . Sheriff? You there?"

The radio clattered once again but it wasn't Ruskin's boss. The dispatcher was reporting that the state police tactical and hostage negotiation teams were on their way but wouldn't arrive for almost an hour.

"Got it, Sally. Thanks."

To Shaw, Ruskin said, "Being out of the way has its disadvantages, time to time." The deputy consulted his GPS. He followed the instructions and raced over shade-filled roads.

He radioed, "This's Pete. Who's on-site?"

"I'm in front of the place. It's George."

Two other deputies reported that they were close.

"Roger that."

Seeing the cruiser ahead, Ruskin slowed and pulled up behind it. George's car was half on, half off the front lawn. The beefy deputy was crouched, taking cover on the driver's side. He looked back as the others pulled up.

All of this was happening in a house typical of the lake houses here. Looked to be about three bedrooms, two story. Give it eighteen hundred square feet. Grass and bushes in the front, parking area to the right side. A battered green Camry with Kansas tags sat within it at an oblique angle. The driver's door was open.

Behind the house was a dock stretching into the still lake beyond.

Ruskin said to Shaw, "I intend not to do anything until the sheriff and the state boys get here. Just contain everything and keep him from hurting anybody. I might need your advice if things get active, if you know what I mean. Unless that happens, I'll ask you to stay out of harm's way."

"My plan too."

The deputies from the other cars approached slowly, crouching. The woman, Harper, carried a shotgun. Shaw guessed she wasn't involved in many physical takedowns; less her short stature than the hoop earrings told him this. They'd be easy for a perp to rip out in a scuffle. She did, however, seem completely comfortable with the short barrel Savage in her hands.

Ruskin looked around. He sent one deputy, Jerry, to clear the houses across the street.

"Circle way 'round. Don't present a target."

"Sure, Pete."

"And get upstairs in one of the houses. I want eyes inside if you can."

The deputy jogged off.

"And keep your head down!"

Shaw asked George, "Whose car?" Nodding at the Camry.

"Ed Whitestone's."

Garner said, "Ed? I know him." A frown. "Owns a farm near the interstate. Never been in trouble that I heard of. Might've been stolen."

Ruskin said, "Bets, get back in the cruiser, go the long way 'round and seal off the street."

The woman jogged back to the car and sped off.

Squinting, Ruskin rose and jockeyed around George's car, trying to get a view. Shaw—not exactly out of harm's way—was watching the windows. Not seeing movement.

Then the crack of a pistol shot rolled through the quiet street. The taker was shooting from a ground floor window toward, but not directly at, the cars. A blue recycling bin, on wheels, shuddered under the impact.

The crouching deputies crouched farther.

A man's voice called, "Don't you assholes try anything!"

Two other squad cars pulled into the street and stopped, well back. The two deputies, young white men with crew cuts, climbed out and jogged forward, keeping low.

They eyed both the house and, with curiosity, Shaw.

Ruskin deployed them, and they jogged to trees nearby and took cover.

The man's hands clenched and unclenched. He looked around uncertainly. He said to Shaw, "Any thoughts, sir?"

"First, I'd secure the site better. That deputy you sent up the street? Make sure she can get a view behind the house. They could get out the back and into a boat."

Ruskin called Harper and relayed the instructions.

Shaw continued, "And I'd say even if he fires our way, don't return. We don't know where the hostage is. If he comes out shooting, alone, that's a different story. I'll leave that up to your rules of engagement."

A brief, humorless laugh from Ruskin. That phrase probably did not appear in the Cimarron County Sheriff's Department handbook.

The deputy gave these orders to the others.

Another mad shout from the window. The law enforcers' heads lowered. There were no more gunshots.

Ruskin looked toward the house. Shaw knew what was in the man's heart. He wanted to act, to do *some-*

*thing* . . . He caught Shaw's gaze—and understood the tacit question. He nodded.

Shaw said, "This is bare bones."

"That's okay. Go ahead."

"It's called the staircase approach—the FBI's strategy with hostage taking."

Shaw's friend and occasional mountain-climbing companion, Tom Pepper, was a former FBI special agent. He'd coached Shaw in these skills.

"First, establish communication. Call back on the hostage's phone. See if he picks up. If it's the hostage, find out if he's all right, who exactly is in there. If the taker's nowhere near, see if he can get out a window. If he's not, have him give the taker the phone.

"Introduce yourself. Not 'deputy.' Just your name. He'll know you're official. But you don't want to make it sound that you're asserting authority over him. Then just talk a little. How's he doing? Is he hurt? What's going on? *Listen* to him. Respond to what he says—doesn't matter how odd or troubling. That's called active listening. Find out where his mind is, what he wants. You're one hundred percent sympathetic. If there's silence, don't jump in. Let him fill it. This is all about him. Don't disagree."

Ruskin and the two deputies nearby, Garner and T. Thornton, a grizzled former soldier, it was easy to see, were paying attention.

"So. Step one, listen. Step two, empathize. He may want to kill every immigrant in the country. He may hate Jews, hate his family, the president, spacemen from Mars. It may sound crazy or repulsive to you, but you put your feelings aside and appreciate his. Everything he says is valid.

"Three. You use the empathy to establish rapport. Make him feel that you really get him. Don't say, 'Sure, that's a good idea,' or he'll see it as manipulation. Tell him that you understand what he's saying . . . and what he's feeling. You're sorry it's upsetting him.

"Four, you influence him. Put the rapport to use. Very subtle. Maybe get him to accept some food and drink—whatever he really likes, though no alcohol. See if there's somebody he'd like to talk to. Never try to get him to do anything he doesn't want, but if you see a chance to guide him in a direction you think he might be inclined to go, then do it. Positive reinforcement.

"Finally, try to change his behavior—that's the big one. Getting him to surrender. You don't do it by saying he's wrong. Tell him that it'll be for his own good. It's the best way to get him to pursue his vision—whatever that is.

"One more thing: use the first name of the hostage a lot. It humanizes them. Makes the taker reluctant to kill."

"Lot to think on," Ruskin said.

"It is . . . But you look like you've got it."

The deputy inhaled.

"A radio call came in."

"Pete. Jerry."

The officer who'd cleared the houses across the street.

"Go ahead."

"Everybody over here's safe. A couple let me upstairs. I can see through windows of the rental. Curtains partly drawn but I got a white male, late forties. Handgun, revolver, I think. He's pacing. Seems to be talking to somebody else. Can't see him."

Another call.

"Pete, it's Sally. I checked with the broker. Rented to a Richard Lansing. From New York. A weeklong rental, starting a couple days ago. Fishing package. Paying extra for the boat and tackle."

"How many people?"

"Broker said two."

"Roger. Where's the sheriff?"

"ETA probably half hour, State tac team, forty minutes."

"'K."

Ruskin glanced at Shaw, who nodded. Meaning: go on.

The deputy asked Sally for the number of the phone the hostage had called 911 on. She gave it to him twice. He memorized it.

Ruskin stared at the house, unmoving, like a pitcher sizing up a batter. Then he tapped in the number and hit speaker.

Two rings, three.

"Who's this?"

"Hey there. My name's Pete. Can I ask who this is?"

"You don't know that from my car? You couldn't read the license plate?"

"Might've been stolen or borrowed."

"Ed Whitestone."

*Never been in trouble . . .*

Ruskin said, "I think I know you."

Whitestone didn't respond.

The deputy was about to speak. Shaw shook his head.

*Don't fill the silence . . .*

The taker said, "No, you *don't* know me. Nobody knows me. Nobody understands. And you don't give a shit."

Shaw gestured his okay.

Ruskin said, "I do care, Ed. I want to hear what you have to say. Really. We've got a situation here and I want to know what you're about. So we can work something out. We don't want anybody to get hurt. That's the last thing we want, right?"

Silence.

"How's a man supposed to live, how's a man supposed to *care* for his family?"

"You having a hard time now, Ed?"

"Hard time? You don't know what hard times is. All this economy crap doesn't affect you. Me? Nobody buying my crops! I got surplus rotting. But do I have to pay the mortgage, do I have to pay the taxes? Hell, yes, I do."

"I was reading about that, Ed. What's happening to the farms. It's terrible, man. Totally unfair."

Shaw nodded. He was doing a good job.

Again. Nothing for a moment.

"If I sell the land, then what'm I going to do? What kind of job could I get?"

"That's tough, Ed. Damn. Hey, you need water, food or anything?"

No answer.

"Anything else? Want you to be comfortable, Ed. I mean it."

"Do you really?" the taker said sarcastically.

Ruskin said firmly, "I do." Then: "I know there's

somebody in there with you. Richard, I think. How's he doing?"

"Fat cat from New York? He's doing just fine, but fuck the rest of us."

"I hear you. You mind if I talk to Richard?"

A debate.

"You're not going to fuck me over, are you, Pete?"

"Oh, no way, Ed. Really. Just my job to make sure everybody's okay. You and Richard."

A long pause.

Then a different male voice came over the phone. Timid. "Yes?"

"Who's this? Richard?"

"Yes."

"I'm Deputy Ruskin with the sheriff's department."

"My buddy, that I'm here with? He's out, buying beer and some food."

"We'll look out for him. We've got the street covered. You okay?"

"Yeah. Sorta."

"Anybody else in the house?"

"No. I—"

Ed's voice raged, "Enough of that. Gimme." Then the taker was speaking directly into the phone: "I think you're trying to fuck with me, Pete."

"No, sir, never."

"I could hear you, you know? Asking how many people're in here. You going to try something."

"No, Ed. I promise. I really do. I'm just trying to do the best I can to see what you're up against."

Shaw whispered, "We should get Ed's family here."

The deputy nodded. "Ed, how'd you like your wife to come out? Can we call her?"

Garner whispered, "Daughter. Twelve."

"And your daughter. She's about in middle school now, isn't she?"

Ed seemed to be muttering to himself.

"Ed, your family?"

A hollow voice. "They left me. They couldn't take it. She's flied off to be with her momma in Boise. This morning. She took Sandy too. That's how loyalty is, right?"

"Oh, man. On top of everything else. I'm sorry."

Ruskin mouthed to Garner, "Call her."

Garner stepped aside, unholstering his phone.

"Listen, Ed, what do you think we could do for you?"

Shaw nodded his approval.

Garner held up the phone and shook his head. He mouthed, "Right to voice mail."

"You can't do shit for me, Pete. But there's somebody who can."

"Who'd that be?"

A pause again. Then Ed said harshly, "Who do you *think*?"

"I don't know, Ed. Tell me. I want to know."

"A fucking banker, who else? They're forgiving all those student loans. Why should farmers be treated worse than punk kids?"

"That's a good question, Ed."

"I want somebody from my bank here. They can forgive *my* debt. I worked hard all my life. Not like those fucking students, learning shit that's useless. And they get *their* loans forgave? It's not fair . . . You want a clue what the problem is? Do you?"

"Sure, Ed. I want to know. What's the clue?"

"It's this saying us farmers have. You want to hear it?"

"I do, Ed."

"It's 'Happiness eludes land-working people.' Me and my family . . . we don't deserve being treated like this." He repeated the line solemnly: "'Happiness eludes land-working people.'" Then he said, "You ever hear that?"

"No, Ed, I didn't. But I want to hear more about your situation. See what we can do."

He fell silent. They could hear indiscernible muttering.

"Ed? Tell me some more—"

"I don't want to tell you anything more," was the snide response. "I want a First Union Trust vice president here in a half hour. If not, this prick dies."

The phone went silent.

# 4.

The Lexus, late model, sparkling white, skidded to a stop behind Ruskin's squad car. Two deputies stepped out of its way, fast.

The driver was big—tall and round and broad—and sported a gunslinger mustache. He hair was thick, salt and pepper. A small scar crescented his right cheek. His uniform was the same as the others: tan slacks and dark green shirt. There was one accessory variation, though. He wore a shiny round badge bearing SHERIFF. It was gold and matched the half-pound Rolex on his wrist. His name plate reported: R. DOBBINS.

The younger deputies glanced his way with a particular look in their eyes. It bordered on evasive. Scared.

The man strode forward to Ruskin and crouched behind the cruiser. He did so stiffly. Shaw put his age at early fifties.

"Sheriff. Let me tell you where we are. Ed Whitestone—"

"Yeah, I know him. Got that farm. Why's he doing this? Not like him."

"It's like he snapped. Money problems and his wife and daughter left this morning."

"Left like in a shopping trip, or left like in left *him*?"

"Him. Went to her mother's."

"You call 'em?"

Garner said, "I did, Sheriff. Went to voice mail. Ed's gotta be pretty gone. Man's a good Christian and he's using words I don't think he's ever said before."

"Hostages?"

"Couple of guys on a fishing trip. Only one of 'em's in the house. He—"

The sheriff waved him silent. "Who's *that*?"

"Name is Colter . . . wait, right?"

A nod.

"Colter Shaw. He was in town looking for a runaway from Topeka. He's had—"

"You law?"

"No, private."

"You can't be at the scene."

"Mr. Shaw was helping us. He's been involved in hostage takings before."

Dobbins had squinty eyes. "So you *were* law." Suggesting Shaw had been lying.

"No." He explained briefly about the rewards.

Dobbins grunted, trying to fathom his career.

"He was helpful, Sheriff," Ruskin said. "Some negotiation things."

"*Things*." Like he was spitting.

This was yet another reminder of why Shaw liked his freelance work. As the son of a survivalist, he'd spent much time by himself in the wilderness around his family's spread near the Sierra Nevada foothills. He'd settled into his rewards-seeking profession because he was beholden to no one. A reward is a unilateral contract; you're not obligated to find the missing person or the escaped prisoner. You can walk away at any time.

"Better you clear out. Liability."

"He doesn't have a car, Sheriff."

Dobbins cocked his head, as he peered at Ruskin. "Oh. You let him drive to a scene with you? Secured in the back of your vehicle?"

"Umm. No, Sheriff."

The man rolled his eyes. "Get up the street," he said impatiently to Shaw. "Now."

Shaw walked a half block up the shoulder—no sidewalks in this neighborhood—and then circled back into the lake house's parking lot. This side was solid clapboard, no windows. He got as close as he could to Ruskin, Garner and Sheriff Dobbins without being seen. Shaw crouched and peered through a thick stand of camellia bushes, dark green leaves, lovely red flowers. He had a good view of the law enforcers. Ruskin was saying, " . . . no, not at anything in particular. The yard and the trash bin."

The sheriff studied the house. "When're the state boys going to get here?"

"'Bout thirty, thirty-five minutes, I make it."

Dobbins grumbled, "You got anybody in that house there, across the street? Or the one next door?"

"Yessir. It's Jerry. He's got eyes inside."

"If he's got eyes inside he can get a slug inside. Boy's a good shot. Been hunting with him. You have too. You gave him a long gun, didn't you?"

Ruskin didn't answer right away. "Sheriff, I think we're a ways from shooting. We just started talking, Ed and me. He's upset, that's the truth. But he's not targeting people. And we're talking. He's responding."

"*Responding.*"

The word was a sneer.

"Did he threaten to kill the hostage?"

"He . . . yes."

"George?"

"Sheriff?"

"There's a Winchester in my trunk. Get it up to Jerry." The sheriff popped the trunk lid remotely. "You scratch that stock, I'll have your hide."

"Yessir, Sheriff. I'll be careful."

The deputy scurried to the car.

Ruskin inhaled long. "All respect, Sheriff, we've got a dialogue going."

"Oh? What's he want?"

"Bank to forgive his loans."

"Who the fuck doesn't? George! What're you doing? Hustle, like you never did with the Tigers."

"I scored four times in a single game, Sheriff."

"Move!"

The young deputy got the rifle out of the trunk carefully and unbagged it. It was a no-nonsense hunting gun. No blade sight at the muzzle. The Nikon telescopic sight was all that would direct the bullet to its target but it would do so with perfect efficiency.

The sheriff sighed. "Don't forget the important part."

The officer stared blankly at his boss.

"Ammunition, son. Bullets. Rounds. Slugs. I have to think of *everything* here?"

"Oh. Sure." George grabbed several boxes, then hustled along the same safe route as Jerry had used to shoo the neighbors off to safety.

The sheriff nodded toward Pete's phone. "You got his number in there?"

"Not his. The hostage's."

Dobbins took the unit and hit REDIAL.

Ed answered. "Is the banker here?" The phone was on speaker.

"The bank isn't coming, Ed. This's Sheriff Dobbins. Listen here: I don't negotiate."

"But he said, Pete said—"

"Quiet up, Ed. Whatever was said before was different from what's going on now."

Even from a distance, Shaw could see Ruskin's lips tighten.

"And what's going on now is you set down that gun of yours and come outside with your hands way up in the sky."

The man's voice was suddenly desperate: "I want my banker."

"No banker."

Ed said, "Then Richard'll die."

"Then you will too."

"Aren't you getting a clue by now? I don't care."

"All the more reason for you to be dead."

The sheriff tossed the unit back to Ruskin.

"Sheriff, look—"

Dobbins cut his deputy off. He gripped his Motorola mic/speaker. "Jerry, you got that Winchester yet?"

"Yeah, Sheriff," was the staticky reply. "I'm chambered."

"You see a target?"

"Off and on. He's pacing a lot."

"Stand by."

"Roger."

Ruskin's face approached disgust.

Shaw stepped away from the tall bushes and walked into the parking area, avoiding the tire-track-laced mud and a large bed of trash. Raccoons, maybe a bear, had been into the trash. Shaw recalled that the renters were from New York, probably the city, since it hadn't occurred to them to bungee the trash can lids.

In the back of the house he noted a dock stretching thirty feet into the smooth lake. A ten-foot outboard motor boat sat covered, winched out of the water. Shaw wasn't much of a boater. His experience with bodies of water while growing up tended to involve getting thrown into icy water by his father, climbing out and fighting hypothermia.

Shaw removed a notebook from his jacket pocket and penned a note. He ripped the page out and walked to the line of squad cars in a wide circle, to avoid being seen by the sheriff. He stepped up to the woman deputy, the one with the accessories, each elegant in its own way: the earrings and the shotgun.

"I ask a favor?"

"Can't give you a ride."

"No. Pete Ruskin was doing a good job negotiating. I've got a few more tips. Could you get him this?" He held up the folded paper. "And maybe keep it quiet? The sheriff's not too kindly disposed toward me."

"Not just you. He's sort of that way most of the time."

"You have a problem delivering it?"

"No problem at all."

# 5.

'm not armed."

Standing in the doorway leading from the kitchen to the living room of the vacation house, Colter Shaw was holding his jacket tails up, revealing his waistband.

Ed spun around. "Who're you?"

The hostage stared, maybe even more shocked than the man with the gun.

"It's all right," Shaw said. He turned to show his back, then completed the circuit and released the sport coat tails. He kept his hands raised.

Ed was in his late forties, balding and well-tanned, as farmers in the month of July will be. He was in jeans and a blue work shirt, his boots were scuffed beyond polishing but in sturdy repair. "Who?" he repeated in a whisper.

"I was in town talking to the sheriff's department on other business. I heard about what was going on. I want to help."

Ed looked past Shaw, into the kitchen.

"You locked the door but not the window. And you

should put that chair under the doorknob. It works well on cork floors."

"You're a fucking undercover cop."

"No. Just a civilian."

"Mister . . . What're you doing?" Richard was compact, dark complexioned and seemed muscular beneath his jeans and untucked tan, Tommy Bahama short-sleeved shirt. His head was crowned with curly dark red hair.

Shaw ignored him for the time being. "Ed, my name's Colter Shaw. My job's being a . . . troubleshooter, you could say. Finding missing persons, things like that."

"Sit the hell down and shut up. You're a fool!" Ed had wild eyes. Red. The gun he was holding was an old revolver, a long-barreled model, probably a .38, like cops in dated movies used to carry. The cylinder held six rounds and Shaw knew at least two slugs had been fired.

Of course there was always reloading.

Shaw sat beside Richard. "There's a sheriff outside who's inclined to start shooting."

"Him, the one who called? I hate him!"

"He's looking for any excuse. If it comes to that, both of you could get hurt. So stay away from the windows and don't act in any way threatening. And stop firing out the window."

"You! Keep your hands where I can see them."

"I'll do that. And, Ed: I heard what you said about the happiness of land-workers. I get it."

For a moment, the man's eyes softened.

Shaw continued, "I grew up in California. My parents had a spread and there were always tax issues."

"Really, man," Richard said. "You shouldn't've done this."

"The state police'll be here soon. Their negotiators'll take over. The sheriff's a hothead, but we'll get it worked out. Now, Ed, I've got a proposition. I want to take Richard's place. Let him go. I'll stay."

Ed looked at Richard, who said angrily, "Nobody needs to take care of me."

"I told you, I do this sort of work for a living." Shaw looked casually over the room, assessing weapons. A baseball bat in the corner. Probably kitchen knives. "Is that okay, Ed? I want you to be okay with it."

He was flustered. "No, I'm not okay with it. Forget it. Is a banker on the way?"

"Let's not worry about the banker right now . . . If you listen to me, Ed, everything's going to be fine. Okay?"

The farmer nodded slowly.

Shaw turned to Richard. "Just hang in there."

"Jesus, mister," he whispered, "you are, plain and simple, crazy."

# 6.

As he surveyed the living room of the lake house once more, Shaw reflected that he'd heard that before.

*You did what? You're crazy, Colter . . .*

A few years ago, a woman he'd been dating offered her assessment of his decision to rappel down a three-hundred-foot cliff in the dead of night. Windy too.

Not like he was asking her to join him. The descent had been the day before what had turned out to be their last date.

*Crazy . . .*

For him, the rappel had been a lark; he was bored, that was all. There's a curious paradox about people who live by a code of survival. The entire concept is about, obviously, staying alive. But that truism misses a key to practitioners: you can never really live unless you confront some danger you *must* survive.

Richard's phone rang again.

"Don't go near the window," Shaw reminded. "He might be trying to draw you into position."

Ed looked at the iPhone. He hit ANSWER. "You have my banker? I'm not—"

"Fuck your banker," Dobbins shouted.

The phone was not on speaker, but Shaw could hear it from across the room.

"I want Shaw," Dobbins belted. "I want him now."

Ed seemed paralyzed. But the gun remained pointed halfway between Richard and Shaw.

Shaw said, "Tell him I'll talk to Ruskin. Only him."

"He said—"

Sheriff Dobbins raged, "I heard and he's not getting to pick and choose who he talks to. Put him on."

Shaw said to Ed, "All right." He held his hand out for the phone.

Ed shook his head, as if worried Shaw would jump him. Shaw pointed to a table. "Leave the phone there."

The farmer set the mobile down and backed away, staying clear of windows. "Hands where I can see them."

Shaw complied and he rose slowly. The gun wasn't pointed directly at him but the hammer was cocked back to single action. The trigger would have an easy pull. A lot of accidents happen when you walk around with a cocked pistol.

Shaw picked up the phone.

"Yes?"

"The fuck do you think you're doing?"

"I've done this before, Sheriff. There's no need for tactical at this point. Ed's being reasonable."

The sheriff growled, "You are going to jail for this. If you even fucking survive. Now I've got *two* hostages to deal with. Thank you very fucking much. It'll be a cold day in hell before the prosecutor gives you a break, I'll see to that."

"When the troopers get here, we'll talk. Until then? No."

"You son of a—"

Shaw disconnected.

He casually handed the phone back to Ed—a natural gesture—and the farmer reached for it instinctively. Then stopped. In the space of one second, Shaw tossed aside the phone and launched himself into Ed, grabbing his gun wrist and driving him into the small parlor off the living room. Rolling on the floor, they grappled and punched and struggled for control of the gun.

The muzzle swung first toward one then the other.

It was as Shaw was struggling to get footing on the gamy, department store oriental carpet, that Ed rolled sideways fast and, hand still on the Colt, the gun went off with a stunning roar.

Shaw left Ed's limp form in the parlor and breathing hard, walked into the living room.

The phone was ringing once more, and Dobbins's voice clattered through the air, via his car's loudspeaker. "What's going on? Shaw? Somebody tell me."

"You all right?" Richard asked. He was on his feet.

Shaw nodded, his face revealing dismay. "Didn't want that to happen. He should've just given up."

"Is he . . ."

"Dead," Shaw said matter-of-factly. He looked around for the ringing phone. "Where'd it fall?"

"Under the couch." Richard pointed.

Shaw set the pistol on the coffee table and walked across the room to find it.

As he crouched, Richard said, "Shaw."

He looked up.

The man had tugged on blue latex gloves. He'd picked up the Colt and was pointing the weapon at Shaw's chest. He pulled the trigger.

# 7.

The EMTs were walking quickly along the mulchy front walk to the lake house.

The technicians, a man and a woman, were in their early thirties, stocky and strong. They wore bulky uniforms, decorated with gear sprouting from many pockets. Both bore tattoos, his on the neck, hers on the back of the hand. His a rock group logo, hers a butterfly wearing sunglasses.

Inside they hurried to the person lying motionless on the floor of the living room. They crouched and did what all EMTs do.

First, clear an airway.

Not really necessary in this case, given the nature of these injuries. But they'd been trained to follow protocol, and so they did.

Sheriff Dobbins strode up to the pair. "Gonna be all right?"

"We'll let you know, Sheriff," Butterfly Lady said.

"You can't tell?" Delivered gutturally, as one impatient word.

"We'll let you know," her male partner added, listening to the heart.

Sheriff Dobbins stepped away and muttered to the person on his right, "Just asked a question. What's the problem with a civil answer?"

Colter Shaw, also looking down at the choreography of the medical techs, said nothing. Ruskin joined them and glanced down at the supine man, the one who'd been claiming to be Richard Lansing. "How is he?"

Dobbins growled, "Don't know. And don't you ask. You'll get your head chewed off."

Both Rock Star and Butterfly were impervious.

Shaw's blows had been delivered fast and hard, but he didn't think the man had been too badly hurt. When Richard had pulled the trigger, the hammer had landed on an empty cylinder. He'd understood instantly that he'd been gamed and that Shaw had emptied the gun in the parlor as he'd stood over Ed.

Shaw had been about to call Dobbins and Ruskin and invite them in for the arrest, when Richard had dropped the Colt and reached for his back waistband.

Shaw hadn't counted on a second weapon. He'd lunged forward and driven an open palm into Richard's jaw. Then he'd turned to the side, ready to slam his elbow into the solar plexus. But the coup de grace was unnecessary. Richard had dropped straight to the floor, a bag of rocks. Collecting and unloading the gun—a baby Glock—Shaw had looked over the man's shallowly breathing body with amusement. He didn't think in his decade as a reward seeker he'd ever knocked anybody out.

Dobbins said, "Clocked him pretty damn good."

"Well, reaching for a gun has consequences."

"Granted that."

Ed Whitestone stood in the corner of the living room, no longer portraying the accidental victim of Colter Shaw's roughhousing—the shot had gone into the floor. The farmer was on the phone. He finished his conversation, then joined the other men.

"God bless you, sir," he said, voice cracking. Then he threw his arms around a startled Colter Shaw and began to sob.

# 8.

Richard's real last name was Quinn.

Yes, he'd driven here from New York but there the facts ended. He'd done time for armed robbery, at juvenile. He'd racked up some drug time over the years and, more recently, at the advanced age of thirty-four, was on the NYPD's and the FBI's radar for his involvement with an East Coast crew.

The buddy he'd come to Humble with probably wasn't much of a fisherman. He was one Terry McNab, a resident of Brooklyn and an enforcer for the same outfit.

For reasons yet to be discovered, it seemed that the pair rented the lake house here to stage a fake kidnapping. Well, Shaw reflected, it was more a *reverse* kidnapping. They'd picked a family at random, the Whitestones, and broken into their house.

McNab stayed with the wife and daughter while Quinn and Ed drove to the lake house, where he was to play the role of a disgruntled farmer who'd taken Quinn—as Richard Lansing—hostage. The man was to do exactly what Quinn said. If he deviated, McNab would torture his wife and daughter.

Earlier, a series of events and observations had led Shaw to conclude that something akin to this was unfolding. The note he'd written to Ruskin had nothing to do with hostage negotiation. It read:

> *You're being scammed. Richard is the taker and Ed is the hostage. Get officers to Ed's house ASAP. Associate of Richard's is there, holding wife and daughter as leverage over Ed. No idea why.*
>
> *I'll go inside lake house. As soon as the family is safe, call me. Use phrase "cold day in hell," and I'll take it from there.*
>
> *Why I'm writing this to you—don't trust sheriff. Too eager to shoot. And Lexus and Rolex? On sheriff's salary? Is he in on it?*

Now, Quinn had been revived, cuffed and stashed in the back of Ruskin's squad car.

The deputy, the sheriff and Shaw were on the front lawn. The sheriff said, "So, didn't trust me?"

There was only one answer: "No."

Ruskin cleared his throat and said, "Sheriff Dobbins's what you might call well-off. Independently. He doesn't even need to work. Puts in long hours and—"

"Give it a rest, Deputy."

The fact that the sheriff had given him the code words about a cold day in hell reassured Shaw that Ruskin was comfortable with Dobbins.

Then to Shaw, "How'd you figure it out?"

"We'll get to that. No time now." His eyes were on Richard Quinn in the back of Ruskin's squad car. The sun made his red ringlets glow an impressive crimson.

"What's the rush?"

"Something's going on." Shaw looked away from the car. "The whole point of this—"

Ruskin snapped his fingers. "—was to get the whole dang sheriff's department here. To keep us out of the way of another thing going down in the county."

Shaw said, "I think so."

"But what?" Dobbins muttered. "Robbery? You've got your well-off folks in the county, but nobody spectacular. There're banks, jewelry stores, like everywhere. No score at any of 'em're worth risking your life for. We're a death penalty state."

Ruskin said, "Cimarron County's mostly a place you drive through."

Shaw said, "That's it. You *have* got something valuable here. The interstate."

The sheriff barked a laugh. "That pair was keeping us busy while some other boys in their crew 'jacked a shipment headed north."

"Drugs." Shaw and Ruskin said simultaneously.

Interstate 35 led straight from Mexico into the heartland.

Nodding, Dobbins said, "They've probably called it off—if they haven't heard from Quinn or McNab by now."

"Possible," Shaw said, "but you can't count on it. Quinn might've given them the go-ahead once he and

Ed were inside and everybody from your department showed up here. Thinking you were monitoring their phones. We need the details of the plan."

Dobbins's head swiveled toward the car containing Quinn. "'Kay," he said in a slow voice. "I'll find out." He started toward the car.

"Sheriff, you want some interrogation help," Ruskin asked. "Maybe Mr. Shaw here—"

"Naw," the big man replied, lifting a hand as he walked away. "I'm good."

# 9.

Near sunset, they were in Dobbins's office: Shaw, Ruskin and the sheriff.

Drinking Budweisers, all three of them. Shaw didn't know the rules regarding alcohol on government property in Cimarron County. Maybe okay or maybe not. In any event, here they were.

The sheriff's conversation with Richard Quinn had been brief. Well, more of a *monologue* than a chat. To the effect: If anyone dies when your asshole crew shoots up the transport truck on the interstate, it'll be like you pulled the trigger. And if any innocents get hurt, the best defense attorneys in the state aren't going to save you from a lethal injection.

But, provide the particulars and Dobbins would go to the DA and recommend a reduced and maybe witness protection after. Quinn had handed over the whole crew—including McNab.

Shaw suspected that Sheriff Dobbins ginned up a whole lot of cooperation this way.

The county deputies and state police intercepted a box truck filled with a hundred tidy packages of opioids and cocaine; the Texans inside, connected to a Chihuahua cartel, went down in the bust, not a shot fired. Quinn's Brooklyn crew—the would-be hijackers—had indeed gotten spooked when he didn't pick up the phone in the lake house. They'd fled just over the Missouri border, where they too were picked up.

The sheriff pointed with a bottle. "Now, Shaw, 'fess up. How'dya figure it out?" The rich, grumpy sheriff apparently considered it a sign of affection to call you by your last name.

"Ed told us himself."

A sip and a grunt. Meaning: explain.

"You didn't hear it, Sheriff. But Ed said there was a clue to his troubles. Used the word *clue* a couple of times. He said, 'Happiness eludes land-working people.' And after that was the phrase 'me and my family.'"

"No, I didn't hear it then and I don't get it now. So what?" One beer vanished. Another was opened.

Ruskin laughed. "Sure. The first letters: *H*, happiness. Then *E*, then *L*, then *P*. Damn. 'Help me and my family.'"

"Jesus Lord. What is he, one of those sudoku players?"

"That's numbers, Sheriff."

"I *know* it's goddamn numbers." Now the bottle poked Ruskin's way. "*You* missed that, boy."

"My first hostage taking, Sheriff. Wasn't really thinking 'bout word games."

Shaw said, "I doubted there was any way it could be a coincidence, that phrase. But there were some other things too: three other tracks of vehicles in the parking area in the past day. The mud, you could see it. One was heavy, a van. And two sedans. Maybe nothing, just seemed curious to me. Why all the visitors, if they'd really been a couple of guys from New York?

"Then, animals'd gotten into the trash. There was at least two days' worth. But Lansing and McNab hadn't used the boat. It was still covered. Why come to a lake house, pay for a boat to fish and not use it?"

Ruskin said, "Bet they *were* going to use it, though. To dump the bodies of Ed and his family in the lake."

"My thinking," Shaw said. "And then there was the question: If Ed'd really snapped, why would he drive seven miles to a house on the lake to ask for a banker? Why not go to his *bank*? And did you notice all those pauses when he was speaking? Quinn was coaching him about what to say to us. Nothing added up, so I figured I had to go inside and see what was what."

In his job as a reward seeker—in fact, in his life—he assessed decisions as his father, the survivalist, had taught him: assign percentage likelihood to each option, and always choose the most logical approach. In this case, he'd figured that it was, as he'd told Ruskin, a ninety percent probability that Ed was innocent. Of course, that left a potentially disastrous ten percent. Still, sometimes you just have to rappel down cliffs on dark windy nights.

Just because.

Sheriff gave a gruff laugh. "Hey, Shaw, you want a job here, you got one."

"Think I'll pass." A moment later: "But I do have a favor . . ."

Ten minutes later, Shaw was in a small room off the main office of the Cimarron County Sheriff's Department. He was sitting beside Peter Ruskin as the deputy was scrolling through videos. The images were the various angles from the traffic cam hovering over the five-way intersection where Shaw had lost the trail of Emma Cummings.

"There," Shaw said. "That's her at the light. The orange Dodge."

"Damn. Girl drives a Charger, and I know that model. It's got some horses under the bonnet."

Red went to green and Emma angled to the right onto Old Highway 47.

"Anything Native American that way? Reservations?"

"Matter of fact, yeah. A small reservation. Museum or two. Casino, of course. 'Bout fifteen miles up the highway."

"Okay. Thanks, Deputy."

Twenty minutes after that, Shaw was in the Winnebago, an aromatic bag of Ling Yu's fried chicken on the passenger seat. He was driving along the route Emma had taken. Was she fifteen miles ahead or fifteen hundred?

In Shaw's pocket was the envelope that her mother wanted him to deliver. He was, naturally, curious what it contained. A letter of apology? A diatribe casting her from the family? And what *was* the small object inside?

In the reward-seeking business, Shaw frequently told

himself, stay at arm's length. Someone made an offer and he pursued it. If he was successful, he moved on.

Never get involved . . .

A good rule.

Occasionally, though, one to be ignored.

He had a feeling this would be one of those jobs.

There was nothing Colter Shaw could do to help Emma and her mother, though, if he didn't find her.

First things first.

In pursuit of two young men accused of terrible hate crimes, Colter Shaw stumbles upon a clue to another mystery. In an effort to save the life of a young woman—and possibly others—he travels to the wilderness of Washington State to investigate a mysterious organization. Is it a community that consoles the bereaved? Or a dangerous cult under the sway of a charismatic leader? As he peels back the layers of truth, Shaw finds that some people will stop at nothing to keep their secrets hidden.

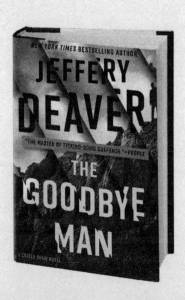

# 1.

## 2 p.m., June 11

Seconds to decide.

Swerve left? Swerve right?

A steep drop into brush? Or a narrow shoulder that ends in a cliff wall?

Left.

Instinct.

Colter Shaw spun the wheel of the rental Kia sedan hard, braking intermittently—he couldn't afford a skid. The vehicle, which had been doing forty along this winding stretch in high mountains, plunged into foliage, narrowly missing a collision with the boulder that had tumbled down a steep hillside and rolled into the middle of road before him. Shaw thought the sound of a two-hundred-pound piece of rock rolling through brush and over gravel would be more dramatic; the transit was virtually silent.

Left was the correct choice.

Had he gone right, the car would have slammed into a granite outcropping hidden by tall, beige grass.

Shaw, who spent much time assessing the percentage

likelihood of harm when making professional decisions, nonetheless knew that sometimes you simply had to roll the dice and see what happened.

No airbags, no injury. He was, however, trapped inside the Kia. To his left was a sea of mahonia, otherwise known as Oregon grape, benign names both, belying the plant's needle-sharp spikes that can handily penetrate shirt sleeves on their effortless way into skin. Not an option for an exit. The passenger side was better, blocked only by insubstantial cinquefoil, in cheerful June bloom, yellow, and a tangle of forsythia tendrils.

Shaw shoved the right-side door open again and again, pushing back the viney plant. As he did this, he noted that the attacker's timing had been good. Had the weapon fallen sooner, Shaw could easily have braked. Any later, he'd have been past it and still on his way.

And a weapon it must have been.

Washington State certainly was home to earthquakes and seismic activity of all sorts, but there'd been no recent shivering in the vicinity. And rocks that are this big usually stay put unless they're leveraged off intentionally— in front of, or onto, cars driven by men in pursuit of an armed, fleeing felon.

After doffing his brown plaid sport coat, Shaw began to leverage himself through the gap between door and frame. He was in trim fit, as one who climbs mountainsides for recreation will be. Still, the opening was only fourteen or so inches, and he was caught. He would shove the door open, retreat, then shove once more. The gap slowly grew wider.

He heard a rustling in the brush across the road. The man who'd tipped the rock into Shaw's path was now scrabbling down the hillside and pressing through the dense growth toward Shaw, who struggled further to free himself. He saw a glint in the man's hand. A pistol.

The son of a survivalist and in a manner of speaking a survivalist himself, Shaw knew myriad ways of cheating death. On the other hand, he was a rock climber, a dirt bike fanatic, a man with a profession that set him against killers and escaped prisoners who'd stop at nothing to stay free. The smoke of death wafted everywhere around him constantly. But it wasn't that finality that troubled him. In death, you had no reckoning. Far worse would be a catastrophic injury to the spine, to the eyes, the ears. Crippling, darkening the world, or muting it forever.

In his youth, Shaw was called "the restless one" among his siblings. Now, having grown into a self-professed restless man, he knew that such incapacity would be pure hell.

He continued to squeeze.

Almost out.

*Come on, come on . . .*

Yes!

No.

Just as he was about to break free, his wallet, in the left rear pocket of his black jeans, caught.

The attacker stopped, leaning through into the brush, and lifted the pistol. Shaw heard it cock. A revolver.

And a big one. When it fired, the muzzle blast blew green leaves from branches.

The bullet went wide, kicking up dust near Shaw.

Another click.

The man fired again.

This bullet hit its mark.

# 2.

Shaw was piloting his thirty-foot Winnebago camper through the winding streets of Gig Harbor, Washington State.

With about seven thousand inhabitants, the place was both charming and scuffed around the edges. It was, to be sure, a harbor, well protected, connected to Puget Sound via a narrow channel through which pleasure and fishing craft now glided. The Winnebago motored past working and long-abandoned factories that manufactured vessels and the countless parts and accessories with which ships were outfitted. To Colter Shaw, never a sailor, it seemed like you could spend every minute of every day maintaining, repairing, polishing and organizing a ship without ever going out to sea.

A sign announced the Blessing of the Fleet in the middle of the harbor, the dates indicating that it had taken place earlier in the month.

PLEASURE CRAFT NOW WELCOME TOO!

Perhaps the industry was now less robust than in the past, and the organizers of the event wanted to beef up its image by letting lawyers and doctors and salesmen edge their cabin cruisers up to the circle of the commercial craft—if that geometry was the configuration for fleet blessing.

Shaw, a professional reward seeker, was here on a job—the word he used to describe what he did. *Cases* were what law enforcement investigated and what prosecutors prosecuted. Although after years of pursuing any number of criminals Shaw might have made a fine detective, he wanted none of the regimen and regulation that went with a full-time job of that sort.

He was free to take on, or reject, any job he wanted. He could chose to abandon the quest at any time.

Freedom meant a lot to Colter Shaw.

He was presently reflecting on the job. In the first page of the notebook he was devoting to the investigation, he'd written down the details that had been provided by one of his business managers:

*Location: Gig Harbor, Pierce County, Washington State.*
*Reward offered for: Information leading to the arrest and conviction of two individuals:*

*— Adam Harper, 27, resident of Tacoma*
*— Erick Young, 20, resident of Gig Harbor*

*Incident: There have been a series of hate crimes in the county, including graffiti of swastikas, the number 88 (Nazi symbol) and the number 666 (sign for the devil) painted on synagogues and a half-dozen churches, pri-*

*marily those with largely black congregations. On June 7, Brethren Baptist Church of Gig Harbor was defaced and a cross burned in the front yard. Original news story was that the church itself was set on fire, but that was found to be inaccurate. A janitor and a lay preacher (William DuBois and Frederick Estes) were inside and ran out to see the two suspects. Either Harper or Young opened fire with a handgun, wounding both men. The preacher has been released from the hospital. The janitor remains in the intensive care unit of a local hospital. The perpetrators fled in a red Toyota pickup, registered to Adam Harper. Law enforcement agency running case: Pierce County Public Safety Office, liaising with U.S. Justice Department, which will investigate to determine if the incident is a federal hate crime.*

*Offerors and amount of reward:*

—*Reward one: $50,000, offered by Pierce County, underwritten by the Western Washington Ecumenical Council (with much of that sum donated by Micro-Enterprises founder Ed Jasper).*

—*Reward two: $900 offered by Erick Young's parents and family.*

*To be aware of: Dalton Crowe is actively pursuing the reward.*

This last bit of intelligence wasn't good.

Crowe was an unpleasant man in his forties. Former military, he opened a security business on the East Coast, though it wasn't successful and he shut it down. His career now was freelance security consultant, mercenary and, from time to time, reward seeker. Shaw's and Crowe's paths had crossed several times, once or twice violently. They approached the profession differently. Crowe rarely went after missing persons; he sought only wanted criminals and escapees. If you shot a fugitive while using a legal weapon in self-defense, you still got the reward and could usually avoid jail. This was Crowe's approach, the antithesis of Shaw's.

Shaw had not been sure he wanted to take the job. The other day, as he sat in a lawn chair in Silicon Valley, he had leaned toward pursuing another matter. That second mission was personal, and it involved his father and a secret from the past—a secret that had nearly gotten Shaw shot in the elbows and kneecaps by a hitman with the unlikely name of Ebbitt Droon.

Risk of bodily harm—*reasonable* risk—didn't deter Shaw, and he truly wanted to pursue his search for his father's hidden treasure.

He'd decided, however, that the capture of two apparent neo-Nazis, armed and willing to kill, took priority.

GPS now directed him through the hilly, winding streets of Gig Harbor until he came to the address he sought, a pleasant single-story home, painted cheerful yellow, a stark contrast to the gray overcast. He glanced in the mirror and brushed smooth his short blond hair, which lay close to his head. It was mussed from a twenty-minute nap, his only rest on the ten-hour drive here from the San Francisco area.

Slinging his computer bag over his shoulder, he climbed from the van and walked to the front door, rang the bell.

Larry and Emma Young admitted him, and he followed the couple into the living room. He assessed their ages to be mid-forties. Erick's father sported sparse gray-brown hair and wore beige slacks and a short-sleeved T-shirt, immaculately white. Emma wore a concealing A-line dress in lavender. She had put on fresh makeup for the visitor, Shaw sensed. Missing children disrupt much, and showers and personal details are often neglected. Not so here. Two pole lamps cast disks of homey light around the room, whose walls were papered with pink and russet flowers and whose floors were covered in dark green carpet, over which sat some Lowe's or Home Depot Oriental rugs. A nice home. Modest. When he'd spoken to them on the phone about stopping by, the Youngs had suggested a café or restaurant. But Shaw had said he'd prefer to meet them in their home. They might have something of their son's that could help him track the young man down, he'd said. This was true, though in his profession Shaw also liked to see where the offerors lived. This helped him assess the job. Had someone run away for safety? Was it possible an offeror had posted a reward for information leading to the discovery of a missing person they had killed? Peering inside homes gave Shaw a better idea of the players involved.

A brown uniform jacket sat on a coat rack near the door. It was thick and stained, with *Larry* stitched on the breast. Shaw guessed the man was a mechanic.

"Sit down, sir," Larry said.

Shaw took a comfortable overstuffed armchair of bright red leather and the couple sat across from him. "Have you heard anything about Erick since we talked?"

"No, sir."

"What's the latest from the police?"

Larry said, "He and that other man, Adam. They're still around the area. The detective, he thinks they're scraping together money, borrowing it, maybe stealing it—"

"He wouldn't," said Emma Young.

"What the police said," Larry explained. "I'm just telling him what they said."

The mother swallowed. "He's . . . never. I mean, I . . ." She began to cry—again. Her eyes had been dry but red and swollen when Shaw arrived.

Shaw removed a notebook from his computer bag, as well as a Delta Titanio Galassia fountain pen, black with three orange rings toward the nib. Writing with the instrument was neither pretense nor luxury for Colter Shaw, who took voluminous notes during the course of his reward jobs. The pen meant less wear and tear on his writing hand. It also was simply a small pleasure to use.

He now wrote the date and the names of the couple. He looked up and asked for details about their son's life. In college and working part-time. On summer break, following the end of term. Lived at home.

"Does Erick have a history of being involved in neo-Nazi or any extremist groups?"

"My God, no," Larry muttered as if exhausted by the familiar question.

"This is all just crazy," said Emma. "He's a good boy. Oh, he's had a little trouble like everybody. Some drug stuff after, well, after what happened, it's understandable. Just tried 'em is all. The school called. No police. They were good about that."

Larry grimaced. "Pierce County, Tacoma? The meth and drug capital of the state. You should read the stories in the paper. Forty percent of all the meth in Washington is produced here."

Shaw nodded. "Was that what Erick did?"

"No, some of that oxy stuff. Just for a while. He took antidepressants too. Still does."

"You said 'after what happened.' After what?"

They looked at each other. "We lost our younger boy sixteen months ago."

"Drugs?"

Emma's hand, resting on her thigh, closed into a fist, bundling the cloth below her fingers. "No. Was on his bike, hit by somebody who was drunk. My, it was hard. So hard. But it hit Erick in particular. It changed him. They were close."

Brothers, Shaw thought, understanding the complex feelings the word implied.

Larry said, "But he wouldn't do anything hurtful. Never anything bad. He never has. 'Cepting for the church."

His wife snapped, "Which he didn't do. You know he didn't."

"I meant what they *claimed* he did." Larry fell silent.

"Does Erick own a weapon? Have access to one?"

"No."

Shaw asked, "So his friend had the gun. Adam."

Larry: "Friend? He wasn't a friend. We never heard of him."

Emma's ruddy fingers twined the dress again. "He's the one did it. I told the police. We both did. Adam kidnapped him. I'm sure that's what happened. *He* had a gun—*he* shot those fellows and made Erick come with him. He was going to take his car, rob him."

"They took Adam's truck, though, not Erick's."

No response to that obvious observation.

"He had his own bank account?"

The boy's father said, "Yes."

So they wouldn't know about withdrawals. The police could get that information, what branches he'd been to. Probably already had.

"You know how much money he has? Enough to get very far?"

"Couple thousand, maybe."

Shaw had been examining the room, observing mostly the pictures of the Youngs' two boys. Erick was a handsome young man with bushy brown hair and an easy smile. Shaw had also seen pictures of Adam Harper, posted as part of the reward announcement. There were no mug shots, though in both of the photos included in the reward announcement he was looking into the camera with caution. The young man, whose crew cut was blond with blue highlights, was gaunt. He was seven years Erick's senior.

"I'm going to pursue this, try to find your son."

Larry said, "Oh, sure. Please. You're nothing like that big guy."

"Didn't like him one bit," Emma muttered.

"Dalton Crowe?"

"That was his name. I told him to leave it be. I wasn't going to pay him any reward. He laughed and said I could stuff it. He was going after the bigger one anyway, you know—the fifty thousand the county offered."

"When was he here?"

"Couple days ago."

In his notebook Shaw wrote, *D.C. present at offerors' house. June 9.*

"Now, let me tell you how I approach this. It won't cost you anything unless I find Erick. No expenses. If I find him, you'll owe me that nine hundred dollars."

Larry said, "It's a thousand sixty now. One of my cousins came through. Wish it was more, but . . ."

"I know you'll want me to talk to him and bring him home to you. But that's not my job. He's a fugitive and I would be breaking the law if I did that."

"Aiding and abetting," Emma said. "I watch all the crime shows."

Colter Shaw tended not to smile, but when meeting offerors, he occasionally did, to put them at ease. "I don't apprehend. I deal in information, not citizen's arrests. But if I can find him, I won't let the police know where he is until there's no chance he or anybody else'll be hurt. You'll get a lawyer. Do you know one?"

The regarded each other. "Fellow did our closing," Larry said.

"No. A criminal lawyer. I'll get you some names."

"Oh, thank you, sir."

Shaw reviewed his notes so far. His handwriting was small and had once been described as balletic, it was so beautifully drawn. This notebook wasn't ruled. Shaw didn't need guidance. Each line was perfectly horizontal.

For another twenty minutes Shaw asked questions and the couple responded. Over the course of the interview, he noted that their adamant view that their son was innocent was objective; they simply could not accept that the son they knew had committed the crime. It had to be Adam Harper. "Or," Shaw had suggested, "someone else altogether."

When he felt he had enough information for the moment, he put away the pen and notebook, rose and walked to the door. The parents agreed to send any new information they heard from the police or friends or relatives Erick had contacted for money or shelter.

"Thank you, sir," Emma said at the doorway, debating hugging him, it seemed. She did not.

It was the husband who was choking up. He fumbled whatever he was going to say and just gripped Shaw's hand. Larry turned back to the house before the first tear appeared.

As Shaw walked to the Winnebago, he was reflecting on the one subject he had not mentioned to Emma and Larry: his policy was not to accept a reward from family members if the search revealed that their missing loved one was dead. No reason to even bring up the possibility, more or less likely, that their second child had been murdered as soon as Adam found he had no more use for the boy.

# NO
# SAFE
# PLACE

## ALSO BY PATRICIA GIBNEY

*The Missing Ones*
*The Stolen Girls*
*The Lost Child*

# NO
# SAFE
# PLACE

## PATRICIA GIBNEY

bookouture

Published by Bookouture

An imprint of StoryFire Ltd.

Carmelite House,
50 Victoria Embankment,
London EC4Y 0DZ

www.bookouture.com

ISBN: 978-1-78681-409-8
eBook ISBN: 978-1-78681-408-1

*For Marie, Gerard and Cathy*
*With love*

## Tuesday 9 February 2016, 3.15 a.m.

Her bare feet stuck to the frost, but still she ran. She thought she was screaming, but there was no sound coming from her throat. Her elbow smashed into granite, the pain minimal in comparison to her fear.

Chancing a glance over her shoulder, she found it was as dark behind her as the blackness that stretched before her. She had unintentionally veered off the path and was now lost among the limestone and granite. Feeling cold stones cutting her soles, she tried to raise herself over the kerb she knew must surely be there, but stubbed her toe and fell head first into the next furrow.

With her mind void of all thoughts except reaching safety, she hauled herself onto her bleeding knees and listened. Silence. No twigs breaking or leaves being thrashed. Had he left her alone? Had he abandoned the chase? Now that she'd stopped running, she shivered violently in the freezing night. A light down the slope to her right caught her eye as she scanned the near horizon. An enclave of bungalows. She knew exactly where she was. And in the distance, she saw the amber hue of street lights. Safety.

A hurried look around. She had to make a run for it. Silently she counted to three, getting ready to make her final dash to safety.

'Now or never,' she whispered, and without a care for her nakedness, she stood up, ready to run like a panther. That was when she saw the breath suspended in the frost of the night.

She felt his arm encircling her throat, crushing her windpipe, and her body being dragged against his jacket. The sweet smell of fabric softener mixed with the sour scent of anger clouded her nostrils. With one last bout of adrenaline, she jabbed her elbow backwards, thrusting it deep and hard into his solar plexus. A gasp of wind escaped his mouth as he loosened his grip, and she was free.

She screamed and ran. Banging and crashing into granite, leaping over frozen stones and low kerbs, she tumbled, still screaming, down the slope towards the light. Almost there. She heard his booted footsteps gaining on her.

No, please God, no. She had to get off this path. Veering to her left, zigzagging, she was almost at the wall when the ground disappeared beneath her. Down she fell, six feet into the cavern, stones and clods of clay tumbling with her.

Excruciating pain shot up her leg, and an agonised scream exploded from her mouth. She knew that the sound she'd heard had not been the breaking of timber but the bone in her left leg shattering with the fall. Biting hard into her knuckles, she tried to be silent. Surely he couldn't find her here, could he?

But as she looked up at the night sky with its twinkling stars heralding further frost, his face appeared at the edge of the hole. All semblance of hope disappeared as the first clatter of clay fell onto her upturned face.

And as she cried, big salty tears mingling with the dirt, she understood with terrible clarity that she was going to die in someone else's grave.

# DAY ONE

Wednesday 10 February 2016

# CHAPTER ONE

Lottie Parker woke to the sound of a child crying. She opened one eye and squinted at the digital clock: 5.30 a.m.

'Oh no, Louis. It's the middle of the night,' she moaned.

Her grandson, at just over four and a half months old, had yet to sleep for longer than two hours straight. Throwing back the duvet, she went to the bedroom next to hers. The night light cast a shadowy hue over her sleeping twenty-year-old daughter. Katie had a pillow over her head, the duvet rising and falling in rhythm with her breathing. Louis stopped crying when Lottie lifted him from his cot. She fetched a nappy and a bottle of formula from the bedside cabinet and left her daughter to her dreams.

Back in her own room, she changed Louis, nestled him into her arms and fed him. She felt the baby's heart beating against her breast. There was something so soothing and at the same time so grounding about it. Adam would have loved him. Her heart constricted when she thought of her husband, dead over four years now. Cancer. The void left after his passing refused to be filled.

She feathered her grandson's soft dark hair with a kiss, and as the baby twisted, pushing the bottle out of his mouth, Lottie winced with the pain in her upper back. She knew she couldn't afford to be off work. Even though things in Ragmullin were unbearably quiet at the moment, it wouldn't stay that way for long.

She winded her little grandson and he smiled up at her. She smiled back.

A good omen for the day ahead.

She hoped.

# CHAPTER TWO

Mollie Hunter settled into her seat. She placed her laptop bag on the table, then rolled up her cotton scarf, scrunched it against the window and rested her head. Her eyelids slid closed, blocking out the impending breakthrough of dawn. Earbuds pumped soft music into her ears, muting the shuffling of her fellow commuters. As the train shunted out of Ragmullin station, she fell back into the sleep she'd risen from just thirty minutes earlier.

Her dreams resurfaced with the rhythm of the wheels, and unconsciously, she smiled.

'What's so funny?'

Mollie heard the question through the haze of sleep, and opened one eye. She hadn't noticed anyone sit down opposite her. But he was there. Again. The second morning in a row he had ignored other empty seats and occupied that one. Straight across from her. Slowly she closed her eyes again, determined to ignore him. Not that he was bad-looking. He appeared to be fairly ordinary, though his mouth wore a smug grin. He was maybe a little older than her twenty-five years. A mental image flared behind her closed eyes and she found herself awakening fully and staring at him.

Who the hell was he?

'What's your name?' he asked.

The cheek of him! There was an unwritten protocol on the six a.m. commuter service. No one annoyed anyone else. They were all in the same predicament. Up at all hours, half asleep, coffee hastily

prepared and poured into travel mugs. Phones, earbuds, laptops and Kindles the only accessories of this tribe. So why the hell couldn't he shut up and let her sleep? Once they reached Maynooth, the carriage would begin to fill up and she could ignore him totally. For now, though, she couldn't.

His eyes were a cool blue. His hair was concealed under a knitted beanie. His fingernails were clean. Manicured? She wondered for a moment if he was a teacher. Or maybe a civil servant or a banker. She couldn't tell whether there was a suit jacket or a sweater under his heavy padded jacket, but she knew from previous mornings that he wore jeans. Blue, with an ironed crease down the centre of the legs. God, who did that any more? His mother? But he looked a little old to be still living with his mother. A wife, then? No ring. Why was she even thinking about it? A tremor of unease shook her shoulders, and immediately she felt afraid of him.

Closing her eyes, she allowed the music to invade her consciousness and the chug of the train to comfort her, hoping for sleep to help her through the next hour and ten minutes. And then she felt his foot touch her boot. Her eyes flew open and she drew back her leg as if scalded.

'What the hell?' she croaked. The first words she'd uttered since awakening that morning.

'Sorry,' he said, his eyes piercing blue darts. His foot didn't move.

And Mollie knew by the tone of his voice that he was anything but sorry.

❋

He looked kind of cute, Grace thought. The way he bugged the woman who just wanted to sleep. She couldn't help smiling at him. He didn't notice her. No one did. But she didn't care. She really didn't.

She curled her fingers in her childish-looking mittens and shrugged her shoulders up to her ears, wishing she could pretend to sleep. But she was never any good at pretending. *What you see is what you get.* That was what her mum always said about her. And now she was stuck living with her brother for a month. Not that he was around too often. Thank God, because he was awfully fussy.

She looked down at the empty seat beside her to make sure her bag was still there. No one ever sat beside her until it was standing room only. I'm not going to bite you, she wanted to say, but she never did. She just smiled her gap-toothed smile and nodded. A nod usually put them at ease. You'd think I was a serial killer, the way some of them look at me, she thought. She couldn't help her anxious fidgeting, and she didn't care about what anyone thought, one way or the other.

I am me, she wanted to shout.

She remained tight-lipped.

# CHAPTER THREE

'Chloe and Sean! Do I have to make myself hoarse every single morning? Up! Now!'

Lottie turned away from the stairs and shook her head. It was getting worse rather than better. At least next week they would be on mid-term break and she could escape to work without ripped vocal cords.

She unloaded the washing machine. The laundry basket was still half full, so she threw in another load and switched on the machine, then lugged the damp clothes to the dryer. At one time, her mother, Rose Fitzpatrick, used to do a little housework for her, but that relationship was more strained than ever before, and now Rose was feeling poorly.

Sipping a cup of coffee, Lottie allowed it to soothe her nerves. She swallowed three painkillers and tried to massage her back where the stab wound was doing its best to heal. Putting the physical injuries aside, she knew the emotional scars were embedded on her psyche forever. As she gazed out at the frosty morning, she wondered if she should fetch a sweater to keep out the cold. She was wearing a black T-shirt with long sleeves, frayed at the cuffs, and a pair of black skinny jeans. She'd dumped her trusty Uggs last week and was wearing Katie's flat-soled black leather ankle boots.

'Here, Mother,' said Chloe, strolling into the kitchen. 'I think you might need this today.'

'Thank you.' Lottie took the blue hoodie from her seventeen-year-old daughter. She noticed that Chloe was wearing pale foundation and a smoky eyeshadow with thick black mascara. Her blonde hair was tied up in a knot on top of her head.

'You know you're not allowed to wear make-up to school.'

'I do. And I'm not.' Chloe fetched a box of cornflakes and began shovelling them into her mouth.

'And that's lip gloss. Come on. You don't want to get into trouble.'

'I won't. It's not make-up. Just a soft sheen to protect my skin from the cold air,' Chloe said, picking cornflake crumbs off her sticky lips.

Lottie shook her head. Too early for an argument. She rinsed her mug under the tap. 'I'm just warning you in case the teachers notice.'

'Right!' Chloe said and turned up her nose. So like her father, Lottie thought.

'I worry about you.'

'Stop fussing. I'm fine.' Chloe picked up her rucksack and headed for the door.

'I can give you a lift if you like.'

'I'll walk, thanks.'

The front door shut loudly. Lottie wasn't at all convinced her daughter *was* fine. Being called Mother still rankled. It grated on her nerves, and Chloe knew it. That was why she did it. Only in times of extreme tenderness did she call Lottie Mum.

'I'd love a pancake,' Sean said, entering the kitchen holding out his school tie.

'Sean, what age are you?' Lottie looped the tie round her neck and began making a knot.

He looked out from under his eyelashes. 'I can't wait to be fifteen in April. Maybe then you might stop treating me like a kid.'

'I've shown you countless times how to knot your tie.' She handed it back.

'Dad never learned how to do it. I remember you always making the knot for him.'

Lottie smiled wistfully. 'You're right. And I'm sorry, but I haven't time to make pancakes. You've been watching too many American TV shows.' She flicked his hair out of his eyes and squeezed his shoulder. 'See you later. Be good at school.'

She zipped up her hoodie, grabbed her bag and coat and escaped towards the front door.

'Any chance of a lift?' Sean said.

'If you hurry up.'

She waited as he took a tub of yoghurt from the fridge and a spoon from a drawer.

Picking up his bag, he said, 'I'm ready when you are.'

Lottie shouted up the stairs. 'See you later, Katie. Give Louis a goodbye kiss from me.' Then, without waiting for her eldest child to reply, she followed her son out the door.

Just another normal morning in the Parker household.

# CHAPTER FOUR

The train stopped at the university town of Maynooth. No one disembarked. Not unusual for the first Ragmullin to Dublin commuter train of the morning. No, the college students would crowd the seven a.m. train. The platform was full, though. Coffee steamed in the frosty air and commuters shuffled towards each other for warmth and seats as they boarded.

Mollie hoped the man sitting opposite her would get out. But she wasn't going to be that lucky. Like the other mornings, he was travelling to Dublin.

With his arms folded and his face turned to the window, she studied him again. Though his eyes were averted, she could feel them on her. Yuck, she thought with a shiver. Rubbing her hands up and down her arms, she tried to ward off the cold. But the feeling was something more than the open doors breathing in the outside air. The chill was emanating from the man sitting across from her.

She watched as he slowly turned away from the window and smiled. Thin pink lips turned up at the corners without the smile reaching his chill blue eyes with their dark pinprick pupils.

'Did you study at Maynooth University?' he asked.

His voice cut a shard into her heart. He sounded different from when he'd spoken earlier. Enquiring yet accusing. Gulping, she shook her head.

'What college did you attend?' he probed.

She really should tell him to bugger off. It was none of his business. Hell, she didn't know who he was. He didn't know her. Or did he? Furrowing her brow, she squinted at him. Was there anything vaguely familiar about him? No, she concluded. Nothing.

'Cat got your tongue?' That smile again. A smile that wasn't a smile at all.

Biting the inside of her mouth, she wished she could get off the damn train. As far away from him as possible. *You're being irrational,* her inner voice warned. *He's just being friendly. Making conversation.* But no one made conversation on the early-morning commute.

Wanting to move away, she looked around, but the train was filling up and she might have to stand. She glanced across the aisle and caught the eye of a young woman sitting beside the opposite window. There was a spare seat beside her. Should she move over there? Would it appear odd given that there was still an empty place right next to her? But she didn't know the man, so what did she care?

Pulling her black laptop bag towards her chest, she stood, grabbing her scarf before it hit the floor. She edged into the aisle and plonked herself down beside the young woman. But even as she exhaled with relief, she felt the cold air dissipate, to be replaced by the heat of an unspoken anger.

Blindly she stared straight ahead, hoping the girl wouldn't try to strike up a conversation. No such luck.

'My name's Grace, what's yours?' The young woman flashed a gap-toothed smile.

Mollie groaned and scrunched her eyes tightly shut. It was definitely one of those mornings.

✳

Two rows down, the man snuggled his chin into his scarf. He'd watched the young woman get up from opposite the annoying

chatty man and sit over beside the gap-toothed girl. He knew it was a good thing that she was on edge. The guy had distracted her. Made her fearful. He smiled into the wool of the scarf. She was playing straight into his hands.

If that other bitch hadn't escaped, he wouldn't have need for her. But he always liked to be one step ahead of himself. His mother used to say that.

The thought of his mother caused his smile to slip, and he shoved his hands deeper into his pockets as the trembling began to shake his joints. It was cold, and the heat was always hit and miss on the train, but now he felt certifiably freezing. Shaking his head, he tried to dislodge the image of his mother and replace it with the girl gripping her laptop to her chest. She'd kept her jacket buttoned up and he wondered what she was wearing beneath it. Did she change her clothes when she arrived at work? He knew a lot about her, but he didn't know what she did once she walked through the doors of the nondescript office building on Townsend Street.

The train stopped and started at all the fiddly suburban stations and the carriage warmed up considerably with the pressing crowd. The aisle was now full of people clutching bags and phones, the air clogged with the smell of feet and body odour. It was so crowded that he could no longer see her. He closed his eyes, conjured her up from memory and touched her straight dark hair with an imaginary finger, all the while stroking himself through the pocket of his coat. He couldn't wait much longer. This evening he would see her again.

The train swayed and chugged, speeded up and then slowed down as it entered Dublin's Connolly station. An air of anticipation rose with the heated breath of the passengers as they readied themselves to disembark. He'd have a long day ahead thinking about her, waiting for her. But it would be worth it. Come 6.30 this evening, she would be his.

# CHAPTER FIVE

At the garda station, Detective Inspector Lottie Parker climbed the stairs and made her way down the corridor. Her refurbished office was to the rear of the general area. The last piece of the puzzle that had involved three years of renovations and extensions. It even had a door that shut properly. But she couldn't get used to it, so she sat down at her old desk in the main office. Detective Sergeant Mark Boyd was seated opposite her in the cluttered space he shared with Detectives Larry Kirby and Maria Lynch.

'I can use it if you don't want to,' he said with a wink, indicating the empty office behind her.

'Not on your life,' she said. 'It's good to retreat in there when I want; to close the door and scream in peace.'

'You scream out here most of the time. We're immune to your outbursts.' He lined pages up in a file and shut it.

'What did you say, Boyd?'

'I'm only expressing out loud what we're all thinking,' he muttered under his breath.

'I know when I'm not wanted.' She picked up her well-worn leather handbag, shrugged it onto her shoulder and marched into her new office, closing the door behind her.

At her desk, she tapped the keyboard and the computer pinged into life. She opened the page she had been viewing the day before, clicked and zoomed up the photograph of twenty-five-year-old Elizabeth Byrne. Not officially classed as missing because it was too

soon. But it was a calm week in Ragmullin, so she'd tasked Boyd with taking a cursory look into Elizabeth's suspected disappearance.

Crooking her chin in her hand, she studied the portrait picture, stared into the shining eyes of the young woman and wondered at the sheen on the auburn hair swept up behind her ear and hanging seductively across one brown eye. Instinctively her hand flew up to her own matted tresses. She needed a colour and cut. Payday was a week away, but she still couldn't afford the eighty-plus euros it would cost.

'Anything else you want me to do regarding Elizabeth Byrne?' Boyd stood half inside, half outside the door.

'I don't bite,' she said, trying to keep the smile from her lips.

'Really? I thought that was you sharpening your teeth a few moments ago.'

'Don't be a smartarse, Boyd. Come in and sit down.'

He closed the door and sat on the grey fabric chair, which she had strategically placed at an angle, ensuring he couldn't see what she was doing. Which wasn't a whole lot, if she was honest.

'Get anything from CCTV?' she asked.

Rustling through the file on his knee, Boyd scanned his eyes over a page then placed a black-and-white image in front of her.

'You know it's not official,' he said.

'I know.'

'It's not yet forty-eight hours.'

She nodded. 'Just tell me what you've got so far.'

'What has you so cranky this morning?'

'Boyd! Just tell me what I'm damn well looking at.'

He scrunched his shoulders and leaned over the desk. 'That's a screenshot of the CCTV from the train station. Taken as she purchased her weekly ticket, Monday morning at 5.55 a.m., before getting on the commuter train to Dublin. She works in the Financial

Services Centre, an administrator at a German bank. According to her colleagues, she was there all day and clocked out at 16.25 in order to get the 17.10 train back to Ragmullin. I asked a friend in Store Street garda station to help. He trawled footage from Connolly station CCTV but as yet he hasn't come across her.'

'Cameras on each platform?'

'Mainly on the DART lines. Other than that, they're focused on the general concourse and ticket offices.'

'Damn.'

'That's mild coming from you.'

'I'm cutting down on swearing. Katie says baby Louis will pick up on it.'

'Ah, for Jaysus' sake,' Boyd laughed. 'Any sign of her going back to college?'

'What do you think?' Lottie shook her head. 'She's hell-bent on heading off to New York to meet up with Tom Rickard, Louis' grandfather.'

'That might be a good thing.'

Mulling over Boyd's words, Lottie was reminded of the trauma her family had suffered the previous year with the death of Rickard's only child, Jason, Katie's boyfriend. A few months later, Katie, then nineteen years old, had discovered she was pregnant with Jason's baby. She'd deferred her college course, and now all her time was consumed with caring for her son.

Lottie had to admit that little Louis was a great tonic for the rest of the family. Chloe and Sean doted on him. But Katie was struggling, while stubbornly refusing all the help Lottie offered. She'd secured a passport for Louis, and was adamant she was heading to New York. There was still the conversation to be had about the cost. Tonight, maybe. Maybe not.

'A trip away might benefit her,' she said. 'But I'm not sure.'

'You're afraid she won't want to come home. Is that it?' he said, seriousness furrowing his brow.

She watched as he leaned back and folded his arms over his pressed blue shirt and immaculate navy tie. His greying hair was cut short as usual, and his leanness verged on being too thin, but not quite. Mid forties suited him better than it suited her, she had to admit. She liked sparring with Boyd and she knew he liked her, but her life was too complicated to embark on anything serious.

'I'm not sure about anything with regards to my children,' she said.

'One day at a time, eh?'

'Sure.' She picked up the CCTV image before Boyd began asking awkward questions. 'A twenty-five-year-old disappears without trace from the 17.10 Dublin to Ragmullin train on Monday evening. Are we positive she actually boarded that train?'

'She was a regular commuter. I talked to a few people leaving the station yesterday evening. Most said they saw her but then weren't sure of the day, but two people swear she was on it. They remembered her standing in the aisle before she secured a seat after Maynooth. Neither of those witnesses can tell us anything further, though, because they both disembarked at the next station, Enfield.'

Lottie said, 'But Elizabeth never arrived home.'

'Exactly.'

'Maybe she got off at Enfield too.'

'Enfield station CCTV confirms she did not.'

'So back to Ragmullin station. You have a CCTV image of her that morning. What about the evening?'

'All the cameras are focused on either the ticket desk or the car park. But we know she has no car so she must have walked to the station Monday morning.'

'She might have stayed on the train and ended up somewhere else.'

Boyd shook his head. 'I've checked with all the stations up to and including Sligo, where the train terminates, and there's no evidence she was on it other than the witnesses who *think* they saw her before Enfield.'

'The media will be calling this "the girl who disappeared from the train".' She printed off the photograph and handed it to Boyd. 'Tell me what you see.'

'A young woman. Hair cut to her shoulders. A scattering of freckles across her nose. Dark brown eyes and full lips. Can I say she's pretty?'

'Boyd! I'm asking about her personality.' She shook her head in exasperation.

'It's just a photograph. I'm not a psychic.'

'Try.'

He sighed. 'She looks sensible enough. No nose or eyebrow piercings. No visible tattoos, though it is only a head shot. Eyes appear clear and bright. Probably no drug use.'

'That's what I thought. Anything show up on her social media accounts?'

'Nothing since Sunday night.'

'What did that say?'

'Just a Facebook post with a GIF of a drowned-looking cat and the caption "Don't tell me tomorrow is Monday. Just don't."'

'Do you think she did a runner?'

'She lives at home and her mother says all her stuff is still in her room.'

Standing up, Lottie grabbed her jacket and bag. 'Come on. Let's have a look round her house and see if we can find out anything.'

'It's not yet forty-eight hours.'

'Are you a parrot? You keep repeating yourself.'

'Elizabeth is an adult. I think you're being a bit premature about this.'

'Oh, for Christ's sake, stop whingeing. Better this than being out in the freezing cold chasing boy racers or trying to get information about illegal bare-knuckle fights.'

'God help me,' he muttered.

She opened the door and looked back over her shoulder as Boyd slowly rose to his feet and joined her. Catching his soapy scent as he passed, she had to stop her hand from reaching out to his. She couldn't do anything that might compromise the contented truce they were experiencing at the moment.

'Why the sour puss?' he asked.

'None of your business,' she said with a smile, and marched through the main office, leaving the jangle of cooling radiators in her wake. In the corridor, she walked straight into Superintendent Corrigan.

'I was just coming to get you,' he said. 'My office. Now.'

Staring after his bulk, Lottie stood open-mouthed. She'd been good recently. Hadn't she?

'What did you do now?' Boyd said, retreating to his office.

'Nothing. I hope.' She crossed her fingers as she took off down the corridor after Corrigan.


'Sit down, Parker. You know it makes me nervous looking at you hopping from foot to foot.'

'I'm not …' Lottie clamped her mouth shut, folded her jacket over her arm and did as her boss commanded.

Superintendent Corrigan pulled his chair into his desk. With his belly suitably comfortable, he tapped a pen on the wood and looked up at her. She stifled a gasp as she noticed the worsening state of his eye. Last summer he'd sported a patch over it, and before Christmas he had declared it better. Better than what, no one asked, but now she thought it looked to have deteriorated considerably.

'Will you stop staring at my eye,' he said, rubbing it viciously, making it tear up and redden further.

'Sorry, sir.'

'Well, actually, it's one of the reasons I called you in.' He paused. 'I had to visit another specialist. He didn't like it. Sent me for a scan. Found a bastard of a tumour sitting on the optic nerve. And ...' His voice cracked and he stood up. She watched him walk to the window. Shit, this was bad news. And she felt there was worse to come.

'I'm going to have to take a break from duty.'

'I'm sorry.'

'Will you stop saying sorry? It's not your fault. One of the only things, I might add, that isn't your fault around here.' He turned around and she saw how much it was annoying him to have to leave work. 'I've contacted head office and they're sending a temporary replacement. No need for interviews or any of that feckin' shite.'

'Really? I thought it was obligatory to hold interviews for replacements, even short-term ones.'

'I've no feckin' idea how short or long my absence will be. My concern is focused on getting this bastard tumour out of my head.'

'I understand. Sorry, sir.'

'Jesus, will you give it up?'

'Sor—' Lottie stopped herself before she said it again. If they weren't holding interviews, shouldn't she get the temporary job of superintendent?

'And before you say another word, you are not going to be my replacement. Apparently your reputation for ballsing things up has reached people higher than me. Much as I try to keep our investigations local.' He took a breath before continuing. 'And how are you feeling since you returned to duty? Better, I hope.'

He wasn't just talking about her physical health. The injury she'd suffered at the hands of a killer had been the catalyst for astonishing revelations about Lottie's family history. Revelations she still couldn't deal with.

'I'm fine, sir. A month at home nearly sent me loopy, but I feel grand now.' She crossed her fingers that he wouldn't dig any deeper.

'That's good.'

'Who is deputising for you, sir? Anyone I know?'

'Detective Inspector David McMahon.'

Lottie shot out of her chair, dropping her jacket and bag to the floor. 'You can't be serious. McMahon! Holy Mother of Jesus, give me a break.' She just about stopped herself stamping her foot like an unruly child. 'If he arrives here, I'm leaving.'

'You're going to do what he says, and you're going to say nothing. Walk the feckin' line. Do you hear me?'

'Sir, you can't let this happen. I'll be the laughing stock of the district. It's preposterous to have an outsider from Dublin coming to deputise for you when I'm already here. It's uncalled for. It's … it's—'

'It's done. No more can be said about it.' Corrigan turned to look out of the window again. 'I hope you won't let me down. I expect you to behave.'

'I'm not five, sir.'

He spun round. 'Well in all honesty, at times you make me wonder.'

Lottie picked up her belongings from the floor. What was she going to do now? This was a disaster. She paused at the door. 'I hope your surgery will be successful, sir. And I promise I'll try to be good while you're gone.'

'Now you definitely sound like a five-year-old. But thanks. And please make McMahon feel welcome,' he added. 'Even though we both know he is an arsehole.'

Outside in the corridor, she leaned against the cool wall. McMahon. What had she done to deserve this? She needed to get out of the station and mull over the implications of the bad news.

She shrugged her jacket on and went in search of Boyd.

# CHAPTER SIX

Boyd hurried through the station and out the front door, but Lottie wasn't so lucky. A commotion at the reception desk warned her to keep going, but curiosity caused her to have a quick look just as the young woman who was shouting turned to face her.

'You there! You seem like someone who will listen to me. Can I talk to you for a minute?' The young woman had voluminous blonde hair with black roots, piled high on her head. Massive hooped earrings hung from her ears, and a child sucking his thumb rested in the crook of her arm.

'What's the matter?' Lottie asked, silently cursing herself for not being quick enough to disappear after Boyd.

In skin-tight jeans and knee-high black leather boots the woman strode towards her.

'That dope behind the counter won't take down what I'm saying. Will you tell her to write it down? I know once it's written you have to investigate it.'

Pointing to the wooden bench inside the front door, Lottie indicated for the woman to sit. She nodded knowingly to Garda Gilly O'Donoghue, who must have drawn the short straw for reception duty.

'What's your name?' Lottie sat beside the woman.

'My name has got nothing to do with anything. I just want to report what I heard, but no one will listen to me!'

'I'm happy to listen to what you have to tell me. But if you want me to take you seriously, I need to know your name and address.' Lottie extracted a notebook and pen from her bag.

'If I tell you that, you definitely won't believe me.' The woman folded her arms tightly around the child.

'Try me.'

'Right then. Let's see how unprejudiced you are. My name is Bridie McWard, and I live on the traveller site.'

'Okay, Bridie,' Lottie said calmly. 'What did you want to tell me?'

The young woman shifted uneasily on the hard seat, seemingly disconcerted that Lottie was prepared to listen.

'Little Tommy is cutting a tooth, see, and wakes up every hour on the hour. And Monday night, he was really bad. The tooth is just out, but all weekend he was a little hoor. Sorry. Don't suppose you'd know about a screaming baby?'

'You'd be wrong there. Go on.'

'Like I said, Monday night, he was a nightmare. I'd got up to him maybe three times, and that was when I heard it.'

'Heard what?'

'The screaming. Like I told that ditsy madam over there.' She pointed at Garda O'Donoghue.

Lottie smiled to herself. Bridie was a mile out in her conclusion. Gilly O'Donoghue was one of the brighter young guards at the station.

'Go on,' she said.

Bridie glanced at her. 'You know where the site is? The temporary accommodation. Temporary my arse. It's been there this twenty-five years. I was born there, and Mammy lived in a caravan on the site all her life, before the wee houses were even built. Reared eight of us, she did, until she had to go into the nursing home. I'm the youngest. Now we have the house. Temporary? No way. Anyway, I live right next door to the graveyard.'

'I know it,' Lottie said. She frequented the cemetery to visit Adam's grave, though not as often as she used to. She should go over soon and leave some red roses for Valentine's Day. Adam would

probably turn in his grave laughing at her. They'd never bothered with Valentine's Day when he was alive.

Bridie continued talking. 'There's a high wall between the houses and the graveyard. And Monday night – well, it was really Tuesday morning – I heard screaming coming from beyond the wall. I thought the dead had risen up to haunt us. It was like a banshee. Mammy told me she heard it once, years ago. I grabbed Tommy out of his cot and turned to wake Paddy, my husband. Except Paddy wasn't there. He does that sometimes. Goes visiting friends and forgets to come home. I know he would've told me I was a stupid woman and to go back to sleep, but how was I supposed to go back to sleep with Tommy awake and someone screaming in the graveyard? Scared shitless I was. Still am, to tell you the truth.' She bit her lip and bowed her head, as if it was a crime to be afraid.

Lottie paused, pen mid-air; the only sound was little Tommy sucking hard on his thumb.

'You heard a scream?'

'You believe me, Guard, don't you?'

'I'm Detective Inspector Parker, and yes, Bridie, I do believe you heard something. But I don't know what. Why didn't you come in yesterday to report this?'

'Had to go to the social, didn't I? To sign on.'

'Right. What time on Monday night did you hear this screaming?'

'I just knew it. You don't believe me.' Bridie jumped up. 'The minute I said where I lived and mentioned the social. You think I'm just one of them time-wasters. Well, Missus High-and-Mighty Detective, you can think what you like. I'm educated. I got my Leaving Cert and a job. Then I got married, had Tommy and gave up work. So I had to sign on.'

'Sit down, Bridie.' Lottie waited a beat as Bridie slumped back onto the bench. 'You're reaching that conclusion about me possibly

because of the way you've been treated in the past. But I do believe you.' She watched the young woman running fingers loaded with gold rings through her son's hair, biting her lip. Deciding what to say next?

'I couldn't see anything,' Bridie said eventually. 'Our windows are right up next to the wall. But the screams, they weren't that far away. Just over the other side somewhere. It was a woman. I'm sure of it. It's usually so quiet at night. Unless there's a row on the site, or ambulance sirens wailing into the hospital. But Monday night it was frosty and silent. Then I heard those screams. It was 3.15 on the clock. I remember seeing the red numbers when I got up with Tommy.'

'How long did the screams last?' Lottie had already decided that Bridie had heard teenagers acting the maggot, running through the graves for kicks and frightening the shite out of themselves in the process.

'Not long. A short burst, followed by silence again.'

'And it was definitely a woman?'

'Yeah. Are you going to go out there and take a look?'

'I'll send someone to scout around. Don't be worrying. It was probably just teenagers playing around.'

'Don't send just anyone. You go. I'd trust you to look properly. And I've heard kids there before. This was different. This was real terror.'

With a sigh, Lottie put her notebook into her bag. 'I'll see what I can do.'

'Promise me. Then I'll know.'

'Know what?'

'If you promise me you'll look yourself, I'll believe you.' Bridie's wide eyes were pleading.

'Okay, okay. I'll take a look myself. But it's now Wednesday, so I can't see what good it will do.'

'I'll feel better. And I'll know Tommy is safe. Promise?'

'I promise.' Lottie thought of crossing her fingers to cover a lie, but didn't. Bridie's sincerity had resonated with her, and she wanted to do what the young woman asked.

'There's a funeral later this morning. You'd want to get in before that.'

'I'll go as soon as I can.'

'Thank you, Missus Detective. The minute I laid eyes on you, I knew you were a lady.'

Bridie bundled up her son, and with a squeak of her leather boots, she was out the door and gone.

'Now you're a lady?' Gilly laughed.

'Could have fooled me,' Lottie said.

# CHAPTER SEVEN

Lottie told Boyd to park outside the cemetery wall, under the CCTV camera. It was trained on one spot, a warning to potential car burglars to move further down the road. The old iron gates through which you could drive were locked with a clumpy chain.

She walked through the side gate, Boyd trotting beside her. The cemetery was eerily quiet.

'They believe in banshees, don't they?' Boyd said.

'Who?'

'The travellers. They believe in curses and fairies and all that shite.'

'And you don't?' Lottie walked swiftly, glancing around for any sign of a screaming woman, almost two days after Bridie McWard had heard the sound. She briefly wondered if it had anything to do with the missing Elizabeth Byrne, but dismissed that notion as ridiculous.

Halfway down the slope, she stopped as a man wearing a yellow workman's jacket stepped out from behind a tree.

'Can I help you at all?' He had a spade in one hand and shears in the other.

'Jesus, you scared me half to death,' Lottie said.

'Sorry, missus. You look lost. Bernard Fahy is the name. Cemetery caretaker.' He moved the shears under his armpit and thrust out a grubby hand. 'Are you looking for any grave in particular?'

'Detective Inspector Lottie Parker, and this is Detective Boyd.'

Lottie's hand came away covered with clay. Looking into the caretaker's yellow-hued face, she noticed that the whites of his eyes

were similarly coloured. 'Have there been any disturbances round here lately?'

'Disturbances? Oh, now I get it. That nosy biddy from the traveller site was on to you, whingeing about banshees screaming in the night.' His laugh was loud and shrill, startling the birds in the bare tree above his head. They fluttered their wings and flew up as one giant black cloud into the cool blue sky. 'Bridie's as mad as old Queenie, her mother. And she's a McWard too. Into all that old witch shite. Know what I mean?'

'Did you investigate Bridie's claims about the screams?' Lottie rubbed her hands together so that she wouldn't get frostbite standing in the freezing air.

'If I was to look into everything reported by that lot living over there, I wouldn't get a single grave dug and you'd have unburied corpses in coffins lined up along with the rubbish at the main gate.'

'You're telling me you didn't investigate it?'

'Dead right I didn't. Isn't that what I just said?'

Lottie shook her head, trying to decipher his cryptic conversation.

'In the last few days, what have you been up to?' she asked.

'Dug a grave on Monday for old Mrs Green from the town centre. Ninety-one she was. The family were waiting for a grandson to come home from Australia. She'll be buried today, beside her late husband.' He pointed down the hill to a mound of clay. 'It's been quiet, to tell you the truth. But this time of year, with the freezing cold weather, you can be sure there'll be a few more kicking the bucket before the week is out.'

'You didn't notice anything out of the ordinary at all? No cider parties? Teenagers running wild through the graves?'

'In this weather? No, that carry-on is reserved for the summer. Those youngsters are at home drinking their parents' gin during the winter. Playing computer games or watching Netflix. Too cold for their young skin.'

As he tugged the shears out from under his arm and back into his hand, Lottie studied Fahy's stubbled face. Pockmarked from teenage acne, she surmised, wisps of hair snaking out around his ears from underneath a black knitted hat. His eyes were inscrutable. She couldn't read what was written in them, and she wondered if she really wanted to.

'We'll have a quick look around if you don't mind,' she said.

'Off you go.' He headed up the way they'd come.

At the bottom of the incline, Boyd said, 'I don't like the look of him.'

Lottie shrugged and glanced over at the houses in the traveller site behind the high wall. Smoke swirled up, then, as if held by an unseen force of frozen air, petered out in straight lines and back down to earth.

There was no way Bridie McWard could have seen anything over the wall in daylight, never mind in the dead of night. As she scanned the headstones in the chilly haze, she glimpsed Adam's granite resting place, on the high ground to her left.

'Isn't Adam buried up there?'

She jumped. 'Jesus, Boyd. For a minute I forgot you were here.'

'Didn't mean to scare you. But it's kind of creepy in this weather.'

'Creepy at the best of times.'

She turned left along the wall, and came to a stop beside the freshly turned clay that Fahy had pointed out. The open grave was covered with slats of timber.

'Mrs Green's new abode, I presume,' she said.

'Dermot Green.' Boyd read the inscription. 'Died September 2001. Aged eighty years. Yes, I'd say this is where she'll be going. To rest beside her late husband.'

'You'll make a good detective someday,' Lottie said with a laugh.

Boyd laughed too. The sound appeared to echo back at them, and she shivered.

Memories of the day Adam had been buried flooded her mind. His body lying in a wooden box with a gold-plated cross on top, interred forever in sacred ground. Dismissing the images, she looked at the area around the Greens' burial plot. The grass outside the kerbstones was flattened, presumably by Fahy and his workmen as they dug the grave. Lottie made her way slowly along the path, stopping at a grave three up from the Greens'.

'Boyd, look at this.' She knelt down. 'Is that blood?'

Boyd leaned over and they stared at the bead of brownish red staining the white pebbles adorning the burial plot.

'Looks like it.' He took a plastic evidence bag from his jacket pocket. 'I'll get it tested.'

'Do that.'

Standing up, she glanced all around. Some of the grass here was flattened too. It could be from the frost, or people visiting buried loved ones, or even the caretaker, she supposed. Or was it something else entirely? And why was there that stain that looked like blood within screaming distance of the traveller site?

She began to think that maybe Bridie McWard hadn't heard a banshee after all. It seemed more likely that someone had indeed screamed while running through the graveyard early on Tuesday morning.

Turning back to Boyd, she said, 'You done yet?'

'I am.'

'I don't like the feeling I'm getting. Let's have another chat with Mr Friendly.'


The caretaker's office was just inside the main gate. The windows were criss-crossed with iron cladding and the roof was shaped like one you'd find on an old country church.

'This used to be living quarters at one time,' Bernard Fahy said.

He'd divested himself of his workman's jacket and was shuffling around the small office. He wore a thin jumper under a pair of dungarees at least two sizes too big for him. His hair had probably once been blonde but had turned yellow. From cigarette smoke, Lottie suspected.

'Does anyone live here now?' She stared at the bare concrete floor, then the cracked walls.

'Not a sinner, except for the poor souls buried six feet beneath us.'

'Really?'

'Not literally.' He laughed, the same harsh sound that had earlier scared the birds.

Lottie felt her skin crawl. She looked up at the tall, thin man. It was hard to tell his age, because his skin was so weather-beaten.

'I've been caretaker here for the last fifteen years, and I could tell you a thing or two about what goes on around here. You wouldn't believe it.'

'I think I would,' Lottie said. She wasn't here for reminiscences. She wanted answers. 'If someone wanted to gain entry to the graveyard at night, is it easy?'

'The main gate is locked, unless a hearse is arriving, but the side gate is left open day and night. And anyone can hop over the wall if they've a mind to. There's a lot of illegal dumping. I work for the council and they won't listen to me about it. Did you see the mound of black bags out there? Don't suppose you can do anything?'

She shook her head. 'Sorry.' Opening her bag, she took out Elizabeth Byrne's photograph. 'Have you ever seen this young woman?'

Fahy picked up the photo and ran a dirty fingernail down Elizabeth's face. 'Pretty girl. What did she do?'

'She didn't *do* anything.' Lottie pulled the photograph from him and wiped it clear of smudges. 'We're trying to locate her.'

'You won't find her here, unless she's dead and buried,' he sniggered.

'Have you seen her?'

'You keep asking the same questions. Must be hard, training to be a guard. No, I never saw that girl before.' He picked up his jacket. 'And if you don't mind, I've Mrs Green's funeral arriving in a few minutes.'

'If you hear anything else from Bridie, or anyone else, please let me know.' Lottie handed him one of her cards.

'I will. If truth be told, she did rattle me a little with her scary stories. I was beginning to believe them myself.' He looked up at the diamond-shaped windows, lost in thought, before adding, 'You sure you don't want to look into that illegal dumping for me?'

'I'm sure.'

'If I catch who's doing it, *they* will be dead and buried,' Fahy said.

Lottie pushed Boyd out the door in front of her and strode to the gate.

'He gives me the creeps,' Boyd said.

Lottie said, 'Dead and buried. I hope not.'

# CHAPTER EIGHT

Boyd started the car, checked his rear-view mirror and prepared to pull out.

'Wait a minute,' Lottie said, putting her hand on the steering wheel to stop him. 'There's the funeral cortège coming up the road. We'd better be respectful and wait until they go in.'

'You're the boss.' He switched off the engine.

She sat back and watched as Fahy unlocked the wrought-iron gates. They swung slowly inwards, and the hearse, containing a simple pine coffin adorned with a spray of lilies, passed through into the cemetery. Eight cars remained outside the gate and parked up on the opposite side of the road.

A priest in a black coat with a purple stole hanging from his shoulders alighted from the first car. He was slightly crouched, as if there was an invisible weight resting on his shoulders.

Shit, Lottie thought.

'Is that who I think it is?' Boyd said.

'Come on,' she said, ignoring the obvious. Father Joe Burke was back. 'There's only a small crowd; we can add to the numbers.'

'We have enough work to be getting on with without gatecrashing a stranger's funeral.'

'Jesus, Boyd, will you ever shut up?' Lottie banged the door on his words and followed the group of about thirty people down the hill to Mrs Green's final resting place.

'This is ridiculous, if you don't mind me saying so.' Boyd kept pace with her.

'I do mind. Keep quiet. I want to see what Mr Fahy gets paid to do.'

'He digs a grave then fills it in when the family leaves. You know that. We're wasting our time here.'

'God give me patience!' she cried. 'Go back to the car and wait for me.'

'No need to be so antsy. Now that I'm here, I might as well go with you.'

She slowed down when the hearse stopped at the end of the narrow roadway. Two undertakers opened the rear door, and the family lined up to receive the coffin. Lottie's shoulders quivered. She hadn't attended a burial since Adam's, except for the interment of her brother's bones. This was a stranger. Someone she had no connection with. She should be okay. But she wasn't.

And there was Father Joe Burke, with his fair hair cut shorter than she remembered, his fringe swept back from his forehead, and his eyes as clear as sapphires. Pulling up the hood of her jacket, she turned away. She wanted to see him, and at the same time she didn't. You're such a contradiction, she told herself. Early last year he had been her friend when things had been tough. He'd even helped her with her investigation into the murder of Susan Sullivan. But he'd left Ragmullin crippled with sorrow when he'd discovered the truth about his parentage and she'd thought she'd never see him again. Now he was back. Was that a good thing? She wasn't at all sure.

Six men, three on either side, laid the coffin down on the laths of timber that Fahy had placed across the open grave. Another man, in a workman's jacket, stood beside Fahy. They both moved to the rear of the sad family gathering.

She watched as a young man in a suit a size too small put the spray of flowers down beside the coffin, on top of the mound of clay. The scent of the lilies was evocative, and she was dragged back

once more to the day she had helped lower her husband into the dead earth. Would she ever be free of the memories? They clung to her like a cold sweat.

With a sprinkling of holy water, Father Joe began the prayers. He was joined in a murmur by the small crowd. Trying to keep her focus off the priest, Lottie found herself wondering about the substance she had found on the pebbles earlier. She was sure it was blood, but it could have come from a child cutting a knee or even one of the workmen as they dug the grave.

More holy water was sprinkled, then six of the mourners, among them the only two women present, took up the leather ropes either side of the opening, rolled them round their hands, knuckles whitening, and pulled them taut. Fahy stepped forward and slid the timber supports away, and the coffin was held aloft above the gaping six-foot hole.

A scream broke from the small assembly, then one of the women let go of the rope and sank to her knees. Such grief, Lottie thought. She watched from a distance as Father Joe gripped the distraught woman's elbow and helped her upright. Fahy and his colleague hurriedly repositioned the timber laths to take the weight of the coffin again.

The woman cried out once more and Lottie pushed her way through the mourners.

'Are you okay?' she asked.

'Lottie!' the priest said. He stared at her open-mouthed, as if to ask a question, but the distressed woman began to speak.

'There's something down there.' She pointed into the grave, her face as white as the blouse peeking out at the collar of her coat.

Peering into the space, Lottie saw only clay. 'What did you see?'

Fahy shimmied in beside them. 'Probably a bird, or vermin. Freshly dug graves can attract them. Especially with an old corpse

already—' He stopped as Lottie speared daggers at him with her eyes. 'Sorry,' he said.

'That's my grandfather you're talking about,' said a stout man who had wrapped his arm about the shoulders of the stricken woman.

'We'll take a break,' Father Joe said with a nod to Lottie, and shepherded the mourners out onto the path, where they huddled at the side of the hearse.

She sensed Boyd at her shoulder.

'Might be the banshee's resting place,' he said.

'Can we have a look?' she asked Fahy.

'There's nothing down there,' he said.

Lottie turned to the sobbing woman. 'What exactly did you see?'

'I'm not entirely sure. Maybe I imagined it, but when we pulled on the rope and the coffin was raised up a bit, I thought I saw what looked like skin poking out of the clay at the bottom of the grave. Human flesh. Good God! Could it be my grandad?' She shook her head wildly. 'But he's been dead fifteen years.'

'Stay right here. All of you.' Lottie marched over to Fahy, who was now standing beside the grave. 'Can you move the coffin so that I can take a look?'

'What? You're not going down there, are you?' Fahy shoved his hands deeper into his pockets.

'I want the coffin moved. Now.' The caretaker was needling her nerves like an irritating itch.

'This is outrageous,' he said.

Boyd edged in between them. 'I think you're overreacting, boss. We should let this family bury their loved one.'

She glared at him before turning back to Fahy. 'You and your colleague push this coffin out of the way. I want a quick look and then you can get on with the ceremony.'

With a theatrical sigh, Fahy called to his workmate. Between them they placed an extra piece of timber underneath the wooden casket and slid it away from the grave.

The air seemed to chill and the sky appeared to darken as Lottie leaned over the edge and peered into the opening.

'Shit,' she said. 'Boyd, get SOCOs here. And call Lynch and Kirby. Quickly.'

# CHAPTER NINE

'What about my funeral?' Fahy asked, as Boyd corralled the mourners and Father Joe with the undertakers on the far side of the hearse.

Lottie squared up to him. 'Mr Fahy, it's not your funeral, it's Mrs Green's, and I want you and your colleague to join the family over there until I can get a cordon in place.'

'We have to bury her,' he said.

'And you will. But not right now. I have a strong suspicion that there's a body in that grave that shouldn't be there, so I'm asking you to move away.'

'Right so.' He grabbed his colleague by the sleeve and took out his phone. 'I'm calling my supervisor about this.'

'You can call whoever you like, just stay out of my crime scene.'

Once she was alone, Lottie stared down into the darkness. Protruding from a thin layer of soil were pink-varnished toenails.

An hour later, the serenity of Ragmullin cemetery was lacerated by a hive of action and noise. Mrs Lorraine Green's coffin had been returned to the hearse and her family members had been whisked away by the undertakers. Much as Lottie would have liked to, she didn't speak to Father Joe, but she registered his sad smile with an inclination of her head.

Eventually the crime-scene tape was in place and the main gate was closed and guarded. A line of spectators perched on the high wall as the scene of crime officers erected a tent over the gaping grave.

'Jim McGlynn is on his way,' Boyd said.

'He'll be delighted to see the pair of us.'

Boyd pulled at his chin, his eyes concerned. 'You think it's her? Our missing woman?'

'There's someone down there and it's not a corpse that's been interred for fifteen years. So, it's possible.' She looked over at the gawkers sitting on the wall. 'We need to speak with Bridie McWard again, plus Fahy and his colleague.'

'Where did they go?'

She pointed to the row of pine trees to her left, where Fahy stood smoking a cigarette. He was flanked by Detectives Larry Kirby and Maria Lynch. As Lottie neared them, Fahy sucked in hard and blew out a stream of smoke.

'I need you down at the station to make a statement,' she said.

'I saw nothing. And I did nothing either, before you go accusing me. Dug the grave on Monday and put the laths on it this morning. I saw only clay down there.'

'We need a formal statement. You're sure you didn't notice anything suspicious over the last few days?'

'I told you already. I didn't see anything.' He lit another cigarette. The smell made Lottie's empty stomach queasy.

'What's your name?' She directed her question to the plump young man with a bad case of acne standing in Fahy's shadow.

'I only started here today. I'm on a scheme.'

'What is your name? Are you deaf?' Lottie said. His teeth were yellow and his skin wan.

'I wear a hearing aid. Deaf in one ear.' He pointed to his right ear. 'But I forgot to put it in today.'

'Sorry.' Lottie positioned herself to talk into his good ear.

'His name is John Gilbey,' Kirby said, his bushy hair standing up on his head and the zip on his jacket straining across his large girth.

Lynch lounged against the wall, pale-faced. Her fair hair, usually tied up in a ponytail, streamed about her shoulders.

'You have to go to the station,' Lottie told Gilbey. 'It's a formality. Nothing to worry about.' She instructed Kirby to take the two men with him.

Lynch said, 'What do you want me to do, boss?'

'Make yourself useful. Help uniforms with the cordon at the front gate.'

As Lynch stomped off up the hill, a silver station wagon rumbled down the slope, slowed and stopped. The driver leaned out of the window.

'Well, if it isn't Inspector Morse and Sergeant Lewis. Disrupting my morning as usual.'

'Jesus, McGlynn. I didn't recognise you with your clothes on.' Lottie smirked. She'd only ever seen the head of the SOCO team in his white protective gear, hood up and mask in place. Two green eyes. That was all she knew about him. Now she could put a face to the ensemble. His craggy features told her he was aged about sixty. And he was in a foul humour, though that was nothing new.

'I'd recognise you in a blackout,' he said, mouth downturned. 'What have you dug up for me this time?'

'Not exactly dug up, though if it wasn't for a bad case of curiosity, I think she would have been interred forever.'

'And you know what curiosity did to the cat, don't you?' McGlynn let the window back up and continued down to the scene.

'Contrary arse,' Lottie said.


Within fifteen minutes, McGlynn had his team in place. They lowered a ladder into the grave, and he climbed to the bottom and stood to one side as pebbles and clay cascaded around him.

'A thin layer of clay and dirt,' he said, hunching down. He used a short-handled, long-bristled brush to carefully sweep it away, working slowly, until a foot emerged from the blackness. Toes painted in a fluorescent pink varnish. The chalky flesh looked paper thin. Brushing away the clay on the opposite side, McGlynn leaned backwards as another foot appeared.

'Can you move up to the area where a head should be?' Lottie was impatient to find out the identity of the buried person.

McGlynn continued his methodical work without reply. As he uncovered the leg, Lottie saw that it was broken, the bone sticking out.

'Tibia open shaft fracture is my initial observation,' McGlynn said. 'Broken through the skin. That's the shin bone. Signs of maggots. No flies. Not been down here long. It's been cold, with no rain, so a day, maybe two at the most.'

Lottie knelt down on the protective covering at the edge of the hole and leaned over further, praying for him to hurry up.

A second leg appeared, and as more of the body was revealed, it became evident that it was definitely a female, and that she was naked.

'No other visible wounds so far,' he muttered.

Eventually the face and hair appeared, and Lottie drew in a breath. McGlynn glanced up, emeralds dancing above the white mask. 'You see what I see, Inspector?'

'She was suffocated with the clay?'

'Even though the layer is thin, I don't think she covered herself with it. Inform the state pathologist that she is needed here.'

'I've already phoned her,' Boyd said. 'She should be here soon.'

Lottie stared down at the victim's mouth, full of clay, and the dirt-encrusted auburn hair.

'Who was the last person you saw?' she asked the lifeless body of Elizabeth Byrne.

# CHAPTER TEN

Lottie left Jane Dore, the state pathologist, with McGlynn to confirm what she already knew. They were dealing with a suspicious death. She sent Lynch to find Bridie McWard so that she could be questioned again, then she and Boyd went back to the station to set up an incident team and to interview the cemetery workers.

Superintendent Corrigan was marching around the incident room when she arrived.

'You found your missing woman?'

'I believe so, sir, but we need to make a positive ID.'

'Did you inform her mother?'

'Not yet.'

'Do it soon, before the media blast it all over Twitter.'

'I intend to.'

'I need to talk to you,' Corrigan said.

Lottie followed him down the corridor and into his office.

'Sit down,' he said, and squeezed in behind his desk.

'Do you want an update, sir? I'll have a full report for a team meeting in the morning.'

'No, I won't be here then, so I'll have to leave it in your hands. In McMahon's hands, I should say. I want to tell you something.'

Oh Lord, Lottie thought. He's going to tell me he's dying and I'll be stuck with McMahon for the rest of my working days. 'Yes, sir?'

'Elizabeth Byrne. She was last seen on the train. Correct?'

'As far as we know. We only have her mother's word that she didn't arrive home.'

'It reminds me of a case I worked ten years ago. In fact, the anniversary is this week. I don't know why I'm even mentioning it, but the train bit – that's what jogged my memory. The difference then was that the young woman was never found. And now I'm wondering, could she have been buried in a grave that was awaiting a coffin?'

'Back up a bit.' Lottie tried to compute what Corrigan was saying but couldn't work it out. 'What woman?'

'Lynn O'Donnell. Aged twenty-four or twenty-five at the time. Last seen on the Dublin to Ragmullin train, but she never arrived home. Valentine's Day 2006. Pull the file if you get time. It's probably nothing to do with this murder, but no harm in knowing about it. I'm sure the media will pick up on it.'

'Thanks, sir, I'll have a look at the file. I do remember it. I was based in Athlone at the time.' She glanced at him. He was rubbing his eye again. 'And you mind yourself. I'll be checking in with you to make sure everything goes well.'

'No need for that. I'm sure McMahon will keep you busy enough.'

'I'm dreading his arrival,' she confessed.

'Stay out of his way, do a good job and he'll have no reason to complain. I'm counting on you to keep up the good name of this district.'

'I'll do my best, sir.'

'Good luck. I think you'll be needing it.'

# CHAPTER ELEVEN

'Do you remember the disappearance of Lynn O'Donnell?' Lottie asked Boyd as they arrived at the home of Elizabeth Byrne.

'Yeah, that rings a bell. A long time ago now, though. Why do you ask?'

'Corrigan mentioned it. She was last seen on a train from Dublin to Ragmullin. Same as Elizabeth.'

'Does he think they might be connected?'

'Not sure. He said to have a look at the cold case file.'

'A giant stretch of the imagination, if you ask me.'

'I'll have a look anyway.' She rang the doorbell.

Elizabeth Byrne had lived with her mother in a detached red-brick house in the Greenway estate. Anna Byrne led them to the kitchen. 'I hope you have news of Elizabeth. I just boiled the kettle. Will you join me in a cup of tea? Coffee? Awful cold out there today.'

As Mrs Byrne busied herself with cups and tea bags, Lottie and Boyd sat at the table, an old-fashioned wooden affair with a red oilcloth covering it. The cooker was a cream-coloured Aga, with a saucepan simmering on top. Glancing at the clock hanging on the wall, Lottie noted that it was just over two hours since they'd discovered the body. She shivered, even though the kitchen was warm.

When Mrs Byrne turned around, Lottie noticed the lines of worry furrowed into her brow. Dressed in jeans and a pink jumper over a white cotton shirt, she wore fluffy socks on her feet. Probably belonged to Elizabeth, Lottie thought. Her heart lurched as

she thought about delivering the news that would shatter this poor woman's hope forever.

'Here, let me give you a hand,' Boyd said, rising to take a jug from her hand. 'You sit and I'll make the tea.'

He knew when to switch on the charm, but Lottie was well aware that he was only putting off the inevitable. Mrs Byrne slumped onto a chair.

'Do you have any news about Elizabeth?'

'Mrs Byrne …' Lottie began.

'Call me Anna.'

'I'm so sorry, Anna … I hate to have to tell you like this, but I'm afraid the news I have is not good.' Shit, this wasn't the way to tell a mother her daughter was dead.

'Would you like a biscuit?' Anna was fussing. 'Ginger nuts. I have a packet somewhere.' She jumped up.

Lottie put a hand on the woman's arm. 'Anna. I'm sorry.'

Anna gnawed at her lip, eyes bulging with unshed tears. Her hand flew to her mouth as if trying to keep back the words she didn't want to utter.

'She's dead, isn't she?' Pulling at her sleeve now. Eyes scrunched up, avoiding Lottie's gaze.

'I'm terribly sorry.'

'Tell me.' The tears now burst forth and spilled down the woman's cheeks, around her streaming nose and over her lips. 'Tell me,' she screamed.

Lottie reached over and put her hand on Anna Byrne's. 'I'm afraid we found the body of a female earlier today.'

'No! I don't believe you. It's not my Elizabeth. She's all I have. Do you understand? It's not her.' Hysteria laced the woman's words.

'We have reason to believe it is Elizabeth. I'm so sorry.'

Anna's body rocked with convulsions, and Lottie jumped up and grabbed a glass from a cupboard. She filled it with water from the tap and held it to Anna's lips.

'Sip this. It might help.' She had delivered bad news many times before, but in the face of naked grief, she was at a loss as to the right approach to use, though if anyone should know, she should.

'Oh God. What happened to her?' A fragile calm settled in the room as Anna looked straight into Lottie's eyes.

She held the gaze. 'All we know at the moment is that the circumstances appear suspicious.'

'Was she murdered?'

'We don't yet know.'

'How did she die? This girl you found.'

'I can't say at the moment. Not until after … after the post-mortem is concluded.'

'Oh my good God!' the woman wailed.

'Can I call someone for you. A friend? Family?'

Anna ignored the question. 'Where did you find her?'

Lottie glanced to Boyd, begging for help. He shook his head slowly. 'In the cemetery,' she said.

'It can't be Elizabeth.' Anna appeared resolute in her conviction as she folded her arms and sniffed back more tears. 'She never goes there.'

'I'm sorry, Anna, I know this is hard for you, but we have reason to believe it may be your daughter. And we need you to formally confirm her identity.'

'I told you she was missing. No one believed me.' The woman's voice was almost inaudible before it rose an octave. 'You said you couldn't look for her because you had to wait forty-eight hours. Well, it's over forty-eight hours since *I* last saw her. You can start searching now.' She unfolded her arms and tore the oilcloth with her nail. Worried the hole larger and dug her finger into the wood of the table.

Lottie stared at Boyd. Come on, she pleaded silently. Time to work some more of his charm.

'Anna,' he said softly. 'We think we've found Elizabeth's body. Do you understand what I'm saying?'

She nodded, and more tears fell from her eyes.

'Please let me call someone to come and sit with you,' Lottie said.

'I'll be fine. Do you want to ask questions about Elizabeth? Go on. Ask me. Better to do it now. Then you'll know you've made a mistake.'

'We can do that another time,' Boyd said quickly.

Anna thumped the table. 'Ask me now. Before it hits me properly.'

'If you're sure?' Lottie said.

The woman nodded.

Lottie lowered her voice, speaking as softly as she could. 'Tell us about your daughter. What was she like? Her friends and—'

'I told that nice young Garda O'Donoghue everything.'

'We need to discover her last movements. Had her mood changed recently?'

'She was the same as usual. On the go. Flitting here and there. She never sits still for two minutes. Always has to be doing something. Do you have children, Inspector?'

'I do,' Lottie said. Anna's description of Elizabeth reminded her of her own Chloe. 'Three teenagers. Well, Katie is twenty now.'

'You know what it's like then. Racing in and out of the house. Changing her clothes a dozen times a day. Out at nightclubs. She goes jogging on Saturday and Sunday mornings. At Rochfort Gardens. During the week, she has to drag herself to the station for the early commuter train.'

Lottie thought this was a world removed from Katie's. 'Did she have many friends?'

'She has a few. No one close comes to mind. She hangs out with Carol O'Grady, even though I don't approve. Not that I'm a snob or anything.'

'You don't like Carol?'

Anna didn't answer the question. She said, 'Elizabeth is an only child, so it's mostly just me and her.'

'Boyfriend?' Boyd asked.

Anna was silent for a moment before she lifted her head. She looked directly at him.

'She had her heart broken a year ago. She was sure he was the one for her. All talk of getting married and looking for a mortgage and the like. No ring ever appeared, though, and then he disappeared from the scene.'

'Disappeared?' Lottie raised a quizzical eyebrow.

'Not like that. He worked in a bank in Dublin and was transferred to a Munich branch. Upped and left my girl with a shattered heart. The bastard. Sorry, I only use bad language where Matt Mullin is concerned.'

Lottie heard Boyd scribble the name in his notebook. She said, 'Did the break-up affect her badly?'

'Very. She started going out with her girlfriends every night. Even on work nights. She'd never done that before. Heartbroken, my poor pet.' Anna wiped away the tears that were dripping down her chin.

Lottie reached out and gripped her hand. 'This Matt guy, is he still in Munich?'

Anna drew back as if Lottie had pinched her. 'Do you think he could be back in town? Do you think he's involved somehow? Did that bastard kill my girl?' Anger rapidly replacing heartache.

'We don't know anything yet,' Lottie said. 'Is he originally from Ragmullin?'

'Yes. He lived on the old Dublin road. I'm sure you can find his address.'

'You gave Garda O'Donoghue a list of Elizabeth's friends. I don't recall this Matt being on it.'

'He's not a friend. I've been trying to forget about him since he dumped my girl. Last Valentine's Day. Can you believe it? She thought he was wining and dining her to present her with a diamond. Some kick in the teeth he presented her with that night.'

'That's awful,' Lottie said. 'I'll definitely contact him.'

'Do that.' Anna was dry-eyed now, glaring. Lottie realised that shock was setting in.

'Did she date anyone after Matt?'

Anna shook her head. 'No. I'd have known.'

'Could she have been dating without telling you?'

'Like I said, I'd have known.'

'Sunday night last. Did she do anything different?'

'She was the same as always.'

'But can you tell me what she did that night?' Lottie knew she appeared heartless, but she had to continue with the questions while Anna was prepared to talk.

'Let me see. Elizabeth doesn't go to mass. She stopped going since all that with Matt. So it was near one o'clock when she got up. Missed her usual run at Rochfort Gardens. She'd been in the Last Hurdle Saturday night and wasn't home until near three. I've got to the stage where I keep my mouth shut. She is twenty-five, after all. An adult, so she keeps telling me. An adult who still wants her dinner cooked and her clothes washed for her. Sometimes I feel more like a servant than a mother.'

'I know the feeling,' Lottie said, noting that Anna was still refer- ring to her daughter in the present tense. 'So on Sunday she got up at one o'clock. What did she do then?'

'We had dinner. A roast. Just the two of us. My husband, Elizabeth's dad, died eight years ago. Cancer.'

A sharp stitch screwed into Lottie's heart. Death did that to you. You never got over it; you just learned to live with it. And she was still learning. She felt Boyd staring at her and raised her head. He nodded, his knowing look.

She turned back to Anna. 'What did Elizabeth do after dinner?'

'Back up to bed she went. Said she was tired, not to disturb her. She had a hangover, so I let her be. She didn't appear downstairs again and I never heard her get up for work Monday morning. Therefore, Inspector, the last time I saw my daughter was around two o'clock on Sunday.'

'Can we see her room?' Lottie asked, thinking it was a bit odd that Anna hadn't checked on Elizabeth. Then again, she herself was guilty of the same inaction from time to time.

'First door at the top of the stairs.' Anna picked up the cups and went to the sink.

'I'll sit with you while Inspector Parker has a look,' Boyd said.

'I'll be fine. Go ahead.'

'You're sure I can't ring someone?' Boyd asked.

'Just do what you have to do.'

Lottie beckoned him to follow and they made their way up the stairs.

'Strange little family,' Lottie whispered.

'You can talk,' Boyd said.


'On first impressions, Elizabeth was a bit like you,' Lottie said to Boyd.

'How do you come to that conclusion?'

'This room screams OCD to me.'

'Maybe her mother cleaned it up.'

'I doubt it, based on what she's just told us.'

As she looked around the room, Lottie was struck by the symmetry of everything. Make-up brushes lined up in a jar by height; perfume bottles in a tidy circle; nail polish in a neat row, the colours of the rainbow. A small bottle of fluorescent pink stood at the end.

She opened the first of three drawers. Underwear, all folded. Running her hand beneath them, it came away empty. The next drawer had a hairdryer, straighteners and brushes. She placed a hairbrush in a plastic evidence bag. The last held a multitude of colourful scarves and socks.

She turned her attention to the wardrobe while Boyd rifled through the bedside cabinet. The clothes were divided neatly down the middle by an IKEA shoe-holder. One side held skirts and jackets – Elizabeth's work clothes; the other side a conglomeration of jeans, some with designer tears and holes. Beside them, a rack of long sleeved T-shirts and blouses, and a selection of Lycra running gear. The top shelf held an assortment of girlie hats, and on the floor of the wardrobe were neatly paired Nike and Adidas runners. All pristine.

'She even cleaned her runners,' Lottie said. She noticed Boyd sitting on the neatly made duvet, thumbing through a flower-covered notebook. 'What's that?'

'Love poems, by the look of it. Mr Matt Mullin broke this girl's heart.'

'Any laptop?'

'No, and no phone either. She must have had them with her.'

Lottie ran her hands under the pillows, finding only folded pyjamas. 'Gosh, I wish my girls could see this.'

'See what?'

'How they should keep their rooms.'

'Not normal, though, is it?' Boyd gestured around. 'For a twenty-five-year-old to be so fastidious.'

'Everyone is different.'

'If you say so.'

Boyd got down on his knees and peered beneath the bed.

'Anything?' Lottie asked.

'Just this.' He pulled out a red cabin-sized suitcase and unzipped it. 'Empty.'

'She hadn't been planning to run away.'

'I'm taking the notebook.'

She watched as he put it into an evidence bag. 'You know what's missing?'

'What?' He secured the flaps.

'Costume jewellery. My girls have drawers full of it.' She pointed to a small selection of silver and gold chains hanging on a plastic stand on the dressing table. 'Why did Elizabeth only have genuine jewellery? I'll ask Anna about it.'

'I think it's more important to find the ex-boyfriend.' Boyd made for the door.

Feeling the tension pushing pinpricks of annoyance up on her skin, Lottie counted to five before following him.

# CHAPTER TWELVE

The box of cornflakes was in the wrong cupboard. Donal O'Donnell shook his head and opened the next cupboard. He took out the packet and got the milk from the fridge, then sat at the table and filled the bowl. Breakfast at lunchtime was becoming a habit. Picking up the spoon, he noticed it was dirty. Caked cereal dotted the handle.

'That's all I need.' His voice echoed around the empty kitchen. 'First the refrigerator packs up, then the dishwasher.' He knew things always came in threes. What would be next?

As he spooned the cereal into his mouth, ignoring the milk dripping down his chin, he realised that the third thing had already occurred. That was, if he could count the death, three weeks ago, of his wife of forty years as a thing going wrong.

Finishing his breakfast, he let the spoon fall noisily into the bowl and carried it to the sink. Then he went to the dresser and struck a match to light the candle. For ten years Maura had lit it daily. Ten years she had yearned for answers. She had always hoped. Hoped for their Lynn to walk through the door; for a guard to ring the doorbell; for someone to tell her ... something. Anything.

He set his lips in a stiff line and sniffed the sob back into his throat. Poor Maura. Consigned to her grave without answers. Breast cancer, the consultant had said. Huh! Donal was one hundred per cent certain his wife had died of a broken heart.

The doorbell rang.

He laced up his shoes before going to answer it. Straightened his shoulders and unhooked the chain.

'Oh, it's you,' he said, turning away, leaving the door swinging open.

'Yes, Dad, it's me. Why aren't you at work?'

'How many times do I have to tell you, Keelan? I am not your dad. To you, I'm Donal. Right?'

It bugged the shite out of him that his daughter-in-law called him Dad. She was a nice girl, trying too hard to be even nicer. But he'd had one daughter and now he had none. No matter how hard she tried, she was just his son's wife. No one could fill the cavernous space left in his heart when his Lynn disappeared.

'I'm sorry, Donal. Do you want a lift anywhere? It's no bother. Saoirse is still at school. I can—'

'No!' He hadn't meant to shout. Easing the harshness from his tone, he said, 'I want to be left alone. Can you understand that? Lynn is gone. Maura is gone. I'm next. You can bugger off home.' Shit, he didn't want to be angry with Keelan. It wasn't her fault.

She was rinsing the bowl under the tap, her shoulders heaving. Christ, he hoped she wasn't crying. He couldn't handle any more tears. Maura's had swallowed him up. In a way, he found it peaceful now to be living in the silence of his own home without sobs shrieking through the air.

'I can do that.' He took the tea towel from her hand. When she turned around, he saw her make-up was streaked. 'Didn't mean to make you cry.'

'It's not your fault.' She was searching up her sleeve and eventually pulled out a tattered tissue. Dabbing at her mascara, she said, 'It's Cillian.'

'What's he done? Has he … has he hurt you?'

'No. Nothing like that. Not physical hurt, if you get me.'

'What do you mean? Come and sit down.'

At the table, Keelan said, 'He's different. Distant. Since Maura died. I know it's probably grief, but he wasn't particularly close to his mother. Was he?'

'Hard to say. Cillian and Finn were both close to their sister. Close in age and close … like friends. When she disappeared, it upset the whole family dynamic. You know what I mean?'

'Tell me.'

'They were only young then, early twenties. They adored Lynn and she doted on them. No fights. No hair-pulling.' He noticed Keelan returning his smile. 'I thought we were the luckiest parents in the world. But you know what? I think Maura was a little resentful of the friendship they shared. It was like they were so close, the three of them, that they shut her out. At times, it led to … I haven't a clue what to call it.'

'Jealousy? Was Maura jealous?'

'I don't rightly know. I was working long hours back then, so I wasn't home a lot. But when Lynn went missing, Maura blamed herself for not caring for the children as much as she should have. And she blamed the boys for not watching out for their sister.'

'But that's illogical. They were all adults.'

Donal slapped the table. Keelan jumped. He reached out to grab her hand, but she pulled away. He noticed a vein of fear in her eyes before they clouded over with tears.

'Silly girl. I was only trying to comfort you. I think Cillian is feeling guilty at his mother's passing. Maybe he thinks he should have been around more to reassure her. To tell her she still had two sons. But he never did. And every time he appeared at that front door, she laid into him. Blaming him. And blaming Finn.'

'He never spoke much about his mother. Always about Lynn. I can tell you, the only guilt he was consumed with was not being there for his sister when she disappeared.'

Donal stood up and put the box of cereal back into the cupboard. 'The anniversary of her disappearance is this Sunday, so tell him to call round. Tell him we need to talk. Will you do that for me?'

'Couldn't you call him yourself?' Keelan stood at the door, wrapping her scarf around her neck.

'He can make the first move,' Donal said. 'My son is lucky to have you. You know what? You look a little how I would imagine Lynn would look if she was still alive. I mean …' He felt bile lurch from his stomach to his mouth. Not once had Maura let him speculate that their daughter might be dead. Not once in the last ten years. Never.

'I'll pass on the message,' Keelan said. 'And there's always hope.' She pulled the door closed behind her.

At the sink, Donal took the bowl from the drainer and put it in the dishwasher. He turned on the machine and listened to it, to work out if anything was amiss with the motor. He stood there for the whole forty-five-minute cycle, water filling and draining. Draining like his life had done since the day Lynn had vanished.

# CHAPTER THIRTEEN

Lottie jumped out of the car at the front of the station and Boyd drove round to the yard. She was considering Anna Byrne's information that Elizabeth had suffered from psoriasis and didn't wear costume jewellery because it exacerbated the complaint, when a woman approached her. She wore a denim jacket over a grey hoodie and jeans; mid forties, Lottie thought as her progress to the steps was blocked.

'Cynthia Rhodes,' the woman said, thrusting out a hand.

Lottie kept her own in her pocket. 'Do I know you?'

'Crime correspondent with national television. I took over after my colleague was murdered.'

Lottie shuddered at the memory but dragged up her professional face. 'How can I help you, Ms Rhodes?'

'The activity at the cemetery. Can you comment on it?'

'Not at this time.'

'Ah, come on, give me a break. I'm new to the job.'

Lottie wasn't going to be taken in that easily. Not now that she recognised Rhodes. A shark with very sharp teeth who had hosted a night-time current affairs television programme a few years ago. Covering crime in the midlands appeared to be a demotion.

'What are you doing in Ragmullin?'

'My job, unlike some I could mention.' Her eyes, shrouded by a tangle of black curls, fired cold warnings to Lottie. Better watch what I say, she thought.

'I'm too busy to talk to you right now.' She made to pass by, but Cynthia held out a hand, halting her escape.

'Not so fast. I know all about you, Lottie Parker. I know about your failings in the past. I know of your husband's death and your brother's manslaughter, and I can tell you, I don't feel one bit sorry for you. If this activity at the cemetery is a murder, mark my words, I'll be walking in your footsteps, waiting for you to trip over and make a mistake.'

'Is that all?' Lottie scooted round the woman and up the steps.

'I'll be watching you. You can bet your life on it.'

'And you can bet your life I won't be watching you on television,' Lottie muttered as she charged into the reception area. She pounded in the code on the inner door.

'Hey, Inspector Parker,' the duty sergeant called out. 'You're wanted in the interview room. Detective Kirby is waiting for you there with Bernard Fahy.'

'Shit.' Lottie flew down the corridor, the door swinging shut behind her.


Kirby stood up as Lottie entered the claustrophobic interview room.

'We're almost finished here, boss. Do you want to read over my notes and ask anything further before Mr Fahy leaves?'

Tearing off her jacket, Lottie sank into a chair and indicated for Kirby to sit back down.

'I've work to be getting on with,' Fahy said. He was leaning across the table, his hands clasped as if in prayer.

'Me too,' Lottie said. 'Can you recount what you've been doing since Monday? Where you've been?'

'He has it written down.' Fahy pointed to Kirby.

Flicking through his notebook, Kirby said, 'I just need to have a word with his wife to confirm she was with him when he says she was.'

'Do you think I'd be stupid enough to bury a woman in my own graveyard?'

'Mr Fahy, I'm just trying to get the facts,' Lottie said, though she had been thinking that exact thing. She turned to Kirby. 'Does Mr Gilbey corroborate everything?'

'Gilbey only started work at the cemetery today. I took his statement and DNA and let him go.' Kirby folded his arms across his bulging stomach.

Lottie read the notes before looking up at Fahy's agitated face. 'The victim broke her leg. Was screaming as she tried to get away from her assailant. A terrified young woman running naked through your cemetery in the dead of night. How does that make you feel?'

He shook his head. 'You're making a big mistake if you think I had anything to do with it. A big mistake.'

'Are you threatening me?' She tried to keep her anger muted. Cynthia Rhodes had already said something similar about mistakes.

'I had nothing to do with it. My wife can vouch for me. I was at home every night. I was at work every day. That's all I have to say. Can I go now?'

'We'll need to take a sample of your DNA first.'

'Why?'

'To rule you in or out of our investigation.'

'I'm sure my DNA is all over the place – I dug the blasted grave.'

'All the same, will you consent to providing us with a sample?'

'Doesn't look like I have much choice in the matter.'

'Interview terminated.' Kirby stood up and sealed the DVD.

Fahy picked up his coat and headed for the door. 'Leave John Gilbey alone. He's not right up here.' He pointed to his temple with a muddy finger. 'I know your reputation, Detective Inspector, and that's the last thing I'm saying about this.'

When he had left, with Kirby in tow, Lottie sat in the humid silence of the room and rested her head in her hands. Thoughts swam in and out of focus. She could do with a Xanax. Half of one, even. She reached into her bag and searched among the till receipts, unopened bills, keys and loose change. Found a blister pack with one pill. Maybe she shouldn't take it. She needed to be alert and focused. Especially with Cynthia Rhodes on her case.

A tap on the door and Boyd entered.

'You okay?' he said.

'Do you really want me to answer that?' She palmed the pill. 'Any word from Lynch on Matt Mullin's whereabouts?'

'Not yet. What next?'

'I need to access the O'Donnell cold case file and speak with Elizabeth's friend. What was her name? The one Anna didn't seem to like.'

Boyd consulted his notebook. 'Carol O'Grady.'

'Address?'

'Will I look it up?'

'That would be a help.'

'The longer this day gets, the shorter your fuse.'

'Boyd, get the address.'

When she was alone, the bang of the door echoing like a gong in her ears, she swallowed the pill and left to find water to wash the chalky taste from her mouth.

# CHAPTER FOURTEEN

Lottie looked at the house beside which Boyd had parked. St Fintan's Road backed onto the old army barracks. Most of the houses were still owned by the local authority. After her encounter with the reporter and then the cemetery caretaker, she'd held an impromptu meeting with Lynch and Kirby in the incident room. She wanted Matt Mullin found. She wanted every piece of information on Elizabeth Byrne, and she wanted Bridie McWard formally interviewed. She wanted results, goddammit.

Boyd glanced at the page in his hand and read, 'Carol O'Grady. Aged twenty-four. She has two younger brothers and lives with her mother and father.' He'd printed off her photograph from her Facebook page. There'd been information about one brother on their PULSE database.

'Let's see what she has to say about Elizabeth,' Lottie said.

Leaving the car, they walked up the short path to the red door of number 36. It was the end house in a terrace of five and looked well maintained, with sparkling clean windows.

The bell appeared broken, so Lottie knocked hard on the glass panel.

The door was opened by a young man. He was the image of the girl in the photograph. Terry, the eighteen-year-old brother they'd read about on PULSE.

'Is Carol at home?' Lottie asked.

'Who wants to know?'

She took out her ID, flashed it in front of his face and watched the complacency fade.

'My apologies,' he said, his tone streaked with sarcasm, 'I didn't know you were the pigs … I mean, the guards. Carol should be at work today but she's off sick. Will I get her for you?'

'Do that and we'll wait inside.' Lottie placed one foot inside the door, in case he slammed it shut.

'I … I'm not sure,' he stammered. 'My mates are here. We're studying. Exams. Leaving Cert. You know.'

'Shouldn't you be at school?'

'Study break.'

'We won't disturb you at all. Just get Carol for us.'

As he flew up the stairs, Lottie reckoned the open door was an invitation to enter. With Boyd behind her, she walked through the small hallway and into the kitchen. There was a scattering of bodies and a scraping of something off the table as she entered.

'No need to leave,' she said.

The three lads halted their progress at the back door, and without turning his head, one of them said, 'We were going anyway.'

'Don't forget this.' Boyd held up a microscopic bag of weed.

'Shit,' said one of the lads.

'Go on, get out,' Boyd said. 'I'll keep it safe for you.'

They kept going.

Lottie smiled. 'That's not enough to lift them two inches off the ground, never mind get them high.'

'Hey, that's mine.' Terry had come into the kitchen. He swiped at Boyd's hand but missed the bag.

'Where's Carol?' Lottie asked.

'She'll be down in a minute. Go on into the good room. Just through there.' He pointed to a glass connecting door.

In the living room, Lottie stood in front of the unlit fireplace. Boyd followed, and sat down on one of the floral-covered armchairs.

'Where's your mum and dad?' he asked.

'At work,' Terry said. 'But they'll be home after six, if you want to come back then.'

'Where do they work?' Lottie said.

'Where's your younger brother?' Boyd said.

'You ask a lot of questions.' Terry threw his hands in the air.

'It's our job,' Lottie said.

The door opened and a young woman entered, wearing a dressing gown. Small and pale. Her hair dyed blonde at the ends. Lottie thought how Chloe had wanted to get her hair styled that way. Balayage, or something weird. It cost nearly one hundred euros, so that put a halt to her gallop.

Lottie produced her ID. 'I'm Detective Inspector Parker, and this is my colleague Detective Sergeant Boyd.'

'I'm Carol. What do you want with me?' Her voice was timid.

'You're not at work today,' Lottie said without preamble. 'Where do you work?' She knew, but she wanted the girl to relax.

'Rochfort Gardens. Why do you want to know? This is the first day I've missed in two years. I don't think that warrants the council calling the guards.' She sank down on the armchair opposite Boyd. 'Are you going to tell me what this is about?'

'It's about Elizabeth Byrne,' Lottie volunteered. 'You're her friend?'

'What if I am? I doubt she's done anything wrong. She's above all that.'

'How do you and Elizabeth get on?'

'Why do you want to know?'

'Answer the question,' Boyd cut in.

'She lives on the good side of town. But we've been friends since school. Her uppity mum doesn't like it, but tough. Life isn't all sweet, is it?'

'No, I don't suppose it is,' Lottie said, sniffing the distinct scent of weed in the coldness of the room. She sat down on the sagging couch. 'When did you last see Elizabeth?'

The girl's eyes skittered around nervously. 'I call her Lizzie, by the way. Her mother rang me on Monday night, asking me the same thing. I'd like to know why you're asking these questions. You're scaring me.'

'We don't mean to scare you. We're trying to trace Elizabeth's movements and we need to backtrack to the last time she was seen.'

'Trace her movements? Is she missing or something?'

'Something like that.' Lottie didn't think the time was right to inform Carol that her friend had been found dead. They needed formal identification first.

Pulling the sides of her dressing gown together, her hands worrying each other, Carol crossed her bare legs at the ankles. Gulping, she said, 'I saw her on Saturday night. We went to the Last Hurdle. That's a nightclub. We had a few drinks here first before we went to the pub. Then to the Hurdle. Sorry, I'm messing this all up.'

'You're doing fine. Did you meet anyone? Friends?'

Carol looked from one to the other. Deciding what to say? Lottie waited her out.

'Loads of people were out, but we stuck together. Lizzie didn't even want to go to the nightclub, but I insisted. I've been trying to boost her up ever since that prick Matt dumped her. We were there until maybe two o'clock. I think. Taxi dropped me off first, then Lizzie, because she said she'd pay. I've heard nothing from her all week, but that's not unusual because she works in Dublin and commutes on the train. Long days. Sometimes we go out during the week, but not that much.'

'No texts or WhatsApp messages? Snapchat?'

'No. Nothing. Like I said, that's not unusual.'

'This boyfriend she had. What do you know about him?' Lottie folded her arms and stared at Carol.

'Matt? Couldn't stand him.'

'Really? Why?'

'The way he treated her. Leading her up the garden path, my mum said.'

'You didn't think he was ever going to put a ring on her finger, then?'

'Not in a million years. Lizzie might be a step above me, but Matt was a flight of stairs above her. The minute he got his transfer to Germany, he was out of here like Usain Bolt.'

'So he's been gone a while?'

'Almost a year. Why are you asking about Lizzie? She seemed fine on Saturday night, just a bit drunker than usual. What's happened?'

'Do you think she was over her relationship with Matt?'

'Well and truly over him. She hates him with a vengeance.'

'And Matt? Know where he might be?'

'Germany?' Carol shrugged her shoulders.

'Anyone else Elizabeth might've been interested in?'

'I'd really like to know what this is about.' Carol folded her arms and stared defiantly.

'Answer the question, please.' Lottie stood up like a military commander conducting a court-martial. Her legs had cramped on the low couch.

Carol appeared to shrink into the folds of her dressing gown. 'I don't think there's anyone in Lizzie's life. The only place she ever goes is her job in Dublin. Talk to her workmates.'

'We'll be interviewing them as soon as possible. So far, we know she was at work on Monday and caught the 17.10 train, but

apparently she never arrived home. We need you to think where she might have gone Monday evening, and who she might have been with.'

'She *is* missing? Oh God. I honestly have no idea. This is so out of character for her. She doesn't even go into town without telling her mother. You'd think she was twelve the way that woman keeps a rein on her.'

'Did she hook up with anyone at the nightclub?' Boyd asked.

Carol shook her head. 'No. She wasn't with anyone. Only me.'

'Your brothers. Were they out Saturday night? Either of them got their eye on Elizabeth?'

'You must be joking me. Terry is gay, and Jake is only fourteen.'

Lottie rubbed her hands together, feeling the cold in the room. 'If you think of anything, will you let us know?'

'I will. Her mother must be out of her mind with worry. Why didn't she tell me Elizabeth was missing when she rang? I'd call over, only she hates the sight of me.'

'Now might not be a good time,' Lottie said. Official confirmation or not, she decided to give Carol the bad news. 'Carol, I'm sorry to have to tell you this, but I think you need to know that we found a body this morning. We have reason to believe it is that of Elizabeth.'

'What? What are you saying?' The girl jumped up, then collapsed back down into the chair. 'You can't be serious. Oh God, you are, aren't you?'

'I'm sorry.'

'I can't believe this. A body? Was it an accident? Where? How … Oh my God, was she murdered?'

'We're not sure what happened yet.'

Carol convulsed into sobs. 'Oh, poor Lizzie. She never hurt anyone in her life.' More sobs. 'Where did you find her?'

'I can't reveal too much at the moment. But a body was found in Ragmullin Cemetery. Would Elizabeth have any reason to be there on Monday night?'

Carol looked up with red-rimmed eyes. 'The graveyard? Lizzie never set foot inside those gates since the day of her father's funeral. She hates the place.' She seemed to realise what she'd said and corrected herself. 'Hated the place.'

'Okay. We have to leave now, but if you think of anything that might help us, please call me.'

Carol took Lottie's card. She looked so small and feeble, her pale cheeks now flushed with the exertion of crying. Lottie felt like giving her a hug.

'Are you off sick today? What's wrong with you? Nothing contagious, I hope?' She was trying to make light of the situation, but her words fell flat.

More tears flowed and Carol's knuckles turned white clutching her dressing gown.

'Hey, I'm sorry.' Lottie sat on the arm of the chair.

'I'm pregnant,' Carol sniffed. 'My mum and dad don't know. I did a test. No one knows.'

'You need to go back to bed,' Lottie said, 'and like I said, call me if you think of anything.' She squeezed the girl's shoulder in a motherly gesture.

Terry stuck his head around the door. 'Can I have my stash back?'

'Not in your lifetime,' Boyd said, patting his pocket. 'You should be glad I'm not taking you to the station. Why don't you do that study you were talking about before we interrupted you?'

'What study?' Carol asked.

'For my Leaving Cert,' Terry said, his eyes boring two holes into her.

'Oh … right,' Carol said, and turned back to Lottie. 'I'll see you out.'

At the front door, Carol said, 'Don't mind Terry. He's a grade A liar. I'm not ... just in case you think ... oh, you know. I told you the truth about Lizzie. I honestly don't know what happened to her. I feel awful now.'

'It's not your fault,' Lottie said.

She had to find out whose fault it was.

\*

Upstairs in the bathroom, Carol threw up the little that remained in her stomach. As she gagged and heaved, Terry banged on the door.

'Have you been smoking my dope? You've been in there puking all day.'

'Fuck off, Terry.'

'Yeah, well I need to have a piss.'

'Give me a minute.'

She heard him thumping back down the stairs, banging the wall as he went, and sat back on her haunches. Her best friend Lizzie. Her only friend. Dead. Murdered? She pulled the inspector's card from her pocket. Should she have told her what Lizzie had said about feeling as though she was being watched by someone on the train last week? Surely that was just Lizzie being Lizzie. Always getting feelings about this and that. But maybe she should have said something.

Putting the card back in her pocket, Carol got up, flushed the toilet and washed her hands. She'd have a think about whether or not to call. First, she needed to put her head on her pillow, and hopefully that would stop the nausea in her stomach.

# CHAPTER FIFTEEN

He walked along O'Connell Street and turned the corner into Talbot Street. Connolly station loomed up in front of him, and as he neared it, he looked up at the black bridge above his head. He felt the vibration of the Dart train as it picked up speed heading for Bray, and breathed in deeply, experiencing the sensation of movement. The sensation of the train and its sounds. He closed his eyes, standing there in the middle of the pavement, lost in a world of his youth.

'You drunk or wha'?'

The man lying in a nearby doorway held out a tattered paper cup. Begging. For drug money? Or a hostel bed for the night? He ignored him and continued towards the station. His mind was filled with expectation for the evening ahead. He was going to do it. Again.

As he waited for the light to turn green to cross the road, he felt a momentary stab of anxiety. Had he been right to leave the woman in the grave? Would her body be discovered? No, surely not. The grave had been open, waiting a burial. And he'd covered her over fully with the clay. He smiled to himself at his ingenuity. Buried in someone else's grave. He'd have to remember that option as a means of disposing of a body. But that wasn't about to happen again. She was a loss, a big loss, and now he had to take the other one. She was his last hope. And this time he wouldn't make the same mistake.

# CHAPTER SIXTEEN

Cafferty's Bar was quiet when Lottie and Boyd entered shortly after 4.30. They sat in a corner and ordered tea and house special sandwiches. The television was showing a soap. A few men sat at the bar slurping soup, thumbing through the local newspapers, pints of Guinness at hand.

'After what I witnessed this morning, I hate this damn town. But you know what?' Lottie said.

'What?' Boyd sipped his tea.

'I hate it but I love it at the same time.'

'Bit like the way you feel about me then?'

'You know what?'

'You're repeating yourself now.'

'It's impossible to have a normal conversation with you.' When their sandwiches arrived, she pushed hers around on the plate until the filling squeezed out of it.

'Right, this is my serious face,' Boyd said. 'I know what you're saying, kind of. I haven't lived here long, so it's not the same for me. But I get it. Ragmullin gets under your skin. Some days you love it, and other days it's just a bitch.'

'Eloquent. As usual.' Picking at the tuna that had spilled out onto the plate, she shoved some of it into her mouth and licked her fingers.

'I'll get you a fork, shall I, or maybe you prefer eating like a baby?'

'Speaking of babies, I must have that conversation with Katie this evening.'

'And what conversation would that be?'

'About visiting Tom Rickard in New York.' Rickard blamed Lottie for the death of his son, but she had never spoken to him about it.

Boyd said, 'Let the girl go. Rickard is the baby's grandfather and it'll be good to have him in Louis' life as he grows up.'

'Why do you say that?'

'One, he's bloody loaded, and two ... he's bloody loaded.'

'It's just ... Oh, I don't know.'

'I think I do.'

'Enlighten me.'

'You're scared of losing Katie and your grandson to Rickard. She didn't travel in November because you were recuperating from that nasty stab wound. But now there's nothing holding her back and you're frightened he will introduce her to a world you can't afford. You're also fearful that she might not want to come home.'

'She has to come home. She only has a holiday visa.'

'Money talks in strange places, and as I said, Tom Rickard is—'

'Bloody loaded. I know. Why do I carry such fear around with me? And before you say it,' she held up her finger in warning, 'don't mention Adam. You've given me that lesson once too often.'

Boyd chewed on a piece of chicken before putting down his sandwich. She didn't like it when he thought things through too seriously. He usually came out with a long-winded notion that ultimately proved correct.

'You're right, I used to think your fear of loss stemmed from Adam's death. But now, with the revelations about your family history, I'm thinking this thing inside of you originates from your childhood.'

'Yes, Sherlock. I lost my father to a suicide that was quite possibly murder, and my brother was murdered in a hellhole of an institution. Then my husband died of cancer and I recently discovered

my mother isn't in fact my biological mother. I may also have a half-sibling whom I know nothing about, and my biological mother was incarcerated … How could I be right in the head?'

'About your biological mother—'

'Shut up. You know that conversation is totally out of bounds. Just eat your sandwich like a good boy.' She really didn't want to go back there. Too many lies.

'Oh Lottie, you wouldn't like me when I'm a good boy.'

'That's enough.' She smiled, despite herself.

Boyd picked up his sandwich and she looked at the mess she'd made of her own. She still felt hungry, but the food now looked so far removed from what she'd ordered, she couldn't face eating it.

'I promised Sean I'd bring him to his hurling training tomorrow evening,' Boyd said with his mouth full. 'Hopefully we'll have this murder solved soon.'

'It's good to see him back at his hurling.'

'And once the evenings get a bit brighter, he wants to join the cycling club with me.'

She looked at him then. Really looked at his thin, finely featured face and his brown eyes with their sparkling flecks of hazel. 'You know more about my own son than I do.'

'He talks to me.'

'When? How?'

'When I take him to his training sessions. Since you were injured. Since Christmas. You know that.'

'I thought you were just giving him a lift, not interrogating him.' She felt her chest tighten with jealousy. She knew she could never be a substitute for the boy's father. But she didn't want Boyd stepping in either. 'What does he talk about?'

'Not much. If he wants to chat, to go training or cycling with me, let him.'

She bit her lip, the silence hanging between them like an invisible sword. Eventually she said, 'It's hard. Damn hard.'

'Nothing in this life is easy.'

'You can say that again. How's Grace getting on with you?' she asked, deflecting the conversation away from her own family.

'You should ask how am I getting on with her. My sister is a tough cookie. Wearing me down, in her own pleasant, unassuming way.'

'When did she arrive?'

'Sunday night. Offloaded by my mother. She's doing a media course in Dublin for four weeks and staying with me during the week until it's finished. She has to go home to Mam at weekends, but she thinks she can stay with me *forever*. Her word, not mine.'

'How old is she again?'

Boyd hesitated before saying, 'Twenty-nine, but she acts younger. She has a lot of anxiety issues.'

'I can't wait to meet her.'

'Look, Lottie, Grace is different. You mightn't like her.'

'Let me be the judge of that. I know so little about you, yet in a perverse sort of way, I know so much. You're a real conundrum, Boyd.'

After a few bites of his sandwich, he looked up at her. 'I'd like to take you out to dinner.'

'What?' Lottie spluttered, drops of tea flying out of her mouth.

'Dinner. You know, what normal people do? Go out at night. Sit in a restaurant and eat delicious food someone else has prepared. Would you like to?'

Gulping down her surprise, Lottie thought about it. It'd be nice for a change. Relieve some of her tension, especially with the murder investigation. No. It was a bad idea.

'Like a date?' she asked.

'Yeah, like a date.'

'I don't think so. No, Boyd. Sorry.'

'Think about it. Maybe tonight? I can pick you up around seven thirty.'

'No … maybe some other time. Not tonight. It's too soon.'

He'd been so good to her since all that heartache last October. A friend. And now Father Joe was back. What had made her think of him? She smiled.

'Ah, that smile. It's agreed so. Tonight. Seven thirty. Now, are you going to eat that mess you've made, before I do?'

She really should set him straight, but she hadn't the energy, so she watched him finish the food instead. When it was time to leave, she felt like she could have sat there all afternoon in the silence. But they had a murderer to find. She needed to go back to the cemetery.

# CHAPTER SEVENTEEN

He bought a takeout coffee and a pastry and stood sipping and eating, looking up at the giant electronic timetable above his head. He knew that plain-clothes gardaí mingled with passengers on the concourse and armed detectives patrolled the main door. In plain sight.

Biting into the crumbling pastry, he turned and scanned the crowd. Watching. Waiting. He was impatient for her to arrive so that he could follow her and sit in the same carriage.

The digital clock clicked over. One minute closer to departure time in four minutes. He walked back to the café and dumped the coffee and paper bag into a flip-top bin inside the door. Licking his lips, he rubbed his hands together. She was late. She would miss the train. He moved towards the gate, careful not to stand under the lens of the camera.

He'd have to wait on the platform. He scanned his ticket and went to Platform 4. The train was waiting. Ready to go. There'd be no seats left. He'd have to stand. He hated standing. Come on, girl, hurry up.

A chill wind gusted from outside and up along the platform as a train entered on Platform 3 and the Belfast express shunted out on the track furthest away. And then he saw her. Desperately trying to scan her ticket. The woman behind her was trying to scan hers at the same time. Eventually they both rushed through, running on the slippery tiles. He knew they'd have to jump onto the last carriage, so he got on just before them.

As he'd thought, the carriage was full. He moved down halfway until he got to the blockage of people standing in the aisle with their technology glued to their hands. He glanced over his shoulder. Three rows down. The two of them were standing in the middle of the aisle.

The train snaked out of Dublin into the dark of the evening, heading for Ragmullin. Over the slow rhythm of the engine his mind whirled with plans. He had to ensure the other woman wasn't going to be a problem. That was Plan A. Plan B was to ensure his target didn't attempt to escape.

He smiled to himself and kept his eyes glued to the two women.

❋

Grace laughed, a nervous reaction to mask her fear. She'd run too quickly. Her breath was catching in the back of her throat.

Fumbling in her pocket, she found her inhaler and, trying to keep the pulsing bodies from touching her, brought it up to her lips. As she inhaled, she felt a slight reduction in the palpitations, but the panic lingered beneath the surface of her skin.

'Are you okay?'

She looked up at Mollie, her new friend.

'I'll be fine once I get to carriage C.'

'Not a hope in hell.'

With her saliva drying up, Grace took another hit from her inhaler. 'But I *have* to sit in carriage C. It's the only way I'll get home safe.'

Mollie laughed. 'You're not *that* superstitious, are you?'

Suddenly Grace found herself in what she called freeze mode. Stock still, only her eyes moving. Slanting to the right, then to the left, then back to Mollie's grinning face. Her lips stuck together, tongue thick and throat closed. As she breathed quickly through her nose, perspiration bubbled on her forehead. She felt it drip down into

her eyes and tasted the saltiness on her lips. Mollie's hand reached out and grabbed hers. No! Don't touch. But her words were lost in the drying mucus.

In, out, in, out. One, two, three, she counted in her head. No use. Ten, nine, eight. Still useless. I can't pass out, she warned herself. There was nowhere for her to fall, nowhere for her to go.

People pushed up against her as the train left the station. Her worst nightmare: physical touch. And the suffocating smell of sweat and last-minute cigarettes. Her hand tightened on the leather strap of her satchel. The numbness began to ebb. Her lips opened, and she exhaled a breath.

'A little colour is coming back to your cheeks,' Mollie said. 'You had me worried for a minute. What came over you?'

Shrugging, Grace clutched her bag tighter to her body. How could she explain to this girl, who was still a stranger, what it was like to live inside her skin? She couldn't, so she remained mute, silently praying for an opportunity to get to carriage C. Only then would she be okay.

# CHAPTER EIGHTEEN

The evening sky was grey-blue. Not quite daylight and not yet night. Dusk. It'd be fully dark soon. February was being a stubbornly cold month, with very little hint of spring appearing. Lottie zipped up her hoodie and then her jacket. The wrought-iron gates were wide open to allow the forensic vehicles entry to the cemetery. Crime-scene tape hung limply across the space, guarded by two uniformed officers.

They signed in and entered the grounds. Lottie stopped to view the caretaker's office, dark and lifeless in the shadow of the trees.

'Jesus, it's cold,' Boyd said.

'Beginning to freeze. Look at that lot. Fahy mentioned illegal dumping.' Lottie scanned the heaving mass of black bags sitting on top of a yellow skip. 'They look like they're moving.' Then she spied the vermin boxes around the house. Ugh!

Boyd said, 'See there. Sacks scattered on the ground. People must drive up outside and hurl their rubbish over the wall.'

'The council need to put up more cameras,' she said. 'Have we got the surveillance footage yet?'

'Kirby's looking after it.'

'Good,' Lottie started down the slope, which was glistening silver with the evening frost. A series of halogen lights on tripods illuminated the forensic tent and cast spectral shadows on the headstones surrounding it. A colony of SOCOs were working systematically, like ants, sifting through the clay and dirt.

She walked towards the wall that backed onto the traveller site. 'How high do you think this is?'

'Must be nine or ten feet.'

'And Bridie's house is just beyond it. She says she heard a scream after three on Tuesday morning. Will you go back up there and scream?' She indicated the direction they'd come from. 'I'll see if I can hear it.'

'You're having me on?'

'I'm serious.'

'Then I'll stand here while *you* go and scream.'

'Maybe I should warn Bridie first.'

'Maybe you should warn the banshee that you intend to take her place.'

'Boyd, I need to confirm one way or the other if someone's screams could be heard the other side of the wall.'

'There are flaws to your plan. Say, if you stand right under the wall, you can be sure you'd be heard.'

Lottie swung her flashlight around the headstones, silently admitting that it had been a half-thought-out plan. But she couldn't shake the feeling that Bridie really had heard the woman's screams. Travellers were renowned for their insights and vision. And if Bridie had heard Elizabeth Byrne screaming, it could tie down time of death.

She went over to the SOCOs. McGlynn was on his knees in the bottom of the grave, brushing and scraping where the body had lain. He looked up.

'Before you even ask,' he said, 'I haven't found much for you to work with. Just flakes of skin, clay, dirt and stones.'

'Blood?' Lottie ventured, peering over the edge.

'Some. It'll be analysed.'

Lottie recalled the spot of blood she'd found on the stone from the neighbouring grave. She'd follow it up in the morning.

'If he covered her with clay, did he use his hands?' she asked.

'How would I know that?' McGlynn said.

Lottie turned to Boyd. 'We need to examine all the tools used around here.'

McGlynn's voice rose from the grave. 'I've taken care of that. You'll have the results as soon as I have them. I'm assuming you took the two workers' DNA and fingerprints.'

'Of course,' she said, hoping Kirby had done his job properly.

'Good.'

'The entire area has been fingertip-searched,' Boyd said. 'When will your work be finished here?'

McGlynn glanced up, his eyes dancing with green fire above his white mouth mask. 'It will be finished when it's finished.'

Lottie looked over at the rows of headstones, misshapen humps on the landscape. The vastness of the resting place for the dead chilled her.

'I don't think this is what the killer intended,' she said. 'It's more than likely the girl escaped from him and he followed. But why were they here in the first place? Were they having sex and it got too rough, or he was raping her and she fled? Where did they come from? He had to have a car, so where was it parked?'

Boyd said, 'We've been assuming this is the work of a man, but it could just as easily have been a woman.'

'True,' Lottie conceded. 'The victim was naked, so that implies something sexual. Hopefully the post-mortem will tell us more about that. And something might show up on the CCTV footage. If it was an accident, why not try to get her out, or call 999? Was the intention all along to kill her? I can't get my head around it. And so far, we haven't one clue. That's unthinkable.'

'Wait for the post-mortem. And the results from McGlynn.'

The embankment to their right lit up with the lights of the Sligo to Dublin train. A horn screeched into the evening air and the inky sky brightened in a V from the light.

'I've to pick up Grace,' Boyd said, and headed up the hill.

Checking the time, Lottie said, 'You've less than fifteen minutes if you want to catch the train coming in from Dublin.'

It was almost dark, and in the cone of light cast by her torch, she noticed crystals of frost on the plastic heads of imitation flowers. White granite sparkled and a blackbird cawed from a branch above her head. She tried to keep up with Boyd's long strides.

When they reached the gate, she looked over at the old office. 'We need to search in there.'

'Once SOCOs finish on site, they can move up here.'

'Did you see that?' She pulled Boyd's sleeve.

'Only thing I saw was a big fat rat crawling out of one of those bags over there.'

'Oh Jesus, let's get out of here.'

They hurried to the car. As Boyd reversed and turned it, Lottie said, 'I hope to God the camera recorded something.'

Boyd said, 'Apart from the front wall, the cemetery is wide open on three sides. The railway tracks at the end plus the traveller site; the old folk's home to one side and a housing estate on the other. Easy access.'

'Nursing home.'

'What?'

'Old folk's home is not a PC term.'

She stared over at the nursing home. A newly built block with floor-to-roof windows facing out over the cemetery. Behind it she could make out the roof of the older building, with its copper roof turned green. Why hadn't anyone heard or seen anything? Why was Elizabeth in the cemetery? Where did she go when she got off the train? If they could figure that out, they might get a direction to follow. But at the moment, they were getting nowhere.

Boyd pulled the car onto the road with a grunt. Lottie was relieved when they sped away from the place of death.

# CHAPTER NINETEEN

'Do you have anything for me, Lynch?' Lottie shouted out to the main office as she flicked through her emails.

Lynch came to stand in the doorway.

'Elizabeth Byrne had very little online presence. She closed down her Twitter account a year ago, hasn't posted on Instagram in that time either. She doesn't appear to use Snapchat at all, and her postings on Facebook are sparse. She used WhatsApp.'

'Check it out. Have you contacted her Facebook friends?'

'Working my way through them.'

'Any joy with Matt Mullin?'

'The bank is to get back to me in the morning. The head of HR wasn't in and no one else would give me details.'

'Get on to that first thing.'

'Boss? This surveillance job that Kirby and myself are working on, I don't think it's getting us anywhere. Do you think it's time we abandoned it?'

They'd had problems recently with illegal bare-knuckle boxing among the traveller community. Vast amounts of money were being wagered, resulting in plenty of injuries. Lottie felt it was only a matter of time before someone died.

'What have you discovered over the last three weeks?'

'Nothing,' Lynch said.

'Just wondering if you found the McWards involved in anything underhand?'

'Don't recall seeing the name anywhere, but I can check.'

'What type of detective are you?'

'A good one,' Lynch said, folding her arms.

'Prove it to me then. I want to know where Matt Mullin is. A banker in Germany can't be that hard to find now, can he?'

Lynch sighed. 'Could I have a few days off, boss? I know it's the start of an investigation, but I really need time to—'

'No. All leave is suspended until this case is solved.'

'But—'

'No buts, Lynch. I need everyone. Is that all?'

Lynch grabbed her coat and was out the door before Lottie could call her back. It really was one of those days.

Lottie phoned the state pathologist.

'Hi, Jane. Did you get to my graveyard victim yet?'

'Sorry. A sudden backlog here. Hypothermia deaths in February are a new thing for me. I've your girl scheduled for the morning. I'll call you with a time so you can attend.'

Hanging up, Lottie went out to the main office and pulled a chair over beside Kirby's desk.

'You were a bit harsh on Lynch,' he said.

'I don't know why, but sparks fly every time we talk recently.'

'Not just recently, boss, it's been going on a long time. And not just with Lynch, if you get my meaning.'

She didn't want to talk about Lynch or Boyd. She'd never really got along with Lynch but she didn't want anyone else knowing.

'Did you interview Bridie McWard?' she said.

'Same as she told you. Heard screams around 3.15 Tuesday morning. Refuses to come in to make a formal statement. I spoke to her at the site.'

'And the footage from the camera at the cemetery. Was there anything useful on it?'

'The tech guys sent me a clip.' He pressed an icon and a grainy grey image appeared in the centre of his screen. Maximising the size, he sat back and let Lottie watch it. 'This is 3.07,' he said.

'I don't see anything.'

'There's nothing to see except for a change in the light. Hold on and I'll rewind it.' He clattered his thick fingers on a couple of keys and the image rolled once more. 'Look carefully at the road. See that? It's the lights of a car approaching, but then they disappear. I'd say he swung the car to park on the opposite side of the road, where there's no camera coverage.'

'Okay. But we can't see any people?'

'No.'

'Might just be someone dumping rubbish over the wall.'

'I don't think so.'

'Why not?'

'Because the footage confirms a vehicle was parked here for twenty-four minutes.' He fast-forwarded to 3.31. 'Look. There's a swerve of light on the road as if a car is turning.'

'And?'

'And that's it.'

'Nothing in between? No other cars?'

'Not a thing. On a Monday night, the town is dead.'

'So it looks like he drove in from town, stopped for nearly half an hour, then turned and went back towards town. Track our own traffic cams around those times and see if you can pick up the car.'

'I'll try.'

Lottie pushed the chair back and moved towards her own office. 'I want all the residents in the nursing home interviewed. Especially those with windows facing the cemetery.'

'Tonight?'

'No. Tomorrow. Did uniforms get anything useful from the housing estate?'

'Database is being compiled, but nothing worth reporting so far.'

'And the residents at the traveller site?'

'No one heard or saw anything.'

'Same old Ragmullin. Squinting windows and silent houses.'

'What?' Kirby scratched his head with the tip of a pen.

'I want an update at our incident team meeting in the morning.'

# CHAPTER TWENTY

He secured a seat once passengers disembarked at Maynooth. The two women got seats also. Now they were sitting opposite him, albeit a few rows down the aisle.

How he wished he was beside her, with her soft flesh trembling beside his own. Skin on skin. Nothing more beautiful, he thought. Unless you counted the rocking motion of the train. Oh, naked flesh on flesh in tune to the motion of the train. That was an image he couldn't stop flitting behind his eyes. How beautiful would that be? The quiver of her lips as he looked down on her, the redness puckered, waiting.

For him.

For no one else.

With the answer he craved.

✳

Ragmullin train station was crumbling under its age. Multiple renovations over the years had done little to enhance its appearance. The fact that it was a protected structure limited the railway company from doing anything major. Protecting it was a paradox, because it was disintegrating before twenty thousand pairs of Ragmullin eyes.

'How's it going, Jimmy? Any news?' Boyd sauntered over to the porter and leaned on the gate to the platform.

'Sure, the only news around here is the weather and late trains.' Jimmy Maguire scratched at a point on his scalp under his cap.

'I hope this one isn't late.'

'Should be in on time. Due at 18.20.'

Boyd smiled as Jimmy made a drama of checking his watch with his gloved fingers. Bright yellow, synthetic fabric. The top of his peaked-capped head only came to Boyd's shoulder, and he looked as weather-beaten as the station.

'In fifty-seven seconds, to be exact.'

'Very precise.'

'It's my job to know these things.'

Boyd stared up along the platform as he heard the train approach.

'She's a little early.' Jimmy straightened up. 'By fifteen seconds.'

Boyd ducked as a pigeon swooped from the gantry that hung over the concrete platform.

The train's hydraulic brakes hissed as it idled to a stop and the doors slid open. Boyd stood to one side to allow the passengers to pour from the carriages, rush to the gate and head for their cars in the overcrowded car park. As quickly as it had arrived, the train departed with a loud rumble along the tracks.

His sister appeared. 'Hi, Mark. You look tired. Is anything wrong?'

'No, just waiting for you. Couldn't see you for a minute.'

'I have a new friend.' Grace looked around. 'She was here a minute ago. I was going to ask if you could give her a lift.'

'Probably went on ahead,' Boyd said, thinking that Grace's new friend wanted to escape his sister's constant chatter. 'Car's outside. On double yellow lines.'

'Breaking the law again?' she said.

'I am the law,' Boyd said.

He pinged the key fob and sat into the car. Grace unwrapped her heavy knitted scarf, folded it neatly on her lap and placed her bag in the footwell, then seemed to think better of it and put it on her knee on top of her scarf.

'Shut the door,' he said. 'It's bloody freezing.'

'You always state the obvious.'

She's worse than Lottie, Boyd thought. He wondered if he had been an insanely bad person in a previous life to be condemned to inhabit the same planet as contrary women.

He swung the car around in a U-turn and nudged into the line of traffic.

'Tell me about your friend.'

'I met her on the train this morning. She told me she always gets the 17.10 home. So I decided to travel with her.'

'In your usual carriage?'

'It got a bit complicated, because she arrived later than me. I had to wait for her and then we had to stand in the wrong carriage. I had a little panic attack, but I'm fine now.'

'Are you sure you're okay?'

'Stop treating me like I'm an imbecile. I might be sixteen years younger than you, but I'm not stupid.'

The traffic lights on the bridge changed to green and Boyd gunned the car to make it through before they flipped again. They were red by the time he was on the crest of the hill, but he kept going.

'You hit it off with her, then?'

'Don't sound so surprised. I can hold conversations with people.'

'That's what worries me.'

'Are you trying to be funny?'

Boyd kicked himself. Grace didn't get jokes. She saw things as either black or white. Straight down the middle. Whatever you wanted to call it, Grace was it. 'On the spectrum' was a phrase he had often heard in the same sentence as her name. He loved his sister, but she tried his patience something terrible. He reminded himself that he'd have to be more careful with his choice of words in her presence. And he'd have to remember she was twenty-nine years old.

'Why are you driving down Main Street?' she asked.

'I'm getting a takeaway for dinner.'

'But I don't eat food made by someone else. You know that.'

'Just this once, Grace. For me? Please?'

'Mark! You have a date.'

'How do you know that?'

'I can read you so well.'

Just like Lottie, he thought, and double-parked outside the Chinese takeaway.

'Don't suppose you'll go in to get it,' he said.

'You suppose absolutely correct.'

Boyd shook his head. He was glad he was going out tonight. Then again, he wondered if it might be frying pan and fire. He hoped Lottie would be in better form than Grace. With all that had happened today, he doubted it.

# CHAPTER TWENTY-ONE

The temperature had dropped to freezing. Windscreens shimmered with a fine coating of hoar frost. A constellation of stars glittered in the clear sky as the commuters exited the station, preceded by their white breath fogging the raw evening air.

Mollie felt a tap on her shoulder as the crowd rushed towards the exit.

'Hi there,' the man said.

The same man whom she had accepted a lift from yesterday evening. He'd been a perfect gentleman, dropping her off outside her apartment. He seemed really nice and sensible. She knew him to see around town but didn't know who he was. They hadn't exchanged names let alone phone numbers. And she was happy enough with that.

'I can give you a lift again,' he said. 'Thought you might want to escape your chatterbox friend.'

She sidestepped around Grace without her noticing. She was chatting with a tall, thin man. Mollie supposed it was the brother she'd heard about on the endless train journey. Feck it, she thought, she had to escape the constant nattering.

'That'd be cool. Thanks,' she said. She felt his hand on her elbow and she was propelled down the steps.

They glided on the frozen ground to the darkness at the left of the car park.

'Your friend is some talker. Never stopped to catch a breath. I'm sure your head must be mithered with her.'

'She's not too bad,' Mollie said. Why was she defending a girl she didn't even know? Why was she taking lifts from a man she didn't know, come to that? The car park was almost empty now. There was only one car parked up against the back wall to the rear of the station. She stopped. He turned to look at her.

'What's up?' he asked. He sounded normal. Not a weirdo, then.

'Thanks for rescuing me. And thanks for the lift yesterday evening, but I think I'd rather walk now. I need some fresh air.'

She stepped back. He walked into the space she had vacated.

'It's no trouble. My car's over there.' He pointed to his dark saloon, out of the range of cameras and lights. This was getting scary. That wasn't where he'd parked yesterday.

'Honestly, I'm grateful for the rescue. I might see you tomorrow?' As she turned, the hand on her elbow tightened, biting through her clothes, hurting her. 'Hey! What are you playing at?'

'I'm not playing, Mollie. That's your name, isn't it? If you walk quickly, I won't have to hurt you. Come along like a good little girl.'

'You're out of your fucking mind.' Mollie opened her mouth to scream, but in that second of hesitation, his gloved hand filled the void and a cloth was stuffed halfway into her mouth. She looked around wildly, but everyone was either in their cars queuing up to exit or rushing away up the hill, heads bent against the biting wind.

'Help.' She thought she said the word, but nothing came out of her mouth because the cloth was there. His arms circled her body, pulling her close to him. The cloth was choking her. And that smell …

'Do what you're told or you die, do you understand?'

The car lock beeped. He opened the door and pushed her inside. She cracked her head against the steering wheel and fell across the two front seats. He lifted her ankles and shoved her legs in behind her. She raised a hand to press the horn before he got in behind her,

but she was too slow. He gripped her fingers and shoved her out of the way, sitting himself into the driver's seat. She lashed out. Her nails snagged on the collar of his shirt.

'Bitch,' he cried, and placed his hand back over her mouth, stuffing the cloth in further. From his pocket he took a plastic bag. She could see another cloth, just like the first one.

'You'll be sorry for trying to hurt me,' he said. 'So fucking sorry, you won't know what's happened to you. You'll beg. Beg, do you hear me? You will beg for your life and do you know what I'll do? No, I don't suppose you do, but you're sure going to find out.'

His hand thumped into her face again and he brought the second cloth to her nose. A sickly-sweet smell filled her senses as darkness fell upon her like a shower of soft rain.

# CHAPTER TWENTY-TWO

'Am I in the right house?' Lottie asked as she hung her jacket on the clutter-free stair post.

The aroma of chilli and cheese drifted in waves from the kitchen. Didn't smell like microwave food. Opening the sitting room door, she was surprised to find it neat, tidy and empty. She walked to the kitchen. The table was set with matching cutlery. There was even a tablecloth that only saw the light on Christmas Day.

'What's going on here?' she said.

Standing in a line at the cupboards to her right were Sean and Chloe, with Katie holding Louis in her arms.

'Surprise!' they cried.

'But why? … What? … I'm stunned.'

'You could try a thank you,' Katie said.

'Thank you. I mean, this is a major shock to the system. I'll have to sit down.'

'Yes, you sit down and I'll take out the lasagne,' Chloe said. 'Do you think it's cooked, Katie?'

'Definitely. Here, Mam, you hold Louis and I'll dish up. There's chilli in it. Sean insisted, hope you don't mind. We found a jar in the cupboard.'

Lottie took Louis in her arms as they began fussing over the food. Her mind went into overdrive mode. They wanted something. Nothing for nothing in her life. What, though? Why had they gone to this much trouble? She glanced around to see if her mother was

commanding the operation. She was nowhere in sight. That figured. Rose was in a lethargic mood recently, feeling unwell all the time, and Lottie was trying her best to call to her with food in the evenings.

Definitely a conspiracy. But she had no idea why, so she decided to play along.

'This is delicious,' she said when they'd finished eating. 'And it's great to sit around the table as a family. We should do it more often.' It was then she caught a look passing between Chloe and Katie.

'I'll take Louis and put on Baby TV.' Sean released the brake on the buggy and pushed it out to the hall, pulling the door behind him.

'Right, tell me what this is about,' Lottie said.

The doorbell rang.

'I'll get it,' Sean shouted from the hallway.

'Oh, shit,' Lottie said, jumping up.

Boyd stood in the doorway, a bunch of six red roses in his hand.

'I see you had dinner without me,' he said.

'Oh God, Boyd. We didn't agree anything, did we? I should have made myself clear. I'm sorry. I didn't …' Shit, she was babbling.

'Let me hang up your jacket,' Sean said.

'No, I'm disturbing a family gathering. I'll leave.'

'It's okay,' Chloe said.

'Bring Boyd into the sitting room for a minute,' Lottie told her. 'I want to have a chat with Katie.'

When they were alone, she looked at her daughter standing with a pile of plates in her hands. 'Sit down and tell me,' she said.

'Mam.' Katie put the dishes on the counter, 'I know you don't agree with me going to New York to visit Louis' grandad, but I want to go. I put it off when you were attacked, and then there was Christmas and … Wait a minute. Don't jump out of your skin yet.'

Lottie sat down again and studied her daughter's beautiful, sad face. Katie had endured so much in her twenty years that maybe it was time to allow her to live for herself. To have a life. Wasn't that what Boyd had said?

'Okay, Katie. I won't argue with you. How much money do you think you'll need?'

'That's the thing. I don't need anything. We cooked the dinner to celebrate … to tell you …'

'Tell me what?'

'Tom Rickard booked the tickets and put money in my bank account. Me and Louis, we're leaving for New York on Friday. I was afraid to tell you before now. Please don't stop me.'

A conflict of emotion surged through Lottie. The hairs on her arms tingled, her tongue stuck to the roof of her mouth, a knot tightened in her chest and tears bulged at the rims of her eyes.

'Say something.' Katie pleaded, widening her eyes. They were crystal clear now that her days of smoking weed with Jason Rickard were behind her. The only thing lurking there was evidence of sleepless nights.

'Which Friday?' Lottie whispered, afraid of the answer.

'This Friday.'

'What? But today is Wednesday … You can't, it's too soon. I need to organise things …'

'You don't have to organise anything. It's all sorted. I couldn't tell you before now, because you'd have time to think up ways of stopping me. I really want this, Mam. Please say it's okay.'

No matter what she said it'd sound wrong, so Lottie kept her mouth shut and nodded. She was suddenly enveloped in a hug. Katie didn't do hugs too often. But now she did.

'You are the best mother ever. This is an amazing opportunity for me. And I know Tom will love Louis just as much as you do.'

'How long will you be away?' Lottie croaked.

'Just for a few weeks.'

'How many is a few?'

'Three.'

'Three?'

'I really want to do this, Mam. For Louis' sake.'

'How much money did Tom send you?' Shit, why had she asked that?

Katie shifted from foot to foot. 'Five thousand euros. Can you believe it?'

'What?' Lottie stared at her daughter. 'Plus the tickets?'

Katie nodded. 'Isn't it great? I'm going into town tomorrow to buy new clothes for myself. I have to look right when I meet him again. It's so exciting. And I have to pack. You'll take me to the airport Friday morning, won't you? Love you, Mam.' She rushed from the kitchen, leaving dishes and cutlery scattered over the worktops.

Lottie had been on the verge of telling her not to forget how badly Tom had treated his son. But there was no point in dampening the happy smile on Katie's face. She stood up wearily and started to load the dishwasher.

'Let me give you a hand.' Boyd joined her and together they cleared the remnants of the meal.

'Thanks,' Lottie said when they were finished. 'You must be starving. Did you cancel the restaurant? Why don't you go on your own? I'm sorry if I gave you the wrong impression. Maybe you should—'

Her arms were gripped by his long, smooth fingers and he looked into her eyes. 'I'm fine. We'll go out tomorrow night instead. Deal?'

'I'm not sure it's a good idea.'

'Deal?'

'No deal,' she said. 'At least not until this murder is solved.'

'I can't win, can I?' Boyd released her arms and leaned against the table. 'Do you want to tell me what that was about with Katie?'

'Not really. It's enough to know she's happy. For now.'

'Are *you* happy?'

'As much as I can be. Sit down and I'll make coffee. Where'd you put the flowers? Thanks, by the way.'

'I left them in the sitting room.'

'Did you collect Grace from the station?' Lottie asked.

'Yes. She's ensconced on my sofa with a Chinese takeaway and Netflix.'

'Sounds like a little bit of heaven.'

'This here, right at this moment, is a little bit of heaven.'

As he smiled at her, Lottie thought of Katie's imminent departure. Then she remembered her mother.

'Shit, Boyd. I'm sorry.'

'What now?'

'I've to go over to Rose with her dinner. I totally forgot.'

He stood. 'You've a tough time trying to keep everything together.'

'I just need to stay focused. I'll try my best to organise things so that we can go out for a meal some night, but …'

'But you can't guarantee it?'

'I can't, so it's a maybe for now.'

'I'll take a maybe.' He smiled. 'Though like I told you before, I won't hang around forever. You know that?' He brushed his lips to her cheek.

The door burst open. Chloe came in and opened the fridge. Then banged it shut and left.

'What was that about?' Boyd asked.

'Teenagers,' Lottie said.

# CHAPTER TWENTY-THREE

'Hi, darling, you're late again. Miss the train?'

Ignoring his wife, Cillian O'Donnell hung his black leather jacket on the back of a chair and bent down to whisk his five-year-old daughter, Saoirse, up into his arms.

'What've you been doing while Daddy was at work, you little minx?'

Saoirse snuggled her curly head into the crook beneath his chin and wrapped her arms and legs about his body. He welcomed the scent of peach shampoo and his daughter's soft skin. Kissing her gently on top of her head, he eased the child to the floor and she dragged him to the kitchen table, where brightly coloured pages were scattered around and brushes stuck out of a jar of water.

'You were painting,' he said. 'Did Mummy help you?'

Saoirse shook her head and stuck her bottom lip out in a scowl.

Keelan said, 'She was a naughty girl at school today, weren't you, honey? I only allowed her to paint for half an hour.'

Cillian lowered his head to the paintings, fearing Keelan would see the torment he was desperately trying to hide. He sensed his wife turn from the stove, felt her stare. She was ordinary. Just plain ordinary. Short-cropped black hair, grey eyes, and the only make-up she wore was so minimal that it was invisible. Her body had failed to regain its slender shape after Saoirse's birth, and he couldn't forgive her for not trying harder. But only in his head. He didn't dare say it out loud.

'Did you forget?' she asked.

'Forget what?'

'The meeting. Tonight. It's at nine. And you're just in the door.' She rubbed her hands dry on a tea towel and sat at the cluttered table. 'Where were you until now?'

'Work was mental. I forgot about the meeting. I'll have a shower, go to the meeting and maybe a bite of dinner before I go to bed.'

'You can't go to sleep on a full stomach. It's bad for you.' She got up and slapped the tea towel against the edge of the table.

Saoirse flinched and scrambled up onto her father's knee.

He knew Keelan had tears of anger in her eyes. She liked everything to be exactly on time, the same day after day, no break from routine. In some ways, though not all, she was a carbon copy of his brother's wife. And both women were copies of Maura, their mother. How did they manage that? He turned his attention to his daughter again.

'Here, pet, use the red. And there's a clean sheet of paper. When Daddy comes down from his shower, I want to see a lovely red steam engine.'

'But I don't know how to do that. Will Mummy help me?'

He physically shuddered at the loud grunt Keelan emitted, standing beside the sink with her back to him.

At the bookcase, he pulled out one of his many train magazines and opened it at the correct page. 'There you are now, Saoirse. Copy that one.'

'It's too advanced for a five-year-old,' Keelan said, facing the window. 'And your father wants you to call him.'

He could see her grimace reflected in the glass. He rolled his hands into fists, quelling the urge to smash them into her face, then turned away and headed for the stairs, pulling off his shirt as he went.

What the hell did his father want with him?

✳

Finn O'Donnell shuffled out of his coat and hung it up on the rack inside the door. One step took him from the hallway into the small living room. Sara was in the scullery. Too small to call a kitchen, she'd said when they moved in with notions that it was only temporary. Five years was too long to live in temporary accommodation, she'd moaned every single bloody night.

'I'm not staying,' he said. 'I've to go to a meeting.'

'You always have something to go to. Can't you sit in for one night?'

He fell into his armchair without bothering to ask if there was anything to eat. He knew the answer by the whiff of alcohol coming from her breath as she squashed into the chair opposite him. He'd get a takeaway later.

The smack of the glass on the coffee table caused him to look up. Sara was round and plump. Fatty blubber. Hair unwashed, hanging about her shoulders, and she'd worn the same clothes for the last three days. God, why had he ever married her? But he knew why. His mother. Maura had forced his hand once Cillian snared Keelan. He hadn't been man enough to handle the jibes, the insinuations she flung at him day after day. Finn knew that no matter what he did, he could never be as good as his brother. Not since Lynn had disappeared. Even before she vanished. He was never good enough in Maura's eyes. And definitely not in his father's. He really should call over and see how Donal was faring. That could be tomorrow night's escape.

'What's going on in that dim brain of yours?' Sara's voice was high and squeaky, like a rat.

'Don't,' he said, standing up. 'Please don't start. I've had a bitch of a day and I'm not listening to you going on and on about shite.'

'Go to your silly meeting then. See if I care.'

As he grabbed his coat and opened the front door, he knew he didn't care either.

✷

The man skulked into the collar of his coat as he drove slowly through the industrial estate then up Gaol Street. He couldn't count how many circuits of the town he'd done since he'd left the train station. He didn't want to go home yet. Maybe if he drove around a bit more she would be in bed by the time he got there.

His eyes were blinded by the tears flowing from his eyes. He hastily wiped them away with his sleeve, like a child. He was no longer a child, but he felt like one. And some days he wished he could go back there and start all over again.

# CHAPTER TWENTY-FOUR

Lottie laid the plate, wrapped in a tea towel, on the table. There was no sign of her mother. 'Anyone home?' she yelled.

'I'm in here.' Rose Fitzpatrick's voice sounded weak.

Lottie went back down the hall and stood at the open door to her mother's bedroom.

'Have you been lying there all day?'

'Nothing to get up for,' Rose said, her mouth turning downwards.

With a disgruntled sigh, Lottie plumped up the pillows and straightened the duvet. Rose didn't move. Stared straight at her. Shrugging off an unwelcome feeling, Lottie took a step away and said, 'I brought over dinner. Are you hungry?'

'Not if it's a fry again.'

'It's lasagne. The kids cooked. It may be a bit hot.'

'Better than being cold like it usually is.'

'I mean spicy. I can throw it in the bin if you don't want it.'

'No need to be so sharp, missy.' Rose dug her elbows into the bed and sat up. 'I'll have it here. And a cup of tea.'

'Right so.' Lottie stomped back down the hall.

The last few months had been difficult, as she tried to come to terms with her mother's cataclysmic revelations. Their relationship had already been flawed, but now Lottie struggled to define exactly what Rose meant to her. If she wasn't her biological mother, then what was she? A liar?

She poured water into a cup with a tea bag, swirled it around with a spoon, slopped in milk, and took it to Rose along with the plate of food.

'Could you not find the tray?'

'Jesus!' Lottie said. 'You ate your food from a plate on your knee yesterday. What's changed?'

Rose was being awkward for the sake of it. To annoy her. Well, you're winning on that score, she thought. She placed the cup on the bedside cabinet and sorted the plate with a knife and fork.

Rose leaned over and sipped the tea. 'You forgot the sugar.'

'You never take sugar.'

'I do now. It might give me energy. Will you get it for me?'

Lottie bit her lip, silencing an impulsive retort. She watched Rose picking at the food. The once tall, vibrant seventy-six-year-old was now a shadow of that woman. Her hair, which used to stand to attention in short silver strands, was plastered to her skull, with white skin peeking out in places. Her head appeared to have shrunk with the rest of her body. Although Lottie tried hard, very hard, she couldn't feel any love for the woman who had raised her, and who she had thought of as her mother for forty-four years. She couldn't find forgiveness in her heart. But she knew it wasn't this woman lying here that she couldn't forgive. It was the woman Rose used to be. And it was the lie. She could never forgive the lie. Of course, she also knew that it was all her father's fault.

Returning with the sugar bowl, she said, 'You need to see a doctor.'

'I'm not changing doctors at this stage of my life. I'll wait until Dr O'Shea comes back to town.'

Lottie sighed. She had no idea when her friend Annabelle O'Shea would return to Ragmullin. She hoped it would be soon; she was running out of pills.

'I don't know how long she'll be away, and this staying in bed all day is not normal for you.'

'Not one day of my life has been normal since I married your father. So off with you. Go home and watch your children. And here.' Rose handed her the plate of food. 'I can't eat this. It's like the hide off a donkey.'

Lottie sighed. She could never win where Rose Fitzpatrick was concerned. 'Do you even know what the hide of a donkey tastes like?'

She left without waiting for an answer.

✳

'You're home early,' Grace said with a smile.

'Change of plans.' Boyd took off his jacket and loosened his tie. 'What are you watching?'

'You're changing the subject.' Grace pressed a button on the remote and folded her arms as the television screen faded to black.

Boyd folded himself into his armchair, pulled off his shoes and nudged them under the coffee table in front of him.

'Would you like—' she began.

'Don't mention tea.'

'I was going to ask if you wanted a drink.'

'Yeah, great. Thanks.'

As Grace went to the kitchenette, she said, 'I can assume things didn't work out with the delightful Lottie Parker. And in case you have forgotten, I have yet to meet her.'

'You don't *have* to meet her. Anyway, her family had other things planned for this evening. I have to reschedule.'

Grace handed him a bottle of Heineken and sat down with a glass of Diet Coke for herself. 'Reschedule? I thought it was a date, not a work meeting.'

'You know what I mean.'

'You should say what you mean.'

'Don't start.'

Grace sipped her drink with a smile. Boyd couldn't help himself. He smiled too. His sister sounded so like Lottie, it was uncanny. And then in other ways she was a million miles removed from his boss.

'You are a very lonely man,' Grace said, pulling at her short brown hair.

Boyd glanced up. She was staring at him over the rim of the glass.

'Where did that come from?' he said.

'I am astute, even though everyone thinks I'm stupid.'

'You're one of the most intelligent people I know.'

'Thank you, brother dear.'

'No need to be cynical.'

'I don't do cynical.'

Boyd sighed and took a swig of his lager. He thought of the way Lottie had rushed him out of her house. No matter what she said about her mother, no matter how confused she was over her parentage, she possessed an innate sense of duty of care to Rose. Family was everything to Lottie Parker, and he despaired that he could ever be part of that family.

'You *are* lonely,' Grace said.

He raised an eyebrow. 'I am not,' he denied, a little too forcefully. 'I like my own company and my own space.'

'I won't be here for long.' Grace put her glass on the coffee table and picked up the remote control again.

'I didn't mean that the way it sounded. Sorry. Believe me, I honestly didn't mean that you're in the way. I love having you here.'

'You're an awful liar.'

'And you can't lie to save your life.'

They both laughed.

'True.' She switched on the television. 'I want to meet Lottie. You better organise it, soon.'

'Okay.'

He sipped his beer. This was only the third day of Grace staying with him; there was still three and a half more weeks to go. He wondered just how he was going to put up with his sister sharing his home.

# CHAPTER TWENTY-FIVE

After the railway preservation meeting, a few of the committee members went to Cafferty's pub, and sat at a round table, pints of Guinness in front of them.

'The station will close down no matter what we do,' the chairman said. 'I'll be out of a job.'

'We have to fight to the bitter end,' Cillian O'Donnell said.

'We need television coverage,' Bernard Fahy suggested.

'I'll see if I can find out anything.' Cillian sipped his pint. He smoothed down his dark hair as the chairman waved a tired hand and headed for the door.

'Thanks for that. Goodnight, lads.'

'Maybe we could have a march on Leinster House,' Cillian said when it was just the three of them left.

'Bit cold for marching this time of year. Very few would turn up,' Bernard said.

'The weather must be good for your business then.' Cillian smirked.

'The graveyard is filling up nicely. Trying to keep the banshees away and all. And the guards.'

'What are you talking about?' Cillian sat up straight and stared at him.

'Oh go on, tell us,' Finn urged. 'Nothing like a few witches to take our minds off the railway bastards.'

'Piss off, the pair of you,' Bernard snorted. 'I'm the one who has to walk around there in the dark.'

'Doing night duty, are you?' Finn straightened his back and gave a mock salute with his dripping pint. 'Keeper of the dead.'

'You're very funny. Ha ha. But I'm not laughing. There's queer things goings on there. Wasn't I trying to get an old woman buried this morning, and this detective was snooping around because of the screams the young traveller one heard—'

'What are you on about?' Cillian said. 'What screams? What happened?'

'All serious now, aren't you? A young woman was found dead in the bottom of the grave.' Bernard put the glass to his lips and drained the black liquid in a single gulp.

'A dead woman? In a grave?' Finn said.

'Jaysus. I've heard it all now.' Cillian sipped his pint.

'Whole place is cordoned off. I can't get in. No one can.' Bernard grabbed his coat. 'I'm off home. See you next Wednesday? Same time?'

'Sure,' the brothers said.

He flattened his cap to his head, pulled on his well-worn black council jacket and headed out into the frost of the night.

'He's a real oddball,' Cillian said. 'A body in a grave? Now that's nothing new, is it?'

Finn stared into the frothy head on his pint, dreading the prospect of going home to Sara. The thought of seeing her frosty face was unappealing. If he could stay out until after eleven, then she would definitely be in bed. Clockwork. That was what she was. He was convinced that a horologist lived inside her ribcage, winding up dials linked to her brain. Time for this. Time for that. You're late for this. You're late for that. For fuck's sake!

'All right there, lads?' Darren, the barman, asked from behind the counter.

'I will be. Just as soon as I finish this,' Finn said.

'Any luck with the plans to keep the station open?' Darren asked as he polished a glass with a tea cloth.

'Ongoing,' Cillian said.

'If anyone can get them to change their minds, you can.' Darren reached up and put the glass on the shelf. 'Awful news about that young woman found murdered in the graveyard.'

'Murdered? I didn't hear that bit.' Finn pulled on his navy anorak and zipped it up. Time to face the clockwork orange once again. The thought filled his stomach with bile.

'Where are you off to?' Cillian said as the brothers left the pub together.

'Home,' Finn said.

'We need to meet with Dad this week.'

'Why?'

'It's Lynn's tenth anniversary. On Sunday.'

'I hadn't forgotten.' Finn looked up at the night sky. 'The first one without Mother. Do you think we should do a fresh appeal?'

'Not going to bring her back, is it?'

'You never know,' Finn said.

'It might send Dad over the edge. According to Keelan, he's lighting candles. She says he's in a bad way.'

'Was he ever any other? The fucking bastard.'

'Hey, keep it down. No need to tell the world.'

'You always did like to bury the truth, didn't you?' Finn pulled his collar tighter to his throat and walked away from his brother.

'You know what, Finn, you're a piece of shit,' Cillian shouted.

'And we both came from the same family.' Finn kept walking, talking over his shoulder. 'You're no angel, Cillian O'Donnell. I know you. Don't ever forget that. I know all about you.'

# CHAPTER TWENTY-SIX

The mirror wasn't doing her any favours tonight. Gilly O'Donoghue wasn't used to the art of applying make-up. A scrape of lipstick was her usual fare. At least she liked the short cut of her hair. It was handy, especially when wearing her peaked garda hat.

'You'll have to do,' she told her reflection.

She was meeting her friend Mollie in Danny's Bar because Kirby had had to cancel their Wednesday-night date due to some surveillance job. She'd rung Mollie, who'd agreed to meet up tonight even though she had to be up early for the train every morning.

Gilly had been going out with Kirby for the last four months and trying to keep it quiet at work. But it was hard to hide a secret from a crew of gardaí. Kirby was at least ten years her senior. It didn't worry her. He actually looked a lot older than that, if she wanted to be totally honest with herself. Probably all the extra weight he carried around his stomach. Could she get him to go jogging with her? She'd ask him.

'I'm running a bit late,' she said to the empty bedroom. Better let Mollie know. Tapping the phone, she called her friend. It rang out. She tried again. Same result. She checked the time: 9.45 p.m. Maybe she was in the pub already and couldn't hear the phone.

Gilly grabbed her coat from the back of the door and left her flat. She hoped Mollie wouldn't be mad at her.

✳

The night was dark. The stars had fled, and the frost had disappeared along with them. It was still cold, but he could feel rain in the air.

He thought about Elizabeth. Dammit, he had thought she'd never be found. Had he been careful enough? He had disposed of her phone. Taken it apart. Dropped pieces of it out of the train window and along the streets of Dublin. He'd dumped her handbag into a rubbish bin behind a pub. Was there anything else he needed to be mindful of?

Her clothes were in the skip inside the cemetery wall. That was the reason he'd been there in the first place. Thought the bitch was still in a flatline state. He'd spent ages at the lake with her, undressing her. Dunking the clothes into the water and putting them into black bin bags, ready for the skip. The guards would probably find them now, but he'd been careful. There shouldn't be any of his DNA on them.

He'd stashed her in one of the caravans at the lake until it was time to move her. He couldn't risk leaving her there. Maybe he should have done, because her escape from the car had changed everything. And directed him to his next conquest.

He smiled when he thought of the new one waiting for him. He still had her belongings. In the morning, her phone would meet the same fate as Elizabeth's, and the laptop would be suitably disposed of on the other side of the city. He'd bagged her clothes and boots, and stuffed them into a charity recycle bin outside Tesco.

All was taken care of.

He was free to play.

✳

Mollie's Canal Drive apartment was in darkness. She hadn't been in the pub, and it was unlike her not to let Gilly know that she'd changed her mind about going out.

When she got no response from ringing the bell, Gilly hammered on the door. Standing on the top step, she looked around at the bleak surroundings. In the distance, she could see the lights of the town shining brighter than the solitary lamp at the corner of the block.

Careful not to slip, she made her way down the steps. That was when she remembered she had a key. Mollie had given it to her a while ago, just in case. You never knew when you might need a bed for a night. She made her way back up to the door.

Surely she was overreacting? But now she was here, she might as well check. It couldn't do any harm, other than wake Mollie up from an early slumber. Rummaging through the multitude of keys on her key ring, she tried two before the door eventually opened inwards.

Stepping inside, she fumbled along the wall for the light switch. 'Mollie? You all right?'

No one in the kitchen. Cereal was caked to a bowl in the sink. No sign of an evening meal having been cooked. Not even takeaway boxes or wrappers. Gilly made her way to the bedrooms. Both empty.

She tried Mollie's number once more. No reply.

Leaving the apartment, she pulled the door shut behind her in frustration. She was a tiny bit angry. First Kirby and then Mollie, who hadn't even had the decency to tell her she wouldn't be around. Some friend.

As she headed along the path, she wondered if perhaps Mollie had missed the last train home and was spending the night in Dublin with one of her colleagues. But wouldn't she have let her know? Wouldn't she answer her phone? Then again, she could be wrapped around a new fellow. Feck you, Mollie.

Now she had to go home and take off her damn make-up. And she hadn't even had a drink.

✽

Mollie's teeth were literally clinking against each other as she tried to recall the sequence of events that had led her here. Her head was woozy and her stomach churning. She'd been drugged, she was sure of it. Her tongue felt like coarse fur was growing on it and her throat was raw.

He had seemed so nice. Offering her a lift. And she hadn't thought twice about taking him up on his offer. After all, he'd brought her home safely yesterday.

Her train companion had been a pain in the butt. Asking a million questions. Did people no longer respect the unspoken rule of commuting? The unwritten law to keep quiet? The continuous talking had caused her to jump at the chance of escape at the station and accept the offer of a lift. Stupid girl. She didn't even know him.

The smell, like sour milk or sick wafted around her. Felt like it was stuck to her face. He'd clamped the cloth against her mouth and nose, and the chemicals had hit her brain. Everything she'd ever heard about accepting lifts from strangers reverberated in her mind. But those were warnings for children. Not for a twenty-five-year-old like herself. She realised she had done the most moronic thing of her whole life.

He was here now, sitting on a chair beside the makeshift bed on which she lay. She tried to cover her nakedness, but her hands wouldn't move. Couldn't move. They were tied to her sides by the rough rope across her waist keeping her horizontal on the dark-coloured sheets. The room was too small. The walls were too close. He was too near.

'Where am I?' she asked. Her vision blurred again before refocusing in the thin light filtering through a hatch in the ceiling.

'You're safe. With me.' He laughed, and the beam from the torch in his hand bumped up and down.

'Come on, this isn't funny. Take me home.'

'Shut your mouth. There'll be time enough for talk.'

When she'd first met him, he'd appeared normal. She'd seen him around town. He was an ordinary-looking commuter taking the train home from work. Was he the reason she'd felt like eyes were following her every move over the last few days?

'I've been watching you,' he said. 'Morning and evening. But you never noticed me. I was either brilliant at concealing my stare, or you had no interest in me. Whatever the case, I can watch you now without disturbance. And you have no choice but to look at me. Just the two of us here. Nice and quiet. The way I like it.'

'You're a fucking pervert. Let me go!' She pulled at the rope, feeling it rip into her skin. But it was the connection of his hand across her cheek that stopped her struggle.

'Take that back! Say you're sorry!' he shouted.

Who the hell was this jerk? No way was she going to apologise to him. Clamping her lips shut, she closed her eyes. Be strong, she willed her bruised body.

Fingers, rough and probing, pulled her eyelids upwards. A sharp scream escaped from her throat before he clamped his other hand over her mouth again.

'Pretty mouth,' he whispered, bringing his face down to hers. 'I have to leave you alone for a while. Don't try to escape like the last bitch. She's dead and buried now, and you don't want that, do you?'

She whimpered and nodded, despite herself.

'When you learn to live by my rules, I will reward you. Little by little.'

'What do you mean?'

'You need food and water, don't you?'

'I'm not going to be here long enough for that,' she spat.

'Let's see how long it takes for that fight to desert you. And when it does, I guarantee you'll beg for the things you've taken for granted all your life.'

'You know nothing about my life.'

'True. But now that I have you here, I've plenty of time to find out, and you will tell me what I want to know.'

'Where are you going?' She tried to lean up on her elbow but flopped back down. She watched as he moved to the iron ladder leading to the opening in the ceiling. Taking the torch with him. 'No! 'Don't leave me here in the dark. Please.'

'Begging already. See, I told you so. You had no one in your life, but now you have me.'

'You're wrong there. I'm supposed to be meeting a friend. She's in the guards. And the girl I met on the train, she has a brother. They'll come looking for me.'

As soon as she'd blurted out the words, Mollie knew she had made a mistake, but she wasn't sure what it was. His eyes darkened and his face took on a ghoulish glow in the semi-darkness.

'You are alone now,' he said flatly.

She watched as he climbed the ladder and hauled himself through the hatch. When the small square door banged shut, she was plunged into darkness.

The night wrapped itself around her cold shoulders, and she cried and cried until her throat was so raw she could hardly breathe.

✳

When he had everything secure, he made his way to his car and sat there thinking. He should have been more careful. He didn't know she had a friend in the guards. Damn. He crashed his fist against the steering wheel. He'd have to find out who that might be and make sure nothing pointed in his direction. But there *was* nothing. He had never come in contact with the girl before, other than giving her one lift and seeing her on the train.

The train!

Who was that gap-toothed girl? What difference did it make if she had a brother or not? What was the significance of that? He was missing something. There was definitely something that Mollie was omitting. He'd have to find out. All this was diverting his attention from getting the answer he needed. If only that bitch hadn't escaped the other night, none of this would be happening now. It was all her fault.

He hadn't even had the time to have fun with her. But this one, yes, he would savour the pleasure of taking her down. He felt the hardness pulse between his legs. She would be just the medicine he needed. And she would give him the answers.

He switched on the ignition and began the drive home.

Slowly. Very slowly.

# CHAPTER TWENTY-SEVEN

Cillian crept into the semi-darkness of the room. The street light cast enough illumination to allow him to undress, fold his clothes and slip naked into bed. Keelan stirred in her sleep. He lay on his back. Stared at the dark ceiling. And he thought of the other woman in his life.

He missed her so much. It was as if someone had taken a bone from his leg and he was forever condemned to walk around in pain, limping on one side. But it's only a bone, people would say, you can still function. Yeah, so what do you know about it?

Keelan rolled over and he knew she was looking at him.

'What did you say?' she asked.

'Nothing. Go back to sleep.'

'You thinking about Lynn?'

'Go to sleep.'

'Did you go to the pub after the meeting?'

'Yes. With Finn.'

He felt her fingers then, lightly feathering the soft hair on his taut belly. Searching lower. And he couldn't help his response. Physically he was ready. But his mind was back there. Back at that time when the darkness descended and his world changed forever.

He felt her shift beneath him.

'Slow down,' she said. 'You're hurting me.'

But he couldn't slow down. His skin slid over hers, up and down, until a soft sheen of sweat built up, oiling their bodies. Maybe tonight he could banish his demons. Shut them away in the closet

and lose the key. Separate his world into two distinct parts. For a while, at least.

As he grunted, teeth gritted, eyes open, he caught sight of the pile of neatly folded clothes on the chair under the window. Everything had to be in its rightful place, like a china dinner service presented as a wedding present. Too good to use, too delicate. Left at the back of the cupboard, only taken out for important people. Like the visit of a priest or the guards …

The thought frustrated his frenzy.

'You stopped at just the wrong time,' she said. 'What's up?'

'Not a lot, by the looks of things.' He lay back on the mattress, sweating, unable to perform his sexual duties.

He was angry.

She was angry.

It wasn't her fault. But he hit her anyway.

❋

'What time of night do you call this?'

Finn shoved past his wife, the talking clock, and made his way down the short, narrow hallway and into the tiny spare room. She followed him.

'What's up with you, baby?'

'Don't you "baby" me,' he said. He lay fully clothed on the single bed and closed his eyes. He still had his coat on. The room was freezing. The whole damn apartment was like an igloo. He wrapped his arms around his body. 'Turn off the light.' If he stretched out his hand, he could switch it off himself. The room was that small.

'Ah, come on. Don't be like that,' she whined and sat on the side of the bed. He rolled away and faced the wall, studying the fungus of damp beneath the windowsill. He didn't need this shit. Still she

rattled on. 'I miss you when you're not here. It's so cold, I could do with a bit of body warmth. Know what I mean?'

'Fuck off,' he growled.

'There's no need for that kind of language.'

'Jesus, you sound just like my mother.'

'Your mother is dead.'

'And I wish you were too. Now turn off the damn light and leave me alone.'

He couldn't talk to her when she was in this mood. When *he* was in this mood. When life was being a complete bitch to him, why did she have to be likewise?

No longer sensing his wife's presence, he sat up and pulled off his boots and clothes. Then he tugged on a T-shirt and jogging pants and slipped under the duvet. He wondered how he was going to get out of the mess he'd made of his life. They had no money, and were still renting this piss-poor two-bed apartment.

At least you have your job, Sara would say. His job. Yeah, right. Working as a clerical officer in the public service, paid just above the minimum wage. No savings, and eighty euros a week train fares.

Why couldn't *she* get a job? No use wandering down that lane, because he knew why. He didn't want to think about Sara's drinking habits now. Things were bad enough. He was thirty-four, for Christ's sake. Wasn't life supposed to be better at his age? He should never have married her, and now he was living with that mistake every single hour of his life.

# CHAPTER TWENTY-EIGHT

Bridie McWard sat up in bed and stared over at her son in his cot. She kept the light on, and Spotify was churning out easy music on her iPhone. Still no sign of Paddy. Every night it was the same. Out until all hours. She hardly saw him any more.

She pulled the sheet up to her chin and folded her legs beneath her. She was too scared to lie down. Too frightened to close her eyes.

The key rattled in the lock and the front door opened. She held her breath, body frozen; her blood seemed to stop flowing. The door to the bedroom was pushed open and she looked up into the sorrowful eyes of her husband.

'I'm sorry,' he said, and sat on the bed to drag off his boots.

'That's what you say all the time.'

She didn't relax until he switched off the light and lay down on the far side of the bed, his breathing lowering into the soft snore of sleep. Only then did she slide down, unfurl her legs and close her eyes.

❋

Lottie felt like she'd been run over by a ten-ton truck. The water pounded down on her as she tried to ease the stress from her mind and body. Her wound had healed well, but the pain nagged at her constantly. And a late-night cold shower wasn't doing her any favours.

She wrapped a towel around herself, smoothed moisturiser onto her skin before pulling on warm pyjamas. She swallowed two paracetamol, then remembered the wash she'd put on that morning.

Everything would be smelly and creased. Unless Katie had looked after the chore. Chances of that were slim to none.

Down in the utility room, she emptied the clothes out of the dryer and folded them into piles, then hefted the damp laundry from the washing machine into the dryer. She switched it on, turned out the light and went back up to bed.

Listening to the sounds of the house settling down and the patter of rain against the window, she thought of Katie heading off to New York with her baby. There was nothing she could do to stop her. Lottie Parker couldn't compete with Tom Rickard. She just hoped he would treat her daughter right and send her home in one piece.

Thoughts of New York reminded her of the unofficial investigation she'd conducted into the murders from last October. She'd got nowhere, but there was a link to New York, for sure. She just had to find it.

She flipped her pillow over, fluffing up the feathers, then twisted and turned, searching for a comfortable position. She thought of poor Anna Byrne, whose daughter was never coming home. Tomorrow she would set about tracking down Elizabeth's killer. And then she remembered.

'Oh no,' she groaned. 'McMahon.'

Somewhere deep in the pit of her stomach, she knew her life was just about to turn very complicated.

✳

Matt Mullin paused the television screen on Elizabeth's photograph, then sat cross-legged on the floor and stared at her. Why had he let her go? Why had he put his job before love? He *had* loved her, hadn't he? And she'd loved him.

He sniffed away his tears and allowed a knot of hate to fill the void in his heart. She had caused his heart to break into tiny pieces, so many that he knew he could never put it back together. Never again.

It was going to be a long night. And still he stared at her face on the television, frozen in time. He remembered that photograph. He remembered it well. Because he had taken it. And now she had been snatched away from him.

'Oh Elizabeth,' he cried. 'What have I done?'

*

Donal O'Donnell switched out the light and went to sit at the table. He couldn't bring himself to make his way up the stairs to his lonely bed.

The flickering of the television highlighted the photograph on the sideboard. The silver frame glistened and the young woman in the picture seemed to come to life.

He stared at her beautiful face. To him she *had* been beautiful. She still was. His princess. But she'd taken Maura away from him. Not just the ten years of yearning for answers, waiting for the knock on the door, mourning without a body. No. Lynn had taken his wife from him the day she was born. It hadn't mattered that they already had two boys; now Maura had a little girl to devote herself to. And she had shut out everyone else. Smothered their daughter with overpowering emotion and attention.

The boys had suffered. He knew that then. He knew it now. But he'd done nothing to stop it. He'd gone along with Maura for fear of losing her altogether. And he'd been complicit in the treatment of his sons. It was wrong, what he and Maura had done, but he'd been powerless to stop it. Once he was in, there was no way out.

Resting his head on his folded arms, he blotted out the image of his daughter in the photograph, but in his mind's eye he could still see her, standing there in the kitchen.

'God in heaven,' he mumbled, 'forgive me. Forgive us all for what we have done.'

But Donal O'Donnell knew his soul was long past the stage of forgiveness.

✳

Bridie felt Paddy leaving their bed. Heard the buzz of his electric razor and the soft thud of the door closing as he went out. He hadn't spoken a word to her. The clock flashed 3.46. She fell back into a fitful sleep.

A loud crack woke her. She sat up. Was it a tree falling down on the roof? But there was no wind and no tree. The clock said 4.25.

Jumping out of bed, she checked on her baby. Tommy was fast asleep. The first night in weeks, and now she was awake. Drawing back the curtain, her eyes met the ugly graveyard wall, but the sky above it was lit up with stars.

The door burst open. She swirled round on the ball of one foot, her mouth open in a silent scream.

A figure stood in the doorway, highlighted by the night light.

'Who … who are you? Fuck off away.'

As Bridie made to rush to the cot, a leather-gloved fist smashed into the side of her face. She raised her arms to shield her head, but the second blow knocked her to the floor. Crouching into a ball, like Paddy had once told her to do if she was ever attacked, she cried, 'Don't touch my baby!'

A boot stamped on her back as she rolled over. When the second boot landed on her stomach, pain flashed up through her chest into her head, and something hard crashed down on her skull.

She thought she heard a voice, somewhere in the distance. What was he saying? If she concentrated, maybe he wouldn't hurt Tommy. But even as his words began to register, the blows continued to rain down in quick succession, and darkness fell.

# DAY TWO

Thursday 11 February 2016

# CHAPTER TWENTY-NINE

He didn't like the reflection he saw in the mirror above the washbasin. Even allowing for the fact that it was cracked, with a brown line cutting diagonally across the glass, splitting his face in two, he knew he looked bad. He leaned in closer and ran a finger under the black bags sagging beneath his tired eyes. His pupils were so dilated they appeared to be dark buttons, masking the true colour of his irises. Not a bad thing in one way, he supposed. Perhaps he could use some of her make-up to lessen the pallor, to add a highlight to otherwise chalk-white cheeks. Perhaps not.

With his teeth brushed and the scum of last night's alcohol swirling down the drain, he splashed water on his face and dried it using the only clean towel he could find. Dressing quickly, he picked up the bundle of flyers from the table and took the stapling gun from the cupboard beneath the sink.

It was 5.25 a.m., and the morning was dark and bitterly cold. Not like spring at all. A shower of rain during the night, followed by frost, had resulted in treacherous footpaths. He parked his car and started walking around town, putting up the A4-sized posters on every lamp post and pole he could find. It was a job he had done at this time every year for the last ten years. And it was one he would continue to do, though he knew there was no prospect of her ever returning. Appearances had to be maintained. And so far, he'd been doing okay on that score.

A car drove by, heading over the bridge towards the train station, lighting up the sheen of ice on the road. With his mind distracted, his

hand slipped and the staple pierced the bridge of her nose, directly between her eyes.

He smirked. That felt good. Too good.

Shaking off the sensation of fire in his belly, he moved on to the next post.

# CHAPTER THIRTY

Grace Boyd settled into her usual seat on the train. Waiting for Mollie, she glanced out of the window, rubbing at the frost stuck to the glass like the spines of dead animals. Mollie would want to hurry up or she'd be late. The whistle sounded. The guard waved a small green baton and the doors whooshed shut.

Maybe she'd got on a different carriage. But no. Grace had been at the station at 5.50 a.m. She had checked the clock in Boyd's car before she got out. She looked at her phone screen: 6.01.

Sighing, she tried to relax. Maybe Mollie was avoiding her. Quite possible, she thought. She'd never had any bother making friends; it was keeping them that was the unworkable trick.

She looked over at the adjacent seats. The man was there again, with his designer stubble, but his eyes looked darker, and red-rimmed. Further down the aisle she noticed another man. The reason she supposed she noticed these two was that they were both wide awake. Everyone else was already asleep.

She rocked in rhythm to the sway of the train, wishing her brain could shut off for at least five minutes. But she knew it never shut off. Not even when she was asleep.

Should she ring her brother? Now why on earth would you do that, Grace? He would say she was nuts. Maybe she was. But she didn't think so. She liked to have silent conversations with herself. They comforted her when no one else would listen.

Grace eyed the man who had sat opposite Mollie yesterday; the man who had caused her to move seats. Maybe she was sick, or had she slept in? Why hadn't she asked for her phone number?

The train stopped at Enfield and more people crowded onto it. Hadn't Mollie said she lived alone? What if she'd fallen down the stairs and no one knew? Stop! Grace didn't even know if there were any stairs in Mollie's house, so why was she thinking these thoughts?

She took her phone from her bag and kept pressing buttons until her contacts appeared. All two of them. Mark and her mother. If she told Mark, at least she would feel better.

*

Detective Inspector David McMahon was already at the station when Lottie arrived. Leaning against the door to her office, arms folded and a smug expression on his square jaw.

She shuffled out of her jacket as slowly as she could manage and hung it on the coat rack. Who the hell does he think he is? With a sigh, she decided she would be nice to him today. If he kept his mouth shut.

His initial mistake was to speak first.

'Well, if it isn't Inspector Clouseau.' He smirked and swiped his black fringe out of his eyes.

She ignored the comment, and brushed past him. Her immediate superior for the foreseeable future was a grade A shithead.

This wasn't a good start to their new working relationship. A relationship that had been soured last October when he'd been sent from Dublin to help with her investigation into a suspected drugs and murder gang. He'd tried to take over, but she'd stood her ground and come out on top in the end. That was then. Now? She'd have to work hard at being civil. God, why had she opened that bottle last night when she couldn't sleep?

'Must be too early for you,' he said. 'I thought you had a sense of humour.' He straightened his back. 'I want you in my office with an update on your current caseload. Let's say five minutes? That should give you time to wake up.'

She watched as he bent his head to leave her office. She had nothing against tall men, but giraffes gave her the shivers.

He turned back. 'And remember this. Corrigan might put up with your bullshit, but I won't.'

Collapsing onto her chair, she glared up at the ceiling. What had she done to deserve McMahon? Scrap that. She had done plenty over the years, and now it was time to prepare her army for battle.

'Boyd!' she called. Where was everyone this morning? There was no one in the office. Shit. She'd have to face the squatter alone. And keep her mouth shut. First, though, she popped in two paracetamol, hoping they'd dull her headache.

'You didn't waste much time,' she said, entering what had been up until yesterday Superintendent Corrigan's office.

'What do you mean?' McMahon looked up with an eyebrow raised in surprise.

'Getting your feet under the table.'

She swept her hand around. McMahon had moved the desk to sit under the window, and the coat rack was now in the furthest corner of the room. Was there a strategy lurking in his actions? She didn't know, but it put her on high alert. No matter how long or short his time in Ragmullin turned out to be, he was evidently intent on making his mark. She hoped she could stay out of the way of the arrow he was staking his claim with.

'Sit, Detective Inspector Parker.' He indicated the chair in front of his desk.

Much as it galled her, Lottie decided compliance was her best option. She sat down.

'Now tell me what you're working on.' He unbuttoned his suit jacket and folded his arms over a double-breasted waistcoat. A red handkerchief poked out of the breast pocket. Jesus! She suddenly missed Corrigan, with his belly carved into the grain of the desk.

'Twenty-five-year-old Elizabeth Byrne went missing on Monday evening having caught the train home from Dublin, where she worked. We found her body yesterday morning in the cemetery. We have reason to believe she was murdered.'

'I saw the skimpy report. How did she die?'

'She had a broken leg and was covered in clay at the bottom of a grave. It appears she was suffocated by the dirt. We believe she was left there to die. I'm waiting for the state pathologist to contact me with a time for the post-mortem.'

'So you don't know for sure that she was murdered?'

'I'm positive she was, sir. Just waiting for confirmation.'

'She might have fallen into a grave, breaking her leg, and in her efforts to get out, dragged clay down on top of herself. Did you think of that?'

'Yes, sir. According to Jim McGlynn, the head of the SOCO team, the amount of clay suggests someone covered her with it deliberately.'

'Hmph. What other investigations do you have on?'

'David—'

'Sir! I am your superior.'

'Don't I just know it,' Lottie muttered.

'What?'

'Thanks for reminding me. Can I speak for a moment about Elizabeth?'

'Who?'

Jesus, this was hard work. She'd rather be outside, sourcing leads. She said, 'The young woman who was murdered. Sir.'

'No wonder Superintendent Corrigan is ill in hospital. You must have worn the poor man to a shell.'

Lottie thought that Corrigan was anything but a shell, but she let it go. She filled McMahon in on the information she had compiled so far.

'Elizabeth worked in Dublin. Her mother hadn't seen her since Sunday lunchtime. The girl caught the six o'clock commuter train each morning. She was at work on Monday and was last seen getting the 17.10 train from Connolly station to Ragmullin. We have a screen grab from Connolly CCTV footage, and two commuters who swear they saw her on the train. But we have no visual of her disembarking at Ragmullin. Then we have a young woman, Bridie McWard, who heard screams from the cemetery at 3.15 on Tuesday morning. Surveillance cameras outside the cemetery gates display the shadow of a car at 3.07 a.m. with similar images twenty-four minutes later. I am treating this as confirmation that the killer drove there with the girl in his car. It is possible she escaped and he followed her. She tripped over something and fell into the open grave, breaking her leg. Her abductor then seized the opportunity to cover her with clay and smother her.'

'You have it all worked out nice and neat. Only two problems with your scenario.'

'What might they be?'

'One, you have no confirmation that she was murdered, and two, that could've been an innocent person's car.'

'I intend to find out. Sir.'

'Do that. And report back to me.'

'I have a team meeting this morning, if you wish to sit in?'

'Didn't you hear what I just said? Report to me.'

Lottie bit her tongue, stalling her reply. 'Anything else? Sir.'

'What other cases are you working on at the moment?'

'Kirby and Lynch have been carrying out a surveillance operation on the traveller community. We believe there is an underground movement of bare-knuckle fights.'

'Fights? Is that all you have to concern yourself with these days?'

'It can be very nasty. Large amounts of money are wagered. And sometimes it turns into a fight-to-the-death kind of thing.'

'Has anyone died?'

'Not yet.'

'Then let them get on with it. I've seen this kind of thing in Dublin. It's all a show of strength.'

Lottie sighed and pulled her sleeves down over her hands, trying desperately to keep herself from fidgeting. God, she needed a Xanax. 'Do you want me to tell Kirby and Lynch to back off, then?'

The suddenness of his movement caught her by surprise. She sank back into her chair as he stood and marched around the small office, coming to a stop in front of her and perching on the edge of the desk. 'I want you to do your job,' he said. 'I don't want you getting stuck in my hair.'

You have enough of it anyway, she thought. As if reading her mind, he brushed his fringe out of his eyes. Shit, she hoped she hadn't spoken aloud.

'Attend the post-mortem and determine whether you are dealing with a murder. Pull your detectives away from the traveller community and present me with a killer. Today, preferably.'

'Right so.' Did he think she was Superwoman or what? 'One other thing,' she said. 'Superintendent Corrigan asked that I look into a cold case.'

'What cold case?'

'A young woman called Lynn O'Donnell, disappeared ten years ago this week.'

'And what has that got to do with anything?'

'I haven't had time to read the file yet, but it appears she was last seen on the commuter train from Dublin. Valentine's Day.'

'Perhaps she eloped?'

'I don't know. She's never been found. I'll read the file and maybe have a chat with her family.'

'I think you've enough to be doing without burying your nose in a ten-year-old case.'

'I'll check it out anyway.'

'Find the Byrne girl's murderer. If she *was* murdered, that is. And that's an order.'

'Yes, sir.' You bollocks, she added in her head.

'You can go,' he said.

Getting up, she edged out past his outstretched legs and left the office without a word. Sometimes it was better to remain silent. Sometimes, but not always.

# CHAPTER THIRTY-ONE

'Where on earth have you been?' Lottie watched Boyd fall into his chair without removing his jacket. 'I needed your support ten minutes ago.'

'Sorry. Grace has my head wrecked. I've been away from home for so long, I'd actually forgotten how much she talks. Non-stop. Never-fecking-ending. I think she's given me a migraine.'

'You don't get migraines,' Lottie scoffed.

'I have one now. I dropped her to the train station early and was at home, standing in the shower, when she rang to tell me her friend wasn't on the train.'

'I thought you said she doesn't have any friends.'

'She doesn't. This is someone she met yesterday. I'd say the poor woman is avoiding her. God forgive me, I know she's my sister, but even I'd want to avoid her.'

'Don't be so mean. I can't wait to meet her.'

'You'll take back those words once you do.'

'Some brother you are.'

Lottie pulled Kirby's chair across and sat down beside Boyd. She thought how she would love to have a brother. She'd had one once, but he'd been murdered when he was just twelve years old. Then she thought about the mysterious half-sibling she had only become aware of during her last murder investigation. The lies. Her life had been built on lies. 'McMahon is on site,' she said.

'That's all we need.'

'My sentiment exactly. He's being a pain about this murder investigation. Won't allow it to be classed as murder until the state pathologist confirms it. I've to report everything to him first. And he wants Kirby and Lynch taken off the fist-fighting investigation.'

Pulling at his chin, Boyd said, 'They haven't had much success. Maybe McMahon is right and it's time they did something new.'

'Whose side are you on?' Lottie stood up, wheeled the chair back to its rightful place and headed for her own office to get her jacket. 'I'm driving to Tullamore for the PM, and after that, we can have our team meeting. Then I'm getting on to the press office.'

'What? After our new acting superintendent told you to report to him first?'

'Starting as I mean to go on,' Lottie said, and kicked the door closed.

Jane Dore was petite and precise. In every way. She nodded as Lottie entered her sterile place of work, aptly called the Dead House.

'Been a few months since you were last here,' she said, pulling down her face mask.

'Thank God, it's been quiet,' Lottie said. 'I was beginning to think all the murderous bastards had hightailed it off to the Costa del Sol.'

'Not quite all of them.'

'What have you found?'

'I've completed the prelims. Elizabeth Byrne was a healthy twenty-five-year-old female. I'd say she looked after her body. Probably did a lot of running, based on her muscle tissue.'

'Maybe that's how she got away from her killer.'

'You're assuming she was murdered?'

'Wasn't she?'

'You'll need forensic evidence to prove it. I can only tell you about the condition of the body and the evidence collected. If you'll allow me?'

'Go ahead.' Lottie perched herself on a high stool, surrounded by white tiles and stainless-steel benches and tables. She couldn't see any bodies. Good.

'She suffered from chronic psoriasis. Her scalp, knees and elbows were badly affected. So badly, in fact, that if she was transported by car, there will be flakes of skin everywhere. Trace evidence.'

Lottie noted this in her notebook. If they ever found a car to check.

Jane continued. 'She had cuts to her right elbow and to the soles of both feet consistent with running barefoot. The hallux on her left foot was fractured – that's her big toe. Also her left leg.'

'Tibia open shaft fracture,' Lottie said.

Jane raised an eyebrow.

'McGlynn told me. Most of this is consistent with what I already know.'

'Her knuckles were bitten by her own teeth, probably from the pain when she suffered the fracture.'

'How did she die?' Lottie was impatient to get this classified as murder.

'To put it bluntly, she was buried alive.'

'That's what I thought.'

'Her assailant grabbed her round the throat from behind with his arm. No fingerprints, but we got some fibres. She fell or was pushed into the grave, and as she lay there, clay either fell down or was thrown in on top of her, smothering her. I can give you the technical details if you like.'

'No, that's fine. So it *was* murder?'

'If I'm being honest, I don't think that amount of clay could have fallen in of its own accord. She died from asphyxiation caused by the clay.'

'McGlynn said there was evidence of maggots.'

'She had an open bleeding wound, so that would be normal, seeing as she was six feet below ground.'

'Time of death?'

'Going by the cold weather, and her lividity, I would estimate she was dead thirty-two to thirty-six hours maximum when you found her.'

'So it's possible she was murdered between three and four on Tuesday morning?'

'I'd agree with that.'

'Any of the killer's trace evidence show up on the body?'

'He wore gloves. As I said, a few fibres on her neck from his coat. It's possible she was drugged. I've sent samples off for toxicology. You will know as soon as I do.'

'Sexual assault?'

'No evidence of any recent sexual activity.'

'Thanks, Jane.'

'One other thing,' the pathologist said.

Lottie waited.

'This girl suffered greatly. Her cheeks, despite the clay, were salty. She'd been crying. Find him, Lottie, before he takes someone else.'

# CHAPTER THIRTY-TWO

The mornings were the longest. When Saoirse was in school. Not for the first time, Keelan O'Donnell wished she had a job. But Cillian said he wanted her at home. He was making enough money; why would she need to work when he was providing for her? She supposed he was right with regards to the money aspect, but she needed to see other human beings during the day. He'd put a stop to her art classes, told her she couldn't paint even when the other women in the group thought her work was good. Then she'd joined a choir in the Arts Centre. Mornings for two hours. He stopped that too. Crows can't sing, he'd said.

Twiddling her phone in her hand, she toyed with the idea of ringing Finn's wife, Sara. Good God, she thought. That confirmed just how lonely she was. She put her phone away. Things weren't that bad. Not yet.

She picked up her coat. She'd see if Donal was coping any better. Glancing in the hall mirror, she checked that the make-up concealed the yellow bruise taking shape on her cheek. Cillian really hadn't been himself since his mother's death.

Why was she always making excuses for him? She had no answer to her own question.

As she lashed on an extra layer of foundation, just to be safe, she caught sight of the little pink umbrella hanging on the hall stand. As long as Cillian kept his anger directed at her, Saoirse should be safe. But the second he stepped over that line, Keelan was taking her daughter, and he would never find them. Ever.

*

Lottie was away from the office no longer than an hour and a half, but on her return to base, she noted the incident boards had filled up. She looked at the list of tools that had been taken from the cemetery for examination. She was particularly interested in getting the results of the analysis from the spade that they'd discovered propped up beside the digger used to excavate the graves. It seemed to be an opportune tool with which to heap clay and dirt on top of Elizabeth.

'I've just come from the Dead House.' She stood in front of the boards, facing her team, and pointed at Elizabeth Byrne's photograph. 'This girl was asphyxiated by clay. Buried alive.' She outlined the injuries Elizabeth had suffered. 'I want to know as soon as DNA and fingerprint results come in for that spade, and also the stone we found with blood on.' She directed her gaze to Kirby. 'You took Bernard Fahy's DNA sample, didn't you?'

'Yes, and also from John Gilbey, the other man who was working there.'

'Any matches?'

'Nothing on PULSE, but we haven't yet run them against the blood and tools found at the scene.' Kirby shifted his buttocks on the narrow creaky chair.

'Did you check their alibis?'

'Fahy's wife confirms he was at home all Monday evening and that night. But wives tend to cover for their husbands. John Gilbey lives in a hostel. I'll follow up on his whereabouts for the relevant time.'

'Okay, do that. The search of the caretaker's office has yielded nothing so far. I didn't expect it would, but I've instructed SOCOs to check it out, and I'll have a nose around later on.'

'It's more likely she was in the car that stopped outside, rather than in the building,' Kirby said.

'Bring up the CCTV footage.'

Kirby tapped the laptop on his knee. Lottie flipped around one of the whiteboards and the grainy images flashed onto it.

'As you can see, there was a car, possibly the killer's, parked there for twenty-four minutes,' Kirby said.

'Our own traffic cams are being checked for the relevant times to see if we can locate the vehicle,' Lottie added.

Lynch said, 'I've assigned a uniform to that. I'll review and report to you if anything turns up.'

Lottie thought Lynch looked considerably paler than yesterday. Hopefully she wasn't coming down with a bug. They needed all the bodies they could get to cover this investigation.

She continued. 'Today, I want the residents at the nursing home interviewed, especially those with rooms facing the cemetery. And the staff. Kirby, have you the data from the house-to-house?'

'I've checked all the reports. No one saw or heard anything. It was the middle of the night, after all. Traveller site residents give the same story, except for Bridie McWard hearing the screaming.'

'Her evidence ties in with the CCTV footage and the pathologist's estimate of time of death. It gives us a time frame to work with. We can deduce that Elizabeth caught the 17.10 from Connolly station, because she was seen by two commuters on the train. They got off at Enfield. To date we've discovered no further sighting. Just the screams heard by Bridie McWard at 3.15 a.m.'

'Maybe Bridie had a nightmare,' Lynch piped up.

'It's possible, but she seemed fairly shaken when I spoke to her,' Lottie said. 'Right, I want you and Kirby to do the interviews at the nursing home. Take uniformed officers with you so that you can get it finished quickly.'

'Boss, we were on stakeout last night. Up in the Munbally estate. Need to get a bit of shut-eye,' Kirby moaned.

'Oh right. On that matter, our *acting* superintendent wants you to cease that operation.'

'But we—'

'I'm just telling you what I've been ordered.'

'Such a waste of time,' Kirby grumbled, patting his pockets. He took out an e-cigarette and jammed it into his mouth.

'You didn't have many results, did you?' Lottie said. 'Now, on to Carol O'Grady. She was Elizabeth's friend so I think we should have another word with her. See if we can find out more about Elizabeth and anyone that might have had an interest in her.'

'Carol's brother is a bit iffy,' Boyd said.

'Terry O'Grady,' Lottie said, checking her notes. 'Pull his details from PULSE, and you and I will chat with Carol. Give her a call to see if she's at home or at work.' She paused and studied the two images of Elizabeth Byrne, dead and alive. 'And Matt Mullin, the ex-boyfriend. Any luck, Lynch?'

'I've been trying to chase him up,' Lynch said, pulling at her eyelids. Just as well McMahon had halted the traveller job. Lottie needed her team awake.

'Did you try the bank again this morning?'

'They were very cagey, but at least they gave me a mobile number for him. He's not answering. I'll get back onto the bank and see what the story is.'

'Check if his family know where he is, and see if his passport has been used.'

'Will do.'

'Anything from Elizabeth's mobile phone?'

'It's inactive. Dead. I'm trying to get the service provider to determine where and when it was last used,' Boyd said.

'I'll get McMahon to organise a press release. He can make an appeal for information. We need to speak with witnesses from the Last Hurdle, where Elizabeth was Saturday night, and witnesses from the train.'

When she had allocated those jobs, she said, 'I'll call to the station again. We need to determine if she actually got off the train at Ragmullin.'

She eyed the team, all ready and eager except Kirby and Lynch.

'You two look like corpses. Go home. Get two hours' sleep, and then I want you both back here.'

She dished out more tasks and said, 'Okay, you all have jobs. Let's catch the bastard who buried this young woman alive.'

✳

'Donal, I know you're in there. Open up.'

Keelan pressed the doorbell again. Peered in through the glass on the upper half of the door. No shadows. No movement. No sound. But his bicycle was parked up under the window and she knew he didn't walk anywhere. Maybe he'd phoned for a taxi.

She turned away from the door and walked down the cracked pathway, avoiding the rambling weeds encroaching from the overgrown winter lawn. Glancing over her shoulder, she looked up at the two-storey terraced house that had been Cillian's childhood home. It was the only house in the line of ten that remained inhabited. The rest were tumbling down around themselves, some with the roofs caved in and others with the bare branches of bushes growing up around the chimney stacks. Most of the windows were boarded up.

Maybe now that Maura was dead, Donal might move out. Ten years waiting for a ghost to appear while the walls crumbled around you was long enough. She would speak with Cillian about it tonight. Maybe he could get his father to see sense.

The rusted gate creaked shut behind her and she made her way under the railway bridge and back into town.

She didn't see the curtain twitch.

# CHAPTER THIRTY-THREE

Kirby smiled as Garda Gilly O'Donoghue walked towards him. He was standing in the covered smoking area at the rear of the station, which doubled as a bicycle rack. He hadn't time to hide the cigar he was puffing.

'Yuck. The smell of that,' Gilly said, indicating the bin of cigarette butts.

'Want one?' Kirby offered.

'No thanks. I knew I'd find you here.'

'How so?'

'Because I was sure you hadn't fully given up smoking. Did you discover anything enlightening last night?'

'Last night?'

'You were working, so you said. You cancelled our date.'

'Sorry, babe.'

'Doesn't suit you.'

'What?'

'The American twang. Even if you could do it correctly.'

'Not making much of an impression this morning, am I?'

'Try a little harder.'

'How about this then?' He reached into the breast pocket of his jacket and handed over an envelope, smiling as Gilly's face lit up.

'Hey, this is the play I wanted to see. You're a star,' she said.

'It's for tonight,' he said.

'Can't wait. And we can go for a drink afterwards.'

Running his hand over his stubbled chin, Kirby shook his head. 'We'll see. I'm absolutely shattered.'

'What are you doing here then, if you've been working nights?'

'On my way home.'

'I'm beginning to think you have another woman.'

'You're woman enough for me.' He stubbed out the cigar and palmed the butt into his pocket. 'How was your evening with that friend of yours?'

'Mollie? She never turned up.'

'That's a bit Irish, isn't it? Being stood up twice the one night.' He grinned.

'It's not funny.' Gilly raised her eyebrows, pocketed the tickets and went to move away.

'Do I not get a good-morning kiss?' Kirby said.

'You won't even get a goodnight kiss if you keep this up.'

'Women!' Kirby said to the empty space Gilly had left in the frosty air. He was debating relighting his cigar when Lynch rounded the side of the building.

'We have a call,' she said.

'No we don't. I need some shut-eye.'

'We have to go to the traveller site. It's urgent. Come on.'

'Maybe our night-time ventures are paying off,' Kirby said, and followed her to the car.

*

Sitting at her computer, Lottie clicked into her email.

'What the hell?' The message in her inbox was from a name she recognised. She blinked and opened a drawer. Had she taken a pill this morning? She couldn't remember, but she found one anyway and gulped it down. If she wasn't careful, she thought, she'd end up as bad as she'd been a year ago.

She was about to call in Boyd but thought that maybe this was too personal. Shit, it *was* personal. Her finger hovered over the mouse. What had prompted this communication? Read it and see, she told herself. With her tongue stuck to the roof of her mouth, her legs jittering, her hand remained frozen in mid-air.

The door opened and Boyd put his head round.

'Kirby needs us at the traveller site.'

She stared at him, unseeing. Lowered her head to the computer.

'Lottie? What's up?' He walked round the side of the desk. 'You have that wild look in your eyes.'

'What look?'

'You know. After a night of drinking.'

'I haven't been drinking,' she lied.

'What has you spooked, then?'

Jerking back to life, she hit the corner tab, minimising her email. 'Nothing.'

Boyd put his hands on the desk. 'I thought you couldn't stand lies, and here you are, lying to me.'

She stood up, knocked the chair out of the way with the back of her legs and sidestepped around him. 'I said it's nothing. None of your business. Butt out. Understood?'

'Loud and clear.' Boyd stood back, bumping against the wall.

Lottie kept walking. 'What's Kirby got himself into this time?'

✳

'Hello? Anyone there?'

Mollie listened. Wind? Or was it an air-conditioning unit? She wasn't sure. But there were no cars or other sounds. Where was she?

It was dark in the room, but a dim light glowed at the edge of the hatch door, high above her head, casting an eerie shadow in a V down to the centre of the floor. She could see the floor was made

of timber, well-worn laths. Knots were feathered along the wood. She looked at the strip of light again and decided it wasn't daylight. It had to come from a light bulb somewhere up above the ceiling.

Her arms were still strapped to her sides, and she badly wanted to pee. Her mouth felt like the internal muscles had swelled, and her throat was constricted with gluey mucus. The hairs in her nostrils were clogged with the fusty, musty smell of the room. And to add to her discomfort, her stomach rumbled with hunger.

A psychotic thought skittered through her brain. What if he never came back? What if he wanted her to starve to death? No. He'd never have gone to this much trouble just to leave her to die. Would he? She knew absolutely nothing about him, and the more she thought about it, the less she wanted to know. She wanted to go home. Now. Before the insane freak returned.

Home. But there was no one there to miss her. She lived alone. Her mother was dead and her father lived in London. She only ever phoned him on Sundays. And today was … Thursday? Wasn't it? She wasn't at all sure. But it didn't feel like much time had passed, unless it was the effects of the drug he'd used on her.

Surely her colleagues would wonder why she hadn't phoned in to say she'd be absent. But perhaps not. You only needed a doctor's certificate if you were going to be off for longer than two days. There was the weekend to come, so they wouldn't start asking questions until Monday.

Gilly! Yes, Gilly would miss her. But how long would that take? They'd been supposed to go out for a drink, but would Gilly wonder at her not turning up? She had no idea one way or the other. All she could do was hope that someone reported her missing.

She tried to raise her head from the rock-like bed. She really needed to pee, but before she could even attempt to wriggle free, warm liquid had seeped down her legs, soaking the mattress.

And that was when she thought she heard a train.

# CHAPTER THIRTY-FOUR

The mid-morning sun, casting a blinding light, had tried its best to melt the hoar frost, but in shaded areas the ground was still hazardous. Boyd parked the car inside the gate and they made their way to where Kirby was lounging against the wall of one of the twelve concrete houses. Lynch stood in front of him, fair hair hanging loose beneath a grey beanie. Both of them were obviously trying to keep themselves awake. A small mobile home was parked in the compact yard.

Kirby moved to one side and filled the space between the house and the mobile home. His blue scarf was wrapped like a noose around his neck and his nose was Christmassy red. His bushy hair looked like he'd been hit with a bolt of lightning. A crowd of onlookers huddled on the other side of the site. Women and children in the centre of a circle of angry-looking men. Their hands were shoved warily in their pockets, but Lottie knew they could strike at any time.

She sniffed the frosty air. 'Tell me about this before I walk into a minefield.'

'It looks like a domestic,' Lynch said. 'But we have to be careful. You know how these situations can be different to how they first appear.' One eyebrow rose in an arch.

Was there a question there somewhere? Sucking in a draught of cold air, Lottie realised Lynch's words were a direct reference to a previous investigation. She decided to let it lie.

'Who lives at this property?' she asked.

'Paddy and Bridie McWard,' Kirby said. 'They have a little boy, called …' He turned the page of his notebook.

'Tommy,' Lottie said.

'Bridie's taken a terrible battering,' Kirby said. 'Go in and see for yourself.'

Inside the house, Bridie was sitting on a white leather sofa. She was holding the little boy in her arms, way too tightly, unshed tears flooding her eyes.

'Jesus, Bridie, are you all right?' Lottie said, shocked. 'You need to see a doctor. The hospital or something.'

'This is your fault,' Bridie yelled.

Was it ever any other way? Lottie sat down and searched for answers in the young woman's eyes. 'Tell me what happened.'

'I told your two monkeys out there.'

'I need to hear it for myself. Did Paddy do this to you?'

A purple bruise had swelled on Bridie's jaw, and dried blood had congealed in her long hair.

'No, but those two don't believe me.' She moaned as she spoke, one hand rubbing her stomach.

The baby began to cry. Lottie thought of Louis, and her heart constricted. Bridie stuck a soother in the little boy's mouth and rocked him close to her chest, wincing with the movement.

'Tell me what happened. You know I'll believe you.' Lottie took her notebook and pen from her bag. 'Do you want Boyd there to hold little Tommy while we talk?'

'You must be joking. No one is taking my baby away.'

'I was only trying to help,' Lottie said. 'You need to clean those wounds up before they get infected.' She handed her notebook to Boyd, indicating with a nod of her head that he was to take notes.

'Do you always talk like this?' Bridie said. 'First you want my story, then you want my child, and now you want me to wash.'

Smiling a little, Lottie nodded. 'You're right. I'm all over the place today. You do what makes you comfortable. When you're ready, tell me what happened to cause those cuts and bruises.'

'Well, it wasn't Paddy, so you can get that notion right out of your head, Missus Detective.'

'Okay. If it wasn't Paddy, who was it? And where *is* Paddy?'

'There you go again. Two questions.'

'I'll shut up and listen.' Lottie set her mouth in a straight line and willed herself to keep it that way.

'At last, a bit of silence.' Bridie rocked Tommy slowly as the child's eyes closed. 'Paddy was here last night for a while. He came to bed but only stayed about an hour before he got up again and left. I don't know where he is, so don't ask me. Right?'

Lottie nodded.

Bridie went on to relate what had happened. Lottie wondered what had prompted the attack on a defenceless young woman with her baby in the room.

'Can you describe your assailant?'

'It was dark, but he was a big fucking monster.'

Lottie waited in silence as sobs broke from Bridie's throat. She was afraid to utter a word in case the young woman refused to carry on talking.

'Leather gloves. He was wearing dark leather gloves. Dressed all in black, now that I think of it. And before you ask, I didn't see his face. Jesus, Paddy will go ballistic when he sees the state of me.'

'Don't worry. Detective Kirby will have a word with him.'

'No one is to talk to Paddy. Not until I do.'

'Have you contacted him?'

'I tried his phone. He must be out of range or something.' Bridie bit her lip as tears slid down her bruised face.

Lottie put out a tentative hand and patted the young woman's knee. 'You're doing fine, Bridie,' she said soothingly. 'Can you remember anything else?'

'That monster hammered the daylights out of me. Kicked me in the stomach. Hit my head with something hard. I could feel the blood flowing. And the pain. God in heaven, it was worse than when I was giving birth to Tommy. Well, maybe not worse. As bad as.'

'Can you remember if he said anything?'

Sniffing now, Bridie said, 'That was the worst thing. He grabbed my hair and twisted it, and said, "Stay away from the guards and the graveyard, if you don't want to end up six feet under like the other one." Oh God.'

Lottie glanced at Boyd. 'What can you recall after he said that?'

'I passed out. I woke up to Tommy screaming in his cot. And every inch of me screaming in pain along with him.'

'Tommy wasn't harmed, though?'

Bridie shook her head. 'He's okay.' She stared into Lottie's eyes, pleading, 'What did he mean? Was it because I told you about the banshee? Something to do with that woman being murdered over there?'

Lottie thought for a moment. Was that the reason Bridie had been attacked? It seemed a little far-fetched. She decided to be honest. 'I don't know, but I'll get the SOCOs in here to see if your assailant left behind any DNA.'

'What's a SOCO?'

'Scene of crime officer.'

'Like the *CSI* crowd on the telly?'

'Something like that,' Lottie said. She nodded at Boyd to make the call.

'They better not leave a mess. It's taken me two hours to wash the floor in the bedroom.'

'You what?' Boyd exclaimed before Lottie could stop him.

Tommy opened his mouth and the soother fell out. He began to roar.

'Now see what you did.' Bridie glared. 'Of course I washed the floor. I couldn't be walking around sticking to all that blood. And there's someone coming to fix the door in a few minutes.'

'Leave it for now,' Lottie said. 'Our people will have a look at it. And don't worry, there'll be a uniformed officer here to keep an eye on you until Paddy returns. Can I have his number?'

'No, you can't. I wouldn't have said anything at all, only those two out there were hanging around here for the last few weeks and I knew they were pigs. *She* even gave me one of those card things with her number. I was going to say nothing to nobody, but sure I was so stressed, I rang her and told her everything before I realised what I was doing.'

'You really need stitches,' Lottie said, noticing fresh blood bubbling through Bridie's hair.

'I'll be grand. I've got plasters somewhere.'

'Can I call someone to come and sit with you?'

'I'm well able to look after myself, thank you very much.'

The irony was lost on Bridie, and Lottie felt a wave of sympathy for the young woman settle in her chest. She took out one of her own cards.

'This is my number. Call me if you remember anything else. Even the smallest detail might be important.'

Bridie took the card. 'I'm warning you lot here and now, my Paddy won't let this pass without blood being spilled. Mark my words.'


After directing the SOCOs into Bridie's house, Lottie instructed Kirby to send the two vans of gardaí who had arrived while they'd been inside back to the station.

'Did you call the riot squad too?' she said drily.

'No, but something like this has the potential to explode.'

'Let's hope not. No need to attract extra attention to Bridie. Locate Paddy McWard and find out where he's been and what he's been up to. Okay?'

'Will do.'

She noticed the houses and caravans all had cameras attached to their outside walls. 'And see if the residents will give you access to their CCTV tapes. There are more cameras here than in all of Ragmullin.'

'Probably just dummies,' Kirby offered.

'Check them out. And it's very quiet around here. Have you scared everyone away?'

'Not my fault.' Kirby slapped a chunky cigar into his mouth without lighting it.

Lowering her voice, Lottie said, 'What's up with Lynch?'

Kirby glanced over her shoulder. Lottie turned, following his gaze. Lynch was walking in small, slow circles with her phone tight to her ear.

'Trouble at home, I think. She hasn't said anything to me, but she's calling her husband every time I turn my back.'

Lottie waited for Boyd to unlock the car. She listened as a train shunted along the tracks on the embankment beyond the cemetery.

'I'm thinking this was probably the work of Elizabeth's killer. Trying to warn Bridie against talking to us,' she said, sitting into the car.

'But she'd already spoken with you,' Boyd said.

'Maybe she saw or heard something else. Something she hasn't told us.'

'I think it's more likely to be related to her own community.'

'We'll see. What do you know about Lynch's husband?'

'Not a lot, why?' he said, turning out onto the main road.

'Just fishing.' Lottie tugged the sleeves of her T-shirt down over her cold hands.

'New hobby?'

'Drive the bloody car.'

'Where to?'

'Wherever we can find Carol O'Grady.'

# CHAPTER THIRTY-FIVE

Nothing was going right for Donal O'Donnell. Not today. Not any day. He had waited fifteen minutes before moving, after Keelan had almost broken his doorbell with her insistent finger.

Shuffling across his kitchen floor, he wished for a day when he could walk around without feeling the emptiness inside of him. He glanced at the radio and considered switching it on. He opened the refrigerator instead. He'd need to go out soon. The milk was two days past its best-before date, and there wasn't anything other than cereal to eat. Perhaps he should have asked Keelan to shop for a few groceries. But then he'd be admitting defeat. And Donal O'Donnell would never give in.

He found the box of matches and lit the candle in front of the photograph. Lynn's smiling face caused him to pause. Reaching out a finger, he traced the flow of her dark hair and the stud in her ear. He wondered at the light in her eyes. How could someone so young, so full of life, so beautiful just evaporate into thin air?

'My pet,' he said.

A cold finger of terror slid down his spine, knocking on each vertebra on its journey. Donal whipped around. No one. No one but himself. Only his shadow inhabited this house now.

He turned back to the photo.

'You broke your mother's heart. You broke this family.' He had no idea if he was talking to Lynn or to himself. He'd never felt more confined by the weight of his own skin. Never more fearful for his

remaining family. Because he knew the evil had returned. Tearing at his hair, he screamed at the walls, 'Leave me be. Leave me be.'

A quiet stillness settled on the kitchen. To dispel it, he turned on the radio and listened to the news. There was never any mention of his Lynn. Not like when she first went missing. When evil had gripped his heart in its claws.

It was true, he thought, as he poured sour milk onto his corn-flakes, the nefarious spirits had returned. And this time he felt powerless to fight them.

# CHAPTER THIRTY-SIX

The Jealous Wall, situated on two hundred acres at Rochfort Gardens, loomed up from the dip in the valley. It was fragmented and falling down. Open spaces marked where windows had never rested, and arches jutted out haphazardly. It had been constructed to resemble the wall of a ruined medieval abbey. With jealousy at its heart.

Lottie walked with Boyd down the sharp incline to the visitor centre and entered through the sliding glass doors. At the reception desk, she hit the bell.

A young woman opened the door behind the desk and stood gawking. 'Oh, it's you.'

'It is me,' Lottie said, and smiled sweetly at Carol O'Grady.

Carol scowled, her face pale and drawn, as she sat down behind the desk. 'What can I do for you?'

'I'd like to have another word with you about your friend Elizabeth. Can you join us for a cup of tea or coffee?'

'Give me a couple of minutes. The café is over there, to your right.'

The scent of freshly brewed coffee permeated the air as the two detectives made their way inside.

'Smells good,' Lottie said. 'I'll have a toasted ham and cheese croissant. And a large coffee.' She sat down on one of the sofas to wait for Carol.

'I'm paying so?' Boyd said, and turned to the counter.

'Looks like it.'

Lottie pulled off her hat and scarf and unbuttoned her jacket. Her hands were as white as a corpse and reminded her of Elizabeth's foot with its pink-painted toenails.

Boyd joined her and sat down. 'They'll bring it over.'

She looked up as a shadow fell across the small table.

Carol said, 'I really have nothing to tell you.'

'We just want to find out a little more about Elizabeth. There has to be something in her life to give us a clue as to why she was killed.'

'I don't want to get into any trouble. I need this job.' Carol's hand flew to her stomach. 'Now more than ever.'

'Sit down,' Lottie said. 'Have a cup of coffee.'

'I really can't leave the front desk.'

'You just have. Isn't there a bell if anyone calls in?'

With a nervous glance out to the foyer, Carol appeared to settle the conflict in her mind and sat down opposite Lottie as Boyd went off to order another coffee.

'Black, no sugar,' Carol called. 'I can't bear anything sweet at the moment.'

'What's it like working here?' Lottie asked.

'It's okay, I suppose. A bit far from town.'

'What did Elizabeth do in her spare time?'

'She hadn't that much spare time with all the commuting.'

'She had time to go out for drinks and clubbing, though. And you mentioned she did some running.'

'Yeah. Out here on Saturdays and Sundays. Lots of locals use the grounds for jogging. We ran together. Don't think I'll be doing too much now.'

'Exercise is good for you, especially while pregnant,' Lottie said, thinking she could do with some herself. 'Was there anyone else that Elizabeth ran with besides yourself?'

'No.'

'Anyone take an interest in her?'

'Not that I know of.'

'How many people would be here on a Saturday morning?'

'Upwards of fifty. I can check the register. Everyone who runs has to sign in. They don't have to pay, you see, but for insurance they have to sign in. I'll get the book.'

'Scare her off already?' Boyd put a tray on the table, then sat down and dished out the coffee.

Carol returned with a ledger. Lottie ran her finger down the mainly illegible signatures. 'Can you copy this for me?'

'Sure. Is this mine?' Carol took the black coffee and blew over the steaming liquid. After only one sip, she said, 'You'll have to excuse me. I need to use the bathroom,' and escaped with her hand clasped to her mouth.

Lottie said, 'When we have this copied, I want you to go through the lists. You're good at that kind of thing.' She handed the book to Boyd.

'This goes back weeks,' he said, flicking through the pages.

'All the better to make a comparison of names each week. We might find something.'

'Or not.' Boyd put the book down and shoved a large portion of croissant into his mouth.

'I thought that was mine.' Lottie rolled her eyes and drank her coffee. Another headache was taking root at the base of her skull. She couldn't shake the feeling that there was something she should be asking Carol.

# CHAPTER THIRTY-SEVEN

Ragmullin train station had stood for over one hundred and fifty years, with the canal on one side and the town on the other. It was situated at the foot of an incline. At one time, it had two viable lines. One carried trains travelling to and from Galway, and the other to Sligo. But now the only remaining line was Dublin to Sligo and vice versa. Part of the old Galway track, along the route of the canal, had been rejuvenated as a cycleway.

'It's great,' Boyd explained to Lottie as they made their way towards the station entrance. 'Very safe. Great for kids. It's always busy, but the good thing is, there's no traffic.'

'Do you use it?'

'At least once a week, when I'm not working a murder investigation. This type of job saps my energy.'

'I'd imagine this type of job would whet your appetite to get out and feel the fresh air in your lungs.'

'There is that too,' he said as they climbed the steps and entered the stone vestibule.

'How are you doing?' Jimmy greeted Boyd. 'No train due in until three.'

'Ah no, I'm not looking for a train this time. Just information.'

'You've come to the right man, then.'

'I know some of our people were asking questions the other day about a young woman, Elizabeth Byrne. But we wanted to see if you've remembered anything since.'

'Oh, the poor unfortunate who went missing and was found dead in a grave. Awful stuff. Shocking. No one is safe in this town any more. No one.'

'We're trying to keep people safe by finding whoever did this,' Lottie said.

Jimmy looked up at her expectantly. She realised he hadn't a clue who she was. She held out her hand in greeting, 'Detective Inspector Lottie Parker.'

'Jimmy Maguire, head guard. Not a guard like you, but I've worked here for the last forty-odd years. Should be retired by now, but I think they've forgotten about me. I'm part of the walls now.' He tried a laugh but it dissolved into a groan.

'Do you have a good knowledge of everyone coming and going through here?'

He pushed his peaked cap back off his forehead and looked up at her.

'One time you could say that. Not now, with all the young ones commuting up and down to Dublin.'

She showed him photographs of Elizabeth. 'This is the girl we're interested in. And we got this one from your ticket office CCTV footage, Monday morning, buying her ticket. Do you recognise her? She took the six a.m. train daily. We believe she arrived back here on the 17.10 from Dublin on Monday evening. Is there any way to verify that?'

Shaking his head, squinting one eye shut, Jimmy said, 'Can't say I recognise her at all, poor soul. They all look the same to me at that age.'

'Any other cameras in place?' Lottie prompted.

'Just in the ticket office and a few in the car park.'

'We have that footage, but there was no sign of her.' Lottie looked around the cold portico where they were standing. 'None on the platform?'

'There was talk at one time of installing more cameras, but then the conversation switched to shutting the place down altogether. It'd be an awful shame if they did that. A committee was set up to try and see if we can keep it open.' He pushed out his chest and straightened his shoulders. 'I'm the chairman.'

Lottie looked at Boyd; from his expression, he seemed to be thinking the same thing. With Jimmy as chairman, the nail might already be in the station's coffin.

'No need to be looking at me like that. I'm passionate about this place. Been standing here since 1848.' Jimmy laughed. 'The station, not me, though some days it feels like it. It's a voluntary group that I set up. Numbers have dwindled away. Only about ten of us active now. More's the pity. There's safety in numbers. Better to have a crowd at your back when you're fighting a battle.'

'You're dead right there,' Lottie said, thinking of the battles she would more than likely have with McMahon while Corrigan was off.

'There are cameras on some of the trains, if you're interested.'

Lottie stepped forward. 'Definitely. Can we access the footage from last Monday?'

'Which train would that be?'

'The six a.m. from Ragmullin to Connolly and all of the evening trains that travelled back here, especially the 17.10.'

'I can tell you here and now, there are no cameras on the morning one. We use an older train for that run. Not much trouble at that hour. You'll have to ring head office for the others.'

'If you give me the details, I'll do that,' Lottie said. 'Can we have a look around while we're here?'

'Be my guest.' Jimmy tipped his cap, opened the gate, and guided them onto the platform. 'I'm around if you need to ask me anything else. God have mercy on her soul, poor lass.'

A sharp breeze cut its way along the platform as Lottie and Boyd walked from one end to the other. There was an old signal box at the far end, and on their right lay the defunct Galway line.

'What are those over there?' She pointed to a series of dilapidated buildings.

'We would have to ask Jimmy that,' Boyd said.

'They were once waiting rooms.'

Lottie jumped as the station guard walked up behind her. 'You frightened me half to death,' she said. Recovering quickly, she added, 'What are they used for now?'

'Nothing. Falling down, overrun with vermin. No one goes near them any more.' He turned around. 'If they close this station, everything will end up in the same state. Our heritage consigned to oblivion by the swish of a pen in some fancy Dublin office.'

'I don't think it will close,' Boyd said.

Jimmy gave him a look as if to say: what would you know about it?

'Well, if this young woman was taken from the train, what do you think that will do to my commuters?'

'We have no evidence she was taken from the train,' Lottie said. 'Or do you know something you're not telling us?'

'I take offence at that remark, so if you won't be minding, I'd like you to move on, because this area is out of bounds. Health and safety. You know the score.'

She took the hint, but not before giving Jimmy a good stare, which he duly returned.

'Were you working here when Lynn O'Donnell disappeared?' she asked.

'What if I was?'

'No need to get defensive. I'm reviewing her case.' Lottie noticed Boyd's eyes questioning her. Feck him. 'Do you remember it?'

'It was a long time ago.'

'Ten years.'

'That's a long time.'

'For someone who's been here for forty?' Lottie said. 'Not that long at all.'

'You need to check your files, because I can't recall it.' He turned to face the disused tracks.

'I will. And I'll be back.'

As she walked back along the platform, Lottie said, 'He knows something.'

'I suspect that as well,' Boyd said.

'We better keep him on our radar.'

'I think he's keeping us on his,' Boyd said, nodding his head to the side.

Maguire was watching them from the old waiting room door. As they left, she could feel his eyes still on her, and she was sorry they'd decided to walk rather than driving. Even as she reached the bridge at the top of the hill, Lottie felt she was being watched.

*

The woman pulled her car into the line of traffic, keeping an eye on the two detectives walking up the hill. She toyed with the notion of returning to the train station to see what they'd found out, but she believed her time would be better utilised by keeping tabs on Lottie Parker.

Because she knew that wherever the detective inspector trod, she always left a murky footprint in her wake. She would make a mistake, that was certain.

And Cynthia Rhodes would be there to swoop in for the kill.

# CHAPTER THIRTY-EIGHT

Lottie squared her shoulders against the cold and walked with Boyd up Main Street. She stopped at a pole and tore off the piece of paper. 'Someone's been putting up flyers looking for information on Lynn O'Donnell.'

'They appear every year,' Boyd said. 'Your current workload already includes a murder, so don't go off on a tangent.'

'There's another one,' she said. 'I'm definitely going to read the cold case file.'

'Lottie!'

'Not on work time; my own time.'

'You don't have any "own" time, I know what you're like. Just drop it.'

'Boyd, would you ever piss off?'

She wouldn't drop it. Not without having a peek at the file first. Superintendent Corrigan would want her to. Just in case there was the possibility of a link to the murder of Elizabeth Byrne.

She walked on ahead of Boyd, wondering why she was so touchy. Perhaps she hadn't taken two pills after all. She was losing track.


The incident room was buzzing. The phones were hopping.

'What's going on?' Lottie said.

Kirby had a phone cradled between his chin and shoulder. 'McMahon made a statement to the media asking for the public's help in tracing the last movements of Elizabeth Byrne.'

'I thought this was my investigation,' Lottie said, hands on hips.

'Something might come of it,' Boyd said.

'He probably ballsed it up and every crank in the town will be phoning in.' She sat on a chair facing the incident board. 'Any luck with the cameras on the trains?'

Boyd said, 'Head office say they only keep the footage for two days, then it's recorded over. But they'll see what they can find.'

'Probably a dead end. Any good news, Kirby?'

He hung up the call and consulted a file. 'The service provider says Elizabeth's phone was last active in the Ragmullin area. They can't give a definite location yet. And it hasn't transmitted a signal since 6.30 Monday evening.'

'The killer has probably dismantled and destroyed it.' Lottie continued to stare at the meagre information on the board. 'Any news on Bridie McWard?'

'Nope.'

'Did she go to hospital for treatment?'

'Refused.'

Lottie turned to Lynch, who was keeping her head down. 'Anything on Matt Mullin?'

Lynch exchanged a glance with Kirby and shrugged her shoulders. 'I'm working on it.'

'What the hell is wrong with you all? I want answers, not dawdling over nonsense phone calls. Get focused on proper work.' She paused to take a breath. 'Shit, I need a coffee.'

She made for the kitchen with Boyd following. Pouring water from the kettle into two mugs, she took one and sipped. Boyd took the other.

'You must have put two spoons of coffee in it,' he said.

'That's mine. Take this one. I need to be alert.'

McMahon walked by, did a double take and came back.

'This area is out of bounds. Use the canteen.'

Lottie lifted her mug to her lips and sipped slowly. 'Says who?'

'Says me. This place is breaking every health and safety regulation.'

'We've used it for the last three years.'

'You have a brand spanking new canteen and that's where you take your breaks. Anyway, I don't agree with this constant stream of tea-making.'

'It's coffee.'

'Are you being smart with me?'

Lottie shook her head, sniffed her mug. 'A bit strong, but it's definitely coffee.'

McMahon puffed out his chest. 'This kitchen will be dismantled before the day is out.'

He took himself off down the corridor. Lottie shook her head and opened her mouth to speak.

'Don't say a word,' Boyd warned.

'Two words then. Complete bollocks.'

She stormed back to her office, slopping coffee everywhere.

The phone rang. McGlynn.

'I've something you'll want to see,' he said. 'In the yard.'

'On my way.' She pulled on her jacket and headed outside.


The yard had been cleared of all vehicles and a tent erected over the skip from the cemetery. A second area for the examination of the rubbish was also covered. Three SOCOs were working their way through the sacks, one by one, as they removed them from the skip.

'It was six of one and half a dozen of the other,' McGlynn explained. 'At least doing it here, we're away from the media circus and the public gawkers.'

'What did you find? Besides rubbish?'

'As you can see, it's mainly domestic waste. People too mean, or too poor, to pay their bin charges must have used the skip as a personal dump. But I have one sack over here that you will certainly be interested in.'

Lottie followed him to the corner of the tent. The smell was worse than anything she had smelled at the Dead House. Rotting detritus. Scraps of waste food, wrappers and everything you were liable to find in a kitchen bin.

'Jesus,' she said. 'This is a horrible job.'

'Give me a decomposing body any day,' McGlynn said. 'Here we are.'

On a fold-out table covered with Teflon, Lottie saw what had made McGlynn so animated.

A black leather jacket. Grey hoodie. Blue checked shirt. Blue jeans. A pair of ankle-length black leather boots. White fluffy socks, pink bra and white knickers.

She went to touch the jacket.

'Wait.' McGlynn handed her a pair of nitrile gloves.

Lottie stared at the clothing. 'These are hers. They have to be. No one would throw out a good leather jacket.'

'Not unless it had come from someone they'd killed or were about to kill.'

'Check for DNA, trace evidence—'

'I know my job, Detective Inspector.'

'No handbag?'

'Not so far.'

'Can I photograph these? I need to show them to her mother for identification purposes.'

'They were all wet.'

'Wet?'

'As if they'd been dunked in a bath of water. I'll test them.'

'Thanks. From the CCTV images, I'm sure Elizabeth was wearing a jacket and jeans similar to these. Good work.'

'Just doing my job. I'll bag these and get them analysed.'

'Let me know as—'

'Yeah, yeah. I'll let you know as soon as I do.'

'He surely left DNA somewhere on the clothes.' Lottie put her feet up on top of her waste-paper basket as she shouted from her office out to the general area.

'This has the markings of an abduction that was well thought out,' Boyd said.

'Do you think he intentionally let her run through the cemetery?'

'Anything is possible.'

'Wish we had some idea of what we're dealing with. Hell, we aren't even sure where she was taken from. There are those unaccounted hours from six in the evening to three in the morning.' Lottie dropped her feet. 'Lynch! I need to know where Matt Mullin is.'

'I've asked for a check on his passport,' Lynch shouted back.

'What did the bank say?'

'They let him go before Christmas.'

'What?' Lottie jumped up and rushed out of her office. 'He has to be at home.'

'There was no answer yesterday.'

'Check again.'

'But I need to—'

'Now. Kirby will go with you.' Lottie turned to Boyd, eyeing his meticulously tidy desk. 'Did you find anything of interest on the list of runners from Rochfort Gardens?'

'Nothing to report. I copied the pages and scanned all the names into the computer, but nothing jumps out at me.'

'Did she run every weekend?'

'These records go back to the week after Christmas. The only day she missed was last Sunday.'

'Dying with a hangover, according to her mother.' Leaning over his shoulder, she squinted at the list on the screen. 'Is it the same crowd every weekend?'

'More or less. I'll collate them into some sort of order.'

'When you've finished that, we'll have to interview each and every person on the list.'

'What about the nursing home interviews?'

'I asked either Lynch or Kirby to do it.' She glanced at the empty desks. 'Shit, I've just sent them looking for Mullin.'

'I checked the uniforms' report from the nursing home. No one heard or saw anything.'

'I'll go over there myself. I want to have a look around anyway.'

'Will I go with you?'

'You keep at that list of runners. I'll grab a sandwich and head over. Then I'll check in with Elizabeth's mother about the clothes.'

'Are you coming back here afterwards?'

'What are you now? My mother?'

'Sorry, just asking.'

Lottie sighed. She'd no idea why Boyd was getting on her nerves today, but he was. 'I'll be going home. Katie is heading off tomorrow and I've to help her pack. I don't want to even think about it.'

'She'll be grand.'

'So you say.' She glanced at the time. 'And don't forget to pick up Grace from the station.'

'As if I'd forget that,' he said.

# CHAPTER THIRTY-NINE

The sandwich was well and truly stuck in her gullet. Shouldn't eat onions, Lottie told herself. God, she'd love a drink. Alcohol. Just to give her a moment of relaxation. One. Only one.

Tonight. Later. Maybe.

'I'm not sure how we can help you.' Peadar Kane, the nursing home manager, led her into his office. He was tall and thin, with a line of hair covering a bald head.

'This is a lovely building. You must enjoy working here.' Lottie didn't do small talk, but as the residents and staff had already been interviewed, she honestly didn't know what she was after.

'Much nicer than the old home, anyway.'

'Is that building still used?'

'No. Health and safety.'

'Health and safety, the bane of my life,' Lottie said, thinking of McMahon and her makeshift canteen.

'Can't be too careful where older people are concerned. They're not as able-bodied as us.'

'I agree.' She wondered how her mother was doing today. Better, she hoped. 'Do you have a Mrs McWard here?'

'Queenie? Yes. Second floor. Do you want to see her?'

'Yes. And I'd like to have a look around.'

'Be my guest. I have a meeting in a few minutes, so I'll give you a visitor's pass then you'll have access to all areas.'

'That'd be brilliant.'

Once she had the pass, and Queenie's room number, he walked her out of the office. A man approached them. His skin was grey, and his eyes were so dark they could only be filled with sadness.

'Ah, Donal. I'm glad you made it in,' Kane said. 'I've been worried about you. Take a seat in my office and I'll be with you in a second.'

The man bowed his head and shuffled into the warm office.

'Poor Donal. He's been a porter at the home since God was a boy. His wife died a few weeks ago and I need to have a word with him to see when he's coming back to work.'

'Don't let me delay you.'

'If there's anything else I can do for you, let me know.'

Kane followed his employee into the office and Lottie headed off on her tour of the facility. She wondered idly if Rose would like it here. But as quickly as the thought entered her head, she dismissed it. Rose Fitzpatrick would die rather than move into a nursing home.

✳

Gilly O'Donoghue handed over the reins to Dan, who was late arriving for his reception desk duty. She picked up her bag and headed for the door, glad that her shift was ended. She'd have to rush home to eat, shower and slap on make-up before the play. Just as she had her coat on, Boyd came rushing down the corridor.

'Hey, Gilly, before you leave, can I have a word?'

'In a bit of a rush this evening. What's it about?'

'I'm not entirely sure. Just a hunch that you might have seen something.' He showed her the copied pages from the Rochfort Gardens sign-in book. 'I notice you go running here.'

'I do. When I'm not on duty. Why?'

'I found your name on a list. Did you know Elizabeth Byrne?'

'The girl who was murdered? No. Why?'

'She ran at Rochfort Gardens every weekend. Just thought you might have seen her, or someone acting suspiciously around her.'

'I saw her photograph on the incident board, but I didn't recognise her. Do you want me to do some undercover work for you?'

'We're trying to contact everyone on the list, and then I think Lottie wants us to interview the remaining people on Saturday morning before their run, so your help would be appreciated with that.'

'Not undercover then?' She would have liked a little detective work. It might help with her aim to become a sergeant.

Boyd shook his head. 'Though if you can remember anything that struck you as being out of the ordinary, let me know.'

'Long shot, isn't it?'

'I'd take any shot that hit the target at this stage.'

As Boyd walked away, Gilly thought of Mollie, who also went running at weekends. She pressed the speed dial on her phone. Nothing. Not even a voice recording. Where was she? She thought of calling round on her way home. Glancing at the clock, she reckoned she was stuck for time as it was. She'd call after Kirby picked her up for their date.

*

She was staring at him again. Carriage C, last seat. He'd watched her get on with her nosy head glancing all around her. Who was she looking for? Surely not the prize he had won yesterday?

He debated sitting beside her. Making conversation. Just to see what he could find out from her. But then he decided life was too short to put himself through such misery. Instead, he focused his mind on visiting his prize later. He ran through the checklist in his brain. The laptop and phone had been disposed of. As had her clothes and bag. Scattered all over Dublin. No way of tracing anything back to her. Or, more importantly, to him.

Allowing a smile of contentment to widen on his face, he immediately dropped it. The little bitch with her piercing eyes was screwing nine-inch nails through him. You better not make a nuisance of yourself, he thought, or I know just the place for you, where no one will ever find you again.

She was annoying him so much, even the rhythm of the train picking up speed couldn't dispel the disturbing feeling of unease hunching his shoulders into each other, bone on bone. He'd have to waste the journey thinking of ways to get rid of her, rather than ways to play with his new toy. You will be sorry, bitch, he vowed silently.

✳

Even though the building was new, the distinct scent of age lingered. Lottie could smell it but couldn't identify it. The rooms were bright and airy and most of the residents seemed contented with their lot.

She took the lift to the top floor and stood at the giant window. The evening was darkening, but she could still see directly into the cemetery from her vantage point.

She stared down to where Elizabeth's body had been discovered. The hole was gaping, uncovered, still awaiting the interment of Mrs Green. An image of Father Joe flashed through her mind and her finger slid to the screen of her phone. She'd love to have a chat with him. But that would be a mistake. They'd both suffered too much pain from their respective families in the past, and she was bad enough now without resurrecting that again.

'It's not a pretty sight,' a voice said from behind her.

She turned around on the ball of her foot. The man she'd seen a little earlier outside Kane's office moved up beside her.

'It's a dark evening,' Lottie ventured.

'All those poor souls buried out there.'

'I'm sorry about your wife. Were you married long?'

'Too long.' He put a heavy hand on Lottie's shoulder blade before heading back the way he had come.

Pain shot along her spine and up to her neck. His hand had landed on the exact spot where she'd suffered the knife wound. But it was the icy tone of his voice that had caused her the most discomfort. A chill trickled down her back as she watched him walk away.

She shook herself. Too long in this job, she thought. Even an old man she didn't know was giving her the shivers.

# CHAPTER FORTY

Matt Mullin's family home was situated on the old Dublin road on the outskirts of Ragmullin. It was a large two-storey affair, with red brick showing signs of damp along the corners of the house and under the windowsills. A narrow avenue led to the front door. The land behind the house had been cleared of trees and was being excavated. Trucks and diggers appeared to be winding down their work for the day.

Lynch pressed the doorbell, half hoping Mrs Mullin wouldn't be in. She was freezing and wanted to get home.

'What's going on there?' Kirby asked.

'Building a new school.' She leaned on the doorbell again.

'Great spot to dump a body.'

'Will you shut up?'

'That girl who disappeared ten years ago,' Kirby said, taking a drag on his cigar before quenching it between thick fingers. 'She could be buried somewhere like that. It was a forest at one time.'

'And you think the builders will suddenly find her body?'

'It's possible.'

She noticed Kirby hiding the cigar butt in the inside pocket of his jacket as the door opened. A woman in her fifties, with an oblong face of fine bones, high forehead and piercing eyes, checked their ID cards.

'You said on the phone that this is about my son.' She twisted her blonde hair and let it fall over one shoulder. Lynch thought it was for effect rather than from anxiety.

'Yes, it is. Can we come in?'

Mrs Mullin turned and headed down a wide hallway. Lynch took in the expensive decor.

'Nice place.'

'We purchased it five years ago. Came on the market after the banking crisis.'

She led them into a living area with two floor-to-ceiling windows. The light in the room was dimmed by the shadow of a large tree outside. She switched on a lamp. 'Sit, please.'

Lynch and Kirby took up positions on armchairs opposite the woman.

'We've been trying to trace Matt but have had no luck so far,' Lynch began. 'Do you know where he might be or how we can get in touch with him?'

'Of course I do.'

'Is he here?' Closing her notebook, Lynch shoved her pen into the knot of her ponytail. 'We thought he was working in Germany, but his bank informed us that he was let go before Christmas. He hasn't returned our calls. I'd like to speak with him.'

'I'm afraid that is out of the question.'

'But it's imperative to our investigation that we confirm a few details with him.'

'What investigation might that be?'

Lynch noted the warning look in Kirby's eyes. This had to be handled tactfully.

'That's something I need to discuss with Matt,' she said. 'Can you confirm whether he's at home at the moment?'

'He's unwell. If you can't discuss it with me, I'm afraid I have nothing further to say.' Mrs Mullin stood up, buttoning her cardigan. Her jeans had a designer look about them.

Lynch remained seated, looking up at the tall woman. 'If he is here, I'm sure he won't mind giving us two minutes. Just to rule him out of our investigation.'

'Since you won't even tell me what the investigation relates to, I can't help.' The narrow face clamped shut.

'It relates to a murder,' Lynch blurted.

Mrs Mullin sat down again. 'Whose murder might that be, and why do you think my son needs to be ruled out of it?'

Lynch sighed. This was seriously hard work. 'The murder of Elizabeth Byrne.'

'I heard about that. Poor girl. But it has absolutely nothing to do with Matt. They split up a year ago. She broke his heart.'

Raising an eyebrow at Kirby, Lynch said, 'We were informed that it was Matt who broke it off with Elizabeth.'

'You were misinformed.'

'So it was Elizabeth who ended the relationship?'

'Correct. On Valentine's Day. How could she have been so cruel?'

'And that's when he went off to Munich?' Lynch had her notebook out again.

'She drove my boy away from me. I'll never forgive her for that.'

'Mrs Mullin, where is Matt?' Lynch had had enough.

'If you wish to speak with him, you may get a court order, a subpoena or whatever you call it.'

'Can't he make the decision himself?'

'I'll show you out.' Mrs Mullin got up and walked to the door.

Kirby cocked his head sideways at Lynch. 'What will we do?' he mouthed.

'Can I use your bathroom before we leave?' Lynch moved to the door. 'I'm really dying to go.'

'That old ploy doesn't wash with me. I'd prefer it if you just fucked off.'

The profanity emanating from such a prim-and-proper mouth caught Lynch off guard. 'What?'

'I'd like you both to leave my home.'

'Tell Matt to call into the station,' Lynch said. 'We need to have that word with him.'

The door closed on her words.

Sitting into the car, Lynch kept her eyes firmly focused on the upstairs windows. Kirby started the engine and drove down the avenue.

'You were a bit cranky back there,' he said.

'I'm pregnant.'

'Piss off! You can't be.'

'I am.'

'Jesus, Lynch. Pregnant?' Kirby checked his pocket for his cigar. 'Well, it's no excuse and you know it. The boss will fry you if Mrs Mullin makes a complaint.'

'Complaint about what? She was the one making the fuss and not answering one bloody question. She isn't going to make a complaint. She doesn't want the attention.'

'Why do you say that?'

'Because we need to speak with her son.'

'He could be anywhere.'

'He was there, I'm sure of it. Now why do you suppose he wouldn't come down and tell us where he was on Monday night?'

'You're imagining things, Lynch.' Kirby slammed his half-smoked cigar between his lips. 'I don't think there was anyone else in that house.'

They drove through the town in silence. As he turned up Main Street, Kirby muttered, 'Pregnant? Jesus, Lynch how did that happen?'

'How do you think?' She got out of the car and left him shaking his head.

*

Bridie's eye was swollen and almost closed up, but baby Tommy was fast asleep in his cot at last. She stood at the window of their tiny house and looked out at the concrete wall.

That poor murdered girl; it had to have been her screams she'd heard the other night. Maybe she should have called the guards at the time. But what could they have done? The poor thing was dead by then. So why was there someone out there who didn't want Bridie saying anything? The body had already been found at that stage. Was her attacker the man who had killed the Byrne girl, or had he come to shut her up about something else entirely?

Paddy.

It must be to do with Paddy. And why wouldn't he answer his phone?

She picked up her iPhone in its glitter case and called again. Still no answer. She left another message for him to contact her immediately.

That was all she could do for now.

# CHAPTER FORTY-ONE

After asking a nurse whether she could speak to Queenie McWard, Lottie found herself sitting by the old woman's bed.

She looked frail, with a pair of thin-framed spectacles perched on her nose, a long gold chain holding them in place. Grey hair, nicely permed, framed her face like a painting. Her wraith-like hands, clutched at her chest, held rosary beads intertwined on her fingers. And her lips were moving rapidly and silently.

'Mrs McWard?' Lottie said. There was no response, though the lips increased their movement. 'Can I have a chat?'

The old woman's eyes flew open and the spectacles fell from her face to her chest, the rosary beads slipping from her fingers.

'Now I've lost my place. I can't remember if that was my fifth Hail Mary or my sixth.' A pair of dark brown eyes cut into Lottie. 'What do you want?'

Queenie's mouth was devoid of teeth and Lottie noticed a set of dentures resting in a glass on the bedside cabinet.

'I'm sorry to disturb you, but I was passing by and thought I'd say hello.' She crossed her fingers.

'That's a lie. Tell me why you're here, young one, and let me get back to my prayers.'

'I was talking to your daughter.'

'Which one?'

'Bridie.'

'What has that husband of hers done now? Hope he didn't beat her. Wouldn't surprise me, though, seeing as his father is a third cousin of my husband, God rest his thieving soul.'

'Ah, I wondered at you and Bridie having the same surname.'

'Wonder no longer, young one.'

'Bridie thought she heard a banshee the other night. Turns out it was the screams of a girl we later found murdered.'

'Then it was the banshee for sure. Heralding the death of the one you speak of. You lot don't believe in the banshee, but my people do. Why are you pestering me?'

'You heard a banshee once before.'

'Says who?'

'Bridie mentioned it.'

'I heard many a banshee in my day. Every time I hear her, someone in the family dies. It's a warning. To be on your guard. She can shriek and keen for nights on end. Never saw one, but my great-grandmother did. Now that wasn't today or yesterday, was it?'

'I don't suppose it was,' Lottie said. She was wasting her time here, like she'd been told once too often. She had to get home and help Katie pack. So much to do.

Queenie was still talking.

'Then there was the time that young woman went missing. Last seen getting off the train. Long time ago. Must be ten years if it's a day. I heard the banshee for seven nights in a row back then. And they never found her.' She paused, placed her spectacles back on her nose and stared at Lottie. 'Don't be looking at me as if you don't believe me. Like I said, they never found her. She was just … gone. Vanished. Disappeared. Mark my words, she's as dead as those buried out there in that graveyard.'

'The anniversary of her disappearance is this weekend.'

'Is it?'

Lottie recalled the flyer she'd found in town. She had it rolled up in her pocket. Taking it out, she flattened it and showed it to the old woman.

'Aye, that's her that went missing all them years ago. Never found. But the banshee found her.'

I'd better read the cold case file, Lottie thought.

# CHAPTER FORTY-TWO

Boyd sat with the engine idling, watching the commuters exit the station. Why had no one noticed Elizabeth Byrne on Monday evening? Where had she been from the time she got off the train until her screams were heard at 3.15 the next morning? She didn't go home. She didn't go to her friend Carol's house. So where? The only obvious conclusion he could reach was that she was taken after she got off the train on her walk home, and held by her abductor until he killed her.

He waved to Grace. She hurried to the car. When she had her seat belt secured and her bag on her lap, she turned to him.

'Mark, I want you to find my friend. She's missing.'

'She's not your friend and she's not missing.'

'You're not much of a detective, are you?'

'What do you mean?'

'You won't take me seriously.'

'Grace, you don't even know the girl's name. You know nothing about her. And we have no reports of anyone missing. Let's go. We need to eat. You must be starving.'

'I was. Now I'm not.'

'I'm going to cook something nice. You might change your mind.'

'Mollie,' Grace said.

'What?'

'Her name is Mollie.'

✳

Mollie still had no idea where she was or what day it was, and now she almost felt like she didn't know *who* she was.

The darkness was propelling her swiftly into madness. No shadows. No sounds apart from her own breathing. Even the strip of light seemed to have vanished. Her brain conjured up her worst fears. Fear of the unknown. Fear of what might be around her. Fear of what was going to happen to her. She tried to dredge up stuff she'd learned on a mindfulness course she'd attended at work. Live in the moment. That was what it professed. A load of bullshit. She certainly did not want to live in this moment. No way. Not a second longer.

With a drought in her eyes, she had no tears to shed. A sweeping gush of anger washed over her. Why had he taken her? What was it about her that had made her a target? Was this her own fault?

Her father had that knack. Making her feel guilty about everything and anything. Spilled milk, mucky boots, her mother's bad moods. Yes, they were all Mollie's fault. One of the reasons she'd refused to move to London was to escape the condemnation that followed every single thing she did. And when her mother died, yes, that was her fault too. If you'd been here, Mollie, she'd still be alive. How did you expect me to care for her on my own? It's all your fault.

Guilty as charged.

But no. She was not going to fall for those mind games. She had to get out of here. And the only way she was going to do that was if she was strong and kept her mind alert. She would have to play the bastard at his own game. Shifting uncomfortably on the bed, she wondered what that game might be.

She had to figure it out before it was too late. Because she knew that there was no one to miss her out there. No one at all.

# CHAPTER FORTY-THREE

'This house is like an ice box,' Lottie said, as she banged the front door behind her. 'Sean? Chloe? Katie?'

She dropped the Lynn O'Donnell file on the table and went to check the boiler in the utility room. The switch was on, but there was no heat. Had it run out of oil? Opening the back door, she glanced out at the darkness. She turned on the exterior light.

Sean slouched into the kitchen. 'What's all the shouting about?'

'Will you put on a pair of shoes and check the oil tank?'

She watched as he climbed up on the concrete wall surrounding the tank and plunged in the measuring rod. He brought it back and she examined it.

'Quarter full,' she said. 'So why is the boiler not working?'

'Turn it off and back on again,' Sean said. 'That's what I do with my computer.'

She tried it. The boiler blasted into life.

Sean smiled. 'Works every time.'

Emptying the washing machine, she piled the laundry into the dryer. Back in the kitchen, she searched the refrigerator for something to cook.

'Mam?' Katie's voice echoed down the stairs. 'Can you give me a hand with this case?'

'In a minute. Just figuring out dinner.' Taking a tray of mince from the fridge, she found a packet of pasta and began to cook.

'I'll have to eat later,' Sean said. 'Boyd is taking me training.'

'Shit, I forgot about that. I'll be up in a minute, Katie.'

Glancing at the file on the table, Lottie knew it had been a mistake to bring it home. She'd try to grab an hour to go through it at some stage.

The doorbell chimed and Sean belted down the stairs to reach it first. Boyd stepped into the hall. 'Well, bud, are you ready?'

'Give me two minutes. Mam's in the kitchen.'

Lottie turned from the stove. 'I'm glad you're taking him.'

'It's no problem. I see you brought work home with you.' She paused, wooden spoon in hand, as he flicked open the file cover. 'I thought you had enough work without this.'

'I want to have a read of it.' Why was she explaining herself to him? 'I went to the nursing home and met Queenie McWard. Don't laugh, but she claims she heard a banshee the night this Lynn O'Donnell went missing. Won't do any harm to have a look at the file.' She knew she was babbling. Shut up, Parker.

'I know you, Lottie, and I don't think you should get stuck into something that will suck the life out of you.'

'I won't.'

He grunted.

'I've to drive Katie to the airport in the morning. I'll be in the office by nine.' She turned to the cooker and stirred the mince vigorously, defences raised. 'Make excuses for me if McMahon asks.'

Her phone vibrated on the table. Boyd picked it up. Snatching it from him, she saw the caller ID and switched it off.

'I saw that,' he said. 'What's he ringing you for?'

'How would I know? I didn't answer it.'

'Why not?'

'Boyd, would you ever—'

'Ready when you are.' Sean arrived with his gear bag on his back and a hurley stick in his hand.

'See you later,' Lottie said, as the door closed.

'Mam!' Katie shouted. 'Chloe is melting my head.'

'Coming.' Lottie gave a final stir, lowered the heat and made her way up the stairs.

Why had Father Joe been ringing her? Should she ring back? No, he would call again if it was something urgent. Probably only wondering when he could inter Mrs Green. She had quite enough problems without Father Joe.

✽

Canal Drive was dark and gloomy as Kirby joined Gilly at the top of the steps to Mollie's apartment. She pressed hard on the bell. No answer. She got out her keys.

'We're going to miss the start of the play,' Kirby said.

'It'll just take a minute.' She turned the key and entered the flat. 'Mollie? It's only me.'

'Come on, this is invasion of privacy.' Kirby edged back down the steps.

'She gave me a key!'

'We have five minutes to get to the Arts Centre or they won't let us in once the play has started.'

'Will you shut up about the stupid play?'

'You're the one that wanted to see it.'

'Come here. Look at this,' Gilly said.

He followed her into the tiny kitchen. 'Doesn't like washing up after herself.'

'Everything's exactly as it was last night. She hasn't been here since yesterday morning.'

'She works in Dublin, you say?'

'Yes. And I'm going to ring her office tomorrow morning to find out what the hell is up.'

'Do that. Now, can we leave?'

Before she followed him out, Gilly tried Mollie's phone once more. It was dead.

'This is not like Mollie at all.'

She was talking to fresh air.

*

Lottie left Katie arguing with Chloe over the ownership of a pair of jeans. Turning the key in the door of Rose's house she said, 'Mother, I brought you dinner.'

'You're stretching that description a little,' Rose said. She was sitting on a chair by the stove. 'Do you know what time it is?'

'I do, and I've been busy.'

'You're always busy.' Rose sniffed. 'Hope it's not that spicy stuff again.'

'Mince and pasta, sorry. I've been helping Katie to pack.'

'Why didn't you ask me to help?'

'You haven't been well.' Lottie put the plate on the table and removed the tea towel. The food looked pretty miserable. She knew criticism would follow. She began making tea.

'I'm not dead. Yet.' Rose shuffled over to the table. 'I could have given my granddaughter a hand if any of you had bothered to ask. And when is she getting that child baptised? He's still in a state of sin until that is done, and it's dangerous to be flying off with sin on your soul.'

The last three and a half months had turned Rose from a raging matriarch into a bitter tyrant. At times, it felt like four years since she had confessed to a lifetime of lies.

Lottie made a cup of tea, battling to keep her temper under control and her tongue silent. No matter what she said, it wouldn't be the right thing.

'Put in three sugars. I think my levels are low.'

'Too much sugar will keep you awake at night.'

'That's my problem, isn't it?'

'Yes, it is.' She put the mug on the table.

'You should have used a teapot. It stews better that way. In my day, we didn't have tea bags.'

'Are you going to eat that or offer it up?' Lottie stood with her back to the stove.

'Hard to do it with an audience, even if it was edible.' Rose put down her knife and fork and sipped the tea. 'You only put in one sugar.'

'That's enough for you.'

Rose turned in her chair, facing Lottie. 'Don't tell me what's enough for me in my own house. I live here, not you.' She pushed the plate into the centre of the table and folded her arms.

Lottie placed her hands on the table and leaned down towards her mother. She could have sworn she heard something physically snap in her brain.

'And I'm glad I *don't* live here, because you know what? My life was a misery when I did, and I hope I never have to live here ever again.'

She picked up her jacket and ran from the house. Definitely the wrong thing to say. But now that it was said, she couldn't take it back.

# CHAPTER FORTY-FOUR

Finn O'Donnell could smell the whiskey on her breath from where she sat eyeing him over the rim of the glass. He was too close, but the room was so small he had nowhere else to go.

'Good day at work, was it?' she said.

'It was fine.' He shook out the newspaper and raised it to his face to keep her out of his line of vision. She was nattering on about someone or other. Doing his head in. He folded the paper and stood up.

'I'm going out.'

'Where?'

'I think I'll pop over to Dad's. See how he's doing.'

'You haven't visited him in ages. Not since the day of your mother's funeral, in fact.'

'All the more reason to go now, isn't it?'

'Do you know what time it is? I don't see why you can't—'

Did he heck know what time it was. Every fifteen minutes she reminded him. He didn't wait for the end of her stupid lecture. He was out the door, down the steps and walking.

❋

Cillian looked up as his wife announced that dinner was ready.

'Saoirse, put your toys away,' he said, and closed the cover on his iPad.

'In a minute, Daddy.' The little girl dug into the page with her red crayon.

'I told you to put that stuff away,' he snapped. He didn't enjoy it when he was like this with his daughter. But he couldn't help himself this evening.

'Hey, that's enough. She's okay for a minute or two.' Keelan stood in the doorway. 'Why don't you help me set the table?'

'Oh, that's priceless, so it is.' He flung the iPad to the coffee table. It teetered on the edge, slipped to the ground with a crash. 'Now see what you made me do!'

He jumped up and snatched the tablet from the floor, ran his finger over the crack on the screen and slammed it back down. He reached the kitchen in two strides.

Keelan backed up against the counter. 'That ... that was your own fault. Don't go blaming me.'

'Oh, so everything is my fault now.' He took a plate from the stack on the counter and threw it on the ground. 'I can tell you, *that* was my fault. And this.' He threw down another one. Waited for effect and flung another.

'Cillian. Stop. You're scaring Saoirse.'

The red mist that had descended lifted as he noticed his daughter poking her head around the doorway.

'Why did you do that, Daddy?'

She sounded just like Keelan. Accusing. Without a thought for what he was doing, he swept the remaining crockery off the counter, then marched through the splinters and grabbed his jacket. He'd leave before he created any real damage. Mortal damage. No, he wouldn't be the cause of that ever again.

*

Paddy couldn't console her. No matter what he did, she shivered and cried.

'Bridie, you need to get stitches. The wound is still bleeding.' He sat beside her on their white couch. 'Here, let me hold Tommy. You go on to bed. I'll feed him and put him down.'

She clutched the boy tighter to her chest, her tears dampening his hair. 'No. You can fuck off. You snuck out in the night and left us here all alone. Some arsehole comes in and beats the shite out of me, and what do you do? Nothing. That's all you're good for, Paddy McWard. Nothing. So fuck off.'

He stood up. What was a man to do? He couldn't bear to see her crying.

'Keep the door locked. I have my key,' he said, and left Bridie alone again in their tiny, immaculate house.

# CHAPTER FORTY-FIVE

Cafferty's Bar was lively for a Thursday night. Beer taps with frosted lights teased the punters. Multiple television sets were showing the dying minutes of a football match.

Kirby ordered a pint and a glass of wine. Gilly sat in the nook furthest from the football activity.

'Bit loud, isn't it?' she said.

'Adds to the atmosphere,' he said.

'Depends on what atmosphere you're expecting.'

The barman arrived with the drinks and Kirby handed over a tenner. 'Keep the change.'

'Play was good. Thanks for bringing me,' Gilly said. 'I thought you might be working tonight.'

'New super called it all off. Tend to agree with him, too. We were getting nowhere. I prefer working on the murder investigation.'

'Boyd was asking me about that this evening. You know I go running at weekends out at Rochfort Gardens? Elizabeth Byrne did too. He asked if I knew her or saw anyone acting suspiciously.'

'And did you?'

'No. The only ones acting suspiciously are the old farts sucking in their bellies trying to look thirty years younger.' She blushed, hoping Kirby didn't think she meant him. 'That's where I first met Mollie.'

Kirby stalled his pint halfway to his mouth. 'The same Mollie you think has disappeared off the face of the earth?'

'One and the same.'

'That's interesting.'

'At last.'

'I'm only saying it's interesting. I'm not making a drama out of it.'

'But she always lets me know if she has to cancel a run or anything. It's a bit out of character, that's all.'

'Give her another ring.'

'I've tried countless times. Her phone's dead now.'

'Did you check if her passport is in her apartment?'

'No, but I think it's unlikely she went off on a holiday. Then again, her father lives in London.'

'There you are. Mystery solved.'

'I'll chase it up tomorrow.'

'Great. Now, let's chill and talk about the play.'

'Maybe we should tell Boyd.'

'Tomorrow.'

'What about now?'

'You're not going to relax, are you?'

'Nope.'

Kirby lifted his pint. 'Drink up so.'

✱

Boyd returned to his apartment, tired from the hurling training and still wondering why Father Joe was ringing Lottie. He was heading for the shower when he remembered Grace. She was sitting on the couch watching television.

'How are you, little sis?' he shouted from the bedroom. Where had he put the clean towels?

The sound of the television disappeared. He looked up. Grace was standing at the door, staring at him. Accusingly?

'I really want you to listen to me, Mark. I'm worried about the girl I met on the train yesterday morning. You know me. I get a

feeling that tells me when something isn't right. Like with you. I sense your loneliness.'

'So?' He pulled out a towel.

'You and I both know you're a lonely middle-aged man.'

'Hey, go easy on the middle-aged bit.'

'You know exactly what I mean.'

'I'm going to have a shower.'

'Will you listen to me? I definitely feel something has happened to Mollie.'

'Grace, she might have had a day off work. Maybe she decided to get a different train.'

'I told you, I know!' Grace stamped her foot. Then, as if realising what she had done, she retreated to the living area and sat down on the couch. 'No one ever listens to me. I'm telling you, if anything has happened to her, at least I warned you.'

'Righto, I'll remember that, but you're being irrational. I'm having my shower now. Is that okay with you? And don't blare the television too loud. I don't want the neighbours complaining.' He was finding it hard to treat his sister as a twenty-nine-year-old adult.

'What neighbours? Do you even know who lives next door? Mark Boyd, you need to get a life.'

With Grace's words ringing in his ears, he slammed the bathroom door, ripped off his sweaty clothes and turned the shower to cold. He needed to cool down in more ways than one. How was he going to last another three weeks with her here? At least she'd be going back to Mam for the weekend. He hoped so, anyway.

As the water chilled his skin, he switched the dial to hot and thought about his life. The years were getting away from him, and what did he have to show for them? Just an estranged wife whom he had yet to divorce. A sister who was getting on his wick. A mother who barely spoke to him. A woman he loved who wouldn't even go out to dinner with him.

Nothing.

Nothing worth talking about, anyway. Nothing to leave to a child. He didn't even have a child. No one to love. His sister, who hadn't been in the town a week, could read the emptiness hollowing out his very heart.

He slapped his hand against the tiles and lifted his face to the pulsing water. If he was a man prone to shedding tears, he would have cried. But it hadn't reached that stage yet. Not quite.

When he switched off the shower, he could hear Grace talking in the bedroom.

'Mark, there's a phone call for you.'

Maybe it was Lottie, he thought, wrapping a towel around his waist. He hoped he had a clean shirt.

By the time he got to the phone, Kirby had hung up. Whatever he wanted could wait until morning. Boyd pulled on a sweatshirt and jogging pants.

'You hungry?'

'Do not try to soft-soap me,' Grace said.

'I think I'll muster up a sandwich. Want one?'

She turned around. 'There are two things I want from you, and a sandwich at this hour of the night is not one of them.'

'Shoot so.' He leaned his damp hair back against the cool upholstery.

'Shoot?'

'What are the two things you want?'

'To meet Lottie Parker, and for you to find out where my friend Mollie is.'

He sat forward in the chair and clenched his hands between his long legs. 'Okay. I'll organise for you to meet Lottie. Happy?'

'And Mollie?'

'I'll do a search on her address tomorrow. What's her surname?'

Grace bit her lip.

'Please tell me you know her full name?'

'Just Mollie. She lives in Ragmullin and works in Dublin.'

'That's not enough.' He shook his head and reached out a hand to her.

'Try? For me?' She gripped his hand so tightly, Boyd thought his fingers must surely be crushed.

'You're asking a lot. A first name and the train she normally takes? But because your smile is so sweet, I'll try.'

He watched as Grace flopped back on the couch, a contented grin spreading across her face. Getting up to make his sandwich, he thought about Elizabeth Byrne. He shook himself. This business with Mollie was probably nothing more than Grace getting caught up in the imaginary world that he remembered her having in childhood.

Searching the refrigerator for sandwich fillings, he noticed there was absolutely nothing to eat.

'Grace, have you been raiding the fridge?'

'You need to shop for two, you know.'

She hadn't answered his question. Bread and butter would have to do until tomorrow.

The doorbell rang.

# CHAPTER FORTY-SIX

The hatch opened and light filled the room. Mollie squeezed her eyes closed against the glare.

'The smell of you.' His voice echoed through the enclosed space.

Her eyes flew open. She slowly moved her head but could still see very little. She needed to orientate herself. It seemed to be a cellar, like one she'd seen in a film. Or some sort of underground bunker. The walls were padded with thick foil, a wrapped pipe snaking up one corner; there was a small square table squashed into the opposite corner, and a short ladder led to the hatch in the ceiling.

Directing her gaze back to him, she said, 'The smell is not my fault.' Her voice was weak from screaming earlier, even though she knew it had been a fruitless exercise.

'I'm going to release your arms. On one condition.'

'What's that?'

'Make a wrong move and I'll leave you here to rot.'

'I'll do what you say.'

'Ah, you've lost your fight.'

Mollie knew she would have to acquiesce to his demands. The knife he was using to cut her bonds was short and sharp. Could she grab it? Not now, when the pain in her released wrists was screaming at her.

'Thank you,' she said, rubbing her wrists.

'There's a bucket there. Use it.'

'I don't need to go. Not now.'

She studied him. Unable to determine his height because he was bent over under the low ceiling, she tried to see his face. The bone structure. The eyes. His features scrunched up suddenly like a squeezed lemon and he sneered at her.

'You pissed yourself. You smell like a dirty cat.'

'What day is it?' she asked tentatively. She knew it'd be wrong to anger him even more.

The slap was quick and fierce. She fell back on the bed, cracking her head against the iron frame.

'Don't speak unless I say so. You hear me?'

She nodded and bit her bottom lip, trying desperately not to cry. With him leaning over her, she couldn't get a decent look at the room again. She needed a good idea of the layout, for when he left her alone. But maybe he'd tie her up again. Maybe he wanted to kill her. She began to cry, the tears that had dried up during the day flowing once more.

'And don't fucking cry. I can't stand whingers.'

'Sorry.' She rubbed her wrists again, trying to get the blood to circulate.

He pulled her by the arms until she was sitting upright. A finger streaked a line down the bones in her jaw, travelled along her throat and caressed the crevice between neck and shoulder blade. She used every inch of willpower not to recoil from his touch. She had to understand what he wanted. Surely he wouldn't have gone to all the trouble of drugging her and hauling her into this cavern if he was going to kill her? Would he?

And then she saw the bones.

# CHAPTER FORTY-SEVEN

Boyd watched Kirby jostling down the narrow hallway with Gilly O'Donoghue behind him.

'This better be important,' he said when they were all seated, with Grace sitting on a chair in the kitchenette watching them. Why couldn't she go to bed? He introduced her and waited to see what Kirby had to say.

'You tell him,' Kirby said.

Gilly tapped her phone and handed it to Boyd.

'Well, that's you at the Jealous Wall. And who's that with you?' Boyd pointed at the photograph.

'She's the reason Gilly dragged me across town to see you.' Kirby grunted and folded his arms.

'I know her through my weekend running,' Gilly said. 'Remember you asked me earlier this evening about Elizabeth Byrne?'

'Yeah.'

'That's Mollie Hunter. We met last year. Joined up for running at the same time. We started going for a drink the odd evening. I think I'm the closest she has to a best friend. Her family moved to London a few years ago.' She glanced at Kirby. 'The thing is, I can't make contact with her.'

'Her name is Mollie?' Grace said.

Boyd looked away from his sister's wide eyes and open mouth, the expression saying, 'I told you so'. Shaking his head, he said, 'Does she commute to work on the train?'

Gilly leaned forward in the armchair. 'She does. And so did Elizabeth Byrne.'

Boyd sighed, getting the insinuation. 'That's a stretch of the imagination. Have you checked out Mollie's home?'

'She gave me her spare key a while back. I've been to her apartment and it looks like the last time she was there was Wednesday morning. Breakfast dishes were in the sink. No coat or handbag lying around.'

'How do you know it was Wednesday?'

'I phoned her Tuesday. We agreed to meet up for a drink Wednesday night. But she didn't turn up and I called to her home.'

'She could have just been out,' Boyd suggested.

'We checked it earlier this evening too,' Kirby said.

Boyd stood. 'I'll do something about it in the morning.'

'Elizabeth Byrne disappeared after getting the train home,' Gilly pointed out.

'You don't know Mollie got on the train. She could be in Dublin,' Kirby said.

'What if she's in the hands of Elizabeth's murderer?'

'Murderer?'

Boyd swung around to see Grace with her hand clasped to her mouth. 'Grace, why don't you go to bed?'

'Tell them what I told you,' she insisted.

Boyd sighed and sat back down. 'According to Grace—'

She interrupted him. 'Mollie sat beside me yesterday morning on the train and we began talking. Then we got the train home together, the 17.10 from Connolly … and now she has vanished.'

Boyd said, 'I'll talk to Lottie tomorrow. We'll see if we can locate Mollie and establish if there is any connection to Elizabeth.'

He watched Gilly linking Kirby's arm as they left.

When Grace had gone to bed and he was alone, the shroud of loneliness settled on his shoulders once more.

# CHAPTER FORTY-EIGHT

Two teenagers crept out of a mobile home and made their way hand in hand down the dark lake road away from the caravan park. He carried a bottle of vodka and she a bottle of Captain Morgan. They drank as they walked, and the more they drank, the more closely entwined they became.

At a cut in the trees, he dragged her by the hand off the road.

'Hey, the branches are snagging my hair.'

'I'll snag your hair in a minute, gorgeous.'

She laughed and allowed him to lead her. They were bent in two, giggling and squealing.

'Ah, Shane, this is too much. I think I'm going to be sick.' She threw the bottle of rum into the undergrowth.

'It's not too bad here. You can see the moon.'

'I can only see trees. This place is scary. It's too dark.'

He pulled her to the ground.

'Shane, it's wet. My jeans …'

His mouth covered hers in a kiss and a smell assaulted her nostrils. Shoving him off, she sat upright.

'Shane! You're rotten. Did you fart?'

'Would you ever shut … You're right. What the hell is that smell?'

She dragged her phone out of her jeans pocket and unlocked it. The light from the screen shone on his face, casting eerie shadows. She swung the phone around.

'There's something over there.'

'Fuck's sake, Jen.' He pulled out his own phone and pressed the flashlight app. 'Oh my God. It's … it's a …'

Jen screamed.

They jumped up and ran, crashing through the forest of briars and bushes.

*

His darn dog wouldn't stop barking. Where was he? Bob Mulligan switched on his flashlight and followed through the undergrowth in the direction the dog had run. Living by Ladystown lake had seemed like an idyllic dream come true for him. Peace, stillness and silence. A stark contrast to city life and all that brought with it. The isolation got to him, though. Days on end, hour after hour. Ticking away with only himself and Mutt. Until youngsters got up to their tricks, drinking and screaming. And tonight they were at it again.

He came out the other side of the clearing with still no sign of Mutt. He stood and listened. The barking had stopped. The screaming had ceased too. The lake was calm, dappled with silver from the moonlight. Stars were shimmering in a constellation against the black sky.

A yelp from his right.

Rustling in the bushes.

Two teenagers ran straight into him.

The girl screamed and pointed behind her. 'In there. It's horrible.'

'Calm down,' Mulligan said. 'What's going on? Did this lad hurt you? Did he do something to you?'

'No! No,' she gasped. 'Don't go in there. Call the guards. Oh God, I'm going to be sick.'

She took off. The young lad shrugged his shoulders and followed her.

Using his stick, Bob tore away at the frozen undergrowth. The clearing was dim, with only the shadowy illumination from the celestial orb in the night sky.

'Hey, boy, what's got you so excited there?'

As he approached, the smell caused him to gag. The dog turned round, tail wagging, something unidentifiable hanging from his jaws.

'Dear God in heaven!' Bob fumbled his phone out of his pocket and grabbed Mutt's collar.

# CHAPTER FORTY-NINE

The large suitcase was packed and Katie's rucksack remained open for last-minute essentials.

Lottie sat on the edge of her daughter's bed and watched her sleep. She turned to the cot. Listened to little Louis breathing. Like she used to do when her own children were babies. Her and Adam. Shushing each other, trying to hear the breaths, to see the little chests rising and falling, before dropping back on their pillows with relief. She supposed every mother on the planet did that at some time in her life, and though her faith had been tested too many times, she prayed that her daughter and grandson would be safe on their travels.

At last she tiptoed out of the room and down to the kitchen. Tiredness chewed sharp bites into her bones as she sat at the table. The cold case file appeared to be tempting her to open it, with its thick sheaf of papers sticking out haphazardly from between the covers. But her shoulder screamed for a painkiller and she remembered the weight of the man's hand on her injury. Thoughts of the nursing home brought her to the argument with her mother.

Rose had always been confrontational, sometimes with good reason, but now she was being plain obstructive. I'm only trying to help, Lottie thought, though she was aware that she was doing it reluctantly. She should have kept her mouth shut. The things she'd said were hurtful. She'd meant them to be at the time. But now? Now she was sorry. Her feelings for Rose were so confused, she couldn't bear to fathom out a solution. Not tonight, in any case. She knew

she was a past master at burying emotional turmoil deep beneath the mundanity of everyday life.

She found a box of paracetamol and swallowed two with a glass of water, then popped a third to be sure the pain would ease enough to allow her a few hours' slumber. She needed a drink. Just one.

She found the vodka at the back of the cupboard, where she'd hidden it, and poured a double measure. The first mouthful made her gag, the second went down more smoothly, and by the third, her head felt lighter.

She glanced at the file. Maybe a few minutes buried in the old case would help her sleep.

As she opened the cover, her phone rang. She jumped up as the vibration filled the kitchen. When she ended the call, she rang Boyd. It was going to be a long night.

# CHAPTER FIFTY

It was gone midnight as Lottie drove with Boyd down the narrow road to Barren Point on the shores of Ladystown lake.

Ladystown was the largest lake bordering Ragmullin. Whereas Lough Cullion was the water source for the town, Ladystown had treated sewage pumped into its depths daily. It was still good for fishing, so Adam had told her years ago.

'Where am I going?' she asked.

'Sharp left,' Boyd said. 'Mind that tree. Jesus. You should have let me drive.'

'I've to be on my way to the airport at six, so it's best I have my own transport.' She hoped he couldn't smell the alcohol on her breath.

'What about me?'

'There's the squad car.'

She parked haphazardly and jumped out. She took her protective suit from the boot and dragged it over her clothes, then got a torch and headed towards a uniformed officer standing beside a crime-scene tape. A man with a dog was there too.

'Who are you?' she asked.

'Bob Mulligan.'

'You're the man who discovered the body?'

'To be honest, I think two teenagers stumbled on it before Mutt here. Don't know how much damage he did to it.'

'Did he dismember it?' She was anxious to see the scene, assess the situation and maybe catch some sleep before she had to be back on the road.

'He had part of a hand in his mouth. I got it out. You'll need to be taking my DNA because I touched it. Isn't that the right procedure?'

'Yes, sir.'

'It can't have been there long.'

'What do you mean?'

'The body. It must have been dumped in the last week. Mutt and I have been away, over in Galway, and he'd have sniffed it out if it had been there before that.'

'Where do you live?'

Mulligan pointed to a light shimmering through the trees. 'Over there.'

'Do you know where these teenagers went?'

'They might be staying at the caravan park.'

'Wrong time of year for holidaymakers.' She instructed two guards to check. 'Mr Mulligan, please stay here. I'm going in to have a look.' She turned to the uniforms. 'Anyone got a torch stronger than this? And call in reinforcements. We need to find the teenagers.'

With an industrial-sized torch in her hand and Boyd behind her, she made her way through the bushes in a crouch, frozen leaves crunching underfoot, until the clearing opened up in front of her.

Though she'd seen a fair number of bodies, her stomach heaved and her skin bumped and crawled. Under the glare of the artificial light, the blue-black body seemed to be heaving too.

'Jesus, Boyd. Tell me what I'm looking at.'

He joined her. 'I hope that isn't Mollie Hunter.'

Lottie took a step back and looked up at him. 'Who?'

'I don't think it can be. This body is too decomposed. She only went missing yesterday evening, if she even is missing.' Boyd was shaking his head.

'What on earth are you on about? Who is Mollie Hunter?' She stepped into his space.

'A young woman who may or may not have disappeared. Gilly O'Donoghue is her friend and she can't locate her. Could be nothing.'

She felt her mouth hanging open and quickly said, 'And when were you going to inform me about this? Jesus, Boyd, sometimes, you know … sometimes I just want to … Oh, I don't know!'

'Why don't we see what we have before you hang me out to dry?'

'Don't touch a thing until the scene is fully cordoned off. Did you contact Kirby and Lynch?'

'Neither of them is answering. McGlynn said to secure the site and he'll be here in the morning.'

'Get a tent erected over the body. And I want those teenagers found.'

As Boyd went off to make more phone calls, Lottie stood at the side of a tree with the light of her torch directed on the body.

'Who are you?' she whispered, then screamed as a rat ran out from beneath the remains.

# DAY THREE

Friday 12 February 2016

# CHAPTER FIFTY-ONE

After the train left Enfield station, Grace realised that the man who had eyed her suspiciously yesterday did not appear to be on the train. Maybe he didn't have to go to Dublin on Fridays, or perhaps he was seated in a different carriage. Was she in the wrong one? She twisted to look at the sign above the door. C. Relief.

The carriage heated up from the extra body warmth as people crowded on. The smell of perfume and hastily sprayed deodorant filled her senses. She avoided breathing in too deeply or her allergies would play up.

Where was Mollie? And where was the man she had seen talking to her at Ragmullin station on Wednesday evening?

It was then that she remembered she hadn't told anyone about him. She must tell Mark. She looked in her bag for her bulky Nokia, but couldn't find it. She'd charged it last night and with all the fussing had forgotten to put it in her bag this morning. Damnation, she thought, she had no way of contacting him. He was expecting her to be heading straight to Galway from Dublin this evening, and she had forgotten to tell him that she'd changed her plans. Late last night she had phoned her mother to say she would be staying in Ragmullin for the weekend. She'd just have to take a taxi to Mark's place this evening.

A knot of anxiety twisted in her stomach. She never forgot things. Her life had to be ordered, otherwise she couldn't cope. Deep breaths. She found her inhaler. At least she had that. A few puffs and the

shaking in her hands ceased. Her throat was still clogged. Another puff and she put the inhaler back in her bag. Searched for her anxiety pills. She'd forgotten those too. With all the talk of Mollie, her mind was not as focused as it should be.

Feeling annoyed with herself, she looked up, and that was when she saw him. Sitting at the other end of the carriage. Staring. As she slipped her bag onto her knee, goose bumps popped up along her arms. Her first thought was that she wished she could call Mark. The second was that she had to find Mollie.

# CHAPTER FIFTY-TWO

At the gates to the airport security area, Katie held out an envelope.

'What's this?' Lottie said.

'I only spent about a hundred euros. I want you to have the rest.' Katie pressed the envelope into her hand. 'I withdrew it from the bank. For you.'

'But you need spending money. You'll be going shopping. Oh Katie, you have to go to Woodbury Common. We were there when you were little. Do you remember?'

'Don't worry about me. I kept a little, and I won't be doing much shopping. Tom says he wants to spend time with his grandson, and of course with me.'

'I can't take this.'

'You can. Treat yourself, and Chloe wants that balayage so badly, and I'm sure Sean could do with new training gear or something. Spend it. Don't feel guilty thinking it's Tom Rickard's money. It's my gift to you for being the best mother ever. You've put up with all the shit I've thrown at you since Dad died; for once, let me do something for you.'

Lottie nodded. 'You have to see the Empire State Building, and don't forget Central Park.' Her voice cracked, and she pushed away memories of her trips to New York with Adam. The time they went on their own, before the children were born. She'd suffered severe vertigo at the top of the Empire State, couldn't look out over the edge of the viewing gantry. Adam had had to practically carry her down in the elevator.

She hugged little Louis, kissed his hair and fingers and nose, inhaling his baby smell, before Chloe took him for her own hugs.

Katie enveloped Lottie in her arms. 'Don't be worrying about me, Mam. I'm only going for three weeks. Love you.'

'Love you too.'

After hugging Chloe, Katie moved to her brother. Tall, awkward Sean hesitated for a moment, then smothered his sister in a bear hug, and suddenly they were all crying, tears of happiness for Katie and loneliness for themselves.

'Ah, guys, come on,' Katie said, taking Louis back and strapping him into his stroller, 'I'll have to do my mascara again.' She fixed the baby bag on the handles and hoisted her rucksack onto her shoulder.

'Drama queen,' Chloe said.

'Look who's talking.' Sean nudged her.

Normal service has resumed, Lottie thought.

As she turned to head for the car park with Chloe and Sean by her side, she felt a hollowness lined with a tinge of fear etch into a corner of her heart. It would not dislodge until her family were all back together, whenever that might be.


She was already late for the team meeting by the time she'd dropped Chloe and Sean at school and returned home to pick up the cold case file. She'd read most of it after returning from the lake last night, managing about an hour's sleep before she had to get up for the airport. Exhaustion gnawed her bones, which didn't bode well for the remainder of the day. Outside the incident room, she swallowed half a Xanax and hoped for the best.

McMahon was at the front of the room, commanding the team meeting, when she blustered in the door.

'At last you decide to grace us with your presence,' he said, gripping his chin with his thumb and index finger.

Lottie glared at Boyd. Had he not made up some plausible excuse for her absence?

'I'm here now,' she said.

Dredging up her confidence, with a buzz in her head from the pill, she marched through the gathered detectives and uniformed officers, stealing a glance at the incident boards. A shadowy photograph of the body found in the woods by the lake had been added.

'So you are,' McMahon said. 'And my arrival in this district has been met with not one but two murders. I'm beginning to believe the media when they say Ragmullin is a nightmare town.'

'And what media would that be?' Lottie asked, trying to gather her thoughts.

McMahon glared. 'I had a visit from the television crime correspondent, Cynthia Rhodes. I believe you've met her. She paints a very dim picture of this town.'

'She must be a damn bad artist then.' Lottie banged her bag onto the floor and bundled her jacket on top of it.

Kirby snickered, and Lottie couldn't help the smile that spread across her face.

'As senior investigating officer, I'll take over here,' she said.

She waited until McMahon had stepped to one side with a smirk on his face. What was that all about? Pointing to the first photograph on the board, she began.

'Elizabeth Byrne. Last physical sighting was on Monday, when she clocked out of her office at 16.00 hours. We have CCTV image from Connolly station placing her there at 17.00. The train departed at 17.10 and arrived in Ragmullin at 18.20. Her body was found on Wednesday morning in the cemetery as a funeral was about to take place. You have the times and details of the relevant interviews. One lead we have is from Bridie McWard, who lives on the traveller site. She claims to have heard screaming at 3.15 a.m. on Tuesday.

The post-mortem findings agree that this was the approximate time of death. Bridie has subsequently been the subject of an attack in her home. Unclear if it is connected or not, but a verbal threat was made during the assault.'

She paused to direct her thoughts back to the murder. 'Elizabeth was more than likely chased through the cemetery, then fell into the grave, breaking her leg, if it hadn't been already broken. She was buried alive. Perhaps the killer hoped she would be entombed with a coffin placed over her that day, Tuesday. As it was, the funeral was delayed until Wednesday, as the deceased's grandson had to fly home from Australia. This meant the loose clay dispersed slightly in the intervening time, leaving part of the body exposed.'

'Do you think any of the Green family was involved?' McMahon asked.

Lottie had forgotten he was still there.

'Kirby, you conducted those interviews.' She turned to the detective. 'What did you come up with?'

'All in the clear. Everything checks out. Also, after the media appeal for information by Acting Superintendent McMahon, I scrutinised the statements of those who came forward having attended the Last Hurdle nightclub on Saturday night and also those who were on the Monday evening train. No one saw anything out of the ordinary. No one remembers Elizabeth, or at least nothing stands out as suspicious. A few commuters said she was a regular on the train but don't recall anything unusual about Monday.'

'Okay. Go back over the station CCTV. Originally we were only looking for Elizabeth. This time check for anyone who might be acting in a suspicious way, anyone who might already be on PULSE.'

'Will do,' Kirby said.

'The only lead we have is a bundle of clothes found in refuse sacks in the cemetery skip. It is possible the killer dumped them there the

same night Elizabeth was murdered. CCTV places a car there for twenty-four minutes. Mrs Byrne has confirmed that this clothing belongs to her daughter. Jim McGlynn says the garments were wet. Are the results of his tests back yet?'

'Not yet,' Kirby said.

'Do Elizabeth's colleagues check out?'

'They can all account for their movements and Elizabeth didn't stay with any of them.' Kirby shuffled a sheaf of papers back into a file.

'The question we have to ask ourselves is this. Where was Elizabeth from the last positive sighting at 17.00 until Bridie heard the screams at 3.15 the following morning? Was she taken from the train at Ragmullin? Or did she get off it safely and was subsequently abducted on her walk home? She doesn't own a car. Have we checked all the town CCTV footage? Businesses along her usual route?'

'All checked and no sign of her,' Kirby said.

'Taxis?'

'No taxi driver recalls her.'

'The ex-boyfriend. Matt Mullin. Did Lynch find him?' Where was Lynch this morning? She couldn't see her in the assembled group.

'Called to his house yesterday,' Kirby said. 'Met with his mother. She was uncooperative to say the least.'

'Why?'

'Refuses to talk without a warrant.'

'So what is she hiding?'

'Matt,' Kirby said. 'He was let go by the bank before Christmas, so he has to be at home.'

'Confirm he's back in town, by whatever means you can. We need to locate him as soon as possible to establish where he was on Monday night. Get his photograph circulated to the media.'

'Bit soon for that,' McMahon interjected.

'He is our *only* suspect,' Lottie emphasised. Why did he have to interrupt her train of thought? 'We can say he's needed to assist our ongoing inquiry.' She folded one arm and rested her other elbow on it, hand under her chin. Thinking. She added, 'Elizabeth's phone hasn't been found. Hound the service provider.'

Boyd said, 'I'm working on it.'

'We have to assume she was on that train. So, what happened to her when the train pulled up in Ragmullin? Come on, guys. That's what we need to discover.'

A muffled murmur rippled through the room.

'Anything else?' Lottie asked.

Kirby piped up. 'The assault on Bridie McWard. SOCOs have finished at her home. They've collected DNA and fibres. We need to speak with her husband, Paddy, to eliminate him from that inquiry.'

McMahon reared up. 'Where is he?'

'Don't know, sir.'

'Find him. Get the registration of his van or car circulated. I don't think Ragmullin is that big a place that you can't find him. Enough of this time-wasting.'

'It's big enough if you don't want to be found,' Lottie said. She noticed that Boyd had his hand tentatively raised. 'Yes, Boyd.'

'We have to consider the possibility that there's also another young woman missing.'

'Who?' Lottie asked.

'Mollie Hunter,' Boyd said. 'I mentioned her to you last night.'

Shit, so he did. 'Is she on the missing persons database?'

'No, not yet. She lives alone in an apartment at Canal Drive. She's a friend of Gilly's. Garda O'Donoghue,' he added for McMahon's benefit. 'Gilly spoke to Mollie on the phone on Tuesday but hasn't been able to contact her since. She has a key to the apartment and checked it twice. No sign of the girl. And this is the interesting bit.

She gets the six o'clock train every morning to her job in Dublin and then the 17.10 home.'

'Have you contacted her employer?' Lottie said.

'Not yet. I only heard about this last night.'

McMahon stepped forward. 'There's no point in flying off on a tangent and—'

'I think we need to follow it up, sir,' Lottie interjected. 'At least to establish that she's not missing.' She noted Kirby was keeping his head studiously stuck in his laptop.

McMahon raised his voice two octaves. 'Why hasn't her family reported this?'

'They're in London, so I think we need to act—' Boyd began.

'She hasn't been reported missing,' McMahon interrupted. 'You have enough to keep you busy with the murder, haven't you, Detective Inspector?'

Lottie was going to fight him but felt if anyone looked crooked at her she might cry – she was that tired, and still emotional over Katie leaving.

'Now what's the story with this body that was found last night?' McMahon pointed to the photograph on the board. 'Could this be your missing Mollie?' He cocked his head at Boyd.

Lottie spoke before Boyd could rise to the provocation. 'We don't know who it is yet. Bob Mulligan, who lives out at Ladystown lake, discovered the body around midnight. Well, his dog did, though that was after two teenagers had already tripped over it.'

'Can you explain what you're talking about?' McMahon swiped his fringe back off his forehead.

Lottie thought she could see a line of pimples pulsing on his furrowed brow as she explained about the situation at the lake.

'I have yet to formally interview Mr Mulligan, but he claims the body can't have been there longer than a week.'

'And how would he know that?'

'He was in Galway from Friday, the fifth, until last night. The dog was with him. He claims the animal would have sniffed it out if it had been there before then.'

'Have you checked his alibi? He could be involved and is trying to put you off his scent. Or the dog's scent.' McMahon laughed.

Lottie ignored him. 'I've to interview the two teenagers this morning. They were in shock last night. They're staying in a mobile home at the caravan park.'

'In this weather?' Kirby piped up.

'They're young, and perhaps squatting. But I'm not concerned about that. The body is still *in situ*. The state pathologist will be there soon, and SOCOs are already at the scene.'

'Follow it up, then.'

Lottie held her breath, counted to five and exhaled slowly. He was going to crack her up. 'Yes, sir.'

'And this Elizabeth Byrne murder. You've told us everything you haven't got; what *have* you got?'

'We spoke to her friend Carol O'Grady. She says Elizabeth went running at Rochfort Gardens every weekend. We have a list of those who participated and are working our way through it. If nothing worthwhile turns up in the meantime, I'll go out there tomorrow and follow up with anyone we haven't made contact with.'

'What good will that do?' McMahon said.

Jesus Christ, she thought. Why doesn't he just fuck off back to Dublin?

'One of them might hold a clue as to what happened. Maybe saw someone acting suspiciously.'

'Could she have been stalked?'

'It's a possibility.'

'I'll tag along then. Tomorrow? Fine. I want to get to know the locality.'

'You do?'

'Of course.'

'Right so.' Holy Jesus, this was going to get worse before it got better.

'And don't waste time on this missing girl who hasn't been reported missing.'

Lottie counted to five again. 'Any further updates, team?'

'John Gilbey is living in a hostel on Kennedy Street,' Kirby said. 'I'm going up there to interview him again after this meeting. And as I mentioned before, Bernard Fahy's wife says he was with her all Monday night.'

'Hmph,' grunted McMahon. 'I'd rattle that alibi good and hard if I were you.'

'I will, sir.'

'I don't think Fahy is involved,' Lottie said.

'No stone and all that,' McMahon said. 'Right. Get to it, everyone. And DI Parker, I want a word. Now. Outside.'

She watched him nod to the team and march out of the incident room. She stayed where she was until he stuck his head back around the door.

'When I say now, I mean now.'

'You better go,' Boyd advised. 'Before he drags you out by the heels.'


McMahon was pacing up and down the corridor.

'Listen here, Parker, I'm getting distinct vibes that you don't want me involved in these investigations.'

'I ...' Lottie clamped her mouth shut. Safer.

'Superintendent Corrigan may have let you run your own one-woman show, but I don't intend to.'

'With all due respect, *sir*, that is untrue. I have a great team in Boyd, Kirby and Lynch.'

'And where is Detective Lynch this morning?'

'Out sick, as far as I know.' She didn't know, but she intended to find out.

'Is everyone in this damn place on sick leave?'

'Only Superintendent Corrigan and Detective Lynch. Sir.'

'You've a smart mouth as well as everything else.' He coiled his large frame and leaned in towards her. 'You have all those men and women in there and you sideline them with the mundane jobs. Glory-hunting, are you?'

Lottie laughed. 'That is one thing I cannot be accused of.'

He seemed to consider that before saying, 'I'm watching you, Parker. Every chip you thought you had on your shoulder is going to be a fully fledged chunk of timber if not a fucking tree by the time I'm finished here. And the shadow you're going to see following you, let me tell you, will be me.'

'Is that all?' Lottie clasped her hands into tight fists, just in case she lashed out at him.

She watched as he strode off down the corridor. This was serious. Kind of. Feck him.

She felt a presence at her shoulder and shivered. What had he said about shadows?

'What did he have to say for himself?' Boyd said.

'Get the car and I'll tell you on the way out to the lake. Do you know where Lynch is?'

# CHAPTER FIFTY-THREE

The lake was a mirror of the sky, silver grey, with the shadows of the clouds rolling across it like steam from an old train engine. On the ground, at the base of the trees, white snowdrops had eased through the hard earth. Birds were singing. A flap of wings and one surged through the branches and soared up into the sky. A sharp wind blew in off the lake, and Lottie zipped her jacket to her throat and hauled the white protective clothing over it.

The area leading to the body had been marked out with tape, and she followed it through the undergrowth with Boyd close behind her. In places, greenery was struggling to bloom against the weather. Overhead, branches dipped and snagged her hair. She pulled up the hood and placed a mask over her mouth before entering the crime scene.

A loud squawk caused her to look upwards. A magpie, black-and-white plumage plumped and ready for flight, observed her as she marched through the inner cordon.

'One for sorrow,' Boyd said, quoting the old saying.

Entering the tent, she looked around the small space and approached McGlynn.

'Have you taken impressions of the footprints?' she asked.

'Everyone and their dog, literally I may add, has tramped around this crime scene.'

'And those branches out there? Perfect for snagging fibres and hair.'

'It'll be done,' he said grumpily.

'Any sign of Jane?' she asked.

'On her way. She was finishing up the paperwork on Elizabeth Byrne. I think she might have some DNA results too.'

'Great. I could do with a break. Anything on the clothes from the skip?'

'If you didn't keep calling me out to dead bodies, I might get to spend some time in my lab.'

'That's a no, then?'

'Yes, it's a no.'

Inching closer to the bloated naked body, Lottie felt, rather than saw, McGlynn's warning eyes.

'I wouldn't go any further,' he said. 'I need the pathologist to have a look at her first.'

'It's a female, then?'

'Yes. But she's been doused with bleach, and vermin have had a good nibble. I'll know more when I get to the lab.'

'How long has she been here?'

'Maybe three or four days. However, she has been deceased longer than that. How long, I don't know.'

'Jane will be able to make the call on time of death,' Lottie said.

'Someone taking my name in vain?' Jane Dore appeared in her protective suit. What she lacked in height, all of five foot nothing, she made up for with her professional and no-nonsense behaviour. 'Good morning, all. Make way.'

Lottie watched with admiration as the pathologist immediately got to work, visually assessing the body, then asking McGlynn to turn it slightly before holding up her hand to halt him.

'Did you move the body?'

'Waiting for you,' he said.

'Turn it so.'

As McGlynn and a technician began to move the body, Jane said, 'Carefully.'

'Of course,' he said.

Lottie smiled wryly. He didn't talk to Jane the way he talked to her. Pecking order sprang to mind.

'No visible sign of wounds,' the pathologist said.

'How did she die, then?' Lottie said.

'I don't make assumptions, as you know. But I'd say foul play is highly likely in some form, given that the body seems to have been washed in bleach.'

'That looks like the remnants of a refuse sack,' Lottie said pointing to two strips of black plastic on the ground.

'Bag it all,' Jane instructed McGlynn. 'She may have been wrapped in it. You might get trace evidence.'

'Good,' Lottie said. 'You'll prioritise this, Jane?'

'I will.'

'What age group are we looking at?'

'Early to mid thirties, I'd say.'

'Thanks.'

Lottie left the tent with Boyd.

'You were fairly quiet in there,' she said.

'You were putting enough feet in it for both of us,' he said, and made off down the trail.

What the hell was eating him? she wondered.

At the outer cordon, they tore off the protective clothing and bagged it.

'Mulligan next on your list?' Boyd said.

'Yes.'

She decided to let him stew in whatever mood he was in. She had enough worries without Boyd. And then she wondered how Katie was doing on her flight. 'Dear God, keep them safe,' she muttered.

# CHAPTER FIFTY-FOUR

The bones. Tiny chips of them lying on the narrow table. And the smallest skull. She should have asked him. Were they real? Had they been left there to frighten her into submission? She didn't know, but she supposed she didn't want to find out either. Best to pretend they were made of plastic. A toy. Yes. No. They were real. Very real.

Sitting on the side of the bed, she took a sip of water from the plastic bottle he'd left her. And still she stared. Why would there be the bones of a child down here? Unburied. Or had they been buried and then excavated? Fear trawled her skin, pricking away like bites from hungry ants. And the odour. The room was filled with it. Like ammonia, or bleach. What had he been cleaning before he'd brought her here? Whatever it was, he hadn't done a very good job. She could smell the underlying scent. Like rotting meat. Like the dead mouse she'd found behind a skirting board once. Much as she feared and detested vermin, she hoped that was what she was now smelling, masked beneath the acidic fumes.

She was weak and tired but knew she wouldn't sleep. Not with those bones over there. On display. Taunting her.

Was she to suffer a similar fate?

No way. She was stronger than this. She wouldn't meet the same fate as … Her throat snagged and she gulped. Were the child's bones challenging her?

✳

A picket fence surrounded Bob Mulligan's home. The prefab house sat in a dip half a mile from the lake shore and about the same from where the body had been found. It was obvious to Lottie that it had been constructed long before more stringent planning laws had been introduced. Then again, maybe Bob Mulligan operated outside the law.

A wire run housed a few hens devoid of most of their feathers, and the dog was tied up with a gnawed rope on a concrete square.

Mulligan brought them into the house and they sat at a table cluttered with the remains of breakfast. No tea was offered, which pleased Lottie. She didn't fancy drinking out of the brown-rimmed mugs.

'How long have you lived here, Mr Mulligan?' she began.

'Thirty years or thereabouts. Inherited from my granny.'

'What do you work at?'

'Retired. I just fish the lake now.'

'It seems very isolated.'

'It's what I like. Me and the animals are happy. Wasn't always so. There was a time, must be fifteen, if not twenty years back, when the travellers threatened to take over with their caravans. But the council moved them to a site in town.'

'Really? Why were they out here?'

'There's that caravan park down the other side of the lake. For holidaymakers, you know. I think the travellers thought they could set up their own park over this side. I didn't have an issue with them, but they had no running water or toilets.'

'That was a long time ago,' Lottie said. 'Has anything other than that ever disturbed you out here?'

'Boy racers from time to time. Lovers in cars with steamed-up windows at night. Other than that, it's nice and quiet.'

'How often do you walk through that particular area where you found the body?' Lottie said, folding her arms.

'I'm not a suspect, am I? I had nothing to do with it.'

'Can you answer the question?' Boyd said.

'I usually walk on the road along the lake, but last night there were those youngsters mucking about. They found the body first. It was the young girl's scream that alerted Mutt. He got the scent and took off. So I followed him.'

'When were you there before last night?' Boyd asked.

'Like I told you already, it was more than a week ago. You can ring my friend in Galway. I went over there Friday last, the fifth.'

'And before that, you were here all the time?'

Lottie watched as Mulligan shuffled on his chair.

'Yes. Doesn't mean I killed anyone.'

'We're just exploring everything until we get the time of death.'

'Was she murdered, do you think?'

'Why would you say that?'

He pointed to the newspaper on the table. The front page carried a report on the murder of Elizabeth Byrne.'

'"Buried in someone else's grave",' Lottie read. 'We'll check with your friend. And I need details of your movements for the last couple of weeks.'

'I'll write it out for you.'

'You can make a formal statement at the station, and give a DNA sample. Sometime today suit you?'

'That's grand.'

'Here's my card. Let me know if you think of anything else that might help us. I'm leaving a uniformed officer at your gate while the forensic examination of the scene is ongoing.'

'So I'm under house arrest?'

'It's for your own safety,' Lottie lied.

✱

Before they got to interview the teenagers, McGlynn sent word for them to come back on site.

'We found this.' He pointed downwards while one of his team stood to one side.

Lottie peered at a piece of upturned earth. 'Someone was digging?'

'Attempting to.'

'The intention may have been to bury the body, but with all the frost, the ground was too hard.'

'So they stripped off the plastic wrapping and left her to the wildlife and the elements.' McGlynn placed a marker beside the hole. 'Hoping that if she was ever found, it would be just a bundle of bones.'

'No sign of a shovel?'

'No.'

'Tyre tracks?'

'None of those either. He probably parked on the road and carried the body over his shoulder. He came in as far as he could before the forest closed over entirely.'

'Has to be a local.'

'Why?'

'To know the area, the lie of the land.'

Boyd said, 'Or he could be from out of town and uses the caravan park.'

'The manager needs to be interviewed.'

'We're trying to make contact with him.'

'And get a list of everyone who has used the park in recent months.'

'You'd have to be mad to live there in this weather,' Boyd said with a shrug.

As they made their way to the car, Lottie said, 'Do you think the person who killed Elizabeth is responsible for this?'

'Hard to know. Wouldn't you think that if he buried Elizabeth in a grave, he'd do the same with this one?'

'That's what I'm thinking. So maybe he tried to dispose of this victim before Elizabeth. And if we agree with Mulligan's hypothesis that his dog would have found her if she'd been here earlier, the body had to have been dumped this week.'

# CHAPTER FIFTY-FIVE

In the incident room, Lottie pinned up another grainy photograph of the body found at the lake, then returned to her own office.

They'd learned nothing new from Shane Timmons or Jen O'Reilly, the two terrified teenagers who had escaped Dublin for a few days to make out in the caravan belonging to Shane's mother.

'Okay, so this body cannot be that of Mollie Hunter, who may or may not be missing. She's aged twenty-five, and it's likely that the body is that of a woman in her mid thirties. She's been dead perhaps a week.' Lottie sat down at her desk. Boyd lounged at the door.

'I'll get someone to go through the national missing persons database, because I don't think anyone local fits that description,' he said.

'We might have her DNA later.'

'In any case, I'll check with Mollie's employer and colleagues to see if they have any notion where she might be.'

'Get Lynch to go through the database.' Lottie strained her neck to see around Boyd. 'Where is she?'

'She called in sick.'

'Shit. We're too busy for anyone to be off.'

'Why don't you give her a call?'

'I don't think so. She might see it as harassment.'

'Is that ugly word rearing its head again?'

'You know what happened before, Boyd. I don't want to go there again.'

Kirby appeared. 'We found Paddy McWard. Do you want to interview him?'

'What grounds did you bring him in on?'

'I didn't bring him in.' Kirby flustered around with a file of papers in his hand. 'He turned up demanding to speak to whoever is in charge. So that's either you or McMahon. Will I get the super to do it, then?'

Lottie stood up.

'The less he's involved in, the better. Which interview room is he in?'

Paddy McWard was standing against the wall, arms by his sides, suppressed rage filling the air. He was wearing a T-shirt, though it was freezing out, and he had a sleeve of coloured tattoos on one arm and a Celtic cross on the other. His voluminous black hair was neatly combed and his hard-blue eyes held a challenge. Lottie was struck by how handsome he looked despite his simmering temper.

She knew from the file she'd read that he was six foot three, thirty-six years old and had two arrests for disturbing the peace. Neither had resulted in a court appearance but both had been logged on PULSE.

'Mr McWard. What brings you here?'

'*You* do.'

'What can I do for you?'

'You can find the bastard who beat the shit out of my wife.'

'Sit down, please.' Lottie didn't like the air of intimidation exuding from him.

'I want to stand. You sit if you like.'

'Mr McWard, this is my interview room. I can bring in a couple of uniforms if you wish.' Lottie smiled sweetly and directed him to the chair on the opposite side of the table.

When he had reluctantly seated himself, she sat down too. He smelled of aftershave and his clothes were fresh. She had dealt with many members of the travelling community during her years in the force, and she knew they were basically good people trying to live their lives the way they wanted and protect their heritage and culture. Like any community, there were always troublemakers, giving everyone a bad name.

'So, Mr McWard, where've you been all week? We've been looking for you.' She folded her arms and rested back in her chair. The effect made him lean forward.

'What are you on about? I came here to talk to you, Missus Detective. You don't be going on about shite, asking me the questions.'

'Your wife was assaulted and you were nowhere to be found. Obviously we want to speak to you about it.'

'And I want to talk to *you* about it.'

'Go ahead.'

'What are you doing to find the bastard who did it? Tell me that.'

'We've carried out forensic analysis of the scene and interviewed everyone on the site, and—'

'This wasn't my own people. This was an outsider.'

'How did they gain access?'

'Through the front gate.'

'I noticed that all the homes, and even the caravans, have cameras. No one was willing to part with their tapes. That's not very helpful.' Lottie had garnered this information from Kirby's investigation.

'There was nothing to see. I checked them out. I want justice for my Bridie. She's a nervous wreck since the attack.'

'Why do you think she was so viciously assaulted?'

'What do you mean by that?' He leaned away from her, eyes wary.

'Are you involved in anything that could have made your wife a target?'

He shoved back the chair and stood up, towering over her.

'This has nothing to do with me.'

Lottie remained seated, unmoving. 'Where were you Monday night and Tuesday morning, Mr McWard?'

'None of your business.' He sat down again.

'You're aware that we found a young woman's body in the cemetery. Your wife heard her screaming. But you weren't at home. So where were you?'

'It's none of your business where I was. You've no right to be asking me these questions.'

'Will you consent to a DNA test?'

'A what? Are you out of your mind?' He slapped the table.

'Can you account for your whereabouts every day and night for the last week?' Lottie kept her voice soft and even.

'This is harassment.' He grimaced, then his lips curled in a smirk. 'Ah, I know. Because I'm a traveller, you think you can harass me.'

'Everyone is being asked the same questions. But you interest me because you don't seem to be very forthcoming with information. Are you going to tell me where you've been and what you've been doing?'

'No, I am not. And if you're not bothered to get off your bony arse and do something about the bollocks who beat my wife, I'll do it myself.'

He hurled the chair back against the wall and strode to the door.

'Mr McWard?' Lottie mustered up her calmest voice. As he turned with his hand on the handle, she said, 'I'll be watching you.'

He flung the door open and stormed out.

Boyd poked his head in.

'Cynthia Rhodes wants a comment from you.'

'Tell her to piss off.'

# CHAPTER FIFTY-SIX

Lottie walked out to the reception area, opened the door to the left of the desk and switched on the light. It was a mirror image of the interview room she'd just left, only smaller. Used mainly for applicants filling up forms. It just about held two people, uncomfortably.

'I'm very busy, as you can imagine,' she said, sitting down and folding her arms.

'I won't take up much of your time. Thank you for agreeing to talk to me.' Cynthia Rhodes pulled out a chair.

'I haven't agreed to anything. Just ticking a box.' Once she'd said the words, Lottie knew she'd succeeded in ruffling Cynthia's journalistic feathers. Paddy McWard's fault. She had yet to digest the interview and identify the source of his anger.

'Will I sit?' Cynthia asked, placing her phone on the tiny desk and opening the recording app. She pushed her black-rimmed spectacles up her nose.

'Two minutes. That's all I can spare.'

'I want to do a feature for the weekend news.'

'Feature on what?'

'The tenth anniversary of the disappearance of Lynn O'Donnell.'

Lottie whistled out a sigh.

'I wasn't based in Ragmullin at that time.' She was determined to say as little as possible.

'Could I speak with Superintendent Corrigan, then? I believe he was the SIO back then.'

'He's on sick leave at the moment.' Come on, Lottie wanted to say, you know that already. Wasting precious time. She had two bodies and a potential missing person to deal with. 'However, we do need media help in seeking information from the public about the last movements of Elizabeth Byrne. That's the young woman we found murdered in—'

'I got the press release and I'm well aware of your current workload,' Cynthia said.

Lottie raised her eyebrows. 'My workload? What's that got to do with you?'

'I had a chat with David.'

David who? Shit. McMahon! Lottie crushed her nails into her hands. 'Maybe *David* can help you with the ten-year-old case then.'

'He said to talk to you.'

'Did he now?' The meddling bastard.

Cynthia was still talking. 'I want to see if Ragmullin gardaí missed something at the time. Especially now that I've discovered that Elizabeth Byrne vanished from a train. Same as Lynn O'Donnell.'

Lottie sighed with relief. At least Cynthia had no inkling about the possible disappearance of Mollie Hunter, also last seen on a train.

'And then there's Mollie Hunter,' Cynthia said with a smile that verged on being sly.

'For Christ's sake,' Lottie exclaimed. 'For your information, we have no missing person report on Mollie Hunter. You've been misinformed.' She stood up and opened the door.

'Shut the door for a moment.'

'What?'

'I said shut—'

'I heard you,' Lottie said, 'and I think it's time you left. When the press office has information to share publicly, I will make sure you are included on the email list.'

'I'm already on the email list. But don't you think it a bit uncanny that almost exactly ten years after Lynn vanished, suddenly you have the murder of a young woman of similar age, and another missing? All disappeared after getting the evening train from Dublin to Ragmullin. Maybe the killer is back on the trail again. Stalking and killing young women. That could spark panic among commuters. To the detriment of a train station already under threat.'

Closing her eyes, Lottie counted to three and opened them again, hoping Cynthia had scuttled out the door. No such luck.

'If you start spreading malicious rumours, causing panic in Ragmullin, I will hold you responsible.'

'I don't mind causing panic if in the process I help save the life of some other unsuspecting young woman. Do you have anything to add?'

'About what?'

'The O'Donnell case?'

'Listen here, Ms Rhodes, you and I both know that the chances of finding Lynn O'Donnell are virtually non-existent. For all we know, the girl was murdered back then and her body dumped in the Dublin mountains. If that is the case, she'll never be found, unless by accident. So please don't go raising the hopes of that poor family when you know there is none.'

'Anything else?'

'Get out.'

'Oh, I'm leaving, but remember, Detective Inspector Parker, your past will catch up with you in the end.'

Lottie stood, open-mouthed. 'What the hell do you mean by that?'

'I think you know right well. The apple doesn't fall far from the tree.'

# CHAPTER FIFTY-SEVEN

Lottie pounded into her office and banged the door shut. She kicked off her boots, swung her feet up on the table and opened the Lynn O'Donnell file. As if she hadn't enough to be doing! Cynthia Rhodes had crawled under her skin and was scratching like vermin trying to suck blood from her veins. She didn't even know the woman and already she hated her.

Before starting on the file, she rooted around in a drawer for a pill. She needed something to slow down her angry heart. Something to ward off the demons of her past. What had Cynthia meant? Was she referring to the fact that Peter Fitzpatrick, Lottie's dad, had been a bent guard? Did she think Lottie was the same? Surely not. Or was it to do with her biological mother? But no one knew about her. Did they? She found a pill and swallowed it dry, gagging at the chalky aftertaste. Was she turning into a replica of her addict mother? God, she hoped not.

Her memory of the file's contents was hazy, the result of a combination of things from last night, including vodka. Shit. She sensed another headache. God help anyone who came in the door.

She focused her eyes on the photograph stapled to the inside cover. Auburn hair, curled around the shoulders. Sky-blue eyes full of life. Lips turned slightly upward in a mischievous smile. Lynn O'Donnell appeared younger than her twenty-five years, and Lottie wondered if it was a photograph taken some time before she vanished.

The file made for sombre reading. The last sighting of the young woman had been on the 5 p.m. Dublin to Ragmullin train. Jimmy Maguire, the station porter, had given a statement saying he came across her after she had disembarked. She had dropped her handbag and he helped her pick up her belongings. After that ... nothing. She simply vanished. There were no CCTV cameras around the station ten years ago, and very few in the town, and even after an intensive investigation the gardaí still had nothing to go on. Lottie could see plenty of areas that hadn't been explored at the time. Things that would be done differently today.

Superintendent Corrigan had written copious amounts of notes at the back of the file. As she scanned them, she remembered the cases of other young women who had disappeared over the years. Some of them had been found. Murdered. But there were still too many unaccounted for. Too many families without answers. Like the O'Donnells.

If there was a remote likelihood that the current cases were linked to Lynn, then Jimmy Maguire would have to be interviewed again. The O'Donnell family members were listed. Maybe she'd have a word with them also.

And as she reached for the phone, an uneasy shiver warned her that Mollie Hunter needed to be found soon.

Before she could lift the phone, it rang.

Jane Dore.

Lottie robed up and joined Jane in the mortuary.

'Thanks for doing this so quickly, Jane,' she said.

'Slow day.' The pathologist opened a file on her computer. 'I have the prelims. A woman in her mid thirties. Extremely undernourished. Verging on malnutrition, I'd say. As you saw, her head

had been shaved, but the follicles tell me her hair had turned grey. Blue eyes, and even though you wouldn't think to look at her now, she was Caucasian.

'She'd been wrapped in some kind of plastic, possibly heavy-duty bin bags. With that and decomposition, it's difficult to pin down time of death. Plus, the use of bleach on the body doesn't help. But the presence of flies and maggots in this cold weather makes me think she's been dead at least a week. Possibly longer. And she may have been held indoors, somewhere warm. Too many unknown variables, I'm afraid. I've further analysis to do, so I may know more later today.'

'Okay.'

'I've taken samples of her DNA, which you should run through the national missing persons database. It might be the only means of identification.'

'Did you do toxicology screens?'

'Yes. On my initial analysis they came up negative, but I've sent them off for more detailed tests.'

'Can you tell me how she died?'

'As I said before, no visible wounds, apart from the obvious vermin activity. The body had been outdoors for around a week. You know I hate making assumptions until I've completed all the tests, but I'm inclined to go with natural causes.'

Lottie widened her eyes. 'But she was wrapped in plastic and dumped in the woods.'

'That suggests foul play after death. At the moment, I can only say that cause of death is inconclusive.'

'Anything else?' Lottie said. 'I'm grasping at fast-disappearing straws now.'

'She'd given birth.'

'Recently?

'No, I'd say five to ten years ago, if not more.' Jane busied herself with a sheaf of paper.

'Any hope of DNA?'

'For the baby? No, but if you find the child, I may be able to match it to the mother.'

'Thanks, Jane.'

'I'll let you have the full report as soon as.'

'And you'll call me if you find anything else?'

'I will.'

Lottie was at the door when Jane said, 'Oh, one other thing.'

Lottie turned around.

'Almost forgot, as I was saving this bit for last. I found a silver Claddagh ring embedded in the junction between the oesophagus and the stomach.'

'What?'

'You heard me. It had been lodged there for some time. Perhaps she swallowed it or it was forced down her throat. But she never passed it.'

'That's terrible. Any inscription?'

'I'll photograph it and send it to you.'

Lottie left Jane to her Dead House. On the drive back to Ragmullin, she wondered who this mystery victim was, and how someone who might have died of natural causes came to be left out in the woods by the lake. And why had she swallowed a ring? Where was her child? Alive or dead? Then another thought struck her. Why had the victim's head been shaved?

# CHAPTER FIFTY-EIGHT

Grace's course finished early. As she left the building, she looked around her. She could feel eyes on her back. She leaned against the wall, letting the rushing crowds file past, then took a deep breath and sniffed away her fear.

She had thought of nothing all day but Mollie. Irrational behaviour was foreign to her. She was a creature of habit. Now she wanted to help a girl she hardly knew. If only she could be brave, if only she could shed her anxiety for a few hours, maybe she could confront the man she'd seen on the train. Would she be able to do that? No, of course not. Yes, Grace, you can. You will.

Shouldering her bag, she tied her scarf around her neck with shaking hands. She really needed her anxiety medication. Taking her first step away from the building, making herself as small as possible to avoid contact with people, she headed for the station. If he was on the train, she was going to approach him. And get him to tell her where he'd taken Mollie.

She headed down Talbot Street, turning her head every few seconds.

Checking.

*

On her return from the Dead House, Lottie bumped into Detective Maria Lynch.

'Sorry about this morning, boss,' Lynch said.

'Not feeling well?' Lottie said. 'Come into my office.'

'I'm a bit nauseous. Mainly in the mornings,' Lynch said when she was seated.

'You're pregnant?'

'I am. I'm thirty-five. I already have two young children and I didn't want any more, and—'

'Congratulations.'

'Thanks.'

'I'm genuinely pleased for you.' Lottie caught the glimmer of something in Lynch's eye. 'You're not happy about it?'

'It wasn't planned. I'm still getting used to the idea. The reason I'm telling you this early is that I may miss a few mornings, but I'll work later in the evenings to make up for it.'

'Don't worry about that.'

'I don't want any preferential treatment. No desk duty.'

'Me? Give preferential treatment? You should know me by now.'

Lynch laughed and the tension eased out of the room. 'Now that the surveillance job has been abandoned, I'll have more energy.'

'Great. Your first priority is to get Matt Mullin in for interview. Can you work on that?'

'Will do. Thanks, boss.'

When Lynch was gone, Lottie felt relieved. She thought it might be the effects of the pill she'd taken earlier, or maybe it was just that she could knock Lynch off the list of people out to get her.


She had just closed the door to try to get a few minutes' peace when there was a knock and Gilly O'Donoghue walked in.

'What's up?' Lottie said, noticing the young woman's pallor. Surely she wasn't pregnant too?

'I want to officially report Mollie Hunter as a missing person.'

'I agree with you, but tell me what's changed.'

'I contacted her office. She works in the Department of Social Welfare on Townsend Street in Dublin. Her line manager says she very rarely misses work. If she has to take a day's sick leave, she always rings in. She hadn't booked any annual leave, so he was particularly worried when he heard she hasn't been seen since Wednesday.'

'Did he confirm she was feeling okay when she finished work on Wednesday? Have you spoken to her colleagues?'

'Not in person. But her manager rang me back and said no one has heard from her. He thinks it's odd.'

'In light of the murder of Elizabeth Byrne, go ahead and file the report. Establish Mollie's last known movements. Talk to anyone who saw her at the station.' This was counteracting McMahon's direct order. Another collision course in the making.

Gilly said, 'I've already put up a personal Facebook appeal, so I'll do an official call-out too. And I'll have a word with Boyd's sister, Grace. She travelled on the train with Mollie on Wednesday.'

'Do that, and keep me up to date on your progress. We need to find Mollie.' As the door shut on Gilly, Lottie whispered, 'Alive.'

# CHAPTER FIFTY-NINE

Lottie gathered the team in the incident room for an impromptu meeting and filled them in on the post-mortem details from the victim found at the lake.

'We need to find a match for her. Kirby, run her DNA through the national database. See what turns up.'

'Will do.' Kirby scribbled on his growing to-do list.

She pinned up a photograph and pointed to it. 'This is a silver Claddagh ring. It was found by the state pathologist in the victim's intestines. Take copies of it. See if you can find out where it came from.'

'Jaysus,' Kirby said.

'It might be a clue to who she was. I can't see any engravings on it, so it may be a lost cause. All the same, we're good at fighting lost causes around here.'

A whisper of laughter before Boyd said, 'It's a symbol of love.'

'What is?'

'The Claddagh. My father gave one to my mother as an engagement ring. It can mean that you're spoken for. It's a traditional ring but nowadays it's mass-produced.'

'That's not much help to us, but bear its significance in mind.' Lottie studied the picture before continuing. 'This victim had a child some years ago. We're looking for a thirty-five-year-old mother. Someone has to be missing her. Her child? Her husband or partner? The man who gave her the ring, perhaps?'

'Someone local?' Boyd piped up.

'The only missing persons we've had in the last couple of weeks are Elizabeth Byrne and now Mollie Hunter,' Lottie said. 'We know Elizabeth is dead and we have her body, but Mollie's age doesn't fit this body and as far as we know she had no children. Therefore it is someone else.

'Mollie Hunter is now officially classed as a missing person. Garda O'Donoghue is organising an appeal for sightings, and we need to track her phone and trace her last movements. See if anything in her life overlaps with Elizabeth Byrne's. It can't be a coincidence that both women were last seen at Ragmullin station. Boyd, you get whatever CCTV footage is available from the station for Wednesday.'

'I'll do my best.'

Lottie patrolled the perimeter of the incident room. 'I don't believe in coincidences, so we need to find Mollie before she ends up like Elizabeth in someone else's grave.'

'Should we warn rail passengers?' Boyd asked.

Lottie cringed, thinking of Cynthia Rhodes' threat. 'I know you're worried for Grace's safety, but I don't think that's warranted at the moment.'

'It's not just Grace I'm worried about.'

'As it stands, we don't know where Elizabeth was actually abducted from. It could have been on her walk home. But we'll put uniforms on the platform this evening. Then we have the weekend to make headway before the Monday commute begins again. All leave is cancelled. Who was taking a second look at Monday's CCTV from the station?'

Kirby raised his hand. 'I was. It's very blurred. No one jumps out at me as recognisable.'

'Check it again.' She pointed to Matt Mullin's photo on the board. 'He is a wanted man. Find him.' Pausing in front of Kirby, she said, 'Any word on John Gilbey?'

'The gravedigger? I interviewed him again and he's in the clear.'

Lottie stopped in front of the incident board. 'Who has the list of names of those who run at Rochfort Gardens?'

'I have it.' Boyd waved it.

'Is Mollie Hunter on there?'

She tapped her foot, waiting as Boyd traced his finger down the list.

'I think this signature is hers.'

'Show me.' Lottie took the page and squinted at it. 'I thought I asked for someone to type this up. Jesus, I can't read it. Whereabouts is her name?'

Boyd pointed to it.

'You're right.' She glanced up at him. 'Has any progress been made with contacting the people on the list?'

'We haven't addresses for all of them.' Boyd dropped his gaze. 'So it's a bit difficult.'

'I don't want to hear about difficult. I want answers.'

'We started on it, but now we have this new body and—'

'Allocate the list to a uniform. Get Gilly O'Donoghue to do it. Which reminds me, Gilly wants to have a word with Grace to see what she remembers about meeting Mollie on the train.'

'I'm not bringing my sister into this.'

'Make some arrangement with her.' Lottie let out an exasperated sigh. 'Do I have to think for you now?'

'Just as well you can't.' Boyd folded up the list and marched out of the room.

*

He was staring at her. Standing there leaning against the door of carriage C. Beads of sweat appeared on her forehead, and her hands were slick and clammy. She took deep breaths, but in the end, she

had to use her inhaler. Thank God she had that with her. At least when she got back to Mark's place she could grab her pills and maybe sleep for a bit. That sounded like heaven. She put her inhaler back in her bag, and when she looked up, he was standing in front of her.

'I think you should sit down,' he said. 'You don't look very well.'

She hadn't noticed him moving. Hadn't noticed the train stopping at Maynooth. Hadn't noticed there were now plenty of seats available.

'I … I'm okay,' she stammered.

'Sit,' he commanded.

She was sure he could see her heart hammering against her chest. Lowering herself onto the seat behind her, she perched on the edge, clutching her bag on her knee. The woman beside her was asleep, head resting against the window, earphones in, oblivious.

He sat down opposite her. Grace held her breath. He leaned over the narrow excuse for a table and said, 'Don't be afraid of me. I can help you.'

Her eyes widened and her mouth seized up. 'What do you mean?'

'I saw you this morning. And yesterday. Looking for your friend.'

She didn't have to ask what he meant. She knew.

'Mollie,' he said. 'She's in a spot of bother. I think she would be happy to see you, even though she told me not to tell anyone.'

As he continued to stare at her, Grace felt her chest tighten and scoured her bag for her inhaler once again. 'Where is she?'

'If you promise not to make a fuss, I'll contact her and find out if she wants to see you.'

Mark wouldn't be at the station to pick her up. What was she going to do? Go with the man and find Mollie, or scream blue murder? Maybe for once in her life she could be brave. She took a quick puff of air and let the thought take root in her anxiety-ridden brain. She would go with him and find Mollie.

'Okay,' she whispered.

# CHAPTER SIXTY

'Are you not supposed to be at the train station?' Lottie checked the time on her phone. 'To pick up Grace?'

'She's heading home to Galway for the weekend.'

'You'll get a break so,' she said. 'Gosh, this day feels as long as a week. I need a coffee. Join me?'

She grabbed her mug and made her way to the makeshift kitchen. Katie should be in New York by now. Still no word. She'd give her an hour, then she was going to ring to make sure they were okay.

'What the hell?' she said. 'Who stole my kitchen?'

The corner was bare, except for pipes with insulating tape around copper nozzles sticking out of the wall.

'McMahon,' Boyd said, stifling a snigger.

'It's not funny.' Lottie turned on her heel and stormed back down the corridor.

'Here, give me your mug,' Boyd said. 'I'll get you some from the canteen.'

'Don't bother. I'm going home.' She went to get her jacket.

Kirby piped up, 'You know what you both need?'

'I know you're going to tell us,' Boyd said, sitting down at his desk.

'A couple of pints.'

'I'm not going drinking with you, Kirby, not on your life.'

'You can come too, boss, and you, Lynch.' Kirby twirled an unlit cigar between his fingers.

'Sorry, I'm not drinking,' Lynch said, keeping her gaze studiously focused on her computer screen.

'Never known you to turn down a drink from Kirby before; not that he offers too often,' Boyd said.

'I'm going home,' Lottie said. 'It's been a long day and I've to be at Rochfort Gardens early in the morning to check out those runners. And you lot better be here bright and early.'

'I might be a bit late,' Lynch offered.

'No worries.' Lottie dragged her jacket over her shoulders and picked up her bag.

Boyd followed her out to the corridor. 'Fancy a bite to eat?'

'I'm starving, but I've a family to feed.'

'Another time maybe?'

'Whenever that may be.' Lottie let the door close behind her.

✳

When the train stopped at Ragmullin station, Grace walked meekly at his side through the throng on the platform. She noticed the uniformed gardaí patrolling up and down and thought of screaming out, but dismissed the notion. She wanted to see Mollie, didn't she? Mark would be proud of her if he could see how brave she was being. Even though he still thought of her as his little sister, she was almost thirty. Time for her to stand on her own two feet.

He had her elbow in a vice. Every muscle in her body blared at the physical contact. She tried to shrug off his hand but he held firm.

At the rear of the station, he opened a car door. 'Won't be long now.'

'What won't be long?' She stalled, uncertainty eroding her earlier bravado.

'Until you see your friend.'

'I thought you had to ring her first,' Grace said.

'I'm sure she won't mind.'

She sat into the car. 'Where are we going?'

'Only a couple of miles along the road. Mollie's nice and comfy and I'm sure you'll both have a great chat.'

Grace clipped on her seat belt and stared out of the window at the street lights vanishing as he drove out of town. She bit her lip and tightened her fingers around the strap of her bag. Maybe this wasn't such a good idea, her inner voice warned. Too late now.

\*

Matt Mullin parked his car around the back of the house. He could see his mother in the kitchen preparing a dinner he didn't want to eat. She mustn't have heard him pull up; she didn't look out the window.

It was no good. He couldn't handle going inside. She'd question him about work. No, I haven't got a new job, Mother. He switched the ignition back on and drove slowly around the house and down the avenue.

He missed Elizabeth. Why had things gone so wrong? It was all her fault. Why had she cut him off? Changed her number, closed down her social media accounts. He couldn't find out what she was up to. But then, just before Christmas, she was back on Facebook. She was reaching out to him. She wanted him home. He'd been sure that was the reason for her going back online.

And then it had all fallen apart again.

He was such a fool. He gripped the steering wheel so hard, his knuckles were in danger of piercing the skin. And he was driving too fast. He slowed down. No point in attracting unwanted attention.

At the Dublin bridge he waited for the lights to change. He looked at the town nestled below him and the canal flowing beneath the bridge. Should he abandon his car and jump into the murky water?

The light flicked to green and he dismissed the thought.

＊

Keelan had put Saoirse to bed early, read her a story and then tidied the kitchen before Cillian arrived home. The row started over nothing.

'You spend more time fussing over Saoirse than me.' Cillian kicked off his shoes and put his feet up on the coffee table.

'And you spend more time giving out about your brother than looking out for him.'

'What's that supposed to mean?'

'Have you not noticed how down he is lately?'

'Down? And how would you know that?'

'I saw him wandering around town. He seems … depressed.'

'Our sister vanished off the face of the earth and it tore our family apart.' He dropped his feet from the table and leaned over with his hands dangling between his legs.

'I know that. I've lived through it with you for the last five years.' Every year it was the same. The week before and the week after the fourteenth of February. And she knew the roses he presented her with annually were really in memory of the sister he had lost.

'Yeah, but you don't know what it did to me, to my family, at the time.'

She placed Saoirse's train book, which Cillian had bought her, back on the shelf and turned to him. 'That's because you won't speak to me about it. You just bottle it all up. Then every so often the cork explodes from the bottle and I have to suffer your temper.'

'I said I was sorry about the plates. Did you buy a new set?'

'I'm not talking about the damn plates. I'm talking about you and me. The way you treat me. It's not right, Cillian. I think you need help.'

He shot up from the chair and grabbed her by the arm. 'Don't you dare say that. First you say my brother is depressed, then you lay all the blame on me.'

'You're hurting me.' She tried to wriggle out of his grasp. He tightened his grip, his fingers digging into her skin, right through to the bone of her arm.

'Hurting? I can hurt you a lot more. Would you like that?'

'Stop!' She snapped his fingers away from her skin one by one. She knew it was anger that drove her strength. He stood looking at her slack-jawed.

She said, 'I've lived with the ghost of your sister haunting me every day since I met you. I thought by now you would have exorcised her spirit. But it gets worse. Every fucking year it gets worse. I've just about had enough of it. Do you get me?'

And then the tears started. She didn't want to cry. She knew it would incense him further. Clenching her fists to keep from lashing out at him, from tearing her nails into his pathetic face, she turned away. Took out the train book and began ripping out the pages, one by one. She had no idea why she was doing it, taking a rise out of him, when he could explode at any minute.

His phone rang, and when he hung up, he said, 'I'm going out.'

She watched him pulling on his shoes. 'Where?' He didn't answer. Helplessly she said, 'Take your coat.'

At the door, he spun round. 'You sound more like my mother every day,' he snarled.

The slam of the door woke Saoirse, and as Keelan rushed to her daughter's room, she wondered if she now possessed the strength to leave Cillian O'Donnell once and for all.

# CHAPTER SIXTY-ONE

The house was unnaturally quiet when Lottie arrived home. Then she remembered that Katie and little Louis were in New York. She pushed the buggy out of the way and wheeled it into the sitting room, glad Katie had the light stroller with her.

'Sean?' she called up the stairs. 'Will you fold up this buggy, please? And where is Chloe?'

Without waiting for a reply, she went to the kitchen and began pulling things from the refrigerator to prepare dinner.

'Can we get takeaway?' Chloe said, walking in behind her.

'I've to cook something for your granny, so I may as well cook for us all.' Lottie turned to find Chloe lounging against the kitchen door, pulling at her sleeves.

'What's up?'

'Nothing. We're on mid-term next week, and with Katie and Louis away I was wondering maybe we could go somewhere for a few days.'

'I'm in the middle of a murder investigation. I can't just up and leave.'

'It's always about you, isn't it?'

'Sorry, Chloe, I didn't mean—'

'Forget it.'

'I'm sorry.' She was talking to fresh air.

Sean shouted from the sitting room, 'I haven't a clue how this thing folds up. I'll just push it in behind the couch.'

Her phone rang. 'Yes, Mother?'

'I roasted a chicken for myself. There's some left over if you want it.'

'No, it's fine. We're getting a takeaway.'

She hung up before her mother could lecture her about the importance of healthy eating for the development of teenagers' brains. At least Rose seemed to be on the mend.

Chloe appeared at the door. 'Will I ring for food, then?'

'Yeah, do.'

But Lottie didn't feel like takeaway. She felt like going out. Somewhere she could get a drink without Chloe finding out.

She rang Boyd.

# CHAPTER SIXTY-TWO

The three men were sitting in the kitchen. The doorbell pierced the silence. Donal got up to answer it.

Cillian eyed his brother across the table. Finn dropped his head and Cillian smiled. He always did have the upper hand where his brother was concerned. His father returned with a woman behind him. Cropped curly hair and black-rimmed spectacles. She was about forty years old. Not much to look at, he thought.

'This is Cynthia Rhodes. She's from the telly,' Donal said.

'Hi, I'm pleased to meet you all.' She shook hands and sat down uninvited.

With the four of them seated around the table, Cillian said, 'Are you going to tell us what this is about?'

'I don't like dredging up sad memories, but I want to do a feature for the news on the tenth anniversary of Lynn's disappearance. It might rekindle an interest in her case.'

'I'm not so sure,' Donal said.

'Do you mind if I record this.' She placed her phone on the table, with its recording app open.

'I do mind,' Cillian said, folding his arms. She took a notebook out of her bag. 'And you can put that away too.'

'Okay.' She put her bag on the floor. 'I've seen the posters around town. I thought you would like some more publicity.'

Finn spoke up. 'Depends on what you mean by publicity.'

Donal said, 'We miss Lynn so much. And my wife Maura … she died …'

Cillian sighed. He hoped his old man wasn't going to start blubbering. He'd seen enough tears to last him forever.

'I'm sorry for your loss,' Cynthia said. 'Maybe something will turn up if I do a particularly good feature? Like *Crimecall*.'

Cillian grunted. 'The authorities seem to think no body, no crime. But we've been without our sister for the last ten years, so in my mind that is a crime.'

'I agree,' Cynthia said.

'Then why are you talking to us?' Cillian said. 'Talk to the guards. See what they can tell you.'

'I tried, but they're very tight-lipped about it. I thought with the murder of a young woman last seen on the train, they would see the similarity to Lynn's disappearance.'

'I heard that. Awful it was,' Donal said.

'So, can you tell me anything that might help jog someone's memory?'

Donal stood up and busied himself folding the newspaper. 'You know the facts. My daughter worked in the civil service in Dublin. Commuted every day. And on the fourteenth of February 2006, she got the train home as usual, only she never arrived. That morning was the last time any of us laid eyes on her.'

'And you boys, when did you last see your sister?'

Cillian observed the reporter taking notes surreptitiously in the notebook on her knee. Does she think I can't see her? 'We all lived at home then. Lynn got up for the early train. There was only the one early train back then. Me and Finn, we saw her the night before, when we were going to bed. Isn't that right?'

Finn grunted, head still bowed. Cillian kicked him under the table. 'That's right,' he said.

Standing up, Cillian said, 'I think the only place you'll get all the information is from the guards. But we'd appreciate it if you could do a new appeal for information.'

He watched as she flattened one of the posters out on the table. 'This phone number, is it one of yours? Can I publicise it?'

'It's a dedicated number. For information. Not that it does much good. Hasn't rung in ten years.' Cillian looked at his father, who by now had the newspaper folded into a small square.

'Aye, that's right,' Donal said.

'Maybe my news feature will throw up some new suspects for the gardaí.'

'They never had any suspects in the first place,' Donal said. 'I'll see you out now, Ms Rhodes.'

After she'd left the house, the three O'Donnell men eyed each other. They knew there was one prime suspect who had never come under garda suspicion. They should have said something back then, but they'd never allow the family to suffer that indignity. Never.

*

Carol lay on her side on her bed. Nausea wended its way up from her stomach and settled at the back of her throat. How had she let this happen? She was a fool. She should have told the guards that Elizabeth knew about her pregnancy and the fact that she was much further on than she had intimated.

She figured she had to talk to him soon. To the father of this child growing in her womb. He had been so nice, hadn't he? After all that had gone before. So understanding of her frustrations with her home life, her gay brother and her dumbass job. Yes, he had been nice to her. But not at the time.

Bloody hell, she thought, it's a freaking mess.

Her phone lay on the pillow beside her. She'd opened his contact details. Saved under a made-up name, just in case. You can never be careful enough, he'd said. Yeah, she knew he was married. But he had a right to know. Hadn't he?

Another wave of nausea released itself from her throat and she retched into the bowl she'd placed beside her bed.

How long was this going to last? As a cold sweat broke out on her forehead, she shut off the contact and locked her phone. Not now. She was too sick.

\*

The traveller site was lit up like Christmas Eve. Paddy McWard parked his Jeep and had a good look around before entering his home.

His dinner was on a plate in the microwave and Bridie was sitting on the couch with Tommy on her knee.

'How's Tommy?' he said.

'My face is very painful, thank you for asking.' Bridie was sulking.

He sat beside her and took his son in his arms. He kissed Tommy's sweet-smelling hair, and the baby nuzzled into his chest. 'I'm sorry I haven't been here for you recently.'

'Why is that, Paddy? Why haven't you been here? Where have you been? Or am I not allowed to ask?'

'Please don't ask and I won't have to lie to you.'

'Like that, is it?' She shuffled away from him but he could see her eyes were on Tommy.

'I'm not going to hurt our son, nor you, for that matter,' he said. She was biting her lip. He knew this was a sign that she was desperately trying not to cry. 'And don't start bawling. I want you to believe that beating you got had nothing to do with me.'

'I'm sure it had something to do with whatever you're involved in. Why else have the guards been swarming around this place for the last few weeks like flies on a shite?'

'They're looking for scapegoats. Someone to blame for every fight or burglary in town. And I can tell you here and now, it has nothing to do with me.'

She inched back closer to him. 'But why would someone break in and beat me up?'

'I don't know. But I'm going to find out.' He could almost feel the heat blazing from her eyes. 'What?'

'If it's nothing to do with you, then it's because someone thinks I saw something at the graveyard. The night that poor girl was murdered.'

He handed the baby over to her and stood up. 'You leave it to me. I've got two of my cousins keeping an eye on this place, and you're not to go anywhere without bringing one or both of them with you.'

'But I did nothing wrong. It's not fair.'

'Listen here, this town is a very dangerous place at the minute, so I don't want you wandering around on your own. I can't afford to lose you too.' He pressed the code on the microwave and watched the plate turn under the light.

'How is your mother?' he asked. He had to change the subject.

'What do you mean, *you too*?' she said from behind him.

He could smell the expensive perfume he'd bought for her. He wanted to tell her everything was going to be okay. But he didn't know how to, and anyway, he couldn't tell her something he didn't believe himself.

✽

They sat in a corner in Cafferty's, nursing pints of Guinness and suffering each other.

'The old man is losing it,' Cillian said.

'I reckon *you're* losing it,' Finn said.

'You can talk. I think I've just gone off my pint. Don't know why I even agreed to come here with you.'

'You know why. You wanted to escape the old man's trip into madness with Lynn's anniversary coming up.'

'He was always mad. Lynn vanishing didn't make him any worse.'

'Maybe not, but Mother did.'

'Don't mention her.' Cillian sipped his pint. The bile rising from his stomach soured the taste in his mouth.

'She adored Lynn.'

'We all did. Me more than anyone.' Cillian shrugged his chin down to his chest. He didn't want to be having this conversation. Least of all with a brother he despised.

'You're the lucky one in all of this. You have Keelan and Saoirse.'

Cillian shot his brother a look that he knew could make milk turn. 'Never, ever talk about my wife and daughter. You made your own bed. Go home and lie in it.'

Finn's jaw crunched up and down as if he was trying to speak but the words were locked in his throat.

After downing his pint in two swallows, Cillian made for the door. 'I don't know how you do it, but every time I have to spend even a minute in your company, I get the urge to kill someone.'

Outside, he stood for a full three minutes in the cold before he could put one foot in front of the other. The collision course that had been mapped out in black and white for them since the day they were born was now flashing in front of his eyes in high definition.

As the chilly air cut through his sweater, he cursed the stubbornness that had made him leave home without his jacket. He didn't want to return to Keelan. Not just yet. There was someone he would much rather be with.

He made his decision and headed for his car.

# CHAPTER SIXTY-THREE

'I remember the last time we were in that restaurant.' Boyd sipped a glass of red wine.

They'd had an exquisite Indian meal and had returned to Boyd's apartment. Lottie didn't need any coercion to come in for a nightcap. Three glasses of wine in the restaurant had done nothing to assuage her thirst. She craved a bottle.

She smiled. 'It was snowing so hard it was a virtual whiteout.'

'And you had to pour me into my car and drive me home. Father Joe was sniffing around you back then.'

'That is such a vulgar comment, Boyd. He was just being a friend.'

'There are friends and … there are friends.'

'Are you sure you didn't have a second bottle of wine while I was eating?'

'Just the one.'

'Liar,' she laughed, feeling more relaxed than she should. 'Do you miss having Grace's company?'

'Nope. What's it like at yours without Katie and Louis?'

'Quiet.'

'And that's a good thing, isn't it?'

'I miss them already. I know, I know. But Chloe's being a drama queen. She wants us to go away for a few days next week because she and Sean have a mid-term break. And I put my big foot in it by using work as an excuse.'

'Knowing you as well as I do, I'd have thought you'd use lack of finance as an excuse.'

Lottie sighed. 'I couldn't play that card. Katie gave me some money before she left.'

'Katie? Where did she get it?' Boyd paused, and opened his mouth in shock. 'Tom Rickard?'

'Yes, and I'm not spending any of his dirty money.'

'I'd spend it.'

'I didn't think you'd be like that.' She sipped her wine, trying to make it last a bit longer, while eyeing the bottle on the table.

'Then again, maybe I'd just burn it,' he said.

'No you wouldn't, and I won't either. Katie will need it when she gets home.'

'How is she getting on?' Boyd rose from the couch and poured himself another glass. She held out her glass and he got the bottle of white for her.

'She sent me a text to let me know they'd arrived safely. I sent back a ton of messages but she hasn't replied yet.'

'Give the girl a chance.'

'Maybe I should call her ...'

'Don't you dare. Let her have a few weeks without you interfering.' He sat down beside her. She noticed he was closer than he had been a moment ago. She drained her glass and poured herself another. Shit, she'd better slow down.

'That's twice in the space of a few minutes you've insulted me.' She shifted to her left and was met by the arm of the couch. She knew he was smirking.

'You fancied him, didn't you?' he said.

'Who?'

'Father Joe.'

'If you keep that up, I'm going home right now.'

'I apologise.'

She felt herself slowly unwind and studied him from the corner of her eye. 'You don't look at all sorry. Actually, you look a bit pale. Are you feeling okay?'

He reached out a hand and caressed her cheek. 'I'm not feeling myself at all.'

'You're such a messer.'

But she didn't spurn his advance. A tingle of anticipation curled around the pit of her stomach, and she welcomed it. Or was it just the wine? If he kisses me now, she thought, I'll end up in his bed.

The clink of his glass on the coffee table jolted her. He took hers and put it down too, then his hand returned to her cheek. She turned to face him.

'Will I put on some soft music?' he asked.

'Soft music? Boyd, you don't even know what soft music is.'

'Can I kiss you, then?' he whispered.

'I thought you'd never ask.'

'That's the corniest line I ever heard.'

'Are you refusing—'

His lips on hers was answer enough.

❋

Grace's eyes flew open. She was shivering uncontrollably. Her skin felt like it had been flayed with a knife. When her chest constricted and the pain shot around her back, she was sure she was having a heart attack. But it was just her anxiety. She couldn't have a panic attack. Not now.

The ground beneath her was damp. Through a boarded-up window, she could make out a weak stream of moonlight. Her breath quickened. This was bad. Very bad. With her hands bound to her sides, she had no way of finding her inhaler. Another few hours like

this and she was sure she would die. He hadn't brought her to Mollie. She had no idea where he'd brought her after he clamped the soaked cloth to her mouth in the car.

How had she been so gullible? Maybe everyone was right. Maybe she was stupid. And now, trussed up like a piece of meat ready for the oven, she had no way to prove them wrong.

# CHAPTER SIXTY-FOUR

Bridie McWard cuddled Tommy to her chest, wrapping the duvet tighter around them both. She had no idea what was eating Paddy the last few weeks. He was like a different man. Hardly ever at home. Angry when he was. Banging and shouting, upsetting Tommy. He was definitely up to something, but she was too afraid to ask. As she smoothed her baby's hair, she realised that whatever Paddy was up to, she really didn't want to know.

When Tommy fell asleep, she lifted him into his cot and returned to bed. Her head still ached from the thumping she'd got. Paddy had been so mad about that too. Maybe he was out trying to chase down her attacker.

As she settled herself in the empty bed, she felt the house shake with a violent bang. Tommy screamed in his cot. Bridie shot upwards, jumped out of bed and grabbed the baby.

Opening the bedroom door, she was flung backwards by a gust of wind. The noise deafened her and the light blinded her. She smelled something in the air, right before she felt the heat.

'No!' she screamed and tried to slam the door shut, but the flames had taken hold of the flimsy wood and she was driven back into her room, chased by the fire.

'Paddy!' she cried as she curled into a corner, shielding her screaming baby. 'Help me. Someone help me.'

The flames rushed along the synthetic carpet, tracking her footprints until they lapped like scalding waves at her feet. She screamed

until the smoke took her voice away and the noxious gases clogged her lungs.

As she buried her face in her son's hair, folding herself into the corner, she thought she heard the sound of the banshee. And in her final moments, she understood that those screams of foreboding had not been for the girl in the cemetery. They'd been for her and her beautiful little boy.

# CHAPTER SIXTY-FIVE

The street light filtering through the slatted wooden blinds was the only illumination in an otherwise dark room. Lottie raised herself on her elbow and glanced around. Where was she? What time was it? God, her head! God, Boyd!

She sat up suddenly, her head spinning, and looked at him lying in the bed beside her. His face was shrouded in darkness except for the horizontal lines of light cast from the blinds. He groaned and opened his eyes.

'Hello, gorgeous,' he said. 'What are you smiling at?'

She lay back down and curled away from him.

'Was my lovemaking that bad?' he said.

'It was sublime, but I have to apologise. I'm so out of practice.'

'You know the saying. Practice makes perfect.'

'Don't ruin the moment with your smartarse comments.'

'You're usually the one with the smart arse—'

'See. I told you. It's ruined now.'

'Let me unruin it.'

'You're talking pure shite.'

'I'll shut up so,' he said, and pulled her beneath him.

She felt the weight of his body and the freshness of his kiss. Her mind told her to stop, to go home, but her body rebelled. Her head was dizzy. From alcohol? Shit. How much had she actually had to drink? Too much.

'You're making my ears ring,' he said softly, his lips moving down her neck towards her nakedness.

'It's my phone!' She shoved him to one side and bolted out of the bed. 'Where's my phone? What time is it? Boyd! Turn on a light.'

'Hold on a minute.'

The room filled with a dim glow as he switched on a lamp. Lottie scrambled around on the floor. Her phone was still ringing. She realised it was out in the living area. Pulling a sheet from the bed, she wrapped it around herself and found her bag beside the couch. The ringing stopped.

'Shit. It might've been Katie. I hope she's okay.'

'Will you stop panicking.'

Glancing back at him silhouetted at the door, she almost abandoned her search for the phone. Almost.

As her fingers found the device, it began to ring again.

'Ah, for feck's sake,' she said, glancing at the caller ID. 'It's only Kirby.'

'I'll wring his neck when I see him. Don't answer it.'

Lottie put the phone to her ear.

# CHAPTER SIXTY-SIX

Boyd drove in silence. Lottie didn't know what to feel, so she just numbed herself into nothingness and let the memories of the evening slip uneasily over her like a shroud. No good was going to come of this, she could feel it in her blood.

Kirby was standing at the entrance to the site. Two trucks were there, fire personnel hosing down the dying blaze.

Jumping from the car almost before Boyd had brought it to a halt, she said, 'I can't believe this, Kirby. I hope Bridie and her family aren't in there.'

'We've evacuated all the residents but there's no sign of the McWards.'

'Has no one seen them? Where is everyone? Can I talk to them?'

'They've been taken to the nursing home around the corner. The staff there are providing blankets and hot tea. Everyone's in shock. The faces on the poor kids. This is bad, boss, very bad.'

'You think the McWards are in there?'

'No idea yet. But they're not among the residents escorted out. I was here almost as soon as the fire crews.'

'How did you manage that?'

'I've a couple of informants who live here. One of them gave me a call. Myself and two uniforms helped everyone to escape while the fire crews got to work.'

'So either the McWards weren't at home or they were in that ...' She took a step forward and was halted by the chief fire officer.

'Sorry, but you'll have to wait until it's safe to enter. There are caravans and gas cylinders around. Everything is combustible in this heat.'

Lottie nodded and turned to Boyd. He gripped her elbow to lead
her away. She shrugged off his concern.

'Take me back to get my car and then return here to Kirby. Erect
a crime-scene cordon until we establish what the hell happened.
Contact me if you find the McWards and call as soon as it's safe to
enter the site.'

The chief fire officer overheard her. 'It'll be morning before we
can deem it safe.'

'All the same,' Lottie said. 'Kirby and Boyd, you coordinate the
uniforms and then interview the survivors. I want to know where
the McWards are, if they're not already dead.'


Even though it was after three a.m., the lights were still on in
her house. Lottie went into the kitchen, but it was empty. She
automatically took clothes, mostly belonging to Louis, from the
washing machine and filled the dryer. Still only the one text from
Katie. Maybe Chloe had heard from her.

At the top of the stairs, she noticed light filtering out from under
Sean's door. She stuck her head inside. He didn't hear her. A massive
set of headphones covered his ears and he was gesticulating wildly at
a screen with a remote control. Opening her mouth to tell him to
get into bed, she stopped and decided to let him off for one night.
There was no school for a week. He'd be grand.

Outside Chloe's door, she hesitated. Her daughter was probably
asleep and she didn't want to wake her, but a nerve tingled at the
base of her skull, so she opened the door.

Chloe was lying in bed, propped up with pillows, her face lit by
the screen of the phone in her hand. The creak of the door had alerted

her and she jumped, dropping her phone. The room was plunged into darkness. Lottie flicked on the light switch.

'I thought you were out for the night,' Chloe said. 'Working. Or something. Oh, or maybe you were *fucking Boyd.*'

'Chloe!' Lottie reeled back on her heels from the venom in her daughter's voice. How the hell was she going to handle this? Carefully. Very carefully. 'We just went for a meal.'

'A very long meal, including alcohol from what I can smell.'

'Chloe, there's no need for that.'

'I think there's every need. You've been drinking. Jesus, have we to go through all this again?'

'Please. I only had the one glass.' Why was she explaining? But she knew her drinking had caused her children suffering in the past. Dear God, she didn't want to go back there again.

'Drinking with Boyd?' Chloe curled up her lip. 'And I thought he was nice. Just shows what I know.'

'It's nothing to do with him.' Lottie let her arms fall limply by her sides. Nothing good could come of sleeping with Boyd. The fire was a warning. Leave him alone, she told herself, or you'll succeed in dragging him down to your level. She had no idea how to explain things to her seventeen-year-old daughter, so she didn't even try.

She said, 'I have to work again in the morning, but ring me any time you want to talk. Please.'

Chloe pulled the duvet to her chin and eyed her. 'So how was Boyd in bed?'

'Goodnight, Chloe.' Lottie switched off the light.

✻

He had left the light on. His 'treat'. Then he'd sat on the small wooden chair, staring at her. She had no idea how long he stayed there before he rose and slowly traced a line down her body with his

finger. She shuddered and cringed, but he had tied her down and she couldn't fight back.

She must have passed out, because when she awoke, he was gone and she was untied. The light was still on and the first thing her eyes focused on were the bones. Laid out on the bench in the form of a skeleton. Fear obstructed her throat and congested her lungs.

Finding the bottle of water and the sandwich he'd left for her, she wondered if she should ration them in case he didn't come back. But he would be back. She knew that as surely as she knew the bones on the bench were human. She knew it from the pain he'd left between her legs. Bile swirled in her stomach.

Closing her eyes, she sucked in a deep breath of stagnant air. When she opened them again, she scanned her surroundings. Then she noticed something she hadn't spotted before. Paintings. Tiny watercolours. Pinned to the wall behind her.

She got up from the bed and gingerly tested the floor with her bare feet. It was cold to the touch. She felt weak from being cooped up. Two steps and she was beside the wall where they hung, faded and grey. Screwing up her eyes, she tried to make out the initials in the corner of one of them. But they were smudged. Even the subject matter was hard to decipher. Once more her eyes were drawn downwards to the bones that had haunted her all day.

Bones that were so small they could only belong to a baby.

# DAY FOUR

Saturday 13 February 2016

# CHAPTER SIXTY-SEVEN

The fire trucks were lined up on the main road and traffic was being diverted. Lottie walked onto the site. The smell of smoke and soot choked the air. Lynch and Garda Gilly O'Donoghue had replaced Boyd and Kirby. Lynch looked worse than yesterday. Lottie was glad she didn't have to face Boyd. The vodka she'd downed after her confrontation with Chloe was lodged in the pit of her stomach. The pill hadn't helped either. No, she didn't want to see Boyd.

She looked up to find Paddy McWard running at her like a bull at a matador. Tears streamed down his face, smeared by his blackened hands.

'This is your fault. Your fucking fault, you pigs.'

'Mr McWard, Paddy, I'm sorry ...' Lottie reached out to him but he swiped her hand away. He'd been nowhere to be found last night. How the hell had he accessed the site?

He kept ranting. 'Don't you dare say you're sorry. Don't even begin to talk to me. Pigs poking around brings nothing but trouble. My wife and my son. Dead. Mark my words, you'll pay for this.' He spat at Lottie's feet, then turned swiftly and stormed back to the smouldering remains of his home.

She couldn't bring herself to move until she felt a hand on her arm. Boyd.

'I thought you'd gone home?' She buried her chin in the collar of her jacket and her hands deep in her pockets.

'Couldn't sleep. Decided I'd be better employed back here.' He dropped his hand.

Had he sidestepped away from her? Shit, her imagination was in overdrive. She turned her attention to the SOCOs. McGlynn and his team were moving about at the periphery of the site, waiting for the fire chief to give them the go-ahead.

'What in God's name happened here, Boyd?' she said.

'Revenge? For something Paddy was involved in?'

'Or for Bridie talking to us?'

'But she didn't tell us anything that could point us to Elizabeth's killer, and the body was found by accident. Don't go blaming yourself for this.'

'A mother and baby. Burned to death in their own home. I can't get my head around it.'

'Don't even try until we have all the facts.'

'She was only a kid herself.' Lottie found herself thinking of Katie and Louis and the text she'd got earlier from her daughter, full of the joys.

The fire chief eventually gave the SOCOs the nod, and they began their work.

'Is Jane Dore on the way?' Lottie asked McGlynn.

'We have to locate the bodies first.'

'We're not even sure anyone was at home,' Boyd said with a shrug.

'The husband says they were here and no one else has seen them since yesterday around five.' McGlynn consulted soot-smeared notes. 'I'm fairly certain we will find the remains.'

Lottie moved away, unable to witness the sight of Paddy kneeling on the wet ground outside the inner cordon, keening. She thought of the young woman who had come to the station and had then suffered an assault in her own home. Bridie, so beautiful, articulate and intelligent. Was Paddy correct in his assessment? Had his wife made herself a target by speaking to the guards? She hoped not, otherwise they'd have a whole new scenario to consider.

She turned to Boyd. 'It must be something Paddy's involved in. And if that's the case, much as I hate to say it, we need to hand it over to another team.'

'Don't go making any assumptions yet. McMahon will have his say on it.'

'Oh no. I'd forgotten we have to pick him up before we head to Rochfort Gardens.'

She instructed Lynch to keep Paddy McWard in her sight at all times and to notify her if McGlynn had anything to report. 'And then find Matt Mullin. I'm sick of waiting for him to crawl out from under a stone when all the time he could be behind this ... this ... catastrophe.'

She shoved her hands into her pockets in exasperation. Or for fear that she might hit someone?

As they made their way out, the hoses were being rolled up and the fire crews were packing away their equipment. A train rumbled and slowed down on the tracks behind the site, making its way into town.

'Still no sign of Mollie Hunter?' Lottie asked.

Boyd shook his head and walked ahead. 'And I've yet to get Wednesday evening's CCTV footage from the train station. Shit.'

It was going to be another one of those days.

# CHAPTER SIXTY-EIGHT

Boyd parked the car, and they made their way down the narrow incline to the visitor centre.

McMahon stopped them before they entered through the sliding glass doors. 'So that's the Jealous Wall.'

'It is.' Lottie hoped she wasn't going to have to give him a lesson in local history.

'I read up about it last night,' he said.

'Thank God for small mercies,' Lottie said.

'What?'

'You found it interesting?' She tried to cover for herself.

'A folly, built like a ruined abbey by an earl in the seventeen hundreds. He was insanely jealous and wanted to keep his brother from spying on his wife. Then he imprisoned her in the manor house.' McMahon looked around. 'Where is that located?'

'Up the hill. It's not too far if you want to take a look.' Maybe he would bugger off and leave them on their own.

'Another time.' McMahon pushed on ahead.

Lottie sighed and followed him inside. A deafening cacophony emanated from the main concourse area.

'How many do you reckon are here?' Lottie whispered to Boyd as she tried to calculate a quick head count.

'About fifty,' Boyd said.

'Are they mad? It must be minus two and they're about to go running,' McMahon said.

'One way to keep warm, I suppose,' Lottie said.

'I can think of better ways,' Boyd murmured.

She caught his grin and blushed uneasily as she consulted the typed list of names Gilly had provided. 'Anyone ever say you have a one-track mind?'

McMahon was standing at the reception desk hitting the bell. Carol O'Grady appeared from the back office. McMahon slapped his ID on the counter.

'I'd like to have a word with the joggers before they go outside. Through here?' He turned on his heel and made for the inner doorway.

'Hey, come back. I don't think that's allowed.' Carol lifted the phone on the desk. 'I need to contact my manager.'

'Already agreed.' McMahon snatched the list out of Lottie's hand. She did her best to keep her mouth shut, and just about succeeded.

The scent of freshly brewed coffee permeated the air as they made their way through the assembled heaving masses of luminous Lycra.

Boyd headed for the door on the opposite side of the large open-plan area. It led to the vast expanse of grounds. He blocked the exit as McMahon attempted to make himself heard.

'Ladies and gentlemen! Just a minute, please. Can I have your attention?'

Gradually the noise descended to a hum of mutterings before silence reigned.

'Thank you,' he said.

Lottie seethed. This was her gig, but she had a feeling McMahon was going to fuck it all up.

'My name is Superintendent McMahon and I have a list of people here with whom my detectives would like to have a few words. Detective Inspector Parker will call out your names, and we'd ask you to wait behind to speak to us.'

There was a murmur of dissenting voices.

'Quiet, please.'

Did he think he was a schoolteacher? Lottie moved up beside him.

'Most of you have already spoken on the phone with my team,' she said, 'but I have a list of fourteen people with whom we haven't made contact. The rest of you are free to head on out for your run. I really appreciate your help in finding anyone who can give us information about the murder of Elizabeth Byrne and the disappearance of Mollie Hunter.'

She took the list back from McMahon and called out the fourteen names. Other runners shuffled out of the way as they made their way forward.

'I only count twelve,' Boyd said.

'Let's get started,' McMahon said, commandeering a table and chairs.

A blast of cold air spread through the high-ceilinged area as the door opened to let the rest of the runners escape.

It didn't take long to interview the twelve. Elizabeth was known by several of them to say hello to, but no one had noticed anything out of the ordinary or anyone acting suspiciously around her. The same was true of Mollie. Lottie looked down at the two names remaining on the list, then glanced up at Boyd.

'See the two who haven't turned up this morning?'

He nodded. 'Do you think they're related to …?'

'I'm sure of it.' She gathered her interview notes and looked around for McMahon. 'Where's the super?'

'Gone to have a snoop around the big house.'

'We haven't time for this.'

'We better go find him.'

'Or maybe abandon him to his fate.'

'Now, Lottie, you can't be like that.'

She hauled on her jacket and shoved the papers into her bag. 'I can, but I don't feel like facing the consequences of his temper.'

Reaching the door, she heard her name being called. Carol came out from behind the desk.

'I was wondering if you found anything helpful? You know, from your interviews.'

'There are two people on the list who don't seem to be here today. Maybe you know them.'

'Who?' Carol wrapped her hands tight around her midriff as if fighting off a bitter wind.

'Cillian and Finn O'Donnell,' Lottie said.

The colour drained from the pregnant girl's face. Boyd reached out a hand to steady her.

'What is it?' he asked.

She shook her head and turned away. Lottie followed.

'Hey, what's up? Do you know them? They're related to the girl who went missing ten years ago, aren't they?'

Carol stopped and turned slowly. Her face was wet with tears, her lips pursed tightly. As if she couldn't trust herself to speak, she nodded, then held her hand to her mouth and ran towards the toilets.

'Being pregnant must be a bitch,' Boyd said.

'And what would you know about it?' Lottie stepped outside, letting the door slide back in his face. She didn't want to be around Boyd today. The tenderness of his caresses was too fresh and too raw, and too wrong.

✻

David McMahon parked in front of the apartment he'd been lucky enough to rent short-term at a knockdown price. On the outskirts of Ragmullin, it was surrounded by trees. Secluded. Anonymous. Great.

He smiled when he saw the car pull in behind him. Stepping out, he leaned back and waited for the occupant to join him.

'Cynthia. What a pleasant surprise.'

'You're such a liar, McMahon.'

'Have you any news for me?'

'I was about to ask you that.' She tried a coy look but he wasn't buying it. He knew what she was like.

'You want to know about the fire?' he said.

'And anything else you can fill me in on.' She took out a pack of mints and offered him one. He shook his head and waited. 'Look, David, I'm digging as much and as quickly as I can. But so far no one will say anything about her.'

'Try Detective Maria Lynch. I get the feeling they're not the best of friends.'

'Right. The fire? Tell me.'

'Not much to tell. Two dead. Mother and her baby. House gutted. All the signs of an arson attack. Have you got anything juicy for me to sink my teeth into?'

'Nothing so far. I told you I'm doing a piece on the missing O'Donnell girl.'

'So you did. An appeal for information?'

'More like a biopic of the effects on Lynn's family. I get the feeling her disappearance ripped them apart.'

'And you intend to rip them wider still?'

'No. This is a human interest piece.' She smiled slyly. 'I'm not all bad, you know.'

'Oh, I think you are.'

He pushed himself away from his BMW, wetted a finger and rubbed away a piece of dirt from the door. Then he walked towards his apartment. Lottie Parker had made a fool of him last October. He was still smarting from the rebuff he'd suffered and he wanted

revenge. He wanted her face in a mire, with his shoe on the back of her neck, holding her down.

'Hey, David?' Cynthia called. 'I need something soon. I'm back in Dublin on Monday.'

'Quid pro quo.'

'Not asking me in for a coffee?' she said.

'I've already had some.'

He disappeared into the apartment wondering if Cynthia Rhodes was worth his trouble.

# CHAPTER SIXTY-NINE

On Lottie's return from Rochfort Gardens, she found Jane Dore seated in her office.

'Jane! Why are you here?'

'I've just left the scene of that awful fire.'

Slumping onto her chair, Lottie said, 'You found a body?'

'Two. What's left of them.'

'Oh God, this is too much.' Lottie pulled at her hair. 'Any hope of identification?'

'DNA, possibly. An adult female and a child.'

'Bridie McWard and her baby.' Trailing her hands up and down her arms, Lottie tried to rub away the feeling of hopelessness.

'Their remains are on the way to the Dead House. I'll know more later.' Jane leaned over the desk, her petite hands joined together. 'What's going on in Ragmullin, Lottie?'

Catching the pathologist's eye, Lottie shook her head. 'I wish I knew. Any evidence of foul play?'

'The fire was started maliciously.'

Lottie flicked through a file on her desk. 'It was reported by a neighbour almost immediately. How could it burn so quickly?'

'McGlynn can fill you in on the details, but it was a fabricated house. Went up like tissue paper.'

'They hadn't a chance.'

'Did you know the victims?'

'I met Bridie a couple of times. I think she heard Elizabeth Byrne's screams the night she was murdered. And she was assaulted in her home the other night.'

Pushing her spectacles up on her nose, Jane said, 'I have some more information on Elizabeth's murder. I emailed it to you early this morning. You may not have accessed it yet. The clothes found in the skip have trace evidence of water.'

'Yes, I knew that.'

'It's a match for water found in Ladystown lake.'

'Where we found the unidentified body. Why was Elizabeth there? How did she get out there?'

'Maybe it was just her clothes. The killer may have dunked the clothes to get rid of evidence of fibres or cells.'

'Christ, this gets weirder by the minute. Had Elizabeth's body any evidence of being in the water?'

'No. And regarding toxicology, I found trace samples of chloroform. Just minute amounts, but it was there.'

'I'm going to string up the bastard when I find him.' Lottie shot up from her chair, pacing the small office before sitting on the edge of the desk. 'And the body at the lake?'

'As you may have noticed, the fingernails were bitten down to the quick. But I found traces of paint embedded in places.'

'Paint? What type of paint?'

'I don't know. I've sent samples for analysis.' Jane stood up. 'Did you find a match for her in missing persons?'

'We checked back a couple of weeks. There's no one. Only Mollie Hunter, and she was around up to Wednesday as far as we can determine. Plus she doesn't fit the age profile.'

'Did you cross-reference on the national database? Run the DNA?'

Lottie shot her a look. 'Of course.' But had they? She needed to double-check.

'A thirty-five-year-old woman, a mother, deceased at least a week and no one has missed her? I don't buy that, Lottie, and I don't think you should either.'

'But you said she died of natural causes.'

'Her heart stopped beating, that's the only natural thing about it. She was malnourished. No food in her system. No drugs. No clothes. No hair. Washed in bleach. Evidence of plastic sacks in the vicinity of the body. No shoes either. No indication that she walked to that location and lay down to die. Who brought her there? That's one of the questions you need to be asking.'

'And who was she?'

Jane stood at the door.

'You need to find out, Lottie. Before someone else ends up dead or missing from Ragmullin.'

While she was still assessing what Jane had told her, her phone rang. Unidentified mobile number. She answered. It was McMahon.

'Sir?'

'Keep me up to date on all your investigations. You can get me on this number.'

'I will.' *Not*, she added silently.

'Might be no harm having a chat with the O'Donnell family. I've heard that Cynthia Rhodes is doing a feature on them. She's already spoken to them, if I'm correct. Bring yourself up to speed.'

'But sir, I've too much—'

'Do it, Parker.'

'And fuck you too,' she said, when she was sure the call was disconnected.

She had enough reason to speak with the O'Donnells without trying to find out what the journalist was up to.

She flicked through the old file for the phone number.

'Boyd! Get your coat on.'

# CHAPTER SEVENTY

After the detectives had left, Carol felt even worse. The nausea continued unabated, and she called her manager and went home.

She switched on her electric blanket and curled into bed, glad that her mother and father were in town doing the weekly grocery shopping. Wrapping her arms around her stomach, she tried to suppress her queasiness. How long would this last? Three months? Longer? She couldn't handle much more.

She'd have to tell him. Soon. Before it was too late. She missed having Lizzie to talk to. If she was here, she would know what to do. That thought offered her no comfort. Her friend was dead. A quiver of fear tensed her muscles. She hadn't told the guards that she also knew Mollie Hunter. Not a friend really, but Mollie had happened to be there that night. The night he had … Anyway, Mollie had helped and now she was missing.

Was this all because of her? Surely it couldn't be.

But as she lay miserably in her bed, Carol couldn't help feeling that it had everything to do with her.

✳

Wind battered the walls of wherever she was being kept. Grace tried to take short, even breaths, but they came out as strangled gasps. Her eyes were gummy and a rash irritated her skin. It felt like someone had pulled a heavy sack over her head and abandoned her.

Trying to drag herself upright was impossible. She lay there, dampness seeping into her pores, ropes cutting into her flesh and her heart thumping in her ears.

It was useless to fight it. Her situation was hopeless. Mark thought she was in Galway and her mother thought she was with Mark. She was at the mercy of the man who'd brought her here.

A wave of nausea crept up her throat and she struggled not to vomit. She knew that if she did, she would choke to death.

# CHAPTER SEVENTY-ONE

The terrace of houses was surrounded by a stone wall with a door cut into the brickwork. Behind it, a path led to a set of steps up to the front door.

Pushing the creaking wooden door inwards, Lottie studied the two-storey house. Most of the pebble-dash had eroded over time, leaving bare cracked concrete to face the elements. A bush, branches bare, peeked out at the side of the chimney, while a satellite dish hung lopsided from a trail of wires on the other side.

'Bit dilapidated for habitation, don't you think?' she said.

'Donal O'Donnell lives alone. Maybe he hasn't the money to relocate to somewhere, let's say, more upmarket.' Boyd quenched his cigarette and doubled up in a fit of coughing.

'You okay?' she said.

'Think I've a bit of a cold.'

'Keep it to yourself. It sounds more than *a bit*. My mother swears by honey and lemon.'

'Your mother doesn't swear.'

'Piss off, Boyd.'

She pressed the doorbell and waited, blowing hot breath into her cupped hands. The door opened.

'Donal O'Donnell?' she said.

'Yes. You must be Detective Inspector Parker. Come to the kitchen.'

He turned and made his way down the dark, narrow hall. Lottie raised an eyebrow at Boyd. He shook his head as if to say, what?

But she'd recognised the man. From the nursing home. He'd been waiting to see Kane and then, up at the glass window, he'd placed a hand on her injured shoulder. She shivered.

'You must be getting a cold now,' Boyd whispered in her ear. She pulled away from him.

The O'Donnell brothers were seated at a table. The kitchen was dull and dusty and Lottie tried to pinpoint the sour smell. The floor had either been washed with a dirty mop or it hadn't been washed in months.

'Thanks for agreeing to speak with us,' she said, and introduced Boyd. With the five of them in the small room, she began to feel claustrophobic. They all shook hands and sat down.

'Is this about our sister?' Cillian O'Donnell was tall and sleek. His black hair was brushed back behind his ears and his leather jacket covered what looked like a blue lambswool sweater, with the collar of a white shirt tight to his neck. When he'd stood to shake her hand, she noticed he was wearing jeans with the requisite tattered designer cuts at the knees.

His brother, on the other hand, had an unkempt appearance, more in line with the look of their father. His sweater sported holes in the sleeves and she was sure they were not there by design. His face was unshaven and his hair unwashed and scraggy.

She struggled to remember the question.

O'Donnell senior said, 'My daughter. Are you here to tell us something about her?'

'No, I'm sorry, I've no news on Lynn's disappearance. We're investigating the murder of a young woman. Her body was found on Tuesday morning in Ragmullin cemetery.'

Cillian shot out of his chair. 'You got us here on false pretences. We thought you had word about Lynn.'

Finn said, 'We know nothing about any murder.'

Lottie thought he'd had his nose broken at some stage in his life; the bone was crooked. His eyes were dark spots of intensity.

'Please sit down and I'll explain,' she said.

'Yes, explain yourself or I'm going to ask you both to leave,' Donal said, nodding his head, agreeing with his own statement.

He appeared to have sunk into himself. He was probably once tall and striking, but a sense of loss pressed on his shoulders like a boulder, weighing him down. A striped shirt hung loose about his skeletal body, and his jaw bones almost jutted out through paper-thin skin. She noticed he continuously screwed his hands into each other, as if the motion could lessen the pain chewing up his heart.

'First of all, I want to thank you, Cillian and Finn, for agreeing to meet us here with your father. It speeds things up greatly,' she said. 'The reason we wish to speak with you is that your names turned up on a list of people who jog around Rochfort Gardens at weekends.'

'But I thought you said the girl was found dead in the graveyard?' Cillian said. Was he taking on the role of spokesperson?

'That's true,' Lottie said. 'But we're talking to anyone who might have known her. One line of inquiry is that she was stalked, perhaps while jogging.'

'Well, you're not pinning anything on my boys,' Donal said, unfurling his hands to slap the table. 'We have enough grief in this family without you dropping more like dog shit on our doorstep.'

'I understand, Mr O'Donnell. We're merely trying to build up a picture of the deceased.'

'You'd do better to find out what happened to my daughter. Her mother went to her grave without any answers and I fear the same will happen to me.'

'Now, Dad, don't go all melancholic,' Cillian said. He twisted in his chair and faced Lottie. 'You're right, Inspector. Finn and I run

most weekends. Not together. We just happen to be there at the same time.'

Placing a photograph of Elizabeth on the table, Lottie watched for their reactions. Finn folded his arms after a quick glance, but Cillian pulled it towards him and studied it.

'I'm sorry, I don't know her.' He pushed the photo back across the table.

'You sure? Take a closer look.' Boyd leaned in and shoved the photo back again.

'I told you, I've no idea who she is. There must be fifty or sixty people out there on a weekend. I go to run, not to admire the women. I'm a happily married man.'

'Me too,' Finn piped up. Was he destined to always be in his older brother's shadow?

Lottie took out another photo. 'Mollie Hunter. She is missing. Also took part in the weekend runs. Recognise her?'

Both men shook their heads. Remained silent. No other discernible reaction.

'If that's all?' Donal rose from his chair, gingerly. He looked so wan, Lottie thought the man might be sick at any minute.

'I'd love a cup of coffee, if you have it?' she said. Why on earth had she said that?

Donal mumbled, 'I've no groceries in. I was writing a list for Keelan. My daughter-in-law.' He remained standing.

Lottie knew when she was being dismissed. She'd have to talk to the brothers individually. Not give them an opportunity to band together. But they had nothing to hide, had they? As she stood, she caught sight of the photograph on the dresser, a candle burning in front of it.

'It's a decade now, isn't it?' she said.

'Ten years tomorrow.' Donal picked up the frame and ran a finger down the face in the picture. 'My pet never came home.'

'She wasn't in any kind of trouble at the time, was she? Any rows at home?'

'What are you accusing me of?' Donal slammed the photo down. The candle flickered and extinguished itself.

'Nothing at all. I read the file and wondered if Lynn had maybe wanted to disappear. Make a new life for herself away from Ragmullin.'

'Why would you even think that?' Cillian now, standing beside his father. 'What brings you to that conclusion?'

'It's not a conclusion, just an observation.' Lottie eyed Boyd for support, but of course he hadn't read the file. 'Had she a boyfriend?'

'Boyfriend?' Finn said, still seated at the table, his eyes dancing balls of intensity. 'Did someone say something? Did you find out something that you didn't tell us?'

'No, no. There is no mention of it in the file. I just thought a beautiful young woman like Lynn might have been in a relationship.'

The temperature in the room appeared to have dropped at least ten degrees, and Lottie had an immediate urge to look through the rest of the house. Not just to escape the closeness of the three men, but to see if some clue had been overlooked ten years ago.

Back then, five adults had lived in this small house. Three men and two women. What had it been like? Cramped and full of hormones. Had they sat around this very table to eat meals as a close, happy family? Or was the tension she felt now even worse back then. Strings pulled so taut that eventually one snapped?

Donal said, 'My daughter could have had any man in the world. Lads were knocking down my front door wanting to bring her out. But no. Lynn was a career woman. She wanted to work her way up the ladder, to the very top. And she wasn't going to be held back by some snot-nosed Ragmullin tosser.'

'Someone from Dublin, maybe? A lad at her office?'

'My girl's life was dissected by you lot. The only thing left unknown by the end of the investigation was her whereabouts.'

Lottie gazed over Donal's shoulder at his two sons. They were standing on opposite sides of the table, glaring.

'And neither of you ever saw Elizabeth Byrne or Mollie Hunter out running?'

'Can't remember everyone we see,' Cillian said.

'Is that a no?'

'It's all you're getting. I'll see you out, Inspector.'

# CHAPTER SEVENTY-TWO

Back at the office, Lottie threw her jacket on the back of a chair. 'I can't figure out whether those three men are just losers in need of sympathy or they're hiding something.'

Kirby raised his head. 'What three men?'

'The two O'Donnell brothers and their father.'

'The family of the girl that's been missing for years?'

'Ten.'

'Right.' Kirby stood and licked his fingers before attempting to calm the bush that was his hair.

'What's up?' Lottie folded her arms, thinking she could do with a ten-minute nap. The chances of that were zero.

'I've a bad feeling about Paddy McWard.'

'We're not in the business of feelings, Kirby. Facts and evidence.'

'You go by your gut, don't you?'

She couldn't argue with that. 'Go on.'

'We, Lynch and I, had been carrying out surveillance on the travelling community for the last few weeks.' He hesitated.

'Jesus, Kirby, spit it out.' She hauled herself out of the chair and headed for her office, beckoning him to follow and shut the door. 'What's bothering you?'

'I've gone back over our notes. I know we did most of our work in the housing estates, but we also covered the traveller site. He hasn't been around any night. I don't know where he goes. But my informant tells me no one else has a clue either.'

'Someone knows.'

'I get that. But he has a wife and young child …'

'Had a wife and child.' Lottie felt a shiver rattling her spine. 'Do you think he killed them?'

'No. Well I'm not sure, but I'm wondering if he was involved in something that went haywire, or he double-crossed someone and this was a revenge attack. A warning to him.'

'Some bloody warning.' She mulled it over. 'Bring him in for questioning. He may or may not have killed his family, but he's guilty of something or other.'

Kirby opened the door before closing it again. 'Lynch is gone home again. Not feeling well. She said to tell you.'

'That's fine. Let me know when McWard is here. And I'm still waiting for someone to locate Matt Mullin!'

'His photo is on social media and we've put out an alert for him.' Kirby scooted out the door.

Once she was alone, Lottie tried to get a handle on McWard. Checking PULSE, she once again scrutinised the entries under his name. Disturbing the peace. A few petty misdemeanours. Then something caught her eye. Something she had missed when she'd checked yesterday. Surely it couldn't mean anything. Then again …

She tugged the sleeves of her sweater and studied the screen. Maybe McWard had some questions to answer besides the obvious one of why his home had been burned to the ground and his family annihilated.


Boyd stopped her at the door.

'I've been going through Elizabeth's notebook.'

'The one you took from her room?'

He nodded and pointed to a page. Lottie looked over his shoulder at the words written in multicoloured gel pens, surrounded with hearts and stars.

'A bit childish for a twenty-five-year-old.'

'The notebook was from years ago. When she was a lot younger. But … here, read it.' He handed it over. 'Look at the name.' He sat back on the edge of his desk and folded his arms.

Scanning down the page, Lottie concluded it was a diary entry. 'She must have been about fifteen when this was written. It's just about school. And exams and stuff. I can't see any name … Jesus, Boyd!'

'Not Jesus, no.'

'Bridie McWard. Was she in Elizabeth's class in school? She told me she finished her Leaving Cert.'

'So, was Elizabeth a friend or a foe?'

'What's up?' Kirby asked.

'I'll read it out.' Lottie squinted at the pink writing. '"Today Bridie McWard got an A for her history essay. I'm so pleased for her. Not."'

'Not what?' Kirby asked, sticking an unlit cigar butt between his lips.

Lottie looked over the edge of the notebook at him and cocked her head to one side. 'She either means she wasn't pleased or she was going to write something else and never finished the sentence.' She flipped over to the next page. It was full of colourful doodles. The following page had a poem. She read aloud, '"He is so near, yet so far, I cannot ever go there. It is taboo. I am forever lost to his undying love. And he can never be mine."'

'That's a bit deep for a fifteen-year-old,' Boyd said.

'Unrequited love, or someone she fancied but was already taken?'

'Could be anything, but it can't possibly have anything to do with her murder. Can it?'

'But there is a connection to Bridie McWard, who is also dead. Has Paddy arrived yet?' she asked Kirby.

He lifted the phone. 'I'll check. And there's still no sign of Matt Mullin or Mollie Hunter, boss.'

'I'm going to have a quick look around Mollie's flat,' Lottie said. 'When I come back, I want McWard in the interview room, waiting to be questioned. Boyd, you come with me.'

She'd got the key from Gilly, and now she stood in Mollie Hunter's tiny kitchenette. Cereal had caked to a rock on the bottom of the breakfast bowl, and a spoon was similarly congealed.

'Not much to see,' Boyd shouted from the bedroom.

'Why didn't she share with someone?' Lottie asked, even though she thought she'd only been thinking it. 'I'm sure the rent around here is high.'

The building shook and a window rattled.

'What the hell …?'

She pierced the wooden blind with her fingers. A train hissed along the tracks. She could see into the carriages as they sped by. It was possible the people on the train could see right back in at her.

Extracting her fingers, she let the wooden slats settle.

'No diaries.' Boyd's voice echoed from the other room.

'Young people nowadays don't write in diaries. Everything is on their phones, Facebook and … That reminds me …' She stood at the door and watched Boyd systematically going through the drawers of the dressing table.

'Reminds you of what?'

'Elizabeth and Mollie's phones. Not a peep from them.'

'Probably in the bottom of the canal.' With gloved fingers, Boyd held up a plastic bag with a red thong inside. 'What is this?'

Lottie shook her head and turned away. 'Sometimes you disgust me, Boyd.'

'No, I'm serious. I know it's a thong. But it doesn't match any other item of underwear in the drawer. Everything is practical and clean. This is not clean and it's the only one. And it's in a plastic bag! If she had underwear for special occasions, don't you think she'd have more than one, even a matching set?'

Returning to the room, Lottie held out an evidence bag and Boyd dropped the bag with the thong into it.

'Maybe it isn't hers,' she said.

'If it isn't hers, why is it here?'

'We'll ask her if we find her.'

'When we find her.'

'Okay, Mr Positivity. When we find her.'

Inside the front door, a line of hooks held jackets and coats. Lottie went through all the pockets and checked the soles of the shoes and boots.

'Anything?' Boyd asked, coming up behind her.

'Not even a tissue.'

'That's what struck me. Her neatness. Everything in order, in its proper place. The only items left unwashed are the cereal bowl and spoon, presumably because she might have been rushing. And the red thong.'

'Still doesn't tell us anything,' Lottie said, then added, 'But Elizabeth was fastidiously neat too. Two similar personalities?'

'What did you make of Bridie McWard?' Boyd asked.

Lottie closed her eyes, recalled the shining table and white leather sofa. 'She was a neat freak also.'

'Not like your kids then.'

'Not like my kids at all. Does it mean anything?'

'I don't think so.'

'But I think something links these three women, and we'd better find out what, because it might give us an answer.'

'Do you think Mollie is dead?'

Lottie shook her head. 'My anxiety levels are at a status red warning level, but I sincerely hope she isn't dead.'

# CHAPTER SEVENTY-THREE

Lottie placed the evidence bag on the desk.

'What is that?' Gilly O'Donoghue said, her eyes widening in shock.

'You know what it is. Why did Mollie have it?'

Gilly turned up her nose. 'How would I know what kind of underwear she likes? We're not that close.'

'It was the only one. No other similar types of underwear. And it was in that plastic freezer bag. Don't you think that's odd?'

Gilly shrugged her shoulders helplessly.

Lottie persisted. 'Why did she give you the key?'

'She lives alone. Her family are in London. I believe I'm her only friend.'

'Did you have any sense that she was in danger? Feared anyone?'

'No. Not at all.'

'Then why the need to give you a key? That puzzles me.' Lottie tapped Mollie's name into PULSE. It came up blank. 'She hasn't even got a parking ticket.'

'She hasn't got a car.'

'When did she give you the key?'

Gilly thought for a moment, brushed her hair behind her ears. 'We'd been friends a good few months, but I think it was sometime before Christmas. Let me think.' She screwed her knuckles into her brow. 'It was mid December. I was pissed at Kirby because he was working on that stakeout thing. Mollie and I went for drinks and

on to a nightclub. She asked if I'd hold onto her spare key in case she ever got locked out or I wanted a bed. I didn't think it odd. I just said, sure.'

'And she gave it to you that night?'

'Yes. We shared a taxi. Dropped her off first, then me. Nothing out of the ordinary. A few drinks, a dance and then home.'

'She had no other friends? No boyfriend?'

Gilly shook her head. 'Not that I know of.'

'Did she know Elizabeth Byrne or Bridie McWard?'

'Sorry, boss, I have no idea.'

'What did you talk about? When you were out?'

Gilly smiled. 'Mainly it was just me giving out about Kirby.'

'That's an—' Lottie clamped her mouth shut before her words hurt the young woman in front of her.

'An odd match?' Gilly laughed. 'You were going to say that and you'd be right. He is a lot older than me, but you know what? We click. I like him. And he's good fun to be with, so I don't care what people say behind my back.'

Lottie returned Gilly's smile and felt a motherly instinct take root. She really liked the young guard. Kirby was branded a lovable rogue, so she could understand how Gilly would be attracted to him.

'I admire you,' Lottie said. 'You're a great worker and I appreciate your help on this case. You'll make a good detective some day soon.'

A smile split Gilly's face. God love her, Lottie thought.

'Thanks,' Gilly said. 'That means a lot to me.'

'You've spoken to Mollie's family?'

'Her dad. He hasn't seen her since Christmas. From what I can gather, they're not in regular communication.'

'Have another word with him. See if you can find out anything, anything that might point us in the right direction.'

'Will do. Straight away.'

When Gilly left, the office felt darker. Lottie wondered what everyone was saying behind *her* back. About her and Boyd. She was not about to give them any reason to talk. Last night was a mistake. A nice one, but a mistake.

Kirby waved at her from the outside office.

She would have to get that glass replaced and a full wooden door installed.

Then she realised he was calling her.

'McWard is here,' he said.


After sending off the red thong for analysis, Lottie made her way to the interview room with Boyd.

'I'm sincerely sorry for your loss,' she said as she sat down in front of Paddy McWard. His jacket was flung across the table. He was wearing jeans and a short-sleeved black T-shirt.

'What are you doing about it, eh? Persecuting me won't help find the bastard who murdered my wife and son.'

'Do you want a solicitor present?' Lottie nodded at Boyd to switch on the recording equipment. 'I've some questions for you and I want you to be clear that you can have a solicitor present if you—'

'I don't want no poxy solicitor.' He folded his bare tattooed arms and leaned back in the chair. 'Get on with it.'

'Right then.' Lottie flicked to the page in her notebook with times and dates given to her by Kirby. 'Where were you last night?'

He unfolded his arms so quickly, she blinked at the sound of the smack he gave the table.

'I'm telling you here and now, you're wasting my time and yours if you think I could do something so ... so horrible as to burn my family alive.'

'Just answer the question,' Boyd said.

With a sigh, McWard appeared to relent. 'I was away.'

'Come on now. I need more.' Lottie was pissed off. So far this morning, they had achieved nothing except for a red thong that probably had absolutely feck all to do with anything.

Tugging at his hair, McWard bit his trembling lip. Jesus, don't cry, she thought.

'I don't want to tell you if I don't have to. Where I was or what I was doing has nothing to do with the fire. Take my word for it.'

'I'm sorry, but that's not enough. I need to know.'

He rubbed his hand over his nose and sniffed. Dear God, the big man was sobbing.

'I loved her. Bridie. In my own way. But she never believed that. When Tommy was born, she locked me out. Not with a key turned in the door, but out of her heart. I'm a good bit older than her. And it was hard for me to be … you know … a loving husband. And the baby, little Tommy, he cried a lot. I couldn't hack it. So I escaped. Every night. I'd drive around for hours and come back in the morning or sometimes in the afternoon, and then I'd disappear again.'

'That's a load of bollocks,' Boyd said.

'It's the truth.'

Lottie didn't know whether to believe him or not. 'Give us an idea of where you drove to last night.'

'Like I said, around.'

Lottie sighed. 'You can make this a lot easier if you just tell us. Otherwise I'll have to keep you here until I can verify that you were nowhere near your home last night when it was torched.'

'You're sure it was arson, then?'

'Yes.'

'Bastards. I knew it. Just knew it.'

'What did you know?' Lottie said.

'They couldn't leave me alone.' He was twisting his hands into knots, his face screwed up. She couldn't determine if it was rage or sorrow causing him to buckle.

'Who are you talking about, Paddy?'

'You wouldn't understand.' He looked up at her, his dark eyes piercing through her. They were unreadable. He intrigued her; not in the same way as the usual criminals who sat across from her, but as a man. She had to physically stop herself reaching out to touch his hand, to tell him it was going to be okay.

'Try us,' Boyd snapped.

'If you're not arresting me, I'm going home.' McWard paused, before crumbling with the realisation that he had no home to go to.

'Did you know Elizabeth Byrne?' Lottie asked.

'Who?' A line of confusion knitted his brow before his hair fell in a black crest over it.

'The woman who was murdered next door to your home. In the cemetery.'

'No, I did not know her.'

'Did Bridie know her?'

'I don't know.' The big man folded up into himself, fingers crunching into his eyes.

There was a knock on the door and Kirby beckoned Lottie outside.

She switched off the recording device. 'Give me a minute. Would you like a coffee?'

McWard recovered some composure and dropped his hands. 'Two minutes. I'm not waiting any longer than that.' The thick tattooed arms were folded once again as he stared at a point on the wall above her head.

Out in the corridor, Lottie took the sheet of paper from Kirby's hand.

'DNA result?' she questioned.

'We found a match on the system.'

'But this sample is from ...' She glanced at the name at the top of the page. 'This can't be ... It doesn't make sense.'

'It doesn't make sense, for sure, but it's been checked twice.'

'Shit, Kirby. This is ... I don't know. What is it?'

'Weird?'

'Yeah. Weird will do for now.'

# CHAPTER SEVENTY-FOUR

They let McWard go. They had nothing to hold him on. But he was issued with a warning not to disappear again.

'I think it's a mistake letting him off like that,' Boyd said. He sat down, crossing one leg over his knee, making himself comfortable in her office.

'I don't think he killed his family. I've sent uniforms to shadow him. He's too distraught to do anything.' She showed him the page Kirby had given her. 'We have something more urgent on our hands than Paddy McWard. The body at the lake.'

'What the hell?' Boyd dropped his leg to the floor. 'Lynn O'Donnell? But she disappeared a decade ago.'

'And now she's turned up dead.'

'But that body at the lake ... it was a woman in her thirties. It can't be Lynn O'Donnell. She was only twenty-five.'

'When she went missing, she was twenty-five then. But this DNA result means she was alive, Boyd. All those years, she was alive!'

'Shit. Where was she all that time?'

'I don't know, but we better find out before her brothers do.' She made her way across the small office, but her arm was pulled back as she opened the door. Boyd was standing into her space, right beside her, and staring into her eyes as she turned around. 'What?' she said.

'Sit down for a minute. You need to think this out clearly. Before McMahon gets on your case.'

Breathing out, Lottie put a hand on his arm. 'You're right. Get Kirby in here too. Then we'll try to regroup.'

She walked away from him and slumped down at her desk. She opened the cold case file. Unclipped the photograph, held it up to the light. 'Where were you?'

'Lottie?'

She dropped the photo. 'The implications of this are huge. Corrigan was the lead detective at the time. Everyone thought Lynn was dead. Only her family believed she could still be alive. The way her body was when she was found can only mean one thing.'

'What?'

'She was held somewhere against her will. Her poor father. How am I going to tell him?' She pursed her lips and gulped. This was a right mess. She'd put a hole through the cuff of her sleeve, she'd poked it so hard with her finger.

'First things first,' Boyd said. 'How are you going to tell Superintendent McMahon?'

'Tell me what?' The voice boomed as the door was opened.

'Oh, shit.' Lottie covered her face with her hands.

'Well at least the media can't blame you for this, Parker.' McMahon had convened them all in the incident room.

'As a force, we failed this girl,' Lottie said.

'Now is not the time for that kind of post-mortem,' McMahon paraded up and down at the front of the room. 'Concentrate. Review the file. Look at the evidence from the body.'

'Ten years, though,' Lottie said. 'Was she at the lake all that time?'

McMahon seemed to consider this. 'Question the geezer who reported the body, and the caravan park manager. You lot missed something.'

Lottie nodded and said, 'Prick' under her breath.

'Heard you,' Boyd whispered.

She looked up at McMahon. 'The state pathologist confirmed that Elizabeth Byrne's clothes were washed in water that came from Ladystown lake. Could her murder and Lynn O'Donnell's disappearance be linked?' As she said the words, she thought how stupid they sounded.

'There's a whole decade separating the two events,' he said.

'But only a few days separating the discovery of their bodies.'

'Who else lives at that location? I want everyone interviewed.'

'We already did that,' Kirby said.

'Do it again, because this time you're looking for somewhere this woman lived for ten years,' McMahon yelled. 'Ten fucking years under your snotty noses.'

'Hey, there's no need to abuse my detectives.' Lottie marched up to him. 'None of us here worked that original case. Superintendent Corrigan was in charge.'

'As you may know, he had surgery yesterday. There's no point bothering him with this.'

'How is he?' Lottie said.

McMahon chewed his bottom lip. 'I don't know. Perhaps you could give Mrs Corrigan a call? When you get time, that is. Don't mention this cock-up.'

'What? Right, sir, but—'

'Was there something you wanted to add?'

'Is there any chance of extra support from another division?'

'Where is Detective Lynch?'

'She's ill at the moment.'

'I'll see what I can do. In the meantime, get uniforms up to speed. Involve every last detective that works at this station. I want answers. Do you hear?'

Nods were accompanied by a blinding silence.

'Am I talking to myself? I want answers and I want them now, and the only way you're going to get them, you dozy lot, is by action. Get out of here.'

'We need to inform the O'Donnells,' Lottie said. 'Before the media get wind of it.'

'Do it. Because I can guarantee that once the media find out, they will push us into a full-on force ten gale.'

# CHAPTER SEVENTY-FIVE

'Back so soon?' Donal O'Donnell led the two detectives into his home.

'Are your sons around?'

'They left shortly after you.'

'Do you think you could ask them to come back again?'

Donal appeared to shudder as he lowered himself onto a chair. 'This is it then. The bad news I've dreaded every day since my little woman went missing. You can tell me. I'll tell the boys.'

Two watery eyes stared up at her and Lottie tried not to avert her own. She was about to crush any remaining hope from the bones of Donal O'Donnell. The kettle whistled and steam rose behind him.

'Better switch that off, love. It'll keep boiling for another two minutes if you don't.'

'Do you want a cup of something?'

'No. I'm okay. Sit down.'

She hated breaking bad news to anyone. But this … this was going to kill the old man. 'You're right, Mr O'Donnell, I do have bad news.'

'Well you're hardly here to tell me I won the lottery, are you?'

'No, I'm not. It's about your Lynn.'

He began refolding the newspaper along the creases where he had folded it previously. 'What about my girl. You find her? I'm guessing she's not alive, or she'd be skipping in the door behind you.'

'I'm so sorry.'

'Don't be sorry. You didn't know her. She was my baby. Now I can finally grieve for her.'

'Are you sure you're okay?'

'Holy God!' The old man stood up suddenly and stretched his arms out wide, like he was welcoming the son of God down on top of him. Or ridding himself of Lucifer, the devil. Lottie had to stop herself squirming. 'The evil that stalks this land is living right here,' he shouted. 'Under this very roof.'

'Hey, steady on,' Boyd said.

'Sit down, please,' Lottie said.

'Piss off, the pair of you.'

'Do you want to know about Lynn?' Lottie asked.

'She's dead. What else can you tell me to ease my pain? Her bones are bare and naked of life. That's all that's left after all this time. I don't need you to tell me. I know.'

'That's not exactly the case,' Lottie said slowly. 'You see, Mr O'Donnell, the thing is, we believe your daughter was alive up to at least two weeks ago.'

The transformation was instantaneous. Donal O'Donnell fell to the floor. A loud wail shattered the silence left in the wake of Lottie's words. Then it was quiet.

\*

Matt Mullin eyed his mother from under his long lashes. She had her arms folded, leaning against his open bedroom door.

'I can't cover for you any longer, Matt. They know you're here. Please, tell me what you've done. I might be able to help you.'

He closed his eyes and curled into the wall, like he used to do when he was nine. 'I don't want to talk about it.'

'If you won't talk to me, call your therapist. Are you taking your medication?'

'Go away. I want to sleep.'

'You were out all night. Where were you?'

Her voice screeched through his skull like chalk on a board.

'Will you shut up with the questions. My head is ready to burst.'

'Did you do something bad, Matt?'

He blew out a breath, opened his eyes and sat up in bed. A pungent sourness swarmed about him. Was it coming from his body, or from her? Cradling the pillow to his chest, he looked over at the woman who'd given birth to him; who had loved and tended to him all his life. And he hated every bone in her body. She was a stranger. All he'd ever wanted was Elizabeth and she hadn't wanted him.

Throwing the pillow to the floor, he pulled on his shoes and walked by his mother, nudging her angrily with his shoulder as he passed.

'Matt? Matt! Where are you going?'

Her voice trailed behind him as he ran from the house.

✳

Grace tried to blink, but her eyes were still glued shut. She couldn't move.

Where was she? She tried to remember.

The train. The man.

She tried to scream, but her lips felt like they were taped shut. She wanted to cry, but no tears could escape. She wanted to shout, but her words were snared deep in her chest.

She grappled against her restraints and struggled with her reality as she drifted back to the darkness.

# CHAPTER SEVENTY-SIX

A magpie eyed Lottie from a bare branch of a tree before extending its wings and flying off.

She was standing on the step waiting for Boyd to finish his cigarette. She dared not ask for a drag. Too many bad habits already. 'They're taking their time.'

'It's not gone five minutes since you phoned them. Patience.'

'I haven't time for patience. We have a mountain of work and this—'

'You want a drag?' He held out the cigarette. 'Calm your nerves?'

She declined the offer with a lie. 'My nerves are very calm. I just want to get over to the nursing home to have a chat with Queenie McWard.'

'Why do you need to do that? She's already been notified of the deaths.'

'I'm not rightly sure, but I want to establish if there was a connection between Elizabeth and Bridie. The notebook. Remember?'

'But what does it matter? It's not going to solve anything even if they did sit beside each other at school.'

'You never know.'

'Here's the cavalry.' Boyd threw down the cigarette and ground it out with the heel of his shoe. The sky had darkened and the air held the impending threat of rain.

They waited as four people came through the wooden door in the outer wall.

'You know he has a bad heart?' one of the brothers said. Cillian. The clean-cut one.

'Your father is in shock,' Lottie said. 'Otherwise he's fine.'

'Fine? Ha, you need to go back to fucking garda school.' That was the untidy one.

'Calm down, Finn.' A dainty little woman in a pink sweater spoke. Her eyes were red-rimmed. From crying, Lottie wondered, or something else?

'Are you his wife?' Lottie asked, nodding towards Finn.

'No, I'm Cillian's wife, Keelan. Sara there is Finn's wife.' She pointed to the overweight woman with hair streeling around the shoulders of a black woollen coat.

'Jesus, this is a right mess,' Cillian snapped.

Lottie recalled thinking the exact same thing earlier that morning. 'Let's go inside and see what needs to be done.'

The family shuffled through the narrow door and down the short hallway. As Lottie followed with Boyd, she noticed that Keelan had held back.

'Are you okay?'

'There are some things you need to know,' Keelan said quietly. 'But I can't talk now. This is my number, please give me a call.'

Lottie took the piece of paper from her and slid it into the pocket of her jeans. Keelan looked up with tired eyes and mouthed a thank you.

'What was that about?' Boyd asked once the woman was out of earshot.

'I have absolutely no idea.'

'Nothing new there so.'

'Shut up, Boyd.'

✳

She had seen one photograph of Lynn on display in the kitchen, but as Lottie entered the living room, she walked into a shrine.

The wall in front of her was covered with photos of the dead woman. All framed, with dust gathering in the corners. She assumed the late Mrs O'Donnell, Donal's wife, had once kept them pristine and dust-free. But the room appeared not to have been used in months, if not years. The furniture was dated, floral and grimy. The fireplace was empty and a two-bar electric heater blazed from a corner after Cillian plugged it in. The smell of burning dust smothered the air in the room.

She tried to imagine how it might have been at one time. Filled with the happiness of children laughing and playing, or watching the battered old television on the corner table. But no, she didn't get that image. A shiver scurried up her spine and rested on the crest of the bones between her shoulder blades.

A hideous brown wallpaper with faded flowers was just about visible behind the multitude of photographs, and a pair of thick velour curtains hung over lacy nets yellow with age and smoke. The carpet was threadbare, so she knew the space had been well used, but she felt like it was a Dickensian room. Dark, dank and dusty.

And then it struck her. Among the photos hanging before her, she could not see one of the two boys, or of the boys with their sister. Odd. She scratched her head trying to figure it out.

The seven adults crowded into the small space and Lottie stood with her back to the mantel beside Boyd. Donal sat in an armchair, while his sons squeezed onto the sofa, bookended by their wives. Lottie was glad no tea had been offered or they'd have to ferry it in on a rota. There was hardly room to raise an elbow.

'Spit it out,' Finn said, his words laced with bitterness.

'We found a body on Thursday night. Out on Barren Point at Ladystown lake.'

'Thursday! And you're only telling us now?' Finn tried to stand up but was wedged between his wife and his brother.

'The body was that of a female in her mid thirties,' Lottie continued, trying to keep her tone sympathetic. 'We found nothing on it to allow us to make a visual identification. It was only this morning that her DNA was matched to a woman on the missing persons list.'

'DNA? What DNA?'

'Shut up, Finn.' Cillian nudged his brother in the chest with his elbow. 'Let her speak. You can ask your questions later.'

Thank God, Lottie thought. Someone talking sense at last.

'Without the DNA match, we had no reason to believe the body was that of Lynn. As you know, ten years missing usually means that the person is deceased.'

'She's deceased now,' Donal muttered.

'But it can't be Lynn,' Cillian said. 'She was only twenty-five. You say this woman was in her thirties.'

'I'm sorry but it is Lynn. We believe she was held somewhere for the last ten years.'

'Where? Where was our Lynn?' Finn said.

'We're trying to find that out.'

'Was she murdered?' He continued with his questions despite the daggers Cillian was throwing at him with his eyes.

'There's no evidence of murder. Not from the preliminary post-mortem results. It's possible she died of natural causes.'

'Nothing natural about being out at Barren Point on a cold February night.' Donal was pulling at his chin.

'It's early days yet—'

'It's a decade too late, that's what it is.'

'Mr O'Donnell, we're doing our best to get answers.'

'You didn't do your best back then; how can we believe you now?'

Lottie sighed and glanced at Boyd for help.

He straightened his back. 'The body was washed in bleach and wrapped in black bin bags, which were then ripped open, leaving her body exposed to the weather and wildlife.'

Jesus, Boyd, Lottie thought, there was no need to be so blunt. But she didn't blame him. The family were not displaying the emotions she would have expected. The overriding emotion in the room, the one she felt more forcefully than any other, was resentment; maybe anger. That usually came a couple of days later. After shock and sorrow. There was something else too. An underlying sensation that she couldn't identify. Not yet. Later, maybe.

'You're a bad bastard,' Finn shouted.

Freeing himself from the constraints of the bodies on the couch, he lunged at Boyd. His fist connected before Lottie could get her hands out of her pockets. As she moved, Cillian grabbed his brother in an armlock and wrestled him to the floor.

'Shut your mouth,' he snarled. 'You're an eejit. Assaulting a guard. What do you think you're doing?'

'I'm going to kill the fucker.'

'Boys! Shut up!' Donal stood and put a foot on Finn's back. 'You're a disgrace to your sister's memory. And to your poor mother.'

When Lottie glanced Boyd's way, he was rubbing his cheek and eye socket, glaring at the men on the floor. She placed a hand on his arm and held him back. Things were bad enough without him retaliating.

'Did Lynn have a baby?' Lottie asked.

Finn got to his feet.

She scanned the men's faces. All three registered varying degrees of the same expression. Horror.

At last, Donal spoke. 'Not that I know of. Why?'

'We suspect she had given birth.'

'This just gets worse,' he said. 'Is there a child out there somewhere?'

'I intend to find out,' Lottie said. 'One final thing.' She opened the flap on her bag and took out a piece of paper. 'This was found … on the body. Do you recognise it?'

'What's that?' Donal said. 'Where did you get it? I don't understand.'

'It's a photograph of a sterling silver Claddagh ring. Does it mean anything to you?'

The O'Donnells remained tight-lipped, shaking their heads. A dead loss to pursue it now, but Lottie knew it meant something to them. Their faces told that story.

'Look, you're all in shock,' she said, though that wasn't the word she wanted to use. 'We'll call back later. Give you time to get your heads around this awful news. Let me know if you remember anything about the ring. Make some tea and talk to each other.'

'Tea? Tea, she says,' Finn said, his voice coming to life. 'I know what I'd like to do with a pot of boiling tea. And drinking it isn't on my agenda.'

The naked anger in his words stunned Lottie. She had to get out, and quickly. Otherwise she, not Boyd, would be the one lashing out.

# CHAPTER SEVENTY-SEVEN

It had started to drizzle while they'd been inside, and the temperature had risen a little.

'I'm going to see Queenie McWard,' Lottie said. 'I'll drop you at the office. Find out what else Kirby has dug up.' She crossed the road to the car park.

'I need a doctor.' Boyd was still rubbing his cheek.

'You won't die. But if you really feel you need one …'

'That lunatic should be locked up.'

'I'll lock you up if you don't shut up.' She unlocked the car. 'Get a grip.'

Boyd stared at her across the roof. 'What's eating you?'

'Something was off in there. Did you feel it?'

'Unsettling.'

'I can't put my finger on it. But it'll come to me.'

'Right. Why did you tell them that Lynn had had a child? That's a bit of a conundrum, isn't it?'

'I wanted to see their reaction.'

She started the car and headed up under the bridge, past the train station. The traffic lights were red. The wipers swished across the windscreen, dragging scum with them, making visibility problematic.

'Those brothers were straining at the leash,' she said. 'It's like they can't stand each other.'

'Most siblings are the same.'

'I loved my brother.'

'He died when you were four. How can you remember that far back? He probably pulled your pigtails and you hated him for it.'

'How'd you know I had—'

'Just saying.'

'Well don't.'

She glanced at Boyd. His head was resting back on the seat, eyes closed, the red mark pulsing on his cheek. She wanted to reach out, to feel the tenderness of last night, but now was a different time. Now it was work. And that was the way it had to stay. Professional. Gripping the steering wheel, leaning over it, trying to see through the film of grease, she waited for the green light. She couldn't start a relationship with Boyd. No way.

'Hate,' she said.

'What?'

'That's what it was.'

'I'm a bit lost.' Boyd ran his fingers over his cheek and winced.

'The tension in that room. Among the O'Donnell family. It was more than anger. It was pure hatred.'

Raindrops trickled down the window. The cemetery looked drab and grey in the distance. Lottie went up in the elevator, then made her way along the corridor to Queenie McWard's room.

The old lady was half sitting up in bed, twiddling her rosary beads. She appeared to have aged thirty years.

'Saw the fire last night. It was one of the *teachíns.*'

'*Teachín?*'

'That's Irish for a little house. Did you not go to school? My Bridie did. Learned a lot. Got a job. Did she tell you that?' Tears rested in the hard crevices of the old woman's face. It was lined like a delta waiting for the tide to come in. 'Until that good-for-nothing

proposed marriage. That was all fine, but he was suffering from a broken heart.'

'You mean Paddy?'

'Yes, Paddy. Good-for-nothing, that's what he is. Did I say that already?'

'I'm sorry to have to ask questions at this sad time, Queenie, but have you any idea why someone would want to burn down their home?'

'And murder my daughter and grandson? We are outcasts in this town …'

'I don't think that's true at all. As long as I can remember, there's been a traveller community in Ragmullin. Of course, there are the usual public order offences, but you get that everywhere and—'

'Prejudice. That's what's rife. Always has been and always will be. That's the reason the *teachín* was burned.'

Lottie sighed and stared at the ceiling.

'Don't be rolling your eyes, young lady. I may be old but I'm not blind. Not yet.'

'I was just thinking. This may have nothing to do with prejudice. I think it might be related to something Paddy's involved in.'

'Paddy's always involved in something or other. But when he married my Bridie, he promised me he was going to be good. I thought he was doing okay for himself and my girl.'

'Doing what?'

'This and that.'

'Queenie, I need to know if he was into dodgy dealings; something that brought the wrath of someone down on his family.'

The old woman tucked an elbow beneath her birdlike frame and tried to raise herself up in the bed. The scent of lavender wafted from the sheets as Lottie leaned over to assist. A hand of bones with a ring on each finger pushed her away. 'Don't need your help.'

Once she was sitting, Queenie squinted over the rim of her spectacles. 'Boxing. That's what he was into.'

'Bare-knuckle fights?' Lottie thought of Kirby and Lynch, trying to get to the root of the activity.

'Nothing illegal, so he said. Travelled the country to boxing clubs. Training young lads.'

That might account for his absences, Lottie thought.

'My Bridie was in here crying like a baby more days than I care to count. Always about him. Her Paddy. She hadn't a clue what he was up to. So I sent for him. Came in here like a lamb to slaughter, he did. I had my say and he had his.' She clamped her lips together.

'And? He told you he was teaching boys to box?'

'He did. Boys *and* girls nowadays.'

'But he was disappearing all night.'

'I know. Told me that sometimes he had to stay over. If it ran late. That's what he said.'

Lottie wondered *where* he stayed over. And why hadn't he told her all this? If it was an innocent activity, surely he wouldn't have been reticent in divulging it. She knew it was unusual for members of the travelling community to be unfaithful, but that was what she was thinking now. She'd have to get Paddy to reveal all, otherwise he was looking at a charge of manslaughter, if not murder.

'He didn't do it, if that's what you're thinking. Not this time, anyway.'

'What's that supposed to mean?'

'Don't get stroppy with me, young lady. I'm just telling it as I see it. Like I said, I'm not blind yet.'

'I'm under a lot of pressure. What with the fire, the murder in the cemetery, a young woman missing after getting the train home, and the body at the lake, it's all—'

'Missing after getting the train? That's what happened to the young lass years ago.'

'I'm talking about Mollie Hunter. She's been missing since Wednesday.'

Queenie slipped down in the bed, appearing to shrink in size as the sheet covered her bony frame.

'What is it?' Lottie asked, alarmed.

'History repeating itself. That's what it is,' the old woman croaked.

'I don't follow you.' Lottie wanted to escape out of the ward. Away from the smell of old people. Away from the creaking bones of Queenie McWard.

The old woman grabbed Lottie's hand. She almost shrieked at the swiftness of the movement.

'That girl was no good. No good for any relation of mine. But that wasn't the real story. They thought *he* was no good for her.' Queenie folded up in a fit of coughing. Foam gathered at the corner of her mouth and a bony ring-clad hand pulled at her lips.

Lottie pressed the call button for a nurse.

Medical staff filled the room, pushing Lottie to one side, and she watched as they worked vigorously on the little old woman.

'Please don't die, Queenie,' she whispered.

She had so many more questions, but it looked like she wouldn't be able to ask them. Not today.

She was moving towards the door when it dawned on her. She glanced back towards the scrum of medical staff. The silver Claddagh ring amid the gold bands on the skeletal hand.

She left the room. Left the hum of machines and the shouts of nurses and doctors. Left Queenie McWard to her fate.

Sitting in her car outside the nursing home, Lottie felt the rusting wheels of her brain begin to turn. Picking up speed. It was there. Within her grasp. She just had to think. Her phone rang.

'This better be good, Boyd, because you've interrupted my thoughts. I was getting somewhere, and now it's gone.'

'You need to get to Carol O'Grady's house now. I'll see you there.'

# CHAPTER SEVENTY-EIGHT

They'd received no response from ringing the bell which appeared broken, and now Lottie was banging on Carol O'Grady's door.

Boyd's eye was beginning to yellow and bruise as a result of the whack he'd taken.

The door opened.

'Terry?' The young man's eyes were sunk in his head. Was he drunk, or high? At this hour of the day?

'Who wants to know?'

'I met you the other day. DI Lottie Parker and DS Boyd. Do you remember?'

'Nah.'

'We want to speak with Carol.'

'She's at work. Ma and Da are in town.'

'I think she's here.' Lottie ducked under the teenager's arm.

'You can't do that,' Terry and Boyd said together.

'I just did.' Lottie stood at the foot of the stairs and shouted up. 'Carol. I want to have a word.'

Footsteps sounded on the landing and Carol appeared. 'What's with all the hammering? I'm trying to sleep.'

Lottie beckoned the young woman down the stairs. 'Would you put the kettle on, Terry?'

'I'm going out.' He bundled past Boyd and down the path.

'You might need a coat,' Lottie shouted after him.

'Fuck the coat.'

Lottie and Boyd followed Carol into the sitting room.

'How are you feeling?'

'Sick as a dog. Had to leave work early.'

'Pregnancy can do that, you know.'

'Shh. Keep your voice down.' Carol swung her head in the direction of the door leading to the kitchen.

'Don't worry. Terry said your parents are in town.'

'What does he know? He's been drinking down the tracks since last night.'

'We want to ask you about Mollie Hunter.' Lottie had had enough of time-wasting for one day.

Carol crossed her arms and tugged at the elbows of her sweater. She pursed her lips tightly shut.

'You know her, don't you?'

'I suppose.'

'No suppose about it. Care to tell us?'

'Not really.'

'I haven't got all day, Carol. I know you're sick, but I'll drag your arse down to the station and put you in a puke-smelling cell and you can vomit your guts up all night. It doesn't really bother me. So tell me.'

'She … she was nice to me.'

'For God's sake. Why did we find an item of your underwear in a plastic bag in Mollie Hunter's flat?'

'What?'

'We fast-tracked a sample of DNA. Your DNA is a match.'

'Match for what? How did you have my DNA?'

'You were arrested with Terry three years ago. Possession of cannabis.'

'The charge was dropped.'

'It was, but your DNA is on file.'

Carol appeared to shrivel up. She sniffed back tears and looked as though she might be sick.

'Tell me,' Lottie said.

'I was raped. There. Now I've said it.' She pulled tighter on her sleeves.

Lottie turned to Boyd. He shrugged. They hadn't considered this scenario at all.

'Tell me, please, Carol.' She spoke more gently.

'It happened near her place. She came along. She was all right, so she was, even though I didn't know her. She found me in a heap on the side of the lane that runs down between two blocks of flats. She brought me into her home. Wanted to call the guards. But I was in shock. Didn't know what I was doing or saying. I must've said not to call anyone.' She sniffed and rubbed the back of her hand beneath her nose.

Lottie widened her eyes at Boyd.

'Who did it, Carol? When?'

'Oh, for Christ's sake. It doesn't matter now. It was over two months ago.'

'Did you recognise him? Someone you knew?'

'I … I'm not sure. I thought he seemed familiar. His voice was gruff, angry. I think he was drunk. I don't know.'

'And the thong. Why had Mollie got it?'

'She took my clothes that night. I was wet and grubby. I was a mess. She said she had a friend in the guards. I got hysterical and said I wanted no guards. She told me if I changed my mind I could talk to this friend. I made her promise not to tell anyone. I don't think she did but she must've kept my clothes for evidence or something. I honestly don't know.' Carol curled into herself, gulping back huge sobs.

Lottie eased back into the armchair, realising she had been coiled, ready to spring forward.

'This man ... this excuse for a man who did this to you, is he the father of the child you're carrying?'

Carol shrugged. 'I'm not sure.'

'Were you in a relationship with someone else at the time?'

A nod.

'Who?'

She shook her head. 'Not saying.'

'Who else knows about the attack?'

'No one.'

'Did Elizabeth know?'

Carol bit her lip, tears coursing down her cheeks. 'Yeah. I told Lizzie.'

'So, two young women who knew that you'd been raped. One is dead – murdered – and the other is missing, quite possibly also murdered. And you didn't think it important enough to tell us? Jesus Christ, where are your brains?'

Lottie felt Boyd touch her arm, restraining her. She let his hand rest. He was right. She was angry with the girl for withholding information, but she was suffering enough. Dear God, she thought for what seemed like the tenth time that day, what a mess.

'You have to report this, Carol.'

'No, I don't. It was just an accident. He didn't mean it. He's a good man.'

'What do you mean?' Lottie reached out and grabbed Carol's hand as the truth dawned on her. 'It *is* someone you know.'

'I didn't say that. Stop putting words in my mouth.'

'I'm sorry. I have to advise you to do the right thing.'

'I'm telling no one. End of. You can go now, before my parents get home.'

Thinking over the girl's words, Lottie said, 'Have you been threatened? By this man?'

Another sniff and a shake of her head.

'Is he married?'

A shrug of shoulders. 'I'm not saying.'

'Are you still in a relationship with him?'

'He thinks so.'

'Does he know you're pregnant?'

'No.' Her eyes, the pupils deep black, glared with terror. 'Don't say a word about any of this. Please. I'm begging you.'

Lottie sighed. 'I'm so sorry this happened to you, Carol, but people will notice you're pregnant eventually.'

'I'm not ready to tell anyone else. The only two people who knew about the rape are … are …' She pulled her legs beneath her and lay in a foetal position on the couch, weeping.

'Give me your brother's number. I'll get him to come back and sit with you.'

'No!' Carol let out a strangled cry. 'Just go. Please. Leave me alone.'

'I'll have to make a report on this, you know that.' Lottie felt sorry for the girl, but she knew she had to do her job too. 'When you're ready, come to the station. There will be trained people available to talk to you. In the meantime, I'll get a liaison officer to stay with you.'

'No fucking way.'

'It's for your own safety. Now give me Terry's number.'

# CHAPTER SEVENTY-NINE

Anna Byrne opened the door and led them inside.

'We're sorry to intrude, but we need to ask a few questions.' Lottie remained standing with Boyd while Anna slumped down on a chair. Her grief was palpable.

'Ask away.'

'Did Elizabeth ever talk about a Mollie Hunter?'

'No, I don't recall that name. She only ever said she was going out to meet Carol O'Grady.'

'You're sure?'

'I can't be sure about anything these days.'

'What about Matt Mullin? We have reason to believe he hasn't been in Munich since Christmas. Did he make any contact with Elizabeth?'

Anna stood. 'I'll put the kettle on.' She was wearing the same clothes as the other day and looked like she had cried non-stop since then.

'We haven't time for tea. Talk to me, please, Anna.'

'I've heard nothing from Matt.' Anna sat back down. 'I don't know if he'd been in contact with Elizabeth. Did you find her phone?'

'There's no trace of it.' Lottie sat down beside the distraught mother. 'I know you've no time for Carol, but is there anything we need to be aware of?'

'Like what?'

'Something she may have got Elizabeth involved in?'

'That tramp. Is it her fault my girl is dead?'

'I'm not saying that at all.' Lottie tilted her head to one side, directing Boyd to work his charm.

'Mrs Byrne,' he said, 'Anna. We're finding very little to lead us to Elizabeth's killer. We think Carol might be a link. A tenuous one, but a link nonetheless. Can you think of anything that was out of the ordinary?'

'Everything was out of the ordinary with that one.'

'Please,' Lottie pleaded.

Anna folded her arms, pulling at the sleeve of her cardigan with her fingers, nails bitten to the quick.

'She was never round here, if that's what you mean. But Elizabeth was always calling round to her. More so in recent weeks. Since Christmas. I've no idea what it was about. Elizabeth never said, but I suspect it was to do with a man. You know what young people are like at that age.'

'I do,' Lottie said.

'Maybe Matt was back in town or something. I don't know.'

'Can we look through Elizabeth's things again? If you don't mind.'

'Your forensic guys have been all over them, but go ahead. Don't take anything without telling me first, though.'

Lottie was glad to escape the sorrow permeating the kitchen walls. Elizabeth's bedroom looked the same as they'd left it.

'What are you hoping to find?' Boyd asked.

'Something to indicate Matt Mullin was in contact with her.'

'But we didn't find anything first time, and neither did SOCOs.'

'We didn't know what we were looking for then.'

'We don't know what we're …' Boyd began. Lottie threw him a warning look. He continued, 'I suppose I'll know it when I see it.'

He brushed by her, and her skin tingled with the touch of his hand as he passed. The slightest connection, but she felt it. Her chest

constricted with anxiety. A pill would help, but there was no way she could sneak one. She willed concentration into her brain. Clues to the fate of Mollie Hunter might be somewhere in this room. They had to be thorough.

'Was there anything in her notebook to give us a hint?' she asked.

'Not unless she was writing in some sort of code.'

After searching the room carefully, Lottie ran her hand through the necklaces hanging on the plastic stand on the dresser. She paused, her fingers snagged in a silver chain.

'Boyd, look at this.' She held up the chain with a ring attached. 'Was this here all the time?'

'Must have been. Ask Anna.'

'Ask me what?' Anna stood at the doorway, clenching and unclenching her fists. Lottie didn't know if it was from anger or a gesture of helplessness.

'Is this Elizabeth's?' She held up the chain and ring, anticipation prickling her skin.

'I've never seen it before.' Anna took a step into the room. 'Are you finished here?'

With a glance at Boyd, Lottie nodded. 'I need to take this.'

'I don't think it belonged to Elizabeth, so you can have it.'

Sliding the jewellery into an evidence bag, Lottie smiled sadly and left the room.

# CHAPTER EIGHTY

The day, if it was still the same day, seemed interminable. Boredom had replaced fear. And the bones, the baby bones, mocked her, lying there on the table as if they expected her to do something.

But what could she do? She was locked up. She had no means of escape. She still had no idea why he'd taken her. But she was sure she had been his target. Not opportune. No. He had sought her out and snatched her. Why?

She'd studied the paintings on the wall, trying to find a clue to who had painted them. To the person who had previously inhabited this prison. Or were the paintings a message? Maybe that was it. Kneeling on the end of the bed, she looked at them, really looked at them. And that was when she saw it. Painted in the tiniest of black letters, along the body of a crooked steam engine, it was there. Hidden in plain sight.

A name.

But it meant absolutely nothing to her.

*

At the office, Boyd plonked two mugs of coffee on Lottie's desk, having first put down coasters.

'Where did you get those?' She opened her eyes wide with amazement.

'The mats? My drawer. You never told me what Queenie said.'

'That feels like two days ago.' She tapped her computer keyboard. 'Wait until I log in here. I want to find a picture of Paddy McWard.'

'Why?'

'To see if he wears any rings.'

She clattered at the keyboard.

'I know we found a ring attached to a chain at Elizabeth's house and a ring in the unidentified female from the lake, but what has McWard got to do with it?'

'Boyd, drink your coffee and shut up for a minute. I'm trying to get my head back in gear.' She brought up a set of photographs and zoomed in on one.

'Is that a recent picture?' Boyd asked.

'It's a few years old. When he was arrested for car theft … There. See his hands?' She turned the screen so that he could see what she was looking at.

'No rings.'

'Right.'

'Right what?

'Most of the traveller community wear jewellery. Thick gold chains, rings and all that shite. But he has no rings.'

'And that proves what?'

'Hold on a minute.' She zoomed the cursor up McWard's arm. 'Jesus, Boyd. Look at that tattoo.'

He stretched across the desk, squinting. 'It's a Celtic cross.'

'Up further. Just below the hem of his sleeve. It's a Claddagh.'

'So it is. So what?'

Lottie thumped a key and the screen turned to black. 'I don't know.'

'What's brought this on?'

'Queenie said that Paddy had a broken heart. We can assume Elizabeth was in school with Bridie. And we've just found a Claddagh ring on a chain in her room. What if there was a love triangle and Paddy was mixed up somehow?'

'And he killed Elizabeth and then his wife? Oh, and I suppose you think he also abducted Lynn O'Donnell and kept her hidden for ten years? And Mollie Hunter too, just for good measure. You need more coffee, Lottie, your brain is dead.'

'My brain is on fire. I need to talk to McWard again.'

She brought two squad cars and Kirby, along with Boyd, for protection. There was no knowing how this was going to pan out. She had a lot of unconnected lines of thought but she knew that somewhere in the maze the answer was waiting to be found. And currently, Matt Mullin aside, all paths were leading her to Paddy McWard.

Crime-scene tape circled the remains of the McWard house. Paddy was at his cousin's mobile home. He stood at the door. No invitation to enter. If that's the way you want it, Lottie thought. We'll do this in front of your relations and neighbours.

'Your mother-in-law passed away an hour ago, Paddy.'

'Good.'

'Good?'

'At least she won't have to mourn her daughter and grandson.'

A pang of fear pierced Lottie's heart as she thought of Katie and Louis so far away from her. She better ring Chloe to make sure she and Sean were okay. As soon as she finished here.

'Did you know Elizabeth Byrne?'

'No.'

'Mollie Hunter?'

'What's this about?'

'Answer the question.'

'Never heard of her.'

Lottie played her trump card. 'What about Lynn O'Donnell?'

'No.'

But his face told the lie. Eyes shrouded over, pupils dilated to black crescents beneath their lids, and the light spilling from the bulb outside the caravan cast a yellow hue on his rapidly tensing skin.

'Come with us, Paddy. We need to have a word down at the station.'

'Again? How many times have I been there and each time it's been a waste of time. So no. You either arrest me or be gone. I've done nothing.'

'We need to speak to you with regards to the arson attack on your home.' She watched as his fists curled. 'We can do this the hard way.'

She took a set of handcuffs from her pocket and pointed to the two squad cars with their flashing lights at the gate.

'This is the last time.' He relented and pushed by her, heading for the nearest car.

Lottie could have sworn there were tears in his eyes.

# CHAPTER EIGHTY-ONE

They followed the two squad cars back to the station, and Lottie jumped out at the front steps. She wanted to be inside when McWard was brought in.

Even though it had started to spill rain, she began pulling off her coat as she ran up the steps.

'Inspector Parker! A word, please.'

Lottie turned to see the reporter, Cynthia Rhodes, complete with a cameraman behind her. A feeling of déjà vu flashed before her eyes. This wasn't going to turn out well.

'What do you want, Cynthia?'

'I believe two complaints have been made against you today. Care to comment?'

'What complaints?'

'I've had a call from a Mrs O'Grady. She says you upset her daughter unnecessarily. Wants to highlight garda insensitivity. The girl's best friend was found murdered and all that.'

'That's a load of bull.' Shut up, Lottie, she chided herself. But she knew it was too late.

Rhodes was in full swing. 'And the O'Donnell family. I've a complaint from them also. DI Parker, can I have a comment about the discovery of Lynn O'Donnell's body two days ago?'

'No, you can't.'

'Why did it take so long to inform her family?'

'None of your business.'

'I think it is the nation's business, Inspector. Was she badly decomposed? Was that the reason for the delay?'

'Why don't you piss off back to Dublin?'

Shit!

Paddy McWard had been taken to a cell by the time Lottie got inside, because there was someone in both interview rooms. She rushed upstairs to find Lynch standing in the middle of the office, wet and bedraggled-looking.

'What now?' Lottie snapped, rolling her coat into a ball and kicking it beneath her desk. Her T-shirt was sopping and her jeans were stuck to her legs. Fuck it, she thought. But she couldn't get Cynthia Rhodes out of her head. She was in deep shit if that toerag excuse for a journalist broadcast … What exactly had she said? She sank into the nearest chair and held her head in her hands.

'Would you like a coffee? A Diet Coke? I've a can in my bag.'

'I thought you were off sick.'

'I'm okay now, boss. This can wait.'

Lottie looked up at her detective. 'I'm sorry. What was it you wanted to say?'

'Matt Mullin. He was with his mother all along.'

'The shite.'

'He's depressed. Actually, he's in a fairly bad way. He's in the interview room.'

'Now?'

'Yeah.'

'Shit.' Running her hand under her nose, Lottie blocked a sneeze.

'You need to go home and change,' Lynch said. 'Did you eat today?'

'Did I eat? You know what? I honestly don't know. I'll be down in five minutes. You stay with him until I get there.'

When Lynch retreated, Lottie searched her pockets for a tissue and found the slip of paper with the phone number Keelan O'Donnell had given her. What could that be about? No time now. She'd call her later. Stuffing it back into her pocket, she squeezed out her dripping hair and figured Matt Mullin would have to take her the way she was.

# CHAPTER EIGHTY-TWO

The man in front of her didn't look anything like his photograph. For a start, he looked much older. Despite black rings beneath red-rimmed eyes, there was a certain smugness to his demeanour. Well, Mr Mullin, we'll see how long that lasts.

Without preamble, Lottie placed Elizabeth's photograph in front of him. The death-mask one. He recoiled instantly. That worked nicely, she thought.

'Was breaking up with Elizabeth a recipe for murder?' she said.

'What are you talking about? I never laid a hand on her.'

'Expect me to believe that? Mr Mullin, I'm in no mood for games. I've had a bitch of a day. Start talking.'

'Talk? About what? I didn't kill Elizabeth. I loved her. I miss her so much. I can't believe she's dead.'

Lottie showed him a photograph of the chain and ring she'd found. He looked up at her with a raised eyebrow. 'Was that Elizabeth's?'

'Was it Elizabeth's?' Lottie mocked. 'You gave it to her, didn't you?'

'Honest to God, I never did. I never saw it before.'

'You think I'm going to believe that?'

'It's the truth.' He bared his teeth, gnawing his bottom lip.

'When did you last see her? And don't tell me it was a year ago, because guess what? I won't believe it.'

He sighed. Considering. 'I found the break-up hard. Once I was in Germany, I knew I'd made a mistake. But she wouldn't listen to me. Blocked my number. Wouldn't talk. It made me ill.'

Was this guy for real? Lottie rolled her eyes and felt Lynch nudge her knee.

'Go on.'

'I got so depressed, I couldn't work and came home to Mum.'

'A thirty-five-year-old banker, jacking in his job and running home to Mummy. Priceless.'

'You're a bit of a bitch, aren't you?'

'Ah, now I'm getting to hear the real Matt Mullin. So you came home. When?'

'Early December.'

'And you met Elizabeth?'

'No. I told you, she wouldn't meet or talk or anything. So I started following her. On the train.'

Lottie let out a low whistle. *Stalker* popped into her mind, quickly followed by *murderer*.

'Did she see you?'

'Probably. But she ignored me. Some days she was sitting beside that other girl.'

'What other girl?'

'The one that's missing. Mollie Hunter.'

Lottie sat up straight. 'You saw Elizabeth sitting on the train with Mollie Hunter?'

'Yeah. Not every day, though. Not like they were friends, just companions.'

'So you killed Elizabeth and then abducted Mollie.'

'I did not.' He looked wildly around the room. 'Am I entitled to a solicitor?'

'If you want one. Might make you look like you have something to hide, though.'

'That's bollocks and you know it.'

'Did you follow Elizabeth out at Rochfort Gardens?'

'I don't know what you're talking about.'

'Running. Jogging. At weekends.'

'No. I didn't. Just on the train.'

'And what did you do all day in Dublin while she was at work?'

'Walked around. Had a coffee at the station and waited.'

'Tell me more.'

'There's nothing to tell. Elizabeth didn't show up on the train on Tuesday or Wednesday and then I heard what happened to her. On the news. Oh God, I can't believe it.' He began to sob.

'What did you do on those days when Elizabeth wasn't on the train?'

'I … I tried to talk to that Mollie girl. But she wouldn't engage with me. Moved off to sit with some nervy young one.'

Wheels clicked in Lottie's brain. Grace!

Could this idiot be telling the truth? She looked to Lynch for some idea of what the detective was thinking, but Lynch was staring at the wall, her face a dreadful shade of grey. That was all she needed, for her detective to puke on a suspect.

Matt stood up, 'I want my solicitor now. Or let me go.'

She really didn't have anything to hold him on. She needed evidence.

'Will you consent to giving a sample of DNA?'

'Get a warrant.'

Christ, he wasn't going to make life any easier for her. 'Okay, I will. You can go, but I want you back here at ten in the morning. With or without your solicitor. Are you agreeable to that?'

He shrugged and left.

'I think I'll join you for that coffee now, Lynch.'

In the hallway, she met Boyd, running.

'Oh, Boyd. The very man. Can you call your mother and get Grace on the phone? She might have seen that Mullin fellow on the train with Mollie.'

'Lottie. The canteen. Now.' He was breathless.

'That's where I'm headed. I'm badly in need of a coffee.'

He was shaking his head. 'You might need something stronger after you see this.'

The canteen had a wall-mounted television, which was usually muted with subtitles. Now, the sound was turned up.

Lottie sat down on one of the new red plastic chairs, open-mouthed.

'This is Cynthia Rhodes reporting from Ragmullin, in the midlands. A town that has seen its fair share of tragedy and murder over the last few years. But now locals are accusing the local Garda Síochána of incompetence.'

'What the hell? Bitch!' Lottie jumped up, rage spiking in her chest.

'The most tragic event to strike the town of Ragmullin concerns the O'Donnell family, who just a few weeks ago buried their wife and mother. Maura O'Donnell battled cancer, but those who knew her say she died of a broken heart. She went to her grave not knowing where her daughter, Lynn O'Donnell, vanished to ten years ago. The gardaí believed Lynn to be dead, possibly buried at an unidentified location in the Dublin mountains, information I got from a detective inspector at Ragmullin garda station.'

'Liar. She's misquoting me.'

'You said that? Out loud?' Boyd asked.

'Kind of.'

'God, Lottie, wait till McMahon finds out.'

'I know.' McMahon's voice boomed out behind her.

'Creep,' Lottie muttered. He had an annoying habit of appearing out of nowhere, silent and sneaky. Or perhaps it was her suspicious mind at work.

'Shh.' Boyd turned the sound up further.

'Turn it down,' Lottie shrieked. 'We can read the subtitles.'

'Turn it up. I want to hear it so I can decide on damage control.' McMahon pulled out a chair, and the plastic squeaked as he sat.

Cynthia was standing outside Donal O'Donnell's home.

'Yesterday I interviewed this heartbroken family. They asked me to highlight the ineptitude of the gardaí and to appeal for information on Lynn's whereabouts. Sadly, I learned today that the body of Ms O'Donnell has been found. And not in the Dublin mountains, but at Ladystown lake, just a few short miles outside Ragmullin.'

A photograph of Lynn appeared on the left-hand side of the screen, with the right-hand side showing the road leading to Barren Point.

'What is more disturbing, my sources tell me that Lynn O'Donnell had not been dead for ten years. She was alive up until a week or two ago. That begs the question, how did local gardaí fail in their efforts to find this beautiful young woman? And where has she been for the last decade? Was she free all that time, or was she the victim of an abduction, held against her will? A short while ago, I attempted to speak with Detective Inspector Parker of Ragmullin garda station.'

The screen cut to the steps of the station, rain spilling down in sheets and Rhodes standing with her microphone in hand. Lottie appeared from the right running up the steps, pulling her coat off.

'Turn it off,' she cried. 'I know where this is leading.'

'What did you say to her?' Boyd whispered. 'Oh God, I hope it isn't anything they can crucify you with.'

'I can't watch this.' She bolted out of her chair, but paused at the door, waiting for the humiliation she was about to suffer on national television.

Cynthia's voice boomed through the canteen. 'DI Parker, can I have a comment about the discovery of Lynn O'Donnell's body two days ago?'

'No, you can't.'

'Why did it take so long to inform her family?'

'None of your business.'

Lottie cringed. Shit, this was worse than she'd feared. She saw McMahon turn his head to face her. Was that a sly smirk snaking across his face?

'I think it is the nation's business, Inspector. Was she badly decomposed? Was that the reason for the delay?'

'Why don't you piss off back to Dublin.'

The image showed Lottie shoving her way past Rhodes. Then the shot returned to a bemused-looking, very damp Cynthia.

'And that is DI Parker, who is heading up two murder investigations and the case of Mollie Hunter, who has been missing since Wednesday.'

Lottie groaned. 'Jesus, if you're going to hang me out to dry, at least get your fucking facts right.'

'What facts?' McMahon rose from his chair as Boyd muted the television.

'Lynn wasn't murdered, she died of natural causes.'

'That, Inspector, is beside the point. Where was she for ten years? If she was being held captive somewhere, don't you think that was a contributing factor to her death?'

'Yeah, well, what do you know?' She leaned back against the door frame and closed her eyes. The day couldn't get any worse, could it?

'My office.' McMahon stormed past her, leaving a trail of sickly aftershave in his wake.

'Will you come with me, Boyd?' she said.

'I think you've dug your own grave on this one, Lottie.'

'Okay. A favour, though, before I throw myself under McMahon's bus. I need you with me while I interview Paddy McWard.'

# CHAPTER EIGHTY-THREE

McWard said he didn't want a solicitor. As Lottie slumped onto a chair, Boyd set up the recording equipment and read out the procedures.

'Get on with it,' McWard said.

'Tell me about your Claddagh tattoo,' Lottie said.

'What?'

'Show it to me.'

He shrugged and held out his arm.

'When did you get that done?'

'Maybe ten years ago. I can't remember.'

'Why that symbol?'

'I liked it. Going to arrest me for it?'

'You don't wear any rings?'

'I don't.'

'Not even a wedding ring?'

'Not a crime. I broke it, if you want to know.'

'Really?'

'My hand swelled up after a fight. Had to get the ring cut off. Satisfied?'

'Not really. Did you know Lynn O'Donnell?'

'I told you already. I didn't know her.'

'I don't believe you.'

He shrugged again.

It was time to play what she thought was her trump card. The photo of the ring Jane Dore had taken from Lynn O'Donnell's

intestine. Her own gut was telling her McWard was involved, but she had no concrete evidence to link him to anything at the moment. Placing the photocopy face down on the table, she waited. Then, slowly, keeping her eyes on his face, she turned it over.

No change in expression.

'So?' he said. 'It's a Claddagh ring. What's it got to do with me?'

'Would you like to know where we found it?'

'Not particularly, but I guess you're going to tell me. Pig.'

'Did you just call me a pig?'

'Oink.'

'For God's sake, stop being childish,' Lottie said. Under the table, she felt Boyd kick her leg. She turned to look at him. A slight shake of his head, warning her to back off. Not on your life.

'This ring was recovered two days ago from the body of a woman who was found dead.'

'Like I said. Nothing to do with me.'

'She went missing ten years ago tomorrow.'

Lottie braced herself for more insults. But instead there was a suffocating silence as McWard's face drained of colour and turned ghost white.

Biting the inside of his cheek, he pulled the photograph towards him and stared. A sob strangled in his throat. 'Lynn?'

Lottie glanced at Boyd. What? He *did* know her.

She gave a little cough. 'Yes, we found the ring inside the body of Lynn O'Donnell.'

He pushed away the photo and folded his arms. 'I know nothing about any Lynn.'

'You're not a great liar, Paddy. You've just said her name. You knew her. Admit it.'

His silence hung in the air like a delicate cobweb. Lottie felt like a fly about to pounce on a spider.

'Paddy. Talk to me, for Christ's sake.'

His eyes were shrouded as he lowered his head. 'I've just lost my wife and my son. And you think I had something to do with that girl? You are the lowest form of scum on the earth.'

'But you knew Lynn O'Donnell. Did you abduct her? Hide her away for ten years and then leave her to die?'

'You're mad, do you know that?'

'Left her to rot out at the lake?'

'I did not.'

Lottie sighed. She had nothing on Paddy McWard. Not a single thing, yet her bones itched with the feeling that he was involved.

'All those days and nights you spend away from home. Where do you go?'

'This again?'

'Yup. I'll find out eventually, so you may as well tell me.'

He folded his arms, put them on the table and laid his head on top of them. 'I must be due a break.' His voice was muffled.

With her own shoulders sagging in defeat, Lottie asked Boyd to terminate the interview.

'As you have no home at the moment, we'll provide you with a nice sterile cell for the night. Give you time to decide to tell us the truth.'

'Bare-knuckle boxing.'

'What?' She nodded to Boyd to continue the recording. She'd seen this on PULSE. He'd been arrested for it eight years ago, but the charges were dropped. Was this all he was guilty of? She needed to find out.

McWard raised his head listlessly. 'I used to be involved in underground bare-knuckle fights. Lost a lot of money. Nearly lost my life.'

'Go on.'

'I had a younger brother who … who died from a kick to the head at one of those fights seven years ago. That changed me.'

'How?'

'Now I try to stop them. I travel the country hunting them down. I try and talk sense into the young lads. Anyone who'll listen, I take them to legit boxing clubs. I even train some of them myself. That's all I've been doing. Nothing suspicious. Just trying to make up for the loss of my brother.'

Was this what Queenie had meant by his broken heart? Glancing sideways at Boyd, Lottie raised a questioning eyebrow before returning her gaze to McWard.

'Can you prove this?'

'I can bring you to some of the clubs. The lads might talk to you. But the illegal stuff, I can't let you in on that. Sure, even your own pigs couldn't uncover anything about them.'

Lottie took a deep breath and expelled it slowly. 'I think you're telling me the truth, but not the whole truth.'

'You've nothing to hold me on. I'm not going to flee, I've funerals to organise. I'll come back tomorrow.'

'You're going nowhere until you tell me the truth. About everything, Paddy.'

Maybe it was the use of his first name that did it, but Lottie watched in wonder as his fingers gripped the image of the ring.

'I loved her so much,' he whispered.

Her breath caught at the back of her throat and her mouth opened without any words escaping.

'My Lynn. I can't believe she's dead. I always thought she'd be found. I searched and searched. We were so in love. But it could never be. Not with that arsehole family of hers. Once they found out, we were finished.'

'Found out what?'

'That we were meeting. That we were lovers.' He looked up at the ceiling, cleared his throat. 'Bridie was only fourteen when I was

betrothed to her. I didn't love her. But that was the way of my people. I'd already met Lynn by then, when I went to Dublin to sort out some welfare stuff at the head office. That was where she worked. She had such a happy smile. I was in love from that first day. And the odd thing was, she felt it too.'

'You had a relationship with Lynn O'Donnell?' Lottie said, incredulous.

'Don't look so shocked. Love happens. I gave her that ring. To show her my loyalty and love.'

'You're sure it's the same one?'

'If you let me see it, I'll know.'

Lottie didn't know if that was a good idea. Was he lying?

'What I can't understand is that your name never appeared anywhere in the original investigation. Why is that?'

'Her family didn't want to suffer the indignity of the whole country knowing their beloved girl was making out with a traveller. The shame of it.' He curled his lip in distaste. 'I hate them. Every last one of them. It's their fault Lynn went missing.'

'I think it's your fault.'

'Maybe you're right there.'

'Where did you keep her for the last ten years, Paddy?'

His eyes, blacker than she'd noticed before, stabbed her with a look of hatred. 'I didn't take her and I didn't keep her anywhere. I want my solicitor. I'm not saying another word.'

With exhaustion eating its way into the core of her being, Lottie wound up the interview, then made arrangements for Paddy's detention to be extended overnight. They needed to run more DNA tests. She hoped that maybe tomorrow she could extract the whole truth from him and, in doing so, find Mollie Hunter.

✳

McMahon's mood had soured considerably in the half-hour she'd left him to stew.

'I thought I told you I wanted to see you immediately. Where the hell were you?'

'I had an interview to conduct. McWard was on a time limit.'

'I'm your superior officer. I come first.'

'Yes, sir.' Too late now, she thought. She'd already relegated him behind Paddy McWard. And there was no way she was telling him about the possible breakthrough in the case of Lynn O'Donnell. He could find out for himself when they filed for an extension of detention time.

'Sit. That debacle of a television interview. What were you thinking?'

'I wasn't thinking, obviously.'

'None of that smart mouth in here.' He slammed his fist on the empty desk.

Lottie slipped down on the chair, hoping it might make her disappear. She was so tired; she couldn't remember the last time she'd slept. She needed to get home.

'I'm exhausted, sir. Can't we do this tomorrow?'

'There's no tomorrow where you're concerned. You're suspended, pending an inquiry into your attitude and behaviour.'

Shit!

'Don't I get a warning first? You can't just suspend me. You have to follow procedure.' She shot forward in the chair, reached out a hand. She didn't do pleading, but she was doing it now.

'And did *you*?' he said.

'What?'

'Follow procedure?'

'That was different. Rhodes hijacked me. I wasn't prepared for—'

'You have to be prepared at all times. Someone in your position knows that.'

'I forgot. I was—'

'Exhausted? No excuse.'

She threw up her hands. 'I've nothing else to offer.'

'Get out, Parker. You're a disgrace to the force.'

She couldn't help rolling her eyes. Incensing him further. Wrong move, Lottie.

He rose from his chair, slow and panther-like. She didn't blink. Wouldn't give him the satisfaction. Remaining seated, she folded her arms.

'Do you know, as bad as that display was on national television, it gave me a quiet moment of satisfaction. Because, Parker, you are nothing but trouble, and I'm making it my one and only aim to have you dismissed from the force.'

'We'll see about that, shall we?' She rose languidly and strolled out of his office.

Hearing the door slam behind her, she stopped and sighed, raising her eyes to the ceiling, then looked around for Boyd. He was nowhere to be seen.

She grabbed her coat and keys and walked out without a backwards glance.

# CHAPTER EIGHTY-FOUR

Chloe cooked dinner. Oven chips and burgers. Lottie wolfed down the food and helped her stack the dishwasher.

'Granny was here earlier,' Chloe said.

'The miraculous recovery.'

'She said she was fed up with your cooking. I don't think she's sick any longer. I helped her tidy up here a bit. She even got the hoover out. Insulted me and Sean in the process.'

'She's definitely better,' Lottie laughed.

Chloe smiled, and Lottie felt the tiredness in her bones ease a little. She pulled her daughter into a hug. Sean strolled into the kitchen but quickly turned on his heel with a 'Yuck!'

'Would you mind if Boyd came over for a while?'

'Work stuff?' Chloe asked.

'Not really.' Lottie released her, then closed the dishwasher door and pressed the button.

'I don't care.'

And before she could reply, the girl had left the room, slamming the door on her way out.

She rang Boyd. They had things to discuss, and it wasn't work-related.


'What are you dressing up for?' Chloe plonked herself down on Lottie's bed. 'It's only Boyd.'

'What about this?' Lottie asked, holding out a cream blouse.

'Try the blue dress.' Chloe folded her arms.

Lottie held it up to her chest. 'I don't think it fits me any more.'

'That's because you've gone to skin and bone. You need to eat.'

'I do eat.'

'Junk food. You're wearing yourself to the bone again.'

'Again?' She pulled the blue dress on over her long grey T-shirt.

'Every time you have a murder case, you forget about yourself. That's too big for you.'

'Any other suggestions?'

'Your jeans and a clean shirt if you can find one.'

'Chloe, don't be so mean.'

'It's only Boyd, for Christ's sake. Not Johnny Depp.'

'I want to look … different from my normal look.'

'Sounds serious.'

'You're right, it's only Boyd.' Lottie pulled two shirts off hangers. 'Which one?'

'The green one.'

'That doesn't go with my eyes.'

'The white one then.'

'What's the matter, Chloe?' Lottie threw the clothes on the floor and sat beside her daughter. She held her hand. 'Boy trouble?'

'Not my boy trouble. Your man trouble.'

'I don't have man trouble.'

'That's the problem. Boyd, well, he's your friend. You can't go on a date with him.'

'For the last time, it's not a date.'

'Why is he down in the sitting room with another bunch of flowers then?'

'He's just being Boyd.' Lottie bit her lip. She hadn't a clue how to handle this awkwardness with her daughter.

'I know you slept with him last night. This is going to end in tears.'

'Hey.' She gripped Chloe's hand tightly. 'I just have things to discuss with him. It's nothing serious.'

'Yeah, but he's your friend. And you're going to ruin that friendship, just like you ruin everything. I miss Dad!'

'Wait a minute …'

But Chloe had fled.

Flopping back on the bed, Lottie stared at a water stain on the ceiling and wondered where she was going wrong.

# CHAPTER EIGHTY-FIVE

In the end, she rushed Boyd out the door and drove over to his apartment behind him.

As usual, the place was clean and quiet. She sat beside him on the couch and sipped a glass of white wine. They had agreed to no work talk.

'Do you miss Grace being around for the weekend?'

'No. I've been on my own for so long, I find it hard to share my space. Anyway, she'll be back tomorrow.'

'No hope for me then,' she laughed. The illicit wine was relaxing her. A little.

'There is always hope for you, Lottie Parker.' He clinked his glass to hers and the hazel in his eyes sparkled with the light. 'I enjoyed having you here last night. In my bed. Our lovemaking.'

'I was only here a couple of hours.' She turned her head to him. How was she going to handle this without ruining their friendship?

'You're beautiful, but you don't realise it.'

'Will you stop!'

'I thought I'd go mental all day, restraining myself.'

'What do you mean?'

'Trying to keep my hands off you and my expression neutral.'

She smiled awkwardly. 'McMahon didn't remain neutral. He's preparing my walking papers. I don't know what I'm going to do.'

'He can't suspend you without consulting the chief super, so don't worry about it.'

'I have to worry about it. I need my job. It's the only thing keeping me half sane.'

'You have your children. They're brilliant kids. I love Sean.'

'Chloe is an enigma, though. If only I could fathom out how her brain works.'

'Problems there?'

'She thinks I'm going to ruin a good friendship.'

'And are you?'

'I ruin everything, according to her.'

'No you don't. She's just a teenager. Afraid she's going to lose her mum.'

'It's more than that, Boyd. I fear for her. She says she misses her dad.'

'Of course she does. Sean too.' He leaned over for the bottle and refilled his glass. 'Another?'

'I shouldn't be drinking at all. I've got to drive home.' As he drew away, she said, 'Well, maybe half a glass.'

They reclined in the silence, their legs touching, her head on his shoulder. She felt that if she sat here long enough, the hassles of her life might just disappear, if only for an hour.

'Do you ever crave sex?' he said.

'Jesus, Boyd. Where did that come from?'

He pointed to the pit of his abs. 'Here. Somewhere down here.'

Lottie stood up and walked to the window. 'That's an odd question.'

He said nothing.

She flicked a slat in the wooden blind, cutting the scene outside in half. She didn't want to turn around. To see him sitting there, hands resting just above the buckle of his belt. His fingers long and lonely. His hair short and damp. And his eyes. Questioning.

'I don't think about it,' she said.

'You must do.'

'Do you?'

'Not as often as you might think,' Boyd said.

She heard him standing up, the glass clinking on the table, the rustle of his trousers, the pad of his feet on the carpet. She sensed his closeness as he stood behind her.

'Do you love me, Lottie?'

That made her take a step away from him. She turned to stare. Side-on, he was even more handsome, because she couldn't see his sticking-out ears.

How to answer him without hurting him. Without hurting herself. Did she love Boyd? Adam had been the only man in her life, all her life, until he got that bastard cancer and died on her. Boyd had always been on hand when she felt her life rug being snatched from beneath her feet. Yes, she'd slept in his bed after bouts of drinking, but last night had felt different. And that was what scared her the most.

As he slowly turned to face her, her breath caught in the back of her throat at the sight of the sadness lurking in the corners of his eyes. She wanted to reach out and touch his cheek, to hold his hand, to tell him what she knew was deep within her heart. But then she might lose him too. Wasn't it safer to keep plodding along, playing the game? But how long could she do that without succumbing to her true feelings? And would Boyd even be around when she faced up to what she knew was the truth?

'This is never going to work,' she said. 'I have to go home.'

He broke away from her.

She left him standing at the window, picked up her coat and bag, and let herself out of his apartment into the loneliness of the night.

# CHAPTER EIGHTY-SIX

It was almost midnight and the house was creaking in silence when she returned home. She automatically sorted the laundry, then put on a wash and placed the damp clothes in the dryer. Upstairs was chilly. She pulled Adam's old fishing jumper out of a drawer and dragged it on over her pyjamas.

Before getting into bed, she checked on Chloe, who was fast asleep. Sean was in bed, headphones on, watching a movie on his laptop. He winked at her when she blew him a kiss and her heart leaped with love as she closed the door.

She fell into bed. She needed sleep to extinguish all thoughts of the problems she now faced with Boyd and her job. She'd worry about murders, missing girls and McMahon tomorrow.

*

Boyd had finished the bottle of wine by the time his mother rang him wondering if Grace needed a new anxiety pill prescription for next week.

Grace? His stomach lurched.

His mother thought Grace was with him. He thought Grace was with his mother. But it turned out she was in neither place. And she wasn't answering her phone. Where the hell was she?

He'd last seen her yesterday morning when he'd dropped her at the train station. Images of Elizabeth Byrne's naked body in the pit of a grave surfaced, and his heart pounded a triple beat in his chest.

As he went into the bedroom, his breathing accelerated and he clutched his chest. He fell back on the bed, his arm dangling. His fingers touched something. Grace's phone, on the floor, her little bottle of anxiety pills lying beside it.

Lottie. He should ring Lottie.

Pain shot up his arm and flew to his chest, and his breath died in his lungs as darkness washed over his eyes.

✳

Smoke. She could smell smoke. Fuck!

Lottie threw back the duvet and sat bolt upright. Flicking on the lamp, she jumped out of bed and opened the door. The landing was filled with thick black smoke. Beyond it, at the bottom of the stairs, flames licked upwards. She grabbed her phone and ran into Chloe's room, hauling the girl out of bed, then did the same to Sean.

'What's going on, Mum?' Sean was bleary-eyed, headphones around his neck.

'Oh God. No! The house is on fire,' Chloe screamed at the top of the stairs.

Lottie pushed her children behind her, her body convulsing in shakes, and with her arm across her nose and mouth placed one foot on the top step.

'No, Mum!' Chloe shouted. 'The smoke. It'll kill you.'

'What are we going to do?' Sean cried.

She descended two steps before smoke threatened to overwhelm her. She ran back up. 'We need to get out of a window.'

'My room.' Chloe turned and ran, Sean behind her. 'I've got out this way before.'

'Wait!' Lottie cried. 'Wet towels. We need wet towels.' All her composure and training evaporated as her lungs clogged with fumes. Was this how Bridie McWard had felt in her dying moments? No,

Lottie wasn't going to let that happen to her family. She quickly followed them into Chloe's room and punched the door shut behind her.

Chloe had opened the window and was sitting out on the ledge. 'You need to jump onto the shed roof. It's not far.'

Staring out, Lottie saw the garden lit up with bright orange flames, smoke billowing from her kitchen. Had some bastard torched the house? She had no time to worry about her possessions burning before her eyes. She had to get her family to safety.

Sean had his phone to his ear, shouting out their address. She hadn't even thought of ringing the emergency services. Focus, Lottie, focus.

'Come on!' Chloe cried, holding out her hand.

Lottie didn't need to give her tall son a leg-up onto the windowsill, but she did anyway, then watched as Chloe jumped onto the shed roof, quickly followed by Sean.

The white paint on the bedroom door was peeling from the heat. Tendrils of black smoke eased through the cracks in the jamb and the bottom of the door. Her breath was almost spent by the time she escaped out the window. Without even worrying about falling and breaking her neck, she leaped down to the roof of the shed. The children had already shimmied down the grassy bank behind it and were huddled together when she joined them.

Arms wrapped around each other, they stared up at their burning home. The wail of sirens pierced the night sky, competing with the crackling and whistling of the flames.

Gone. Lost.

She had lost everything.

And then she heard the soft sobs of her children.

*

The cold and wet had eaten into her bones. She couldn't open her eyes, no matter how she tried. The voices in her head came and went, trickling away like froth on a wave.

Her body shook incessantly, her lips trembled and her teeth ground against each other. Who was she?

Grace. That was her name. What had happened? The man on the train. Had he brought her here? Where?

And a name flitted into her consciousness. Mollie. She hadn't found Mollie. Would anyone find her?

❉

Wrapping the thin blanket around her shoulders, Mollie lay back on the bed and wished she had the means to turn off the light. It was blinding her. Keeping her awake. There was no night or day in this place. Only long, unending hours.

She had no notion of when he had last been with her. It seemed like an eternity. Had he forgotten about her? Had he left her here to die? Would she end up like the bones on the table? Rotted bare of all flesh. Unburied and unblessed.

Surely someone had missed her by now?

Her throat was raw from screaming and her eyes had dried up like gravel had taken root behind them. And she was hungry and thirsty. She had nothing left.

She turned onto her side.

No one was coming.

She was alone.

She would never be found.

There was nothing she could do.

She was going to die.

Alone.

# DAY FIVE

Sunday 14 February 2016

# CHAPTER EIGHTY-SEVEN

Lottie awoke to a soft light filtering through thin cotton curtains. She shot up in the bed. Where the hell was she?

Looking around the room, it all came crashing back to her. Her throat was clogged with a taste like the aftermath of smoking one too many cigarettes, and she smelled of smoke.

She hadn't slept in this room since she'd married Adam, but now memories of her childhood flowed about her like a waterfall. As a child, she'd felt safe here, but now she was like an interloper. A giant in a miniature world. Not nostalgia, just sadness. She didn't belong here. The only place she could truly call home was now a smouldering mound of ash.

All her memories of her husband and their life together had gone with the house. Disintegrated to ash. Tugging Adam's sweater to her body, she realised it was the only thing of meaning she had left of him.

The door opened. Lottie hastily wiped the tears from her face and watched her mother place a mug of coffee on the bedside locker.

Rose Fitzpatrick looked healthier than she had in months. Hair washed and standing to attention. Clothes sharply ironed. A mask of yellow still lingered on her skin and her eyes held that sorrowful, dry look you often saw in people who had grieved so long they'd no tears left to shed. Still, it was as if last night's fire had acted as a catalyst for Rose, causing her to take on the role of Lazarus and rise from the dead.

In that instant, Lottie realised how much she wanted her mother to take control of things. Not that she was going to let it get out of hand. But for now, she was glad of it. Maybe some day soon they might be able to deal with the complexities of their past.

'Chloe and Sean? Are they okay?' she asked.

'Still asleep, poor pets. Awful thing to happen to anyone.'

'Thanks,' Lottie said.

'For what?'

'Taking us in.'

'Don't be acting the lady now, Lottie Parker. Taking you in? Isn't that what a mother is for? Looking after her family.'

Somewhere in that statement there was a slight on Lottie's ability to care for her own family, but she let it pass. Slurped the coffee, trying to kick-start her brain.

'I need to go down to the house. Get some clothes.' She sensed her mother's stare. 'What?'

'There's nothing left. You know that.'

'I didn't …' She quickly swallowed a mouthful of coffee, to mask the sob gaining traction in her throat.

'You need to think, Lottie, long and hard. You and my grand-children are welcome to stay here. I know you won't want to do that for very long, but in the meantime, can we at least be civil to each other? Do you think you can manage that?'

Lottie held her tongue. It wasn't her that was always throwing out snide remarks. Or was it?

'Okay. Thank you.'

Rose nodded and left the room, closing the door with a soft thud.

'What am I going to do?' Lottie cried at the four walls.

She needed air. Shit, she needed clothes.

And then her phone beeped with a message.

# CHAPTER EIGHTY-EIGHT

Last night, once he'd got over his panic attack, Boyd had scoured the town. Grace was nowhere to be found. He'd rounded up Kirby, Lynch and Gilly to start phoning. Store Street garda station, Garda HQ. The rail company. Anyone and everyone. Someone must know where she was.

It was fruitless. He knew that. Look at Mollie Hunter. No sighting of her since Wednesday. And Grace had been on that train with her. So where was she?

When he'd heard about the fire at Lottie's house, he'd rushed there to see what he could do to help, and had made sure she and the children were safely ensconced at her mother's. Now SOCOs were sifting through the embers for clues to what had happened. Had Lottie and her family become the target of whoever had murdered Bridie McWard and her child? The only variable in that synopsis was that Paddy McWard had been detained in a cell all night.

Boyd paced the incident room. He needed to get into his car and do something. Go somewhere. But where?

Right now, he could do with some of Lottie's gut instinct.

Right now, he could do with Lottie by his side, full stop.

# CHAPTER EIGHTY-NINE

Standing at the corner by the caretaker's office, Lottie looked down the hill at the small gathering. Father Joe was sprinkling holy water from a narrow hand-held brass bucket. She wanted to walk away from this intimate activity, from the tranquillity of the morning after the mayhem of the last twelve hours, but she'd been drawn here and now she couldn't move her feet.

She shuffled her hands up the sleeves of her mother's coat for warmth and bit her lip as the mourners passed by, arms linked, heads bowed. She felt awkward in Rose's boots, trousers and shirt. All too big, hanging off her body, but beggars can't be choosers, Rose had said. Gilly had come over with stuff she thought might fit Chloe and said she'd bring her to town later to buy clothes for Sean. A squad car with two officers was parked outside Rose's house with orders to keep watch.

Father Joe stopped when he saw her. His face wore a tormented expression, like the look you'd see imprinted on the faces of people who'd suffered tragedy in their lives. That look. Lottie knew exactly what Father Joe Burke had suffered. The loss of a mother he never knew. A mother whom he'd been taken from against her will. And then her murder. Too much suffering for one man.

'Hello again,' she said.

He smiled, and she noticed that single act could still light up his face, though now it was full of sadness. The blonde hair that used to fall into his once-mischievous blue eyes was gone, replaced

by a tightly shorn head. Was it a form of self-flagellation? Was he divesting himself of who he thought he was? She knew that feeling well.

He moved into her space, placed a hand lightly on her elbow, and she bit harder into her lip.

'You got my text,' he stated. 'Are you okay? The children?'

She shrugged. 'I suppose so.'

'You need to talk to someone, Lottie. Will you come up to the house for a chat?'

'I've things to sort,' she said, feeling foolish for having come.

'Let's walk then.'

She felt his arm link hers and allowed herself to be led.

Halfway down the hill, she felt dizzy and they sat on a steel bench.

'It's all a bit mad,' she said, watching Bernard Fahy filling in Mrs Green's grave.

'Isn't it always?'

She laughed sadly. 'You'll be having a few more funerals in the coming days. I was with Queenie McWard just before she died.'

'Very sad.'

The sun glinted off the copper roof of the old nursing home nestled behind the new building. 'Do you ever visit the residents in the home?'

'Sometimes. But I only came back just before Christmas.'

'Thought you were gone for good.'

'I had a change of heart. This is where I belong.'

'I thought I did too. Belonged. Now I'm not so sure.'

'You're in shock, Lottie. It was an awful thing to happen.'

'The fire?'

'Yes. Are there other things?'

'Plenty. I think I'll be suspended from my job. One daughter hates me; the other's flown to New York to stay with her son's

grandfather for a while. Sean is Sean, and my mother … That's a story for another day.'

'What about Boyd?'

'What about him?' And as she said the words, Lottie felt a longing in her heart. She wanted to speak with him. Knowing Boyd, he was giving her space. 'I like Boyd.'

'I think you need a comforting arm around you. And not just a priestly one.'

'You are so good, Joe. I'm sorry for all the things that happened to you.'

'Not your fault. I'm working my way through the pain.'

'So am I. But now I might have no job.' She found herself explaining to him how her investigations had led to her being in danger of suspension.

'I've been following the news. Do you think the current cases are linked to Lynn O'Donnell?'

'I'm beginning to think so.'

'I was thinking that maybe Mollie Hunter is being held where Lynn was held for ten years,' he said.

'It's possible. But we have no clue where that might be.'

'Go back to when it all started. Today, ten years ago.'

Lottie shivered as a bird flapped its wings above her head to the sound of a train slowing down on the tracks as it headed for the station. 'You always were good at detective work.'

He smiled.

The train blasted its horn and disappeared from view.

# CHAPTER NINETY

After she left Father Joe at the cemetery, Lottie went into town and grabbed a coffee, then walked slowly up Main Street, ignoring the shop windows full of red hearts. She found herself at the train station without really knowing that was where she'd been headed.

She doubted Jimmy Maguire would be around on Sunday morning, and it was half an hour since she'd heard the Sligo train. But as she stood in the portico, just outside the ticket office, she saw his capped head approaching.

'The lovely Detective Inspector Parker.'

'I wanted to have a word with you.'

He directed her towards the ticket office. 'There's a vending machine inside if you'd like a hot drink.'

'No thanks. I've just had a coffee.'

She sat on the wooden bench outside the door and felt the cold wind whistle around her ears. She nestled her chin into the wool of her mother's coat as he joined her.

'What did you want to ask me? I can't remember anything else about those two lassies. Terrible. One murdered and the other missing. Shocking business.'

'This is about Lynn O'Donnell.'

His face paled and he bit the inside of his cheek. 'What about her?'

'Did you know her?'

'No.'

'Did you see her the day she disappeared?'

'I'm presuming you read up on the case, so you know I saw her that evening when she got off the train.'

'She dropped her bag on the platform.'

'I helped her pick up her belongings. That's the last I saw of her.'

'Did you know her before then?'

He seemed to digest that, perhaps wondering if it was a trick question. But she was throwing out a line, hoping something might bite.

'I knew her a little. Knew her brothers. They were avid train watchers. Obsessed with trains, those boys were. Still are. Both are on the railway preservation committee.'

Lottie filed away that snippet. 'How did Lynn seem that day?'

'Ah, sure it was a long time ago.'

'Try to remember.'

He closed his eyes. 'Flustered. She dropped her bag, didn't she?' He opened one eye and squinted at Lottie.

'Was there any reason for that? Did she see someone or something to make her flustered?'

He closed his eyes again. Imagining that day ten years ago?

'The platform was packed,' he said. 'Busy. Not as many trains running back then. There were more people crowded onto the few that were operating. All the men were flitting about with bunches of roses. Probably got them cheap on Moore Street.'

'After you helped her repack her handbag,' Lottie probed, 'did you notice where she went?'

'What did I say in the report?'

'I want to know what you can remember.'

He sighed and looked up at pigeons nesting on a rafter. 'My memory is not as good as it used to be.'

'I'm sure it's just fine.'

He smiled at the compliment.

'She was red-faced. Embarrassed? I don't know. She rushed through that gate from the platform and went outside. Most of the crowd had dispersed by then. I flagged the train on its way and closed the gate. I remember standing on the steps there, thinking I was almost finished for the day. That was the last train. And …'

'And what?'

'I never said anything before.' He clasped his hands tightly, as if the gesture might keep his tongue quiet.

Lottie placed a hand on his arm. 'You can tell me.'

'I … I couldn't tell anyone. You see a small fire started. I think it blurred my memory. The old waiting rooms round the back. It was beginning to blaze. I never told anyone. It was my responsibility. I was terrified of losing my job.'

'What was your responsibility?

'Keeping the place clean and free of rubbish.'

Lottie sighed. He was trekking off on a tangent. 'Jimmy, you were telling me about Lynn O'Donnell?'

'There's nothing to tell.'

'Was it a big fire?'

'I thought so at first. But I put it out quick enough.'

'How did it start?'

'A build-up of rubbish caught light at the side of the building.' He wrung his hands together, his lips quivering. 'I never reported it as it was my job on the line. Can you understand that?'

She could, but she said, 'What aren't you telling me?'

'I couldn't say anything back then. And I can't now.'

'We found her body. Lynn. Did you know that? We think someone abducted her that day and hid her away for ten years until she died. Can you imagine anything worse? Was your job worth the heartache that family had to go through?'

'He said nothing either. So it wasn't all my fault.'

'Who are you talking about?' Lottie sat up straight. This was certainly new.

'He helped me. To put out the fire. I couldn't say anything or he might have dropped me in the shit, you know.'

'Jimmy, you have to tell me what you mean.'

He stood up, pushed his cap back and scratched his forehead. He had his back to her, and his voice was so low she had to stand up to hear him.

'You see, he was with her, collecting her or something. They were in the car. I think he saw the flames starting around the same time I did, because he came to help me. When we got it quenched with the extinguishers, I shook his hand to thank him and asked him to say nothing to no one, and he said …'

'Go on, Jimmy.'

'He said, I expect the same from you. Then he joined her in the car.'

'Jesus!' Lottie felt a tingle of anticipation catching fire in her belly. This had not appeared anywhere in Lynn O'Donnell's file. 'Who? Who was it?'

He looked back at her, his eyes half closed with sadness.

'Her brother.'

Lottie gulped down her surprise.

'Which one, Jimmy? Tell me! Which brother?'

# CHAPTER NINETY-ONE

'Carol?' Terry's voice echoed up the stairs.

If he wakes Mum and Dad, I'm going to kill him, she thought as she jumped out of bed. The contents of her stomach rose to her mouth. Grabbing a tissue, she threw up in the bowl beside the bed. When would it ever stop?

'Carol, get down here.'

'I'm coming, you moron.' Maybe it was a delivery of flowers for Valentine's Day. That would be great. Maybe he was leaving his wife.

'What's all the racket?'

Now her dad was awake.

'It's for me. Go back to sleep, Dad. It's Sunday,' she said.

At the bottom of the stairs, Terry stood with the door open. 'Someone wants to talk to you.'

'You!' Carol said, her jaw dropping almost to her chest. 'What are you doing here?'

'We need to talk,' the man said, and turned away. 'I'm parked around the corner.'

'Give me five minutes. I better get dressed.'

*

The office was in uproar when Lottie entered. Desks were littered with mugs of coffee and half-eaten croissants, crumbs everywhere. People eating on the go.

'What's going on?' she asked, stretching her arms out, imploring an answer from her animated team.

'What are you doing here?' Boyd jumped up from his desk and dragged her into her office. 'Jesus, Lottie, you look a sight. You should be at home in bed.'

'I don't have a home, never mind a bed.'

'And didn't McMahon suspend you?'

'He only thinks he did. I don't care about him. Anyway, the chief super won't want to get rid of me. Someone tried to murder my family last night. That's all I care about. As soon as McGlynn has the evidence, I'm going to swing for the bastard who did it. So tell me, what's all this about?' She slammed the table, immediately wincing with pain. Her own news would have to wait until she found out what was going on.

'Your hand, it's hurt.'

She held up her bandaged left hand. 'So it is, Sherlock. I didn't realise how quickly flames could climb stairs.'

'At least you got some clothes, even if they are a bit vintage.'

She studied Boyd's haggard face. 'You look awful. What's going on?'

'It's Grace. She's missing.'

'What? Tell me.'

He explained about his mother's phone call, and all they'd done so far without finding a trace of his sister.

'She'll be fine. Don't fret.' Lottie didn't believe her own words.

Boyd's breaths came in short puffs as he said, 'She can't be fine. Her phone and medication are at my place and I'm sure she's wherever Mollie Hunter is. And if Mollie is already dead, then I'll never see Grace again.'

'One step at a time, Boyd. Breathe before you have a panic attack.'

'Had one already. Passed out.'

'See a doctor. Get checked out.'

'Look who's talking. I'll be fine. Once I find Grace.'

'Have you followed the protocol for a missing person?'

'Yes, and more. I asked McMahon to talk to the media. In the light of all that's happened this last week, he agreed.'

'Okay. If Grace is linked to the current cases, we need to retrace our steps on Mollie Hunter's disappearance and maybe that way we'll find your sister. Agree?'

'I suppose so. Are Chloe and Sean okay?'

'They're with my mother. Gilly is there. They're fine.'

'You should be with them.'

'I know. But I'll be like a hen on an egg if we don't find Grace, so I'm better off here. My kids know me well; they understand.'

'McWard is still refusing to say anything,' he said. 'We have him for another few hours and then it's either charge or release.'

'Forget McWard for the moment. I made a discovery earlier. It might throw new light on our investigation. The day Lynn O'Donnell vanished, there was a fire in the old waiting rooms over on the disused platform.'

'What's that got to do with her disappearance?'

'When I gave him a nudge, Jimmy Maguire remembered that a man met her that evening at the station.'

'Paddy McWard?'

'Nope. Her brother.'

*

Carol pulled the collar of her coat tight to her neck and settled into the passenger seat of his car. She shoved her hands into her pockets defiantly.

'You have some nerve coming round to my house. My brother will kill you.'

'I'll kill the little shit first. Fucking dope head.'

'What do you want? I don't see any flowers, so that's not a good start.'

'I can give you something much better than flowers. I missed you. Just wanted to see you.'

'And risk my dad seeing you? What is this really about, Cillian?' She twisted in the seat to get a good look at him. He appeared strained, his hands tense on the steering wheel. His eyes were rimmed with black circles. But he still looked stunningly handsome.

'Let's go for a drive,' he said. 'I know a quiet spot at the lake.' He turned on the ignition without waiting for her reply. 'There's something important I need to tell you.'

Fuck it, thought Carol, she could do with a hug. She slipped her hand out of her pocket and caressed his leg as he drove out of the estate, down the road and on towards the lake.

# CHAPTER NINETY-TWO

Lottie watched as Boyd digested the information.

'Okay, so we don't know which brother it was,' he said. 'Maguire won't tell and he says he's never raised it with whichever one it was over the last ten years. That doesn't make sense.'

'Dealing with covering up for the fire tainted his judgement. So he says. I was lucky to get that much out of him.'

'And there's no mention in the file of either brother meeting her that day?'

'Not a dicky bird.'

'We better get them in.'

'Wait, Boyd. There may be no connection to Lynn's case but if we do that, and he's the one who's taken Mollie and Grace, he might never tell us where they are. We need a strategy.'

He let out a sigh. His hands were trembling and sweat bubbled on his brow. She reached over but he folded his arms.

He said, 'We've searched the town high up and low down for Mollie, without a result.'

'What about Rochfort Gardens? That's where the girls ran.'

'There are acres out there.'

'Exactly. And an old house and all those ridiculous follies.'

Boyd got on the phone and organised a search team and the garda helicopter.

'Where else?' he said as he hung up.

'The train station and surrounding areas have already been searched. Including the old buildings. So that's out.'

'What about that terrace of dilapidated houses where Donal O'Donnell lives?'

'Another possibility,' she said.

Boyd lifted the phone to organize that search.

'Just a minute.' Lottie halted him. He was moving too fast. They needed to think. 'We don't want to spook anyone. Maybe we should get Donal out of there first.'

'How can we do that without causing suspicion?'

'I'll say we have new evidence on Lynn and need him to identify something.'

'He might've been in on it.'

She paused. She hadn't considered that.

'Makes sense. A family thing. Hiding the possibility that Lynn got pregnant with a traveller.'

Once she'd said the words, Lottie realised something.

'Shit, Boyd. What happened to her baby?'

# CHAPTER NINETY-THREE

When Donal O'Donnell refused to come to the station. Lottie decided to go to him.

In the car, her phone rang.

'Is that Inspector Lottie Parker?'

'Yes. Who's this?'

'Keelan. Keelan O'Donnell.'

'What can I do for you?'

'You never contacted me.'

'Sorry. Things are hectic.' And that was putting it mildly, Lottie thought. 'What's up?'

'It's Cillian. I don't know where he is. And …'

'And?'

'Things are bad at home. Very bad, the last few months. That's why I wanted to talk to you. I think he's up to something.'

'Something?' Lottie rolled her eyes over at Boyd. 'Like what?'

'I think he's seeing someone else. Look, the reason … I'm scared, Inspector. He's become a bit violent. I'm terrified he'll do something to me, to Saoirse.'

'Keelan, I'm on my way to your father-in-law's place. Why don't you meet me there?'

The television was on, the sound muted. The candle on the dresser in front of Lynn's photograph remained unlit. Donal sat at the table with his hands clenched in fists. Opposite him, Lottie sat with Boyd.

'Mr O'Donnell. Donal. Can you tell us about the day Lynn disappeared?'

'Jesus. Now you've found her body, all you have are questions. It's all in the file. I'm sure it's a big fat file. You can't miss it.' He pulled the newspaper towards him and began to fold it.

'We have new information.'

'You have her body.'

'We believe Lynn got off the train this day ten years ago and was met by her brother. Did she come home? Did something happen? A family row because she was in love with a traveller? Something like that, huh?'

The paper-folding exercise halted, his hand in the air. 'What makes you say that?'

'Remember I told you about the ring the pathologist found inside Lynn's body?'

'What about it?'

'It was given to Lynn by Paddy McWard.'

His lip curled up to his nose. 'That piece of scum. I wouldn't let him near my sons, never mind my daughter.'

'But he *was* near your daughter. According to Paddy, they were in love. Probably would've run off together to get married if someone hadn't stopped that happening.'

She recoiled as Donal spat on the kitchen floor. 'He wasn't near my girl.'

Deciding offence was the best option, she said, 'I have reason to believe one of her brothers picked her up from the train. Did they come back here? A big row broke out. Then what?'

'Fuck off, devil woman. Talking evil in my house. I won't have it.'

The doorbell chimed.

'I'll get it,' Boyd said, and escaped.

He returned a few seconds later followed by Keelan and a little girl.

'Hey, Dad, what's going on?'

'I'm not your dad! What do you want?'

Lottie noticed Keelan shrinking back and her daughter cowering behind her legs.

'I'm … I'm looking for Cillian.'

'He's not here. You can bugger off.'

Lottie interjected. 'Sit down, Keelan.' The woman was so scared, she might as well have had the word FEAR written in bold letters on her face.

'I'll just let Saoirse play in the living room.'

When she returned, she sat at the end of the table.

Lottie said, 'Donal, this is serious. Please tell us what happened this day ten years ago.'

The lids of his watery eyes rose slightly before he looked down at his hands and shook his head.

'It was bad. Evil. My girl brought a curse on this family. Cavorting with the likes of them, living in caravans with their spells and curses. Can you imagine how my poor Maura would have felt if she'd found out about it? Devastated she'd have been.'

'Was Lynn planning on telling her mother?' Lottie said.

'She told Cillian. He was always her favourite. She never got on with Finn. Think the lad was mighty jealous of his brother. But that's beside the point. Cillian knew she intended to tell all that day, it being Valentine's, and she'd planned to meet the tinker fellow.' He paused as if the word caused his mouth to dry up. 'I was just in from work when the boys sat me down. She stood there.' He pointed to the dresser. 'Stood there like a hussy and told me she was pregnant.'

'Where was your wife?'

'She was still at work. We worked hard for our kids. Day and night. And that's how the girl repaid us. Slut. That's what she was. A fucking slut.'

'There's no need to speak ill of your daughter like that.' Keelan hugged her arms to her chest, her features incredulous.

'Please continue, Donal,' Lottie said. She didn't want him to clam up, or they might never find out what had happened; might never find Grace and Mollie. That is, if they were linked at all.

Donal eyed her before continuing. 'You've no idea what it was like. I nearly died, right where I was sitting. That's the kind of shock it was. But when she said who she'd been whoring around with, I lost it. Jumped up and hit her smack in the face. She fell back and Cillian caught her. He started shouting at me, and Finn stood there with his mouth open like the big eejit he was and always will be.'

'And then?'

'And then I stormed out of the house. Went to the pub. Must have drunk ten pints, and when I got home, there was no Lynn.'

'What had happened? What did your sons say?'

'Cillian said Lynn had run off. He told me he'd driven round to the site, where that yoke lived, but she wasn't there and the tinker hadn't a clue.'

'And did you believe him, that she'd run off?'

'What else could I believe? That he'd killed her and hidden her body? That's what I believed for the last ten years. That's why I never mentioned the McWard fellow. There was enough disgrace hanging like a noose around my family without that.'

'And your wife. What did you tell Maura?'

'Finn told her that Lynn never came home. And that's what we stuck to. That's the story we told all those years. He covered up for Cillian, like brothers do.'

'But Lynn wasn't dead. Where was she?'

'I've no idea. I convinced myself she was dead since that day, and now she is.'

'Where's Cillian now?' Lottie turned to Keelan.

'I don't know. He was out half the night. Like he is most of the time.' Keelan paused, struggling to get the words out. 'We had another blazing row this morning and he stormed off. But he said something that frightened me.'

'What did he say?'

'He told me I was a jealous bitch. Then he said that jealousy took his sister from him and got her killed, and if I didn't shut up, he'd kill me.'

'Any idea where he goes at night?' Boyd asked.

Lottie glanced at his anxious face, etched with concern for his sister. 'Keelan, do you know where he might have kept Lynn hidden all these years? Where he might be keeping Mollie Hunter and possibly Grace Boyd?'

'Oh God. You don't think … He couldn't. Not Cillian.' Keelan stood up, her hands pulling at her hair.

'Please think,' Lottie said. She turned to Donal. 'Is there anywhere your sons went to when they were younger? Someplace no one would think of looking?'

'All the houses beside us are empty, ten if not eleven years. Maura wouldn't let us move in case Lynn came home and couldn't find us.'

'Okay. I want you to come to the station. We'll organise a search.'

'I'm going nowhere,' Donal said.

'Mr O'Donnell, you've been complicit in covering up a crime. You're coming with us.'

'You'll have to handcuff me.'

'I will.' Boyd pulled a set from his pocket and clicked them open.

'Wait a minute,' Lottie said. She turned to Keelan. 'We need to get Finn and his wife into protective custody. Are they at home?'

'I imagine so.'

Lottie phoned Kirby to get there straight away with a squad car. She left Boyd with Donal and ushered Keelan into the sitting room to collect Saoirse. The room exuded misery and loss.

'Inspector?' Keelan said.

Lottie looked at her.

'I don't think my Cillian could do that to his sister. He loved her.'

'Love can do strange things to people,' Lottie said.

# CHAPTER NINETY-FOUR

The car windows were fogged up from their lovemaking. Carol straightened her clothes, glad that her nausea seemed to have waned. She ran a finger down Cillian's face. 'You look sad.'

'I love you, Carol,' he said. 'I know a horrible thing happened to you. But I need to know if the baby you're carrying is mine or from the bastard who raped you.'

Carol turned away. Why was he saying this? It was him, wasn't it? She couldn't tell him that she knew he was her rapist. That he'd got drunk and followed her and attacked her that night. She'd been fairly drunk too, so what would that make her? Complicit? The only thing keeping her going was the fact that it could only be Cillian's baby. She hadn't had sex with anyone else. How could she convince him?

She wanted to be angry at him, but her heart was filled with love. And sorrow for her dead friend. Lizzie, who had held onto the chain and ring she'd pulled from her rapist's neck. The same one that Cillian had always worn but no longer did. Oh, why could she not remember more? Why had she been drinking so much that night?

'Answer me,' he said, leaning over her, his mouth so close she was swallowing his words. 'I'll tear him apart with my bare hands. Who was the bollocks who did it to you?'

'I'm not sure.'

'But you have an idea?'

'Yes.'

'Tell me.' His face was hard and his eyes darker than she'd ever noticed before.

'First I need to know that you're going to leave your wife,' she blurted, clasping her fingers into each other.

He pulled away from her and she felt a cold void spring up between them. And something else. Something that was consuming the cramped space in the car.

And then she knew.

It was her own fear.

\*

Kirby took Keelan, Saoirse and Donal to the garda station. Donal was raving and shouting about evil spirits, so Lottie told Kirby to call a doctor. She was in enough trouble without being the cause of a suspect dying.

'I need to find Grace,' Boyd said as they finished searching the old man's house.

'The search team are working their way through the terrace. So far we have nothing.'

'Where could he keep a girl hidden for ten years? Never mind the why.'

'There must be a clue in this house. This is the last place we know where Lynn was.'

'You'd think she'd be safe in her own home.'

'A house with a demented father and two brothers oozing hormones, and God knows what the mother was like. Then Lynn brings home news that in Donal's mind was the ultimate taboo. Pregnant by a traveller. Prejudice is an awful thing, Boyd.'

'So is keeping a young woman hidden for ten years. Do you think when Lynn died he went over the edge and took Elizabeth to replace her?'

'That's what I suspect. Then Elizabeth escapes, and he kills her and has to find another replacement. Where the hell did he keep them?'

Lottie entered Donal's small bedroom again. It was suffused with such a thick, fusty smell that she felt she could touch it if she put out her hand. She didn't dare. Beside the bed was a small bookcase, folders sticking out haphazardly.

'I already looked there,' Boyd said. 'Seems to be old work stuff. Mainly relates to the nursing home.'

'That's where he works.'

'The boys worked with him for a while. I saw invoices. Donal was a cute fucker. Billed the health board for his sons doing a bit of painting.'

'Where did you see that?'

Boyd tugged a black A4 ring binder from the shelf and two others slipped to the floor.

'Jesus, leave them there,' Lottie said as he bent to tidy up. 'Which page? Show me.'

He leaned over her shoulder and flipped through. 'There. Fixing up a boiler room and painting some corridor or other. February 2001.'

'This relates to the old nursing home. It closed down maybe a year after that. Could that be it?'

'What?'

'I think it might be where he kept Elizabeth.' Lottie made for the door.

'Jesus, that's a long shot,' Boyd shouted.

She kept running.

*

'Carol, you have to tell me what you suspect. I can't promise you anything until I know.'

She looked out the window at the ripples roughing up the lake. 'You used to wear a ring on a chain round your neck. But you don't wear it any more. Why?'

'I don't know what that's got to do with anything. But to satisfy you, I'll tell you.' He turned around to face her. 'I had a row with my brother one night. I can't even remember the exact thing we fought over. Something to do with the railway preservation committee, I think. But fight we did. Down and dirty. Like we used to when we were kids. He pulled the chain off me. It got lost. Searched the ground for it when he was gone. Never found it. Are you saying the rapist had it?'

'You don't know where it might be?'

'No and I don't care any more. It was a Claddagh ring. Lynn had one just like it … when she vanished. I bought a similar one and wore it around my neck to remind me of her.'

Carol twisted away from the window and faced him.

'The night I was attacked, my rapist was wearing one exactly like it. I pulled it from his neck.'

'What?' The realisation of what she was saying began to dawn on him. 'You thought it was me. All these weeks, you still met up with me, thinking I might have attacked and raped you. How could you?'

She shrugged. 'I just did. The ring was yours. I was sure of it. I gave it to a friend to mind for me, in case I ever reported the rape and needed evidence.'

'You what? Jesus, Carol. I could never …' He stopped. 'I don't think I could … you know, be violent like that. But I've been so stressed recently, I'm not myself. I actually hit Keelan one night, and another evening I broke every plate in the house.'

Tears streamed down his cheeks. She reached up and wiped them. 'I'm sorry. I love you and didn't want to believe it was you.'

'I don't really blame you.'

'Cillian.' Her voice dropped to a whisper. 'The man who attacked me, could it have been, you know, your brother?'

'Finn? No!' he cried.

She watched him and saw his expression changing.

'Oh God,' she said.

Banging his head against the steering wheel, Cillian wailed at the waters rising on the lake.

And in that moment, Carol feared for her life and that of the baby growing in her womb.

# CHAPTER NINETY-FIVE

The door of the hatch opened and his legs appeared, climbing down the ladder. Why hadn't she thought of whacking him before? A day or two ago, when she still had the strength? But now hunger gnawed at her stomach like a rat, and she could hardly move.

When he jumped off the last rung onto the floor, she saw he held scissors in one hand, and a battery-powered razor in the other.

'Time for a haircut,' he said. 'Or maybe you'd like to tell me where you hid it first?'

'Hid what?'

'Oh, don't go all coy on me, pretty girl. I know you were friends with that slut. Took her in the night she was attacked. Didn't I tell you? I did that to her. She was some fighter. A terrible vixen.'

Was he talking about the girl who was raped? What was her name? Carol O'Grady? But Mollie hardly knew her. 'What am I supposed to have hidden?'

'So that's the way you want to play it? I thought a few days of confinement might loosen your tongue, but it seems I have to use brutal measures. Poor old Lynn. She didn't like getting her head shaved. But I had to do it. The creepy-crawly lice would've torn her scalp to shreds in this place. See, I'm not all bad.'

Before she realised what he was doing, he had pulled her upright by her hair. Gripped it in a tight knot around his fingers and sliced through with the scissors. She watched helplessly as it fell to the ground at her bare feet.

'No!'

The buzz of the razor drowned out her sobs as it sliced close to her scalp, shaving her hair clean from her head. It nicked a spot that had erupted over the last day, and blood seeped down her forehead into her eyes.

'What do you want?' she cried.

'The silver chain with the ring. The one your raped friend gave you to mind.'

'I don't know what you're talking about.' She honestly hadn't a clue.

'Come on. I'm not stupid. She either gave it to that Elizabeth bitch or she gave it to you. That cow died before I could get the information from her, so I'm back to thinking you must have it. Now where the fuck is it?'

Mollie crumpled in a heap on the floor in the midst of her shorn hair and tried to remember. She had Carol's clothes. Nothing else. No chain. No ring. But he wasn't going to believe that. As he hunkered down to continue shaving, she knew she had to come up with a plan. And mighty quick. Otherwise she'd end up fermenting beside the bones on the table.

# CHAPTER NINETY-SIX

On the way, Boyd checked in with the other search teams. Still ongoing at Rochfort Gardens, but nothing had been found. Yet. As they drove towards the old nursing home, Kirby came on the radio.

'Dropped the O'Donnells at the station. Heading to pick up Finn and Sara, then I'm going to join the search at the Ladystown caravan park.'

Boyd clicked him off.

'They'll find her,' Lottie said. 'Are you okay?'

'I will be once this is all over.'

He drove up to the front of the old home and parked. Lottie got out of the car and walked between two buildings leaning in over her until she came to the oldest structure.

'It dates back to the famine,' she said as Boyd joined her.

'I thought Lynch was our local history fanatic.'

She pointed to a plaque above the black timber door. 'Says it right there.' Pushing against the door, she found it was firmly closed. 'Let's have a look further back.'

Rusting oil tanks and odds and ends of machinery were lined up against the ancient wall behind which the current nursing home was housed. She continued walking to her right, with Boyd by her side. They turned another corner and stopped. A car was parked haphazardly.

'Who owns that, then?' Boyd asked, taking out his phone.

'My bet is Cillian O'Donnell. Check the registration.'

He was already on the phone as she made her way past the car and behind a mound of rubble to the side of another building.

'Is that a boiler house?' she said.

'I'd say so but look at the chimney.' He pointed upwards. 'There must have been an incinerator here.'

To the rear, a door. Lottie nudged it with the knuckles of her good hand and it swung inwards. She raised her eyebrows at Boyd.

'That's a stroke of good luck,' he said.

'You always can read my mind. Pull on gloves, just in case this leads to anything.'

They moved inside.

'I think you're right, Boyd. This was an incinerator. You go that way and I'll take this side.'

They spent five minutes looking, searching and listening. Nothing.

'There's a car out back, so someone must be here,' Lottie said.

'Maybe he's avoiding parking charges at the nursing home. Just dropped the car there and headed off.'

She ignored him and opened the door to the oven-like structure built into a brick chimney breast. Leaned over the edge and peered in.

'Holy fuck, Boyd. There's a hatch built into the floor.'

# CHAPTER NINETY-SEVEN

Was that a voice?

Sounded like one. Up high.

He was so busy scalping her bald, he mustn't have heard it. She was sure someone was there above them. Someone with him? Or help for her? She had to distract him.

'The bones,' she said. 'Where did they come from?'

'Why do you want to know?'

'They scare me a little.'

'I can scare you a whole lot more than bones.'

'I'm not afraid of you.' The hope that rescue might be close gave her a smidgen of courage.

He let go of her head and sat back on the floor. She twisted round and faced him.

'Who do you think I'm going to tell, locked up here?' she said.

'You have a smart mouth on you, for a pretty girl.'

'Oh, don't bother telling me. I don't want to know.'

He stared at her, chewing the inside of his cheek. Weighing it up. Was she getting to him? She hoped so.

'They belong to a baby,' he said.

'Whose baby? And who was Lynn that you mentioned?'

'Now you want to chat. I don't have time for this.' He raised the scissors.

'I'll tell you where the chain and ring are if you tell me about her.' Mollie had no idea where she was getting the strength from,

but deep down she knew this might be her last chance. If she kept him talking, whoever was up above might hear them.

'You playing games with me?'

'No.'

'My nutjob of a wife does that to me.'

'I'm sorry about that,' she lied, trying to be convincing with her sympathy.

'The bones. That was my sister's baby. Lynn was pregnant when I took her. Took her away from her loving brother. She always had more time for him. He was always getting me into trouble. Blaming me for things. She was the star of our family show and everyone doted on her, and I was left out. The middle child, that was me. Left behind.' He set his mouth in a grim line and Mollie saw his fingers whiten as they clenched the scissors.

'That's awful,' she soothed and wondered if she could grab the scissors.

'Not fair,' he said. 'She came home that day, the whore, and announced in front of my excuse for a father and my brother that she was pregnant with a tinker's child. I knew she was finished then. The golden girl was tarnished and I saw my chance. I took her for myself.'

'How did you manage that?' Keep talking, Mollie prayed. Silence from above. Was it a good or a bad sign? As long as she could keep him talking, there was hope.

'The old man stormed off to the pub, my brother was broken before my eyes, and Mother was due home. I knew I'd be blamed, because, sweetheart, I got blamed for everything. Lynn fled the house, scared shitless. I followed her. Picked her up. Sweet-talked her. Told her a pack of lies and brought her here.'

'Was this place always here?'

'This place is a stroke of genius on my part.'

'You must be very clever.'

'I think I am actually.' He smirked. 'I held her upstairs in the old incinerator room, but over a few weeks I built a false bottom in the chamber with an entrance down here. All this is part of the original boiler house. I helped renovate it one summer. I blocked off the door and put in the hatch and steps. Yes, I am very clever. Anyone who decided to search was never going to find her. And they never did. I finally had something my brother couldn't have. I had her to myself.'

'What happened to her … baby?' Mollie couldn't help her eyes being drawn to the stark whiteness of the tiny bones.

'He was born dead, the little bastard. I left him upstairs to rot. Thought of burying him. But it was a better idea to leave his bones out for her to see every day of her miserable life.'

Mollie felt sick to her stomach. The mental torture that poor girl must have suffered. 'Where is she now?'

'Who?'

She noticed his eyes glazing over, a film of insanity shrouding the whites, the pupils dark rings of hate. She struggled to keep her voice even.

'Your sister.'

'She died. It was such fun, every year, watching them all wallowing in grief, wondering where she was.' He laughed, a strange, screechy sound. 'They never told a living soul about the traveller. She had this ring. A Claddagh or something. Swallowed it, she did. Stupid bitch. Don't know if it got stuck in her gullet, poisoned her or what, but when I told her that Mother had died without ever finding out she was still alive, it was like Lynn couldn't hack it any longer. Or maybe it was because I was busy with the funeral, relations and all that shite. It went on for a week, the wake, the funeral, the afters. I forgot to come with food and water. So maybe she starved. I don't really care. I was left with the bother of getting rid of her body.'

'You could have left her here,' Mollie ventured. 'With her baby.'

'I wasn't able for the smell. And I wanted to have this space free in case I needed it. And I did.'

Mollie was afraid to ask, but she got the words out, 'What did you do with her body?'

'Doused her in bleach, wrapped her up in bin bags and dumped her out at the lake for the rats and wild birds to feast on. But some teenage trash found her before she was eaten to the bone. So, pretty girl, I'm done with talking. Your turn. Tell me, where is the chain with the ring?'

\*

Lottie held a finger to her lips. 'Shh. I hear voices. There's someone down there.'

Boyd leaned into the cavernous space with her. 'You're right. I'm going down.'

'No, you need to call for backup. And have a good look around outside. There might be another way in. This building is next to the boiler house. Have a look there. But do it quietly.'

'I'm not leaving you alone.'

'Why not?'

'Because it might be my sister down there and you'll do something stupid.'

'I won't. I'll just guard this door. Go. Make the call.'

She watched him reluctantly leave, then put her ear to the wooden hatch in the oven floor. The sound was muffled, but she could make out some of the words. She switched her phone to record and pushed it over the widest gap in the timber that she could find.

She had been listening for about five minutes, with no sign of Boyd returning, when she heard the scream.

Without further thought, she slid her phone away, pulled the hatch door open and jumped down.

# CHAPTER NINETY-EIGHT

Lottie hit the floor with a thud, having missed most of the rungs on the ladder.

'Drop your weapon, Finn. Step away from Mollie.'

Two sets of wild eyes gaped back at her, Mollie's with terror and Finn's with confusion. The air was filled with the scent of claustrophobic fear. It dripped down the walls and rested like a sheen on the skin of the naked girl.

She was on her knees, her head haphazardly shaven. He stood behind her, one arm around her waist, pulling her into his body, the other about her neck. A pair of scissors in his hand was pointing directly at her eye.

'Stay there,' he growled. 'I'll do her, I swear I will.'

'That's not a good move.' Still on the floor, Lottie tried to see something in her vicinity that she could use as a weapon. She had no bag and no gun, but Mollie was in danger and she had to do something. Where the hell was Boyd?

'Oh, I think it is a good move. I outsmarted the lot of you.'

A noise above them caused Lottie to look up. But it wasn't Boyd. It was Cillian O'Donnell. Where the hell had he come from? This was not good.

A wild laugh broke from Finn. 'Now we can play happy families, dear brother.'

Cillian stepped off the ladder, then reached down and pulled Lottie to her feet. Shit, she thought. The two of them are involved in this together. Where the fuck was Boyd?

'It's okay, Finn, I have the guard now,' he said. 'Put down the scissors. You don't want another murder on your head, do you?'

'Another murder? What are you talking about.'

'We can do this together. Me and you. Like old times.'

Lottie felt the hairs on her arms sizzle. How was she going to take down the two of them? Mollie looked in no shape to help. Boyd better be quick.

'Yes, Finn,' she said. 'Put down the scissors.'

'Shut her up,' Finn shouted.

'I have her. No need to shout,' Cillian said, and Lottie felt his arm loop around her neck.

Finn snarled. 'What do you care? You never thought about me before; you're not going to change now.'

'But I do care,' Cillian said. 'I want to help you. Like you helped me with Lynn.'

'What do you mean?' The hand holding the scissors wavered.

Mollie was as still as a statue, only her eyes giving away that she was alive. Darting from Cillian to Lottie, pleading for help. Lottie scanned the room once again for a weapon. The space was so confined, they were virtually on top of each other, but at the same time Finn seemed to be miles from her reach.

'You took her away, didn't you?' Cillian said. 'Before she could disgrace our family. You saved us a shitload of heartache, bro.'

Was he inverting the truth, trying to get Finn to believe he was the good guy in all this? Smart move if that was the case. But maybe it was a ploy. With exhaustion and the effects of the last twenty-four hours, Lottie felt her gut instinct had deserted her. She couldn't read the situation. She needed Boyd.

'You really think so?' Finn said, his hand falling lower. It was now at Mollie's neck. She still hadn't moved.

'Sure. And that traveller,' Cillian said, 'he got what he deserved.'

'He sure did. I burned his hovel to the ground. Now he's got nothing. Living there all that time, laughing at us, and he never knew how close he was to Lynn. I thought that was funny.'

'Finn?' Cillian said.

'Yeah, bro?'

'You took Lynn, I can understand that. But Carol. Why'd you have to take her from me too?'

'What're you talking about?' Finn said, his brow tightening in two straight lines.

Yeah, what are you talking about? Lottie thought.

'You raped her. Why?'

With her body pressed to Cillian's, his arm still around her neck, Lottie sensed the tears streaming down his face. She glanced down at his other hand, to see if he held a weapon, but saw nothing. She had to hear this.

'Rape? I didn't …' Finn's eyes flared at his brother.

'You did. I know you did. Why?'

'So you know everything, as usual.' He pointed the scissors at Cillian, away from Mollie, though he still had his other arm around her waist. 'You had Keelan and Saoirse. You had everything and you went and ruined it. Going around sticking it in that Carol slut. And me at home with fucking Sara the cuckoo clock. Tick tock. Time's up.'

He moved swiftly. Lottie was quicker. She rammed her elbow into Cillian's stomach, shoving him back against the steps. Lunging forward, she kicked Finn in the groin and wrestled the weapon from his hand as he doubled over. Mollie fell back and rolled under the bed.

Footsteps hammered on the ladder and Boyd vaulted over the prostrate Cillian, landing on top of Finn. Lottie squirmed as she heard the whirr of a motor. Finn brought the razor up to Boyd's

face, shredding his cheek. But he held on to Finn's wrists until the razor dropped to the ground.

Lottie snapped a set of handcuffs on the abductor and blew out a sigh of relief. Then she coaxed Mollie from beneath the bed and hugged her. Boyd pulled Cillian's hands together and cuffed him.

Before reading the two men their rights, Lottie glanced around the hovel and noticed the little paintings on the walls. Saw the name on them.

Then she saw the bones.

# CHAPTER NINETY-NINE

Kirby scratched his head and shoved a cigar into his mouth. The lake was churning waves in the wind.

'Don't you dare light that,' Lynch said as she pulled open the door of a mobile home.

'This must be the fiftieth door we've opened today,' he said, looking longingly at the cigar in his hand before consigning it to his pocket.

Lynch said. 'It's the tenth. Nothing here. Have you the key to the next one?'

Kirby checked the bundle of keys they'd found in the unattended caretaker's hut. So much for security. 'This is a waste of time. There's no one in any of them.'

'Give me the key.' Lynch marched over to number eleven.

'What's that over there?' Kirby approached a small caravan surrounded by bushes at the end of the row. The windows were boarded up and the step broken. No sign of any gas cylinder or rubbish bins.

'How the hell do I know?' Lynch snapped the bundle of keys from his hand. 'Maybe the owner died and it's been left to rot.'

She went off with the keys and Kirby made to follow, but paused when he noticed a new lock on the door.

'Lynch. This looks odd.'

'Everything looks odd to you today,' she called back.

He moved closer, tried to see in through the boards nailed to the windows. No cracks. He could see nothing. He rattled the handle of the door. 'Anyone in there?'

He stuck his ear to the timber. Not a sound. Still, his gut told him to investigate further. A vice grip would be handy, he thought.

'Any padlock keys on that ring?' he yelled to Lynch.

'No.' She joined him.

Kirby thought for a minute. 'Stand back.'

The wood splintered as his boot went through the rotten timber. The lock held firm, but he tore with his bare hands to make space to enter. The light cast shadows on a shape on the floor.

'Call an ambulance,' he whispered.

✱

Crime-scene tape fluttered around his burned-out home. Paddy McWard shoved his hands deep into his jacket pockets and blinked away his tears. All his life he'd stood up to discrimination and prejudice, but he'd never got a chance to stand up for Lynn. And because of his love for her, he'd never allowed himself to love Bridie. But his son, little Tommy …

He choked the sob back down his throat.

He had fought long and hard to rescue young lads from the dangerous underworld after he lost his brother. Now he had to do something about the ill his people were suffering. He didn't know what yet, but he would not be broken completely.

He turned at the sound of footsteps behind him. A priest stood there, his eyes twinkling in the light of the moon.

'Hello, Paddy. I'm Father Joe Burke. I know something of the torment you're suffering. I'm a good listener if you'd like to talk.'

'You know what, Father, I think that would be a good thing.'

# CHAPTER ONE HUNDRED

Boyd had a large white plaster taped down his jaw.

'Goes well with the bruise on the other side,' Lottie said. 'That Finn really didn't like you.'

'It's not funny. It's painful.' Boyd looked up as an ambulance siren wailed outside the A&E before cutting out.

Lottie checked the message on her phone again. 'That should be them.'

Boyd rushed forward as the paramedics unloaded the stretcher, secured the wheels and pushed past them. Boyd grabbed Grace's hand and followed the stretcher inside.

'She's going to be okay,' Lottie said.

But Boyd was gone.


Back in the office, Lottie tried to make sense of what had happened in the old nursing home. Finn and Cillian had been arrested, though she now suspected that Cillian had not been involved in the abduction of their sister. That was all Finn. And he had wreaked havoc on the McWards because of his insane jealousy. She still had to interview Carol and take her statement. But once Finn started talking, he would be charged with rape along with his other crimes.

Mollie was in hospital, as was Grace, and both were expected to recover physically. Their mental health was another issue. Boyd's mother had arrived from Galway, so Lottie expected him to return to the office any minute.

The door opened and in he walked.

'You look like shit,' he said and pulled out a chair and flopped down.

'You can talk,' Lottie said. 'Is Grace okay? Are you okay?'

'She'll be fine. It's hard when your family is involved,' he said.

'You can say that again.'

'It's hard—'

'Boyd!' She stretched her legs out under her desk. Her foot snagged on the strap of her bag and she dragged it towards her. She'd forgotten to bring it home last night, so she still had the envelope containing Katie's money. One thing that had survived the fire.

'That O'Donnell family was seriously dysfunctional,' she said.

'I can't help thinking that Carol could have prevented Elizabeth's death if she had reported the rape.'

'Wasn't her fault. She was terrified. Like a lot of rape victims, she thought it was her own fault, and to complicate things, she believed it was her lover, Cillian, who'd raped her. She kept quiet thinking she was protecting him.'

'Poor girl.'

'And when his nut of a brother realised he'd lost the chain and ring, he started searching and questioning, seeking out anyone Carol was in contact with.' Lottie sighed.

'But it all started with Lynn falling in love with Paddy McWard, whose only crime was being born into a community despised by the O'Donnell men.' Boyd slammed the desk in frustration. 'Prejudice!'

'No, it started before then. Jealousy between two brothers. Jealousy within their family.'

Kirby barged in the door. 'Sorry, boss. We found a body.'

'Where? Who? Everyone is accounted for.'

'On the train tracks. Just by the cemetery. Reports came in a half-hour ago.' Kirby was out of breath.

'Who is it?'

Kirby placed a photo on Lottie's desk. 'That's his photo, from the incident board. He was hit by the evening train.'

'Matt Mullin,' Lottie said. 'Poor man.'

'When Grace is well enough, I'll get her to have a look at his photograph,' Boyd said. 'It was probably Mullin who caused Mollie to move seats and sit beside her.'

'Thanks, Kirby,' Lottie said. 'Will you inform his mother? Take a family liaison officer with you.'

'Will do. Oh, one other thing, boss. SOCOs have been going over Finn O'Donnell's car. Found flecks of skin in the footwell and on the front and back seats.'

'Links Finn directly to Elizabeth Byrne. She suffered from psoriasis.'

'DNA should link him to Carol's rape,' Boyd said. 'Where's his brother now?'

'We released him on bail, so he's probably at home, either patching things up with Keelan or packing his bags. Either way, Cillian did nothing wrong that we can prove, yet.'

'Not unless Keelan makes an official complaint for domestic abuse.'

'Time will tell,' Lottie said.

'But how did he know Finn was at the old nursing home?' Boyd rubbed his jaw, and winced as his fingers snagged on the plaster.

'His story is that he was out at the lake with Carol and she told him about being raped. When she mentioned the chain with the ring, he immediately suspected his brother. He knew there were only two places Finn had an interest in. One was the old railway, so he checked that first, and then he made his way to Finn's other favourite haunt. The old nursing home.'

'Had he not been there before? Surely he would have come across Lynn?'

'He says he never went there, but both of them had worked there when they were younger. He said Finn often talked about the old incinerator and how one day he wanted to restore it.'

'I still believe Cillian was involved.'

'I don't think so,' Lottie said, just as her desk phone lit up with a call. She answered it, her head as weary as her hands. Last night's fire drama seemed to have shrivelled her brain.

It was Jim McGlynn.

'Any news on who tried to murder my family?' Lottie asked.

'Fire started in your utility room. Probably a clothes dryer.'

'That can't be right.' Lottie felt her cheeks burn with embarrassment. 'It can't be my fault.'

'We're still working on it. We may find something else. Just wanted to let you know that.'

'Thanks, Jim.'

'You'd want to check your insurance, though.'

'Oh, won't it cover the fire?'

'How would I know?' McGlynn hung up.

Lottie glanced up. 'What?'

'Your fault?' Boyd said.

Feeling tears building up, Lottie sniffed them away. 'Jesus, Boyd. What have I done to my family? I never have time for maintenance or household stuff. It's always rush and fuss. Oh God. It's all my fault.' She laid her head on the desk and wrapped her hands about it.

'Shush, Lottie,' Boyd said. 'Don't blame yourself. It might still turn out to be the work of that bastard Finn O'Donnell.'

She raised her head. 'Maybe you're right. I don't know which is worse. Thinking it's my fault, or that someone targeted me and my family.'

Kirby stuck his head around the door. 'Lynch is buying the first round in Cafferty's. That right, Lynch?'

'Piss off, Kirby. I can't drink and you know it.'

'Why not?' Boyd said.

'I'm pregnant,' Lynch said, her cheeks flaring.

'Ah, a bit of good news at last,' Boyd said.

'Grace doing okay?' Lynch said.

'She'll be fine. My mother is with her. I better get back to the hospital.'

'Suppose I should give Gilly a call,' Kirby said. 'Don't like celebrating the end of a case on my own.'

When the office emptied and she was alone, Lottie called Chloe.

'Hey, hun. You and Sean okay?'

'Fine. Had a fab day with Gilly. She's cool. Bought loads of clothes in town. Wait till I show you. And we got Sean a hoodie and shirts and a pair of jeans. He's going around in his bare feet, though. We forgot to buy him shoes.'

'I'll get him some tomorrow.'

'He spent all day watching old films on the telly with Granny. You know what? He actually enjoyed it.'

'That's great.' Lottie felt a stab of jealousy. 'Will I bring a take-away?'

'Is Boyd paying?'

'No, I found my handbag with Katie's money.'

'Only joking. About Boyd, I mean. Bring him round. Granny wants a word with him.'

'Really?'

'No, not really.' Chloe's voice dropped to a whisper. 'We can't live here, Mum. She's going to drive me mad, and by tomorrow Sean will be bored of movies. And we have a week off school. What are we going to do?'

'I'm sorry, Chloe, but we'll have to stay there for a little while. At least until I sort out somewhere to rent.'

'Granny wants to speak to you.'

'No, Chloe, I have to run.'

Too late.

'You're always running.' Rose Fitzpatrick had her mojo back. 'You don't have to bring any takeaway into my house. I've cooked a turkey and a ham.'

'But it's not Christmas.'

'It's Valentine's Day. About time we had a little love around here. And bring along that lad with the big ears.'

'Who? Boyd?'

'Yes. I like him. Are you on your way?'

Lottie hung up and noticed Boyd lounging in the doorway.

'I thought you were gone to the hospital,' she said, moving files around her desk. She found the little paintings in their plastic evidence bag.

'Wanted to make sure you weren't staying here all night.'

'It must have been hell for Lynn being held in that tiny space for ten years. And the bones of her baby beside her. How cruel can people be?' Lottie wondered.

'The baby can be buried with his mother, once Jane runs the DNA tests.'

'I'm trying to make out the signature.' She picked up another painting, one of a train. She glanced up with tears in her eyes.

'What is it, Lottie?' Boyd leaned over the desk and gripped her hand.

She welcomed the contact, needing to feel the touch of a good human being. There was too much evil in the world. But she pulled her hand away all the same.

'Lynn never stopped loving the father of her child.' She turned the painting around for Boyd to read. 'See the word on the train. It's his name. Paddy.'

'Poor bastard. He's off organising funerals. But he probably won't get to attend Lynn's. Donal O'Donnell won't have him near it.'

'If Keelan has anything to do with it, Paddy will be there. I'd say she's sick of their jealousy and prejudice. And frankly, so am I.'

Kirby rushed in, his unlit cigar hanging from his lips.

'What now?' Lottie said.

'McMahon. He's on the warpath. Worse than Corrigan ever was. Coming this way. I'd make a quick exit if I was you.'

'Arsehole,' Boyd said.

'Shit,' Lottie muttered.

# EPILOGUE

With Boyd by her side, Lottie stood in the road, looking at the remains of her burned-out house. It was dark, and the heavens were in a tormented mood.

'Why do the gods continue to conspire against me to take everything away?'

'You have your family and you still have your job,' Boyd said. 'You're lucky McMahon's not pursuing your television debacle any further.'

'It's only so he can wallow in the success of closing the murder investigation so quickly. I wonder if Cynthia Rhodes is sticking around.'

'I'm sure she will.'

'Any word on Corrigan?' Lottie said. 'Never thought I'd say this, but I miss him.'

'His surgery was a success, but I don't know when he'll be back, if ever.'

'That means I'll have to suffer McMahon!'

'Or he'll have to suffer you,' Boyd laughed.

'Boyd, I've no home. It's been swallowed up in black smoke and flames. It's all ashes.'

'You have Katie's money from Tom Rickard,' he said with a laugh.

'It's not funny.' She shoved her hands deeper into her mother's wool coat.

'I know, but sometimes you have to laugh or you might cry,' he said.

Her phone vibrated in her pocket as rain began to come down in a diagonal line, cutting her face like shards of glass.

She answered the unknown number.

'Am I speaking to Lottie Parker?'

'Yes.' She walked in small circles. 'Who is this?'

'Captain Leo Belfield. I'm with the NYPD. New York Police Department.'

Lottie dropped to her knees on the hard tarmac, rainwater flowing around her. She clenched the phone to her ear.

'What's happened? Oh God Almighty. Please tell me they're all right?' Boyd bent down and wrapped his arms about her. She shrugged him off.

'Sorry, I don't follow you,' the caller said. 'Slow down.'

'My daughter and grandson are in New York,' she sobbed, all control draining away. 'Tell me nothing has happened to them. Dear God, Jesus ...'

'Eh, not that I'm aware of, ma'am.'

'Oh.' She slumped down on the kerb, oblivious to her saturated clothes. 'Why are you calling me then?'

'I found your number among my mother's things.'

'Your mother? What's this about? You scared me half to death.'

'My mother's name is Alexis Belfield. She's suffered a heart attack, though it's nothing to worry about. The doctor says she's going to be fine, with medication. I had to look through her papers and computer files to locate her medical insurance details. I sent you an email, but you didn't reply. After some detective work, I found your number and decided to ring. I don't think I was ever intended to see some of those files ...'

'Hey, slow down there. Did you say Alexis Belfield?'

'One and the same. My Mom.'

'Oh!' Lottie stared up at Boyd, wide-eyed, her heart crashing against her chest.

'So I just wanted to introduce myself and say hello. I believe we are related, if I can believe this stuff I've read here.'

'What did you say your name was again?'

'Leo Belfield. You know what, Lottie Parker, I believe I may be your half-brother.'

'What?' She almost dropped the phone.

'Are you coming to the States any time soon? Or hey, I can come visit you. I'm sure Mom would love that.'

I'm sure she wouldn't, Lottie thought.

'Are you for real?' she said.

He hesitated for the first time. 'Sorry, have I upset you? I know a phone call isn't the best way to do introductions, but I was excited and—'

'I need to digest this.' The words tumbled from her mouth. 'You see, my house burned to the ground last night. I'm living with my two teenagers in my mother's house and she isn't the easiest person in the world to get along with, but that's another story. My eldest is in New York with her son, my grandson, and that's why you scared the shit out of me. I've just solved a major case and I'm sitting in the rain, on the side of the road, and I don't know what the future holds for me. I need time to think. Please, Leo, don't come here. Not just yet, anyway.'

She hung up and stared at Boyd.

'I don't believe it,' she said.

'Neither do I. What was that all about?'

Lottie looked up at the sky as the rain turned to sleet.

'I thought ... I thought something had happened to Katie and Louis ...'

'But they're just fine.'

'Yes. But he said … this Leo guy on the phone … he said he might be my half-brother. Jesus, Boyd. What am I going to do?'

'You're going to get up out of that puddle. Here, grab my hand. You need to go to your mother's and hug your children. And you don't have to meet this Leo if you don't want to.'

'This will finish Rose off.' Lottie pulled away from him. 'I'm not going to tell her. And you're not to either.'

'I won't. But Lottie … you need to think seriously about the implications of that phone call.'

'I will.' She caught the look of hurt skimming across his eyes. 'Just not tonight.'

She linked her arm through his and, leaning into his shoulder, walked away from what had once been her home.

And she truly had no idea where she was going.

# A LETTER FROM PATRICIA

Hello dear reader,

I wish to sincerely thank you for reading my fourth novel, *No Safe Place*.

I'm so grateful to you for sharing your precious time with Lottie Parker, her family and team. If you enjoyed it you might like to follow Lottie throughout the series of novels. To those of you who have already read the first three Lottie Parker books, *The Missing Ones, The Stolen Girls*, and *The Lost Child*, I thank you for your support and reviews.

If you would like to join my mailing list to be kept informed of my new releases, please click here:

www.bookouture.com/patricia-gibney

All characters in this story are fictional, as is the town of Ragmullin, though life events have deeply influenced my writing.

If you enjoyed *No Safe Place*, I would love if you could post a review online. It would mean so much to me. The amazing reviews my books have received to date inspire me to believe in myself and to keep writing.

You can connect with me on my Facebook Author page and Twitter. I also have a blog (which I try to keep up to date).

Thanks again, and I hope you will join me for book five in the series.

Love,
Patricia

www.patriciagibney.com

trisha460/

@trisha460

# ACKNOWLEDGEMENTS

This is my fourth book in the Lottie Parker series, following on from *The Missing Ones*, *The Stolen Girls* and *The Lost Child*. As a writer, I am dependent on many people, and I'm grateful to have a great team working with me.

But first let me say, *you* are the most important person in my writing journey. You have bought my books and read them. I hope you enjoy *No Safe Place*. Readers give me the confidence to keep on writing. Thank you.

To me, Bookouture is more than a just a publishing house. It's like a family, where everyone supports each other and offers advice. My writing and editing are a lot more manageable because of it.

Helen Jenner and Lydia Vassar Smith were my editors on *No Safe Place*, and I want to thank you both for your insight into my writing and for guiding me in producing a book I am proud of. To everyone else from Bookouture who worked on *No Safe Place*, thank you. I want to give special mention to Kim Nash and Noelle Holten for their incredible media work and for organising blog tours. Kim, thank you for always being there for me and checking up on me. I really appreciate it.

Thank you also to those who work directly on my books: Lauren Finger (production), Jen Hunt (publishing), Alex Crow and Jules McAdam (marketing) and Jane Selley.

All my books are published in audio format, so I want to thank Michele Moran for her magnificent narration, giving voice to Lottie

and my cast of characters, as well as Adam Helal at The Audiobook Producers.

Fellow Bookouture authors, you are the most supportive group of people I know. Special thanks to Angie Marsons for all your support and advice.

Thank you to each and every blogger and reviewer who has read and reviewed *The Missing Ones*, *The Stolen Girls*, *The Lost Child* and *No Safe Place*. I hope I can continue to keep you busy!

Thanks to my agent, Ger Nichol of The Book Bureau, for looking out for me and promoting my interests.

To my sister Marie Brennan, thanks a million for taking the time to read early drafts of my work and for your insightful comments and support.

John Quinn, you're always available to advise me on policing matters. I take huge liberties with most of it, so I take full responsibility for the fiction!

Thank you to my friends. Jo and Antoinette for always being there. Jackie for the writing escapes. Niamh for your informative phone calls. Grainne for your calming influence.

Others in the writing world who inspire and motivate me are: Louise Phillips, Liz Nugent, Vanessa O'Loughlin, Arlene Hunt, Carolann Copeland, Laurence O'Bryan, Sean O'Farrell and many more.

To local and national media, I cannot thank you enough for the coverage you have given me and my books. Olga Aughey, Claire Corrigan and Claire O'Brien, thank you.

Thanks to Dr Clodagh Brennan, Eric Smyth, Kevin Monaghan, Sean Lynch, Rita Gilmartin, Marty Mulligan and Shane Barkey. Also Stella Lynch of Just Books, and a special thanks to libraries and their staff everywhere.

Thanks to Lily Gibney and family for always supporting me.

To my mother and father, William and Kathleen Ward, for many years of listening to my dreams and believing in me.

I am so proud of my three children, Aisling, Orla and Cathal. You three have proved time and again how strong you are. Your dad, Aidan, would be so proud of how you are now coping following his untimely death. And Daisy and Shay have brought oodles of joy and love into my life. Love you both.

Finally, I dedicate *No Safe Place* to my sisters Marie and Cathy, and my brother Gerard. This book touches on the relationship between brothers and sisters. And mine are the best.